# STORM FROM THE
# SHADOWS

# STORM FROM THE SHADOWS

BY

# DAVID WEBER

STORM FROM THE SHADOWS

This is a work of fiction. All the characters and events portrayed in this book are fictional, and any resemblance to real people or incidents is purely coincidental.

A Baen Books Original

Baen Publishing Enterprises
P.O. Box 1403
Riverdale, NY 10471
www.baen.com

ISBN 10: 1-4165-9147-8
ISBN 13: 978-1-4165-9147-4

Cover art by David Mattingly
Interior schematics by Thomas Marrone, Thomas Pope and William H. Edwards

First printing, March 2009

Distributed by Simon & Schuster
1230 Avenue of the Americas
New York, NY 10020

Library of Congress Cataloging-in-Publication Data

Weber, David, 1952–
Storm from the shadows / David Weber.
        p. cm.
ISBN-13: 978-1-4165-9147-4
ISBN-10: 1-4165-9147-8
1. Harrington, Honor (Fictitious character)—Fiction. 2. Space warfare—Fiction. 3. Women soldiers—Fiction. I. Title.

PS3573.E217S76 2009
813'.54—dc22

                                                         2008042780

10   9   8   7   6   5   4   3   2   1

Pages by Joy Freeman (www.pagesbyjoy.com)
Printed in the United States of America

Always for Sharon.

# Contents

# An Authorial Note

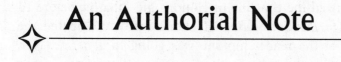

MANY READERS WILL NOTICE that some of the earlier chapters in this book retell, or fill in between, events which occurred in *At All Costs*. The retold material constitutes a very small portion of the entire book, and there is a definite method to my madness in taking this approach.

Once upon a time, in the simpler days of yore when I first began the Honor Harrington series, I hadn't quite visualized the scale of the project upon which I'd embarked. I always knew the story that I wanted to tell, and I'd always intended to arrive at the portion of the story line of which this book is a part. What I *hadn't* really counted on was the degree of detail, the number of characters, and the sheer size of the canvas I was going to end up with.

It isn't often that a writer is blessed with the response the Honor Harrington books have generated. When it happened to me, I was deeply gratified, and that's still true today. I also think that when readers are kind enough to support a series as strongly as these books have been supported, the writer has not only a special relationship with his readers, but also a special responsibility to them. At the same time, when a series extends through as many novels (thirteen, including *Shadow of Saganami* and *Crown of Slaves*) and anthologies, the writer sometimes finds himself forced to consider taking the storyline in directions of which not all of his readers are likely to approve. There's a fine balance between going where you know you *have* to go with a book and worrying about how you meet that special responsibility to your readership. And, to be honest, the Honor books reached that point about two novels ago.

Some of my readers who have spoken to me at conventions know that Honor was supposed to be killed in *At All Costs* under my version of what Mentor of Arisia used to refer to as his "visualization of the cosmic all." I always knew that killing Honor would have been a high-risk move, and that many readers of the series would have been very angry with me, but at the time I'd organized the timeline of Honor's life—that is, before I'd even begun *On Basilisk Station*—I hadn't really anticipated the fierce loyalty of the readership she was going to generate. Nor, for that matter, had I fully realized just how fond *I* was going to become of the character. Nonetheless, I remained steadfastly determined (my wife Sharon will tell you that I can sometimes be just a tad stubborn) to hew to my original plan. The fact that I'd always visualized Honor as being based on Horatio Nelson only reinforced my determination, since the Battle of Manticore was supposed to be the equivalent of his Battle of Trafalgar. Like Nelson, Honor had been supposed to fall in battle at the moment of victory in the climactic battle which saved the Star Kingdom of Manticore and ratified her as the Royal Manticoran Navy's greatest heroine.

At the same time, however, I had always intended to continue writing books in the "Honorverse." The great challenge of the later books was supposed to emerge about twenty-five or thirty years after Honor's death, and the primary viewpoint characters would have been her children, Raoul and Katherine. Unfortunately—or fortunately, depending upon your viewpoint—Eric Flint screwed up my original timetable when he introduced the character of Victor Cachat and asked me for an enemy which Manticoran and Havenite secret agents could agree to fight as allies, despite the fact that their star nations were at war. I suggested Manpower, which worked very well for Eric's story. But, especially when I incorporated Eric's characters into the mainstream novels, and when Eric and I decided to do *Crown of Slaves*, it also pulled the entire storyline forward by two or three decades. Which meant I wasn't going to have time to kill Honor off and get her children grown up before the Manpower challenge hit Manticore.

I wasn't precisely heartbroken when I realized I no longer had any choice about granting Honor a reprieve. Not only did I think her fans would be less likely to come looking for me with pitchforks and ropes, but the closer I'd come to actually killing her, the less and less I'd liked the thought myself.

This still left me with something of a problem, however, since Honor had grown too senior to be sent on any more "death rides." I needed some additional, less senior officers who could become the fresh viewpoint figures on the front lines that Raoul and Katherine had originally been supposed to provide. So, I wrote *Shadow of Saganami*, and it and *Crown of Slaves* were supposed to be the lead books in two separate, subsidiary series. They were supposed to proceed separately from but in parallel with the "main stem" novels in which Honor would continue to be a primary viewpoint character. I actually intended for one of her kids to take the lead in the military portion of the storyline and for the other to become the "spymaster," which would have permitted a logical division of the Honorverse into two separate but related storylines. And these two new series were also supposed to be a device which would allow me to cut down on the amount of "back story" which had to be included in each of those "main stem" books.

To some extent, that original plan continues to hold good, but I've found myself forced to modify it. What I've discovered over the last two or three novels is that incorporating those two subsidiary series much more closely into the main series permits me to advance the story line on a broader front and focus on specific *areas* of the *same* story in separate novels. Thus, *Shadow of Saganami* and *Storm from the Shadows* both focus primarily on the events in and around the Talbott Cluster, and *Crown of Slaves* and *Torch of Freedom* focus on the "covert war" between the two sides and on the moral issues of genetic slavery. And *Mission of Honor*, the next "main stem" book, will weave events from both of those areas together and advance the general storyline towards its final destination. (Which does not now necessarily include the demise of Honor Alexander-Harrington.)

Both *Torch of Freedom* and *Mission of Honor* have been delivered and are currently in the production pipeline, so hopefully readers won't be left too long between books.

One aspect of this new master scheme of mine, however, is

that scenes which have appeared in one book may very well appear—usually from another character's point of view—in another book. This is not an effort simply to increase word count. It is intended to serve the function of more fully developing additional characters, giving different perspectives on the events they observe and participate in, filling in missing details, and—perhaps most importantly of all—nailing down exactly *when* these books' events occur relative to one another.

So far, this seems to be working out fairly well. That doesn't necessarily mean it will continue to do so, or that something won't come along to send me off in yet another direction, but at this moment, I don't expect that to happen. So for the foreseeable future, at least, expect this pattern to continue.

And I suppose I should also warn you that the ride is going to get a lot rougher for the good guys over the next few books.

Take care,

David Weber

# Chapter One

"TALK TO ME, JOHN!"

Rear Admiral Michelle Henke's husky contralto came sharp and crisp as the information on her repeater tactical display shifted catastrophically.

"It's still coming in from the Flag, Ma'am," Commander Oliver Manfredi, Battlecruiser Squadron Eighty-One's golden-haired chief of staff, replied for the squadron's operations officer, Lieutenant Commander John Stackpole. Manfredi was standing behind Stackpole, watching the ops section's more detailed displays, and he had considerably more attention to spare for updates at the moment than Stackpole did. "I'm not sure, but it looks—"

Manfredi broke off, and his jaw clenched. Then his nostrils flared and he squeezed Stackpole's shoulder before he turned his head to look at his admiral.

"It would appear the Peeps have taken Her Grace's lessons to heart, Ma'am," he said grimly. "They've arranged a Sidemore all their own for us."

Michelle looked at him for a moment, and her expression tightened.

"Oliver's right, Ma'am," Stackpole said, looking up from his own display as the changing light codes finally restabilized. "They've got us boxed."

"How bad is it?" she asked.

"They've sent in three separate groups," Stackpole replied. "One dead astern of us, one at polar north, and one at polar south. The Flag is designating the in-system force we already knew about as Bogey One. The task group to system north is Bogey Two; the one to system south is Bogey Three; and the one directly astern is Bogey Four. Our velocity relative to Bogey Four is just over twenty-two thousand kilometers per second, but range is less than thirty-one million klicks."

"Understood."

Michelle looked back at her own, smaller, display. At the moment, it was configured to show the entire Solon System, which meant, by definition, that it was nowhere as detailed as Stackpole's. There wasn't room for that on a plot small enough to deploy from a command chair—not when it was displaying the volume of something the size of a star system, at any rate. But it was more than detailed enough to confirm what Stackpole had just told her. The Peeps had just duplicated exactly what had happened to *them* at the Battle of Sidemore, and managed to do it on a more sophisticated scale, to boot. Unless something reduced Task Force Eighty-Two's rate of acceleration, none of the three forces which had just dropped out of hyperspace to ambush it could hope to overtake it. Unfortunately, they didn't need to physically overtake the task force in order to engage it—not when current-generation Havenite multidrive missiles had a maximum powered range from rest of over sixty million kilometers.

And, of course, there was always the possibility that there was yet *another* Havenite task group waiting in hyper, prepared to drop back into normal space right in their faces as they approached the system hyper limit . . .

*No,* she decided after a moment. *If they had the hulls for a fourth force, it would have already translated in, as well. They'd really have us in a rat trap if they'd been able to box us from four directions. I suppose it's possible that they* do *have another force in reserve—that they decided to double-think us and hold number four until they've had a chance to see which way we run. But that'd be a violation of the KISS principle, and this generation of Peeps doesn't go in much for that sort of thing, damn it.*

She grimaced at the thought, but it was certainly true.

*Honor's been warning us all that* these *Peeps aren't exactly stupid,* she reflected. *Not that any of us should've needed reminding after what they did to us in Thunderbolt! But I could wish that just this once she'd been wrong.*

Her lips twitched in a humorless smile, but she felt herself coming back on balance mentally, and her brain whirred as tactical possibilities and decision trees spilled through it. Not that the primary responsibility was hers. No, that weight rested on the shoulders of her best friend, and despite herself, Michelle was grateful that it *wasn't* hers . . . a fact which made her feel more than a little guilty.

One thing was painfully evident. Eighth Fleet's entire operational strategy for the last three and a half months had been dedicated to convincing the numerically superior navy of the Republic of Haven to redeploy, adopt a more defensive stance while the desperately off-balance Manticoran Alliance got its own feet back under it. Judging by the ambush into which the task force had sailed, that strategy was obviously succeeding. In fact, it looked like it was succeeding entirely too well.

*It was so much easier when we could keep their command teams pruned back . . . or count on State Security to do it for us. Unfortunately, Saint-Just's not around anymore to shoot any admiral whose initiative might make her dangerous to the régime, is he?* Her lips twitched with bitterly sardonic amusement as she recalled the relief with which Manticore's pundits, as well as the woman in the street, had greeted the news of the Committee of Public Safety's final overthrow. *Maybe we were just a little premature about that,* she thought, *since it means that this time around, we don't have anywhere near the same edge in operational experience, and it shows. This batch of Peeps actually knows what it's doing. Damn it.*

"Course change from the Flag, Ma'am," Lieutenant Commander Braga, her staff astrogator announced. "Two-niner-three, zero-zero-five, six-point-zero-one KPS squared."

"Understood," Michelle repeated, and nodded approvingly as the new vector projection stretched itself across her plot and she recognized Honor's intention. The task force was breaking to system south at its maximum acceleration on a course that would take it as far away from Bogey Two as possible while maintaining at least the current separation from Bogey Four. Their new course would still take them deep into the missile envelope of Bogey One, the detachment covering the planet Arthur, whose orbital infrastructure had been the task force's original target. But Bogey One consisted of only two superdreadnoughts and seven battlecruisers, supported by less than two hundred LACs, and from their emissions signatures and maneuvers, Bogey One's wallers were pre-pod designs. Compared to the six obviously modern superdreadnoughts and two LAC carriers in each of the three ambush forces, Bogey One's threat was minimal. Even if all nine of its hyper-capable combatants had heavy pod loads on tow, its older ships would lack the fire control to pose a significant threat to Task Force Eighty-Two's missile defenses. Under the circumstances, it was the same option Michelle would have chosen if she'd been in Honor's shoes.

*I wonder if they've been able to ID her flagship?* Michelle wondered. *It wouldn't have been all that hard, given the news coverage and her "negotiations" in Hera.*

That, too, of course, had been part of the strategy. Putting Admiral Lady Dame Honor Harrington, Duchess and Steadholder Harrington, in command of Eighth Fleet had been a carefully calculated decision on the Admiralty's part. In Michelle's opinion, Honor was obviously the best person for the command anyway, but the appointment had been made in a glare of publicity for the express purpose of letting the Republic of Haven know that "the Salamander" was the person who'd been chosen to systematically demolish its rear-area industry.

*One way to make sure they honored the threat,* Michelle thought wryly as the task force came to its new heading in obedience to the commands emanating from HMS *Imperator,* Honor's SD(P) flagship. *After all, she's been their personal nightmare ever since Basilisk station! But I wonder if they got a fingerprint on Imperator at Hera or Augusta? Probably—they knew which ship she was aboard at Hera, at least. Which probably means they know who it is they've just mousetrapped, too.*

Michelle grimaced at the thought. It was unlikely any Havenite flag officer would have required extra incentive to trash the task force if she could, especially after Eighth Fleet's unbroken string of victories. But knowing whose command they were about to hammer certainly couldn't make them any *less* eager to drive home their attack.

"Missile defense Plan Romeo, Ma'am," Stackpole said. "Formation Charlie."

"Defense only?" Michelle asked. "No orders to roll pods?"

"No, Ma'am. Not yet."

"Thank you."

Michelle's frown deepened thoughtfully. Her own battlecruisers' pods were loaded with Mark 16 dual-drive missiles. That gave her far more missiles per pod, but Mark 16s were both smaller, with lighter laser heads, and shorter-legged than a ship of the wall's multidrive missiles like the Mark 23s aboard Honor's superdreadnoughts. They would have been forced to adopt an attack profile with a lengthy ballistic flight, and the biggest tactical weakness of a pod battlecruiser design was that it simply couldn't carry as many pods as a true capital ship like *Imperator*. It made sense not to waste BCS 81's limited ammunition supply at a range so extended as to guarantee a low percentage of hits, but in Honor's place, Michelle would have been sorely tempted to throw at least a few salvos of all-up MDMs from her two superdreadnoughts back into Bogey Four's face, if only to keep them honest. On the other hand . . .

*Well, she's the four-star admiral, not me. And I suppose*—she smiled again at the tartness of her own mental tone—*that she's demonstrated at least a* modicum *of tactical insight from time to time.*

"Missile separation!" Stackpole announced suddenly. "Multiple missile separations! Estimate twenty-one hundred—two-one-zero-zero—inbound. Time to attack range seven minutes!"

Each of the six Havenite superdreadnoughts in the group which had been designated Bogey Four could roll six pods simultaneously, one pattern every twelve seconds, and each pod contained ten missiles. Given the fact that Havenite fire control systems remained inferior to Manticoran ones, accuracy was going to be poor, to say the least. Which was why the admiral commanding that group had opted to stack six full patterns from each superdreadnought, programmed for staggered launch to bring all of their missiles simultaneously in on their targets. It took seventy-two seconds to deploy them, but then just over a thousand MDMs hurled themselves after Task force Eighty-Two.

Seventy-two seconds after that, a second, equally massive salvo launched. Then a third. A fourth. In the space of just over seven minutes, the Havenites fired just under thirteen thousand missiles—almost a third of Bogey Four's total missile loadout—at the task force's twenty starships.

✧        ✧        ✧

As little as three or four T-years ago, any one of those ava-
lanches of fire would have been lethally effective against so few
targets, and Michelle felt her stomach muscles tightening as the
tempest swept towards her. But this *wasn't* three or four T-years
ago. The Royal Manticoran Navy's missile defense doctrine was
in a constant state of evolution, continually revised in the face
of new threats and the opportunities of new technology, and
it had been vastly improved even in the six months since the
Battle of Marsh. The *Katana*-class LACs deployed to cover the
task force maneuvered to bring their missile launchers to bear
on the incoming fire, but their counter-missiles weren't required
yet. Not in an era when the Royal Navy had developed Keyhole
and the Mark 31 counter-missile.

Each superdreadnought and battlecruiser deployed two Keyhole
control platforms, one through each sidewall, and each of those
platforms had sufficient telemetry links to control the fire of *all* of
its mother ship's counter-missile launchers simultaneously. Equally
important, they allowed the task force's units to roll sideways in
space, interposing the impenetrable shields of their impeller wedges
against the most dangerous threat axes without compromising their
defensive fire control in the least. Each Keyhole also served as a
highly sophisticated electronics warfare platform, liberally provided
with its own close-in point defense clusters, as well. And as an
added bonus, rolling ship gave the platforms sufficient "vertical"
separation to see past the interference generated by the impeller
wedges of subsequent counter-missile salvos, which made it possible to fire those salvos at far tighter intervals than anyone had
ever been able to manage before.

The Havenites hadn't made sufficient allowance for how badly
Keyhole's EW capability was going to affect their attack missiles' accuracy. Worse, they'd anticipated no more than five CM
launches against each of their salvos, and since they'd anticipated
facing only the limited fire control arcs of their fleeing targets'
after hammerheads, they'd allowed for an average of only ten
counter-missiles per ship per launch. Their fire plans had been
based on the assumption that they would face somewhere around
a thousand ship-launched counter-missiles, and perhaps another
thousand or so Mark 31-based Vipers from the *Katanas*.

Michelle Henke had no way of knowing what the enemy's
tactical assumptions might have been, but she was reasonably

certain they hadn't expected to see over *seven* thousand counter-missiles from Honor's starships, alone.

"That's a lot of counter-missiles, Ma'am," Commander Manfredi remarked quietly.

The chief of staff had paused beside Michelle's command chair on his way back to his own command station, and she glanced up at him, one eyebrow quirked.

"I know we've increased our magazine space to accommodate them," he replied to the unspoken question. "Even so, we don't have enough to maintain this volume of defensive fire forever. And they're not exactly inexpensive, either."

*Either we're both confident as hell, or else we're certifiable lunatics with nothing better to do than* pretend *we are so we can impress each other with our steely nerve,* Michelle thought wryly.

"They may not be cheap," she said out loud, returning her attention to her display, "but they're a hell of a lot less expensive than a new ship would be. Not to mention the cost of replacing our own personal hides."

"There is that, Ma'am," Manfredi agreed with a lopsided smile. "There is that."

"And," Michelle continued with a considerably nastier smile of her own as the leading salvo of Havenite MDMs vanished under the weight of the task force's defensive fire, "I'm willing to bet Mark 31s cost one hell of a lot less than all those *attack* missiles did, too."

The second attack salvo followed the first one into oblivion well short of the inner defensive perimeter. So did the third. And the fourth.

"They've ceased fire, Ma'am," Stackpole announced.

"I'm not surprised," Michelle murmured. Indeed, if anything surprised her, it was that the Havenites hadn't ceased fire even sooner. On the other hand, maybe she wasn't being fair to her opponents. It had taken seven minutes for the first salvo to enter engagement range, long enough for six more salvos to be launched on its heels. And the effectiveness of the task force's defenses had surpassed even BuWeaps' estimates. If it had come as as big a surprise to the bad guys as she rather expected it had, it was probably unreasonable to expect the other side to realize instantly just how hard to penetrate that defensive wall was. And the only way they had to measure its toughness was to actually hammer at it with their missiles, of course. Still, she liked to think that it wouldn't have taken a full additional six minutes for *her* to figure out she was throwing good money after bad.

*On the* other *other hand, there are those other nine salvos still on the way*, she reminded herself. *Let's not get too carried away with our own self-confidence, Mike! The last few waves will have had at least a little time to adjust to our EW, won't they? And it only takes one leaker in the wrong place to knock out an alpha node . . . or even some overly optimistic rear admiral's command deck.*

"What do you think they're going to try next, Ma'am?" Manfredi asked as the fifth, sixth, and seventh salvos vanished equally ineffectually.

"Well, they've had a chance now to get a feel for just how tough our new doctrine really is," she replied, leaning back in her command chair, eyes still on her tactical repeater. "If it were me over there, I'd be thinking in terms of a really massive salvo. Something big enough to swamp our defenses by literally running us out of control channels for the CMs, no matter how many of them we have."

"But they couldn't possibly control something that big, either," Manfredi protested.

"We don't *think* they could control something that big," Michelle corrected almost absently, watching the eighth and ninth missile waves being wiped away. "Mind you, I think you're probably right, but we don't have any way of knowing that . . . yet. We could be wrong. And even if we aren't, how much accuracy would they really be giving up at this range, even if they completely cut the control links early and let the birds rely on just their on-board sensors? They wouldn't get very good targeting solutions without shipboard guidance to refine them, but they aren't going to get *good* solutions at this range anyway, whatever they do, and enough *bad* solutions to actually break through are likely to be just a bit more useful than perfect solutions that can't get past their targets' defenses, wouldn't you say?"

"Put that way, I suppose it does make sense," Manfredi agreed, but it was apparent to Michelle that her chief of staff's sense of professionalism was offended by the idea of relying on what was essentially unaimed fire. The notion's sheer crudity clearly said volumes about the competence (or lack thereof) of any navy which had to rely upon it, as far as he was concerned.

Michelle started to twit him for it, then paused with a mental frown. Just how much of a blind spot on Manfredi's part—or on her own, for that matter—did that kind of thinking really represent? Manticoran officers were accustomed to looking down their noses at Havenite technology and the crudity of technique its limitations enforced. But there was nothing wrong with a crude technique if it was also an *effective* one. The Republican Navy had already administered several painful demonstrations of that minor fact, and it was about time officers like Oliver Manfredi—or Michelle Henke, for that matter—stopped letting themselves be surprised each time it happened.

"I didn't say it would be pretty, Oliver." She allowed the merest hint of reprimand into her tone. "But we don't get paid for 'pretty,' do we?"

"No, Ma'am," Manfredi said just a bit more crisply.

"Well, neither do they, I feel fairly confident." She smiled, taking the possible sting out of the sentence. "And let's face it, they're still holding the short and smelly end of the hardware stick. Under the circumstances, they've made damned effective use of the capabilities they have this time around. Remember Admiral Bellefeuille? If you don't, *I* certainly do!" She shook her head wryly. "That woman is *devious*, and she certainly made the best use of everything she had. I'm afraid I don't see any reason to assume the rest of their flag officers won't go right on doing the same thing, unfortunately."

"You're right, Ma'am." Manfredi twitched a smile of his own. "I'll try to bear that in mind next time."

"'Next time,'" Michelle repeated, and chuckled. "I like the implication there, Oliver."

"*Imperator* and *Intolerant* are rolling pods, Ma'am," Stackpole reported.

"Sounds like Her Grace's come to the same conclusion you have, Ma'am," Manfredi observed. "That should be one way to keep them from stacking *too* big a salvo to throw at us!"

"Maybe," Michelle replied.

The great weakness of missile pods was their vulnerability to proximity kills once they were deployed and outside their mother ship's passive defenses, and Manfredi had a point that incoming

Manticoran missiles might well be able to wreak havoc on the Havenite pods. On the other hand, they'd already had time to stack quite a few of them, and it would take Honor's missiles almost eight more minutes to reach their targets across the steadily opening range between the task force and Bogey Four. But at least they were on notice that those missiles were coming.

The Havenite commander didn't wait for the task force's fire to reach him. In fact, he fired at almost the same instant Honor's first salvo launched against *him*, and whereas Task Force Eighty-Two had fired just under three hundred missiles at him, he fired the next best thing to eleven thousand in reply.

"Damn," Commander Manfredi said almost mildly as the enemy returned more than thirty-six missiles for each one TF 82 had just fired at him, then shook his head and glanced at Michelle. "Under normal circumstances, Ma'am, it's reassuring to work for a boss who's good at reading the other side's mind. Just this once, though, I really wish you'd been wrong."

"You and I, both," Michelle replied. She studied the data side-bars for several seconds, then turned her command chair to face Stackpole.

"Is it my imagination, John, or does their fire control seem just a bit better than it ought to be?"

"I'm afraid you're not imagining things, Ma'am," Stackpole replied grimly. "It's a single salvo, all right, and it's going to come in as a single wave. But they've divided it into several 'clumps,' and the clumps appear to be under tighter control than *I* would have antici-pated out of them. If I had to guess, I'd say they've spread them to clear their telemetry paths to each clump and they're using rotating control links, jumping back and forth between each group."

"They'd need a lot more bandwidth than they've shown so far," Manfredi said. It wasn't a disagreement with Stackpole, only thoughtful, and Michelle shrugged.

"Probably," she said. "But maybe not, too. We don't know enough about what they're doing to decide that."

"Without it, they're going to be running the risk of completely dropping control linkages in mid-flight," Manfredi pointed out.

"Probably," Michelle repeated. This was no time, she decided, to mention certain recent missile fire control developments Sonja Hemphill and BuWeaps were pursuing. Besides, Manfredi was right.

"On the other hand," she continued, "this salvo is five times the size of anything they've tried before, isn't it? Even if they dropped twenty-five or thirty percent of them, it would still be a hell of a lot heavier weight of fire."

"Yes, Ma'am," Manfredi agreed, and smiled crookedly. "More of those bad solutions you were talking about before."

"Exactly," Michelle said grimly as the oncoming torrent of Havenite missiles swept into the outermost counter-missile zone.

"It looks like they've decided to target us this time, too, Ma'am," Stackpole said, and she nodded.

TF 82's opening missile salvo reached its target first.

Unlike the Havenites, Duchess Harrington had opted to concentrate all of her fire on a single target, and Bogey Four's missile defenses opened fire as the Manticoran MDMs swept towards it. The Manticoran electronic warfare platforms scattered among the attack missiles carried far more effective penetration aids than anything the Republic of Haven had, but Haven's defenses had improved even more radically than Manticore's since the last war. They remained substantially inferior to the Star Kingdom's in absolute terms, but the relative improvement was still enormous, and the gap between TF 82's performance and what *they* could achieve was far narrower than it once would have been. Shannon Foraker's "layered defense" couldn't count on the same sort of accuracy and technological sophistication Manticore could produce, so it depended on sheer weight of fire, instead. And an incredible storm front of counter-missiles raced to meet the threat, fired from the starships' escorting LACs, as well as from the superdreadnoughts themselves. There was so much wedge interference that anything resembling precise control of all that defensive fire was impossible, but with so many counter-missiles in space simultaneously, some of them simply *had* to hit something.

They did. In fact, they hit quite a few "somethings." Of the two hundred and eighty-eight MDMs *Intolerant* and *Imperator* had fired at RHNS *Conquete*, the counter-missiles killed a hundred and thirty-two, and then it was the laser clusters' turn. Each of those clusters had time for only a single shot each, given the missiles' closing speed. At sixty-two percent of light-speed, it took barely half a second from the instant they entered the laser clusters' range for the Manticoran laser heads to reach their own attack range of *Conquete*. But there were literally thousands of those clusters aboard the superdreadnoughts and their escorting *Cimeterre*-class light attack craft.

Despite everything the superior Manticoran EW could do, Shannon Foraker's defensive doctrine worked. Only eight of TF 82's missiles survived to attack their target. Two of them detonated late, wasting their power on the roof of *Conquete*'s impenetrable impeller wedge. The other six detonated between fifteen and twenty thousand kilometers off the ship's port bow, and massive bomb-pumped lasers punched brutally through her sidewall.

Alarms screamed aboard the Havenite ship as armor shattered, weapons—and the men and women who manned them—were wiped out of existence, and atmosphere streamed from *Conquete*'s lacerated flanks. But superdreadnoughts were designed to survive precisely that kind of damage, and the big ship didn't even falter. She maintained her position in Bogey Four's defensive formation, and her counter-missile launchers were already firing against TF 82's second salvo.

"It looks like we got at least a few through, Ma'am," Stackpole reported, his eyes intent as the studied the reports coming back from the FTL Ghost Rider reconnaissance platforms.

"Good," Michelle replied. Of course, "a few" hits probably hadn't done a lot more than scratch their target's paint, but she could always hope, and some damage was a hell of a lot better than no damage at all. Unfortunately . . .

"And here comes their reply," Manfredi muttered. Which, Michelle thought, was something of an . . . understatement.

Six hundred of the Havenite MDMs had simply become lost and wandered away, demonstrating the validity of Manfredi's prediction about dropped control links. But that was less than six percent of the total . . . which demonstrated the accuracy of Michelle's counterpoint.

The task force's counter-missiles killed almost nine thousand of the missiles which *didn't* get lost, and the last-ditch fire of the task force's laser clusters and the *Katana*-class LACs killed nine hundred more.

Which left "only" three hundred and seventy-two.

Five of them attacked *Ajax*.

Captain Diego Mikhailov rolled ship, twisting his command farther over onto her side relative to the incoming fire, fighting to interpose the defensive barrier of his wedge, and the sensor reach of his Keyhole platforms gave him a marked maneuver advantage, as well as improving his fire control. He could see threats more clearly and from a greater range, which gave him more time to react to them, and most of the incoming X-ray lasers wasted themselves against the floor of his wedge. One of the attacking missiles managed to avoid that fate, however. It swept past *Ajax* and detonated less than five thousand kilometers from her port sidewall.

The battlecruiser twitched as two of the missile's lasers blasted through that sidewall. By the nature of things, battlecruiser armor was far thinner than superdreadnoughts could carry, and Havenite laser heads were heavier than matching Manticoran weapons as a deliberate compensation for their lower base accuracy. Battle steel shattered and alarms howled. Patches of ominous crimson appeared on the damage control schematics, yet given the original size of that mighty salvo, *Ajax*'s actual damage was remarkably light.

"Two hits, Ma'am," Stackpole announced. "We've lost Graser Five and a couple of point defense clusters, and Medical reports seven wounded."

Michelle nodded. She hoped none of those seven crewmen were badly wounded. No one ever liked to take casualties, but at the same time, only seven—none of them fatal, so far at least—was an almost incredibly light loss rate.

"The rest of the squadron?" she asked sharply.

"Not a scratch, Ma'am!" Manfredi replied jubilantly from his own command station, and Michelle felt herself beginning to smile. But then—

"Multiple hits on both SDs," Stackpole reported in a much grimmer voice, and Michelle's smile died stillborn. "*Imperator*'s lost two or three grasers, but she's essentially intact."

"And *Intolerant*?" Michelle demanded harshly when the ops officer paused.

"Not good," Manfredi replied as the information scrolled across his display from the task force data net. "She must have taken two or three dozen hits . . . and at least one of them blew straight into the missile core. She's got heavy casualties, Ma'am, including Admiral Morowitz and most of his staff. And it looks like all of her pod rails are down."

"The Flag is terminating the missile engagement, Ma'am," Stackpole said quietly.

He looked up from his display to meet her eyes, and she nodded in bitter understanding. The task force's sustainable long-range firepower had just been cut in half. Not even Manticoran fire control was going to accomplish much at the next best thing to two light-minutes with salvoes the size a single SD(P) could throw, and Honor wasn't going to waste ammunition trying to do the impossible.

*Which, unfortunately, leaves the question of just what we are going to do wide open, doesn't it?* she thought.

Several minutes passed, and Michelle listened to the background flow of clipped, professional voices as her staff officers and their assistants continued refining their assessment of what had just happened. It wasn't getting much better, she reflected, watching the data bars shift as more detailed damage reports flowed in.

As Manfredi had already reported, her own squadron—aside from her flagship—had suffered no damage at all, but it was beginning to look as if Stackpole's initial assessment of HMS *Intolerant*'s damages had actually been optimistic.

"Admiral," Lieutenant Kaminski said suddenly. Michelle turned towards her staff communications officer, one eyebrow raised. "Duchess Harrington wants to speak to you," he said.

"Put her through," Michelle said quickly, and turned back to her own small com screen. A familiar, almond-eyed face appeared upon it almost instantly.

"Mike," Honor Alexander-Harrington began without preamble, her crisp, Sphinxian accent only a shade more pronounced than usual, "*Intolerant*'s in trouble. Her missile defenses are way below par, and we're headed into the planetary pods' envelope. I know *Ajax*'s taken a few licks of her own, but I want your squadron moved out on our flank. I need to interpose your point defense between *Intolerant* and Arthur. Are you in shape for that?"

"Of course we are." Henke nodded vigorously. Putting something as fragile as a battlecruiser between a wounded superdreadnought and a planet surrounded by missile pods wasn't something to be approached lightly. On the other hand, screening ships of the wall was one of the functions battlecruisers had been designed to fulfill, and at least, given the relative dearth of missile pods their scouts had reported in Arthur orbit, they wouldn't be looking at another missile hurricane like the one which had just roared through the task force.

"*Ajax*'s the only one who's been kissed," Michelle continued, "and our damage is all pretty much superficial. None of it'll have any effect on our missile defense."

"Good! Andrea and I will shift the LACs as well, but they've expended a lot of CMs." Honor shook her head. "I didn't think they could stack that many pods without completely saturating their own fire control. It looks like we're going to have to rethink a few things."

"That's the nature of the beast, isn't it?" Michelle responded with a shrug. "We live and learn."

"Those of us fortunate enough to survive," Honor agreed, a bit grimly. "All right, Mike. Get your people moving. Clear."

"Clear," Michelle acknowledged, then turned her chair to face Stackpole and Braga. "You heard the lady," she said. "Let's get them moving."

BCS 81 moved out on Task force Eighty-Two's flank as the Manticoran force continued accelerating steadily away from its pursuers. The final damage reports came in, and Michelle grimaced as she considered how the task force's commanding officer was undoubtedly feeling about those reports. She'd known Honor Harrington since Honor had been a tall, skinny first-form midshipwoman at Saganami Island. It wasn't Honor's fault the Havenites had managed to mousetrap her command, but that wasn't going to matter. Not to Honor Harrington. Those were her ships which had been damaged, her people who had been killed, and at this moment, Michelle Henke knew, she was feeling the hits her task force had taken as if every one of them had landed directly on her.

*No, that isn't what she's feeling*, Michelle told herself. *What she's doing right now is wishing that every one of them* had *landed on her, and she's not going to forgive herself for walking into this. Not for a long time, if I know her. But she's not going to let it affect her decisions, either.*

She shook her head. It was a pity Honor was so much better at forgiving her subordinates for disasters she knew perfectly well weren't their fault than she was at forgiving herself. Unfortunately, it was too late to change her now.

*And, truth to tell, I don't think any of us would want to go screwing around* trying *to change her*, Michelle thought wryly.

"We'll be entering the estimated range of Arthur's pods in another thirty seconds, Ma'am," Stackpole said quietly, breaking in on her thoughts.

"Thank you." Michelle shook herself, then settled herself more solidly into her command chair.

"Stand by missile defense," she said.

The seconds trickled by, and then—

"Missile launch!" Stackpole announced. "Multiple missile launches, *multiple sources!*"

His voice sharpened with the last two words, and Michelle's head snapped around.

"Estimate seventeen thousand, Ma'am!"

"Repeat that!" Michelle snapped, certain for an instant that she must have misunderstood him somehow.

"CIC says seventeen thousand, Ma'am," Stackpole told her harshly, turning to look at her. "Time to attack range, seven minutes."

Michelle stared at him while her mind tried to grapple with the impossible numbers. The remote arrays deployed by the task force's pre-attack scout ships had detected barely four hundred pods in orbit around Arthur. That should have meant a maximum of only *four* thousand missiles, so where the hell—?

"We've got at least thirteen thousand coming in from Bogey One," Stackpole said, as if he'd just read her mind. His tone was more than a little incredulous, and her own eyes widened in shock. That was even more preposterous. Two superdreadnoughts and seven battlecruisers couldn't possibly have the fire control for that many missiles, even if they'd all been pod designs!

"How could—?" someone began.

"Those aren't *battlecruisers*," Oliver Manfredi said suddenly. "They're frigging *minelayers!*"

Michelle understood him instantly, and her mouth tightened in agreement. Just like the Royal Manticoran Navy, the Republic of Haven built its fast minelayers on battlecruiser hulls. And Manfredi was undoubtedly correct. Instead of normal loads of mines, those ships had been stuffed to the deckhead with missile pods. The whole time they'd been sitting there, watching the task force flee away from Bogey Four and directly towards *them*, they'd been rolling those pods, stacking them into the horrendous salvo which had just come screaming straight at TF 82.

"Well," she said, hearing the harshness in her own voice, "now we understand how they did it. Which still leaves us with the little problem of what we do *about* it. Execute Hotel, John!"

"Defense Plan Hotel, aye, Ma'am," Stackpole acknowledged,

and orders began to stream out from HMS *Ajax* to the rest of her squadron.

Michelle watched her plot. There wasn't time for her to adjust her formation significantly, but she'd already set up for Hotel, even though it had seemed unlikely the Havenites' fire could be heavy enough to require it. Her ships' primary responsibility was to protect *Intolerant*. Looking out for themselves came fairly high on their list of priorities as well, of course, but the superdreadnought represented more combat power—and almost as much total tonnage—as her entire squadron combined. That was why Missile Defense Plan Hotel had stacked her battlecruisers vertically in space, like a mobile wall between the planet Arthur and *Intolerant*. They were perfectly placed to intercept the incoming fire . . . which, unfortunately, meant that they were completely exposed *to* that fire, as well.

"Signal from the Flag, Ma'am," Stackpole said suddenly. "Fire Plan Gamma."

"Acknowledged. Execute Fire Plan Gamma," Michelle said tersely.

"Aye, aye, Ma'am. Executing Fire Plan Gamma," Stackpole said, and Battlecruiser Squadron Eighty-One began to roll pods at last.

It wasn't going to be much of a response compared to the amount of fire coming at the task force, but Michelle felt her lips drawing back from her teeth in satisfaction anyway. The gamma sequence Honor and her tactical staff had worked out months ago was designed to coordinate the battlecruisers' shorter-legged Mark 16s with the superdreadnoughts' MDMs. It would take a Mark 16 over thirteen minutes to reach Bogey One, as compared to the *seven* minutes one of *Imperator*'s Mark 23s would require. Both missiles used fusion-powered impeller drives, but there was no physical way to squeeze three complete drives into the smaller missile's tighter dimensions, which meant it simply could not accelerate as long as its bigger brother.

So, under Fire Plan Gamma *Imperator*'s first half-dozen patterns of pod-launched Mark 23s' drive settings had been stepped down to match those of the *Agamemnons*' less capable missiles. It let the task force put six salvos of almost three hundred mixed Mark 16 and Mark 23 missiles each into space before the superdreadnought began firing hundred-and-twenty-bird salvos at the Mark 23's maximum power settings.

*All of which is very fine*, Michelle thought grimly, watching the icons of the attack missiles go streaking away from the task force. *Unfortunately, it doesn't do much about the birds they've already launched.*

As if to punctuate her thought, *Ajax* began to quiver with the sharp vibration of outgoing waves of *counter*-missiles as her launchers went to sustained rapid fire.

The Grayson-designed *Katana*-class LACs were firing, as well, sending their own counter-missiles screaming to meet the attack, but no one in her worst nightmare had ever envisioned facing a single salvo this massive.

"It's coming through, Ma'am," Manfredi said quietly.

She looked back up from her plot, and her lips tightened as she saw him standing beside her command chair once more. Given what was headed towards them at the moment, he really ought to have been back in the shock frame and protective armored shell of his own chair. *And he damned well* knows *it, too*, she thought in familiar, sharp-edged irritation. But he'd always been a roamer, and she'd finally given up yelling at him for it. He was one of those people who *needed* to move around to keep their brains running at the maximum possible RPM. Now his voice was too low pitched for anyone else to have heard as he gazed down into her repeater plot with her, but his eyes were bleak.

"Of course it is," she replied, equally quietly. The task force simply didn't have the firepower to stop that many missiles in the time available to it.

"How the *hell* are they managing to control that many birds?" Manfredi continued, never looking away from the plot. "Look at that pattern. Those aren't blind-fired shots; they're under tight control, for now at least. So where in hell did they find that many control channels?"

"Don't have a clue," Michelle admitted, her tone almost absent as she watched the defenders' fire ripping huge holes in the cloud of incoming missiles. "I think we'd better figure it out, though. Don't you?"

"You've got that right, Ma'am," he agreed with a mirthless smile.

No one in Task force Eighty-Two—or anyone in the rest of the Royal Manticoran Navy, for that matter—had ever heard of the control system Shannon Foraker had dubbed "Moriarty" after a pre-space fictional character. If they had, and if they'd understood the reference, they probably would have agreed that it was appropriate, however.

One thing of which no one would ever be able to accuse Foraker was thinking small. Faced with the problem of controlling a big enough missile salvo to break through the steadily improving Manticoran missile defenses, she'd been forced to accept that Havenite ships of the wall, even the latest podnoughts, simply lacked the necessary fire control channels. So, she'd set out to solve the problem. Unable to match the technological capability to shoehorn the control systems she needed into something like Manticore's Keyhole, she'd simply accepted that she had to build something bigger. *Much* bigger. And while she'd been at it, she'd decided, she might as well figure out how to integrate that "something bigger" into an entire star system's defenses.

Moriarty was the answer she'd come up with. It consisted of remotely deployed platforms which existed for the sole purpose of providing telemetry relays and control channels. They were distributed throughout the entire volume of space inside Solon's hyper limit, and every one of them reported to a single control station which was about the size of a heavy cruiser . . . and contained nothing except the very best fire control computers and software the Republic of Haven could build.

She couldn't do anything about the light-speed limitations of the control channels themselves, but she'd finally found a way to provide enough of those channels to handle truly massive salvos. In fact, although TF 82 had no way of knowing it, the wave of missiles coming at it was less than half of Moriarty's maximum capacity.

Of course, even if the task force's tactical officers had known that, they might have felt less than completely grateful, given the weight of fire which *was* coming at them.

Michelle never knew how many of the incoming missiles were destroyed short of their targets, or how many simply got lost, despite all Moriarty could do, and wandered off or acquired targets other than the ones they'd originally been assigned. It was obvious that the task force's defenses managed to stop an enormous percentage of them. Unfortunately, it was even more obvious that they hadn't stopped *enough* of them.

Hundreds of them hurled themselves at the LACs—not because anyone had wanted to waste MDMs on something as small as a LAC, but because missiles which had lost their original targets as they spread beyond the reach of Moriarty's light-speed commands had acquired them, instead. LACs, and especially Manticoran and Grayson LACs, were very difficult for missiles to hit. Which was not to say that they were *impossible* to hit, however, and over two hundred of them were blown out of space as the tornado of missiles ripped into the task force.

Most of the rest of Moriarty's missiles had been targeted on the two superdreadnoughts, and they howled in on their targets like demons. Captain Rafe Cardones maneuvered Honor's flagship as if the stupendous superdreadnought were a heavy cruiser, twisting around to interpose his wedge while jammers and decoys joined with laser clusters in a last-ditch, point-blank defense. *Imperator* shuddered and bucked as laser heads blasted through her sidewalls, but despite grievous wounds, she actually got off lightly. Not even her massive armor was impervious to such a concentrated rain of destruction, but it did its job, preserving her core hull and essential systems intact, and her human casualties were minuscule in proportion to the amount of fire scorching in upon her.

*Intolerant* was less fortunate.

The earlier damage to *Imperator*'s sister ship was simply too severe. She'd lost both of her Keyholes and all too many of her counter-missile launchers and laser clusters in the last attack. Her sensors had been battered, leaving holes in her own close-in coverage, and her electronic warfare systems were far below par. She was simply the biggest, most visible, most vulnerable target in the entire task force, and despite everything BCS 81 could do, droves of myopic end-of-run Havenite MDMs hurled themselves at the clearest target they could see.

The superdreadnought was trapped at the heart of a maelstrom of detonating laser heads, hurling X-ray lasers like vicious harpoons. They slammed into her again and again and again, ripping and maiming, tearing steadily deeper while the big ship shuddered and bucked in agony. And then, finally, one of those lasers found something fatal and HMS *Intolerant* and her entire company vanished into a glaring fireball.

Nor did she die alone.

✧　　✧　　✧

HMS *Ajax* heaved indescribably as the universe went mad.

Compared to the torrent of fire streaming in on the two super-dreadnoughts, only a handful of missiles attacked the battlecruisers. But that "handful" was still numbered in the hundreds, and they were much more fragile targets. Alarms screamed as deadly lasers ripped deep into far more lightly armored hulls, and the *Agamemnon*-class were podlayers. They had the hollow cores of their type, and that made them even more fragile than other, older battlecruisers little more than half their size. Michelle had always wondered if that aspect of their design was as great a vulnerability as the BC(P)'s critics had always contended.

It looked like they—and she—were about to find out.

Oliver Manfredi was hurled from his feet as *Ajax* lurched, and Michelle felt her command chair's shock frame hammering viciously at her. Urgent voices, high-pitched and distorted despite the professionalism trained bone-deep into their owners, filled the com channels with messages of devastation—announcements of casualties, of destroyed systems, which ended all too often in mid-syllable as death came for the men and women making those reports.

Even through the pounding, Michelle saw the icons of both of her second division's ships—*Priam* and *Patrocles*—disappear abruptly from her plot, and other icons disappeared or flashed critical damage codes throughout the task force's formation. The light cruisers *Fury*, *Buckler*, and *Atum* vanished in glaring flashes of destruction, and the heavy cruisers *Star Ranger* and *Blackstone* were transformed into crippled hulks, coasting onward ballistically without power or impeller wedges. And then—

"Direct hit on the command deck!" one of Stackpole's ratings announced. "No survivors, Sir! Heavy damage to Boat Bay Two, and Boat Bay One's been completely destroyed! Engineering reports—"

Michelle felt it in her own flesh as HMS *Ajax* faltered suddenly.

"We've lost the after ring, Ma'am!" Stackpole said harshly. "*All* of it."

Michelle bit the inside of her lower lip so hard she tasted blood. Solon lay in the heart of a hyper-space gravity wave. No ship could enter, navigate, or long survive in a gravity wave without both Warshawski sails . . . and without the after impeller ring's alpha nodes, *Ajax* could no longer generate an after sail.

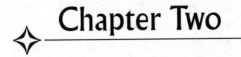

# Chapter Two

"IT'S HER GRACE, MA'AM," Lieutenant Kaminski said quietly, and Michelle stood, rising from where she'd knelt on the decksole beside the sick-berth attendant working on an unconscious Manfredi.

"I'll take it there, Albert," she said, crossing quickly to the communications officer's station. She leaned over his shoulder, looking into the pickup, and saw Honor on the display.

"How bad is it, Mike?" Honor asked quickly.

"That's an interesting question." Michelle managed a twisted smile. "Captain Mikhailov is dead, and things are . . . a bit confused over here, just now. Our rails and pods are still intact, and our fire control looks pretty good, but our point defense and energy armament took a real beating. The worst of it seems to be the after impeller ring, though. It's completely down."

"Can you restore it?" Honor asked urgently.

"We're working on it. The good news is that the damage appears to be in the control runs; the nodes themselves look like they're still intact, including the Alphas. The bad news is that we've got one hell of a lot of structural damage aft, and just locating where the runs are broken is going to be a copperplated bitch."

"Can you get her out?" Honor's voice was suddenly softer as she asked the only question that really mattered, and Michelle looked into best friend's eyes for perhaps three heartbeats, then shrugged.

"I don't know," she admitted. "Frankly, it doesn't look good, but

I'm not prepared to just write her off yet. Besides," she managed another smile, "we can't abandon very well."

"What do you mean?" Honor demanded quickly.

"Both boat bays are trashed, Honor. The bosun says she thinks she can get the after bay cleared, but it's going to take at least a half-hour. Without that—"

Michelle shrugged, wondering if she looked as stricken as Honor did. Not that Honor's expression would have given anything away to most people, but Michelle knew her too well.

They looked at one another for several seconds, neither of them willing to say what they both knew. Without at least one functional boat bay, small craft couldn't dock with *Ajax* to take her crew off, and she carried enough emergency life pods for a little more than half her total complement. There wasn't much point in carrying more than that, since only half her battle stations were close enough to the skin of her hull to make a life pod practical.

And her flag bridge was far too deeply buried to be one of them.

"Mike, I—"

Honor's voice seemed to fray around the edges, and Michelle shook her head quickly.

"Don't say it," she said, almost gently. "If we can get the after ring back, we can probably play hide and seek with anything heavy enough to kill us. If we *don't* get it back, we're not getting out. It's that simple, Honor. And you know as well as I do that you can't hold the rest of the task force back to cover us. Not with Bogey Three still closing. Even just hanging around for a half-hour while we try to make repairs would bring you into their envelope, and your missile defense has been shot to shit."

She could see it in Honor's eyes. See that Honor wanted to argue, to protest. But she couldn't.

"You're right," she said quietly. "I wish you weren't, but you are."

"I know." Michelle's lips twitched again. "And at least we're in better shape than *Necromancer*," she observed. "Although I think her boat bays are at least intact."

"Well, yes," Honor said. "There is that minor difference. Rafe's coordinating the evacuation of her personnel now."

"Good for Rafe," Michelle replied.

"Break north," Honor told her. "I'm going to drop our acceleration for about fifteen minutes."

Michelle opened her mouth to protest, but Honor shook her head quickly.

"Only fifteen minutes, Mike. If we go back to the best acceleration we can sustain at that point and maintain heading, we'll still scrape past Bogey Three at least eighty thousand kilometers outside its powered missile range."

"That's cutting it too close, Honor!" Michelle said sharply.

"No," Honor said flatly, "it isn't, Admiral Henke. And not just because *Ajax* is your ship. There are seven hundred and fifty *other* men and women aboard her."

Michelle started to protest again, then stopped, inhaled sharply, and nodded. She still didn't like it, still suspected that Honor's friendship for her was affecting the other woman's judgment. But it was also possible that that same friendship was affecting her *own* judgment, and Honor was right about how many other people were at risk aboard *Ajax*.

"When they see our accel drop, they'll have to act on the assumption *Imperator* has enough impeller damage to slow the rest of the task force," Honor continued. "Bogey Three should continue to pursue *us* on that basis. If you can get the after ring back within the next forty-five minutes to an hour, you should still be able to stay clear of Bogey Two, and Bogey One is pretty much scrap metal at this point. But if you don't get it back—"

"If we don't get it back, we can't get into hyper anyway," Michelle interrupted her. "I think it's the best we can do, Honor. Thank you."

Honor's mouth tightened on Michelle's com screen, but she only nodded.

"Give Beth my best, just in case," Michelle added.

"Do it yourself," Honor shot back.

"I will, of course," Michelle said. Then, more softly, "Take care, Honor."

"God bless, Mike," Honor said equally quietly. "Clear."

"Ma'am, it's Commander Horn," Lieutenant Kaminski said quietly. Commander Manfredi had been taken off to sickbay, and the communications officer had taken over Manfredi's duties as chief of staff. He was scarcely the most senior of her staffers still on his feet, but his official duties left him with the least to do, under the circumstances . . . and it wasn't as if Michelle any longer had a squadron which really needed a chief of staff.

"Thanks, Al," she said, and turned quickly to her own com screen as a face materialized upon it.

Commander Alexandra Horn was a stocky, short-haired, gray-eyed brunette. She'd been HMS *Ajax*'s executive officer, up until the moment the death of Diego Mikhailov and every other officer and rating who'd been on his command deck changed that. Now she was the ship's commanding officer, and behind her, Henke could see the backup command crew in the battlecruiser's Auxiliary Control, located at the far end of *Ajax*'s core hull from her normal command deck, as they bent over their command stations, working frantically.

"Yes, Alex?"

"Admiral," Horn's voice was hoarse, her face tight with strain and fatigue, "I think it's time to start evacuating everyone who has access to a life pod."

Michelle felt her own face turn masklike, but managed to hold her voice to an almost normal conversational pitch.

"It's that bad, is it?" she asked.

"Maybe worse than that, Ma'am." Horn rubbed her eyes for a moment, then looked back out of the display at Michelle. "There's just too much wreckage in the way. God only knows how all four rails can still be up, because we've got breaches clear through to the missile core in at least four places. Maybe as many as six. Commander Tigh still can't even tell us where the control runs are broken, much less when he might be able to get the after ring back up."

*Well, that seems to be a fairly emphatic answer to the great fragility debate, doesn't it, Mike?* a small voice said in the back of Michelle's head. *Under the circumstances, it's a mystery to me why we didn't go up right along with* Patrocles *and* Priam. *What was that phrase Honor used? "Eggshells armed with sledgehammers," wasn't it? Of course, she was talking about LACs at the time, not battlecruisers, but still . . .*

She gazed at the other woman for several seconds while her mind raced down the same logic trees Horn must already have worked through. Lieutenant Commander William Tigh was *Ajax*'s chief engineer, and she knew he and his damage control crews had been prying, battering, and cutting their way through the wreckage aft of midships in their frantic search for the damage which had taken the after alpha nodes off-line. She couldn't say she was particularly surprised by what Horn had just told her, but that didn't make the news one bit more welcome.

Nor could she misunderstand what Horn was thinking now. They couldn't afford to let the technology aboard *Ajax* fall into Havenite hands. Haven had captured more than enough examples of Manticoran weapons and electronics tech at the outbreak of the war, but the systems aboard *Ajax* and her sisters now were substantially more advanced than anything they might have captured then, and the Alliance had already suffered graphic evidence of just how quickly Haven had managed to put anything they'd captured to good use. The Navy had built in the very best safeguards it could to make sure that as little as possible of that tech would be recoverable if a ship was lost, and virtually all of her molycircs could be wiped with the entry of the proper command codes, but no possible system was perfect. And if Tigh couldn't get the after ring back on-line, there was only one way to prevent *Ajax* and everything aboard her from falling into Havenite hands.

"What about the after boat bay?" Michelle asked after several moments.

"The Bosun's still working at clearing away the wreckage, Ma'am. At the moment, it looks like it's a horse race—at best."

Michelle nodded in understanding. Master Chief Alice MaGuire was *Ajax*'s boatswain, her senior noncommissioned officer. At the moment, MaGuire and her own repair teams were laboring with frantic discipline to get at least one of the battlecruiser's boat bay's operational again. Unless they could manage to do that, there was no way anyone without an operational life pod was getting off the ship.

Technically, the decision was now Horn's, not Michelle's. The commander was *Ajax*'s captain; what happened to her ship and her crew was her responsibility, not that of the admiral who simply happened to be aboard at the moment. Nor did Michelle think for a moment that Horn was trying to get her to take the weight of decision off of the other woman's shoulders. Which wasn't quite the same thing as saying she wouldn't be grateful for any advice Michelle might be able to contribute.

"Assuming you get the pods off, will you still have enough personnel to fight the ship?" she asked quietly.

"I'm afraid the answer to that question is yes, Ma'am," Horn said bitterly. "We'll lose most of our on-mount backup crews for the energy weapons and point defense clusters, but none of our remaining mounts are in local control at the moment, anyway. And, of course, our rails won't be affected at all. Within those limits, we'll still have more people than we need to fight her."

Michelle nodded again. The on-mount crews were there primarily to take over the weapons should they be cut off from the centralized control of the tactical officer on the ship's command deck. The probability that they'd be able to do any good—especially against the threat which had been rumbling steadily towards *Ajax* at almost twice the lamed battlecruiser's current maximum acceleration ever since Bogey Two abandoned its pursuit of the rest of the task force—was minute. The ship's primary armament, her missile pods, on the other hand, were buried deep at her core. The men and women responsible for overseeing *them* were much too far inside the core hull for any possible life pod to carry them to safety.

What it really came down to, Michelle thought sadly, was the fact that it was now too late to save the ship even if Tigh somehow managed to get the after ring back. They'd lost too much lead on Bogey Two. In less than twenty minutes, those six modern superdreadnoughts were going to enter their own MDM range from *Ajax*. When they did that, the ship was going to die, one way or the other. The only way to prevent that would have been to surrender her to the enemy, which would just happen to hand all of that invaluable technological data and examples of modern systems over to Haven.

*I wonder if Horn's cold-blooded enough to give the scuttle order? Could she really order the ship blown up knowing over half her crew would go with her?*

The fact that no court of inquiry or court-martial convened in Manticore would ever condemn her for honorably surrendering her vessel made the commander's dilemma even more hellish. For that matter, if she *didn't* surrender—if she went ahead and destroyed her own ship, with so many of her people still aboard—her name would undoubtedly be vilified by any number of people who hadn't been there, hadn't had to face the same decision or make the same call.

*But she's not going to have to do that*, Michelle thought almost calmly. *If she tries to fight that much firepower, the Peeps will take care of it for her.*

"If your ship will still be combat capable, Captain," she said formally to Horn, "then by all means, I concur. Given the tactical situation, evacuating everyone you can by pod is clearly the right decision."

"Thank you, Ma'am," Horn said softly. The decision had been hers, but her gratitude for Michelle's concurrence was both obvious and deep. Then she drew a deep breath. "If you and your staff will evacuate Flag Bridge now, Ma'am, there'll be time—"

"No, Captain," Michelle interrupted quietly. Horn looked at her, and she shook her head. "Those pods will be used by the personnel assigned to them or closest to them at the moment the evacuation order is given," Michelle continued steadily.

For a moment, she thought Horn was going to argue. For that matter, Horn had the authority to *order* Michelle and her staff off the ship, and to use force to accomplish that end, if necessary. But as she looked into the commander's eyes, she saw that Horn understood. If Michelle Henke's flagship was going to die with people trapped aboard it, then she was going to be one of those people. It made absolutely no sense from any logical perspective, but that didn't matter.

"Yes, Ma'am," Horn said, and produced something almost like a smile. "Now, if you'll excuse me, Admiral, I have some orders to issue," she said.

"By all means, Captain. Clear."

"You know," Lieutenant Commander Stackpole said, "I know we're pretty much screwed, Ma'am, but I really would like to take some of them with us."

There was something remarkably like whimsy in his tone, and Michelle wondered if he was aware of that . . . or how ironic it was.

Ironic or not, a part of her agreed with him. Bogey Two had continued its pursuit of the rest of the task force only until it became obvious that it would be impossible to overtake *Imperator* and the other ships in company with her. At that point, Bogey Two—*all* of Bogey Two—had altered course to pursue *Ajax*, instead, with acceleration advantage of almost 2.5 $KPS^2$. Thanks to her own damage, and the fact that Bogey Two had been able to begin cutting the chord of *Ajax*'s course after abandoning the pursuit of the rest of the task force, the pursuing Havenites had already been able to build a velocity advantage of over two thousand KPS. With that sort of overtake velocity and such an acceleration advantage over a ship which couldn't escape into hyper even if she managed to get across the hyper limit before she was intercepted, this chase could have only one outcome.

Maximum range for Havenite MDMs was just under sixty-one million kilometers, and the range was already down to little more than sixty-three million. It wouldn't be long now, unless . . .

"You know," Michelle said, "I wonder just how close these people are willing to come before they pull the trigger?"

"Well, they must know we've loaded our battlecruiser pods with Mark 16s," Stackpole pointed out, turning to look over his shoulder at her. "I can't believe they'd be interested in coming into *our* range!"

"I certainly wouldn't be, in their place," Michelle agreed. "Still, their hard numbers on the Mark 16's performance have to be a little iffy. Oh," she waved one hand in the air before her, "I know we've used them before, but the only time they've ever seen them used at maximum powered range was right here, in Fire Plan Gamma, and that had that ballistic component right in the middle of it. It's remotely possible Bogey Two hasn't had the benefit of a full tactical analysis yet."

"You're suggesting they might just come into our range, after all, Ma'am?" Stackpole sounded like a junior officer doing his best not to sound overtly dubious.

"It's possible, I suppose," Michelle said. Then she snorted. "On the other hand, it's entirely possible I'm grasping at straws, too!"

"Well, Ma'am," Stackpole said, "I hate to rain on your parade, but I can think of at least one damned good reason for them to be doing what they're doing." She cocked an eyebrow at him, and he shrugged. "If *I* were them, and if I did have a pretty good idea what our maximum powered envelope was, I wouldn't be in any hurry. I'd want to get as close as I could and still stay outside our envelope before I fired. Of course, if we want to start engaging them at longer ranges, with a ballistic component in the flight, they'll probably shoot back pretty damned fast."

"I know," Michelle said.

She smiled thinly, then tipped back in her command chair. It was remarkable, actually, she mused. Whatever the Peeps were up to, she was going to die sometime in the next hour or so, and yet she felt oddly calm. She hadn't resigned herself to death, didn't *want* to die—perhaps, deep down inside, some survival center simply refuse to accept the possibility, even now—and yet her forebrain knew it was going to happen. And despite that, her mind was clear, with a sort of bittersweet serenity. There were a lot of things she'd meant to do that she'd never have the chance to get around to now, and she felt a deep surge of regret for that. And, for that matter, she felt an even deeper, darker regret for the other men and women trapped aboard *Ajax* with her. Yet this was a possible ending she'd accepted the day she entered the Academy, the day she swore her oath as an officer in the Royal Manticoran Navy. She couldn't pretend she hadn't known it might come, and if she had to die, she could not have done it in better company than with the crew of HMS *Ajax*.

She considered the men and women who'd escaped aboard the battlecruiser's remaining operational life pods, wondered what they were thinking as they awaited rescue by their enemies. There'd been a time when the Manticoran Navy had been none too sure Havenite ships would bother with search-and-rescue after a battle, yet despite the sneak attack with which the Republic had opened this war, no one on either side had ever doubted that the victor in any engagement would do her very best to rescue as many survivors from *both* sides as possible.

*So we've made some progress, at least,* she told herself sardonically. Then she gave herself a mental shake. The last thing she should be doing at a moment like this was feeling anything except gratitude that the people Commander Horn had gotten off *Ajax* were going to survive!

*We really* have *come a long way since Basilisk Station and First Hancock,* she told herself. *In fact—*

"John." She let her command chair snap back upright and turned it to face the tac officer.

"Yes, Ma'am?" Something about her tone brought his own chair around to face her squarely, and his eyes narrowed.

"These people just finished borrowing Her Grace's tactics from Sidemore, right?"

"That's one way to put it," Stackpole agreed, his eyes narrowing further.

"Well, in that case," Michelle said with a razor-like smile, "I think it just might be time for *us* to borrow her tactics from Hancock Station. Why don't you and I kick this idea around with Commander Horn for a couple of minutes? After all," her smile grew thinner yet, "it's not like any of us have anything better to do, is it?"

"I like it, Your Grace," Alexandra Horn said grimly from Michelle's com screen.

"According to our best figures from here," Michelle said, "we've got roughly three hundred pods still on the rails."

"Three hundred and six, Admiral," Commander Dwayne Harrison, who had become *Ajax*'s tactical officer in the same instant Horn had become the battlecruiser's captain, said from behind Horn.

"Just over fifteen minutes to roll all of them, then."

"Yes, Ma'am," Horn agreed. "Use their tractors to limpet them to the hull until we're ready to drop all of them in a single clutch?"

"Exactly. And if we're going to do this, we'd better get started pretty quick," Michelle said.

"Agreed." Horn frowned for a moment, then grimaced. "I've got too much else on my plate right now, Admiral. I think this is something for you and Commander Stackpole to work out with Dwayne while I concentrate on pushing the repair parties."

"I agree, Alex." Michelle nodded firmly, even though she knew Horn was as well aware as she was that all the repairs in the world weren't going to make much difference. Master Chief MaGuire and her repair parties were still fighting to get at least one boat bay cleared, but the bosun's last estimate was that she'd need at least another hour, and probably at least a little longer. It was . . . unlikely, to say the least, that *Ajax* was going to have that hour.

"Very well, Ma'am." Horn nodded back. "Clear," she said, and Harrison's face replaced hers on both Michelle's and Stackpole's com screens.

The grim pursuit was coming to its inevitable conclusion, Michelle thought. Her belly was like a lump of congealed iron, and she felt almost lightheaded. Fear was a huge part of it, of course—she wasn't insane, after all. And yet excitement, *anticipation*, gripped her almost as tightly as the fear.

*If it's the final shot I'm ever going to get, at least it's going to be a doozy,* she told herself tautly. *And it looks like I'm actually going to get to see it fired, after all. Hard to believe.*

It had become only too evident over the last forty-seven minutes that Stackpole's assessment of the Peep commander's intentions had been accurate. That was how long it had been since Bogey Two had entered its own extreme missile range of *Ajax*, but the enemy was clearly in no hurry to pull the trigger.

And rightly so, Michelle thought. The Peeps had every advantage there was—numbers, acceleration rate, firepower, counter-missile launchers and laser clusters, and missile range—and they were using them ruthlessly. She was a bit surprised, to be honest, that the enemy had managed to resist the temptation to start firing sooner, but she understood the logic perfectly. As Stackpole had suggested, the Peeps would close to a range at which they remained just outside the powered envelope of *Ajax*'s Mark 16s, *then* open fire. Or, perhaps, call upon *Ajax* to surrender, since the situation would have become hopeless. There would have been just about zero probability of even Manticoran missiles getting through Bogey Two's defenses in salvos the size a single *Agamemnon* could throw and control at any range, but with the need for them to incorporate at least a brief ballistic phase in their approach, the probability would shrink still further. And no matter how good *Ajax*'s missile defenses might be, she was still only a single battlecruiser, and she would be thirty million kilometers inside Bogey Two's maximum range. Light-speed communication lags would be far lower, which would improve both the enemy's fire control and its ability to compensate for Manticore's superior EW.

*Of course, there* could *be a few minor difficulties hidden in that tactical situation, couldn't there?* Michelle thought.

She turned her command chair back towards Stackpole once again. Her tactical officer's shoulders were tight, his attention totally focused on his displays, and she smiled at him with a sort of bittersweet regret. He and Harrison had implemented Michelle's brainstorm quickly and efficiently. Now—

Michelle's com beeped softly at her. The sound startled her, and she twitched before she reached down and pressed the acceptance key. Alexandra Horn appeared on her display, and this time there was something very different about the commander's gray eyes. They literally glowed, and she smiled hugely at Michelle.

"Master Chief MaGuire's cleared the after bay, Ma'am!" she announced before her admiral could even speak, and Michelle jerked upright. The bosun and her work parties had continued laboring heroically, but after so long, Michelle—like everyone else aboard *Ajax*, she was certain—had come to the conclusion that there was simply no way MaGuire's people were going to succeed.

Michelle's eyes darted to the countdown clock blinking steadily towards zero in the corner of her tactical plot, then back to Horn.

"In that case, Alex," she said, "I suggest you start getting our people off right now. Somehow, I don't think the other side's going to be very happy with us in about seven minutes."

No one aboard *Ajax* had needed their admiral's observation.

The range between the battlecruiser and her overwhelming adversaries was down to little more than 48,600,000 kilometers, which put them far inside the Havenites' engagement envelope. No doubt those SD(P)s astern of them had already deployed multiple patterns of pods, tractored to their hulls inside their wedges, where they wouldn't degrade anyone's acceleration. The Peep commander was no doubt watching his own tactical displays intently, waiting for the first sign that *Ajax* might change her mind and attempt a long-range missile launch. If he saw one, he would undoubtedly roll his own pods, immediately. And if he *didn't* see one, he would probably roll them anyway within the next ten to twelve minutes.

Small craft began to launch from the boat bay Master Chief MaGuire and her people had managed—somehow—to get back into service. The bad news was that there weren't very many of those small craft available. The good news was that there were barely three hundred people still aboard the battlecruiser. Of course, for some of those people, getting *to* the boat bay was going to take a bit longer than for others.

"Admiral," a voice said from Michelle Henke's com. "It's time for you to go, Ma'am."

It was Commander Horn, and Michelle glanced at the display, then shook her head.

"I don't think so, Alex," she said. "I'm a little busy just now."

"Bullshit." The single, succinct word snapped her head back around, and Horn shook her own head, her expression stern. "You don't have a damned thing to do, Admiral. Not anymore. So get your ass off my ship—now!"

"I don't think—" Michelle began once more, but Horn cut her off abruptly.

"That's right, Ma'am. You *aren't* thinking. Sure, it was your idea, but you don't even have a tactical link to the pods from Flag Bridge. That means it up to me and Dwayne, and you know it. Staying behind at this point isn't your duty, Admiral. And it doesn't have anything to do with courage or cowardice."

Michelle stared at her, wanting to argue. But she couldn't—not logically. Not rationally. Yet her own need to stay with *Ajax* to the very end had very little to do with logic, or reason. Her eyes locked with those of the woman who was effectively ordering her to abandon her and her tactical officer to certain death, and the fact that *no one* had expected to have the opportunity to escape only made her own sense of guilt cut deeper and harder.

"I can't," she said softly.

"Don't be stupid, Ma'am!" Horn said sharply. Then her expression softened. "I know what you're feeling," she said, "but forget it. I doubt Dwayne or I could get to the boat bay in time, anyway. And whether we can or not, it doesn't change a thing I just said to you. Besides, it's your duty to get off if you can and look after my people for me."

Michelle had opened her mouth again, but Horn's last seven words shut it abruptly. She looked at the other woman, her eyes burning, then inhaled deeply.

"You're right," she said softly. "Wish you weren't, Alex."

"So do I." Horn managed a smile. "Unfortunately, I'm not. Now go. That's an order, Admiral."

"Aye, aye, Captain." Michelle's answering smile was crooked, and she knew it. "God bless, Vicky."

"And you, Ma'am."

The screen blanked, and Michelle looked at her staff officers and their assistants.

"You heard the Captain, people!" she said, her husky contralto harsh and rasping. "Let's go!"

Bogey Two kept charging after HMS *Ajax*. The Havenites' sensor resolution was problematical at best against something as small as a pinnace or a cutter at such an extended range, but the remote arrays they'd sent ahead of them were another matter. Less capable, and with much shorter endurance than their Manticoran counterparts, they'd still had *Ajax* under close observation for the last half-hour. They were close enough to recognize the impeller wedges of small craft, and to confirm that they *were* small craft, and not missile pods.

"They're abandoning, Sir."

Admiral Pierre Redmont turned to his tactical officer, one eyebrow quirked.

"It's confirmed, Sir," the tac officer said.

"Damn." The admiral's lips twisted as if he'd just tasted something sour, but he couldn't pretend it was a surprise. Under the circumstances the only thing that qualified as a *surprise* was that the Manties had waited so long. Obviously, they didn't intend to let him take that ship intact, after all. They were getting their people off before they scuttled.

"We could always order them not to abandon, Sir," the tac officer said quietly. Redmont shot him a sharp look, and the tac officer shrugged. "They're deep inside our range, Sir."

"Yes, they are, Commander," the admiral said just a bit testily. "And they also aren't shooting at us. In fact, they *can't* shoot at us from here—not effectively enough to make us break a sweat, anyway. And just how do you think Admiral Giscard—or, worse, Admiral Theisman—is going to react if I open fire on a ship that can't even return fire just to keep them from abandoning?"

"Not well, Sir," the commander said after a moment. Then he shook his head with a wry smile. "Not one of my better suggestions, Admiral."

"No, it wasn't," Redmont agreed, but a brief smile of his own took most of the sting from it, and he returned his own attention to his displays.

Michelle Henke and her staff made their way quickly down the passage towards the lift tubes. The passageway itself was already deserted, hatches standing open. The ship was running almost entirely on her remotes as her remaining personnel hurried towards the restored boat bay, and a spike of worry stabbed suddenly through her.

*Oh, Jesus! What if the Peeps decide all of this was nothing but a* trick? *That we could have abandoned any time, but we didn't because—*

She started to turn around, reaching for her personal communicator, but it was too late.

✧     ✧     ✧

An alarm shrilled suddenly.

The flagship's tactical officer's head jerked up in astonishment as he recognized the sound. It was the *proximity* alarm, and that was ridiculous! The thought flashed through his brain, but he was an experienced professional. His automatic incredulity didn't keep him from turning almost instantly towards his active sensor section.

"Radar contact!" one of his ratings snapped, but it was too late for the warning to make any difference at all.

Current-generation Manticoran missile pods were extraordinarily stealthy. Against a powered-down missile, active radar detection range was around a million kilometers, give or take. But then, missiles weren't designed to be as stealthy as the pods that carried them, because any attack missile was going to be picked up and tracked on passives with ludicrous ease thanks to the glaring signature of its impeller wedge. Which meant stealth wasn't going to help it very much.

But a missile *pod* was something else entirely. Especially a pod like the current-generation Manticoran "flatpack" pods with their on-board fusion plants. They'd been designed to be deployed in the system-defense role, as well as in ship-to-ship combat. After all, BuWeaps had decided, it made more sense to build a single pod with the features for both, as long as neither function was compromised. It hugely simplified production and reduced expense, which was a not insignificant consideration in an era of MDM combat.

All of which meant the Havenite radar crews had done extraordinarily well in the first place just to pick up the missile pods HMS *Ajax* had deployed in a single, massive salvo. The sheer size of the radar target helped, no doubt, despite the stealthiness of the individual pods of which the salvo consisted, and the range was just under nine hundred thousand kilometers when the alarms went off.

Unfortunately, Bogey Two's velocity was up to over twenty-seven thousand kilometers per second, and its starships had been charging directly up *Ajax*'s wake for well over an hour now. The missile pods had been continuing onward at the speed *Ajax*'s velocity had imparted to them at launch, which meant the steadily accelerating units of Bogey Two overflew them at a relative velocity of 19,838 KPS. At that closure rate, Bogey Two had exactly 1.2 minutes to detect and react to them before they found themselves half a million kilometers behind Bogey Two . . . and launched.

There were three hundred and six pods, each loaded with fourteen Mark 16 missiles. Of those forty-two-hundred-plus missiles, a quarter were EW platforms. The remaining thirty-two hundred laser heads were far lighter than the laser heads mounted by capital ship missiles. In fact, they were *too* light to pose any significant threat to something as heavily armored and protected as a ship of the wall. But Bogey Two's SD(P)s were screened by battlecruisers, and *battlecruisers* didn't carry that sort of armor.

The Havenite tactical officers had eighty-four seconds to recognize what had happened. Eighty-four seconds to see their displays come alive with thousands of attacking missiles. Despite the stunning surprise, they actually managed to implement their defensive doctrine, but there simply wasn't enough time for that doctrine to be effective.

The hurricane of missiles tore into the Havenite formation. Michelle Henke had indeed taken a page from Honor Harrington's and Mark Sarnow's tactics at the Battle of Hancock Station, and her weapons were far more capable than the ones Manticore had possessed then. Although the Mark 16 hadn't really been designed for use in any area-defense mine role, its sensors were actually superior to those carried by most mines. And Henke had taken advantage of the improvements in reconnaissance platforms and communications links, as well. Along with the missile pods, *Ajax* had deployed half a dozen Hermes buoys—communications platforms equipped with FTL grav-pulse receivers and light-speed communications lasers. Ghost Rider recon platforms had kept the Havenites under close observation, reporting in near real-time to *Ajax*, and *Ajax* had used her own FTL com and the Hermes buoys to feed continuous updates to her waiting missile pods.

Any sort of precise fire control over such a jury rigged control link, with its limited bandwidth and cobbled-up target selection, was impossible, of course. But it was good enough to ensure that each of those missiles had been fed the emissions signatures of the battlecruisers it was supposed to attack. Accuracy might be poor, compared to a standard missile engagement, and the EW platforms and penetration aids were far less effective without proper shipboard updates, but the range was also incredibly short, which gave the defense no time to react. Despite any shortcomings, that huge salvo's accuracy was far greater than anything Haven could possibly have anticipated . . . and not one of its missiles wasted itself against a ship of the wall.

Admiral Redmont swore savagely as the missile storm rampaged through his screen. The missile defense computers did the best they could, and considering how completely surprised their human masters had been and the attack's deadly geometry, that best was actually amazingly good. Which, unfortunately, didn't mean it was even remotely good *enough*.

There was no time for a counter-missile launch, and the attack from almost directly astern minimized the number of laser clusters which could defend any of the Manticorans' targets. Hundreds of incoming missiles were destroyed, but there were *thousands* of them, and their targets heaved in agony as lasers stabbed through their sidewalls or blasted directly up the kilts of their wedges. Hulls shattered, belching atmosphere and debris, and the fragile humans crewing those ships burned like straw in a furnace.

Two of Bogey Two's eight battlecruisers died spectacularly, vanishing into blinding fireballs with every single man and woman of their crews as the demonic bomb-pumped lasers stabbed through them again and again and again. The other six survived, but four of *them* were little more than broken and battered wrecks, wedges down, coasting onward while shocked and stunned survivors fought their way through the wreckage, searching frantically for other survivors in the ruin.

The admiral's jaw muscles ridged as his battlecruisers died. Then he twisted around to glare at his tac officer.

"*Open fire!*" he snapped.

# Chapter Three

"ADMIRAL HENKE."

Michelle Henke opened her eyes, then struggled hastily upright in the hospital bed as she saw the person who'd spoken her name. It wasn't easy, with her left leg still in traction while the quick heal rebuilt the shattered bone. But although they'd never met, she'd seen more than enough publicity imagery to recognize the platinum-haired, topaz-eyed woman standing at the foot of her bed.

"Don't bother, Admiral," Eloise Pritchart said. "You've been hurt, and this isn't really an official visit."

"You're a head of state, Madam President," Michelle said dryly, getting herself upright and then settling back in relief as the elevating upper end of the bed caught up with her shoulders. "That means it *is* an official visit."

"Well, perhaps you're right," Pritchart acknowledged with a charming smile. Then she gestured at the chair beside the bed. "May I?"

"Of course. After all, it's your chair. In fact," Michelle waved at the pleasant, if not precisely luxurious, room, "this is your entire hospital."

"In a manner of speaking, I suppose."

Pritchart seated herself gracefully, then sat for several seconds, her head cocked slightly to the side, her expression thoughtful. Michelle looked back at her, wondering what had brought her to a prisoner-of-war's bedside. As Michelle had just pointed out, this hospital—which, she'd been forced to admit, had been a much less unpleasant experience than she'd anticipated—belonged to the Republic of Haven. In point of fact, it belonged to the Republican Navy, and for all of its airiness and pastel color scheme, it was as much a prisoner-of-war camp as the more outwardly guarded facilities in which the rest of her personnel were confined.

She felt her facial muscles tightening ever so slightly as she remembered her flagship's final moments. The fact that *Ajax* hadn't gone alone was cold comfort beside the loss of two thirds of the ship's remaining company.

*Me and my goddamned brilliant idea,* she thought harshly. *Sure, we ripped them a new one, but my God! No wonder they thought we'd deliberately sucked them in, then timed our evacuation of the ship perfectly to put them off guard! God knows I would've thought exactly the same thing in their place.*

It wasn't the first time she'd battered herself with those thoughts. Nor, she knew, would it be the last. When her conscience wasn't prepared to savage her, the coldly logical strategist and tactician within her knew that in the merciless calculation of war, the complete destruction of two enemy battlecruisers and the reduction of at least three more into wrecks fit only for the breakers, was well worth the loss of so many men and women.

*And,* she thought harshly, *at least these people believed me in the end. I think they did, anyway. I may have gotten Alex and way too many of her people killed, but at least no one even suggested the possibility of some sort of "reprisal." Which probably wouldn't have come as such a surprise to me if I'd paid more attention to what Honor had to say about Theisman and Tourville.*

She still didn't remember exactly how Stackpole and Braga had gotten her into the boat bay and away from *Ajax* before the tornado of vengeful Havenite MDMs tore the battlecruiser the pieces. The first wave of lasers had slammed into the ship like sledgehammers before they ever reached the bay, and one of those hits had picked Michelle up and tossed her into a bulkhead like a toy. Somehow Stackpole and Braga had dragged her the rest of the way into the boat bay and gotten her aboard the last pinnace to clear the ship, and they were the only two members of her staff to survive *Ajax*'s destruction.

*I sure as hell hope keeping her systems out of Peep hands was worth it,* she thought bitterly. But then she reminded herself that she had other things to worry about at this particular moment.

"To what do I owe the honor, Madam President?" she asked, shoving the useless "what ifs" and self-blame ruthlessly aside once more.

"Several things. First, you're our senior POW, in several senses. You're the highest ranking, militarily speaking, and you're also—what? Fifth in the line of succession?"

"Since my older brother was murdered, yes," Michelle said levelly, and had the satisfaction of seeing Pritchart flinch ever so slightly.

"I'm most sincerely sorry about the death of your father and your brother, Admiral Henke," she said, her voice equally level, meeting Michelle's eyes squarely as she spoke. "We've determined from our own records that StateSec was, in fact, directly responsible for that assassination. The fanatics who actually carried it out may have been Masadans, but StateSec effectively recruited them and provided the weapons. As far as we're able to determine, all the individuals directly involved in the decision to carry out that operation are either dead or in prison. Not," she continued as Michelle's eyebrows began to arch in disbelief, "because of that particular operation, but because of an entire catalog of crimes they'd committed against the people of their own star nation. In fact, while I'm sure it won't do anything to alleviate your own grief and anger, I'd simply point out that the same people were responsible for the deaths of untold thousands—no, millions—of their own citizens. The Republic of Haven has had more than enough of men and women like that."

"I'm sure you have," Michelle said, watching the other woman carefully. "But you don't seem to have completely renounced their methods."

"In what way?" Pritchart asked a bit sharply, her eyes narrowing.

"I could bring up the little matter of your immediately prewar diplomacy, except that I'm reasonably certain we wouldn't agree on that point," Michelle said. "So instead, I'll restrict myself to pointing out your attempt to assassinate Duchess Harrington. Who, I might remind you, happens to be a personal friend of mine."

Michelle's brown eyes bored into Pritchart's topaz gaze. Somewhat to her surprise, the Havenite President didn't even attempt to look away.

"I'm aware of your close relationship with the Duchess," Pritchart said. "In fact, that's one of the several reasons I mentioned for this conversation. Some of my senior officers, including Secretary of War Theisman and Admiral Tourville and Admiral Foraker have met your 'Salamander.' They think very highly of her. And if they believed for a moment that my administration had ordered her assassination, they'd be very, very displeased with me."

"Forgive me, Madam President, but that's not exactly the same thing as saying you *didn't* authorize it."

"No, it isn't, is it?" Pritchart smiled with what certainly appeared to be genuine amusement. "I'd forgotten for a moment that you're used to moving at the highest levels of politics in the Star Kingdom. You have a politician's ear, even if you are 'only a naval officer.' However, I'll be clearer. Neither I, nor anyone else in my administration, ordered or authorized an attempt to assassinate Duchess Harrington."

It was Michelle's eyes' turn to narrow. As Pritchart said, she was accustomed to dealing with Manticoran *politicians*, if not politics per se. In point of fact, she didn't like politics, which was why she was content to leave her mother, the Dowager Countess of Gold Peak, to act as her proxy in the House of Lords. Still, no one could stand as close to the crown as Michelle did without being forced to let politicians into hand-shaking range at least occasionally, and in her time, she'd met some extraordinarily adroit and polished liars. But if Eloise Pritchart was another of them, it didn't show.

"That's an interesting statement, Madam President," she said after a moment. "Unfortunately, with all due respect, I have no way to know it's accurate. And even if you think it is, that doesn't necessarily mean some rogue element in your administration didn't order it."

"I'm not surprised you feel that way, and we here in the Republic have certainly had more than enough experience with operations mounted by 'rogue elements.' I can only say I believe very strongly that the statement I just made is accurate. And I'll also say I've replaced both my external and internal security chiefs with men I've known for years, and in whom I have the greatest personal confidence. If any rogue operation was mounted against Duchess Harrington, it was mounted without their knowledge or approval. Of that much, I'm absolutely positive."

*Oh, of* course *you are*, Michelle thought sardonically. *No Peep would ever dream of assassinating an opposing fleet commander! And, I'm sure, none of them would ever decide it might be easier to get forgiveness afterward than permission ahead of time and fire away at Honor on her own hook. What was that line Honor quoted to me . . . ? Something about 'Will no one rid me of this pestilential priest?' or something like that, I think.*

"And who else would you suggest might have a motive for wanting her dead?" Michelle asked aloud. "Or the resources to try to kill her in that particular fashion?"

"We don't have many specific details about how the attempt was made," Pritchart countered. "From what we have seen, however, speculation seems to be centering on the possibility that her young officer—a Lieutenant Meares, I believe—was somehow adjusted to make the attempt on her life. If that's the case, *we* don't have the resources to have done it. Certainly not in the time window which appears to have been available to whoever carried out the adjustment. Assuming that's what it was, of course."

"I hope you'll forgive me, Madam President, if I reserve judgment in this case," Michelle said after a moment. "You're very convincing. On the other hand, like me, you operate at the highest level of politics, and politicians at that level *have* to be convincing. I will, however, take what you've said under advisement. Should I assume you're telling me this in hopes I'll pass your message along to Queen Elizabeth?"

"From what I've heard of your cousin, Admiral Henke," Pritchart said wryly, "I doubt very much that she'd believe *any* statement of mine, including a declaration that water is wet."

"I see you've got a fairly accurate profile of Her Majesty," Michelle observed. "Although that's probably actually something of an understatement," she added.

"I know. Nonetheless, if you get the opportunity, I wish you'd tell her that for me. You may not believe this, Admiral, but I didn't really want this war, either. Oh," Pritchart went on quickly as Michelle began to open her mouth, "I'll freely admit I fired the first shot. And I'll also admit that, given what I knew then, I'd do the same thing again. That's not the same thing as *wanting* to do it, and I deeply regret all the men and women who have been killed or, like yourself, wounded. I can't undo that. But I would like to think it's possible for us to find an end to the fighting short of one of us killing *everyone* on the other side."

"So would I," Michelle said levelly. "Unfortunately, whatever happened to our diplomatic correspondence, you did fire the first shot. Elizabeth isn't the only Manticoran or Grayson—or Andermani—who's going to find that difficult to forget or overlook."

"And are you one of them, Admiral?"

"Yes, Madam President, I am," Michelle said quietly.

"I see. And I appreciate your honesty. Still, it does rather underscore the nature of our quandary, doesn't it?"

"I suppose it does."

Silence fell in the sunlit hospital room. Oddly enough, it was an almost companionable silence, Michelle discovered. She remembered again what Honor had told her about Thomas Theisman and about Lester Tourville, and she reminded herself that whatever else Eloise Pritchart might be, she was the duly elected president both of those men had chosen to serve. Maybe she was actually telling the truth about not having authorized the assassination attempt against Honor.

*And maybe she isn't, too. Not every evil, conniving politico in the universe goes around with a holo sign that says "I'm the Bad Guy!" For that matter, there's no rule that requires them all to look like that son-of-a-bitch High Ridge, either. It'd be nice if all the bad guys did look like bad guys, or acted like bad guys, but that's not the way things work outside really bad holo drama. I'm sure Adolf Hitler's and Rob Pierre's inner circles all thought they were just real sweethearts.*

After perhaps three minutes, Pritchart straightened, inhaled crisply, and stood.

"I'll let you get back to the business of healing, Admiral. The doctors assure me you're doing well. They anticipate a full recovery, and they tell me you can be discharged from the hospital in another week or so."

"At which point it's off to the stalag?" Michelle said with a smile. She waved one hand at the unbarred windows of the hospital room. "I can't say I'm looking forward to the change of view."

"I think we can probably do better than a miserable hut behind a tangle of razor wire, Admiral." There was actually a twinkle in Pritchart's topaz eyes. "Tom Theisman has strong views on the proper treatment of prisoners of war—as Duchess Harrington may remember from the day they met in Yeltsin. I assure you that all our POWs are being properly provided for. Not only that,

I'm hoping it may be possible to set up regular prisoner of war exchanges, perhaps on some sort of parole basis."

"Really?" Michelle was surprised, and she knew it showed in her voice.

"Really." Pritchart smiled again, this time a bit sadly. "Whatever else, Admiral, and however hardly your Queen may be thinking about us just now, we really aren't Rob Pierre or Oscar Saint-Just. We have our faults, don't get me wrong. But I'd like to think one of them isn't an ability to forget that even enemies are human beings. Good day, Admiral Henke."

Michelle put down her book viewer as the admittance chime on her hospital door sounded quietly.

"Yes?" she said, depressing the key on her bedside com.

"Secretary of War Theisman is here, Admiral," the voice of Lieutenant Jasmine Coatsworth, the senior floor nurse said, just a little bit nervously. "He'd like a few minutes of your time, if that would be convenient."

Both of Michelle's eyebrows rose. Just over a week had passed since her unexpected encounter with Eloise Pritchart. She'd had a handful of other visitors during that time, but most of them had been relatively junior officers, there to report to her in her role as the senior Manticoran POW about the status of her people and the other prisoners in Havenite hands. All of them had been professional and courteous, although she'd sensed a certain inevitable restraint which went beyond the normal restraint of a junior officer in the presence of a flag officer. No one had mentioned the possibility of a visit from Thomas Theisman himself, however.

"Well, Jasmine," she replied after a moment, with a smile she couldn't quite suppress (not that she tried all that hard, to be fair), "let me check my calendar." She paused for a single breath, eyes dancing with amusement, then cleared her throat. "By the strangest coincidence, I happen to be free this afternoon," she said. "Please, ask the Secretary to come in."

There was a moment of intense silence. Then the door slid open, and Lieutenant Coatsworth looked in. The expression on her face almost broke Michelle's self-control and sent her off in peals of laughter, but she managed to restrain herself. Then her eyes went past the nurse to the stocky, brown-haired man in civilian dress, accompanied by a dark-haired Navy captain with the shoulder rope which denoted her status as a senior officer's personal aide.

"I'm glad you were able to find time in your schedule for me, Admiral," the brown-haired man said dryly. His own lips appeared to hover on the edge of smiling, and Michelle shook her head.

"Forgive me, Mr. Secretary," she said. "I've been told I have a peculiar sense of humor. I couldn't quite resist the temptation, under the circumstances."

"Which is probably a sign that I'm not going to have to discipline anyone for mistreating or browbeating our POW patients."

"On the contrary, Mr. Secretary," Michelle said in a rather more serious tone, "everyone here in the hospital—especially Lieutenant Coatsworth—has treated our wounded people exactly the same way, I'm sure, that they would have treated any of *your* people. I've been very impressed with their professionalism and their courtesy."

"Good."

Theisman stepped into the room, looked around once as if personally assuring himself of its adequacy, then gestured at the bedside chair.

"May I?"

"Of course. As I pointed out to President Pritchart when she asked the same question, it's *your* hospital, Mr. Secretary."

"She didn't tell me you'd said that," he said as he seated himself in the chair, leaned back, and crossed his legs comfortably. "Still, you do have a point, I suppose."

He smiled, and, almost despite herself, Michelle smiled back.

Thomas Theisman reminded her a lot of Alastair McKeon, she thought as she studied the man leaning back in the chair while his aide tried not to hover too obviously over a boss of whom she was clearly more than just fond. Neither Theisman nor McKeon was exactly a towering giant of a man . . . physically, at least. But both of them had steady eyes: Thesiman's brown and McKeon's gray. Both of them radiated that sense of tough competence, and both of them—little as she'd wanted to admit it—projected that same aura of quiet, unflinching integrity.

*It was a lot easier when all the Peeps I knew anything about were slime,* she reflected. *And it makes bearing in mind that they're the ones who lied about all our prewar diplomacy harder.*

"I suppose the real reason I came by, Admiral Henke—" the

Secretary of War began, then paused. "I'm sorry, Admiral, but it just occurred to me. Are you still properly addressed as 'Admiral Henke,' or should I be calling you 'Admiral Gold Peak'?"

"Technically, I've been 'Admiral Gold Peak' ever since my father and my brother were murdered," Michelle told him levelly. The look in his eyes acknowledged her unstated point, but he gazed back at her without flinching, and she continued in that same, level tone. "I'm still much more comfortable with 'Henke,' however. That's who I've been ever since the Academy."

She started to add something more, then stopped herself with a tiny headshake. There was no need to tell him a tiny part of her still insisted that as long as she could put off formally claiming the title in all aspects of her life, her father and her brother wouldn't truly be gone.

"I understand," Theisman told her, and cleared his throat. "As I was saying, then, Admiral Henke, the real reason I came by was to add my own reassurances to President Pritchart's. I know she's already told you your people are being well taken care of. On the other hand, I also know you and I are both fully aware of how seldom that was the case during the last war. So I decided I should probably come by and put in my own two-credits worth. After all," even his *smile* reminded her of McKeon, "in this instance, at least, we're the leopard who has to prove he's changed his spots."

"I appreciate that, Mr. Secretary," Michelle replied after a moment. "And I also appreciate the fact that I've already been allowed to communicate with the senior POWs. Who, I hasten to add, have confirmed everything you and President Pritchart have told me. Duchess Harrington's been assuring everyone that your attitude towards captured personnel isn't exactly the same as Cordelia Ransom's or Oscar Saint-Just's. While I won't pretend I wouldn't rather be sitting down to dinner at Cosmo's in Landing just now instead of enjoying your hospitality, I'm glad to see just how right she was."

"Thank you." Theisman looked away for a moment and cleared his throat again, harder this time, before he looked back at her. "Thank you," he repeated. "That means a lot to me—knowing Lady Harrington's said that, I mean. Especially given the circumstances the only two times we've actually met."

"No one in the Star Kingdom blames you for what those Masadan lunatics did on Blackbird, Mr. Secretary. And we remember who told Honor—Duchess Harrington, I mean—about what was happening. And who testified for the prosecution at the trials." She shook her head. "That took more than just integrity, Sir."

"Not as much more as I'd like to take credit for." Theisman's smile was off-center but genuine.

"No?" Michelle cocked her head. "Let's just say that *I* wouldn't have wanted to be the officer who stood up and painted a great big bull's-eye on her own chest when I knew a senior officer corps full of Legislaturalists was going to be looking for a scapegoat for a busted operation."

"That thought did cross my mind," Theisman admitted. "Then again, the fact that the Masadans really are the lunatics you just called them didn't hurt. In a way, my testimony only underscored the fact that it was their idiocy in seizing '*Thunder of God*' that really blew the operation wide open. Well, that and Lady Harrington. Besides," he smiled again, "Alfredo Yu made a much better—and more senior—scapegoat than I could have."

"I suppose. Oh, and while I'm at it, I should probably say that Admiral Yu's also been one of the senior officers on our side who's spoken well of you."

"I'm glad." Theisman's face softened at the mention of his old mentor. Then it tightened again. "I'm glad," he repeated, "but I wouldn't have blamed Lady Harrington for changing any positive impression she might have had of me when I just stood there and watched Ransom drag her off to Cerberus."

"And just what were you supposed to do to keep that from happening, Sir?" Michelle asked. He looked at her, as if surprised to hear her say that, and she snorted. "Don't forget that Warner Caslet came home from Cerberus with her, Mr. Secretary. From everything he's said, it's pretty evident Ransom was only looking for an excuse to 'make an example' out of you, as well as Admiral Tourville. And Nimitz—" she'd caught herself just in time to substitute the treecat's name for Honor's "—could 'taste' enough of your emotions to know how you felt about what was happening."

His eyes narrowed, and she watched him digesting her confirmation of the ability of the telempathic 'cats to reliably detect the emotions of those in their vicinity. She had no doubt Havenite intelligence had been passing on the revelations from the Star Kingdom's newscasts about treecat intelligence since Nimitz and his mate Samantha had learned to communicate using sign language, but that wasn't quite the same thing as firsthand, independent confirmation.

*Of course, I don't imagine any of those reports have mentioned the minor fact that* Honor's *become an empath herself,* she reflected. *And I don't have any intention of telling them about that, either.*

"I'm glad," he said, after a moment. "Not that knowing she understands and sympathizes makes me feel any better about the entire Navy's failure to meet its obligations under interstellar law under the old régime."

"Maybe not," Michelle replied, "but, then, you had a little bit to do with the reason that it is the *'old* régime,' too. And with Chairman Saint-Just's rather abrupt . . . retirement. Or so I've heard, at any rate."

The captain standing at Theisman's shoulder stiffened, her expression more than a little outraged at the obvious reference to the reports (unconfirmed, of course) that then-Citizen Admiral Theisman had shot Saint-Just out of hand during his successful coup, but the Secretary of War only chuckled.

"I suppose you could put it that way," he acknowledged, then sobered just a bit. "On the other hand, I didn't help overthrow Saint-Just just so we could go back to shooting at one another again."

"Sir, with all due respect, I don't think that's going to be a particularly profitable topic," Michelle said, meeting his eye steadily. "I can't begin to tell you how glad I am to learn how humanely your POWs are being treated, but the accusations and actions which led to the resumption of hostilities aren't something I'm really prepared to discuss. Nor," she ended unflinchingly, "is that topic one upon which I believe you and I are likely to find ourselves in agreement."

"No?" Theisman gazed at her calmly, almost speculatively, while his aide bridled behind him. Then the Secretary of War shook his head. "Very well, Admiral Henke. If it's a topic you'd prefer not to discuss at this time, I'm entirely prepared to defer to your wishes. Perhaps another time. And," there was something odd about the look in his eyes, Michelle thought, "you might be surprised at just how close to agreement we might be able to come."

He paused, as if waiting to see if she would rise to the bait of his final sentence. And, truth to tell, she was tempted—*very* tempted. But one thing of which she was painfully aware was just how totally unsuited she was to the role of diplomat.

Honor *might be the right woman for that, these days, at least,* she thought. *But the best I can say about me is that I'm smart enough to know that I'm most definitely* not *the right woman for it.*

"Well, at any rate," Theisman resumed a bit more briskly, "I understand from the doctors that they're going to be moving you out of the hospital the day after tomorrow. I trust you'll find your new accommodations as comfortable as could be expected, under the circumstances, and I'd also like to extend a formal invitation to join me for supper before we send you off to durance vile. I promise there won't be any truth drugs in the wine, and there are a few other officers I'd like you to meet. Admiral Giscard, Admiral Tourville, and Admiral Redmont, among others."

"Admiral Redmont and I have already met, Mr. Secretary," Michelle told him.

"So I understand." Theisman smiled thinly. "On the other hand, a little more time has passed since then, and Admiral Redmont and I have had the opportunity to . . . discuss his actions at Solon."

"Sir, Admiral Redmont didn't—"

"I didn't say I didn't understand what happened, Admiral," Theisman told her. "And, if we're going to be honest, I might very well have reacted the same way if I'd thought you'd deliberately waited to abandon ship until you knew I'd sailed into your ambush. But if we're going to keep a handle on atrocities and counter-atrocities, then anytime something like this comes along, it needs to be addressed squarely. I don't doubt that Admiral Redmont acted correctly after he'd picked up your surviving people. And I don't doubt that the two of you handled yourselves with proper professional courtesy. I hope, however, that you'll accept my invitation and give all of us an opportunity to discuss the incident and our reactions to it in a less . . . charged atmosphere, shall we say?"

"Very well, Mr. Secretary," Michelle said. "Of course I'll accept your invitation."

"Excellent." Theisman rose and extended his hand to her. They shook, and he maintained his grip for a heartbeat or two afterward. Then he released her hand and nodded to his aide.

"We'd better be going, Alenka," he said.

"Yes, Sir." The captain opened the hospital room door, then stood waiting at a position of semi-attention for her superior to proceed her through it.

"Until tomorrow night, then, Admiral," Theisman said to Michelle, and he was gone.

# Chapter Four

"—THIS MORNING, SO I think that situation's under control, Milady."

"I see." Michelle tipped back in the chair behind the desk and contemplated Commodore Arlo Turner with a hidden smile of mingled satisfaction and exasperation.

Turner, a heavyset, fair-haired man in his mid-fifties, was, like Michelle, from the planet of Manticore itself. More than that, he was from the City of Landing, the Star Kingdom's capital, and she suspected that he'd always been one of those people who followed the daily newsfaxes expressly so he could keep up with the doings of what was still called "the rich and famous." When she first realized that, she'd been tempted to write him off as an inept, would-be social climber, but she'd quickly realized that would have been doing him a disservice he didn't deserve. He might be fascinated by the social gossip columns, and she didn't doubt he cherished a slightly wistful hope of someday attaining at least a knighthood of his very own, yet he was anything but inept. In fact, he was one of the more efficient administrators she'd ever worked with, and she had no doubt he was a competent tactician, too, despite his present residence in one of the Republic of Haven's prisoner-of-war camps. After all, she considered herself a reasonably competent tactician, and look where she'd ended up.

Her lips twitched, the hidden smile almost breaking free, as that thought flickered through her mind, but it wasn't what had awakened her exasperation. Despite his efficiency, and despite her rather pointed hints to the contrary, he simply could not forget that she was Queen Elizabeth's first cousin and the Countess of Gold Peak in her own right. It would be grossly unfair to accuse him of anything remotely like fawning, yet he insisted upon addressing her as "Admiral Gold Peak," and instead of the sturdy, serviceable naval "Ma'am" she would really have preferred, he insisted upon the technically correct "Milady" whenever he addressed her.

*I suppose if that's the only thing I can find to worry about where he's concerned, I don't have any real room for complaint,* she reflected, and glanced sideways for a moment at Lieutenant Colonel Ivan McGregor.

McGregor, who had been born and raised on the planet of Gryphon, less than five hundred kilometers from what had since become the Duchy of Harrington, was Turner's antithesis in almost every way. Where Turner was fair-haired and blue-eyed, McGregor had black hair, dark brown eyes, and a swarthy complexion. Where Turner was heavyset—chunky, not overweight—and stood only a little more than a hundred and sixty-two centimeters in height, McGregor had a runner's build and topped a hundred and ninety-three centimeters. And if Turner was a gossip junkie, McGregor had every bit of the native Gryphon's distrust for the majority of the Star Kingdom's aristocracy, and his eyes reflected an echo of Michelle's own exasperation with Turner's choice of address at the moment.

Despite which, the two men were fast friends and worked smoothly together.

Until her own unanticipated arrival, Turner had been the senior officer of Camp Charlie-Seven, and McGregor, as the senior Marine officer in the camp, had been his adjutant and the commander of Camp Charlie's internal police service. He continued to hold both of those posts, and Turner had become Michelle's executive officer.

If she were going to be completely honest, she had to admit her own duties consisted primarily of standing back and letting the two of them get on with the smoothly oiled partnership they'd built up during their thirteen months in captivity. Both of them had been captured in the opening stages of Operation Thunderbolt, and she was impressed by their joint refusal to allow the fact that they had been captured so early in the war, through no fault of their own, to embitter them.

*There's a lesson there I'd probably better learn for myself, the way this war seems to be going.* Her temptation to smile disappeared with the thought.

"So you're satisfied, then, Arlo?"

"Yes, Milady." The commodore nodded. "It was only a misunderstanding. The kitchens screwed up their records—it looks like a simple data-entry error. According to them, we still had plenty of fresh vegetables. I think Captain Bouvier's a little ticked that he didn't realize the reports *had* to be in error, given the delivery schedule, and he assures me we can expect delivery within the next few hours."

"Good." Michelle nodded.

Captain Adelbert Bouvier was the Republican Navy's designated "liaison officer" to its prisoner-of-war camps here on the Republic's capital world. Frankly, she found the Havenites' arrangements a bit . . . peculiar. Technically, Bouvier should probably have been considered Camp Charlie-Seven's commanding officer, although he wasn't called that. He was the Havenite officer with command authority over the camp and its inhabitants, at any rate, but he and his superiors seemed prepared to allow Camp Charlie to function with a sort of semi-autonomy which had astounded Michelle when she first encountered it.

Right off the top of her head, she couldn't think of another example of a star nation which didn't bother to post its own personnel on the ground, as it were, to at least keep an eye on a camp full of prisoners of war, all of whom could be presumed to be trained military personnel with a distinct interest in being elsewhere. On the other hand, it wasn't exactly as if they needed to put a lot of boots on the ground here at Charlie-Seven.

*Reminds me a little of what Honor had to say about Cerberus,* she reflected, glancing out the window of her office in the camp's main administration building. *Not that it has anything in common with the way those motherless StateSec bastards treated their prisoners, thank God! But the Peeps—no, Honor was right about that, too; the Havenites—do seem to have a thing about islands.*

Camp Charlie-Seven occupied the entirety of a relatively small, somewhat chilly island in the planet of Haven's Vaillancourt Sea. It was almost eight hundred kilometers to the nearest body of land in any direction, which provided what Michelle had to concede was a reasonably effective moat. And if there were no guards actually on the ground, everyone in the camp knew their island was under permanent, round-the-clock surveillance by dedicated satellites and ground-based remote sensors. Even assuming that anyone on the island had been able to cobble up some sort of boat that actually stood a chance of crossing to the mainland across all that water, the sensor nets and satellites would have detected the attempt to launch said boat quickly, and Republican Marines could be on the ground on the island within fifteen minutes, if they really needed to.

With that sort of security available, Secretary of War Theisman had opted to allow his prisoners to manage their own affairs, subject to a sort of distant oversight by officers like Captain Bouvier, as long as they kept things running relatively smoothly. It might be an unheard-of technique, but it appeared to be an effective one, and it was about as far as it was possible to get from the horror stories Michelle Henke heard from Manticorans unfortunate enough to fall into Havenite custody in the previous war.

*Which is undoubtedly the reason he did it.* She shook her head mentally. *There's a man who still thinks he has a lot to make up for. And not for anything* he *did, either. Honor was right—he is a decent man.*

In fact, she'd come to the conclusion that most of the Havenites she'd met were decent people. In a way, she wished that weren't the case. It was always simpler when one could think of the enemy as the scum of the galaxy. Reflecting on the fact that the people who were firing missiles at you—and who you were firing missiles back at—were just as decent as anyone you knew on your side could be . . . uncomfortable.

She thought about Theisman's dinner party. As promised, Admiral Redmont had been present, and under Theisman's watchful eye, Redmont had actually unbent to the point of telling a few modest jokes over the post-dinner wine. Michelle realized she still wasn't very high on his list of favorite people—not surprisingly, when *Ajax* had killed almost six thousand of his personnel—and he wasn't exactly likely to become her lifetime pen pal, either, given what had happened to her flagship. But at least the two of them had acquired a sense of mutual respect, and she was a bit surprised by how little bitterness there truly was in her feelings where he was concerned.

She hadn't had that sort of baggage with the other dinner guests. Admiral Lester Tourville had been something of a surprise. According to all of the reports she'd ever seen, he was supposed to be something of a loose warhead—one of those colorful, larger-than-life people who would always be far more at home on the command deck of a single battlecruiser fighting a ship-to-ship action somewhere (assuming he couldn't find the eyepatch, cutlass, and flintlock pistols he *really* wanted) rather than commanding a task force or a fleet. She should have realized those reports could scarcely be accurate, given his string of successes commanding those task forces and fleets. In fact, the only person who'd ever bloodied his nose was Honor, and as nearly as Michelle could tell, honors were about even between the two of them. A point which became much easier to understand when she finally had the opportunity to look into his eyes and see the shrewd, cool, calculating tactician hiding behind what she'd come to suspect was a carefully cultivated façade. In fact, she'd discovered she rather liked him, which she hadn't really expected to.

All things being equal, she was just as happy that she hadn't heard—then—about the masterful job Tourville had done of thoroughly trashing the Zanzibar System and its defenses.

Theisman's other two dinner guests—Vice Admiral Linda Trenis and Rear Admiral Victor Lewis—had also been pleasant enough dinner companions, although she'd found herself feeling definitely grateful for Theisman's promise the meal's beverages would be truth-drug-free. She was reasonably confident the Navy's anti-drug protocols would have worked, but even without that, Trenis and Lewis—especially Lewis—would have made formidable interrogators if Theisman hadn't quietly reminded them this was a social occasion. Given the fact that Trenis commanded the Republican Navy's Bureau of Planning, which made her the equivalent of Second Space Lord Patricia Givens, the commander of the Manticoran Navy's Office of Naval Intelligence, and that Lewis commanded the Office of Operational Research, the Bureau of Planning's primary analysis agency, their ability to put even small fragments together shouldn't have surprised her, she supposed. It was still impressive, though. In fact, pleasant though the evening had been, she'd come to the conclusion that the Republic of Haven's senior command staff had a depressingly high level of general competence.

Most of the time, it was hard to believe that dinner party had been a full six weeks ago. She managed to stay busy here on the island—with a total prisoner population of almost nine thousand, there was always something that needed her attention, despite Turner's efficiency—which kept boredom at bay most days. And Charlie-Seven's island home was far enough north to provide the occasional interesting storm, now that this hemisphere's autumn was well advanced. Some of the POWs, she knew, found those storms less than reassuring. She wasn't one of them, however. The camp's sturdy, storm-tight buildings stood up to the howling wind without any particular difficulty, and the surf on the island's rocky southern beaches was truly spectacular. In fact, she found the local storms invigorating, although McGregor insisted they were mere zephyrs compared to a real *Gryphon* storm.

Still, there were days when the fact of her captivity, however little like the brutality of StateSec from the last war it might be, ground down upon her. When she looked out the window of her office and saw not sky and sea, but an enemy planet, where she was held prisoner, powerless, unable to protect the Star Kingdom she loved. And that, she knew, was going to get only worse in the days, weeks, and months ahead.

*Before too long, I'm probably going to be* grateful *for the distraction of snafus in the vegetable deliveries*, she reflected. *Golly! Isn't that something to look forward to?*

"Excuse me, Ma'am."

Michelle twitched and looked up quickly from her reverie as a head poked in through her office door. The head in question belonged to one of the very few men she'd ever met who'd probably been in the Service as long as—and, she suspected, racked up more demerits in his youth as—Chief Warrant Officer Sir Horace Harkness.

"Yes, Chris?" Michelle's tone was pleasant, although she felt an inner pang every time she looked at Master Steward Chris Billingsley.

Her steward of many years, Clarissa Arbuckle, had never cleared *Ajax*. Billingsley had been provided as Clarissa's replacement once Michelle arrived at Charlie-Seven. The good news was that, physically, Billingsley reminded her as little as anyone possibly could of Clarissa. He was about James MacGuiness' age, and—like MacGuiness—a first-generation prolong recipient. And, unlike Clarissa, he was not simply male but solidly, if compactly, built with a rather luxuriant beard he'd grown since his capture. That would have been more than enough to differentiate him from Clarissa in Michelle's mind even without . . . certain other differences. Obviously, as a prisoner-of-war, his personnel file hadn't followed him to Charlie-Seven, which was probably not a bad thing in his case, since he was undoubtedly what the Service had always described as A Character.

Actually, the Service had a great many serviceable—and quite probably more accurate—terms for describing someone like Master Steward Billingsley. It was just that he was far too likable for Michelle to have the heart to apply them to him. And, in all fairness, he seemed to have mostly reformed his more questionable ways. To be sure, Michelle suspected that he had, upon occasion, during his stay here on Nouveau Paris, supplied certain minor but highly desired luxuries to his fellow POWs by way of not quite legal transactions with the Peeps. And if there were a game of chance—especially one involving dice—within a half light-year, Master Steward Billingsley knew where it was, knew who was playing, and had a reserved seat. Then there was that minor matter of the distillery he'd once been involved with, purely as a part of his social responsibility to help provide the camp medical staff with medicinal alcohol.

Despite his various shenanigans, and what Michelle was sure a novelist fond of clichés would have described as "a checkered past," he was one of those people who was always popular with the officers he served under and the enlisted personnel he served with. Almost despite herself, Michelle had found herself warming to his undeniable charm, despite the fact that the mere fact of his presence reminded her of Clarissa's *absence*, like a wound which refused to truly heal. That wasn't even remotely *Billingsley's* fault, though, and Michelle more than suspected that he'd figured out what she felt, and why, for he was surprisingly sensitive and considerate of her wounds.

"I'm sorry to disturb you, Ma'am," he said now, "but there's an air car inbound, ETA twenty minutes, and we've just received a message from Captain Bouvier's office. For you, Ma'am."

"What sort of message?" Michelle's eyes narrowed speculatively.

"Ma'am, Captain Bouvier presents Secretary Theisman's compliments and requests that you make yourself available to the Secretary at your earliest convenience."

The eyes which had narrowed widened abruptly, and she glanced quickly at Turner and McGregor. They looked as surprised as she felt.

"And may I presume," she said, turning back to Billingsley, "that the imminent arrival of the air car you mentioned has something to do with my 'earliest convenience'?"

"I'd say that's a fairly safe conclusion, Ma'am," Billingsley said gravely. "Especially since the same message from Captain Bouvier specifically requested that I pack a bag for you, and one for myself."

"I see." Michelle looked at him for a moment longer, then inhaled. "All right, Chris. If you'll see to that, Commodore Turner and Colonel McGregor and I have a few details we should probably discuss before I go haring off to wherever it is we're going."

"Yes, Ma'am."

The air car arrived almost exactly on schedule, and under the circumstances, Michelle felt she and Billingsley were doing rather well to keep her chauffeur waiting for less than ten minutes. She didn't know if the air car's pilot was aware of just how little notice she'd had of his impending arrival, but he and the neatly uniformed Navy commander accompanying him—and the two well armed Marines who'd been sent along to help discourage any of the POWs' temptation towards hijacking the vehicle—waited respectfully for her. She limped across to the hatch (her injured leg was still well short of completely recovered), and the commander came to attention as she approached.

"Secretary Theisman instructed me to apologize for the lack of warning, Admiral Henke," he said as he opened the hatch courteously for her. Michelle nodded her thanks and settled into her seat while Billingsley stowed the luggage in the cargo compartment. The steward climbed into the rearmost seat at the commander's gesture. Then the Havenite officer followed, closing the hatch and settling into the seat facing Michelle's as the car leapt back into the air.

"The Secretary also instructed me to tell you that he believes you'll understand the reason for his haste in arranging this after you and he have had an opportunity to talk, Ma'am," he added.

"May I conclude from that, Commander," Michelle said, cocking her head with a slight smile, "that we are even now bound to meet the Secretary?"

"Yes, Ma'am. I believe the Admiral may safely conclude that," the commander replied.

"And the flight to this meeting will take about how long?"

"Ma'am," the commander glanced at his chrono, then back at her, "I believe our ETA is approximately forty-three minutes from now."

"I see." Michelle nodded. Forty-three minutes wasn't long enough for a return flight clear to Nouveau Paris, which presented several interesting questions. Not that it seemed likely the courteous young commander knew the answers to those questions. Or, at least, that he was prepared to admit it, if he did.

"Thank you, Commander," she said, then leaned back in the comfortable seat, gazing out through the armorplast canopy as the wind-ruffled blue and white water of the Vaillancourt Sea rushed past below them.

Despite the courtesy with which she had been treated since her capture, Michelle felt her nerves tightening as the air car settled onto a landing pad on the grounds of a large, sprawling estate perched on a craggy headland above the Vaillancourt. Surf pounded at the headland's sheer face, sending geysers of white surging far up its steepness while seabirds—or their local analogues, at least—wheeled and darted on the brawny breeze. It wasn't the surf, or the seabirds, which set her nerves on edge, however. No, it was the sting ships parked to one side, and the light armored vehicles positioned to keep a watchful eye on the estate's landward approaches.

As the air car touched down with delicate precision, she looked up through the canopy and realized that in addition to the pair of sting ships on the pad, there was at least one more of them in the air above the estate, hovering watchfully on counter-grav. That degree of ostentatious security would have been enough to make anyone nervous, she decided, even if the anyone in question hadn't happened to be a prisoner of war.

"If you'll follow me, please, Admiral," the commander murmured as the air car hatch opened and the boarding ramp extended itself.

"And Master Steward Billingsley?" She was pleased to note that there was no nervousness in her tone, at least.

"My understanding, Ma'am, is that you'll probably be spending at least the evening here, and Master Steward Billingsley will be escorted to your assigned quarters to see that everything is properly settled by the time you get there. If that will be convenient, Ma'am?"

He managed to ask the question as if she actually had a choice, Michelle noticed, and smiled slightly.

"That sounds quite convenient, Commander. Thank you," she said gravely.

"Of course, Admiral. This way, please?"

He gestured gracefully towards the main building of the estate, and she nodded.

"Lead the way, Commander," she said.

The commander led her across a carefully manicured lawn, through a pair of old-fashioned, unpowered double doors—watched over by an obviously competent security guard in civilian clothing, not uniform—and down a short hallway. He paused outside another set of double doors—this one of some exotic, hand-polished wood which Michelle had no doubt was native to Haven—and rapped gently.

"Yes?" a voice inquired from the other side of the door.

"Admiral Henke is here," the commander replied.

"Then ask her to come in," the voice said.

The voice didn't belong to Thomas Theisman. It was female, and although it was muffled by the closed door, it sounded vaguely familiar. Then the door opened, Michelle stepped through it, and found herself face to face with President Eloise Pritchart.

Surprise made Michelle hesitate for a moment, but then she shook herself and continued forward into the room. She was aware of at least one more civilian-clothed bodyguard, this one female, and given Pritchart's presence, all of the security around the estate suddenly made perfectly good sense. That thought ran through the back of Michelle's brain as Pritchart extended her hand in greeting and Thomas Theisman rose from a chair behind the standing President.

"Madame President," Michelle murmured, and allowed one eyebrow to arch as she gripped the offered hand.

"I'm sorry about the minor deception, Admiral," Pritchart replied with a charming smile. "It wasn't really directed at you so much as at anyone else who might be wondering where you were, or who you might be talking to. And, in all honesty, it *probably* wasn't really necessary. Under the circumstances, however, I'd prefer to err on the side of caution."

"I trust you'll forgive me, Madame President, if I point out that all of that sounds suitably mysterious."

"I'm sure it does." Pritchart smiled again and released Michelle's hand to wave invitingly at the pair of comfortable armchairs arranged to face the one Theisman had just climbed out of. "Please, sit down, and I'll try to make things at least a little less mysterious."

Michelle obeyed the polite command. The chair was just as comfortable as it had looked, and she leaned back into its embrace, looking back and forth between Theisman and Pritchart. The President returned her gaze for a few moments, then turned her head to look at the bodyguard standing behind her.

"Turn off the recorders, Sheila," she said.

"Madame President, the recorders have already—" the bodyguard began, but Pritchart shook her head with a smile.

"Sheila," she said chidingly, "I know perfectly well that your personal recorder is still switched on." The bodyguard looked at her, and the President waved a gently admonishing finger in her direction. "I don't believe for a moment that you're a spy, Sheila," she said dryly. "But I do know SOP for the Detachment is to record everything that happens in my presence so there's a record just in case I happen to be killed by a stray micro-meteorite or some crazed, rampaging seagull manages to get past my intrepid guardians and hurl itself ferociously upon me. In this case, though, I think we'll dispense with that."

"Yes, Ma'am," the bodyguard said after a moment, with manifest reluctance. She touched a spot on her lapel, then folded her hands behind her and settled into a position the military would have called parade rest.

"Thank you," Pritchart said, and turned back to Michelle.

"If your object was to make sure you have my full attention, Madame President, you've succeeded," Michelle said dryly.

"That wasn't really the reason I did it, but I'm not going to complain if it had that effect," Pritchart replied.

"Then may I ask exactly what this is all about?"

"Certainly, but I'm afraid it's going to be just a little bit complicated."

"Somehow, I'm not terribly surprised to hear that, Madame President."

"No, I suppose you aren't." Pritchart settled back in her own chair, topaz-colored eyes intent while she gazed at Michelle for another few seconds, as if organizing her thoughts. Then she gave herself a little shake.

"I hope you remember our conversation in your hospital room, Admiral," she began. "At the time, if you'll recall, I told you I'd like to think we might somehow find an end to the fighting short of one side killing everyone on the other side."

She paused, and Michelle nodded.

"Well, I think it may be possible for us to do that. Or that there's a chance we can do that, at least," the President said quietly.

"I beg your pardon?" Michelle sat forward in her chair, her eyes suddenly very narrow.

"Admiral Henke, we've recently received certain reports about events in the Talbott Cluster." Michelle's expression showed her confusion at Pritchart's apparent non sequitur, and the President shook her head. "Bear with me, Admiral. It's relevant, I assure you."

"If you say so, of course, Madame President," Michelle responded a bit doubtfully.

"As I say, we've received certain reports about events in the Talbott Cluster," Pritchart resumed. "I'm afraid they aren't exactly pleasant news, from your perspective, Admiral. I'm sure that, prior to your capture, you were far better aware than any of us of the so-called 'resistance movements' springing up on two or three of the planets in the Cluster. We've been doing our best to monitor the situation, of course, since anything that distracts your Star Kingdom's attention and resources has obvious benefits for us. It hasn't had the priority other intelligence-gathering activities have had, though, and we don't have complete information, by any stretch of the imagination. Our priorities have shifted rather dramatically in the last few days, however."

"And that would be because—?" Michelle prompted obediently when the President paused.

"That, Admiral, would be because according to the information sources we have been able to cultivate, one of your captains has uncovered evidence which he believes demonstrates that someone outside the Cluster has been manipulating and supplying those 'resistance movements.' Apparently, he believes the Union of Monica is directly implicated in that manipulation, and he's launched an unauthorized preemptive operation against Monica to bring it to an end."

Michelle stared at the other woman, unable to conceal her astonishment.

"Despite the fact that our information is so incomplete," Pritchart continued, "a few facts are quite clear to us. One, of course, is that Monica has a long history of acting as a proxy for the Office of Frontier Security, which strongly suggests OFS is also directly implicated in whatever is going on. Assuming, of course, that your captain's suspicions prove accurate, that is. And the second, I'm afraid, is that if, in fact, he launches some sort of preemptive strike against Monica, your Star Kingdom will find itself facing the very real prospect of a shooting incident with the Solarian League Navy."

The President paused, crossed her legs, and sat back, head cocked to one side, obviously giving Michelle time to get past the worst of her initial shock and absorb the implications of what she'd just said, and Michelle forced herself not to swallow as those implications went through her. She couldn't imagine what sort of evidence chain could have sent any reasonably sane captain in the Royal Manticoran Navy into what could so readily turn into an eyeball-to-eyeball confrontation with the most powerful navy in the history of mankind.

*Well, the* biggest, *at any rate,* a stubborn little voice said in the back of her mind. *ONI's reports all insist the SLN still doesn't have the new compensators, FTL coms, decent missile pods or pod-layers, or—especially—MDMs. But what they* do *have is something like twenty-one hundred superdreadnoughts in active commission, a reserve fleet at least two or three times that size, the biggest industrial and technological base in existence . . . and something like two thousand fully developed star systems. Plus, of course, the entire Verge to exploit at will.*

She was well aware that some of the RMN's more . . . enthusiastic tactical thinkers had been arguing for years that the advances in military technology produced by the Star Kingdom's half-century and more of arms race and open warfare with Haven had rendered the entire League Navy hopelessly obsolete. Personally, she was less confident than the majority of those enthusiasts that Manticore's clear advantages in many areas translated into advantages in *all* areas. Even so, she was entirely confident that any Manticoran task force or fleet could handily polish off any comparable Solarian force, probably without even breaking a sweat. Unlike those enthusiasts, however, she strongly doubted (to put it mildly) that all of Manticore's tactical advantages put together could possibly overcome the enormous strategic *disadvantage* of the difference between the Manticoran and Solarian populations and resource and industrial bases.

*There's nothing wrong with the Sollies' general tech base, either. We probably have a slight edge overall, thanks to the way the war's pressurized every area of R&D for the last fifty years or so, but if we do, it's fingernail-thin. And once their navy wakes up and smells the coffee, they've got lots of people to put to work closing the gap. Not to mention the building capacity, if they ever get organized. For that matter, some of the League members' system defense forces have been a lot more innovative than the SLN's senior officer corps for as long as anyone can remember. There's no telling what some of them have been up to, or how quickly any little surprises one of them may have developed for us could be gotten into general service once we bloodied the SLN's nose a time or three. And some of the SDFs are damned near as big—or bigger—in their own right than our entire Navy was before Uncle Roger started his buildup.*

She felt herself coming back on balance as the first shock of Pritchart's information began to ease just a bit. Still, what sort of lunatic—?

"Excuse me, Madame President," she said after a moment, "but you said one of our captains was involved in this. Would you happen to know *which* captain?"

"Thomas?" Pritchart looked at Theisman, one eyebrow arched, and the Secretary of War smiled a bit tartly.

"According to our reports, Admiral, I suspect it's a name you'll recognize as well as I did. It's Terekhov—Aivars Terekhov."

Despite herself, Michelle felt her eyes widen once again. She'd never actually met Aivars Aleksovitch Terekhov, but she certainly did recognize the name. And she wasn't a bit surprised Theisman had, either, given Terekhov's performance in the Battle of Hyacinth and the Secretary of War's personal apology for the atrocities State Security had perpetrated against Terekhov's surviving personnel after their capture. But what could possibly have possessed a man with Terekhov's record and experience to court active hostilities with the Solarian League?

"I think, given the fact that it's Captain Terekhov," Theisman continued, as if he'd read her mind, "we have to assume first, that he thinks his evidence is absolutely conclusive, and, second, that his assessment of that evidence has convinced him that only quick, decisive action—presumably intended to nip whatever is happening in the bud—can prevent something even worse. From your perspective, that is."

*Oh, thank you for that little qualifier, Mr. Secretary!* Michelle thought tartly.

Pritchart gave Theisman a moderately severe glance, as if rebuking him for the boorishness of his last sentence. Or, Michelle thought, as if she wanted her "guest" to *think* she was rebuking the Secretary of War for a carefully preplanned comment. None of which affected the accuracy of anything he'd said, assuming they were both telling her the truth. And any questions about their prewar diplomatic exchanges aside, she couldn't imagine any possible advantage they might see in lying to a prisoner of war.

"May I ask exactly why you're telling me this?" she asked after a handful of seconds.

"Because I want you to understand exactly how grave the Star Kingdom's strategic position has just become, Admiral," Pritchart said levelly, looking back at her. Michelle bristled slightly internally, but Pritchart continued in that same, level tone. "I strongly suspect, Admiral Henke, that an officer of your seniority, serving directly under Duchess Harrington and with your close family relationship to your Queen, has access to intelligence reports indicating the numerical superiority we currently possess. I fully realize that your Manticoran Alliance's war fighting technology is still substantially in advance of our own, and I would be lying if I told you Thomas and I are completely confident our advantage in numbers is sufficient to offset your advantage in quality. We believe it is, or shortly will be; both of us, however, have had entirely too much personal and distinctly unpleasant experience of your Navy's . . . resilience, shall we say.

"But now this new element has been added to the equation. Neither you nor I have any idea at this time what consequences—long term or short term—your Captain Terekhov's actions are going to produce. Given the general arrogance quotient of the Solarian League where 'neobarbs' like the Star Kingdom and the Republic are concerned, however, I believe it's entirely possible local League administrators and admirals are likely to react without any concept of just how devastating your Navy's quality advantage would prove where *they* were concerned. In other words, the potential for Manticore to find itself in an ultimately fatal confrontation with the League is, in my judgment, very real."

"And," Michelle said, trying very hard to keep an edge of bitterness out of her tone, "given the distraction potential of all this, no doubt your calculations about your numerical superiority have revised your own prospects upwards, Madame President."

"To be perfectly honest, Admiral," Theisman said, "the first reaction of most of my analysts over at the New Octagon was that the only question was whether or not we should press the offensive immediately or wait a bit longer in hopes a worsening situation in Talbott will force you to weaken yourself still further on our front and *then* hit you."

He met her gaze unflinchingly, and she didn't blame him. In the Republic's position, exactly the same thoughts would have occurred to her, after all.

"That was the analysts' first thought," Pritchart agreed. "And mine, for that matter, I'm afraid. I spent too many years as a People's Commissioner for the People's Navy under the old régime not to think first in those terms. But then another thought occurred to me . . . Lady Gold Peak."

The abrupt change in the President's chosen form of address took Michelle offguard, and she sat back, pushing herself deep into her chair's physically comforting embrace, while she wondered what it portended.

"And that thought was, Madame President—?" she asked after a moment, her tone wary.

"Milady, I was completely candid with you in your hospital room. I want a way to end this war, and I would genuinely prefer to do it without killing any more people—on either side—than we have to. And because that's what I would prefer to do, I have a proposal for you."

"What sort of 'proposal'?" Michelle asked, watching her expression narrowly.

"I've already told you we've been considering proposing the possibility of prisoner exchanges. What I have in mind is to offer to release you and return you to the Star Kingdom, if you're willing to give us your parole to take no further part in active operations against the Republic until you are properly exchanged for one of our own officers in Manticoran custody."

"Why?" Michelle asked tersely.

"Because, frankly, I need an envoy your Queen might actually pay attention to. Someone close enough to her to deliver a message she'll at least listen to, even if it comes from me."

"And that message would be?"

Michelle braced herself. Her cousin Elizabeth's temper was justly famous . . . or perhaps *in*famous. It was one of her strengths, in many ways—part of what made her as effective as she was, part of what had won her her treecat name of "Soul of Steel." It was also, in Michelle's opinion, her greatest weakness. And Michelle had few illusions about how Elizabeth III was going to react when the Republic of Haven politely pointed out that her position had just become hopeless and it was time for her to consider surrendering.

"That message would be, Milady, that I wish to formally propose, as the Republic's head of state, a summit meeting between the two of us. A meeting to be held at a neutral location, to be chosen by her, for the purpose of discussing both possible ways to end the current conflict between our two star nations and also, if she so desires, the circumstances and content of our prewar diplomatic correspondence. In addition, I will be prepared to discuss any other matter she wishes to place upon the agenda. I will declare an offensive stand down of the Republic's forces, to begin the moment you agree to carry our message to the Queen, and I will not resume offensive operations, under any circumstances, until your Queen's response has reached me here in Nouveau Paris."

Somehow, Michelle managed to keep her jaw from dropping, but something very like a faint twinkle in the President's striking eyes suggested to her that she shouldn't consider a career change to diplomat or professional gambler.

"I realize this has come as . . . something of a surprise, Milady," Pritchart said with what Michelle considered to be massive understatement. "Frankly, though, I don't see that you have any option but to agree to take my message to Queen Elizabeth, for a lot of reasons."

"Oh, I think you can safely take that as a given, Madame President," Michelle said dryly.

"I rather thought I could." Pritchart smiled slightly, then glanced at Theisman and looked back at Michelle.

"For the most part, Her Majesty should feel free to include anyone she chooses in our meetings. I hope we'll be able to restrict staff and advisers to a manageable number for the direct, face-to-face conversations I hope to hold. We do, however, have one specific request in regard to the advisers she might choose to bring with her."

"Which is, Madame President?" Michelle asked just a bit cautiously.

"We would like to stipulate that Duchess Harrington be present."

Michelle blinked. She couldn't help it, although she managed—somehow—to keep her eyes from darting to Theisman to see his reaction to what the President had just said. At that moment, Michelle Henke wished, with a burning intensity, that she were a treecat, able to peek inside Eloise Pritchart's mind. From her own conversation with Theisman, it was evident to her that the Republic of Haven—or its intelligence services, at least—had, indeed, been aware for some time of the Manticoran media's reports about the 'cats and their recently confirmed abilities. And they must know that even if Elizabeth would be willing to leave her Ariel home, Honor most definitely would *not* agree to leave Nimitz home. Indeed, Theisman had personally seen just what the level of attachment between Honor and Nimitz was. Which meant Pritchart was deliberately inviting someone with a living lie detector to sit in on her personal conversations with the monarch of the star nation with which she was currently at war. Unless, of course, Michelle wanted to assume that someone as obviously competent as Pritchart, with advisers as competent as Thomas Theisman, was somehow unaware of what she'd just done.

"If the Queen accepts your proposal, Madame President," Michelle said, "I can't imagine that she would have any objection to including Duchess Harrington in her official delegation to any such talks. For that matter, while this is only my own opinion, you understand, I think Her Grace's unique status in both the Star Kingdom and Grayson would make her an ideal candidate for any such summit."

"And do you think Her Majesty will accept my proposal, Admiral Gold Peak?"

"That, Madame President," Michelle said frankly, "is something about which I'm not prepared even to speculate."

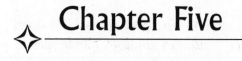

# Chapter Five

THE FACE IN AIVARS TEREKHOV'S mirror was thinner and gaunter than the one he remembered. In fact, it reminded him of the one he'd seen when he'd been repatriated to Manticore as a returning prisoner-of-war. The last few months might not have been as bad as that nightmare experience, but they—and especially the six weeks since leaving Montana—had still left their imprint, and his blue eyes searched their own reflection as if seeking some omen of the future.

Whatever he was looking for, he didn't find it . . . again. His nostrils flared as he snorted in mordant amusement at his own thoughts, and he splashed cold water across his face. Then he straightened, dried his face, and reached for the fresh uniform blouse Chief Steward Joanna Agnelli had laid out for him. He slid into it, feeling the sensual warmth of it as it slid across his skin, then sealed it and examined himself in the mirror one more time.

*No change*, he thought. *Just a man with a shirt on this time.*

But the man in the mirror wasn't really "just a man with a shirt on," and Terekhov knew it. He was once again *Captain* Terekhov, commanding officer of Her Manticoran Majesty's heavy cruiser *Hexapuma.*

*For now, at least*, he reminded himself, and watched his mirror's lips twitch in a brief almost-smile.

He turned away from the mirror and stepped out of his private head into his sleeping cabin. The door to his day cabin was slightly open, and he could just see Commander Ginger Lewis, his acting executive officer, and Lieutenant Commander Amal Nagchaudhuri, *Hexapuma*'s communications officer, waiting for him. He paused for just a moment longer, then drew a deep breath, made sure his "confident CO" expression was in place, and went out to meet them.

"Good morning," he said, waving for them to remain seated when they started to rise.

"Good morning, Sir," Lewis replied for both of them.

"I assume you've both had breakfast already?"

"Yes, Sir."

"Well, I'm afraid I haven't, and Joanna gets cranky if I don't eat. So if the two of you don't mind, I'm going to nibble like an obedient little captain while we go over the morning reports."

"Far be it from me to try to get between Chief Agnelli and her notion of the proper feeding of captains, Sir," Lewis said, and grinned broadly. So did Nagchaudhuri, although not every acting exec would have been comfortable making jokes at what could have been construed as the captain's expense, and Terekhov chuckled.

"I see you're a wise woman," he observed, and sat down behind his desk. The terminal was folded down, giving him a level work surface or—in this case—a surface for something else, and Chief Steward Agnelli appeared as quickly and silently as if the captain had rubbed a lamp to summon her.

With a brisk efficiency that always reminded Terekhov of a stage magician bedazzling his audience, Agnelli whisked a white linen cloth across the desktop, added a plate with a bowl of cold cereal and fruit precisely centered upon it, set out a small pitcher of milk, a plate of steamy hot muffins, a butter dish, a tall glass of chilled tomato juice, a coffee cup, a steaming carafe, silverware, and a snowy napkin. She considered her handiwork for a moment or two, then minutely readjusted the silverware.

"Buzz when you're finished, Sir," she said, and withdrew.

Terekhov found himself once more searching for the puff of smoke into which his resident djinn had just disappeared. Then he shook his head, reached for the milk, and poured it over the waiting cereal.

"With all due respect, Sir, that doesn't look like a particularly huge breakfast to me," Lewis observed.

"Maybe not," Terekhov acknowledged, then gave her a sharp

glance. "On the other hand, this is about what I usually have for breakfast, Ginger. I'm not exactly off my feed, if that's what you were subtly asking."

"I suppose I was, actually."

If Lewis felt particularly abashed, she showed no signs of it, and Terekhov shook his head. Ginger Lewis looked a great deal like a younger version of his wife, Sinead, whose portrait hung on the wall behind the commander even now. She was just as self-confident as Sinead, as well. In fact, Terekhov sometimes felt as if she were *channeling* Sinead, and he more than suspected that she'd decided it was more important than ever that someone aboard *Hexapuma* be willing to admit she was mother-henning the captain.

*Although, between her and Joanna, it's not likely I could miss the point, now is it?*

"Well, consider yourself not so subtly answered," he said aloud, his tone making it obvious that it was not a rebuke. "And while I crunch away at my modest—but healthy, *very* healthy—repast, why don't the two of you get started telling me all the things I need to know?"

"Yes, Sir."

Lewis pulled out her personal minicomp and called up the first of the several memos to herself which she had composed.

"First," she said, "there's the sick report. Lieutenant Sarkozy still has twenty-seven patients in sickbay, but she expects to discharge three more of them today. That will be . . . eight of our own people and twelve more from *Warlock* and *Aria* who've returned to duty so far. And she says that Lajos should be returning to duty in the next two or three days."

"Good," Terekhov said. Surgeon Lieutenant Ruth Sarkozy had been HMS *Vigilant's* ship's surgeon before the brutal Battle of Monica. *Vigilant* was one of the six ships Terekhov had lost in that engagement, but Sarkozy had survived, which had turned out to be an extraordinarily good thing for a lot of reasons, including the fact that Surgeon Commander Lajos Orban, *Hexapuma's* own surgeon, had been one of *Hexapuma's* thirty-two wounded. Sarkozy had turned out to be an outstanding substitute for him—a point Terekhov had emphasized in the post-battle reports he'd already drafted—but like all too many of his surviving personnel, she was obviously feeling the strain of doing too many people's duty. She had to be even more relieved than anyone else to see Orban recovered enough to leave sickbay! It was fortunate that his injuries, while messy, had been less severe than they'd originally appeared. With quick-heal, Sarkozy had gotten him back on his feet (although he'd remained very shaky) in less than a week, which made him far luckier than people like Naomi Kaplan, *Hexapuma*'s tactical officer, who was still conscious only intermittently.

And Lajos was a *hell* of a lot luckier than the seventy-four members of the ship's company who'd been killed in action, Terekhov thought grimly.

"Ansten isn't going to be back on his feet again for a while, according to Sarkozy's current reports," Lewis continued. "Of course, *he* claims he'll be ready to resume his duties 'any time now.'" She glanced up and looked Terekhov in the eye. "Despite any rumors to the contrary, I'm not so drunk with power that I want to stay on as acting XO any longer than I have to, but somehow I don't think that's going to happen. Lieutenant Sarkozy's let him move out of sickbay and back to his own quarters, but I think that was only because she needed the bed. And probably partly because he was driving her towards raving lunacy." Her lips twitched. "He's not exactly . . . the best patient in the recorded history of the galaxy."

Terekhov was drinking tomato juice at that particular moment, and his involuntary snort of amusement came very close to sparking sartorial catastrophe. Fortunately, he managed to get the glass lowered in time without quite spraying juice all over his uniform blouse.

Calling Ansten FitzGerald "not the best patient" was one of the finest examples of gross understatement to come his way in quite some time. *Hexapuma*'s executive officer was constitutionally incapable of taking a single moment longer from his duties than he absolutely had to. He was also one of those people who deeply resented the discovery that in the face of sufficient physical trauma his body was prepared to *demand* he take some time to recover while it got itself back into proper running order.

"Part of it," Terekhov said as severely as he could as he wiped his lips with the napkin, "is that Ansten is aware of how shorthanded we are. How shorthanded all of us are. And, of course," he lowered the napkin and smiled crookedly, "he's also got enough sheer, bullheaded stubbornness for any three people I could think of right offhand."

"Should I take that as an indication that you don't want me handing the job back over to him this afternoon, Sir?"

"Frankly, nothing would please me more than to have you hand it over to him," Terekhov told her. "Believe me, Ginger, I know you've got plenty to do down in Engineering without adding this to the load. But I'm not prepared to put Ansten back into harness until Sarkozy—or Lajos—is ready to sign off on it, whatever *he* thinks."

"I can't pretend I wouldn't rather go back to Engineering full-time," Lewis said, "but I agree with you where Ansten is concerned. Do you want me to break it gently to him, Sir, or will you tell him yourself?"

"The cowardly part of me wants to leave it to you. Unfortunately, I believe they told me at Saganami Island that there were certain responsibilities a commanding officer wasn't allowed to shuffle off on to a subordinate. I suspect facing Ansten under these circumstances qualifies."

"I stand in awe of your courage, Sir."

"And well you should." Terekhov said with an air of becoming modesty, then turned to Nagchaudhuri.

"Anything new from the Monicans this morning, Amal?"

"No, Sir." The tall, almost albino-pale communications officer grimaced. "They've repeated their demand that we evacuate the system immediately right on schedule, but that's about all. So far."

"Nothing more about that 'medical necessity' civilian evacuation of Eroica they trotted out yesterday?"

"No, Sir. Or not yet, at least. After all, the day's still young in Estelle."

Terekhov smiled in sour amusement, although it wasn't really particularly funny.

There was no doubt in his mind that he was the most hated man in the Monica System, and with good reason. He and the ten warships under his command had killed or wounded something like seventy-five percent of the total personnel strength of the Monica System Navy. They'd also destroyed the Monicans' main naval shipyard, killed several thousand yard workers, and wiped out at least two or three decades of infrastructure investment in the process. Not to mention destroying or permanently disabling twelve of the fourteen Solarian battlecruisers with which Monica had been supplied. He still wasn't certain exactly how those ships had factored into the elaborate plans someone had worked out to sabotage the Star Kingdom's annexation of the Talbott Cluster, but all the evidence he'd so far been able to collect from the wreckage of Eroica Station only served to further underscore the fact that those plans had required a sponsor with very deep pockets . . . and very few scruples against killing people in job lots.

At the moment, however, he and Roberto Tyler, President of the Union of Monica, were both rather more preoccupied, although from different perspectives, with a more pressing concern. Aivars Terekhov had lost sixty percent of his hastily improvised squadron, and more like three-quarters of his personnel, in destroying those ships and the military component of Eroica Station. His four surviving ships were all severely damaged. Only two of them remained hyper-capable, at least until they'd been able to make major repairs, and those two offered far too little life-support capacity for all of his surviving personnel. Which meant he *couldn't* pull out of Monica, even if he'd been inclined to do so. Which he wasn't, since he had no intention of allowing Tyler and his people to "vanish" any inconvenient evidence before someone arrived from Manticore to examine it more fully and systematically than Terekhov's own resources permitted.

So far, there was no reason to believe Tyler suspected that half of the Manticoran intruders were too crippled to withdraw. And, fortunately, there was also no evidence to suggest he intended to push Terekhov into making good on his threat where the remaining pair of *Indefatigable*-class battlecruisers were concerned. Those two ships had been moored in *civilian* shipyard slips on the far side of Eroica Station's sprawling industrial complex. Terekhov had declined to target them in his initial attack, given the horrendous number of civilian casualties that would have entailed. But when the surviving units of the Monican Navy had demanded he surrender or face destruction, he'd given them back an ultimatum of his own.

If his ships were attacked, he would destroy those remaining battlecruisers with a saturation nuclear bombardment . . . and he would not permit the evacuation of civilians from Eroica Station first.

It was entirely possible some members of Tyler's administration thought he was bluffing. If so, however, the President remained unwilling to call that bluff. Which was a very good thing for everyone concerned, Terekhov thought grimly, since the one thing he *wasn't* doing was bluffing.

"Do you think there's any truth to Tyler's 'medical emergency' claims, Sir?" Lewis' question pulled Terekhov back up out of his thoughts and he gave himself a mental shake, followed by a physical shake of his head.

"I won't completely rule out the possibility. If it is a genuine emergency, though, it's a very conveniently *timed* one, don't you think?"

"Yes, Sir." Lewis rubbed the tip of her nose for a moment, then shrugged. "The only thing that struck me as just a bit odd about it is that he's waited this long to trot it out."

"Well, he's already used the running-out-of-food argument, and the life-support-emergency claim, and the damaged-power-systems claim, Ginger," Nagchaudhuri pointed out. "That old fairytale about the boy that cried wolf comes to mind now."

"That it does," Terekhov agreed. "On the other hand, this one *is* a bit different in that we can't verify—or disprove—his claims as easily as we did the others."

Nagchaudhuri nodded, and Terekhov busied himself spreading butter across a warm muffin while he pondered.

It had been relatively simple to dispose of most of the Monicans' so-called emergencies. Although *Hexapuma*'s shipboard sensors had been severely mauled, Terekhov still had more than enough highly capable remote reconnaissance platforms to keep an eye on everything happening in the Monica System. Those same platforms had been able to monitor the surviving components of Eroica Station and disprove Tyler's claims about things like power spikes or atmospheric leaks caused by collateral damage from the bombardment of the station's military component. But claims of disease among the station's inhabitants were something else.

"I think we're going to have to arrange an examination of some of these conveniently sick Monicans," he said after a moment. "Which probably means it's a good thing Lajos is just about fit for duty again."

"Sir, with all due respect, I'm not sure offering the Monicans hostages of their own is the best move," Lewis said, rather more diffidently than usual. "Once we send—"

"Don't worry, Ginger."

Terekhov's voice was a bit indistinct as he spoke around a bite of buttered muffin. He chewed, swallowed, and cleared his throat.

"Don't worry," he repeated in a clearer tone, shaking his head.

"I'm not about to send Lieutenant Sarkozy or Lajos aboard Eroica Station. If they're prepared to put some of their deathly ill patients aboard a shuttle and send it out to us, we'll examine them here. And if they aren't willing to, I'll take that as evidence they know we'd see through their bogus claims."

"Yes, Sir." Lewis nodded.

"In the meantime, what's the latest from Commander Lignos about *Aegis'* fire control?"

"They're making at least some progress, Sir," Lewis said, accessing another of her memos. "It's not anything the yard dogs back home would be ready to sign off on, but by swapping out those components with *Aria*, Commander Lignos should be able to get at least her forward lidar back on-line. That's still going to leave—"

"So Tyler turned down your invitation to offer his sick citizens free medical care, did he?" Bernardus Van Dort said dryly. He and Terekhov sat in the captain's briefing room later that morning, chairs tipped back, nursing cups of coffee, and Terekhov snorted.

"You might say that." He shook his head. "There are times I wish I hadn't stopped you from presenting your credentials as Baroness Medusa's personal representative. If I had, at least all of this diplomatic crap would be landing on your plate, instead of mine."

"If you think—" Van Dort began, but Terekhov shook his head again, harder.

"Forget it. I didn't spend all those years in Foreign Office service without learning a little bit about how the game's played, Bernardus! The minute you open your mouth as Medusa's officially accredited representative, this stops being a case of a single rogue officer Her Majesty can disavow if she has to. We can't afford to give Tyler and his crew any basis to attack the notion that I acted independently of any orders from any higher authority. Especially since I did!"

Van Dort started to open his mouth, then closed it. Much as he hated to admit it, Terekhov was right. Van Dort's own experience in the politics of his home system of Rembrandt, his decades of work as the founding CEO of the multi-system Rembrandt Trade Union, and his experience working to set up the annexation plebiscite for the entire Talbott Cluster all supported the same conclusion.

Which didn't mean he had to like it.

He sipped from his own coffee cup, savoring its rich, strong taste, and hoped Terekhov couldn't see how worried he was becoming. Not over the political and military situation here in Monica, although either of those would have provided ample justification for two or three T-years' worth of normal anxiety, but over Terekhov himself. The captain was the glue which held the entire squadron together, and the burden of command pressed down on him like a two or three-gravity field. It didn't go away, either. It was always there, always weighing down upon him, and there was nothing any of his officers—or Van Dort—could do to relieve that constant, grinding pressure, however much they might have wished to. Not that knowing they couldn't kept anyone from trying, of course.

"What about Bourmont's units?" he asked after a moment.

Gregoire Bourmont was the Monican Navy's chief of naval operations. He was the one who'd issued the demand for Terekhov's surrender after the Battle of Monica, and from the tone of the handful of messages which had passed between the two sides since, his continued inability to compel that surrender was only making him more belligerent.

*Unless, of course, it's all an act,* Van Dort reminded himself. *Aivars isn't the only one who understands "plausible deniability," after all. If Tyler lets Bourmont play the part of the saber-rattling military hard ass, then* he *can play the role of conciliating statesman. Or try to, anyway. And if anything goes wrong in the end, he can always try to head off the consequences by offering Bourmont up to Aivars as a sacrificial lamb and sacking the "hothead" who pushed things ever so much further than his civilian superiors would ever have authorized.*

"All of his ships—such as they are and what there are of them—are still sitting in orbit around Monica," Terekhov said. "From all appearances, they plan to go right on sitting there, too."

"Have there been any more departures from the system?" Van Dort's tone was almost painfully neutral, but Terekhov snorted again, more harshly than before.

"No," he said. "Of course, that's not a lot of comfort, given how many ships definitely did 'depart from the system' before I sent my little explanatory note to Admiral Bourmont."

Van Dort nodded. That was the real source of the anxiety

gnawing at the nerves of every surviving man and woman of Terekhov's battered squadron. The truth was that Terekhov's threat to nuke Eroica Station wasn't actually necessary any longer. *Hexapuma*, the light cruiser *Aegis*, and the older (and even more heavily damaged) *Star Knight*-class heavy cruiser *Warlock* had managed to restore enough of their fire control to manage several dozen of the Royal Manticoran Navy's new "flat pack" missile pods, and the ammunition ship *Volcano* had delivered over two hundred of them to the squadron. With those pods full of MDMs, Terekhov could have annihilated Bourmont's entire remaining naval strength long before those ships were able to get into their own range of *his* units.

Unfortunately, Bourmont might not realize that. Or, for that matter, believe it, despite the evidence of what similar pods had done at Eroica Station. The fact that no one outside Eroica Station appeared to have seen any of the tracking or tactical data from the opening phase of the engagement actually worked against Terekhov in that respect. Bourmont literally hadn't seen any hard evidence of what the Manticoran squadron had done, or how. In fact, it very much looked as if the only people who really *had* seen any of that evidence were either dead or among the tiny handful of survivors Terekhov's small craft had plucked from the shattered ruins of the station's military component and the hulked wreckage of two of the battlecruisers his squadron had engaged.

Personally, Van Dort had come to the conclusion that Terekhov *probably* wouldn't nuke the civilian portion of the station no matter what happened. Or not any longer, at least. Given his range and accuracy advantage, he was far more likely to settle for picking off Bourmont's cruisers and destroyers, instead. In fact, Van Dort thought, the threat against Eroica's civilians had actually become the way Terekhov was avoiding the necessity of killing any more of the Monican Navy's uniformed personnel, since it prevented Bourmont from pushing him into doing just that.

*Of course it does, Bernardus,* the businessman-turned-statesman told himself. *And one reason you want it to be true is that you don't really want to think your friend Aivars really would kill all of those civilians.*

But the truth of the matter was that Bourmont and the entire surviving Monican Navy had never posed the real threat. No, the real threat, the one which menaced not just Terekhov's squadron but the entire Star Kingdom of Manticore, lay in that handful of ships which had fled into hyper-space in the aftermath of the short, brutal battle. What had made the Union of Monica a viable threat to the annexation of the Talbott Cluster in the first place was its status as a client of the Solarian League's Office of Frontier Security. Neither Van Dort nor anyone else in Terekhov's squadron knew the actual content of any of the treaties or formal agreements defining Monica's relationship with Frontier Security. It was more than likely, however, that those agreements included a "mutual defense" clause. And if they did, and if one of those fleeing starships had headed for Meyers, where the local Frontier Security commissioner hung his hat, it was entirely possible that a *Solarian* squadron—or even a light task force—was headed for Monica at this very moment.

*And a Solly flag officer, especially one working for OFS, isn't going to shed a lot of tears over the deaths of a few hundred—or even a few thousand—neobarbs,* Van Dort thought grimly. *Even if those neobarbs are citizens of the star nation he's supposedly there to support. Can't make an omelet without cracking a few eggs, after all. And he's not going to believe any wild stories about Manticoran "super missiles," either. So if a Frontier Fleet detachment does turn up, Aivars is either going to have to surrender after all . . . or else start a shooting war directly with the Solarian League.*

"So the situation's pretty much unchanged," he said out loud, and Terekhov nodded.

"We did let the pregnant workers from Eroica return to the planet," he said, and made a face. "I can't imagine what these people were thinking about letting them work in an environment like that in the first place! Every extra-atmospheric work contract in the Star Kingdom contains specific provisions to prevent exposing fetuses to the sorts of radiation hazards aboard a station like that."

"Rembrandt, too," Van Dort agreed. "But a lot of the star nations out here, especially the poorer ones, don't seem to think they have that luxury."

"*Luxury!*" Terekhov snorted. "You mean they aren't going to enforce proper liability laws against their local employers, don't you? After all, insurance drives up overhead, right? And if they aren't going to be liable—legally, at least—anyway, then why should any of them worry about a little thing like what happens to their workers or their workers' children?"

Van Dort contented himself with a nod of agreement, although Terekhov's vehemence worried him. It wasn't because he disagreed with anything the captain had just said, but the raw anger—and the contempt—glittering in Terekhov's blue eyes was a far cry from the Manticoran's normal demeanor of cool self-control. His anger was one more indication of the pressure he was under, and Van Dort didn't even want to think about what would happen if Aivars Terekhov suddenly crumbled.

*But that isn't going to happen,* he told himself. *In fact, the way you're worrying about it is probably an indication of the pressure you're* under, *when you come right down to it. Aivars is one of the least likely to crack people you've ever met. In fact, the real reason you're worrying about him is because of how much you like him, isn't it?*

"Well, letting them go back dirt-side ought to earn us at least a little good press," he observed out loud.

"Oh, don't be silly, Bernardus." Terekhov waved his coffee cup. "You know as well as I do how it's going to be presented. President Tyler's tireless efforts on behalf of his citizens have finally borne at least partial fruit in convincing the heartless Manticoran tyrant and murderer Terekhov to allow these poor, pregnant women—the women the wicked Manties have been callously exposing to all the threats of a space station environment, along with the rest of their hostages, as part of their barbarous threat to massacre helpless civilians—to return to safety." He shook his head. "If there's any 'good press' going around, trust me, Tyler and his toadies will see to it that all of it focuses on *him.*"

"After reaching his hand into a trash disposer like this one, he probably needs all the good press he can get!" Van Dort replied.

"Assuming he ever stops playing the victimized total innocent and admits that's what he did. Which he doesn't seem to be in any hurry to do."

"No, but—"

"Excuse me, Sir."

Both men turned their heads to look at the briefing room hatch as the youthful voice spoke. Midshipwoman Helen Zilwicki, one of *Hexapuma*'s "snotties," looked back at them, and Terekhov arched an eyebrow.

"And just which 'sir' are you asking to excuse you, Ms. Zilwicki?" he inquired mildly. Under most circumstances, there wouldn't have been any question who a midshipwoman under his command was addressing, but Helen had been assigned as Van Dort's personal aide, in addition to her other duties, ever since he'd come aboard ship.

"Sorry, Sir." Helen's smile was fleeting, but genuine. "I meant you, Captain," she said, and her smile disappeared as quickly as it had come. "CIC's just detected a hyper footprint, Sir. A big one."

# Chapter Six

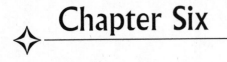

HEXAPUMA'S BRIDGE WAS FULLY manned when Terekhov stepped onto it. The ship's casualties left her short of all the officers she truly needed, but the damage to Auxiliary Control and the backup bridge there had been far too severe to be repaired out of *Hexapuma*'s shipboard resources. That meant there was no tactical crew to take over if anything happened to the bridge proper, but it also meant there was no need for an entire backup set of officers, either, which at least eased the pressure on the survivors. And that there was no reason Ginger Lewis shouldn't man her customary battle stations position in Engineering rather than haring off as acting exec to take charge of AuxCon.

Midshipwoman Zilwicki stepped around Terekhov and walked quickly to her own position at missile defense. She seated herself at the elbow of Lieutenant Abigail Hearns, the Grayson born (and extremely youthful) young woman who had replaced Naomi Kaplan as *Hexapuma*'s tactical officer.

*I wonder if any other heavy cruiser in the entire Queen's Navy's ever had a pair that young in charge of its tactical section?* a corner of Terekhov's mind wondered. *They can't have much more than forty-five T-years between them!*

Maybe not, he reflected, but the job that youthful pair had already done during the Battle of Monica left him without any qualms about relying on them now.

"Any IDs?" he asked.

"Not yet, Sir," Abigail replied without ever looking up from her own displays while her long, slender fingers played across her console, working to refine the data. "Whoever it is, they opted for an almost polar approach, and we don't have any platforms in position for a close look at them. We're redeploying now, but it's going to take a while."

"Understood."

Terekhov crossed to his own command chair, settled into it, and deployed its displays. There were several possible explanations for why someone might have opted to approach a star system from well above the ecliptic, but aside from gross astrogational error, very few of those explanations would have applied to merchant shipping. Most of a merchant ship's likely destinations in any star system lay in the plane of the system's ecliptic, so translating into hyper in that plane and on the same side of the system as the destination in question required the shortest normal-space flight to reach it. Then, too, crossing a star's hyper limit from significantly above or below the plane of the ecliptic also imposed greater wear and tear—which equated to higher maintenance and replacement costs—on a freighter's hyper generator and alpha nodes. That was true for warships, too, of course . . . but maintenance costs ran a poor second to tactical considerations where they were concerned.

The most likely reason for a polar approach by a warship or a squadron of warships would be to avoid any nasty little surprises a defender might have attempted to arrange on a more conventional approach vector. The fact that it also gave better sensor coverage of the entire system (or, at least, of the entire ecliptic) wasn't anything to sneer at, either. A defender could still hide on the far side of the system's central star, or in the shadow of one or more of its planets or even moons, but it got harder against someone looking down—or up—from system north or south.

"Sir," Abigail said after several more tense moments, "CIC's managed to isolate a count on the footprints. They make it ten. Best estimate is that five of them are in the four million-plus tonnage range."

"Thank you." Terekhov's tone was calm, almost absent, as he studied his own repeater displays, and no one else had to know how difficult it was for him to keep it that way.

If CIC's estimate was accurate, then five of the unknowns fell squarely into the tonnage bracket for ships of the wall. And if that was what they actually were, their arrival could be nothing but bad news for HMS *Hexapuma* and the rest of her squadron, because there weren't five *Manticoran* wallers in the entire Talbott Cluster. So if five of them were turning up now, they had to belong to someone else . . . like the Solarian League.

*Although, now that I come to think about it, just what the hell would* Solly *wallers be doing way out here? This is Frontier Fleet's bailiwick, not Battle Fleet's, so they shouldn't have anything bigger than battlecruisers in the vicinity, either. On the other hand, none of the local systems have anything the size of a dreadnought or a superdreadnought in inventory. So . . .*

"Bring the Squadron to readiness, Mr. Nagchaudhuri," he said.

"Aye, aye, Sir," the communications officer replied, and sent the order (which Terekhov was quite certain was thoroughly unnecessary) to the other three ships of his battered "squadron."

The good news, such as it was and what there was of it, was that the missile pods deployed about his ships contained all-up Mark 23s, not the Mark 16s which normally lived in *Hexapuma's* magazines. The Mark 16's laser heads produced greater destructive power than almost anything else below the wall of battle, but they'd never been intended to take on superdreadnought armor. They could inflict a lot of superficial damage, possibly even cripple the heavier ship's sensor suites or rip up the vulnerable nodes of its impeller rings, but good as they were, they had far too little punch to actually *stop* a waller.

But the Mark 23 was a very different proposition, he thought grimly. His control links were still too badly damaged to manage more than a few dozen pods simultaneously. Certainly he couldn't come close to matching the multi-thousand-missile salvos the Manticoran Alliance and the Republic of Haven had become accustomed to throwing at one another! But he could still fire almost four hundred attack birds in a single launch, and if those *were* Solly dreadnoughts or superdreadnoughts, they were in for an extraordinarily unpleasant surprise when three badly mauled cruisers and a single destroyer opened fire on them with that many capital missiles from well outside their own engagement range.

*And what if they are?* that corner of his mind jeered. *Even if you destroy all five of them outright, so what? Great! You'll begin the war with the Sollies with a resounding triumph. That should be plenty of comfort when two or three thousand ships of the wall head for Manticore with blood in their eyes!*

At least he'd have four or five hours before he had to start making any irrevocable decisions. Not that—

"Sir, we're being hailed!" Nagchaudhuri said suddenly, spinning his chair to face his captain. "It's FTL, Sir!"

Terekhov twitched upright in his own chair. If the unknowns were transmitting using FTL grav-pulses, then they damned well weren't *Sollies*! In fact, if they were transmitting FTL, the only people they *could* be were—

"Put it on my display," he said.

"Yes, Sir!" Nagchaudhuri said with a huge grin, and punched in a command.

A face appeared on the small com display by Terekhov's knee. It was a dark-complexioned face, with a strong nose and chin and thinning hair, and Terekhov's eyes widened in surprise as he saw it.

"This is Admiral Khumalo," the owner of that face said. "I am approaching Monica with a relief force. If Captain Terekhov is available, I need to speak to him immediately."

"*Available,*" Terekhov thought with a sort of lunatic glee as the first outriders of almost unimaginable relief crashed through him. *Now, there's a word choice for you! He probably thinks it would have been bad for morale to say "if he's still alive," instead.*

"Put me through, Amal," he said.

"Aye, aye, Sir." Nagchaudhuri punched in another command. "Live mike, Sir."

"Terekhov here, Admiral Khumalo," Terekhov said into his com pickup. "It's good to see you, Sir."

Their relative positions put *Hexapuma* and Khumalo's flagship the better part of thirty light-minutes apart, and even with a grav-pulse com, that imposed a transmission delay of over twenty-seven seconds. Terekhov waited patiently for fifty-four seconds, and then Khumalo's eyes sharpened.

"I don't doubt that it is, Captain," he said. "May I assume there's a reason your ships are sitting where they are?"

"Yes, Sir, there is. We found it necessary to remain close enough to Eroica Station to keep an eye on the evidence and, ah, present President Tyler with an argument sufficient to prevent any hastiness on the part of his surviving navy."

"'*Surviving* navy'?" Khumalo repeated the better part of a minute later. "It would appear you've been quite busy out here, Captain Terekhov." His smile was decidedly on the wintry side.

Terekhov thought about replying, then thought better of it and simply sat there, waiting.

"May I assume you've already written up your reports on this . . . incident?" Khumalo asked after several more moments.

"Yes, Sir. I have."

"Good. Let me have them now then, if you would. I should have ample time to review them, since my astrogator makes it roughly seven and a half hours for us to reach your current position. At that time, please be prepared to come aboard *Hercules*."

"Of course, Sir."

"In that case, Captain, I'll see you then, when we don't have to worry about transmission lag. Khumalo, clear."

Seven hours and forty-five minutes later, Aivars Terekhov's pinnace drifted out of *Hexapuma*'s boat bay on reaction thrusters, rolled on gyros, reoriented itself, and accelerated smoothly towards HMS *Hercules*. The trip was short enough that there was no point bringing up the small craft's impeller wedge, and Terekhov sat back in his comfortable seat, watching the view screen on the forward bulkhead as the superdreadnought grew steadily larger.

Khumalo must have pulled out of the Spindle System literally within hours of the arrival of Terekhov's dispatch informing him of his plans. In fact, Terekhov was frankly astonished that the rear admiral had obviously responded so promptly and decisively. It was clear he hadn't waited to call in a single additional ship; he must have simply ordered every hyper-capable hull in the star system to rendezvous with his flagship and headed straight for Monica.

His scratch-built force was even more lopsided and ill-balanced than Terekhov's "squadron" had been. Aside from *Hercules*—which, for all her impressively massive tonnage was still one of the only two or three sadly obsolescent *Samothrace*-class ships lingering on in commission as little more than depot ships on distant stations—it consisted solely of the light cruisers *Devastation* and *Intrepid*, and the three destroyers *Victorious*, *Ironside*, and *Domino*. Aside from *Victorious*, not a one of them was less than twenty T-years old, although that still made them considerably more modern and lethal than anything Monica had possessed before the sudden and mysterious infusion of modern battlecruisers.

The other four "superdreadnought-range" hyper footprints had belonged to the ammunition ships *Petard* and *Holocaust* and the repair ships *Ericsson* and *White*. Terekhov was relieved to see all of them, but especially the two repair ships, given the state of his own command.

*Not that it's likely to be "my command" much longer*, he reflected as the pinnace sped towards *Hercules*.

All of his reports had been burst-transmitted to *Hercules* within minutes of his conversation with Khumalo, but so far, the rear admiral hadn't said another word to him. Under the circumstances, Terekhov found that more than a bit ominous. There were several reasons Khumalo might have hastened off to Monica, and one of the ones that came most forcibly to mind, given the admiral's lack of combat experience and general "by The Book" attitude, was a desire to sit on Terekhov before he got the Star Kingdom into even worse trouble. In fact, Terekhov wouldn't blame him a bit if that *was* the reason he was here. Augustus Khumalo hadn't been assigned to the Talbott Cluster because of his brilliant combat record and demonstrated ability to think outside the box. The real reasons he'd been sent to Talbott by the High Ridge Government were his connections to the Conservative Party . . . and the fact that no one in High Ridge's cabinet had ever dreamed Talbott might turn into a critical flashpoint. They'd wanted a reliable administrator for a post of decidedly secondary importance, not a warrior, and that was precisely what Khumalo had given them.

And the truth was that Terekhov could see any number of perfectly good and valid reasons for Khumalo to repudiate Terekhov's own actions, and not just from the personal perspective of the admiral's career. Stopping whatever plot had been set in motion by the provider of those battlecruisers had been absolutely essential, but avoiding an open conflict with the Solarian League was equally vital. That was the entire reason Terekhov had set himself up to be publicly disavowed by the Star Kingdom as a sacrifice to placate the Solarians. If Khumalo was as politically aware as Terekhov suspected he was, then the admiral would no doubt recognize the advantages in disavowing him immediately. Khumalo could always stay exactly where he was, maintaining the status quo in Monica until the more powerful relief force which had undoubtedly been dispatched directly from Manticore arrived, on the grounds that the situation, while not of his own or the Star Kingdom's official making, still had to be stabilized until an impartial investigation could get to the bottom of what had really happened. If it should happen that the Queen and the Grantville Government chose *not* to disavow Terekhov after all of the reports were in, there would always be time for Khumalo's repudiation to be withdrawn.

*And besides all of those perfectly good and logical reasons of state*, Terekhov thought with a sour grin, *on a personal level, he's got to be totally and completely pissed off with me for putting him in this situation in the first place, no matter* how *good my reasons turn out to've been! I know* I'd *be royally pissed at me if I* were him, *anyway.*

He glanced at the time display ticking steadily down in one corner of the visual display and shrugged mentally. Another eighteen minutes, and he'd have the chance to observe Rear Admiral Augustus Khumalo's reaction firsthand.

It promised to be an interesting experience.

HMS *Hercules'* forward boat bay was considerably larger than *Hexapuma's*, and it seemed oddly quiet as Terekhov swam the personnel tube from his pinnace, then swung himself into the boat bay's regulation one standard gravity.

"*Hexapuma*, arriving!" the bay speakers intoned, and the side party came to attention as Terekhov landed just outside the painted line on the deck.

"Permission to come aboard, Ma'am?" he asked the boat bay officer of the deck.

"Permission granted, Sir," the youthful lieutenant in question replied, returning his salute, then stepped back to clear the way for Captain Victoria Saunders, *Hercules's* commanding officer.

"Captain," Terekhov said, saluting her in turn.

"Welcome aboard, Captain Terekhov," Saunders replied, returning the courtesy. The auburn-haired captain was a good fifteen T-years older than Terekhov, and her expression gave very little indication of her emotions. Her crisp, Sphinxian accent might have been just a bit more taut than usual, but her handshake, when she offered it a moment later, was firm.

"Thank you, Ma'am." Terekhov was unusually aware of the white beret which marked Saunders as the commander of a hyper-capable unit of the Royal Manticoran Navy. His own matching beret was tucked neatly under one of his epaulets, since courtesy precluded his wearing it aboard another captain's command, and he wondered if he was so aware of Saunders' because the odds were so good that he himself would never again be permitted to wear it.

"If you'll come with me, Captain," Saunders continued, "Admiral Khumalo is waiting for you in his day cabin."

"Of course, Ma'am."

Terekhov fell in beside Saunders as *Hercules'* captain escorted him to the lifts. Saunders made no particular effort to make small talk, for which Terekhov was grateful. There was no point pretending this was a normal courtesy call by one captain upon another, and trying to would only have twisted his own nerves more tightly.

It was odd, he reflected, as he followed Saunders into the lift car and she punched in the proper destination code. He'd thought about this moment literally for months—now it was here, and his stomach muscles were tense and he seemed preternaturally aware of every air current, every tiny scratch on the lift car's control panel. The fact that Khumalo had arrived before any Solarian response was an unspeakable relief, and he was guiltily aware that the knowledge that Khumalo's seniority would make whatever happened from here out *his* responsibility was an almost equal relief. But Khumalo's arrival also meant Terekhov's personal day of reckoning was at hand. He felt the consequences of his own actions race towards him, and he was far too honest with himself to pretend they didn't frighten him in a way facing the Monican Navy hadn't. This fear lacked the sharp, jagged spikes and raw terror of facing the enemy's fire, but in many ways, that only made it worse. At least in combat there was the illusion that his fate hung upon his own decisions, his own actions. In this case, that fate now hung upon the decisions and actions of others, and nothing he could possibly do at this point would affect those decisions one way or the other.

And yet despite the fear, he felt . . . content. That was what was so odd about it. It wasn't that he felt *happy*, or that he would have no regrets if it turned out his naval career was, in fact, over. It was simply that he knew, with a certainty which admitted of no doubts at all, that the decisions he'd made and the actions he'd taken were the only ones he *could* have taken and still been the man Sinead Terekhov loved.

And beside that, he realized, all of the other consequences in the universe were secondary.

The lift car delivered them to their destination, and Terekhov followed Saunders down a passage to the cabin door guarded by the traditional Marine sentry.

"Captain Saunders and Captain Terekhov to see the admiral," Saunders told the Marine.

"Yes, Ma'am. Thank you, Ma'am," the Marine corporal replied, as if he hadn't already known perfectly well who the two naval officers were. He reached down and keyed the bulkhead intercom switch. "Captain Saunders and Captain Terekhov to see the admiral," he announced.

The door slid open immediately, and Captain Loretta Shoupe, Augustus Khumalo's chief of staff, looked out at them.

"Come in," she invited, standing back to clear the way, and then led them across a truly stupendous dining cabin into the only moderately smaller day cabin where Khumalo awaited them.

The admiral remained seated behind his desk as the trio of captains entered.

"Find seats," he said before any formal military courtesies could be exchanged, and Terekhov and the two women settled into three of the day cabin's comfortable chairs.

Khumalo tipped back in his own chair, gazing at Terekhov with a thoughtful expression while several seconds trickled past. Then he shook his head slowly.

"What *am* I supposed to do with you, Captain Terekhov?" he said finally, still shaking his head. Terekhov started to open his mouth, but Khumalo waved one hand before he could speak.

"That was in the nature of a rhetorical question, Captain," he said. "It does, however, rather neatly sum up my current dilemma, doesn't it? I doubt even someone with your own obviously extraordinarily active imagination is truly up to visualizing the reactions of myself and Baroness Medusa when *Ericsson* delivered your, ah, *missive* to us. Mr. O'Shaughnessy, in particular, seemed quite . . . perturbed by your conclusions and projected course of action."

Gregor O'Shaughnessy, Baroness Medusa's senior civilian intelligence analyst, was not one of the military's most uncritical admirers, Terekhov knew.

"Frankly, despite any past differences of opinion with Mr. O'Shaughnessy, I found it just a bit difficult not to sympathize with his reaction," Khumalo continued. "Let's see now. First, there was that little act of piracy in the Montana System when you stole *Copenhagen*—from no less than Heinrich Kalokainos—to use as your forward scout here in Monica. Kalokainos has never been particularly fond of the Star Kingdom, and he has quite a few Solarian assemblymen and, even more importantly, Frontier Security bureaucrats in his hip pocket, as I'm sure I don't have to tell an officer with your own Foreign Service background. Then there was the way you induced President Suttles to incarcerate *Copenhagen*'s entire crew so you could steal their ship. Somehow, I don't think Frontier Security will be exactly enthralled with *his* actions when news of this little escapade gets back to Commissioner Verrochio, which could still have unfortunate consequences for Montana.

"And let's not forget the fashion in which you completely demolished my own deployment plans by appropriating control of every unit of the Southern Patrol which was *supposed* to be covering the Cluster's entire flank. Or the fact that you deliberately chose to inform me—who, if memory serves, is your superior officer, nominally, at least—of your plans in a manner which would completely preclude any attempt on my part to countermand your intentions.

"Which brings me to the *consequences* of those intentions."

He smiled thinly.

"According to your report, you've destroyed an even dozen Solarian-built battlecruisers in the service of a Solarian client state without benefit of any orders to do so *or* of any formal declaration of hostilities between the Star Kingdom and the client state in question. In the course of accomplishing that destruction, you've also killed several thousand Monican military personnel and an as yet undetermined—but undoubtedly very large—number of Solarian and Monican shipyard techs, many of whom were undoubtedly civilians. You've lost six of Her Majesty's warships, along with sixty-odd percent of their ship's' companies, and suffered crippling damage to the only four survivors of your original force. And, according to both your own report and the rather vociferous complaints I've already received from President Tyler, not content with all of that, you've used the threat of destroying the *civilian* components of Eroica Station—and, just incidentally, killing all of the civilians aboard those components—to hold the surviving Monican Navy at bay and prevent the removal of any personnel or possibly incriminating evidence from the two remaining battlecruisers."

He rocked his chair gently from side to side, contemplating Terekhov for several more seconds, then raised one eyebrow.

"Would that seem to you to constitute a reasonably accurate summation of your energetic activities over the last two or three T-months, Captain?"

"Yes, Sir," Terekhov heard his own voice reply with unreasonable steadiness.

"And would you care to offer any . . . explanations or justifications for those actions, other than those contained in your reports?"

"No, Sir," Terekhov said, meeting the admiral's eyes levelly.

"Well."

Khumalo studied his face without speaking for perhaps ten seconds, then shrugged.

"I can't say I'm incredibly surprised to hear that, Captain," he said. "Under the circumstances, however, I thought you might care to be present when I record my official response to President Tyler's demands that I immediately disavow your actions, relieve you of command, place you under arrest pending a well-deserved court-martial, apologize to the sovereign Union of Monica, and agree to submit this entire matter to the 'impartial' investigation and arbitration of the Office of Frontier Security."

Terekhov wondered if the admiral actually expected a response. Under the circumstances, making one didn't strike Terekhov as the wisest possible course of action, even if he did.

Khumalo produced another of those thin smiles at Terekhov's silence, then tapped a key at his workstation.

"Communications," a voice said. "Lieutenant Masters."

"This is the admiral, Lieutenant. I need to record a message to President Roberto Tyler."

"Yes, Sir. Just a moment." There was a brief pause, then Masters spoke again. "Live mike, Admiral. Go ahead."

"President Tyler," Khumalo said, looking into the com pickup at his terminal, "I apologize for not getting back to you more promptly. As you know, the current one-way transmission lag to Eroica Station is well over forty minutes. Given that inevitable delay in our communications loop, I judged it would be wiser to speak directly to Captain Terekhov and hear his version of the unfortunate events here in Monica in person before speaking to you again."

*Hear* my *version of events, is it?* Terekhov thought with a mental snort.

"Obviously, I am deeply distressed by the loss of life, both Monican and Manticoran," Khumalo continued gravely. "The destruction of so many ships, and so much damage to the public property of the Union, are also deeply distressing to me. And I must inform you that Captain Terekhov, by his own admission to me in his formal reports, acknowledges that his actions were completely unauthorized by any higher authority."

The rear admiral shook his head, his expression solemn.

"I have carefully considered your requests that I disavow his actions, remove him from his command, formally apologize to your government for his actions, and agree to submit this entire tragic affair to the investigation and arbitration of the Office of Frontier Security. And I am certain my Queen could desire very few things more than a speedy, just, and fair resolution to all of the myriad questions, accusations, and claims and counter-claims arising from events here in Monica."

Khumalo's eyes glanced sideways at Terekhov's masklike, impassive features, then went back to the pickup.

"Unfortunately, Mr. President," he said, "while all of that is true, I am also of the opinion that what my Queen would even *more* strongly desire is for you and your government to explain to her why you have been directly assisting efforts to recruit, support, encourage, and arm terrorist organizations engaged in active campaigns of assassination, murder, and destruction against the citizens of *other* sovereign star nations who have requested membership in the Star Kingdom of Manticore. I am further of the opinion that she would argue that my first responsibility is to protect those citizens from future attack and determine precisely who supplied those responsible for the attacks already carried out with the several tons of modern *Solarian* weapons Captain Terekhov confiscated in the Split System. Moreover, I fear Her Majesty is unlikely to repose the most lively possible confidence in the impartiality of any investigation by the Solarian League's Office of Frontier Security, and that she would be most displeased if the two surviving battlecruisers obviously provided to you by *Solarian* interests should mysteriously disappear before that investigation could be completed to everyone's satisfaction."

Terekhov felt his jaw trying to drop and restrained it firmly.

"Obviously, at this great distance from Manticore, I cannot know for certain what Her Majesty will ultimately decide when she considers these weighty matters," Khumalo continued. "It is my judgment, however, as the senior officer present of the Queen's Navy, that until I do know what her decision is, it is my duty and responsibility to maintain the status quo in this star system pending the arrival of the substantial reinforcements I have requested from Home Fleet, which will undoubtedly arrive with dispatches directly from Manticore. At that time, should my Queen instruct me to comply with your requests, I will, of course, be only too happy to do so. Until that time, however, I must unreservedly *endorse* Captain Terekhov's actions and inform you that I concur entirely in his conclusions and have every intention of continuing the policy and the military stance he has adopted since the unfortunate engagement with your naval units.

"It is my earnest hope that this entire situation can be resolved as amicably as possible, between the diplomatic representatives of two civilized star nations, with no further loss of life or damage to property, public or private. If, however, you should choose—as is your undoubted right—to use the military force remaining under your command against any unit of the Royal Manticoran Navy, or should I have any reason to believe you are taking steps to destroy, conceal, or remove evidence from Eroica Station, I will not hesitate to act precisely as Captain Terekhov has already informed you *he* would act."

Augustus Khumalo gazed directly into the pickup, and his deep voice was very level.

"The decision, Mr. President, is up to you. I trust you will choose wisely."

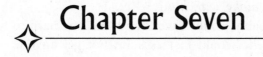

# Chapter Seven

MICHELLE HENKE MADE HERSELF look up from her book reader calmly, with no sign of burning anticipation or nervousness, as Master Steward Billingsley cleared his throat politely in the open hatch.

"Yes, Chris?"

"Sorry to disturb you, Ma'am," Billingsley said gravely, dutifully allowing her to pretend she felt neither of those emotions, "but the captain asked me to tell you we'll be dropping out of hyper in another twenty minutes. He requests that you join him on the command deck at your earliest convenience."

"I see." Michelle carefully bookmarked her place, then tucked the reader away, and stood. "Please inform the captain that I'll join him there in fifteen minutes. In the meantime, I'm going to freshen up just a bit."

"Yes, Ma'am."

Billingsley disappeared, and Michelle crossed to her minuscule cabin's even tinier head and allowed herself to smile wryly into the mirror over the small lavatory.

She knew perfectly well she hadn't fooled Billingsley. For that matter, she hadn't really been trying to. She'd simply been dutifully playing the roles their respective ranks had assigned to them, and Lieutenant Toussaint Brangeard, the CO of RHNS *Comet*, was playing by the same rules.

*And all of us are as nervous as treecats trying to sneak up on a hexapuma with a sore foot.* She shook her head at the reflected admiral in the mirror. *I'm damned sure I'm not the only one aboard who wishes there'd been time to set this up through the regular diplomatic channels instead of making this dramatic dash. Dropping in all unannounced is certainly one way to be sure we get Pritchart's message delivered in time to do some good, but only if we survive the experience. Under the circumstances, I wonder whether Brangeard is more nervous about being blown out of space by one of our pickets or of going down in history as the skipper who let the Queen of Manticore's cousin—and his President's diplomatic mission—get blown away along with him?*

Brangeard himself probably would have found that one hard to answer. Personally, Michelle would just as soon not get anyone killed, herself included, and she'd been extremely tempted to steer Brangeard towards one of the Hermes buoys seeded around the perimeter of Trevor's Star. As yet, however, there was no indication the Havenites were aware of that particular adaptation of Manticore's superior FTL communications technology. The system was still on the Official Secrets List but she'd come very close to telling Brangeard about it on the theory that the message she carried was far more important than preserving the secret of the Hermes buoy's existence. Always assuming, of course, that it really was still a secret.

In the end, she'd decided against it for three reasons. First, it was entirely possible that seeing an unidentified hyper transit close to one of the buoys might prompt a shoot-first, ask-questions-later response from some overeager destroyer or light cruiser skipper. It wasn't supposed to, and neither Honor nor Theodosia Kuzak would be particularly pleased with the skipper in question. All of which would no doubt be very satisfying to the ghosts of the unarmed dispatch boat's passengers and crew. Second, she'd realized, was the fact that deep inside, she was still afraid to let herself believe her mission—or Pritchart's mission, perhaps, if she was going to be totally accurate—was going to succeed. It was almost as if a part of her had decided that she dared not do anything that might tempt a capricious fate into punishing her hubris. Which was undoubtedly about as dumb as it got, but was unfortunately also the truth. And, third, was the fact that the quicker communication the FTL relay would have permitted probably wouldn't really have had that much effect on the system defense forces' response to the sudden emergence of an unidentified ship from hyper. The fact that the entire star system had been declared closed military space gave any of its defenders the legal right to shoot first and try to identify the bodies—if any—afterwards, although she rather doubted any Manticoran squadron commander was likely to do anything of the sort.

*You* hope, *anyway*, she told herself dryly.

She checked her appearance carefully, making certain it was as close to perfect as humanly possible, then drew a deep breath and straightened her shoulders.

*Time to stop wasting time pretending Chris would let you leave this cabin looking anything* but *perfect, girl. You told him to tell Brangeard you'd join him on the flight deck. Now do it.*

"Good morning, Admiral Gold Peak," Lieutenant Brangeard said, standing respectfully as Michelle stepped onto *Comet*'s thumbnail-sized command deck.

"Thank you, Captain," Michelle replied. She'd tried, for the first couple of days, to break Brangeard of the habit of addressing her by her title, but she'd met with no more success than she had with Arlo Tanner, although the reasons were quite different, she felt certain.

"You timed it pretty well, Milady," he said, and nodded to the digital display on the bulkhead which showed the remaining time until *Comet* dropped back out of hyper-space again. As Michelle glanced at the display, it slipped over to show exactly four minutes, and she chuckled. Brangeard raised a polite eyebrow at her, and her chuckle turned into a snort.

"I was just contemplating the perversity of the universe, Captain," Michelle told him. "A rather close friend of mine once did something very similar to this, although on a substantially grander scale."

"Oh?" Brangeard cocked his head for a moment, then snorted himself. "You mean Duchess Harrington after she got away from StateSec at Cerberus, Milady?"

"That's exactly who I mean," Michelle agreed. "As I say, though, she managed her arrival quite a bit more flamboyantly than we're about to. For one thing, she wasn't a paroled prisoner of war on someone else's command deck. And she had at least a half-dozen battlecruisers, which was probably enough firepower to give anyone pause long enough for her to establish communications."

"I suppose that's true, Milady. On the other hand, the fact that *Comet's* only a dispatch boat is probably going to keep anyone from thinking we're any kind of significant threat. Which ought to keep any fingers off the launch button at least long enough to ask us what we think we're doing."

"I keep telling myself that, Captain. Fervently and often," Michelle told him only half humorously. "Of course, there was one other small difference about Her Grace's arrival and ours." Brangeard looked at her, and she smiled. "At that point, no one had MDMs. So she had a lot more distance to play with before anyone could get into range of her ships."

"Milady, I could've gone all morning without your reminding me of that particular little difference," Brangeard said in a desert-dry tone. "Let me thank you for drawing it to my attention."

Michelle laughed and started to reply, but before she could, a soft tone chimed and *Comet* dropped back into normal-space just outside the Trevor's Star hyper limit.

"Skipper, we've got an unscheduled hyper footprint at six million kilometers!"

Captain Jane Timmons, CO, HMS *Andromeda*, spun her command chair towards her tactical officer. Six million kilometers was inside *single*-drive missile range!

She opened her mouth to demand more information, but the tac officer was already providing it.

"It's a single footprint, Ma'am. Very small. Probably a dispatch boat."

"Anything from it?" Timmons asked.

"Not FTL, Ma'am. And we wouldn't have anything light-speed for another—" he glanced at the time chop on the initial detection "—another couple of seconds. In fact—"

"Captain," the com officer said in a very careful voice, "I have a communications request I think you'd better take."

"Excuse me," the extremely suspicious looking woman in the uniform of a Royal Manticoran Navy captain of the list said from the smallish com screen on *Comet's* command deck, "but you're going to have to do a bit better than *that*, Captain . . . Brangeard, was it? There are proper channels for diplomatic exchanges. Ones that don't let Havenite dispatch boats into sensor range of sensitive installations. So I recommend you try a bit harder to convince me not to open fire."

"All right, Captain," Michelle said, stepping into the range of the visual pickup. "Let's see if *I* can't just do that little thing for the captain."

Michelle hadn't realized just how badly the Manticoran Alliance's FTL com had spoiled her until she found herself forced to put up once again with the limitations of purely light-speed communications at such piddling little ranges. She stood there, waiting while her transmission crossed the twenty light-seconds to the other ship, then for *another* twenty seconds while the response from the other end crossed back to *Comet*.

In the end, she decided, it was worth the wait.

Forty seconds after she'd first spoken, a spike of heightened suspicion flashed across the face on *Comet*'s com display as the other woman saw Michelle's immaculate *Manticoran* uniform on someone speaking to her from aboard a Havenite vessel. But then *Andromeda*'s captain looked past the uniform, and the suspicion turned into something very different. Michelle knew from personal experience that the RMN didn't exactly pick people it expected to be easily confounded to command its battlecruisers, but the other woman's jaw actually dropped.

*Well,* Michelle thought, *I do have the Winton nose. And aside from the fact that my complexion's about twelve shades darker than Beth's, we really do favor. Or so I've been told, anyway.*

"I suppose this is all a bit irregular," she said dryly as recognition flared across the captain's face, "but I have a message for Her Majesty from the President of the Republic of Haven."

Michelle made herself sit very still as thrusters flared, easing *Andromeda*'s number one pinnace into the boat bay of the stupendous superdreadnought. It was hard. Too many emotions, too many conflicting tides of relief, surprise, hope, and anxiety were washing through her. The last time she'd seen this ship's icon on a tactical display, she'd known she would never see it or the admiral whose lights it flew again. Yet here she was, turning up once again, like the proverbial bad penny.

*And with such an . . . interesting message to deliver, too,* she reflected. *But it's really not fair. When* Honor *came back from the dead, I was nowhere in the vicinity. At least we'd both gotten a chance to get our emotions back under control before we came face-to-face again.*

The pinnace settled into the docking arms, and the personnel tube and service umbilicals ran out and mated with the access points on its hull. The flight engineer checked the hatch telltales.

"Good seal, Flight," he reported to the flight deck. "Cracking the hatch."

The hatch slid open, and the petty officer who'd opened it stood aside and braced to attention.

"Welcome home, Admiral," he said with an enormous smile, and Michelle smiled back at him.

"Thank you, PO Gervais," she said, reading his name off the nameplate on the breast of his uniform. The petty officer's smile grew even broader, and then she nodded to him and launched herself into the personnel tube's zero-gravity.

The distance from the pinnace's passenger compartment to HMS *Imperator* was no more than a few meters, but she relished the brief zero-gee passage. Her leg hadn't been simply broken when *Ajax* was destroyed. "Shattered" would have been a more accurate choice of verb, or even "pulverized," and quick-heal always slowed down on bone repairs, anyway. The leg was perfectly capable of supporting her weight now, at least as long as she took it easy, but it still tended to ache most unpleasantly if she pushed it too hard.

She reached the inboard end of the tube, caught the red grab bar, and swung herself back out of the tube's microgravity and into the standard one-gravity field of Eighth Fleet's flagship. She landed more than a bit gingerly—sudden impacts pushed the nerve messages from her broken leg beyond unpleasant to acutely painful—and came to attention and saluted through the twitter of bosun's pipes.

"Battlecruiser Squadron Eighty-One, arriving!"

The announcement she'd expected never to hear again came over the bay's speakers, and the side party snapped to attention, returning her salute sharply.

"Permission to come aboard, Sir?" she requested from the lieutenant who wore the black brassard of the boat bay officer of the deck.

"Permission granted, Admiral Henke!"

Both hands fell from the salute, and Michelle stepped past the

BBOD, trying not to limp too noticeably as she found herself face-to-face with the tall, almond-eyed woman in the uniform of a full admiral and the cream and gray treecat riding on her shoulder.

"Mike," Honor Alexander-Harrington said, very quietly, taking her offered hand in a firm clasp. "It's good to see you again."

"And you, Your Grace." Michelle tried to keep her voice from wavering, but she knew she hadn't quite pulled it off, and Honor's grip on her hand tightened ever so briefly. Then Honor released her and stepped back a bit.

"Well," she said, "I believe you said something about a message?"

"Yes, I did."

"Should I get Admiral Kuzak out here?"

"I don't believe that will be necessary, Ma'am." Michelle had her voice back under control, and she kept her tone formal, aware of the spectators surrounding them.

"Then why don't you accompany me to my quarters?"

"Of course, Your Grace."

Honor led the way to the lift shaft, and Colonel Andrew LaFollet, her personal armsman, followed alertly behind them in his Harrington green uniform. No one else accompanied them, however, and Honor personally pressed the button, then smiled faintly and waved Michelle through the opening door. She and LaFollet followed, and as the door slid shut behind them, she reached out and gripped Michelle's upper arms.

"My God," she said softly. "It *is* good to see you, Mike!"

Michelle started to reply, but before she could think of something suitably flippant, Honor swept her suddenly into a bear hug. Michelle's eyes widened. Honor had never been one for easy embraces, and even now, Michelle hadn't really expected one. Nor, she thought an instant later, had she ever truly appreciated just how strong Honor's genetically-engineered, Sphinx-bred muscles actually were.

"Easy! *Easy!*" she gasped, returning the embrace. "The leg's bad enough, woman! Don't add crushed ribs to the list!"

"Sorry," Honor said huskily, then stood back and cleared her throat while Nimitz buzzed a happy, welcoming purr from her shoulder.

"Sorry," she repeated after moment. "It's just that I thought you were dead. And then, when we found out you weren't, I still expected months, or years, to pass before I saw you again."

"Then I guess we're even over that little Cerberus trip you took," Michelle replied with a smile.

"I guess we are," Honor acknowledged, then chuckled suddenly. "Although *you* at least weren't dead long enough for them to throw an entire state funeral for you!"

"Pity." Michelle grinned at her. "I would've loved to watch the HD of it."

"Yes, you probably would have. You always have been just a bit peculiar, Mike Henke."

"You only say that because of my taste in friends."

"No doubt," Honor agreed as the lift doors opened on the passageway outside her quarters. Spencer Hawke, the junior member of her permanent personal security team, stood guard just outside them, and she paused and looked back at LaFollet.

"Andrew, you and Spencer can't keep this up forever. We've got to get at least one other armsman up here to give the two of you some relief."

"My Lady, I've been thinking about that, but I haven't had the time to select someone," LaFollet replied. There was something odd about his tone, something Michelle had never before heard in it when he spoke to Honor. It wasn't a note of disagreement, or even of evasiveness—not quite—and yet . . .

"I'd have to go back to Grayson, My Lady," LaFollet continued, "and—"

"No, Andrew, you wouldn't," Honor interrupted with a moderately stern look. "Two points," she continued. "First, my son will be born in another month. Second, Brigadier Hill is quite capable of selecting a suitable pool of candidates back on Grayson and sending them to us for you and me to consider together. I know you have a lot on your mind, and I know there are aspects of the situation you don't really like. But this needs to be attended to."

He looked back at her for a few seconds, then sighed.

"Yes, My Lady. I'll send the dispatch to Brigadier Hill on the morning shuttle."

"Thank you," she said, and touched him lightly on the arm, then turned back to Michelle.

"I believe someone else is waiting to welcome you back," she said, and the hatch slid open to show a beaming James MacGuiness.

"Mac," Michelle said, reaching out to grip McGuinness' hand. Then she decided that wasn't enough, and swept him into an embrace almost as crushing as the one Honor had just inflicted upon her. The older man's eyes widened very briefly. Technically, Michelle supposed, a rear admiral wasn't supposed to go around hugging mere stewards, but she really didn't give much of a damn. She'd known MacGuiness for almost twenty years, and he'd become part of Honor's extended family—just as Michelle herself had—long ago. Besides, there were stewards, and then there were stewards, and there was nothing in the least "mere" about James MacGuiness.

"May I say, Admiral, that it's one of the greatest pleasures of my life to welcome you home," he said as the strength of her embrace eased and he stood back a few centimeters. "Indeed, it's given me almost as much pleasure as it did to welcome someone else home, some years ago."

"And who could *that* possibly have been, Mac?" Michelle asked, rounding her eyes innocently.

The steward chuckled and shook his head, then looked across at Honor.

"I've taken the liberty of preparing a few snacks, Your Grace," he told her. "I've set them out in your day cabin. If you should require anything else, just buzz."

"Mac, it's the middle of the *night*," Honor pointed out with fond exasperation. "I realize Admiral Henke is still on a Nouveau Paris time schedule, but *we* aren't. So go back to bed. Get some sleep!"

"Just buzz, Your Grace," he told her with a slight smile and withdrew.

LaFollet did the same thing, leaving Honor and Michelle alone, and Michelle quirked an eyebrow.

"Andrew is leaving me alone with you?" she asked quizzically as Honor led the way into her day cabin and waved her into one of the comfortable chairs.

"Yes, he is," Honor confirmed.

"Are you sure that's wise?" Michelle's voice was entirely serious, and Honor arched an eyebrow of her own as she settled into a facing chair. Nimitz flowed down from his person's shoulder and curled his long, sinuous body length around behind her on the armchair's upholstered back.

"I just got back from a stint as a Havenite prisoner-of-war," Michelle pointed out. "I don't *think* their medicos did anything except take really good care of me and all my survivors, Honor, but Tim didn't think anything had been done to *him* before he tried to kill you, either. And given the fact that it was almost certainly the Peeps who programmed him, however the hell they did it . . ."

She let her voice trail off, and Honor's nostrils flared. She didn't—quite—snort, but her body language and expression gave the impression she had.

"First," she said, "you aren't armed, unless they also managed to tuck some sort of weapon away inside you, and the scans aboard *Andromeda* would have picked that up. And, with all due respect, Mike, I'm not really concerned about your managing to kill me with your bare hands before Andrew gets back in here to rescue me."

Despite her own genuine concern, Michelle's lips twitched. Unlike her, Honor Alexander-Harrington had spent the better part of fifty T-years training in *coup de vitesse*. Even without the hidden pulser Michelle knew her father had built into Honor's artificial left hand, Honor wouldn't find it particularly difficult to fend off any bare-handed assault Michelle might launch.

"And, second," Honor continued, "both Nimitz and I know what to watch for now. I feel fairly confident we'd realize something was taking over at least as quickly as you did, and this time, Mike," she looked directly into Michelle's eyes, "I am *not* going to kill another friend as the only way to stop her. Nor am I going to take a chance on Andrew's doing the same thing. So if it should happen that anyone on the planet of Haven slipped any new lines of code into your programming, the sooner it kicks in, the better, as far as I'm concerned.

"Besides," she grinned suddenly, breaking the tension of the moment, "I can't believe anyone in the Republic would be crazy enough to deliberately send another programmed assassin after me, especially after releasing the aforesaid assassin from prison and providing her with transportation home! I think they must have a pretty shrewd notion of how Elizabeth would react to that."

"If you're sure," Michelle said.

"Positive," Honor replied firmly, and reached for the coffee pot on the tray MacGuiness had set up. She poured a cup for

Michelle, poured a cup of hot, steaming cocoa from a second carafe for herself, then settled back in her chair.

For several minutes, neither of them spoke. They only sat there, sipping their beverages of choice while Honor nibbled idly on a sandwich—taking the opportunity to stoke her genetically-modified metabolism—and handed Nimitz a stick of celery. The 'cat chewed blissfully—and messily—on the treat, and the crunching sound of his dining sounded unnaturally loud in the day cabin's quiet.

It was odd, Michelle reflected. She supposed most people in their position would have been busy filling the silence with small talk, or at least telling one another all over again how glad they were to see each other. But neither she nor Honor felt the need to do that. They'd known each other much too long to need to manufacture chatter just to be saying something, after all.

*Besides*, Michelle thought with an internal flicker of amusement, *we've already done this once before, from the* other *side. We're all practiced up!*

"So, Mike," Honor said finally, "just what induced the Havenites to send you home?"

"That's an interesting question." Michelle cradled her cup in both hands, gazing at Honor across it. "I think mostly they picked me because I'm Beth's cousin. They figured she'd have to listen to a message from me. And, I imagine, they hoped the fact that they'd given me back to her would at least tempt her to listen seriously to what they had to say."

"Which is? Or is it privileged information you can't share with me?"

"Oh, it's privileged all right—for now, at least," Michelle told her wryly. She kept her expression suitably solemn, although she was perfectly well aware that Honor's empathic sense could taste her impish amusement. "But I was specifically told I could share it with you, since it also concerns you."

"Mike," Honor informed her, "if you don't come clean with me and quit tossing out tidbits, I'm going to choke it out of you. You do realize that, don't you?"

"Home less than an hour, and already threatened with physical violence." Michelle shook her head sadly, then shrank back into her chair as Honor started to stand up and Nimitz bleeked a laugh from his chair-back perch.

"All right, all right! I'll talk!"

"Good." Honor settled back. "And," she added, "I'm still waiting."

"Yes, well," Michelle straightened in her own chair, "it's not really a laughing matter, I suppose. But put most simply, Pritchart is using me as her messenger to suggest to Beth that the two of them meet in a face-to-face summit to discuss a negotiated settlement."

Honor's eyes flickered. That was the only sign of surprise Michelle saw out of her, but that very lack of expression was its own revelation. Then Honor drew a deep breath and cocked her head to one side.

"That's a very interesting offer. Do you think she really means it?"

"Oh, I think she definitely wants to meet with Beth. Just what she intends to offer is another matter. On that front, I wish you'd been the one talking to her."

"What sort of agenda did she propose?" Honor asked.

"That's one of the odd parts about the offer." Michelle shook her head. "Basically, she left it wide open. Obviously, she wants a peace treaty, but she didn't list any specific set of terms. Apparently, she's willing to throw everything into the melting pot if Beth will agree to negotiate with her one-on-one."

"That's a significant change from their previous stance, at least as I understand it," Honor said thoughtfully, and Michelle shrugged.

"I hate to say it, but you're probably in a better position to know that than I am," she admitted. "I've been trying to pay more attention to politics since you tore a strip off me, but it's still not really a primary interest of mine."

Honor gave her an exasperated look and shook her head. Michelle only looked back, essentially unrepentant, even though she had to admit Honor's annoyance was amply justified. For a moment, she thought Honor was going to read her the riot act all over again, but then her friend only shrugged for her to continue.

"Actually," Michelle told her, "it's probably a good thing you *are* more interested in politics and diplomacy than I am."

"Why?"

"Because one specific element of Pritchart's proposal is a request that you also attend the conference she wants to set up."

"Me?" This time Honor's surprise was evident, and Michelle nodded.

"You. I got the impression the original suggestion to include you may have come from Thomas Theisman, but I'm not sure about that. Pritchart did assure me, however, that neither she nor anyone in her administration had anything to do with your attempted assassination. And you can believe however much of that you want to."

"She'd almost have to say that, I suppose," Honor said. Clearly, she was thinking hard. Several seconds passed in silence before she cocked her head again. "Did she say anything about Ariel or Nimitz?"

"No, she didn't . . . and I thought that was probably significant. They know both you and Beth have been adopted, of course, and it was obvious that they have extensive dossiers on both of you. I'm sure they've been following the articles and other presentations on the 'cats' capabilities since they decided to come out of the closet, too."

"Which means, in effect, that she's inviting us to bring a pair of furry lie detectors to this summit of hers."

"That's what I think." Michelle nodded. "I guess it's always possible they haven't made that connection after all, but I think it's unlikely."

"So do I." Honor gazed off into the distance, once again clearly thinking hard. Then she looked back at Michelle.

"The timing on this is interesting. We've got several factors working here."

"I know," Michelle said. "And so does Pritchart." Honor's eyebrows rose, and Michelle snorted. "She made very certain I knew about that business in Talbott. She made the specific point that her offer of a summit is being made at a time when she and her advisers are fully aware of how tightly stretched we are. The unstated implication was that instead of an invitation to talk, they might have sent a battle fleet."

"Yes, they certainly could have," Honor agreed grimly.

"Have we heard any more from the Cluster?" Michelle asked, unable to keep the anxiety she'd felt ever since Pritchart told her about the initial reports out of her voice.

"No. And we won't hear anything back from Monica for at least another ten or eleven days. And that's one reason I said the timing on this was interesting. On the chance that the news we get may be good, I've been ordered to update our plans for Operation Sanskrit—that's the successor to the Cutworm raids—with a tentative execution date twelve days from tomorrow. Well, from today, actually, now."

"You're thinking about the way Saint-Just derailed Buttercup by suggesting a cease-fire to High Ridge," Michelle said, shaking her head. After all, the same thought had crossed her own mind more than once, although the strategic momentum seemed to be on the other side, this time around.

"Actually," Honor replied, shaking her own head, "I'm thinking about the fact that *Elizabeth* is going to remember it. Unless they've got a lot more penetration of our security than I believe they do, they can't know what our operational schedule is. Oh, they've probably surmised that Eighth Fleet was just about ready to resume offensive operations, assuming we were going to do that at all, when Khumalo's dispatch arrived. And if they've done the math, they probably know we're about due to hear back from him. But they must have packed you off home almost the same day word of our diversions from Home Fleet could have reached them. To me, that sounds like they moved as quickly as possible to take advantage of an opportunity to negotiate seriously. I'm just afraid it's going to resonate with Buttercup in Elizabeth's thoughts."

"She's not entirely rational where Peeps are concerned," Michelle agreed.

"With justification I'm afraid." Honor sighed, and Michelle looked at her in mild surprise. Honor, she knew, had been a persistent voice of moderation in the Queen's inner circle. In fact, she'd been just about the *only* persistent voice of moderation, after the surprise attack with which the Republic of Haven had recommenced hostilities. So why was she suggesting that Elizabeth's fiery intransigence might be justified?

Michelle thought about asking exactly that, then changed her mind.

"Well, I hope she doesn't get her dander up this time," she said instead. "God knows I love her, and she's one of the strongest monarchs we've ever had, but that temper of hers—!"

She shook her head, and Honor grimaced.

"I know everyone thinks she's a warhead with a hairtrigger," she said with more than a hint of annoyance. "I'll even acknowledge that she's one of the best grudge-holders I know. But she isn't really blind to her responsibilities as a head of state, you know!"

"You don't have to defend her to *me*, Honor!" Michelle raised both hands, palms towards her friend in a warding off gesture. "I'm just trying to be realistic. The fact is that she's got a temper from the dark side of Hell, when it's roused, and you know as well as I do how she hates yielding to pressure, even from people she knows are giving her their best advice. And speaking of pressure, Pritchart was careful to make sure I knew *she* knew the goings on in the Cluster have given the Republic the whip hand, diplomatically speaking. Not only that, she told me to inform Beth that she's releasing an official statement tomorrow in Nouveau Paris informing the Republic and the galaxy at large that she's issued her invitation."

"Oh, lovely." Honor leaned back. "That was a smart move. And you're right, Elizabeth is going to resent it. But she's played the interstellar diplomacy game herself—quite well, in fact. I don't think she'll be surprised by it. And I doubt very much that any resentment she feels over it would have a decisive impact on her decision."

"I hope you're right." Michelle sipped from her coffee cup, then lowered it. "I hope you're right, because hard as I tried to stay cynical, I think Pritchart really means it. She really wants to sit down with Beth and negotiate peace."

"Then let's hope she manages to pull it off," Honor said softly.

# Chapter Eight

"LIEUTENANT ARCHER?"

Lieutenant Gervais Archer turned quickly from his contemplation of the luxuriantly bright beds of terrestrial flowers on the far side of the picture window to the even more luxuriantly bearded master steward in the doorway.

"Yes, Master Steward?"

"The admiral will see you now, Sir."

"Thank you."

Archer suppressed an urge to straighten his beret nervously as he followed the steward through the doorway and down a tastefully—and expensively—furnished hallway. He also attempted, less successfully, to suppress the thought of how his parents, and especially his mother, would have reacted to an invitation to this Landing townhouse. And how unlikely it was that they would ever receive one.

The steward glanced back over his shoulder at him as they approached another, open doorway, then coughed gently, in an attention-gathering sort of way.

"Yes, Chris?" a throaty, almost furry-sounding contralto responded.

"Lieutenant Archer is here, Ma'am."

"I see. Ask him to step in, please."

"Yes, Ma'am."

The bearded steward stepped to one side and nodded courteously

114

for Archer to step past him. Which, with a certain trepidation, the lieutenant did.

The room beyond the door was a combination library and office. It was a large room, and he felt his eyes widen very slightly as he saw towering shelves filled with what certainly appeared to be old-style printed books. For most people, that sort of collection would have been pure ostentation, or at least window dressing, at best. *These* books, though, weren't. He couldn't have said exactly how he knew that, but he did. Perhaps it was the fact that their spines had that slightly worn, almost matte-polished look that human hands left on things they actually handled.

In sharp contrast to the archaic books, the room also boasted a sleekly modern and efficient workstation. It was the woman seated at that workstation Archer had come to see, and he crossed to it, then braced to attention.

"Lieutenant Archer, Ma'am," he said.

"So I see, Lieutenant," she said, standing and extending her hand through the insubstantial holo of the display she'd been perusing when he arrived.

He took the hand, which gripped his firmly, and let his spine and shoulders relax at the handshake's unstated command to settle into a more comfortable stance.

"Have a seat," she invited, and he settled into the indicated chair just a bit gingerly.

She sat down behind her own desk again, this time deactivating the holo display, and leaned back slightly, regarding him intently. He looked back, hoping he didn't look nervous . . . especially since he *was* nervous.

"So," she said after a moment or two, "you were in *Necromancer* at Solon."

Her tone made the statement a question, although he wasn't certain exactly what the question *was*. Still . . .

"Yes, Ma'am. I was."

His voice came out sounding level, he noted with a certain almost distant surprise. Surprise because it didn't *feel* level. Nothing felt "level" whenever he thought about Solon. Thought about the screaming hurricane of missiles, about the way his ship had heaved and twisted indescribably under the pounding of the bomb-pumped lasers. Remembered the howling alarms, the screams over the intercom, the sudden silences where voices used to be, the bodies of two of his best friends . . .

"Pretty bad, wasn't it?"

His eyes snapped back into focus, and he blinked in surprise. Surprise that she should broach the subject so openly when everyone else had tried so hard to avoid talking about it at all. And surprise at the understanding—the sympathy born of mutual experience, not saccharine pity—in her quiet question.

"Yes, Ma'am, it was," he heard himself say, equally quietly.

Michelle Henke gazed at the young man on the other side of her desk. She'd had her doubts when Honor had recommended young Archer as her new flag lieutenant. Of course, part of that was because she'd wondered whether she'd even *need* a new flag lieutenant.

*Getting just a bit ahead of yourself going ahead and interviewing candidates when the Admiralty hasn't even told you it's going to find you a command, aren't you, girl?* she reflected. *On the other hand, it's not like good flag lieutenants are a-dime-a-dozen, either. And even an admiral who doesn't have a command needs a good aide.*

Indeed they weren't, and indeed she did. And it wasn't many lieutenants who were likely to gain the recommendation of someone like Honor Harrington without ever having served directly under her.

"He's been through hell, Mike," she remembered Honor saying, reaching up to touch Nimitz's ears. "His efficiency reports are top-notch, and I know Captain Cruickshank thought the world of him. He 'tastes' a lot like another Tim Meares, to be honest. But there's a lot of pain locked up inside him at the moment, too. I think part of its probably survivor's guilt." Those almond-shaped eyes had bored into Michelle's. "Almost like he did something wrong surviving when his ship didn't. Sound familiar?"

*Yeah, Honor,* she thought now. *Yeah, it does.*

"Well, Lieutenant," she said aloud, "when that kind of thing happens, it leaves marks. They don't go away, either. Believe me, I know firsthand. The question is whether or not we let it change who we are."

Gervais twitched. He'd come here expecting to answer the standard questions, to summarize his experience, demonstrate his expertise. He hadn't expected to find an admiral he'd never even met before talking about memories. About the bleak sense of loss, the gnawing question of why *he'd* survived when so many others hadn't.

"Change who we are, Ma'am?" he heard himself reply. "I'm not sure that's the right question. Isn't 'who we are' the result of everything that *does* change us? I mean, if we don't change, then we don't learn, either, do we?"

*Whoa! Didn't see* that *one coming*, Michelle thought. She managed not to blink or to narrow her eyes in surprise, but she did tip her chair back a bit further and purse her lips thoughtfully.

"That's an excellent point, Lieutenant," she conceded. "And I'm not usually guilty of such imprecise language. What I meant, I suppose, is that the question is whether or not we allow the changes to deflect us from who we want to be, change what we want to *accomplish* with our lives. Do we let them . . . diminish us, or do we accept the scars and continue growing?"

*She's not talking just to me.* Gervais had no idea where that flash of insight could come from, but he knew, without question, that it was true. *She's talking to herself. Or, no, that's not quite right either. . . . She's talking about us. About all of us survivors. And she's talking to both of us about it.*

"I don't know, Ma'am," he said. "Whether or not it's going to deflect me, I mean. I don't want it to. I don't *think* it's going to. But, I have to admit, it hurts so much sometimes that I'm not sure about that."

Michelle nodded slowly. She didn't need Honor's empathic sense to recognize the painful honesty behind that response, and she respected young Archer for it. In fact, a part of her was astonished that he could confront it that openly and honestly in front of a total stranger.

*Maybe Honor was right about this one's metal*, she thought, then chuckled silently to herself. *Wouldn't exactly be the first time she'd been right about something, would it?*

"That's something I'm not always as confident about as I'd like to be, either, Lieutenant," she said, returning honesty for honesty. "And, unfortunately, I only know one way for either of us to find out. So, tell me, are you game to climb back onto the horse?"

The young man gazed at her for several seconds, then nodded back to her, as slowly as she'd nodded to him.

"Yes, Ma'am," he said. "I am."

"And would you be interested in doing that as my flag lieutenant?" she asked. He started to reply, but her raised hand stopped him. "Before you answer that question, understand that at this particular point in time, I don't even know if I'm going to have a command. The doctors still haven't officially cleared me to return to duty, and I understand Admiralty House is having a fairly lively internal debate about exactly what the terms of my parole require. So it's entirely possible that if you do sign on as my flag lieutenant, we're not going to be offered any horses to climb back *onto* any time soon."

"Ma'am," Archer felt his lips trying to twitch into a half-smile, "somehow I don't really see that being a big problem. I don't know what the terms of your 'parole' were, but I'd be really surprised if the Admiralty wasn't willing to be fairly . . . creative in its interpretation, if that's what it takes to get you back on a flag deck."

"Obviously, Lieutenant, you have a high opinion of my abilities," Michelle said dryly.

She also watched Archer's expression carefully as she said it, but she saw neither surprise, nor chagrin, nor sycophancy. Nor, for that matter, did he appear to feel any compulsion to reply just to be replying or to explain—which she was confident would be completely honest—that he'd had no intention of flattering her. A most self-possessed young man, Lieutenant Archer, she reflected.

"I see from your file," she continued in a deliberately brisker tone, "that you and I are related, Lieutenant."

"Ah, not really—" he began, then stopped himself. For the first time since he'd entered her office, he sounded genuinely flustered, Michelle thought with a carefully hidden mental smile. "What I meant to say, Ma'am," he resumed after a moment, "is that the relationship is . . . very distant."

He really hadn't had to tell her that, Michelle thought with another silent chuckle, looking at his flaming red hair, green eyes, and snub nose. Anything less like the Winton genotype would have been difficult to imagine. In fact, young Archer was at best an exceedingly remote cousin. A point of which his mother appeared to have been unaware when it came time to name her infant son.

"I see." Despite herself, her lips twitched very slightly, and when she glanced up, she saw something she hadn't really expected. A sparkle of amusement of his own had displaced at least some of the shadows in those green eyes.

Gervais saw her tiny smile, and felt his own mouth trying to smile back. Somehow, especially after all of his mother's childhood tales about the Wintons, he hadn't expected the woman who stood fifth in line for the crown to be quite so approachable, so ... human. For the first time, almost to his own surprise, he found himself looking forward to the possibility of this assignment in something more than merely professional terms.

"My mother always thought of the relationship as being just a bit *closer* than my father ever did, Ma'am," he heard himself saying. "That's how I ended up with my name. If you noticed, of course."

His last sentence came out so demurely that Michelle chuckled out loud this time, and shook her head at him.

"Actually, I did notice," she told him in a moderately reproving tone. Then she grinned. "Gervais Winton Erwin Neville Archer. Now that's a mouthful. Almost as bad as Gloria Michelle Samantha Evelyn Henke. There's a reason my friends call me Michelle or Mike, Lieutenant."

"I'm not surprised, Ma'am," he replied, and she chuckled again.

"No, I don't imagine you are," she agreed, tapping the record chip on her desk which contained his personal file. "I noticed that you were nicknamed 'Gwen' at the Academy—from your initials, as my keen intellect speedily deduced."

"Yes, Ma'am," Gervais agreed. "Mom never did understand why I preferred it to Gervais, either. Don't get me wrong—I love my mother, and she's a brilliant woman. One of the Star Kingdom's top molecular chemists. There's just this one point where she's ... well, 'marching to another drum' is the way Dad's always put it."

"I see." Michelle regarded him for several more seconds, then reached a decision. She stood once more, holding out her hand again.

"Well, 'Gwen,' I suppose that since every flag lieutenant is part of his admiral's official family, our relationship is going to get a bit closer. Welcome aboard, Lieutenant."

# Chapter Nine

MICHELLE ACCEPTED HER BERET from Master Steward Billingsley and started to turn towards the door and the waiting Admiralty air car when she paused suddenly.

"And what, Master Steward, might *that* be?" she asked.

"I beg the Admiral's pardon?" Billingsley said innocently. "What 'that' would the Admiral be referring to?"

"The Admiral would be referring to *that* 'that,'" Michelle replied, one forefinger indicating the broad, prick-eared head which had just poked itself exploringly around the corner of a door.

"Oh, *that* 'that'!"

"Precisely," Michelle said, folding her arms and regarding him ominously.

"That's a cat, Ma'am," Billingsley told her. "Not a treecat, a *cat*—an Old Earth cat. It's called a 'Maine Coon.'"

"I'm well aware of what an Old Earth cat looks like, Chris," Michelle said repressively, never unfolding her arms. "I don't believe I've ever seen one quite that *large*, but I do know what they are. What I *don't* know is what it's doing in my mother's townhouse."

Actually, the townhouse and its landscaped grounds belonged to Michelle now, not to her mother, but it was Caitrin Winton-Henke's *home*, even if Michelle did have most of a wing reserved for her private use whenever she was on Manticore.

"Well, actually, Ma'am, he's mine," Billingsley said with the air of someone making a clean breast of it.

120

"And just when did this monumental change in your status as a parent take place?" Michelle inquired just a bit acidly as the rest of the impressively large feline ambled into the foyer.

"Day before yesterday," Billingsley said. "I . . . found him wandering around over near the Master Chiefs' Club. He looked like he needed a home, and he walked right up to me, and I *couldn't* just leave him there, Ma'am!"

"I see," Michelle said, looking into his guilelessly wide and innocent eyes. "And would it happen that this hulking menace to all mice, hamsters, chipmunks, and unwary small children has a name?"

"Yes, Ma'am. I call him 'Dicey.' "

" 'Dicey,' " Michelle replied with long-suffering resignation. "Of course."

Billingsley continued to look as if butter would not melt in his mouth, but the name was a dead giveaway of how his new pet had really come into his possession, Michelle thought, looking at the enormous cat. It was the first terrestrial cat she'd ever seen who looked like he probably came close to matching Nimitz's mass. Not only that, but 'Dicey' was a good twenty centimeters shorter overall than Nimitz, and although he was definitely a long hair, he was nowhere near as fluffy as a treecat, which made him substantially bulkier. One ear had a notch that looked like someone else had taken a bite out of it, and a scar across the back of his burly neck left a visible furrow in his fur. There were a couple of more of those on the left side of his face, as well, she noticed. Obviously, he'd been to the wars, yet there was something about him that reminded her irresistibly of Billingsley himself, now that she thought about it. A certain endearing disreputability, perhaps.

She glanced at her new flag lieutenant, who was observing the entire scene with a laudably professional and serene expression. There was, however, a certain almost subliminal twinkle in Lieutenant Archer's green eyes. One that boded ill, she decided. Clearly "Gwen" was already succumbing to Billingsley's incorrigible charm.

*Much like a certain admiral you know, perhaps?* she reflected.

"You do realize how many regulations there are against having a pet on board one of her Majesty's starships?" she inquired out loud after a moment.

"Regulations, Ma'am?" Billingsley repeated blankly, as if he'd never heard the word before.

Michelle started to open her mouth again, then gave up. A wise woman knew when to cut her losses, and she didn't begin to have the time it would take to make a dent in Billingsley's bland innocence. Besides, she didn't have the heart for it.

"As long as you understand that *I'm* not going to put any pressure on anyone to allow you to bring that beast along on our next deployment," she said, trying womanfully to sound firm.

"Oh, yes, Ma'am. I understand *that*," Billingsley assured her without a trace of triumph.

They'd managed to arrive almost twenty minutes early.

*Not exactly the best way to look like I'm not champing at the bit for another assignment, I suppose*, Michelle had mused as she and Archer were ushered into the waiting room. *On the other hand, it's probably a little late to try to convince anyone I'm not doing exactly that. Besides,* she looked around the spacious waiting room, *it gives me more time to appreciate the "new air car smell," doesn't it?*

Admiralty House's latest expansion project had been authorized less than a month after the High Ridge Government took office. The previous one had been completed—on time and under budget—just over a T-year before that by a subsidiary of the Hauptman Cartel. Obviously, an administration which had based its domestic policies so firmly on the time-honored, well-tested device of the support-buying boondoggle couldn't have such a potentially lucrative avenue for . . . creative capital flow sitting around unutilized, however. So another expansion had promptly been authorized . . . despite the fact that the Janacek Admiralty had been so busily downsizing the Navy. This one was going to add another forty floors when it was finished sometime in the next few months, and Michelle didn't like to think about how much it had contributed to the bottom line of Apex Industrial Group.

*I probably wouldn't mind as much if Apex didn't belong to a bottom-feeder like dear, dear Cousin Freddy*, she thought.

There'd never been any real likelihood that someone as strongly and openly opposed to High Ridge as Klaus Hauptman was going to get the contract for this expansion. Aside from his political views, Hauptman was known for a certain ruthless concentration on holding down little things like creative cost overruns, and his accountants were sudden death on anything that even looked like kickbacks or "comfortable" little relationships with corrupt politicians.

The Honorable Frederick James Winton-Travis, CEO and majority stockholder of the Apex Industrial Group, was a far smaller fish than Hauptman, but he'd been much more to the High Ridge crowd's taste. First, he was a card-carrying member of the Conservative Association who'd contributed in excess of three million Manticoran dollars to the political coffers of one Michael Janvier, also known as the Baron of High Ridge. There was no law against his doing that, of course, as long as the contributions were a matter of public record, and there was no doubt—unfortunately—that the contributions had reflected Winton-Travis' actual political convictions. Such as they were and what there was of them. Michelle would have found the political convictions in question distasteful enough on their own merits, however. The fact that the most recent Admiralty House "renovation project" had obviously been a way for High Ridge to pay back the contribution—with hefty interest—had simply added a particularly repulsive taste to the entire transaction, as far as she was concerned.

*Being related to the scummy bastard doesn't help, either,* she admitted to herself. *Still, I don't think I'd mind quite as much if it wasn't something everyone* knows *about but no one can* prove. *If there was at least a chance of sending dear Freddy to prison for a decade or two, I'd be able to think about this much more philosophically. It's not even as if we didn't really need the extra space, because we do. But that doesn't make it any less of a boondoggle, because no one involved in deciding to build it could possibly have believed we actually ever would. And every time I think about the way the contracts were handled my blood pressure goes—*

"Excuse me, Admiral."

Michelle turned from her study of the streets and green belts of the City of Landing, two hundred floors below her crystoplast window viewpoint, as the Admiralty yeoman spoke.

"Yes, Chief?"

"Sir Lucian is ready for you now, Ma'am."

"Thank you, Chief."

She managed to restrain the almost overpowering impulse to let nervous fingers check her appearance one last time, nor did she lick her lips anxiously or whistle a merry tune to disguise her nervousness. Despite which, unusually large butterflies seemed to be waltzing about in her midsection as the yeoman pressed the button which opened the door to Sir Lucian Cortez's palatial Admiralty House office.

She nodded her thanks and stepped through the waiting portal, with Archer on her heels.

"Admiral Gold Peak!"

Cortez was a smallish man who wore the uniform of an admiral of the green. In many ways, he looked more like a successful schoolteacher, or perhaps a bank bureaucrat, than a naval officer, despite the uniform. And in many ways, Michelle supposed, he *was* a bureaucrat. But he was a very important bureaucrat—the Royal Manticoran Navy's Fifth Space Lord and the commanding officer of the Bureau of Personnel. It was his job to meet the unending appetite of the frantically expanding, brutally overworked Navy, and no one—including Michelle—quite knew how he had done that so well, for so long. Under the prewar system of rotating senior officers regularly through fleet commands and then back to desk jobs in order to see to it that they stayed operationally current, Cortez would have been replaced in his present position long since. No one in her right mind was going to suggest replacing him under *wartime* conditions, however.

Now he came to his feet, smiling in welcome, and extended his hand to her across the desk as the other man, a commander wearing the insignia of the Judge Advocate's Corps, who'd been sitting beside the office's coffee table also stood respectfully.

"Good morning, My Lord," Michelle responded to Cortez's greeting, and clasped his hand firmly. Then she quirked one eyebrow politely at the waiting commander, and Cortez smiled.

"No, you're not going to need legal representation, Milady," he assured her. "This is Commander Hal Roach, and he *is* here because of you, but not because of anything you've done. Unless, of course, you have a guilty conscience I didn't know anything about?"

"My Lord, my conscience is as pure as the driven snow," she replied, holding out her hand to Roach, and the commander smiled in appreciation as he took it. He was a solidly built fellow, with dark hair, and probably somewhere in his mid-forties, Michelle estimated.

"It's a pleasure to meet you, Milady," he assured her.

"A lawyer, and tactful, too," Michelle observed, and nodded her head at Lieutenant Archer. "My Lord, Commander, this is Gervais Archer, my flag lieutenant."

"Lieutenant," Cortez said, acknowledging him with another nod, and then gestured at the comfortable chairs which faced his desk.

"Please," he said. "Have a seat. Both of you."

"Thank you, My Lord," Michelle murmured, and settled herself in the indicated chair. Archer, with a junior aide's unfailing instincts, took another one, set slightly behind and to the left of Michelle's, and Roach resumed his own chair after Cortez seated himself behind his desk once more. Then the admiral tipped back slightly and cocked his head to one side as he regarded Michelle with deep-set dark eyes gleaming with intelligence.

"I understand you've been pestering Captain Shaw, Milady," he said.

"I'd hardly call it 'pestering,' My Lord," she replied. "I may have contacted the captain a time or two."

Captain Terrence Shaw was Cortez's chief of staff, which made him the ultimate keeper of the keys where BuPers was concerned.

"Captain Shaw didn't call it that, either," Cortez said with a twinkle. "On the other hand, Milady, seven com calls in eight days does seem just a tad . . . energetic."

"Did I really screen him that many times?" Michelle blinked, honestly surprised by the total, and Cortez snorted.

"Yes, Milady. You did. One would almost think that you were eager to get off-world again. Surely there's something you could think of to do with your convalescent leave?"

"Probably, My Lord," Michelle conceded. "On the other hand, I really wasn't gone all *that* long, and it wasn't particularly difficult to get things sorted back out after I got home. And," a smile softened her expression, "I made it in time for the one thing I really wanted to do."

"The birth of Lady Alexander-Harrington's son, Milady?" Cortez asked in a considerably gentler tone.

"Yes." Michelle's nostrils flared as she inhaled deeply, remembering that moment, once again seeing Honor's transcendent happiness and reliving her own joy as she shared that joyous experience with her best friend.

"Yes, My Lord," she repeated. "Mind you, I missed the wedding, along with all the rest of the Star Kingdom, but at least I did make it home for Raoul's birth."

"And then promptly began hounding BuMed again," Cortez observed. "So, tell me, Milady—how's the leg?"

"Fine, My Lord," she replied just a bit warily.

"BuMed agrees with you," he said, swinging his chair gently from side to side. "In fact, they've endorsed your fitness report in very positive terms." Michelle began to exhale a surreptitious sigh of relief, but amusement flickered in Cortez's eyes as he continued, "Although Captain Montoya did point out that you've been persistently . . . less than completely candid, shall we say, about the amount of physical discomfort you're continuing to experience."

"My Lord," she began, but Cortez shook his head.

"Believe me, Milady," he told her, his eyes now deadly serious, "Montoya would have to be reporting something a lot more serious than a case of someone who's too stubborn to take the convalescent leave to which she's entitled before we worried about it at this point."

"I'm . . . relieved to hear that, Sir," Michelle said frankly, and Cortez snorted.

"I'm going to assume that what you mean is that you're relieved we have a command for you, rather than that we're so desperately pressed for personnel we're cutting corners where medical considerations are concerned, Milady."

*Well,* there's *something there's no good response to,* Michelle thought, and Cortez chuckled.

"Forgive me, Milady. I'm afraid my sense of humor has gotten itself a bit skewed over the last T-year or so."

He gave himself a shake and let his chair come fully back upright once again.

"In fact," he told her, "the real reason I've been ducking your calls—and I *have* been, if I'm going to be honest—is that we've had quite a problem deciding exactly what to do about that parole of yours. No one here at Admiralty House has any qualms about your having given President Pritchart your parole, especially under the circumstances that obtained," he said quickly, as she started to open her mouth. "It's more a matter of our needing to figure out which precedents apply. Which is what Commander Roach is here to explain to you."

He looked at Roach and raised one hand. "Commander?"

"Of course, My Lord," Roach replied, then turned his attention to Michelle.

"For fairly obvious reasons, Milady, there weren't any paroles during the last war, and I'm afraid we've never set up the proper channels between us and the Repulic since the fall of the Committee of Public Safety, either. An oversight we ought to have rectified long since, once we were rid of StateSec. Unfortunately, it would appear the previous government had other things on its mind, such as it was and what there was of it, and we've been just a bit *busy* ourselves since Baron High Ridge's . . . departure. So, frankly, we've been going around in circles over in the JAG's office, trying to decide how to handle your case."

"Not just over at the JAG's office, either," Cortez added. "Public Affairs has been dithering about it, too, I'm afraid, because of all of the interstellar news coverage this whole summit meeting proposal has spawned. Given your close relationship to Her Majesty and the glare of publicity which has accompanied your return, it's particularly important that we get it right, as I trust you understand."

"Yes, Sir. Of course," Michelle agreed.

"There was a minority opinion," Roach told her when Cortez nodded for him to resume, "that the exact wording of your parole technically disqualifies you from active service anywhere until you've been properly exchanged, on the basis that allowing you to serve somewhere besides directly against Haven would still free up another officer for that service. That's a very strict interpretation of the Deneb Accords, however, and it's one the Star Kingdom has never formally accepted. It was also, frankly, an interpretation that Admiral Cortez didn't much care for, so I was asked to do some additional research, probably because I'm currently the executive officer over at the Charleston Center for Admiralty Law."

Michelle nodded. The Charleston Center was recognized as one of the galaxy's premier authorities on interstellar admiralty law. Its original reason for being when it was initially established a hundred and sixty T-years ago had been to deal specifically with the military implications of the customary legal practices which had grown up over the centuries of the Diaspora. But despite the fact that it remained a Navy command, the sheer size of the Star

Kingdom's merchant marine gave its decisions enormous impact where *civilian* interstellar traffic was concerned, as well.

"Like any good lawyer, I went looking for the precedents most favorable to my client's case—the stronger and more specific the better—and I found what I was looking for in a decision from the old Greenbriar-Chanticleer War. In 1843, they agreed to submit a dispute over officers' paroles for Solarian League binding arbitration. The decision of the arbitrator was that any legally paroled officer could be utilized for any duty in which he or she was not personally and directly engaged against the enemy who had paroled him or her. Staff, logistic, and medical services assignments for any unit directly committed against the enemy who had paroled him or her were held to be unlawful, but service in another astrographic area, or against another opponent, was specifically held to be a lawful employment of paroled officers. In other words, Milady, as long as you aren't actively shooting at the Peeps or helping someone else do the same thing, the Admiralty can send you anywhere it wants."

"Which is exactly what he told us, in considerably more detail, when he wrote the final decision that we can legally and honorably employ you in either Silesia or the Talbott Cluster, even if that does let us send some other rear admiral to go beat on Haven in your place," Cortez said. "And, frankly, it's a damned good thing we can, too, under the circumstances."

"I understand, My Lord," Michelle said when he paused, and she did.

It didn't seem possible that she'd been back in the Star Kingdom for the better part of two T-months. News of Captain Aivars Terekhov's stunning—and costly—victory at the Battle of Monica had arrived only nine days after she had, and the entire Star Kingdom had experienced a spasm of almost unendurable relief. The price his scratch-built squadron had paid might have been agonizing, but no one had any illusions about what would have happened if he'd failed to demolish the battlecruisers which had been supplied to the Union of Monica. Nor did anyone doubt that those ships had been supplied by someone who clearly did not have the Star Kingdom's best interests at heart, although just what the full ramifications of that "someone's" plans might have been was still being unraveled. Frankly, Michelle was one of those who doubted that even Patricia Givens would ever manage to dig all the bits and pieces of the plot out from under their concealing rocks. But the intelligence people reporting to Rear Admiral Khumalo, Vice Admiral O'Malley, and Special Minister Amandine Corvisart had already dug out enough to validate all of Terekhov's suspicions . . . and actions.

Unfortunately, anyone who thought the Star Kingdom was out of the woods probably enjoyed only intermittent contact with reality, she thought grimly. True, the Monican Navy had been completely removed from the board, but Monica had never been the true threat, anyway. It had always been Monica's status as a client state of the Solarian League which posed the real danger, and it was still far too early to predict how the League was going to react. The government of Baron Grantville and the Navy's officer corps had always realized that, and over the last month, that same awareness had begun sinking in for the average woman-in-the-street, as well.

*It's a hell of a galaxy when Frontier Security can use a bunch of criminals like Manpower and come this damned close to getting us into war with the most powerful star nation in existence,* she thought. *And it's even more of a pain in the ass when we can't be certain they won't succeed in the end anyway, even after we've started turning over the rocks and exposing the slime underneath them. No wonder everyone's so relieved by the thought that we're at least going to be talking to Haven again!*

"I know you've been briefed by Admiral Givens and her people," Cortez continued. "Since they've brought you up to date on the basic political and deployment aspects of the overall situation, I'm going to concentrate on the nuts and bolts of our manning requirements and the problems directly related to them.

"You may not be aware that the first wave of our emergency superdreadnought construction programs will be commissioning over the next several months," he said, and Michelle's eyes narrowed. He saw it, and snorted. "I see you weren't. Good. They've worked some not so minor miracles in the shipyards—and, to be frank, cut some corners in ways we would never have accepted in peacetime—to telescope construction times, and we're substantially ahead of schedule on most of the ships. We've done our best to conceal the extent to which that's true, and we sincerely hope Haven hasn't picked up on it yet, either. But, to be perfectly honest, that's one reason everyone here at Admiralty House heaved such a huge sigh of relief when Her Majesty agreed to meet with Pritchart and Theisman. Obviously, we'll all be delighted if some sort of peace settlement emerges from this summit. But, frankly, even if nothing at all comes of it in that regard, we should be able to string the talks out for at least a couple of months, even after Her Majesty and Pritchart reach Torch. And that doesn't even consider all the messages which are going to have to be sent back and forth to set something like this up in the first place. Just all of the physical coming and going involved is going to buy us *time*. Time enough for us to get a lot of those new wallers into service. And that, Admiral Gold Peak, coupled with the new weapons and control systems which are also coming into service, means the Republic's numerical advantage is going to be a lot less crushing than anyone in Nouveau Paris thinks it is."

He smiled thinly at her, but then the smile vanished, and he shook his head.

"That's all well and good where Haven is concerned, of course. But if we find ourselves at war with the Solarian League, it's going to be a very different story. As my mother always used to warn me, every silver lining has a cloud, and that's certainly true in this case. Given the situation vis-a-vis the League, we have no choice but to continue to tweak our recruiting, training, *and* building programs whenever and wherever we can, despite the summit and any respite it might offer on the Haven front. And despite all of the advances in automation and reductions in manpower requirements, crewing that much new construction is stretching our personnel strength right to the breaking point. For example, most of the new superdreadnoughts are close enough to completion at this point that we're already assembling cadre and assigning them to their new ships. Fortunately, we've been able to decommission many of the old-style ships of the wall we were forced to put back into service after Grendelsbane, and that's freed up a lot of trained manpower. And we've recovered from Janacek and High Ridge's build-down. But we're still short of all the people we need, and the situation is even worse for our lighter units. Like—" he gave her a sharp, level look "—the new battlecruisers."

He paused, and Michelle nodded. The most urgent priorities of the new war emergency construction programs had focused on producing as many ships of the wall, pod-laying superdreadnoughts like Honor's *Imperator*, as was physically possible. It couldn't have been any other way, given the overwhelming primacy the new "podnoughts" had attained. Because of that emphasis, lighter ships, like cruisers and destroyers, had been assigned a much lower building priority. Large numbers had been projected, and, indeed, laid down, but only after the needs of the superdreadnought-building programs had already been met. And only after additional dispersed yards in which to *do* the laying down could be thrown together, as well. As a result, construction had been much slower to begin on those smaller, lighter units.

On the other hand, it took much less time to build a destroyer or a cruiser—or even one of the new battlecruisers—than it did to build a ship of the wall. Which meant there'd been time to refine their designs and get classes like the new *Nike*-class battlecruisers and *Roland*-class destroyers into the pipeline. And it also meant that, despite their later start, truly enormous numbers of brand-new ships "below the wall" were already in the process of working up for service. But although the adoption of such vastly increased automation meant the once vast gulf between the absolute numbers of noncommissioned and enlisted personnel required by a superdreadnought and a mere battlecruiser had shrunk substantially, a battlecruiser still required almost as many *officers* as a superdreadnought. And while the new LACs might free up large numbers of starships which might once have been tied down on picket, patrol, or anti-piracy system security, each of *them* required its own slice of officers and enlisted, as well, which, in turn, put an even greater strain on the available supply of trained personnel.

"Here's what we have in mind, Milady," Cortez said, leaning forward and folding his hands on his desk blotter. "Initially, we'd earmarked somewhere around two thirds of the new cruisers and battlecruisers for Admiral Sarnow's command in Silesia. That, unfortunately, was before the situation in Talbott blew up in our faces. So now it looks as if we're basically going to be reversing the proportions we'd originally projected and sending two thirds of them to Talbott, instead. Including you, Admiral."

"Me, My Lord?" she asked when he paused as if to invite comment.

"You," he confirmed. "We're giving you the 106th."

For a moment, it failed to register. Then her eyes flared in astonishment. He couldn't be serious! That was her first thought. And on its heels, came another.

"Sir Lucian," she began, "I don't—"

"We're not going to have that particular discussion, Milady," Cortez interrupted her. She closed her mouth, sitting back in her chair, and he gazed at her sternly. "You've been not-pestering Captain Shaw for a billet, and now you've got one, and this decision has nothing to do with the fact that you're the Queen's cousin. It has to do with the fact that you are a highly experienced officer, who has just returned from demonstrating exactly how capable you are, and who—to be frank—we can't use where we'd most *like* to use you. But if we can't give you a superdreadnought division or squadron and send you back to Eighth Fleet, the 106th is, in the Admiralty's considered opinion, absolutely the next best use we can make of you."

Michelle bit her tongue rather firmly, remembering a conversation with Honor on this same topic. Despite Cortez's explanation, she remained less than fully convinced favoritism had played no part at all in the Admiralty's decision. Still, she had to admit Honor had also had a point. The fact that Michelle had spent so long guarding against even the appearance of playing the patronage game which had so bedeviled the prewar Manticoran officer corps might, indeed, have made her overly sensitive in some respects.

"Having said that, however," Cortez continued, "and to be completely honest, there are some factors in your orders which don't relate directly to your demonstrated capabilities as a combat commander. Not to the decision to give you the 106th, but to the decision as to where to *send* you—and it—after giving it to you."

Michelle's eyes narrowed as she sensed the impending fall of the second shoe, and Cortez smiled a bit crookedly.

"No, Milady, we didn't make any deals with Mount Royal Palace," he told her. "But the fact is that we've known from the beginning that we couldn't permanently leave Vice Admiral O'Malley in Talbott, for a lot of reasons. Among them, the fact that he's just about due for his third star. Another is that we have a task group of *Invictus*-class SD(P)s waiting for him when he gets it. So, as soon as possible, we need to recall him to the Lynx Terminus and get Admiral Blaine's screening units back to the rest of his task force. But we're going to need someone to replace O'Malley

in Talbott proper, and we're going to be recalling the pod battlecruisers we borrowed from Grayson when we deployed him in
the first place. We're replacing them with the 106th, and we're
replacing *him* with you . . . Vice Admiral Gold Peak."

Michelle stiffened in her chair, and Cortez's smile grew broader.

"You were already on the list before Solon," he told her. "In fact,
the promotion board had acted before *Ajax* was lost, although
the paperwork was still being processed. And then things got a
little complicated when we thought you were dead, of course.
That's been straightened out, however, and some of those factors
other than your combat skills are coming into play here, as well.
For one thing, it's been decided Admiral Khumalo will also be
promoted. In fact, he's already been notified of his promotion to
vice admiral. His date of rank precedes your own, so he'll still
be senior to you, and he'll be staying on as the Talbott Station
commander."

Michelle kept her mouth shut . . . not without difficulty, and
this time Cortez allowed his smile to slide over into a chuckle.
Then he sobered.

"I'm sorry, Milady. I shouldn't have laughed, but your expression . . ."

He shook his head.

"No, My Lord, *I'm* sorry," she said. "I didn't mean—"

"Milady, you aren't the only one who's been . . . under-impressed
by Augustus Khumalo over the years. To be honest, there'd been
serious consideration of recalling him from Talbott before this
situation with Monica blew up. And, the truth is, he's always been
more of an administrator than a combat officer. But he demonstrated a lot of moral courage—more, to be honest, than I, for
one, ever really thought he had, I'm a bit ashamed to admit—when
he backed Terekhov to the hilt. His instincts turned out to be
very sound in that instance, and he really is a superior administrator. Hopefully that's going to be more important than tactical
acumen, assuming we can avoid a war with the League. And his
and Terekhov's response to what every Talbotter is convinced
was an OFS plot to annex the entire Cluster has made both of
them *extremely* popular in Talbott. A lot of people would be very
unhappy if we recalled him and replaced him with someone else
at this particular time.

"All of that's true, but it still seems to us here at Admiralty House that he's going to need someone as his second-in-command who has the combat experience he lacks. Given your availability—and the fact that you *aren't* available for service with Eighth Fleet any longer—you're well suited to provide that for him. And, quite frankly, the fact that you stand so high in the succession, not to mention the fact that he's directly related to you through the Wintons, should give you an extra handle for influence with him. Not to mention the fact that your relationship to Her Majesty should also help to underscore the Government's support for the Cluster under the new constitution."

Michelle nodded slowly. In a sense, what Cortez had just said demonstrated that politics and her birth had, indeed, helped to dictate the Admiralty's policy. On the other hand, she couldn't disagree with a single one of the points he'd made, and little though she might *like* politics, she'd always known political and military strategy were inextricably entwined. As that ancient Old Earth military historian Honor was so fond of quoting had put it, the setting of national goals was a political decision, and war represented the pursuit of those same political goals by nonpolitical means.

"I know this doesn't constitute much warning," Cortez continued. "And I'm afraid you aren't going to have time to assemble your own staff. For that matter, you're not going to have time to properly work up your new squadron, either. From the last report I received, I'm not even sure all of your ships will have completed their acceptance trials before you have to depart. I've done my best to pull together as strong a team for you as I could, however."

He took a document viewer from his desk drawer and passed it across to her. She keyed it and pursed her lips thoughtfully as she scanned the information. She didn't recognize many of the names, but she did recognize some of them.

"Captain Lecter became available almost as unexpectedly as you did, Milady," Cortez said. "At least a half-dozen flag officers requested her services, but I felt she'd fit best as your chief of staff."

Michelle nodded in mingled understanding and gratitude. Captain Cynthia Lecter—only she'd been *Commander* Cynthia Lecter, at the time—had been the best executive officer Michelle had ever had. She was delighted Cynthia's promotion had come through, and she had no qualms at all about her suitability for the chief of the squadron command staff she'd had no idea she was about to inherit.

"I don't believe you've ever served with Commander Adenauer," Cortez continued, "but she's compiled a very impressive record."

Michelle nodded again. As far as she was aware, she'd never even met Commander Dominica Adenauer, much less served with her, but the bare synopsis of the combat record appended to the file Cortez had handed her was impressive. Not every skilled tactical officer worked out well as a squadron operations officer, but at first glance, at least, Adenauer looked promising. And Cortez did have that knack for putting the right officer into the right slot.

"I think you'll be pleased with Commander Casterlin and Lieutenant Commander Edwards, as well," Cortez told her.

"I know Commander Casterlin," Michelle said, looking up from the document. "Not as well as I'd like to, under the circumstances, but what I do know about him, I like. I don't know anything about Edwards, though."

"He's young," Cortez replied. "In fact, he just made lieutenant commander about two months ago, but I was impressed when I interviewed him. And he's just finished a stint with BuWeaps as one of Admiral Hemphill's assistants. He's too junior to hold down the ops officer's slot, and even if he wasn't, he's a communications specialist, not a tac officer. That's why Adenauer got Operations and Edwards got Communications. But he's been hands-on with both laser head development and the new command and control systems, and I think you—and Commander Adenauer—will find his familiarity with the admiral's newest toys very useful."

"I'm sure we will," Michelle agreed.

"I'm still trying to find you a good logistics officer, and I still need a staff EW expert for you. Edwards' experience could probably be helpful in that area, as well, but, again, it's not something he's really trained for. Hopefully, I'll have both Logistics and Electronic Warfare covered by the end of the day. Obviously, all of these are suggestions at this point, and if you do have any serious reservations or objections to my nominations, we'll do everything we can to accommodate you. I'm afraid, however, that time's so short we may not have a lot of flex."

"Understood, My Lord," Michelle said in a voice that sounded more cheerful than she actually felt. The Manticoran tradition had always been that BuPers tried hard to meet any flag officer's reasonable requests for staffers, and no squadron or task force commander was ever happy to find herself stuck with someone else's choices for her own staff officers. She couldn't pretend *she* was exactly delighted to find herself in that position, but she suspected that quite a few other flag officers were finding themselves in very similar circumstances at the moment.

*With Cindy to ride herd on them, we should be all right,* she told herself. *I wish I'd ever at least* met *Adenauer, though. Her record looks* good, *from what I've been able to see of it so far, at least, but that's all on paper as far as I'm concerned. And Edwards looks like he'd be happier as a research weenie somewhere. God, I hope appearances are deceiving in that respect, anyway! But Casterlin's a good, solid choice for astrogator. Between them, he and Cindy should at least be able to keep things running on an even keel. And if there are any problems, it'll just be my job to make sure they . . . go away.*

"I understand, My Lord," she said again, a bit more firmly. "I do have one additional question, however."

"Of course, Milady."

"From everything you've said, I assume you're planning on deploying the squadron as soon as possible."

"Actually, Milady, I'm planning on deploying the squadron even sooner than that," Cortez said with a tight smile. "That's what I meant when I said you might even be pulling out for Talbott before all of your ships have completed their acceptance trials. You do remember what I said about the shipyards cutting corners to streamline production, don't you? Well, one of the things we've dispensed with is the full spectrum of acceptance trials and pre-trial testing."

Michelle's eyes widened in the first real alarm she'd felt since entering Cortez's office, and he shrugged.

"Milady, we're between the proverbial rock and the hard place, and we've simply had no choice but to make some . . . accommodations. I won't pretend anyone's delighted by it, but we've tried to compensate by putting even more emphasis on quality control in the construction process. So far, we haven't had any major component failures, but I'd be misleading you if I didn't admit we have had some minor to even moderately severe problems which had to be worked out using on-board resources after a ship left the yard. I hope that won't be the case where your squadron is concerned, but I can't guarantee it. And if we have to deploy you with builder's reps still on board, we will. So, in answer to the question I'm sure you were about to ask, your deployment date is one T-week from today."

Despite herself, Michelle's lips tightened. Cortez saw it, and shook his head.

"I'm genuinely sorry, Milady. I fully realize one week isn't even long enough for you to complete straightening out the details of your personal affairs, far less long enough to develop any feel for your ship commanders, or even the members of your own staff. If we could give you longer, we would. But whatever may be happening where *Haven* is concerned, the Talbott Cluster is still a powder keg waiting for a single spark in the wrong place. A powder keg someone's already tried their damnedest to touch off for reasons we're still only guessing at. We need a powerful, sustained presence there, and we need it in place before any Solarian redeployments in response to events in Monica shift the balance. God knows there are enough arrogant Solly COs and squadron commanders out there, even without the little matter of the fact that we're still trying to figure out exactly who—besides Manpower—was doing what to whom until Terekhov spoked their wheel. I hope we'll all breathe a sigh of relief when we do figure that out, but I'm not planning on putting down any bets on that outcome. And one thing we *don't* need while we work on that little problem is for some Solly commodore or admiral to decide he has a big enough advantage in combat power to do something stupid that we'll all regret."

"I understand, Sir," Michelle said yet again. "I can't say I expected any of this when I walked into your office, but I understand."

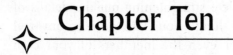

# Chapter Ten

A CONCEALED DOOR SLID silently open, and three men stepped through it into the luxurious office. They looked remarkably like younger versions of the fourth man, already sitting behind the desk in that office. They had the same dark hair, the same dark eyes, the same high cheekbones, and the same strong nose, and for good reason.

They crossed to the chairs arranged in a loose semicircle facing the desk and settled into them. One of them selected the chair in which one of the two women who'd just left had been seated, and the older man behind the desk smiled at them with remarkably little humor.

"Well?" Albrecht Detweiler said after a moment, tipping back his own chair as he regarded the newcomers.

"It would appear," the one who'd chosen the previously occupied chair said, in a voice which sounded eerily like Albrecht's, "that we've hit an air pocket."

"Really?" Albrecht raised his eyebrows in mock amazement. "And what, pray tell, might have led you to that conclusion, Benjamin?"

Benjamin showed very little sign of the sort of apprehension Albrecht's irony evoked in most of the people who knew of his existence. Perhaps that was because his own last name was also Detweiler . . . as was the last name of both of his companions, as well.

"That was what's known as a prefatory remark, Father," he replied.

"Ah, I see. In that case, why don't you go ahead and elucidate?"

Benjamin smiled and shook his head, then leaned back in his chair.

"Father, you know as well as I do—*better* than I do—that at least part of this is the result of how thoroughly we've compartmentalized. Personally, I think Anisimovna might have done a marginally better job if she'd known what our real objectives were, but that may be because I've been arguing for years now that we need to bring more of the Strategy Council fully inside. As it is, though, I think her and Bardasano's analysis of what went wrong in Talbott is probably essentially accurate. No one could have allowed for the sort of freak occurrence which apparently led this Terekhov into stumbling across the connection to Frontier Security and Monica. Nor, I think, could anyone have legitimately expected him to launch some sort of unauthorized preemptive strike even if they'd expected him to uncover whatever it was he uncovered. And, unlike us, Anisimovna didn't have our latest appreciation on Manty capabilities. Let's be honest—what they did to Monica's new battlecruisers surprised even us, and she didn't have as much inside information as we did to begin with. Besides that, she didn't know that what we really wanted all along was for Verrochio and Frontier Fleet to get reamed, even if we did plan for it to happen considerably later in the process. If Bardasano had been allowed to tell her *everything*, it's possible—not likely, but *possible*—that the two of them could have designed in a fallback position for something like this."

He shrugged.

"Things like this happen sometimes. It's not exactly as if it's the first time it's happened to *us*, after all. The fact that Pritchart was able to turn what happened into an opening wedge for this summit of hers is a lot more painful, of course, but we've had at least a few other setbacks which have been just as severe. The thing that makes *this* one smart as much as it does is that we're moving into the endgame phase, and that reduces our margin to recover from missteps. Which," he added just a bit pointedly, "is one reason I think we may need to reconsider how tightly we do compartmentalize things."

Albrecht frowned. It was a less than fully happy expression, yet it was a thoughtful frown, not an angry one. His reputation (among those who knew he existed at all) for ruthlessness was well-deserved, and he'd carefully cultivated a matching reputation for the shortness and ferocity of his temper. That second reputation, however, was more useful than accurate.

"I understand what you're saying, Ben," he said, after a moment. "God knows you've said it often enough!"

A grin robbed his last sentence of any potential air of complaint, but then the grin faded back into thoughtfulness.

"The problem is that the onion's served us so well for so long," he said. "I'm not prepared to just throw all of that away, especially when the consequences could be so severe if anyone we decide has the need to know screws up. It's one of those 'if it isn't broken, don't fix it' sorts of things."

"I'm not suggesting 'throwing it away,' Father. I'm only suggesting . . . peeling it back a little for the people trying to coordinate and carry out critical operations. And I agree with you that we shouldn't fix things that aren't broken, as a general rule. Unfortunately, I think there's a possibility that it *is* broken—or, at least, sufficiently inefficient to be getting dangerous—in this regard," Benjamin pointed out respectfully but firmly, and Albrecht grimaced at the validity of the qualification. It was entirely possible Benjamin was right, after all.

The problem with a conspiracy embracing a multi-century schedule, he reflected, was that nobody, however gifted at skulduggery and paranoia they might be, could operate on that scale for that long without having the occasional operational *faux pas* stray into sight. So the approach which had been adopted by the Mesan Alignment all those centuries ago had been to establish what one of Albrecht's direct ancestors had christened the "onion strategy."

So far as the galaxy at large was aware, the planet Mesa was simply an outlaw world, home to ruthless and corrupt corporations from throughout the Solarian League's huge volume. Not a member of the League itself, Mesa nonetheless had lucrative contacts with many League worlds, which protected it and its "outlaw" owners from Solarian intervention. And, of course, the worst of the outlaws in question was none other than Manpower Incorporated, the galaxy's leading producer of genetic slaves, which had been founded by Leonard Detweiler the better part of six hundred T-years before. There were others, some of them equally disreputable and "evil" by other peoples' standards, but Manpower was clearly the standardbearer for Mesa's incredibly wealthy—and thoroughly corrupt—elite. And Manpower, equally clearly, was ruthlessly determined to protect its economic interests at any cost. Any and all of its *political* contacts, objectives, and strategies were obviously subordinated to that purpose.

Which was where the "onion" came in. Although Albrecht himself had often thought it would have been more appropriate to describe Manpower as the stage magician's left hand, moving in dramatic passes to fix the audience's attention upon it while his *right* hand performed the critical manipulation the Alignment wanted no one else to notice.

Manpower and its genetic slaves remained, in fact, immensely profitable, but these days that was actually only a happy secondary benefit of Manpower's existence. In fact, as the Alignment fully recognized, genetic slavery had long since ceased to be a truly competitive way to supply labor forces, except under highly specialized circumstances. Fortunately many of its customers failed to grasp that same point, and Manpower's marketing department went to considerable lengths to encourage that failure of understanding wherever possible. And, possibly even more fortunately, *other* aspects of genetic slavery, particularly those associated with the vices to which humanity had always been prey, made rather more economic sense. Not only were the profits higher for Manpower's customers, the frailties of human nature and appetites being what they were, but the various types of pleasure slave Manpower provided were enormously more profitable for it, on a per-slave basis, as well. Yet the truth was that although the vast amounts the slave trade earned remained extremely welcome and useful, the main purposes which today's Manpower truly served were quite different from anything directly related to money.

First, Manpower and its genetic research facilities provided the perfect cover for the experimentation and development which were the true focus of the Mesan Alignment and its goals. Second, the need to protect Manpower explained why Mesa, although not a member of the League itself, was so heavily plugged into the League's political and economic structures. Third, the perversions to which genetic slavery pandered provided ready-made "hooks" by which Manpower's proprietors could . . . influence decisionmakers throughout the League and beyond. Fourth, the nature of the slave trade itself turned Manpower—and thus, by extension, all of Mesa's ruling corporations—into obvious *criminals*, with an instinctive imperative to maintain the current system as it was so that they could continue to feed in its comfortably corrupt depths, which distracted anyone from considering the possibility that Mesa might actually want to *change* the current system, instead. And, fifth, it provided a ready-made excuse—or plausible cover, at least—for almost any covert operation the Alignment might undertake if details of that operation should stray into sight.

There were, however, some unfortunate downsides to that otherwise highly satisfactory state of affairs. Three of them, in fact, came rather pointedly to mind, given what he'd just been discussing with Aldona Anisimovna and Isabel Bardasano: Beowulf, Manticore, and Haven.

It would no doubt have helped, in some ways, at least, if Leonard Detweiler had fully worked out his grand concept before establishing Manpower. No one could think of everything, unfortunately, and one thing Mesa's geneticists still hadn't been able to produce was prescience. Besides, he'd been provoked. His Detweiler Consortium had first settled Mesa in 1460 PD, migrating to its new home from Beowulf following the discovery of the Visigoth System's wormhole junction six T-years earlier. The Mesa System itself had first been surveyed in 1398, but until the astrogators discovered that it was home to one of the two secondary termini of the Visigoth Wormhole, it had been too far out in the back of beyond to attract development.

That changed when the Visigoth Wormhole survey was completed, and Detweiler had acquired the development rights from the system's original surveyors. The fact that the planet Mesa, despite having quite a nice climate, also possessed a biosystem poorly suited to terrestrial physiology helped lower the price, given the expenses involved in terraforming. But Detweiler hadn't intended to terraform Mesa. Instead, he'd opted to "mesaform" the colonists through genetic engineering. That decision had been inevitable in light of Detweiler's condemnation of the "illogical, ignorant, unthinking, hysterical, Frankenstein fear" of the genetic modification of human beings which had hardened into almost instinctual repugnance over the five hundred T-years between Old Earth's

Final War and his departure for Mesa. Still, however inevitable it might have been, it had *not* been popular with the Beowulf medical establishment of the time. Worse, the fact that Visigoth was barely sixty light-years from Beowulf had guaranteed that Mesa and Beowulf would remain close enough together (despite the hundreds of light-years between them through normal-space) to be a continuous irritant to one another, and Beowulf's unceasing condemnation of Detweiler's faith in the genetic perfectability of humanity had infuriated him. It was, after all, the entire reason he and those members of the Beowulf genetic establishment who shared his views had left Beowulf in the first place.

It was quite clear that Leonard's decision to rename the Detweiler Consortium "Manpower, Incorporated," had been intended as a thumb in the eye to the entire Beowulf establishment, and that thumb had landed exactly where he'd aimed it. And if Beowulf had been . . . upset by the Detweiler Consortium's practice of wholesale genetic modification of colonists to suit hostile environments like Mesa, it was infuriated when Manpower began producing "indentured servants" genetically designed for specific environments or specific tasks. At first, periods of indenturement on Mesa itself had been limited to no more than twenty-five T-years, although even after completing their indentures, the "genetic clients" had been denied the franchise and generally treated as second-class citizens. As they became an increasing percentage of the planetary population, however, the planetary constitution had been modified to make "indenturement" a lifelong condition. Technically, Mesa and Manpower continued to insist that there were no such things as "slaves," only "indentured servants," but while that distinction might offer at least some useful smokescreen for Mesa's allies and paid mouthpieces in places like the Solarian League's Assembly, it was meaningless to the institution's opponents.

The hostility between Beowulf and Mesa had grown unspeakably bitter over the past four and a half centuries, and the anti-slavery Cherwell Convention which had been created by Beowulf had produced enormous headaches for Manpower, Mesa, and the Mesan Alignment. That was unfortunate, and it had posed some significant problems for the Alignment's overall strategy. The ferocity with which the Star Kingdom of Manticore and the Republic of Haven harassed Manpower's operations, for example, had clearly presented a long-term threat. While both of those star nations combined constituted little more than a flyspeck compared to the Solarian League, their loathing for genetic slavery had made them implacable foes, and the Republic of Haven's vibrant economy and steady expansion had caused the Alignment considerable anxiety. Haven had been colonized over a hundred and fifty T-years before Mesa, and while it had lacked the enormous financial "nest egg" Leonard Detweiler had brought with him to Mesa, it had created a powerful, self-fueling economic base which promised to do nothing but continue to grow. And that had made the Haven Quadrant loom large in the Alignment's thinking, especially following the discovery of the Manticoran Wormhole Junction in 1585.

It was the Manticoran Junction and the way it moved the entire Haven Quadrant to within shouting distance of the Sol System itself which had made a pair of insignificant, far off neobarb star nations a matter of major concern to the Alignment. Their direct connection to the League ran through the Beowulf System, and both the Republic and the Star Kingdom had fully imbibed the Beowulfan attitudes towards genetic slavery.

Although Manpower had found the Star Kingdom's deep involvement in the League's merchant shipping made possible by the Junction inconvenient in the extreme, the Alignment had actually been much more concerned by the Republic's existence. After all, although the official Republic of Haven had consisted only of the Haven System itself and a handful of its oldest daughter colonies, its influence had pervaded the whole Haven Quadrant, making Nouveau Paris the natural leader of that entire volume, and the Quadrant had been growing steadily in both size and economic and industrial power. There'd been no doubt in the mind of the Alignment that the Republic would stand staunchly by the historic Beowulfan position in any open conflict, and it promised to form a power bloc poised to come to Beowulf's aid from well beyond Mesa's reach. Manticore, on the other hand, had been only a single star system—although it was in the process of becoming an extraordinarily rich one—with a tradition of powerful domestic opposition to territorial expansion. Which was why the Alignment's initial attention had been focused on crippling the Republic of Haven as expeditiously as possible, and the subtle encouragement of certain domestic philosophies and political machinations—and machines—had offered Mesa a pry bar.

That particular effort had worked out rather well ... except, of course, for the unfortunate side effect it had produced where *Manticore* was concerned. The Legislaturalist régime and its policies had transformed Haven from a shining example into a vast, voracious, shambling, ramshackle entity, thoroughly detested by its neighbors and the majority of its involuntary citizens and perpetually hovering on the brink of outright collapse. As such, it had scarcely constituted any sort of threat ... until, that was, it turned its sights upon Manticore, at which point, things had departed drastically from the Alignment's strategic playbook.

Manticore had declined to be absorbed. In fact, it had resisted so strongly and successfully—and had embraced so many military innovations in the process—that it had come within a hair's breadth of toppling the People's Republic, instead. In fact, it *had* toppled the *People's* Republic ... which had not only threatened to resurrect the old Republic of Haven, but also provided both Haven and Manticore with an enormous military edge over any potential opponent. Not to mention the fact that the previously anti-expansion Star Kingdom was busily converting itself into a star *empire*, instead.

*The thing that makes it so damned irritating,* Albrecht reflected, *is that everything else is going so well. In a lot of ways, Manticore and Haven shouldn't matter a fart in a windstorm, given their limited size and how far away they are. Unfortunately, not only are they both likely to grow nothing but bigger and stronger if we don't take steps, but the wormhole network gives Manticore the ability to reach almost any part of the Solarian League quickly, in theory, at least. And they aren't really that damned far away from us, either. Talbott is bad enough in normal-space terms, but the entire Manty home fleet is only sixty light-years—and two junction transits—away from Mesa by way of Beowulf. And the Manties keep right on introducing new pieces of hardware at the most inconvenient times. Not to mention pushing the damned Havenites into following their lead!*

"I don't think we want to abandon the onion at this particular moment," he said finally. Benjamin started to say something more, then closed his mouth and nodded, accepting the decision, and Albrecht smiled at him.

"I understand that you're thinking about our internal arrangements and the way we compartmentalize information and operations, not the face we present to the galaxy at large, Ben," he said.

"And I'm not saying I disagree with you in theory. In fact, I don't disagree with you in practice, either. It's just a matter of timing. We've always intended to bring the entire Strategy Council fully inside well before we actually push the button, after all. It may well be that we need to reconsider our decision trees and pull that moment further forward, too. I don't want to do that precipitously, without considering all of the implications—and without carefully considering which of the Council members might pose additional security risks—but I'm perfectly willing to concede that this is something we should be looking at very seriously."

"I'm glad to hear you say that, Father," Collin Detweiler said. Albrecht glanced at him, and Collin smiled a bit crookedly. "I think Ben feels his shoes pinching a bit harder than the rest of us because his emphasis is so much on the military side of things. But I have to say that my toes are feeling a little squeezed, too."

"They are?"

"Oh, yes." Collin shook his head. "I'm glad you've at least let me bring Bardasano most of the way inside. That makes coordinating covert ops a lot simpler and cleaner. But that's not quite the same thing as making them easy and efficient, and now that we're ramping up to the main event, its inconvenient as hell when the *only* person I've been allowed to bring that far inside has to spend so much of her time hundreds of light-years away."

"How serious a problem is that, really?" Albrecht asked, his eyes narrowing intensely.

"So far, it hasn't been all that bad," Collin admitted. "It's cumbersome, of course. And to be perfectly honest, the need to keep coming up with convincing rationales for why we're doing some of the things we're doing can get pretty exhausting. I'm talking about internal rationales, for the people we actually have doing them. You don't want idiots planning and executing black operations, and the non-idiots you need are likely to start wondering why you're doing things that don't logically support the objectives they think you're trying to accomplish. Finding ways to prevent that from happening uses up almost as much energy as figuring out what it is we really do need to accomplish. Not to mention creating all sorts of possibilities for dropped stitches or embarrassing gaffes."

"Daniel?" Albrecht looked at the third younger man. "What about your side of things?"

"It doesn't really matter very much one way or the other from where I sit, Father," Daniel Detweiler replied. "Unlike Benjamin and Collin, Everett and I have been openly involved with our R and D programs all along, and no one questions how thoroughly we compartmentalize on that side. Obviously, everyone knows some R and D has to be kept 'black,' and that helps a lot from our perspective. We can set up quiet little projects whenever we feel like it, and no one asks very many questions. At the same time, I have to agree with Collin that bringing Bardasano this far inside has been a considerable help, even for us. We can use her to handle the security on anything we need kept really well hidden while we get on with the business of coordinating the programs themselves. It would help if we could bring people like Kyprianou all the way in, though."

Albrecht nodded slowly. Renzo Kyprianou was in charge of bio-weapons research and development and a member of the Mesan Strategy Council. At the moment, however, not even the Strategy Council knew everything the Alignment was up to.

*Not surprisingly, I suppose,* he mused, *given that the Alignment's always been so much of a . . . family business.*

His lips twitched in an almost-smile at the thought, and he wondered how many members of the Strategy Council had figured out just how close he truly was to his "sons."

The official demise of the Detweiler line had been part of the strategy designed to divert the galaxy's—and especially Beowulf's—attention from Leonard Detweiler's determination to uplift human genetics in general. The Detweilers had been too strongly and fiercely devoted to that goal for too long, and the apparent—and spectacular—assassination of the "last" Detweiler heir by greedy elements on the Manpower Incorporated board of directors had punctuated the fact that the increasingly criminal Mesans no longer shared that lofty aspiration. It had also served to get Leonard's descendants safely beneath anyone else's radar, of course, but its most useful function had been to help explain and justify Mesa's switch to the full-bore exploitation of genetic slavery by Manpower. The steady, ongoing improvement of the alignment's own genomes had been buried under Manpower's R&D programs and camouflaged as little more than surface improvements in physical beauty.

But whatever the rest of humanity might have thought, the Detweiler line was far from extinct. In fact, the Detweiler genome was one of the—if not *the*—most improved within the entire Alignment. And Albrecht Detweiler's "sons" were also his genetic clones. Bardasano, for one, he felt certain, had figured that out, despite how closely held a secret it was supposed to be. It was possible Kyprianou had, as well, given how closely he worked with Daniel. For that matter, Jerome Sandusky might cherish a few suspicions of his own, not that any of that trio was going to breathe a word of any such suspicions to anyone else.

"All right," he said. "As soon as Everett, Franklin, and Gervais get back to Mesa, we'll all sit down and discuss this. As I say, my only reservation has to do with the timing. We all know we're getting close—*very* close—and I don't want last-minute impatience to push us into making a wrong decision at this point."

"None of us want that, Father," Benjamin agreed, and the other two nodded. Taking the time to think things through had always been a fundamental principle of the Alignment's operational planning.

"Good. In the meantime, though, what's your impression of Anisimovna and Bardasano's report?"

"I think Bardasano's probably put her finger on what happened," Benjamin said. He cocked an eyebrow at Collin, and his brother nodded.

"And whether she's right about what caused the operation to blow up is really beside the point," Benjamin continued, turning back to Albrecht. "We've lost Monica; Verrochio is going to pull in his horns, exactly as Anisimovna's predicted; the entire Technodyne connection's been shot right in the head, at least for now; and Manticore's accepted Pritchart's invitation. Leaving summit meetings aside for the moment, we're still going to have to rethink our entire approach to Talbott, at the very least. And we're going to have to find some other way to get through to those idiots in Battle Fleet."

"Well, Monica's not that big a loss," Albrecht observed. "It was never more than a cat's-paw in the first place, and I'm confident we can find another one of those if we need it. Having Verrochio go all gutless on us, now . . . *That's* more than a little irritating. Especially after all the investment we made in Crandall and Filareta."

"Why is that a problem, Father?" Daniel asked after a moment. Albrecht looked at him, and Daniel shrugged. "I know neither of them came cheap, but it's not as if we don't have fairly deep pockets."

"That's not the problem, Dan," Collin said before Albrecht could reply. "The problem is that now that we've used them, we're going to have to get rid of them."

Daniel looked at him for several seconds, then shook his head with a pursed-lip sigh.

"I know I'm only the family tech weenie, not an expert in covert ops like you and Benjamin," he said, "but usually I can at least follow your logic. This time, though, I don't really understand why we need to do that."

"Collin's right, Daniel," Albrecht said. "We can't afford to have either of them asking questions—or, even worse, shooting off his or her mouth and starting someone *else* asking questions." He snorted. "Both of them had the authority to choose their own training problems and deploy their squadrons where they wanted to for the exercises, so that's not a problem. But now that the entire Talbott operation's gone sour on us, we can't have anyone wondering—or, worse, actually asking—why both of them chose such obscure locations. Locations which just *happened* to move their task forces so close to Talbott and Manticore itself just when things were coming to a head at Monica . . . almost as if they knew something was going to happen ahead of time.

"Oh," he waved one hand, "it's unlikely anyone's even going to notice, much less ask questions. But unlikely isn't the same thing as impossible, and you know our policy about eliminating risks, however remote, whenever possible. Which means Crandall and Filareta are both going to have to suffer fatal accidents. Even if someone finds all of their hidden accounts, the money passed through enough cutouts no one will ever be able to tie it to us, but if they should happen to mention that Manpower suggested their exercise areas to them, it could start the damned Manties or Havenites asking questions of their own. Like how even Manpower could have the resources to put so many pieces into play simultaneously."

"I don't think we need to worry about acting immediately, though, Father," Benjamin said. Albrecht looked at him, and it was his turn to shrug. "Trying to get to either of them while they're still out with their fleets would be a royal pain in the ass, even if everything went perfectly. And the odds are that it *wouldn't* go perfectly, either. Much better to let them go ahead, carry out their planned exercises, and then head on home. Both of them are very fond of our pleasure resorts, after all. It won't be too difficult to convince them to drop by for a complimentary visit as a way of expressing our thanks for their efforts, will it? They'll take their own precautions to cover any connection between us before they avail themselves of our generosity, too. And when they do, Collin can arrange things quietly and discreetly."

"Or Bardasano can, anyway," Collin agreed.

"And it's still remotely possible we can somehow prod Verrochio into providing the shooting incident we need," Benjamin added. He saw Albrecht's expression and chuckled. "I didn't say I thought it was *likely*, Father. Frankly, at the moment, I can't think of anything that could possibly have that effect. But if it should happen to happen, we're going to need Crandall and Filareta in place to exploit it. And as you've always told us, never throw away an asset until you're positive it's about to become a liability."

"I can see that," Albrecht acknowledged. "But while we're on the topic of removing liabilities, Collin, what do you think about Webster and Rat Poison?"

"I agree with your decision, Father. And Bardasano's suggestion that we combine the two operations is an indication of why it's been so useful to have her so far inside. I don't know that it's going to have the effect we all hope it will, but I don't see anything else we can do in the available timeframe with a realistic chance of derailing this summit. And, frankly, I can't think of anything that would be likely to make more waves for us than having Elizabeth and Pritchart sit down across a table from each other and figure out someone's been manipulating them both. My only possible quibble would be with just how obvious we want to make the Havenite connection."

"Well, like you and Benjamin, I think Anisimovna's and Bardasano's analysis of how much *Ambassador* Webster is hurting us on Old Terra is reasonably accurate," Albrecht said more than a little sourly. "And, frankly, I got pissed. I know—I know! I'm not supposed to do that. But I did, and, to be honest, it felt good to vent a little. Obviously, calling the Manties 'neobarbs,' however satisfying, isn't something we want to allow to shape the way we think about them, of course. Despite which, I do think we need to make it very clear Haven was behind the assassination."

"I don't disagree with you there," Collin said. "But let me think about this. I'll call Bardasano in and discuss it with her, too. We probably do need something fairly glaring to focus the Manties' attention on Haven. Normally, they'd be inclined to do that anyway, given who they're at war with at the moment and the Havenite tradition of eliminating problems through assassination. But, like you, I'm a little anxious about their connecting it with Monica instead of Haven, now that the wheels have come off that particular operation. Rat Poison could very easily start them thinking in Manpower's direction, as well, given the target. And, frankly, however reluctantly Elizabeth may have agreed to sit down with Pritchart, she has agreed. Logically, that's likely to make them question why anyone on Pritchart's side would try something like this. Bearing all of that in mind, we probably *do* need something to point them rather firmly in Haven's direction. On the other hand, much as we'd prefer for them to be stupid, they aren't. In particular, Givens is especially not-stupid, and she's managed some pretty fair disinformation schemes of her own over the last couple of decades, which means she's probably especially wary of having someone else do the same thing to *her*. So if we *do* build in a direct Havenite connection, we've got to make it look like one Haven's done it's damnedest to erase or conceal."

"I'll leave the tactical decisions up to you," Albrecht said. He sat for a few more seconds, obviously thinking hard, then shrugged.

"I suppose that's just about everything for this afternoon, then. But I'd like for you and Daniel to brief me on the current status of the spider and Oyster Bay sometime in the next few days, Benjamin."

"Of course. I can tell you now, though, that we're still well short of being able to implement Oyster Harbor, Father. We've only got thirty or so of the *Sharks*, and they were never intended to be much more than prototypes and training ships to prove the concept. They've got decent capability for their size, but they're certainly not wallers! We're not even scheduled to lay down the first of the *real* attack ships for another three or four T-months."

"Oh, I know that. I just want a better feel for where we are on producing the actual hardware. But as Collin's just pointed out, it's entirely possible that we're not going to manage to short-circuit this summit of Pritchart's after all. If we can't, and if the frigging Sollies keep falling over their own feet this way, we may have to take things into our own hands earlier in the process than we wanted to. And if that looks like happening, I'll need to know our exact status when we think about timing."

# Chapter Eleven

"WELCOME ABOARD, ADMIRAL," Captain of the List Victoria Armstrong said as Michelle stepped across the decksole line that marked the official boundary between Her Majesty's Space Station *Hephaestus* and HMS *Artemis*, which had just become her flagship.

The outsized personnel tube connecting the battlecruiser's number two boat bay to the space station had been crowded when she arrived. It was amazing how that had changed when the PA had informed everyone *she* was headed down-tube, however. The flow in and out of the tube had stopped almost immediately, and those souls who'd been unable to get out of it had shrunk back against the tube walls as Michelle made her way down its center with Gervais Archer and Chris Billingsley at her heels.

*It's good to be the admiral,* she'd thought to herself, working hard at maintaining a properly solemn expression. The temptation to laugh, however, had faded abruptly as she stepped out of the tube and the bosun's pipes began to shrill. The ancient boarding ceremony's salutes and formalities had flowed around her, and she'd felt her nerves tightening in a combination of anticipation, excitement, and nervousness. Now she reached out and clasped the hand Armstrong was offering her.

"Thank you, Captain," she told her brand new flag captain . . . whom she'd never met before in her life.

Armstrong was on the tall side, somewhere between Michelle and Honor for height, with a strong face, dark green eyes, and chestnut hair, She was young for her rank, even after a half T-century of naval expansion and twenty-plus years of war—just over twenty-five T-years younger than Michelle, in fact—and no one would ever consider her beautiful, or even exceptionally pretty. But there was character in that face, and intelligence, and the green eyes looked lively.

"As you can see, Milady," the flag captain continued, waving her free hand at the bustling activity and seeming chaos which engulfed her boat bay, "we're still just a little busy." She had to raise her voice to be heard over the noise level, which had surged back up as soon as the new admiral's official welcoming was out of the way. "In fact, we've got yard dogs hanging from the deckhead, I'm afraid," she said with a smile.

"So I can see," Michelle agreed. "Is there a particular problem?"

"Tons of them," Armstrong said cheerfully. "But if you're asking if there's a problem that's going to delay our departure, the answer is no. At least, I'm pretty sure the answer is no. Engineering is the most buttoned up department, and I'm confident the ship will move when we step on the hydrogen, anyway. I may have my doubts about some of the *other* systems, but one way or the other, we will make our schedule, Milady. I've already warned Hephaesteus Central that if I have to, I'm taking their yard dogs with me when I go."

"I see." Michelle shook her head, smiling. Her first suspicion— that Armstrong was drawing attention to the yard workers still thronging her boat bay as a preliminary for explaining why it wasn't *her* fault they couldn't pull out on time—had obviously been misplaced.

"What I thought would probably be best, Milady," Armstrong continued, "was to get you onto the lift and out of this bedlam. Once we've got the doors closed and we can hear ourselves think, you can tell me where you want to go. Captain Lecter and Commander Adenauer are on Flag Deck at the moment. Cindy—I mean, Captain Lecter—asked me to tell you she knew you wouldn't be able to get anything done in the middle of all this racket, so she's waiting for you to decide where you want her. If you want her and Adenauer—and me, for that matter—in your day cabin instead of on Flag Deck, they'll be there by the time we could get there from here."

"I would like to see my quarters," Michelle admitted, "but I'd like to see Flag Deck even more." She pointed over her shoulder at Chris Billingsley, who stood beside Lieutenant Archer a respectful three paces behind her. "If you could detail a guide for Chris here, and see to it that *he* gets to our quarters, I'd really prefer to head on up to Flag Deck. It's one way to stay out from underfoot while he fusses around and gets everything arranged perfectly."

Armstrong glanced at the steward, one eyebrow rising as she noticed the out-sized animal carrier in his right hand, then shrugged, chuckled, and nodded.

"Of course, Milady. Would you object if I had my XO and tac officer join us there, as well?"

"On the contrary, I was just about to ask you to invite them to do that."

"Good. In that case, Admiral, I believe the lifts are on the other side of that heap of engineering spares somewhere."

It was indeed much quieter once the lift doors had closed behind them, and Michelle's nostrils flared as she inhaled the new-ship smell. There was nothing else quite like it. The environmental plants aboard the Navy's warships were extremely efficient at filtering out the more objectionable aromas a starship's closed environment generated so effortlessly. But there was a difference between air that was inoffensively clean and air that carried that indefinable perfume of newness. Before Michelle's Uncle Roger had begun his military buildup in response to the People's Republic of Haven's remorseless expansionism, some naval personnel had served their entire careers without smelling that perfume more than once. Some of them had never smelled it at all, for that matter.

Michelle, on the other hand, had actually lost track of the number of times *she'd* smelled it. It was a small thing, perhaps, but it was the sort of small thing that put the enormous investment in money, resources, industrial effort, and trained personnel into stark perspective. The Star Kingdom of Manticore, for its size, might well be the wealthiest political entity in the entire galaxy, yet Michelle hated to think about the deficit the Star Kingdom was running up as it strained every sinew to survive.

*It's cheaper than buying a new kingdom, Mike,* she told herself grimly, then gave herself a mental shake. *And only you are perverse enough to go from "Gosh this ship smells wonderful!" to worrying about the national debt in point-three seconds flat. What you need is a treecat of your own. Someone like Nimitz to kick you in the ass—or bite you on the ear, or something—when you start doing crap like this.*

"Despite all of the yard dogs and loose parts scattered around, she looks like a beautiful ship, Captain," she said to Armstrong.

"Oh, she is. She is!" Armstrong agreed. "And I only had to contract three murders to be sure I got her, too," she added cheerfully.

"Only three?"

"Well, there was that one other candidate," Armstrong said thoughtfully. "But he requested assignment somewhere else after I pointed out what had happened to the other three. Tactfully, of course."

"Oh, of course."

Michelle managed not to chuckle again, although it was difficult. Not many captains would have been prepared to wax quite that cheerful with a vice admiral they'd never met before. Especially not a vice admiral whose flag captain they'd just become. Armstrong, obviously, was, and that said interesting things about her. Either she was a buffoon, or else she was sufficiently confident of her own competence to be who she was and let the chips fall wherever they fell.

Somehow she didn't strike Michelle as the buffoon type.

*In fact, what she* strikes *me as is the Michelle Henke type,* she admitted to herself. *God. I wonder if the squadron's going to be able to survive two of us?*

"Ah, here we are," Armstrong observed as the lift slid to a halt and the door opened.

They passed two more yard dogs in the very brief walk between the lift shaft and the armored hatch protecting *Artemis'* flag deck, and Michelle shook her head mentally. A lot of what was being done seemed to come under the heading of "cosmetic"—closing up interior bulkheads around circuitry runs, painting, lighting fixtures, that sort of thing—but she doubted that she could have been as cheerful as Armstrong if she'd been the captain of a ship due to deploy into a potential war zone in less than one week now and still buried under such swarms of yard workers.

That thought carried her through the hatch, and the spacious, dimly lit coolness of her flag deck spread about her.

Four people had been waiting for her there, and all four of them came to attention as she appeared.

"Rule Number One," she said pleasantly. "Unless we're trying to impress some foreign potentate or convince some newsy we're really earning our lordly salaries, we all have better things to do than spend our time bowing and scraping before my towering presence."

"Yes, Milady," a trim blonde at least twelve or thirteen centimeters shorter than Michelle replied.

"Rule Number Two," Michelle continued, reaching out to shake the smaller woman's hand. "It's 'Ma'am,' not 'Milady,' unless the aforementioned foreign potentate or newsy is present."

"Aye, aye, Ma'am," the other woman said.

"And it's good to see you, too, Cindy," Michelle told her.

"Thank you. Although," Captain (junior-grade) Cynthia Lecter told her, "after what happened at Solon, I didn't think I was going to be seeing you again quite this soon."

"Which makes two of us," Michelle agreed. "This," she continued, waving Archer forward, "is Gwen Archer, my flag lieutenant." She grinned as Lecter quirked an eyebrow at the first name. "Don't let that innocent expression of his fool you, either. He graduated fourteenth in his class in Tactics, and he's just finished a deployment as JTO on a heavy cruiser."

She decided against explaining exactly how and when that deployment had ended. Cindy was more than good enough at her job to discover that information—as well as the reason for Archer's nickname—without having it handed to her on a plate. Besides, the practice would do her good.

Lecter didn't seem particularly perturbed by Michelle's failure to provide the information. She only nodded and smiled at Archer, who smiled back, and Michelle looked past Lecter at a considerably taller dark-haired commander.

"And this must be Commander Adenauer," she observed.

"Yes, Ma'am," Adenauer confirmed as she shook Michelle's hand in turn. Adenauer was obviously from Sphinx, and her accent reminded Michelle strongly of Honor's, although Adenauer's voice was considerably deeper than her own contralto, far less Honor's soprano.

"I hope you don't mind me mentioning this, Commander," Michelle said, "but your accent sounds awfully familiar."

"Probably because I was raised about thirty kilometers outside Twin Forks, Ma'am," Adenauer replied with a grin. "The other side of the city from Duchess Harrington. But she's my ... um ... fifth cousin, I think. Something like that, anyway. I'd have to ask my mom to nail it down any closer than that, but just about everyone born in Duvalier is related to everyone else, one way or another."

"I see." Michelle nodded. "Well, I've met Her Grace's mother and father, and if their level of competence runs in the family, I think you and I should get along just fine, Commander."

"Being related to 'the Salamander' is actually something of a karmic burden, Ma'am," Adenauer said. "Especially for a tac officer."

"Really?" Michelle chuckled. "Well, so is being *her* tac officer or XO. Both of which positions I happen to have held in the dim shades of my own youth."

"And speaking of tactical officers," Armstrong put in, "may I introduce Wilton Diego, *my* tac officer?"

"Commander Diego." Michelle offered her hand once again and hoped he hadn't noticed the sharp, biting flicker of pain she'd felt when Armstrong introduced him. It wasn't Diego's fault, but simply hearing his last name reminded her of her last flag captain, Diego Mikhailov.

Fortunately, the stocky, broad-shouldered commander was as fair-skinned as Lecter and as red-haired as Archer. He didn't look a thing like Mikhailov, and if he'd noticed her tiny twitch, he gave no sign of it.

"Admiral," he said, returning her grip firmly.

"I'm sure you're looking—that you and the captain both are looking—forward to getting the yard dogs out of your hair, Commander," she said.

"You've got that right, Mil—I mean, Ma'am," Diego said fervently. "Actually, Tactical is in pretty good shape. If it weren't for the traffic passing through at the most inopportune possible moments, I'd be a lot happier, though. It sort of takes the edge off a simulation when some yard dog cuts power at the critical moment because he has to change a heating element in the air scrubbers."

"I know," Michelle said with carefully metered sympathy.

"And this," Armstrong continued, waving the fourth and final officer forward, "is Ron Larson, my exec."

"Commander Larson."

Larson's handshake was as firm as Armstrong's own, although he was half a head shorter than the flag captain. He was as dark-haired as Adenauer, but his eyes were a curious slate-gray, not brown, and he sported a luxuriant but neatly trimmed beard that made him look vaguely piratical. There was something about him that reminded Michelle of Michael Oversteegen, though she couldn't put her finger on what it was. Hopefully it wouldn't turn out to be Oversteegen's cheerfully unquenchable arrogance. Michelle had always rather liked Oversteegen, and she respected his abilities, but that didn't mean she liked *everything* about him.

"Admiral Gold Peak," Larson replied while that thought was still running through the back of her brain, and it became instantly obvious that whatever the similarity to Oversteegen might be, it wasn't going to be Oversteegen's aristocratic sense of who he was. Not with that highland Gryphon burr. It was strong enough Michelle could have used it to saw wood.

"Let me guess," she said with a chuckle. "Commander Adenauer was raised fifty kilometers from Duchess Harrington and *you* were raised fifty kilometers outside what's become the Duchy of Harrington, right?"

"No, Ma'am," Larson said, shaking his head with a smile of his own. "As a matter of fact, I was born and raised on the other side of the planet. On the other hand, it's a fairly *small* planet, I suppose."

"Almost neighbors, in fact," Michelle agreed. Then she released his hand and stood back, gazing at the other officers.

"In a few minutes," she told them, "I'm going to want the ten-dollar tour. I had Michael Oversteegen and the original *Nike* in my last squadron, briefly at least, so I'm generally familiar with the class, but I'm sure *Artemis* has her own brand new bells and whistles, and I want to see all of them. First, though, I'd like to say a couple of things about our mission, as I understand it at this time."

The smiles had disappeared into sober, focused expressions, and she gave a mental nod of approval as they shifted gears right along with her.

"I have another briefing scheduled with Admiral Givens' people tomorrow morning at Admiralty House," she continued. "Cindy, I'd like you and Captain Armstrong to accompany me for that one. And I have another briefing, this one with Admiral Hemphill at BuWeaps, the day after that."

"Yes, Ma'am," Lecter agreed, and Armstrong nodded.

"I don't expect any major surprises," Michelle told them. "On the other hand, I've been surprised anyway, a time or two in the past. In fact, I've been bitten right on the ass a time or two, if we're going to be honest about it. Assuming that doesn't happen in this case, however, the basic parameters of our orders are clear enough. I'm sure all of us hope the summit meeting between Her Majesty and President Pritchart will actually do some good. Unfortunately, we can't count on that. And, equally unfortunately, we're not going to be here while that happens—*if* that happens. Instead, we're going to be off in the Talbott Quadrant, showing the flag and generally making certain no ill-intentioned souls make any more trouble for us.

"I'm confident all of you have taken steps to keep yourself abreast of events in Talbott. In light of the domestic political changes there, I think we all need to get into the habit of thinking of the Cluster by its new name, the Quadrant, but that isn't going to change any of the unpalatable realities about the region, I'm afraid. Until the rest of the staff assembles and we receive our actual instructions, we can't really get into a lot of detailed planning, but I learned a long time ago that the more people you can involve in actually thinking about a problem, the more likely someone is to come up with something that hadn't occurred to *you*. So here's what I want you to be thinking about.

"Militarily, our first responsibility is going to be to secure the physical integrity of the Quadrant and the lives, persons, and property of Her Majesty's new subjects. And, ladies and gentlemen, our responsibility is to secure those things against *any* threat, no matter who—or where—it may have come from. And lest anyone misunderstand me, let me make it very clear that that specifically includes the Solarian League."

She met each set of eyes in turn, and there were no smiles at all on Flag Bridge any longer.

"Admiral Caparelli, Earl White Haven, and Baron Grantville have made that perfectly clear to me," she continued after a moment. "No one wants a shooting incident with the League. God knows the *last* thing we need is a war with the Sollies. But the Constitutional Convention in Spindle has ratified the Cluster's new constitution and enacted all of the amendments Her Majesty requested. That means the citizens represented by that convention are now *Manticoran* citizens, ladies and gentlemen, and they will be defended by Her Majesty's Navy as such."

She paused once more to let that sink in, then shrugged.

"Our second military responsibility will be to provide support, as directed by Vice Admiral Khumalo, if, as, and when requested by Baroness Medusa or any of the planetary governments in the Quadrant. Despite the ratification, there are strong indications that the terrorist campaign in the Split System is still with us. They've been pruned back drastically, and they've become increasingly irrelevant, but those are some very *angry* people. The terrorists themselves—especially their leadership and central cadre—are probably even angrier than they were, now that the constitution's been ratified by their parliament, and that's scarcely likely to make people who've already picked up guns behave themselves. On the other hand, I expect much of the anger that drove anyone outside that central cadre to begin fading once the new civil rights provisions of the constitution work their way down to the grassroots level. And, frankly, I expect the upturn the entire Quadrant's economy is going to experience in the very near future will go even further towards eroding support for Nordbrandt and her FAK lunatics among anyone in the general population who was prepared to see them as some sort of freedom fighters or liberation movement instead of cold-blooded murderers. That, however, is going to take some time, and I'm sure Her Majesty would prefer for us to arrange things so that no more of her new subjects get killed by these idiots in the meantime than we can possibly avoid.

"Our third responsibility is going to be the fulfillment of our role as Baroness Medusa's and Vice Admiral Khumalo's primary fire brigade. The good news is that we're going to see a steady increase in light units in the Cluster. Plans are already afoot to forward deploy enough LACs to provide at least one LAC group to each system in the Quadrant to provide basic security against piracy and backup for local customs efforts in light of the increase in traffic we're expecting in the area. It's going to take a while to get all of that moving, especially with the call for LAC carriers for Eighth Fleet and system defense closer to home, but as soon as the CLACs can be freed up, they'll start moving forward. In the meantime, it's going to be up to our available starships to cover the most exposed systems.

"That's almost certainly going to lead to a certain inevitable dispersal of force, but it can't be helped for the immediate future. For that matter, despite all the Navy's experience in commerce protection and system defense, we've never before been responsible for the security of a single star nation spread out over this large a volume of space, so we're making some of this up as we go. That's going to pinch our toes harder than just about anyone else's in the immediate future, but at least everyone knows it, which is why the Admiralty's trying so hard to give us the tools we'll need . . . and why we're expecting at least two full flotillas of the new *Roland*-class ships, as well as additional *Saganami-Cs* and *Nikes*. The *Agamemnons* are going to be going to Home Fleet, Third Fleet, and—especially—Eighth Fleet, but we'll be getting the *Nikes* in compensation."

She paused as Adenauer half-raised a hand.

"Yes, Dominica?"

"It sounds like you're saying *all* the *Agamemnons* are being retained here at the front, Ma'am."

"That's exactly what I *am* saying," Michelle agreed. "The *Nikes* were designed for this sort of duty from the beginning. We're bigger than the *Agamemnons*, we've got larger crews, and we've got more Marines. And we're not a pod design. Unlike us, the *Agamemnons* can load their pods with all-up Mark 23s, whereas we're limited to the Mark 16."

Adenauer nodded, although it was evident she didn't see exactly why that was particularly significant, given the traditional battlecruiser's role and tactical doctrine. Then again, Commander Adenauer knew even less about a fire control system called Apollo than then-Rear Admiral Henke had known prior to the Battle of Solon . . . and *considerably* less than Vice Admiral Henke hoped to know about it in about two days' time.

*And this isn't the time to tell her about it, either*, Michelle thought.

"I'm sure another aspect of the Admiralty's thinking is that the Havenites have MDMs of their own, whereas the *Sollies*—as far as all of our intelligence sources know, at any rate—don't. The new laser head modifications are going to turn the Mark 16 into a much heavier hitter, and if we do find ourselves in a shooting situation with the Sollies, the Mark 16 is also going to outrange anything they've got. Which, unfortunately, is not the case where Haven is concerned."

Adenauer nodded again, this time more firmly, and Michelle shrugged.

"Unless present plans change—and Lord knows they're entirely likely to do just that—we'll be seeing a total of at least two and probably three squadrons of *Nikes* in the Cluster within the next few months. And, also unless present plans change, those squadrons will be integrated into a new fleet, designated Tenth Fleet. My understanding is that Vice Admiral Khumalo will remain Talbott Station SO, and that the entire Cluster will be integrated into that station. Tenth Fleet will be his primary naval component, and *Artemis* will become Tenth Fleet's flagship when it's formally activated."

Cynthia Lecter's eyes widened, and Michelle restrained an urge to chuckle at her expression. Michele's own expression when Cortez and First Space Lord Caparelli had sprung that additional little surprise upon her had been considerably more flabbergasted than Lecter's was.

*From prisoner-of-war to fleet commander in one easy jump,* she thought. *What would life be like without these little surprises to keep us on our toes?*

"That's, ah, the first I've heard of that, Ma'am," Captain Armstrong said after a moment, and Michelle snorted softly.

"I did say plans are likely to be subject to change, Captain," she pointed out. "Despite that caveat, however, I also have to say Admiral Caparelli and Admiral Cortez made it quite clear they don't expect this particular plan to change. The reason I'm mentioning it at this point is that we all need to be thinking outside the 'single-squadron' box. That's where our thinking has to be right now, of course, for a lot of reasons, but I want all of us to remember what's coming at us from the other side of the horizon. Not just because of its implications for our own responsibilities, either. When we begin interacting with the Talbotters—and, for that matter, with any Sollies in the vicinity—it should be with the understanding that in a very short time you people are going to be the staffers and flag captain, respectively, not of a single battlecruiser squadron, but of an entire *fleet*. We need to be careful about the sort of relationships we establish with the Talbotters, and we need to be both firm and cautious from the outset where the Sollies are concerned."

Heads nodded soberly, and she nodded back.

"In addition to the purely military dimensions of our duties in Talbott," she continued, "there are the diplomatic dimensions. At the moment, unfortunately, our military and diplomatic responsibilities are rather . . . intimately interwoven, one might say. Not only that, but the entire Quadrant is in a transitional stage. We're still going to be involved in what are essentially diplomatic missions, even though officially all of the ratifying star systems are now member systems of the Star Empire of Manticore."

She wondered for a moment if those last four words sounded as bizarre to the others as they still did to her.

"It's going to take some time for them to settle into their new relationships with one another and with us," she went on. "While that's happening, we're still going to be acting much more in the role of someone refereeing disputes between independent entities. At the same time, however, we have to act in a fashion which clearly indicates that as far as we're concerned, the annexation is an accomplished fact. And it's just as important we indicate that to the star systems—and the navies—of anyone who *hasn't* ratified the new constitution. I'm thinking in particular of systems like New Tuscany, but that also applies to the Office of Frontier Security and to the Solarian League in general.

"And, of course, in our copious free time, we'll be doing all those other little things navies do. Chasing down pirates, interdicting the slave trade and generally making ourselves pains where those bastards on Mesa are concerned, updating charts, surveying for dangers to navigation, rendering assistance to ships in distress, disaster relief, and anything else that comes along.

"Any questions?"

The other five officers looked at one another speculatively for several seconds, then returned their attention to her.

"I think that's all reasonably clear, Ma'am," Armstrong told her. "Please note that I didn't say that it sounds *easy*, just that it's clear," she added.

"Oh, believe me, Captain, any suspicion I might have cherished that the Admiralty, in the kindness of its heart, was trying to find some simple, uncomplicated billet for a recently released prisoner-of-war to fill went right out the airlock at Admiral Givens' first briefing. And I'm sure that, after tomorrow's briefing, the rest of you are going to be just as well aware as I am of the dimensions of the job waiting for us. Mind you, getting to play with all of the new ships as they become available is going to be fun, I'm sure. Unfortunately, this time around, one *other* thing I'm sure of is that we're all going to be earning our pay."

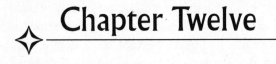

# Chapter Twelve

MICHELLE HENKE LEANED BACK in her comfortable seat beside Gervais Archer as her pinnace separated from HMS *Artemis'* number one boat bay, rolled on gyros and maneuvering thrusters, aligned its nose on the planet Manticore, and went to main thrusters. It had no option but to use reaction drive, since *Artemis* was still wedded to HMSS *Hephaestus* by the entire complex tapestry of personnel and equipment tubes and current traffic control regulations prohibited the use of even small craft impellers until the small craft in question was at least five hundred kilometers clear of the space station. That was many times the pinnace's impeller wedge's threat perimeter, but no one was inclined to take any chances with the Star Kingdom's premier orbital industrial node. For that matter, *inbound* small craft (and larger vessels) were now required to shift to thrusters while still ten *thousand* kilometers out.

Michelle could remember when *Hephaestus* had been little more than twenty kilometers in length, but those days were long gone. The ungainly, lumpy conglomeration of cargo platforms, personnel sections, heavy fabrication modules, and associated shipyards, all clustered around the station's central spine, now stretched for over a hundred and ten kilometers along its main axis. Something better than three quarters of a million people—not including ship crews and other transients—lived and worked aboard the station these days, and the hectic pace of its activity had to be

164

experienced to be believed. *Vulcan*, in orbit around Sphinx, was almost as large, and just as busy. *Weyland*, the smallest of the Star Kingdom's space stations, orbited Gryphon, and was actually the busiest of the three, given the amount of highly classified research and development which was carried out there.

Those three space stations represented the heart and soul of the Manticore Binary System's industrial muscle. The resource extraction ships which plied the system's asteroid belts, and the deep-space smelters and refiners which processed those resources, were scattered about the system's vast volume, but the space stations housed the production lines, the fabrication centers, and the highly trained labor force who made them all work. The mere thought of what an active impeller wedge could do to something like that was enough to cause anyone the occasional nightmare. Michelle might not care very much for the way traffic control's restrictions extended her flight time, but she wasn't about to complain, and she had remarkably little sympathy for people who did moan about it.

There were some of those, of course. There always were, and some of them wore the same uniform Michelle did and damned well ought to understand why those restrictions were in place. More of them were civilians, though, and she'd heard more than one upper-level civilian executive venting about the *Hephaestus* approach rules and Planetary Approach's new rules in general.

*Idiots*, she thought, gazing out the viewport as the shuttle's fusion-powered thrusters moved it Manticoreward at a steady (if pokey) ninety gravities. *All we need is some lunatic, like one of those Masadan fanatics who attacked Ruth in Erewhon, to get a shuttle with an active impeller wedge into ramming range of the station! And,* she added unhappily, glancing briefly at the youthful lieutenant beside her, *until we can figure out how the hell Haven got to Tim Meares, we can't be sure they couldn't get to a shuttle pilot, either. Which means the poor son-of-a-bitch at the controls wouldn't even have to be a volunteer. Hell, he probably wouldn't even realize he was doing it until it was too late!*

The thought had no sooner crossed her mind than her eye caught the subtle distortion of an impeller wedge a hell of a lot bigger than any pinnace's. In fact, it was at least the size of a superdreadnought's wedge ... and it couldn't be more than a couple of hundred kilometers outside its threat perimeter from the station. She tensed internally, then relaxed almost as quickly as she saw the second ship moving steadily—and rapidly—away from *Hephaestus* behind whoever was generating that wedge and realized what it must be.

*Well, I suppose there have to be some exceptions to any rule,* she reflected. *But even the tugs have been required to make a few operational changes since Haven tried to kill Honor.*

The Royal Astrogation Control Service's tugs were the only type of ship which was allowed that close to a space station under impeller drive. They were also the only ships, aside from warships of Her Majesty's Navy, which were permitted to enter or leave planetary orbit under impellers. Manticoran registered and crewed merchant traffic could approach to within ten thousand kilometers of Manticore, Sphinx, or Gryphon under impellers, *if* their ACS certification was current. Even they were required to have reduced their closing velocity to a maximum of no more than fifty thousand KPS while still two light-minutes out, however, and no one was allowed to use impeller drive outbound until they were at least ten thousand kilometers clear of their parking orbital radius. No one *else's* merchant vessels—not even those of such close allies as Grayson—were allowed to approach within two and a half light-minutes without first having gone to reaction drive, however, and there had been absolutely no exceptions to that policy since the attack on Honor.

*Which has led to a few pissed-off exchanges between ACS and some of the "regulars" on the Manticore-Grayson run,* Michelle thought. *More from our side than anybody else's, from what Admiral Grimm was saying.*

Admiral Stephania Grimm was the current commanding officer of the Junction ACS. She was also ex-Navy, and her younger brother had served with Michelle aboard the old dreadnought *Perseus* far too many years ago. Michelle had run into her at a dinner party three or four weeks after her return from Haven, and the two of them—inevitably—had ended up in a corner talking shop.

Grimm didn't have to put up with anywhere near the crap Planetary Traffic Control did, of course, but to make up for that, she had many times the amount of traffic to keep track of. Actually, for a star nation whose preposterous wealth was so heavily based upon its merchant marine, there were usually remarkably few hyper-capable ships anywhere near Manticore or Sphinx, even under normal conditions. It made far more sense for cargoes bound in or out of the Manticore System to take advantage of the stupendous warehousing and service platforms associated with the Junction itself. It was much more time and cost effective, even for ships which weren't using the Junction—and there were some of those, headed for more local destinations—to use its facilities, which were undoubtedly the biggest, most efficient, and most capable in the entire galaxy. The ships and cargo shuttles which plied back and forth between the Junction and the star system's planets were far smaller than the leviathans which traveled between stars, and they were a far more efficient way for most shipments to complete the final transition to their destinations.

It was those freight-haulers who were complaining most vociferously about ACS' new rules and attitude, according to Grimm. After all, before a shuttle pilot or, even more, the astrogators and helmsmen aboard one of the bigger, short-haul freighters were certified for planetary approach, they had to clear dozens of certifications, background checks, and routine physical and mental evaluations, and all of those certifications and evaluations had to be kept current, as well. Given all of that, some of them seemed to deeply resent the fact that they were no longer trusted to make those approaches under impeller drive. And some of the owners of those vessels clearly resented the way the new requirement to have two fully certified planetary approach pilots on the bridge at all times was increasing their overhead.

*Well, I can live with that,* Michelle reflected. *I think sometimes they forget just how frigging* dangerous *an impeller-drive ship is. Maybe it's because they spend so much time in space themselves that for them it's all just routine, but they might want to remember that even a fairly small ship could turn itself into a dinosaur-killer from hell if it really wanted to.*

She shuddered inside at the thought of what a mere hundred thousand-ton short-haul freighter could do if it hit, say, Manticore, at twenty or thirty thousand kilometers per second. A tenteraton explosion would pretty much ruin the local real estate values. Michelle was no historian herself, certainly not to the extent Honor was, but Admiral Grimm, who'd seen all the ACS threat analyses and recommendations, had told her that an impact like that represented something like sixteen times the destructive power of the meteor impact which was supposed to have killed off Old Earth's dinosaurs. Given the fact that the danger represented by her ship was pounded into the head of every ACS-certified planetary approach pilot from Day One of her training, the idiots who were complaining certainly ought to understand why the new rules—including the "two-man" rule—were in place.

Especially after what had happened to Tim Meares.

*I wish we knew more—hell, I wish we knew anything!—about how they got to him. And not just because of how much I liked him,* Michelle thought for far from the first time, glancing again at the young man sitting beside her and remembering all the youthful, murdered zest and promise of *Honor's* flag lieutenant. *And I wish we knew whether or not the same "programming" could have made him do something else . . . like flying a pinnace into downtown Landing at a few thousand KPS. But until we have the answers to both of those questions, I don't think anyone's going to be venturing into or out of Manticore orbit under impellers. Or no one except Navy ships and the tugs, that is.*

There never had been enough tugs, of course, and the situation was even worse now. Traditionally, three ready-duty tugs had been assigned to each of Manticore's space stations. Actually, there'd been seven—enough to keep three continually on call, three more at standby as backups, and one down for mantenance or overhaul. Despite the wear and tear on their impeller nodes, the trio of ready-duty tugs' nodes were *always* hot, ready for instant use. And, despite their relatively diminutive size, they had hugely powerful wedges, as well as gargantuan tractors. One of them could easily handle the unpowered mass of two, or even three, superdreadnoughts if it had to. And the reason their nodes were always hot was that one of their responsibilities was to maintain a safety watch over the space stations. Even without some sort of esoteric mind control to create a *deliberate* collision, there was always the possibility of an accidental collision as ships maneuvered under thrusters to dock with the station. So whenever a ship approached or departed from *Hephaestus*, *Vulcan*, or *Weyland*, one of the duty tugs was ready to intervene. And they were always ready to pounce on any random bits of space debris, as well.

Only the most experienced captains and helmsmen were allowed to command the ACS tugs, and they'd *always* used the "two-man" rule, for reasons Michelle had always found self-evident. But these days, with all of the new, additional restrictions, the demand for their services had risen astronomically.

Michelle winced internally as she recognized the word play she had just inflicted upon herself, but that didn't make the thought inaccurate. According to Grimm, her Planetary Control counterparts needed at least half again the number of tugs they actually had. The good news was that even with the press of warship construction, at least some vital auxiliaries were still being laid down, and eight new tugs were set to commission over the next couple of T-months. The *bad* news was that despite the newly commissioned units, the number of ships which were going to be leaving the near-Manticore dispersed building slips over the next several months meant the need for still *more* tugs was going to get even worse quite soon now.

*Fortunately, I'm not going to be here when it does. But I do wish we could figure out how they got to Tim.*

"Twenty minutes from the pad, Milady," the flight engineer informed her, and she looked up with a nod.

"Thank you, PO."


"Admiral Gold Peak!"

Admiral Sonja Hemphill held out her hand with a smile as Michelle and Gervais Archer were ushered into the Admiralty House conference room. Hemphill—who had somehow managed, Michelle reflected sourly, to avoid being addressed as "Admiral Low Delhi," despite her succession to the Barony of Low Delhi—was the Fourth Space Lord of the Royal Manticoran Navy.

There were those, and Michelle had been one of them, who'd been astounded (to put it mildly) when the First Lord of Admiralty, Hamish Alexander-Harrington (although he'd been only Hamish *Alexander* at the time), had selected Hemphill for her present position. Alexander-Harrington, the Earl of White Haven, and Hemphill had been bitter opponents for decades. White Haven had been the champion and leader of the "historical school," which had argued that changes in technology could only shift the relative values of strategic and tactical realities which were themselves constant. That being so, the true art of strategy and naval command had lain in understanding what those realities were and applying them in the most effective manner possible with the available tools, not in looking for some sort of magical gimmick which would make them all go away.

Hemphill, on the other hand, although substantially junior to

White Haven, had been the leader of the "*jeune ecole*." The *jeune ecole* had argued that the plateau—or, as they preferred to call it, "stagnation"—in military technology over the past couple of centuries had led to a matching stagnation in strategic and tactical thinking. The answer, as far as the *jeune ecole*'s members were concerned, was to follow the pattern established (sort of) by the introduction of the laser head and break the hardware stagnation, thus completely restructuring strategy and tactics. Or even making conventional tactics—and strategy—completely irrelevant.

The internecine warfare between the supporters of the two schools had been . . . vigorous. It had also, upon occasion, been highly personal, and possibly just a little less than professionally correct. In light of the fact that the Star Kingdom's survival had probably hinged on getting the answer right, it wasn't surprising tempers had run high, Michelle supposed. And the White Haven temper had been famous throughout the Navy even before combat was joined. Nor had Hemphill exactly been a shrinking violet, and despite the fact that the Alexanders and the Hemphills had moved in the same social circles for generations, there'd been a time when the hostesses of Landing had gone to great lengths to make sure they did *not* invite both of them to the same party.

In the end, they'd both turned out to be right . . . and wrong. Hemphill's near-obsession with new weapons and command-and-control systems might have left people feeling as if they'd been "run down by an air lorry without being physically injured," as one of her contemporaries had put it, but it had also led directly to the FTL com, the new missile pods, the new LACs, Ghost Rider, and, ultimately, to the multidrive missile and the podnought. Yet for all of the huge increases in lethality which those new systems had made possible, the strategic and tactical constraints faced by military commanders had not magically disappeared. At the same time, however, the historical school had been forced to admit that the new technology had fundamentally transformed the *parameters* of those constraints to an extent which had created a radically new tactical paradigm.

And it seemed that, along the way, White Haven and Hemphill had learned to tolerate one another again. Or, at least, to recognize that each of them had vital contributions to make.

*And it probably helps that Hamish is First Lord, not First* Space *Lord, too*, Michelle thought wryly as she gripped Hemphill's proffered hand. *He's the Admiralty's political head these days. I know he hates it, feels like he's out of the loop—or even out to pasture—but it also means the two of them are a lot less likely to lock horns than they might have been. Still, the idea to move her up to the head of BuWeaps came from* him, *not from Tom Caparelli or Pat Givens, so maybe he really is mellowing under Honor's influence. I suppose* something more unlikely *has to have happened somewhere* in the galaxy. Maybe.

"I'm glad you could make it," Hemphill continued, escorting Michelle around the conference table to the waiting chair. "I was afraid there wouldn't be time in your schedule, given your deployment date."

Archer trailed along behind, carrying the small hand case which contained his minicomp. Michelle had been more than a little surprised when neither Commander Hennessy, Hemphill's chief of staff, nor the admiral's personal yeoman had objected to the minicomp's presence. One of a flag lieutenant's normal responsibilities was to record and annotate a record of her admiral's meetings, conferences, and calendar, but the subject of this particular conference was so highly classified Michelle had half-assumed she wouldn't be permitted to tell *herself* about it, far less keep any notes.

Apparently, she'd been wrong.

"I'm glad there was time, too, Ma'am," Michelle replied, and shook her head with a slightly lopsided smile. "Fortunately, it's turning out that I have a pretty fair staff, so I've been able to steal the occasional few hours here and there instead of wrestling personally with all the squadron's problems. They're clubbing most of the hexapumas as they come out of the shrubbery all on their own now."

Hemphill smiled back, and gestured for Michelle to sit down, then sat in her own chair at the head of the conference table. Lieutenant Archer waited until both flag officers were seated, then sat himself, and Hemphill didn't turn a hair as the lieutenant uncased his minicomp and configured it to record mode.

"I'm glad to hear that," the admiral told Michelle, without so much as glancing in Archer's direction. "I understand Bill Edwards wound up working for you?"

"Yes, he did." Michelle nodded. "Admiral Cortez told me I was lucky to get him, and I've come to the conclusion that—as usual—the admiral was right."

"Good!" Hemphill's smile got considerably broader, and she leaned back in her chair and swung it at a slight angle to the round table so that she could face Michelle squarely.

"Bill is good, *very* good," she said. "I really wanted to go on hang-ing onto him, but I couldn't justify it. Or, rather, I couldn't justify doing that *to him*. He's been with BuWeaps ever since he was an ensign—as Vice Admiral Adcock's flag lieutenant, originally—and he's way overdue for a rotation. In fact, he's at the point where he needs a shipboard deployment in his File 210 if he doesn't want to get stuck dirt-side *permanently*. Besides, I know how badly he's wanted one for years, even if he didn't exactly sit around crying about it. And, as I say, he's always been very good at whatever we've asked him to do."

"That was my impression of him, too," Michelle agreed, but she was watching Hemphill's expression a bit more closely than she had been. The last three hectic days seemed to have confirmed her initial concern that Edwards was more of a techno-type than a combat officer. In many ways, that was fine, since the communications department was a lot less likely than others to find itself making tactical decisions, and there was absolutely no question of Edwards' outstanding competence where hardware and administration were concerned. Still, Michelle had continued to cherish a few concerns.

"I sometimes think Bill would have been happier in the tactical track," Hemphill continued, rather to Michelle's surprise, given what she'd just been thinking. "I think he probably would have done quite well there, in fact. The problem is that while he might have done well there, he's done *outstandingly* on the development side. He's nowhere near as strong on pure theory as some of my people are, and I don't think he'd ever have been happy at all on the research side of things. But where *development* is concerned, he has an abso-lute talent for recognizing possible applications and seeing what he calls 'the shooters' perspective' on what we need to be doing. In fact, he had quite a lot to do with what we're going to be discussing today. Which," she shook her head, her expression suddenly wry, "undoubtedly explains why he's being sent in the opposite direc-tion from where the new systems are actually likely to get used!"

"I hadn't realized he was directly involved in developing Apollo," Michelle said. "He hasn't even twitched a muscle the time or two I've wandered a bit too close to mentioning it to the rest of the staff."

"He wouldn't have," Hemphill agreed. "One thing about Bill; he knows how—and when—to keep his mouth shut."

"So I've just discovered, Ma'am."

"Well," Hemphill shrugged, "I know Bill doesn't exactly come off looking like a classic warrior, Admiral. Not until you get to know him, at least. And, as I say, he knows how to keep his mouth shut, which means he's not going to be polishing his image by dropping hints about all of the wonderful things he did for the Fleet's tactical sorts while he was over here at BuWeaps. To be honest, though, he did do some pretty good things while he was here, which is why I took it upon myself to mention that to you. I'm sure he'd be upset if he found out I had, but, well . . ."

She let her voice trail off with another shrug, and Michelle nodded once more. Much as she despised the patronage game herself, she had no problem with anything Hemphill had just said. Making certain the admiral a subordinate who'd served you well was now serving was aware of your high opinion of the subordinate in question was light-seconds away from the kind of self-serving horse-trading of favors which had so bedeviled the prewar RMN.

"I won't mention this conversation to him, Ma'am," she assured Hemphill. "On the other hand, I'm glad you told me."

"Good," Hemphill said again, then gave herself a little shake, as if to shift mental gears.

"Tell me, Admiral Gold Peak. Just how much do you already know about Apollo?"

"Very little, really," Michelle replied. "As one of Duchess Harrington's squadron commanders, I was briefed—very generally—on what the tech people were trying to accomplish, but that was about as far as it went. Just far enough to make me really nervous about the possibility of spilling something while I was the Havenites' . . . guest, you might say."

Hemphill snorted at Michelle's wry tone and shook her head.

"I imagine I'd probably have worried about the same thing myself, in your place," she said. "On the other hand, when we're done here today, you're *definitely* going to know enough to be nervous about 'spilling something.'"

"Oh, thank you, Ma'am," Michelle said, and this time Hemphill laughed out loud.

"Seriously, Ma'am," Michelle continued after a moment, "I'm not at all sure that giving me any sort of a detailed briefing at this point is a good idea. I mean, don't get me wrong, I'm curious as hell. But like Commander Edwards, I'm headed in the opposite direction from where it's likely to get used. Do I really have the need to know any of the details about it?"

"That's an excellent question," Hemphill conceded. "And, to be honest, I'd really like to keep this whole thing closed up in a dark little cupboard somewhere—preferably under my bed—until we've actually used it. The tests we've carried out with it have made it clear we substantially underestimated the tactical implications in our original projections, and I've had more than a few bad dreams about the secret getting out. But there actually is a method to our apparent madness in briefing you fully on the system capabilities."

"There is?" Michelle tried not to sound dubious, but she suspected she hadn't fully succeeded.

"Given the possibilities offered by this summit between Her Majesty and Pritchart, it's at least possible we're going to see a cease-fire, maybe even a long-term peace agreement, with Haven," Hemphill said. "In that case, we're not going to need Apollo against the Republic. But it's entirely possible we *will* need it in Talbott if the situation there turns as nasty as it still could. And you, Admiral Gold Peak, are the designated commander for Tenth Fleet. So the feeling here at Admiralty House is that if we suddenly find ourselves able to begin transferring Apollo-capable ships to Talbott, it would be nice if the Fleet commander who's going to be using them was already aware of the system's capabilities."

Michelle's eyes had narrowed while Hemphill was speaking. She hadn't really thought about that possibility, because there were no ships of the wall on Tenth Fleet's planned order of battle. Her admittedly incomplete knowledge of Apollo had suggested to her that it could be used only by Keyhole-equipped *ships of the wall*. The *Nikes* and the second-flight *Agamemnons* were both Keyhole-capable, but their platforms were rather smaller than those of superdreadnoughts, and her impression had been that only wallers were big enough to carry the refitted, FTL-capable Keyhole platforms the new system required. Since she didn't *have* any wallers, it had followed that she wouldn't be using Apollo. But now she found herself nodding in understanding.

"I hadn't thought about it that way," she admitted. "Would it happen that one reason Commander Edwards found himself available for service on my staff was that same possibility?"

"It . . . had a bearing," Hemphill replied.

"And will I be authorized to fully brief the rest of my staff on it, as well?"

"You will," Hemphill said firmly, and grimaced. "The object is for you to begin familiarizing yourself with Apollo's capabilities and tactical possibilities. To do that, you're going to have to play around with those capabilities, game them out in the simulators, at the very least. You can't do that without bringing your staff, and for that matter, your flag captain and her tactical department, fully on board. And, of course," she glanced in Archer's direction for a moment, "if an admiral and her staff know about anything, her flag lieutenant probably knew about it first."

Archer's head came up and he looked quickly at Hemphill, but the admiral only chuckled and shook her head.

"Don't worry about it, Lieutenant. You're doing exactly what you're supposed to do—assuming that minicomp is as secure as I expect it is. And it's hardly going to be the only electronic record about Apollo aboard *Artemis*." She looked back at Michelle. "Before your squadron actually deploys, Admiral, we'll be uploading the same sims Duchess Harrington is using with Eighth Fleet to *Artemis'* tactical department."

"Good," Michelle said, not even trying to hide her relief. "Of course, from the little I already know, I sort of suspect that having the sims to play around with when I don't have the actual hardware is going to get just a *bit* frustrating. I have to admit, Admiral—you've come up with some really neat toys."

"One tries, Milady." Hemphill waved one hand modestly, but Michelle could see the comment had pleased her. Which was fair enough, given the fact that those "neat toys" of Hemphill's were one of the main reasons there was still a Royal Manticoran Navy and a Star Kingdom for it to serve.

"It's just about time," Hemphill continued, glancing at her chrono, and tapped a brief command into the conference table console. The holo imager built into the tabletop came to life, projecting the images of a dozen or so Navy officers manning a tactical simulator's command deck. The senior-grade captain in the command chair looked up as he realized the electronic conference connection had come on-line.

"Good morning, Captain Halsted," Hemphill said.

"Good morning, Ma'am."

"This is Vice Admiral Gold Peak, Captain," Hemphill told Halstead. "We're going to be giving her the inside story on Apollo this morning."

"So I understood, Ma'am," he said, and looked respectfully at Henke. "Good morning, Ma'am."

"Captain," Michelle acknowledged with a nod.

"I think, Captain," Hemphill said, "that we should start with a general description of Apollo's capabilities. Once we've done that, we can run through a couple of the simulations for the admiral."

"Of course, Admiral." Halsted turned his command chair so his holo image was directly facing Michelle.

"Essentially, Admiral Gold Peak," he began, "Apollo is a new step in missile command and control. It's a logical extension of other things we've already been doing, which marries the existing Ghost Rider technology with the Keyhole platforms and the MDM by using the newest generation of grav-pulse transceivers. What it does is to establish near-real-time control linkages for MDMs at extended ranges. At three light-minutes, the command and control transmission delay for Apollo is only three *seconds*, one-way, and it's turned out that we've been able to provide significantly more bandwidth than we'd projected as little as seven months ago. In fact, we have enough that we can actually reprogram electronic warfare birds and input new attack profiles on the fly. In effect, we have a *reactive* EW and target selection capability, managed by the full capability of a ship of the wall's computational capacity, with a shorter control loop than the shipboard systems trying to defeat it."

Despite herself, Michelle's eyebrows rose. Unlike Bill Edwards, she *was* a trained and experienced tactical officer, and the possibilities Halstead seemed to be suggesting . . .

"Our initial projections were based on trying to install the new transceivers in each MDM," Halstead continued. "Originally, we saw no other option, and doing things that way would have made each MDM an individual unit, independent of any other missile, which seemed to offer us the most tactical flexibility *and* would have meant we could fire them from standard MDM launchers and the Mark 15 and Mark 17 pods. Unfortunately, putting independent links in each bird would have required us to remove one entire drive stage because of volume constraints. That would still have been worthwhile, given the increased accuracy and penetration ability we anticipated, but the development team's feeling was that we would be giving away too much range performance."

"That was one of Bill's suggestions, Admiral," Hemphill said quietly.

"Once we'd taken up ways to deal with that particular objection," Halstead went on, "it became evident that our only choices were to either strip the drive stage out of the birds, as we'd originally planned, or else to add a dedicated missile. One whose sole function would be to provide the FTL link between the firing ship and the attack birds. There were some potential drawbacks to that, but it allowed us not only to retain the full range of the MDM, but actually required very few modifications to the existing Mark 23. And, somewhat to the surprise of several members of our team, using a dedicated control missile actually *increased* tactical flexibility enormously. It let us put in a significantly more capable—and longer-ranged—transciever, and we were also able to fit in a much more capable data processing and AI node. The Mark 23s are slaved to the control bird—the real 'Apollo' missile—using their standard light-speed systems, reconfigured for maximum bandwidth rather than maximum sensitivity, and the Apollo's internal AI manages its slaved attack birds while simultaneously collecting and analyzing the data from all of their on-board sensors. It transmits the consolidated output from *all* of its slaved missiles to the firing vessel, which gives the ship's tactical department a real-time, close-up and personal view of the tactical environment.

"It works the same way on the command side, as well. The firing vessel tells the Apollo *what* to do, based on the sensor data coming in from it, and the on-board AI decides how to tell its Mark 23s *how* to do it. That's the real reason our effective bandwidth's gone up so significantly; we're not trying to individually micromanage hundreds or even thousands of missiles. Instead, we're relying on a dispersed network of control nodes, each of which is far more capable of thinking for itself than any previous missile has been. In fact, if we lose the FTL link for any reason, the Apollo drops into autonomous mode, based on the prelaunch attack profiles loaded to it and the most recent commands it's received. It's actually capable of generating entirely new targeting and penetration commands on its own. They're not going to be as good as the ones a waller's tac department could generate for it if the link were still up, but we're estimating something like a forty-two percent increase in terminal performance at extreme range as compared to any previous missile or, for that matter, our own Mark 23s with purely sub-light telemetry links, even if the Apollo bird is operating entirely on its own."

Michelle nodded, her eyes intent, and Halstead touched a button on his command chair's arm. A side-by-side schematic of two large—and one *very large*—missiles appeared above the conference table, between Michelle and the simulator command deck, and he indicated one of them with a flashing cursor.

"The Apollo itself is an almost entirely new design, but, as you can see, the only modifications the Mark 23 required were relatively minor and could be easily incorporated without any break in production schedules."

The cursor moved to the very largest missile.

"This is the system-defense variant, the Mark 23-D, for the moment, although it's probably going to end up redesignated the Mark 25. It's basically an elongated Mark 23 to accommodate both a fourth impeller drive *and* longer lasing rods with more powerful grav focusing to push the directed yield still higher. Aside from the grav units and laser rods, this is all off-the-shelf hardware, so production shouldn't be a problem, although at the moment the ship-launched system has priority.

"With the Apollo missile itself—we've officially designated the ship-launched version the Mark 23-E, partly in an attempt to convince anyone who hears about it that it's only an attack bird upgrade—" the cursor moved to the third missile "—the situation's a bit more complicated. As I say, it's an entirely new design, and we're looking at some bottlenecks in getting it into volume production. The system-defense variant—the Mark 23-F—is another all-new design. Aside from the drives and the fusion bottle, we had to start with a blank piece of paper in each case, and we hit some snags getting the new transceiver squared away. We're on top of those, now, but we're still only beginning to ramp up production. The 23-F is lagging behind the 23-E, mostly because we've tweaked the transceiver's sensitivity even higher in light of the longer anticipated engagement ranges, which increased volume requirements more dramatically than we'd expected, but even the Echo model is coming off the lines more slowly than we'd like. When you factor in the need for the original Keyhole control platforms to be refitted to the Keyhole-Two standard, this isn't something we're going to be able to put into fleet-wide deployment overnight. On the other hand—"

# Chapter Thirteen

"WE'RE CLEARED FOR STATION DEPARTURE, Ma'am," Captain Lecter reported.

Michelle nodded as serenely as possible and wondered if she was doing a better job of hiding her relief than Cindy was.

*Go ahead, admit it—to yourself, at least. You didn't think you were going to make it on deadline after all, did you?*

*Of course I did*, she told herself astringently. *Now shut up and go away!*

"Very well," she said aloud, and touched a stud on the arm of her flag deck command chair. The small com display came to life almost instantly with Captain Armstrong's face.

"*Hephaestus* Control says we can leave now, Captain," she said.

"Did they happen to mention anything about missing personnel, Ma'am?" Armstrong inquired in an innocent tone.

"As a matter of fact, no. Why? Is there something I should know about?"

"Oh, no, Admiral. Nothing at all."

"I'm relieved to hear it. In that case, however, I believe Admiral Blaine is expecting us at the Lynx Terminus."

"Yes, Ma'am." Armstrong's expression turned much more serious, and she nodded. "I'll see to it."

"Good. I'll let you be about it, then. Henke, clear."

She touched the stud again, and the display blanked. Then she turned her command chair, once again admiring the magnificent spaciousness of *Artemis'* flag deck, and moved her attention to the huge tactical plot. Normally, that was configured into a schematic representation of the volume about the ship, spangled with the light codes of tactical icons, but at the moment, it was configured for direct visual from the optical heads spotted about the huge battlecruiser's hull, instead, and Michelle watched as *Artemis'* bow thrusters awoke. She felt the faint vibration transmitted through the ship's two and a half million tons of battle steel, armor, and weapons, and the big ship began to back slowly and smoothly out of the docking arms.

The moment when a starship actually began her very first deployment was always special. Michelle doubted she would ever truly be able to describe that specialness to someone who hadn't actually experienced it, but for someone who had, there was no other moment quite like it. That sense of newness, of being present at the birth of a living creature, of watching the Star Kingdom's newest warrior take her very first step. A keel-plate owner understood without any need of explanations, knew that whatever fate ultimately awaited the ship, he or she was a part of it. And knew that the reputation of that ship, for good or ill, would stem from the actions and attitudes of her very first crew.

And yet, this moment was different for Michelle Henke. *Artemis* was her flagship, but she wasn't *her* ship. She belonged to Victoria Armstrong and her crew, not to the admiral who simply happened to fly her flag aboard her.

She remembered something her mother had once said—"From those to whom much is given, much is taken, as well." It was odd how accurate that had proved since Michelle had attained flag rank herself. At the Academy, she'd known flag rank was what she wanted. That squadron, task force, or even fleet command was where she wanted to apply her talents, test herself. But she hadn't known then what she'd have to give up to get it. Not really. She'd never realized how much it would hurt to realize she would never again command a Queen's ship herself. Never again wear the white beret of a starship commander.

*Oh, stop being maudlin!* she told herself as the gap between *Artemis'* bow and the space station widened steadily. *Next thing you know, you're going to be asking them to take the squadron back!*

She snorted in amusement, and leaned back in her command chair as one of the waiting tugs moved in.

*Artemis'* thrusters shut down, and the ship quivered again—a subtly different quiver, this time—as the tug's tractors locked onto her. Nothing happened for a moment, and then she began to accelerate again, much more rapidly, although nowhere near so rapidly as she could have accelerated under her own power if she'd been permitted to use her impeller wedge this close to the station. Or, for that matter, as rapidly as the tug could have moved her, if not for niggling little considerations like, oh, keeping the crew alive. Without the wedge, there was no handy sump for the inertial compensator, which limited the ship's protoplasmic crew to an acceleration her internal grav plates could handle. If they'd really wanted to push the envelope, and if the squadron had been prepared to secure for heavy acceleration, they could have pulled at least a hundred gravities, but there wasn't really much point in that. No one was in that big a hurry, and modern starships weren't really designed to handle heavy accelerations for any extended period of time. The ships themselves might not have minded particularly, but their personnel was another matter entirely.

*At least* Artemis, Romulus, *and* Theseus *were the only ones still docked at one of the stations, so you didn't have to worry about tug availability*, she reminded herself.

She tapped a control on her chair arm and her repeater plot deployed from the chair base. It configured itself into standard tactical format, and she watched the icons representing the three battlecruisers moving steadily away from the purple anchor which had been used for generations to represent space stations like *Hephaestus*. HMS *Stevedore*, the single tug towing all of them, showed as a purple arrowhead pointed directly at the five icons of the rest of the squadron, waiting under their own power for their last three consorts to make rendezvous.

Michelle didn't know whether or not the Admiralty intended to completely scrap the squadron reorganization plan the Janacek Admiralty had put into place. There were some advantages to the six-ship squadron format Janacek had adopted, much though it galled Michelle to admit that anything that ham-fisted idiot had done could possibly have *any* beneficial consequences. Fortunately for her blood pressure, if not for the Star Kingdom's wellbeing, there weren't very many instances in which she had to. But even though the smaller-sized squadrons offered at least some additional tactical flexibility, they also required twenty-five percent more admirals—and admirals' staffs—for the same number of ships. Personally, Michelle suspected that had been part of the attraction for Janacek and his partisans. After all, it had provided so many more flag slots into which he could plug sycophants, despite the way he'd downsized the fleet. Those of his cronies who hadn't been removed by the Havenites in the course of Operation Thunderbolt (she supposed *any* cloud had to have at least some silver lining) had been ruthlessly purged by the White Haven Admiralty, yet that had left a tiny problem. Finding that many *competent* admirals was a not so minor concern in a navy expanding as rapidly and hugely as the present Royal Manticoran Navy. Just as even the new, highly automated designs still needed complete bridge crews, complete engineering officer complements, admirals still needed staffs, and there simply weren't that many experienced staff officers to go around. For example, Michelle herself still didn't have a staff intelligence officer. At the moment, Cynthia Lecter was wearing that hat as well as holding down the chief of staff's slot, which was rather unfair to her. On the other hand, at least she'd spent a tour with ONI two deployments ago, so she knew what she was doing in *both* slots. And it didn't hurt that Gervais Archer was turning out to be a surprisingly competent *assistant* intelligence officer.

There were undoubtedly other reasons for the White Haven Admiralty's new thinking, as well, but in combination, they explained why the 106th Battlecruiser Squadron consisted of *eight* units, not six. And, to be perfectly frank, Michelle didn't really care what other reasons there might have been. She was too busy gloating over the possession of those two additional battlecruisers.

*Not that most other navies would consider them "battlecruisers," I suppose,* she told herself. At two and a half million tons, the new *Nike*-class ships were closing in on the size of the old battleships no one had built for the last fifty or sixty T-years, and some navies—*like the Sollies,* she thought sourly—still defined ship types by tonnage brackets which had become obsolete even before the First Havenite War. But even though the *Nikes* were the next best thing to half again the size of her dead *Ajax*, *Artemis* was capable of almost seven hundred gravities' acceleration at maximum military power. And her magazines were crammed with over six thousand Mark 16 dual-drive missiles.

*I don't care how big she is, she's still a battlecruiser, though,*
Michelle thought. *It's the function, the doctrine, that counts, not
just tonnage. And by that meter stick, she's a battlecruiser, all right.
One from the dark side of Hell, maybe, but still a battlecruiser.
And I've got* eight *of her.*

It was possible, she admitted to herself, watching the plot as
the tugs moved her new command steadily away from *Hephaestus*,
that flag rank did have its own compensations.

"We're being hailed, Ma'am," Lieutenant Commander Edwards
reported.

"Well, that was prompt," Michelle observed dryly. *Artemis* had
just emerged from the Lynx Terminus, a bit over six hundred
light-years from the Manticore Binary System. In fact, she'd barely
finished reconfiguring her Warshawski sails into a normal-space
impeller wedge, and none of the other ships of the squadron had
yet transited the junction behind her.

Edwards' only response to her comment was a smile, and she
grinned back, then shrugged philosophically.

"Go ahead, Bill."

"Yes, Ma'am."

Edwards input the command that triggered *Artemis'* transponder,
identifying her to the mostly-completed forts and the two squadrons of Home Fleet ships of the wall holding station here.

"Acknowledged, Ma'am," he said a moment later.

"Good," Michelle replied. And it *was* good that the local picket
was obviously on its toes, she reflected. To be sure, no hostile
force was likely to be coming through from Manticore. Or, if
one was, the Star Kingdom would have to be so well and truly
screwed that it really wouldn't matter how alert anyone in the
Talbott Quadrant might be. Still, alertness was a state of mind,
and anyone who let herself grow slack and sloppy in one aspect
of her duties was only too likely to let the same thing happen
in *all* aspects. Not that any Manticoran admiral was likely to let
that happen after the reaming Thomas Theisman's navy had given
them in Operation Thunderbolt.

*Or we'd* better *not be, at least,* she thought grimly, then shook
herself. *Time to make our manners.*

"Raise *Lysander*, please, Bill," she said, walking back across the
bridge to her command chair. Gervais Archer looked up from his

own bridge station to one side of her chair as she seated herself. "My compliments to Vice Admiral Blaine," she continued, "and inquire if it would be convenient for him to speak with me."

"Aye, aye, Ma'am," Edwards replied, exactly as if he hadn't known she was going to say exactly that . . . and exactly as if there were, in fact, the remotest possibility that Vice Admiral Blaine would *not* find it convenient to speak to a newly arrived admiral passing through his bailiwick.

"I have Admiral Blaine, Ma'am," Edwards said a handful of minutes later.

"Put him on my display, please."

"Yes, Ma'am."

Vice Admiral Jessup Blaine was a tallish, bland-faced man with thinning hair and a thick beard. The beard was neatly trimmed, but the contrast between it and his far sparser hair made him look vaguely lopsided and scruffy, and she wondered why he'd grown it.

"Welcome to Lynx, Milady." Blaine's voice was deeper, and much more smoothly modulated than she had allowed herself to expect from his appearance.

"Thank you, Admiral," she replied.

"I'm glad to see you," Blaine continued. "For a lot of reasons, although, to be honest, the biggest one from *my* perspective is because it means I'll probably be getting Quentin O'Malley back from Monica sometime soon."

*That's coming right to the point of things*, Michelle thought dryly.

"We'll get him back to you as quickly as we can, Admiral," she assured him out loud.

"It's not that I'm not glad to see you for all those other reasons, as well, Milady," Blaine told her with a quick smile. "It's just that, technically, I'm still one of the reserve forces for the home system, and Quentin is supposed to be my screening element. I'd really like to have him back just to give me a little extra depth here in Lynx until the forts come on-line. And if things go so wrong they do call me back to Manticore, I think I can assume I'll need all the screening support I can get."

"I understand," Michelle assured him, and she did. "On the other hand, according to my last briefing at Admiralty House, there should be quite a few additional forces headed this way shortly."

"And not a moment too soon."

Blaine's fervent approval was evident, and Michelle smiled slightly. She doubted that they'd pulled Blaine's name out of a hat when they decided they had to dispatch reinforcements to Talbott, which argued that there was a very competent officer under that bland exterior. But even the most competent officer had to feel the occasional moment of . . . loneliness when he found himself hanging out at the far end of the Manticoran Wormhole Junction waiting for a possible attack by the Solarian League. No wonder Blaine wanted to see all the friendly faces he could find.

"Do you know Rear Admiral Oversteegen, Admiral?" she asked.

"*Michael* Oversteegen?" Blaine frowned. "Last I heard, he was a *captain*." He sounded a bit plaintive, and Michelle chuckled.

"And I was a rear admiral up until a week ago," she said. "I'm afraid they're going to be pushing a lot of us up quickly, with all the new construction coming out of the yards. But my point, Sir, was that they've given Michael the 108th. And assuming he makes his deployment schedule, he should be following along behind me within a couple of months or so. And the first squadron of *Rolands* is about ready to start working up. In fact, it may already have begun the process."

"That, Milady, is very good news," Blaine said frankly. "Now, if this cease-fire only lasts long enough to get all that new construction deployed."

"We can hope, Sir."

"Yes. Yes, we can." Blaine seemed to give himself a mental shake, then smiled. "I appear to have forgotten my manners, though. Would you and your captains have time to join me for dinner, Milady?"

"I'm afraid not," Michelle said with genuine regret. Like Honor, she believed personal, face-to-face contact was the best way for officers who might have to work together to feel confident they actually knew one another.

"I'm under orders to expedite my arrival in Spindle by all possible means, Sir," she continued. "As a matter of fact, *Artemis* still has over a dozen of *Hephaestus*' yard dogs on board, working at adjusting this and that. And Captain Duchovny has even more than that aboard *Horatius*."

"And the station commander let you go without opening fire,

did she?" Blaine inquired with something suspiciously like a chuckle.

"I don't think she would have without Admiral D'Orville standing behind me with his energy batteries cleared away," Michelle replied.

"Actually, I don't find that particularly hard to believe. I've had my own dealings with yard dogs over the years, Milady. The stories I could tell you!"

"As could we all, Sir."

"True." Blaine smiled at her, then inhaled with an air of finality. "Well, in that case, Milady, we won't delay you. Please give my respects to Admiral Khumalo when you reach Spindle."

"I will, Sir."

"Thank you, Milady, And on that note, I'll wish you a speedy voyage and let you be on your way. Blaine, clear."

The display blanked, and Michelle looked back up at the tactical plot.

While she'd been talking to Blaine, *Artemis'* division mates in BCS 106's first division—*Penelope, Romulus,* and *Horatius*—had followed her through the terminus. As she watched, Filipa Alcoforado's *Theseus,* the flagship of Commodore Shulamit Onasis, who commanded the squadron's second division, erupted from the invisible flaw in space, radiating the blue glory of transit energy from her sails.

Not much longer, she thought, and glanced at Commander Sterling Casterlin. As she'd told Cortez, she'd met Casterlin before, although they'd never served together until now. They'd *almost* served on the old *Bryan Knight* together, but she'd just been leaving the ship when he came on board. She actually knew his cousin, Commodore Jake Casterlin, better, and from what she'd seen of Sterling already, she was willing to bet that Jake's Liberal Party sympathies drove the far more conservative Sterling bananas.

She might be wrong, though, since it looked to her as if it would probably take quite a bit to shake Commander Casterlin's equanimity. He'd been late arriving aboard, through no fault of his own, but he hadn't even turned a hair at the prospect of having less than forty hours to "settle in" with an entirely new department, aboard an entirely new ship, under an entirely new vice admiral, before departing for a possible combat deployment. Under the circumstances, he'd shown remarkable aplomb, she thought.

"It seems we'll be leaving soon," she observed.

"Yes, Ma'am," he replied without turning a hair. "I've just passed our heading and course to Commander Bouchard."

"Good," she said.

He looked over his shoulder at her, and she smiled. She'd known she wasn't going to catch him out without a course already figured, but he'd quietly one-upped her by going ahead and passing the course to Jerod Bouchard, *Artemis'* astrogator, before she asked.

"I believe he'd already worked out approximately the same course, Ma'am," Casterlin observed.

"No, really?" Michelle rounded her eyes in innocent astonishment, then chuckled as Casterlin shook his head.

*Daedalus* and *Jason* had followed *Theseus* through the Junction, now. All they still needed was Captain Esmerelda Dunne's *Perseus*, and they could be on their way, and Michelle was looking forward to the voyage. It was sixteen days from the Lynx Terminus to the Spindle System, and just as Spindle had been the site of the Constitutional Convention, it had been chosen—at least provisionally—as the Talbott Quadrant's capital system. Which meant that was where she was going to find Baroness Medusa and Vice Admiral Khumalo. When she did, she'd finally be able to begin forming a realistic idea of what she was going to have to do and what she was going to do it with. Under normal circumstances, her desire to hit the ground running would have left her feeling impatient and antsy, but not this time. The sixteen days' passage would undoubtedly be welcome to her captains, even though it would be only ten days for them, given the relativistic effect, since it would give them additional time to complete bringing their ships' hardware to full readiness. And, of course, getting their ships' companies trained up to something approaching the standard expected out of a Queen's ship.

"Remind me to invite Captain Conner and Commodore Onasis to dine with me tonight, Gwen," she said.

"Yes, Ma'am," Archer replied. "Should we invite Commander Houseman and Commander McIver, as well?"

"An excellent thought, Gwen," Michelle approved with a smile. "For that matter let's get Captain Armstrong, Cindy, Dominica, and Commander Dallas and Commander Diego on the guest list, as well. And you can drop them a little hint—unofficially, of course—that we'll be talking about training schedules."

"Yes, Ma'am." Archer made a note to himself, and Michelle smiled at him. The youngster was working out even better than she'd hoped he would, and it looked as if at least some of the ghosts of Solon were fading out of the backs of his eyes. She hoped so, anyway. It was obvious that nature had intended him to be a cheerful extrovert, and she was pleased to see him shedding the . . . somberness which had been so much a part of him at their first meeting.

He was quick, too. His suggestion that Conner and Onasis bring along their chiefs of staff was an excellent one, and exactly the sort of anticipation and thinking ahead a good flag lieutenant was supposed to provide to her admiral. And it probably represented his own experience aboard *Necromancer*, as well. Obviously, Gervais was aware of the squadron's rough edges and recognized the need to start filing them down.

Her nostrils flared at that thought. Those rough edges weren't her captains' fault, any more than they were hers. In fact, they weren't *anyone's* fault. Despite which, Michelle was uncomfortably aware of just how unprepared for battle her command truly was, and that was precisely why she, too, was looking forward to those ten days of exercises. *Hard* exercises, she thought—as demanding as she and her captains could make them. Given the situation she might well find herself facing in the very near future, it was time she and her officers started finding the problems, figuring out what to do about them, and doing it.

*And the sooner the better*, she reflected grimly. *The sooner the better.*

The range-to-target sidebar on the tactical display was preposterous.

The missile salvo was sixty-eight million kilometers from *Artemis*, speeding steadily onward at 150,029 KPS. Its birds had been ballistic for four and a half minutes, ever since the second drive system had burned out, and they were still ninety-three seconds—almost fourteen million kilometers—from their target, even at half the speed of light.

And the attack missiles still hadn't been assigned targets.

Michelle Henke sat quietly to one side, playing the umpire's role as she watched Dominica Adenauer, Wilton Diego, and Victoria Armstrong work the simulation. It felt just plain *wrong* to have attack birds that far out at all, she reflected, far less have them swanning around without targets already locked into their cybernetic brains. And yet, what was happening was only a logical consequence of the new technology.

Admiral Hemphill, she'd decided, had been absolutely right about Bill Edwards. The "communications" officer's intimate knowledge of the entire Apollo project had proved invaluable when she and her staff started kicking around the new system's potentialities. In fact, Adenauer and he had spent hours off to one side, talking animatedly, scribbling on napkins (or any other unwary surface which made itself available), and tweaking the simulation software. Michelle had been relieved to see that. Some tactical specialists would undoubtedly have rebuffed a mere communications type's suggestions, *wherever* he might have spent his last tour. Adenauer, on the other hand, was sufficiently self-confident to welcome insight, regardless of its source, and over the last six days of ship's time, she and Edwards had established not simply a sound working relationship, but a warm friendship. And the fruits of their efforts were readily apparent. In fact, Michelle suspected that the two of them had come up with at least a few wrinkles which hadn't occurred to anyone at BuWeaps.

"Coming up on Point Alpha," Diego said quietly.

"Acknowledged," Adenauer replied.

The actual firing and management of the missiles was Diego's responsibility as *Artemis'* tactical officer, but the management and distribution of the squadron's massed firepower was a function of its operations officer. Normally, Adenauer would have given Diego Michelle's attack criteria and established general attack profiles before the first missile was launched. Diego would have taken things from there, assigning individual missiles to specific targets and—with Lieutenant Isaiah Maslov, *Artemis'* electronics warfare officer—slotting them into the attack, EW, and penetration profiles Adenaur had laid down.

But today, they were examining a completely different capability. A capability no squadron commander in history had ever before enjoyed. For the purposes of today's simulation, HMS *Artemis* had been promoted from a battlecruiser to an *Invictus*-class SD(P). Every unit of the squadron had undergone a similar transformation, which meant that instead of the sixty Mark 16s each ship could normally fire in a single double-broadside salvo, each of them could deploy six full pods of Mark 23s. Normally, that would have meant that each ship rolled one pattern of Mark 17 "flat pack" missile pods, each of which contained ten Mark 23s, every twelve seconds. In this case, however, they were rolling the Mark 17, Mod D, which contained only *eight* Mark 23s . . . and a single Mark 23-*E*.

So instead of sixty Mark 16s every eighteen seconds, with a maximum powered attack range (without a ballistic segment, at least) of only a shade over twenty-seven million kilometers and "cruiser range" laser heads, they were firing forty-eight attack and dedicated EW Mark 23s every *twelve* seconds.

That was a sufficiently heady increase in firepower, Michelle thought dryly, but the technique which she and Adenauer—and Edwards—had come up with for today made it even sweeter.

One of the Manticoran Alliance's most telling advantages was Ghost Rider, the highly developed—and constantly evolving—family of FTL recon and EW platforms. Deployed in a shell around a single ship, squadron, or task force, they gave an Alliance CO a degree of situational awareness no one else could match. Alliance starships could simply see farther, faster, and better than anyone else, and their recon platforms could deliver their take in real-time or near real-time, which no one else—not even the Republic of Haven—could do.

But there were still drawbacks. It was still entirely possible to detect the impeller signatures of a potentially hostile force and not have a recon platform in position to run and find out who the newcomers were. Even if a tactical officer had very good reason to believe the newcomers in question cherished ill intentions, she still had to get one of her platforms into position to look them over from relatively close range before she could be positive of that. Or, for that matter, before she could be positive that what she was seeing were really starships and not electronic warfare drones *pretending* to be starships. And it was generally considered to be a good idea to have that sort of information in hand before one sent an entire salvo of attack missiles screaming in on what might, after all, turn out to be a neutral merchant convoy.

In one of Adenauer's and Edwards' brainstorming sessions with Michelle, however, Edwards had pointed out a new possibility which Apollo made possible. Fast as the Ghost Rider platforms were, they were immensely slower than an MDM. They had to be, since stealth and long endurance were completely incompatible with the massive acceleration rates produced by an attack missile's impeller wedge in its brief, incredibly *un*-stealthy lifetime. But Apollo was designed to combine and analyze the readings from the attack missiles slaved to it . . . and to transmit that analysis back to the launching ship at FTL speed. Michelle and Adenauer had grasped his point immediately and run with it, and this simulation was designed to test what they'd come up with. What Adenauer had done was to fire a single Apollo pod thirty seconds before they fired a complete squadron salvo. And that pod was now one minute's flight from the "unknown impeller wedges" *eighty-two million* kilometers from *Artemis.*

"Jettisoning the shrouds now," Diego reported as the first pod's missiles reached Point Alpha.

"Acknowledged," Adenauer replied.

The shroud-jettisoning maneuver had been programmed into the missiles before launch. Unlike any previous attack missile, the Mark 23s in an Apollo pod were fitted with protective shrouds intended to shield their sensors from the particle erosion of extended ballistic flight profiles at relativistic speeds. Most missiles didn't really need anything of the sort, since their impeller wedges incorporated particle screening. They were capable of maintaining a separate particle screen—briefly, at least—as long as they retained on-board power, even after the wedge went down, but that screening was far less efficient than a starship's particle screens. For the most part, that hadn't mattered, since any ballistic component of a "standard" attack profile was going to be brief, at best. But with Apollo, very long-range attacks, with lengthy ballistic components built into them, had suddenly become feasible. That capability, however, would be of limited usefulness if particle erosion had blinded the missiles before they ever got a chance to see their targets.

Now the jettisoning command blew the shrouds, and the sensors they had protected came on-line. Of course, the missiles were 72,998,260 kilometers from *Artemis.* That was over four light-minutes, which in the old days (like five or six T-years ago) would have meant any transmission from them would take four minutes to reach *Artemis.*

With the FTL grav-pulse transceiver built into the Mark 23-E, however, it took barely four *seconds.*

The display in front of Adenauer blossomed suddenly with icons as the first missile pod's Apollo faithfully reported what its brood could see, now that their eyes had been opened. The light codes of three hostile superdreadnoughts, screened by three light cruisers and a quartet of destroyers, burned crisp and clear, and for a heartbeat, the tactical officer did absolutely nothing. She simply sat there, gazing at the display, her face expressionless. But Michelle had come to know Adenauer better, especially over the last six days. She knew the commander was operating almost in fugue state. She wasn't actually even looking at the plot. She was simply . . . absorbing it. And then, suddenly, her hands came to life on her console.

The missiles in the attack salvo had been preloaded with dozens of possible attack and EW profiles. Now Adenauer's flying fingers transmitted a series of commands which selected from the menu of preprogrammed options. One command designated the superdreadnoughts as the attack missiles' targets. Another told the Dazzlers and Dragon's Teeth seeded into the salvo when to bring their EW systems up, and in what sequence. A third told the attack missiles when to bring up their final drive stages and what penetration profile to adopt when they hit the enemy force's missile-defense envelope. And a fourth told the Mark 23-Es when and how they should take over and restructure her commands if the enemy suddenly did something outside the parameters of her chosen attack patterns.

Entering those commands took her twenty-five seconds, in which the attack missiles traveled another 3,451,000 kilometers. It took just under four seconds for her commands to reach from *Artemis* to the Apollos. It took another twelve seconds for her instructions to be receipted, triple-checked, and confirmed by the Apollo AIs while the shrouds on the attack missiles were jettisoned. Forty-five seconds after the first pod's missiles had jettisoned *their* shrouds, the follow-on salvo opened its eyes, looked ahead, and saw its targets, still two and a quarter million kilometers in front of it. They were 4.4 light-minutes from *Artemis* . . . but their targeting orders were less than sixty seconds old, and the computers which had further refined and analyzed the reports from the first pod's Apollo were those of a *superdreadnought*, not a missile, however capable.

The simulated targets' fire control had only a relatively imprecise idea of where to look for the attack missiles before their third-stage drives came suddenly on-line. They'd still been so far out when they shut down for the ballistic leg of their flight that the defenders' on-board sensors hadn't been able to fully localize them. The target ships had gotten enough to predict their positions to within only a few percentage points of error, but at those velocities, and on such an enormous "battlefield," even tiny uncertainties made precise targeting impossible. And precise targeting was exactly what was necessary for a counter-missile to hit an attack missile at extended range.

The defenders saw the Mark 23s clearly when the attack missiles' final stages came suddenly and abruptly to life, but by then it was already too late. There was no time for any long-range counter-missile launch, and even the short-range CMs had rushed targeting solutions. Worse, the EW platforms supporting the attack came on-line at the worst possible moment for the defenders. The counter-missiles' rudimentary sensors were totally outclassed, and there was no time for missile-defense officers to analyze the Manticoran EW patterns. Point defense clusters blazed desperately in a last-ditch effort to stop the MDMs hurtling in on the superdreadnoughts, but there were too many of them, they were closing too quickly, and the ballistic approach had robbed the defenders of too much tracking time. Many of the Mark 23s were destroyed short of target, but not enough.

The imagery on Adenauer's plot froze abruptly as the attack missiles and their Apollos slammed into their targets, were picked off by the defenses, or self-destructed at the end of their programmed runs. For an instant or two, the plot simply stayed that way. But then it came abruptly back to life once more. Just as a single pod had preceded the attack wave, *another* single pod followed in its wake. Its missiles had jettisoned their shrouds at the same moment the attack missiles executed their final runs, and Michelle watched in something very like disbelief, even now, as the results of the initial strike reached *Artemis* in less than five seconds.

One of the superdreadnoughts was obviously gone. Her wedge was down, she was streaming atmosphere and shedding debris, and the transponders of her crew's escape pods burned clear and sharp on the plot. One of her sisters was clearly in serious trouble, as well. From her impeller signature, she'd taken massive damage to her forward ring, and her emission signature showed heavy damage to the active sensors necessary for effective close-ranged missile-defense. The third superdreadnought appeared to have gotten off more lightly, but even she showed evidence of significant damage, and a second, equally massive attack wave was already tearing down on her.

*My God,* Michelle thought quietly. *My God, it really works. It not only* works, *but I'll bet we've still only begun to scratch the surface of what this means. Hemphill told me it would be a force multiplier, and, Jesus, was she right!*

She watched the second salvo bearing down on its victims, and even though it was only a simulation, she shivered at the thought of what it would be like to know that wave of destruction was coming.

*Lord, if Haven knew about this, they'd be* begging *for a peace treaty!* she thought shakenly.

She remembered something White Haven had said after Operation Buttercup, the offensive which had driven Oscar Saint-Just's People's Republic to its knees. "It made me feel . . . dirty. Like I was drowning baby chicks," he'd said, and for the first time, she fully understood what he'd meant.

# Chapter Fourteen

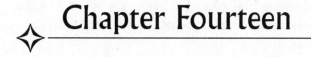

AUGUSTUS KHUMALO WAS GRAYER than Michelle remembered.

He was some sort of distant cousin of hers, although she had only the vaguest idea of exactly how and through whom they were related, and she'd met him in passing half a dozen times. This was the first time she'd ever really spoken to him, though, and as she followed his chief of staff, Captain Loretta Shoupe, into his day cabin aboard HMS *Hercules*, she found herself looking into his eyes, searching for some sign of the moral courage he'd displayed when he received Aivars Terekhov's bombshell dispatch.

She didn't see it. Not surprisingly, perhaps. She'd discovered long since that people who looked like warriors too often proved to be Elvis Santinos or Pavel Youngs, while the most outwardly unprepossessing people frequently turned out to have nerves of steel.

*I wonder if I'm looking so hard because I feel guilty about the way I've always dismissed him in the past?*

"Vice Admiral Gold Peak, Sir," Shoupe announced quietly.

"Welcome to Spindle, Milady," Khumalo held out a large, rather beefy hand, and Michelle shook it firmly. The Talbott Station commander was a large man, with powerful shoulders and a middle which was beginning to thicken. His complexion was considerably lighter than Michelle's own—in fact, it was almost as light as the Queen's—but there was no mistaking the Winton chin. Michelle knew there wasn't; she had it herself, if in a thankfully somewhat more delicate version.

"Thank you, Sir," she replied, then released his hand to indicate the two officers who had accompanied her. "Captain Armstrong, my flag captain, Sir. And Lieutenant Archer, my flag lieutenant."

"Captain," Khumalo said, offering his hand to Armstrong in turn, and then nodded in Gervais Archer's direction. "Lieutenant."

"Admiral," Armstrong replied, shaking his hand, and Archer returned his nod with a respectful half-bow.

"Please," Khumalo said then, gesturing at the chairs arranged in a comfortable, conversational circle in front of his desk. "Find seats. I'm sure we've got quite a lot to talk about."

That, Michelle reflected, as she settled back into one of the indicated chairs, was undoubtedly one of the greater understatements she'd heard lately.

Archer waited until all of his seniors had seated themselves before he found a chair of his own, and Michelle watched out of the corner of her eye as her flag lieutenant touched his cased minicomp and raised one eyebrow at Shoupe. The chief of staff nodded permission, and Archer uncased the minicomp and configured it to record.

"We're due to dine with Baroness Medusa and Mr. Van Dort this evening, Milady," Khumalo said. "At that time, I have no doubt that she and Mr. O'Shaughnessy—and Commander Chandler, my intelligence officer—will be as eager as I am to hear everything you can tell us about the situation at home and this proposed summit meeting between Her Majesty and Pritchart. And I'm also confident that the baroness and Mr. O'Shaughnessy will have a rather more detailed briefing for you on the political side of events here in the Cluster. I mean, Quadrant."

His lips twitched sourly but briefly as he corrected himself, and Michelle smiled. No doubt the change in nomenclature was going to take some getting used to for everyone involved, but as she'd warned her own staff, it was important. Words had power of their own, and remembering to get it right was one way of helping to assure everyone out here in Talbott that they'd done the right thing when they requested annexation by the Star Kingdom.

Of course, it was probable that they'd envisioned things working out just a little differently than they actually had. Not that anyone in Talbott was likely to complain about the final outcome . . . assuming they'd thought annexation was a good idea in the first place, that was. Some of them, like that lunatic Nordbrandt in

Kornati, obviously hadn't, and Michelle had no doubt that those Talbotters who continued to object were *vociferously* unhappy about that same "final outcome."

The entire annexation debate had posed serious domestic political questions for the Star Kingdom, as well, however, and the answers to those questions had dictated the conditions under which it could go forward. The original proposal hadn't been Manticore's in the first place, and more than one member of Parliament had thought it was a terrible idea. In many ways, Michelle had actually found herself in agreement with those who had objected to the entire concept. Although she'd always felt the advantages outweighed her concerns, she'd still had a high anxiety quotient where some aspects of the proposal were concerned.

The Star Kingdom of Manticore had been in existence for four hundred and fifty years, during which it had evolved and grown into its own unique identity and galactic position. It was incredibly wealthy, especially for a star nation with such a small population, but the point was that its population was *small* by the standards of any multisystem star nation. It was also politically stable, with a system which—despite its occasional blemishes, like the disastrous High Ridge Government, and monumentally nasty political infighting—enshrined the rule of law. Manticorans were no more likely to be candidates for sainthood than anyone else, and there were those—like High Ridge, Janacek, her own Cousin Freddy, or the Earls of North Hollow—who were perfectly willing to evade or even outright break the law in pursuit of their own ends. But when they got caught, they were just as accountable in the eyes of the law as anyone else, and the Star Kingdom enshrined both transparency and accountability in government. It also enshrined the orderly, *legal* exchange of power, even between the most bitter of political enemies, through the electoral process, and it possessed a highly educated, politically active electorate.

That was why the notion of adding more than a dozen additional star systems whose individual average populations at least matched that of the Manticore Binary System had been dismaying to Michelle, in many respects. Especially given how poor—and poorly educated (by Manticoran standards, at least)—all of those prospective new citizens were. Some Manticorans had been nervous enough about admitting San Martin, the inhabited world of Trevor's Star, to the Star Kingdom, and San Martin had been an entirely different kettle of fish, despite its years as a Havenite "protectorate" under the People's Republic. Its population was still that of a first-rank star nation, with decent educational, medical, and industrial bases, and it had always been Manticore's immediate astrographic neighbor. Manticorans and San Martinos had known each other for a long, long time; they'd known how one another's governments and societies worked, and shared many more similarities than they had differences. But the Talbott Cluster was typical of the Verge, that vast belt of sparsely settled, economically depressed, technically backward star systems which surrounded the slowly but inexorably expanding sphere of the Solarian League.

Michelle, like many people in the Star Kingdom, had found the idea of adding that many voters with absolutely no experience in the Star Kingdom's political traditions alarming. Some of those alarmed souls had been none too shy about calling the Talbotters "neobarbs," which Michelle, despite her own concerns, had found decidedly ironic, given the fact that Sollies routinely applied that pejorative to the same citizens of the Star Kingdom who were now using it about someone else. Yet even those who would never have dreamed of using that particular term, and who were prepared to accept that their new fellow citizens would have the best intentions in the universe, had to wonder if those new citizens would have time to absorb the instruction manual before they tried to take over the air car's controls. And, of course, there was always the concern—the legitimate concern, in Michelle's view—of what destination a bunch of voters from outside the Manticoran tradition might choose for all of them.

There'd been concerns on the Talbott side, as well, and not just from people like Nordbrandt. Or, for that matter, like Stephen Westman, although from what Michelle had heard so far, Westman seemed to have seen the light. Those with the deepest concerns appeared to have been worried about losing their own identity, although what many of them—especially among the Cluster's traditional power elites—had *really* meant when they'd said that was that they were worried about losing control.

In the end, however, the Constitutional Convention here on the planet Flax in the Spindle System had worked out an approach that actually seemed to satisfy just about everyone. *Nothing* could have satisfied absolutely everyone, of course, and some of the local potentates—like the oligarchs of New Tuscany—had opted out in the end and refused to ratify the new constitution. And, to be perfectly fair, it was unlikely that *anyone* was completely satisfied with the new arrangements. But that, after all, was the definition of a successful political compromise, wasn't it?

*Of course it is,* she thought. *That's one reason I've never liked politics. Still, in this case I've got to admit it looks like something that will actually work.*

For all intents and purposes, the approved constitution had established what bade fair to become a model for future annexations. For example, the political future of the systems which had fallen into the Star Kingdom's sphere in the now defunct Silesian Confederacy was going to have to be resolved eventually, and it looked like Talbott was going to be the example for that resolution, as well. Assuming, of course, that it actually worked in Talbott's case.

Instead of adding all of those systems, and all of those voters, directly to the Star Kingdom, the Flax Constitutional Convention had recognized that the sheer distance between the planets of the Cluster—not to mention the entire Cluster's distance from the Manticore Binary System—would have made that sort of close, seamless integration impossible. So the convention had proposed a more federal model for the new "Star Empire of Manticore."

The Talbott Quadrant was a political unit consisting of the sixteen Cluster star systems which had ratified the proposed constitution. It would have its own local Parliament, and after a certain degree of bloody infighting, it had been agreed that that Parliament would be located here on Flax, in the planetary capital of Thimble. And when it came to electing that Parliament's members, the Quadrant franchise would, at the insistence of Prime Minister Grantville's government (and Queen Elizabeth III), be granted on the same terms and conditions as the Star Kingdom's franchise, which had probably had quite a bit to do with New Tuscany's decision to go home and play with its own marbles.

The Quadrant and the Star Kingdom (which some people were already beginning to refer to as "the Old Star Kingdom," even though Trevor's Star and the Lynx System had scarcely been charter members of the original Star Kingdom) would both be units of a new realm known as the Star Empire of Manticore. Both would recognize Queen Elizabeth of Manticore as Empress, and both would send representatives to a new Imperial Parliament, which would be located on the planet of Manticore. An imperial governor would be appointed (and there'd never been any real doubt about *who* that would be) as the Empress' direct representative and viceroy here in the Quadrant. The armed forces, economic policy, and foreign policy of the Empire would be established and unified under the new imperial government. The imperial currency would be the existing Manticoran dollar, no internal economic trade barriers would be tolerated, and the citizens of the Talbott Quadrant and of the Star Kingdom would pay both local taxes and imperial taxes. The fundamental citizens' rights of the Star Kingdom would be extended to every citizen of the Talbott Quadrant, although the Quadrant's member planets were free to extend additional, purely local citizens' rights, if they so chose. The new imperial judiciary would be based upon the Star Kingdom's existing constitutional law, and its justices would be drawn, initially, at least, from the Star Kingdom, although the new constitution contained specific provisions for integrating justices from outside the Old Star Kingdom as quickly as possible, and local constitutional traditions within the Quadrant would be tolerated so long as they did not conflict with imperial ones. And every citizen of the Quadrant and the Old Star Kingdom would hold imperial citizenship.

Although the Star Kingdom of Manticore had always eschewed any sort of progressive income tax except under the most dire of emergency conditions, the Old Star Kingdom had agreed (not without a certain degree of domestic protest) that imperial taxation would be progressive at the federal level—that is, the degree of the imperial tax bill to be footed by each subunit of the Empire would be based upon that subunit's proportional share of the entire Empire's gross product. Everyone was perfectly well aware that that particular provision meant the Old Star Kingdom would be footing the lion's share of the imperial treasury's bills for the foreseeable future. In return for accepting that provision, however, the Star Kingdom had won agreement to a phased-in representation within the Imperial Parliament.

For the first fifteen years of the Empire's existence, the Star Kingdom would elect seventy-five percent of the Imperial Parliament's membership, and all other subunits of the Empire would elect the other twenty-five percent. For the next fifteen years, the Star

Kingdom would elect sixty percent of Parliament's members. And for the next twenty-five years, the Star Kingdom would elect fifty percent. Thereafter, membership in the Imperial House of Commons would be directly proportional to each subunit's population. The theory was that that fifty-five T-years of dominance by the established political system of the Old Star Kingdom would give the citizens of the Quadrant time to master the instruction manual. It would also give them time for the stupendous potential industrial and economic power of the Quadrant to be developed. At the same time, the gradual phasing in of full parliamentary representation for the Quadrant (and, presumably, for the Silesian systems, as well, when it was their turn) would reassure the citizens of the Old Star Kingdom that Manticore wasn't going to find itself suddenly haring off in some totally bizarre direction. And the fact that the Imperial Constitution guaranteed local autonomy to each recognized subunit of the Empire ought to preserve the individual identities of the various worlds and societies which had agreed to unite under the imperial framework.

Since one of the Star Kingdom's basic citizens' rights was access to the prolong therapies, the fifty-five-T-year ramp up to full representation in the Imperial Parliament wasn't going to be quite the hardship for most of the Talbott Cluster's citizens that it might have been once upon a time. True, it would hit some member systems harder than others (which had required some serious horse trading at the Constitutional Convention), because their poverty-stricken economies hadn't already made prolong available. That meant any of their citizens more than twenty-five T-years old would never receive it . . . and that a sizable portion of their present electorate would die of old age, even with modern medical care, before the Quadrant received its full representation. No arrangement could be perfect, however, and the Star Kingdom had pledged to put those systems first on the list to receive the prolong therapies, while the Constitutional Convention had pledged some *very* hefty financial incentives to bring their economies up to the standards of their neighbors as quickly as possible.

With those arrangements to offset some of the representational sacrifice of those "graying" voters, most people were prepared to call the arrangement as fair as could be contrived. It offered a roadmap to a reasonably orderly transition, anyway. And just as the security umbrella of the Royal Manticoran Navy would discourage piracy, instability, and bloodshed in both Silesia and Talbott, the importance of annexing additional star systems—and the population and resources they represented—in order to bolster Manticore's economic, industrial, and military muscle had become evident to most Manticoran strategists. In light of which, it appeared to be fairly obvious to everyone involved that the tremendous advantages inherent in the new arrangement vastly outweighed any *dis*advantages.

*One can* hope *so, at any rate,* Michelle thought dryly. *Although, given the Sollies' present antics, I suppose someone could be pardoned for wondering just how sound that logic actually is.*

"Speaking purely from a naval perspective, Milady," Khumalo said, recalling Michelle's attention from the political ramifications of the creation of a brand-new Empire, "I am delighted to see you." He smiled more than a little crookedly. "I remember when Captain Terekhov first reported to Talbott—it doesn't seem possible that that was only eight T-months ago!—I was complaining to him about how few Queen's ships had been assigned to the Cluster. To be perfectly honest, I wish we could have found something just a little less traumatic than the Battle of Monica to convince the Admiralty to turn the tap on."

"I won't mention any squeaky wheels, Sir," Michelle said with an answering smile. "On the other hand, I think you can take it as a given that the 'tap' is going to be opened even wider in the next few months. Especially if anything comes of this summit meeting."

"According to my most recent dispatches from the Admiralty, at least," Khumalo agreed. "And frankly, even without the situation vis-à-vis the League and OFS, I'm sure I'll be able to make good use of every hull they can send me. I believe it's important to establish a naval presence in every one of the Quadrant's member star systems as quickly as possible. Her Majesty's new subjects have the right to call upon her navy's protection, and until they can get their local law enforcement organizations integrated into the new system, and until we can get on-call Marine or Army units into position to assist them in dealing locally with imperial problems, it's going to be up to the Navy to do that, too. Not to mention disaster relief, assistance to navigation, and all those other things we always find ourselves doing."

"I certainly can't argue with any of that, Sir," Michelle said soberly.

"Still, I'm inclined to suspect that my position as the CO of Tenth Fleet, once we get organized, is bound to leave me whining and complaining about all the diversions you and Baroness Medusa want me to make. I know we have an absolute responsibility to do exactly what you've just described, but I'm afraid my own focus, for the foreseeable future at least, is probably going to be pretty thoroughly locked in on OFS and the League."

"Oh, that's a given, Milady," Khumalo told her with a genuine smile. "It always works that way. In fact, there'd probably be something seriously broken about the system if you *weren't* whining and complaining! Which doesn't mean the baroness and I are going to let you talk us out of doing it anyway, of course."

"Somehow, I find that depressingly easy to believe," Michelle observed, and Khumalo chuckled. It was, Michelle noticed, a very genuine chuckle.

Whatever else had happened in the last eight months, she reflected, Augustus Khumalo appeared to have found his niche. All of the reports from the Quadrant had emphasized how the general Talbotter opinion of Khumalo had changed in the wake of the Battle of Monica. As far as Michelle could tell, most Talbotters appeared to believe that the only reason Khumalo and Terekhov didn't routinely walk across swimming pools was because they didn't like wet shoes. To give him credit, Khumalo's aura of confidence and assurance didn't seem to owe itself to a head swelled by popular adulation, however. In fact, it appeared to Michelle that what had actually happened was that his own performance had surprised him as much as it had surprised so many other people. And, in the process, he'd grown into the full dimension of his responsibilities.

*Which could, of course, just be my own way of pretending that he* had *to grow into them instead of just admitting that we'd all underestimated his abilities from the beginning.*

"At the moment, Sir," she continued out loud, "my gravest concern is the readiness state of my units. The shipyards back home are pushing so hard, that—"

"There's no need to explain, Milady," Khumalo interrupted. "I've been kept updated. I know they rushed all of your battlecruisers out of the yard, and I also know what short notice you received when they handed you this particular hot potato. I'm not at all surprised if you have readiness problems, and we'll try to give you as much time as we can to deal with them. And, of course, all of the assistance we can. Speaking of which, is there anything we can do to help with your current problems?"

"At this point, I genuinely don't think so," Michelle said. "We deployed with almost eighty of *Hephaestus'* yard dogs on board, and over the last couple of weeks they've dealt with most of our hardware problems. We do have a couple of minor faults we haven't been able to deal with out of shipboard resources, but I'm confident your repair ships can set all of them right fairly quickly and easily. What no one else can do for us, though, is to bring our people's cohesiveness and training up to Fleet standards."

"How bad is it?" There was no impatience or condemnation in Khumalo's question, only understanding, and Michelle felt herself warming further towards him.

"Honestly, it's not good, Sir," she said frankly. "And it's not my captains' fault, either. We simply haven't had time to deal with the problems that normally get handled in a routine working-up period. We've got a few weak spots among our officers—more than I'd like, really, if I'm going to be honest—thanks to the manning pressures Admiral Cortez has to deal with. And some of our ratings are a lot greener than I'd really like. On the other hand, I've just come from a tour with Eighth Fleet, and that's probably enough to give me a jaundiced view of just about anybody else's training and experience. I don't think we have any problems that can't be set right by a few more weeks—a T-month, if I can get it—of good, hard drill. Well, that and, possibly, a little judicious personnel reassignment."

"A month we can probably give you," Khumalo said, glancing at Shoupe as he spoke. "I'm not sure how much more than that's going to be possible, though. Both Admiral Blaine and Admiral O'Malley are under pressure to get their commands concentrated at the Lynx Terminus as soon as possible, for reasons I'm sure you understand at least as well as I do. That puts us under pressure of our own to get O'Malley relieved down on the 'southern frontier.' At the moment, he's still at Monica, but we've redeployed a support squadron to Tillerman. That's close enough to Monica—and to Meyers—to keep an eye on the Sollies without staying any more obviously in their faces than we have to. So as soon as our damaged units at Monica have managed to complete enough repairs to get underway for home—which will probably take another six to eight T-weeks—and Ambassador Corvisart completes the . . . treaty negotiations, we'll be withdrawing our forces as far as Tillerman."

"I'm confident of the month, Sir," Captain Shoupe said, answering his unasked question. "And I think we can probably squeeze out at least a few more weeks. As you say, it's going to be at least another month or two before Admiral O'Malley is going to be able to withdraw from Monica, anyway."

"Should we think about deploying my squadron—or some of it, at least—forward to Monica to support O'Malley, Sir?" Michelle asked.

"As a show of force for the Sollies, you mean?" Khumalo raised an eyebrow, and Michelle nodded. "I don't think that's really imperative at this point, Milady," he said then. "Frankly, if two squadrons of modern battlecruisers aren't enough to deter Solarian thoughts of aggression, then I don't see how three squadrons would have that effect. Unfortunately, it's entirely possible that a *dozen* squadrons—of anything less than wallers, at least—wouldn't deter some of the idiots we've seen out here. Even Sollies ought to be beginning to figure out that they don't want to tangle with Her Majesty's Navy on anything like even terms, but I'd be disinclined to risk any money betting on that possibility." He grimaced. "You'd think what Terekhov did at Monica would begin hammering at least a little sense into their brains, but I've come to the conclusion that their skulls are better armored than their wallers are."

His expression was profoundly disgusted looking, and Captain Shoupe looked, if possible, even more disgusted than he was.

"Is it really that bad, Sir?"

"It's probably *worse*, Milady," Khumalo growled. "I don't doubt you've had your own run-ins with League arrogance over the years. I don't know any serving officer who hasn't. But we've been rather more . . . irritating to them since the Talbotters applied for admission to the Star Kingdom. Or Star Empire, or whatever." He waved one hand. "I don't think there's much doubt Frontier Security was completely confident Talbott was just one more cluster they'd get around to gobbling up whenever they decided it was convenient. Instead, *we* turned up, and that really, *really* pissed them off. Which has only made them even more arrogant pains in the arse."

"You mentioned Ambassador Corvisart, Sir," Captain Armstrong observed quietly. "When we left the Star Kingdom, we were only beginning to get reports on what she was finding out there. May I assume she's dug a little deeper in the meantime?"

"Oh, yes, Captain." Khumalo showed his teeth in a tight smile. "I think you could safely say that. And the deeper she gets, the worse it smells."

"Was OFS directly involved, Sir?" Michelle asked.

"Of course it was, Milady." Khumalo snorted. "There's no need for any 'investigation' to tell us that! *Proving* it—especially to the satisfaction of the notoriously and scrupulously impartial League legal system—is something else, of course." The irony in his tone could have withered an entire forest of Sphinxian picket-wood. "Nothing happens in the Verge—nothing that could possibly have an impact on the League, at any rate—without Frontier Security's involvement. In this case, though, it's actually beginning to look like OFS wasn't the primary player."

"They weren't, Sir?" There was surprise in Michelle's voice, and Khumalo smiled again, grimly, as he heard it.

"That's what it's beginning to look like," he repeated. "As a matter of fact, most of the straws in the wind, including President Tyler's testimony, suggest that the prime mover was Manpower."

Michelle's eyes widened, and Khumalo shrugged.

"Commander Chandler and Mr. O'Shaughnessy will be able to give you a lot more detail on this than I can, Milady. But according to Ambassador Corvisart and her on-site investigators, our original theory that Manpower and the Jessyk Combine were being used as cat's-paws by Frontier Security had things reversed. We've known from the beginning that Commissioner Verrochio has a very . . . comfortable relationship with Manpower and several other Mesan 'corporations.' We assumed—wrongly, apparently—that it was him using that relationship to convince Manpower to serve as his deniable conduit to Nordbrandt and the other terrorist movements here in the Quadrant. From what Corvisart is turning up now, though, it looks like it was actually the other way around."

"*Manpower* wanted control of the Lynx Terminus?" Michelle shook her head. "I can understand why they'd want us as far away from their home system as they could get us. We've never made any secret of how we feel about the slave trade, after all.

But my understanding was that the entire objective of the operation was for Monica to end up controlling the Cluster and the Lynx Terminus as a front for Frontier Security. That would suit Manpower a lot better than what's actually happening, of course, but going about it this way sounds awfully ambitious for a bunch of criminals."

"'Ambitious' is actually a pretty severe understatement, Milady. They've tried a few other high-stakes maneuvers in the past, but right offhand, I can't think of another one that was this risky and 'ambitious' of them, either. Still, that's the way it's beginning to look. And, considered from one perspective, it's a perfectly logical extension of their usual mode of operation. Not only would it have pushed us six hundred-plus light-years farther away from their headquarters, but it would have given them another set of hooks, this time into Tyler and Monica. I'm sure they would have shown a substantial profit, over the long term, on their ability to manipulate traffic through the terminus, as well, and they didn't even have to come up with the battlecruisers they supplied. *Those* came from Technodyne."

"That's been confirmed, Sir?"

"It has." Khumalo nodded. "Apparently, they were officially stricken from the Sollies' shiplist to make room for the new *Nevadas*, and Technodyne saw a way to turn an extra profit on them. We've recovered some electronic records which make it pretty clear Technodyne, at least, has been paying some attention to the rumors about our new systems. It looks as if they expected to get the chance for a close look at our hardware when the unfinished terminus forts had to surrender to Tyler. And they were probably slated for their own share of the income Manpower expected to be raking off from Jessyk's manipulation of the terminus traffic."

Michelle nodded slowly. What Khumalo had just said made plenty of sense, but the notion was going to take some getting used to.

*It does hang together, though,* she reflected. *And poking the Star Kingdom in the eye really isn't as risky for them as it would be for someone else. After all, we're already effectively at war with them over the slave trade. I suppose that from their perspective it was a question of how much worse it could get. And looked at that way, running even a fairly substantial risk to keep our frontiers from moving six hundred light-years closer to them would have an awful lot to recommend it.*

"Well, whoever was really in charge, and wherever they were really headed," Khumalo continued, "I'm sure Ambassador Corvisart is going to uncover quite a few more things our good friend Commissioner Verrochio would just as soon stayed buried. But Monica and the Solarian League aren't our sole concerns here in the Quadrant, Milady."

He leaned back in his chair, his expression intent.

"As Captain Terekhov discovered during his *brief* tour with us before he went trotting off to Monica," Khumalo's smile was quirky, "the new influx of merchant shipping being attracted into the Quadrant by the Lynx Terminus is attracting pirates right along with it. We need to make it clear that this isn't going to be a healthy place for them to operate. That's going to get easier when those light attack craft everyone keeps promising me actually get here, of course. A couple of squadrons of LACs will keep just about any pirate *I* can imagine out of the star system they're patrolling, at any rate. And having 'their' LAC groups assigned to each new member system will help them realize we're really serious about integrating them into a Cluster-wide security system.

"At the same time, there are threats LACs alone aren't going to be able to deter, and we have to be aware of other potential flash points, whether with OFS or with one of the other single-system star nations out here. Her Majesty has made it quite clear that we're supposed to convince the locals that the Star Empire is going to be a good neighbor. I think she's right that, over time, quite a few more of the local star systems are going to recognize a good thing when they see it and seek admission to the Quadrant. That's for the future, though. For right now, it's our job to make it plain to them that while we're perfectly willing to assist them in dealing with mutual problems—like piracy—we aren't using that assistance as a way to wedge our foot into their doors so we can gobble them up more easily.

"And, of course, there are our equally good friends on New Tuscany."

"I gathered from Admiral Givens' briefings that New Tuscany wasn't exactly likely to be very happy with us," Michelle said.

"No, they aren't. And the fact that Joachim Alquezar's Constitutional Union Party has a clear majority in the new Quadrant

Parliament isn't making them any happier. Andrieaux Yvernau hates his guts, and vice versa. In fact, probably the only person in the entire cluster Yvernau hates more than he hates Alquezar is Bernardus Van Dort . . . and the first thing *Prime Minister* Alquezar did was to name Van Dort a special minister without portfolio as soon as he got back from Monica aboard *Hercules*."

"I have to admit that I'm more than a little surprised Yvernau could have survived politically after the Convention repudiated his position so thoroughly, Sir," Michelle said cautiously, venturing warily into the political waters she normally kept her toes well clear of.

"I wouldn't say he came through it unscathed, Milady," Khumalo replied. "He didn't get hammered as badly as Tonkovic, of course, but he probably burned twenty or thirty T-years worth of political favors salvaging his position back home."

Shoupe stirred in her chair, and Khumalo glanced at her.

"I know that expression, Loretta," he said. "I take it you disagree?"

"Not entirely, Sir," his chief of staff replied. "I think O'Shaughnessy has a point, though. The real reason Yvernau's political career didn't come to a screeching halt is that a majority of his friends and neighbors back home agree with him."

Shoupe looked at Michelle.

"It's evident that Yvernau and those who think like him decided the citizens' rights provisions of the new constitution would upset their self-serving little applecart on New Tuscany. They aren't prepared to have that happen, so they opted out of the annexation. But one of the reasons they did that was because they figure they'll share in any general economic improvement in the Cluster due to simple proximity, and that our mere presence will protect them from Frontier Security whether that's what we're setting out to do, or not."

"I know that's what Yvernau thought, and I suppose I can't really dispute O'Shaughnessy's belief that quite a few of his fellow oligarchs think the same way," Khumalo said. It was obvious to Michelle that he was discussing the situation with Shoupe, and the fact that she seemed comfortable maintaining a contrary viewpoint—and that he wasn't hammering her for it—said good things about their working relationship, in her opinion.

"But even if that's what Yvernau and some of the others think," the vice admiral continued, "it's not what *all* of them think. Some of them are royally pissed that the Convention didn't do things Yvernau's way in the first place. Quite a few of them blame *us*—well, Baroness Medusa, at least—just as much as they do Alquezar and Van Dort. And for a lot of the others, the danger the example of the Quadrant and the Star Empire poses is going to far outweigh any trade advantages or protection against OFS. Nordbrandt's terror campaign against her own oligarchs on Kornati scares the stuffing out of that crew. What they're going to see is that their own lower class is going to be watching the example of what's happening to their counterparts here in the Quadrant. Which isn't exactly likely to contribute to the oligarchs' efforts to keep the lid screwed down."

"Which means exactly what for us, Sir?" Michelle asked, and he snorted.

"If I knew the answer to *that* question, I wouldn't need to work for a living. I'd just sit around picking winners in the local air car races! I know the baroness, Mr. O'Shaughnessy, Prime Minister Alquezar, and Mr. Van Dort—all of whom, frankly, are much better than I am at political analysis—are all thinking hard about that same question, and I don't believe they've come up with an answer for it yet, either. The thing I can't quite get out of my own mind, though, is that Yvernau and his crew were stupid enough to cut off their noses to spite their own faces when they couldn't get the Convention to swallow their line. I'm afraid I'm not prepared to put anything past anyone who's *that* stupid, and we're not exactly the favorite people on their list, either. So I just can't shake the suspicion that they're going to be looking for anything they can do to cause problems. The only real question in my mind where that's concerned is how much risk they're willing to run in the process. How far are they actually prepared to push us in order to demonstrate that we don't scare *them*?"

Michelle nodded again. If *she'd* been one of the chief crooks in one of the local kleptocracies, she would have been doing everything she could to avoid ticking off Manticore, whether it was the Old Star Kingdom or this newfangled Star Empire. The *last* thing she'd have done would be to risk goading it into some sort of unfortunately permanent reaction. Then again, she *wasn't* one of the chief crooks, and even if she had been, she wouldn't have been stupid enough to have embraced Andrieaux Yvernau's political strategy in the first place. Which meant she had no idea how valid Khumalo's concerns might be.

"Even if my concerns prove totally unfounded," the Talbott Station CO continued, "and, to be honest, nothing would please me more than to see exactly that happen, New Tuscany is still going to be one of our more potentially sensitive concerns. The disappearance of the various protective tariffs and other trade barriers here in the Quadrant is going to have a significant impact on local shipping patterns, and New Tuscany is probably going to be one of the major outside players in those patterns, at least in local terms. We're going to have to be careful about how we handle New Tuscan-registry merchant vessels, and I won't be a bit surprised if we encounter all kinds of customs disputes. So we're going to require at least some naval presence permanently in the vicinity of New Tuscany, Marian, Scarlet, and Pequod."

"Yes, Sir," Michelle agreed.

Khumalo started to say something more, but Shoupe cleared her throat quietly. He glanced at her, and she tapped one fingertip on her chrono.

"Point taken, Loretta," he said with a smile, and returned his attention to Michelle.

"What Captain Shoupe has just tactfully reminded me of is that dinner engagement with Baroness Medusa I mentioned to you. She's expecting us in Thimble in about three hours, and I imagine you and Captain Armstrong would like to return to *Artemis* to prepare. Mess dress, I'm afraid, since Prime Minister Alquezar will also be present. And the baroness also asked me to extend an invitation to all of your captains and their senior officers."

"That's rather a large number of people Sir," Michelle pointed out diffidently, and he chuckled.

"Believe me, Milady, Baroness Medusa is aware of that. She has rather a large banquet room in her official residence, and I believe she visualizes this as an opportunity for the Prime Minister and several other important local political figures to meet your personnel. She sees it as a major first step in fostering their confidence in us, and I think she has a point."

"That makes perfectly good sense to me, Sir. As long as she's got that large banquet room to fit us all into."

"I believe we'll manage, Admiral Gold Peak," Khumalo assured her.

# Chapter Fifteen

"AND THIS, ADMIRAL GOLD PEAK, is Prime Minister Alquezar," Lady Dame Estelle Matsuko, Baroness Medusa, and Her Majesty Elizabeth III's Imperial Governor for the Talbott Quadrant, said. "Prime Minister, Countess Gold Peak."

"Welcome to the Quadrant, Countess," the red-haired, improbably tall and slender Alquezar said, shaking Micehlle's hand with a smile. Despite the low-gravity homeworld which had produced his physique, his grip was firm and strong. Then he glanced over her shoulder at Khumalo, and his smile took on a wicked edge. "It's one of my traditions to ask newly arrived officers in Her Majesty's Navy for their impression of the Cluster's political complexion."

Khumalo smiled back at the Prime Minister, shaking his head, and Baroness Medusa chuckled.

"Now, now, Joachim! None of that," she admonished. "You promised you were going to behave yourself tonight."

"True." Alquezar nodded gravely. "On the other hand, I *am* a politician."

"And the sort of politician who gives *other* politicians a bad name," another man said. Michelle recognized him from the newsfaxes. He was shorter than Alquezar—who had to be at least a full two meters tall—but still considerably taller than Michelle. He was also fair-haired and blue-eyed, and his Standard English had a distinctly different accent from Alquezar's.

"Well, of course, Bernardus," Alquezar said to him. "Now that I've been able to secure my grip on power, it's time for my megalomania to begin coming to the surface, isn't it?"

"Only if you really like being chased around Thimble by assassins," the fair-haired man said. "Trust me—I'm sure I can find a dozen or so of them if I really need to."

"Admiral Gold Peak, allow me to introduce Special Minister Bernardus Van Dort." Medusa shook her head, and her tone took on just an edge of tolerant resignation as she waved gracefully at the newcomer.

"I'm very pleased to meet you, Mr. Van Dort," Michelle said with quiet sincerity, shaking his hand firmly. "From everything I've read and heard, none of this—" she swept her free hand around the luxurious banquet room in a gesture which included everything outside its walls, as well "—would have happened without you."

"I wouldn't go that far, Admiral," Van Dort began. "There were—"

"*I'd* go that far, Admiral," Alquezar interrupted, his tone and expression both completely serious.

"As would I," Medusa said firmly. Van Dort looked more than a little uncomfortable, but it was obvious the others weren't going to let him off the hook if he continued to protest, so he only shook his head, instead.

"There are several other people you need to meet tonight, Milady," Medusa said to Michelle. "I believe Commodore Lázló is around somewhere. He's the senior officer of the Spindle System Navy, and I'm sure he has quite a lot he'd like to discuss with you. And there are at least half a dozen more senior members of the Quadrant political establishment, as well."

"Of course, Governor," Michelle murmured, trying to look pleased.

There was no point protesting. She'd known that the instant Khumalo informed her about the banquet. For that matter, she even understood the logic, however little she might have liked the consequences. Not only was she the proof the Quadrant's new Empress and her government took the protection of her new subjects seriously, but she also stood far too close to the royal—and now imperial—succession for her to be able to hide aboard ship. And since it couldn't be avoided, the only thing to do was to pretend she was actually enjoying herself.

She thought she saw a glimmer of sympathy in Van Dort's eyes as Medusa shepherded her away, but the special minister only bowed with a murmured pleasantry and abandoned her to her fate.

"And this, Lieutenant Archer, is Helga Boltitz," Paul Van Scheldt said, and Gervais Archer turned to find himself face-to-face with one of the most attractive women he'd ever seen.

"Ms. Boltitz," he said, holding out his hand and smiling, which wasn't exactly the hardest thing he'd ever had to do in his life.

"Lieutenant Archer," she replied, and took his hand in a brief, decidedly pro forma handshake. There was not, he noticed, a smile in her blue eyes, and her voice, with its harsh, sharp-edged accent, was unmistakably cool. Indeed, "frosty" might have been a better choice of adverb.

"Helga is Minister Krietzmann's personal aide," Van Scheldt explained. Gervais was scarcely surprised by that announcement, given the similarity between her accent and Krietzmann's, but there was a none too deeply hidden sparkle of malicious delight in Van Scheldt's tone as he added in his own smoothly urbane accent, "She's from Dresden."

"I see," Gervais was very careful to keep any hint that he'd detected Van Scheldt's amusement out of his own response.

The suave, dark-haired Rembrandter was Joachim Alquezar's appointments secretary. The Prime Minister had sent him off with a wave of his hand to introduce Gervais to "the other youngsters," as Alquezar had put it. Unless Gervais was sadly mistaken, Van Scheldt had been less than delighted by his assignment. The Rembrandter, despite his youthful appearance, was at least ten or fifteen T-years older than Gervais, and there was an undeniable edge to his personality, a sort of supercilious arrogance, of knowing he was naturally and inevitably superior to those of lesser birth or wealth. It was a personality type Gervais had seen entirely too frequently back home, especially when someone afflicted by it realized he himself was at least distantly related to the Queen of Manticore. The people who had it frequently demonstrated an appalling desire to do what his father had always described as "sucking up" as soon as they realized the possibility of doing so existed. Gervais had come up with several rather more colorful descriptions of his own over the past few years, but he had to admit that Sir Roger Archer's was still the best.

Fortunately, Van Scheldt appeared not to have made that particular connection just yet. Which left Gervais wondering exactly at whose expense the appointments secretary had decided to amuse himself—Gervais' or Ms. Boltitz's?

"I imagine you and the lieutenant will be seeing quite a bit of one another, Helga," Van Scheldt continued now, smiling at Boltitz. "He's Admiral Gold Peak's flag lieutenant."

"So I understood," Boltitz replied, and her voice, Gervais noted, was even frostier as she turned her attention to the Rembrandter. Then she looked back at Gervais. "I'm sure we'll work well together, Lieutenant." Her tone said that she anticipated exactly the opposite. "For now, however, if you'll excuse me, someone is expecting me elsewhere."

She gave Gervais and Van Scheldt a rather brusque little nod, then turned and made her way purposefully off through the clusters of guests. She moved with a natural, instinctive grace, yet it was obvious to Gervais that she lacked the social polish Van Scheldt exuded from his very pores.

Or *thought* he did, at any rate.

"My," the Rembrandter observed. "*That* didn't seem to go very well, did it, Lieutenant?"

"No, it didn't," Gervais agreed. He considered the appointments secretary thoughtfully, then crooked one eyebrow. "Is there a particular reason why it didn't?"

For a moment, Van Scheldt seemed a bit taken aback by the directness of the question. Then he produced a smiling snort of amusement.

"Helga doesn't much care for what she calls 'oligarchs,'" he explained. "I'm afraid that means she and I got off on the wrong foot from the very beginning. Don't get me wrong—she's very good at what she does. Very smart, very dedicated. Possibly a little too intense, I think sometimes, but that's probably why she's so effective. Still, she's also very . . . parochial one might say, I suppose. And despite her position over at the War Ministry, I suspect her heart isn't fully in this annexation business."

"I see." Gervais glanced after the now-vanished Boltitz with that same thoughtful expression. Personally, he empathized with her a lot more than he did with Van Scheldt. After all, the appointments secretary hadn't exactly gotten off on the right foot with *him*, whether he realized it or not.

"I suppose I really shouldn't hold it against her," Van Scheldt sighed. "After all, she's not exactly from the upper crust of Dresden. For that matter, I'm not at all sure Dresden *has* an upper crust, now that I think about it. If it does, though, she probably despises it almost as much as she automatically despises anyone from Rembrandt."

*I wonder if you realize you're letting a genuine streak of venom show?* Gervais thought. *And I also wonder exactly what Ms. Boltitz did to piss you off so thoroughly? From what I've seen of you so far, it probably wouldn't have taken much. On the other hand, I can always at least hope it was something suitably publicly humiliating.*

"That's unfortunate," he said out loud, and turned back to the task at hand as Van Scheldt spotted someone else who needed to be introduced to the new Manticoran admiral's flag lieutenant.

"Ms. Boltitz?"

Helga Boltitz twitched in surprise and looked up quickly from the wrist chrono she'd been studying hopefully. Unfortunately, it hadn't magically sped ahead to a point which would let her disappear, but that wasn't the source of her surprise.

"Yes, Lieutenant . . . Archer, wasn't it?" she said. She tried to say it tactfully—she really did—but she knew it hadn't come out that way.

"Yes," the red-haired, green-eyed young man replied. The single word came out with a polished, aristocratic smoothness not even that cretin Van Scheldt could have rivaled, she reflected. Despite her innate distaste for the wealth and arrogance which had created it, it actually had a sort of beauty.

"What can I do for you, Lieutenant?" she asked a bit impatiently, and his educated accent made her even more aware than usual of the harshness of her own. Dresdeners weren't exactly noted for the beauty of *their* speech, she reflected sourly.

"Actually," the Manticoran said, "I was wondering if you could explain to me exactly what that unmitigated jerk Van Scheldt did to . . . irritate you so thoroughly?"

"I beg your pardon?" Despite herself, Helga felt her eyes widen in surprise.

"Well," Gervais said, "it was pretty obvious you weren't what someone might call delighted to see him. And since whatever it was about him that irritated you seemed to be splashing onto me, as well, I thought it might be a good idea to find out what it was. After all, he may be an ass, but he had a point about how much we're likely to be seeing of one another, and I'd just as soon not inadvertently offend you in the same way."

Helga blinked, then felt herself settling back on her heels, head cocking to one side as she looked at—*really* looked at—Archer for the first time.

What she saw was a tallish young man, a good quarter-meter taller than her own hundred and sixty-two centimeters, although he was nowhere near the height of someone like Alquezar or someone else from San Miguel. He was built more for speed than brute strength—he looked like he'd probably make a decent wing—and his face was pleasantly ordinary looking. But there was something about those green eyes . . .

"I must say, that's a conversational gambit I haven't encountered before, Lieutenant," she told him after a moment.

"I imagine people both here in the Quadrant and back home are going to be encountering all sorts of things we haven't encountered before over the next few years," he replied. "On the other hand, I think it's a valid concern, don't you?"

"However little I may like Mr. Van Scheldt, I don't allow it to color my professional relationship with him," she shot back a bit sharply.

"Probably not. On the other hand, he's only an appointments secretary, and I'm the flag lieutenant of the second-ranking naval officer here in the Quadrant," Gervais pointed out. "I'd say that probably means you and I are going to be running into one another quite a bit more frequently than you run into him. Which brings me back to my original question."

"And if I pointed out to you that my personal relationship—or lack thereof—with Mr. Van Scheldt is none of your affair?" Helga inquired, her tone no more pleasant than it had to be.

"I'd agree that you're entirely correct," Gervais replied calmly. "And then I'd go on to say that, speaking in a purely professional sense, I think it's important that I know how he contrived to give offense—not that I can't think of at least a dozen probable scenarios right off hand, you understand, even on this short an acquaintance with him—so I can manage not to follow in his footsteps. To be perfectly frank, Ms. Boltitz, I don't care what your personal relationship with him or anyone else might be. I'm simply concerned with potential consequences to our own *professional* relationship."

*And you can believe as much of that as you'd like to, lady,* he reflected. *Not that there isn't quite a bit of truth in it, but still . . .*

"I see."

Helga considered Lieutenant Archer thoughtfully. He was a prolong recipient, of course—probably at least a second-generation recipient, given the background of wealth and privilege his accent clearly denoted—which meant he was also very probably quite a bit older than she'd originally thought. There weren't enough Dresdeners who'd received prolong for her people to be particularly good at estimating the age of people who had, she reflected bitterly. But despite the way his confident, sophisticated attitude made Van Scheldt's look like the provincial façade it actually was, there was still that hint of a twinkle in his eyes. And his tone, though amused, wasn't patronizing or dismissive. It was more as if he were inviting her to share his own amusement at *Van Scheldt* than as if he were mocking her.

*Sure it is. You just go right ahead and assume that and see what it gets you, Helga!*

Still, he did have a point about how likely they were to find themselves working together, or at least in close proximity to one another. And Minister Krietzmann, despite his own deep-seated aversion to oligarchs, wasn't likely to thank her for generating any more friction with the Manties than she had to.

"Actually, Lieutenant Archer," she heard herself say, "I rather doubt you're going to be as offensive as Mr. Van Scheldt. I hope not, at least, since I don't see how anyone possibly could be without deliberately working at it."

"From what I've seen of him so far," Gervais told her, "I imagine that's exactly what he did—work at it, I mean." He saw her blue eyes widen slightly in fresh surprise and smiled faintly at her. "We're not exactly unfamiliar with the type back home," he added.

"Really?" Helga was a bit surprised by the cold edge of her own voice, but she couldn't help it. "I rather doubt that, Lieutenant. His 'type,' as you put it, has had a bit more of an impact on Dresden than I imagine it's ever had on *you*."

Gervais managed not to blink in surprise or raise any eyebrows, but the harshness, the sudden, unmistakable anger, in her response took him more than a little aback.

*This isn't just a case of Van Scheldt personally being an asshole,* he realized. *I don't know what the hell it is, but it's more than that. And now that I've so nonchalantly wandered out into this particular minefield, what do I do about it?*

He gazed at her for several seconds, and as he did, he realized there was a darkness behind the anger in her eyes. A darkness put there by some memory, some personal experience. He felt certain somehow that this wasn't a woman who lightly succumbed to prejudice or permitted it to rule her life, and if that was true, there had to be more to the bitterness, the shadows of pain, than the mere casual arrogance and amused malice of a drone like Van Scheldt.

"I don't doubt that that's true," he said finally. "I've done my best to bone up on Talbott since Lady Gold Peak picked me as her flag lieutenant and we both found out we were headed this way, but I can't pretend to really know very much about the way things have been out here in the past. I'm working on it, but there's an awful lot of information involved and I simply haven't had time to make very much of a dent in it. It's obvious to me that you and Van Scheldt don't exactly get along like a house on fire, but I'd assumed he must have personally done something to offend you. Lord knows he's obviously the sort of jackass who could do something like that as easily as breathing! But from what you've just said, I'm beginning to realize there's more to it. I'm not trying to be flip, and if you'd rather not talk about it, I'll accept that. On the other hand, if it's something I should know—something my admiral should be aware of—so that we don't inadvertently do the same thing, I'd really appreciate it if you could help further my education about the Quadrant."

*My God, I think he actually means it!* Helga thought. She gazed at him for several heartbeats, frowning ever so slightly, then felt the decision make itself.

*He wants to know why I feel the way I feel? Wants to understand why not all of us are ready to start dancing in the streets just because another batch of oligarchs thinks it can make a profit off of us? All right. I'll tell him.*

"All right, Lieutenant," she said. "You want to know why Van

Scheldt and I don't like each other? Try this on for size." She folded her arms in front of her, standing hip-shot, her blue eyes glittering, and looked up at him. "I'm twenty-six T-years old, and I only received my very first prolong treatments when I went to work for Minister Krietzmann last year. If I'd been three T-months older, I'd have been too old for even the first-generation treatment . . . just like my parents. Just like my two older brothers and my three older sisters. Just like all but six of my cousins and every one of my aunts and uncles. But not Mr. Van Scheldt. Oh, no! *He's* from Rembrandt! He got it just because of where he was born, who his parents were, what planet he came from—just like *you* did, Lieutenant. And so did his parents, and all of his sisters and brothers. Just like they got decent medical care and a balanced diet."

Her eyes were no longer merely glittering. They *blazed*, now, and her voice was far harsher than her accent alone could ever have explained.

"We don't like Frontier Security on Dresden any more than anyone else in the Cluster. And, sure, everything we've heard about Manticore suggests we'll get a better deal out of your Star Kingdom than we ever would out of OFS. But we know all about being ignored, Lieutenant Archer, and most of us on Dresden don't have any illusions. I doubt the Star Kingdom is going to gouge us the way Frontier Security, the League, and the Rembrandt Trade Union have, but most of us take all those 'economic incentives' the Convention promised us with a very large grain of salt. We'd like to think at least *some* of our neighbors were sincere about it, but we're not stupid enough to believe in altruism or the tooth fairy. And if any of us might've been tempted to, there are enough Paul Van Scheldts in the Cluster to teach us better. His family was deeply invested in Dresden even before the Annexation, you know. They hold majority interests in three of our major construction companies, and they could care less about the people who work for them. About the building site injuries, or the long-term health problems, or providing their employees' families—their children, at least, for God's sake!—with access to prolong."

The depth of her anger swept over Gervais with a pure and consuming power, and it took everything he had not to flinch from it. No wonder Van Scheldt had found it so easy to flick her on the raw!

*And the fact that he obviously enjoys doing it so much suggests he's an even nastier piece of work than I thought he was. He probably spends his free time pulling the wings off flies.*

"I'm sorry to hear that, especially about your family," he said quietly. "And you're right—it's not something I can really imagine or share from my own experience. My brothers and sisters, my parents—even my *grandparents*—are all prolong recipients. I can't begin to imagine how I'd feel if I'd gotten it and none of them had. If I knew I was going to lose every single one of them before I was even 'middle aged.'" He shook his head, his own eyes dark. "But I can understand why an asshole like Van Scheldt would be able to get to you. And even if I can't really say I 'know' him yet I don't *need* to know him to recognize how much he enjoys doing just that. Which, given what you've just said about his family's involvement in your planet's economy, makes him an even sicker bastard than I'd already thought."

Helga twitched as she heard the hard, cold disgust—the contempt—in his voice. She'd heard plenty of contempt from people like Van Scheldt, but this was different. It wasn't directed at the speaker's "natural inferiors," and it wasn't petty and denigrating. More than that, it was born of *anger*, not arrogance. Of outrage, not disdain.

Or, at least, it sounded as if it were. But Dresden had learned the hard way that appearances could be deceiving, she cautioned herself.

"Really?" she said.

"Really," he replied, and he felt a distant sort of wonder at the rock-ribbed certitude of his own tone.

The back of his brain wondered what the hell he thought he was doing, using terms like "sick bastard" to describe someone he hardly knew to someone he'd barely even spoken to. Yet there it was. He did recognize the self-indulgent sadism required for someone to enjoy mocking the victim of his own family's exploitative greed and neglect.

"I'd like to believe that," she said finally, slowly. Her Dresden accent was as harsh as ever, yet that harshness was oddly smoothed, he thought. Or perhaps the word he really wanted was "gentled," instead. "I'd like to. But we've believed people on Dresden before. In fact, it took us far too long to realize we shouldn't have. We've accomplished a lot in the last couple of generations, but only because people like Minister Krietzmann realized we had to do it ourselves. Realized that no one else gave a solitary damn what happened to us.

"Don't get me wrong." She shook her head, and her voice was calmer, as if she were reasserting control over her own passions. "There's no reason why anyone off Dresden should have given us a free ride. We understand that. Charity begins at home, they say, and Dresden is *our* home, not Rembrandt's, or San Miguel's, or Manticore's. It's not so much that no one came and invested in free clinics or schools for us, but that we had to fight other people tooth and nail to somehow hang onto enough of the profit of our own labor, our own industrial structure—such as it was, and what there was of it—to begin building our *own* clinics and schools.

"We'd figured that out by the time the RTU finally got around to us, which is why one of the things we insisted on, if they wanted trade deals with us, was that they had to clean their own house where people like the Van Scheldts were concerned—had to put at least some limits on the kind of crap they could get away with. And, to Mr. Van Dort's credit, I suppose, the RTU did just that. Of course, the extent of the limits they could impose was limited by the domestic pull of their own oligarchs who were already invested in Dresden, but they still managed to do a lot. Which is probably one of the reasons Van Scheldt is such a pain where *I'm* concerned, I suppose, since his family got whacked harder than most . . . since they'd been even *worse* than most. But even with Van Dort on our side—and I think he really is" she sounded almost as if she wished she could believe otherwise, Gervais thought "—we're still a *long* way from where we could have been. It's hard to stand on your own two feet when someone else owns the carpet and keeps trying to jerk it out from under you."

The party's background noise seemed distant, like the sound of surf rolling up onto a far-off beach. It was no longer part of Gervais' world—or hers, he realized. It was no more than a frame, something which enclosed her intensity, whose contrasting banality underscored the raw honesty in her voice.

"That's one thing that isn't going to be happening again," he told her quietly. "Not on our watch. Her Majesty won't stand for it—not for a heartbeat."

"I hope you'll pardon me for saying that Dresden's going to be taking *that* with a grain of salt, too, Lieutenant." Her voice was flatter, no less passionate but with something far worse than anger, he thought. It was flat with the bitterness of experience. With disillusionment so deep, so intense, that it couldn't—dared not—expose itself to the risk of optimism.

He felt a stab of quick, fierce anger of his own—anger directed at her for daring to prejudge the Star Kingdom of Manticore. Daring to prejudge *him*, simply because he'd been fortunate enough to be born into a wealthier, less constrained world than she. Who was she to look at him with such distrust? Such bitterness and anger born of the actions of *others*? He'd told her nothing but the simple truth, and she'd rejected it. It was as if she'd looked him straight in the eye and told him that he'd *lied* to her.

Yet even as he thought that, even as the anger flared, he knew it was at least as irrational—and unfair—as anything *she* might have felt.

"It's obvious I have even more to learn about the Talbott Quadrant than I thought I did," he said after several moments. "In fact, at the moment, I'm feeling pretty stupid for not having realized it had to be that way." He shook his head. "Trying to get some sort of 'quick fix' on sixteen different inhabited star systems is guaranteed to be an exercise in futility, isn't it? I guess nobody's really immune to the idea that everyone else has to be 'just like them' even when intellectually they know better."

She was looking at him now with a slightly puzzled expression, and he grinned crookedly at her.

"I promise I'll try to do my homework better, Ms. Boltitz. I know Lady Gold Peak will be doing the same, and I don't doubt that Baroness Medusa's been working at it the entire time she's been out here. But while I'm doing that, do you think you could do a little homework on the Star Kingdom? I'm not going to say Manticore doesn't have its own share of warts, because God knows we do. And I don't blame you a bit for taking the Star Kingdom's promises with—what was it you called it? 'A grain of salt'?—but when Queen Elizabeth gives her word to someone, she keeps it. *We* keep it for her."

"That sounds good. And I'd like to believe it," she replied. "I doubt you have any idea how *much* I'd like to believe it. And if a part of me didn't, I wouldn't be here, wouldn't be working with

Minister Krietzmann to try to *make* it be true. But when you've been kicked often enough, it's hard to trust someone you don't even know. Especially when he's wearing the biggest, heaviest boots you've ever seen in your life."

"I'll try to bear that in mind, too," he assured her. "Do you think you can give me—give us—at least a little bit of the benefit of the doubt, as well?" He smiled at her. "At least for a little while, long enough to see how well we do at living up to our promises?"

Helga looked at that smile, and its warmth, the empathy and the concern—the *personal* concern—behind it amazed her. He meant it, she realized, and wondered how he could possibly be that naïve. How could he believe, even for a moment, that the oligarchs who must infest an economic power like the Star Kingdom of Manticore would care for a moment about any political "promises" someone else had made?

Yet he did. He might be—almost certainly was—wrong, yet he wasn't lying. There were many things in those green eyes that she couldn't read, but deceit wasn't one of them. And so, despite herself, she felt a small stir of hope. Felt herself daring to believe that perhaps, just perhaps, he might *not* be wrong.

Bitter experience and the cynicism of self preservation roused instantly, horrified by the possibility of opening such a breach in her defenses. She started to speak quickly, to make her rejection of his overture's false hope clear. But that wasn't what came out of her mouth.

"All right, Lieutenant," she heard herself say instead. "I'll do my 'homework' while you do yours. And at the end of the day, we'll see who's right. And," she realized *she* was actually smiling slightly, "believe it or not, I hope it turns out *you* are."

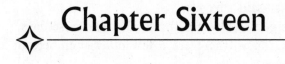

# Chapter Sixteen

TOO MANY HOURS LATER for Michelle's taste, she found herself sitting in a pleasant study sipping an excellent local cognac from a large, tulip-shaped glass. She was thoroughly exhausted, and she had that stuffed-too-tightly feeling that all too often followed state dinners . . . and always made her envy Honor Harrington's genetically enhanced metabolism. But she also felt a sense of accomplishment. However little she liked formal political dinners, she felt reasonably confident she'd carried off her part in this one successfully.

She wasn't alone in the study. Baroness Medusa sat behind the desk, and Gregor O'Shaughnessy sat in a chair to her right, at the end of the desk. O'Shaughnessy, Medusa's senior intelligence analyst, was slightly built and a good ten centimeters shorter than Augustus Khumalo, with thinning gray hair. Khumalo, Alquezar, Van Dort, and the Quadrant's minister of war, Henri Krietzmann, sat in a semicircle with Michelle, facing the desk. Krietzmann was a short, compact, solid-looking man with brown hair and gray eyes. His left hand had been mangled in some long-ago accident, and although Michelle knew he was actually the youngest person in the room, he looked like the oldest, because prolong had been unavailable on his native planet of Dresden in his youth. In fact, it *still* wasn't generally available the way it ought to be.

"Well," Medusa tipped back in her chair, and Michelle strongly suspected that the baroness had just toed off her shoes underneath her desk. "I'm glad *that's* over. For tonight, at least."

"As are we all, I'm sure," Alquezar agreed, passing his own glass appreciatively back and forth under his nose.

"Not me," Krietzmann announced. He and Van Dort, unlike anyone else in the study, nursed moisture-beaded tankards of beer rather than some effete beverage like cognac. "I *love* evenings like tonight."

"Yes, but that's because of how much you enjoy pissing off people like Samiha Lababibi by putting on your crude, unlettered barbarian act," Alquezar said severely.

"Nonsense. Samiha's getting along with me just fine these days," Krietzmann shot back. "Now, there are a few *other* members of the political establishment . . ."

He let his voice trail off provocatively, and Van Dort snorted. Then he looked across Krietzmann at Michelle.

"Henri takes a certain perverse pleasure in irritating us oligarchs, Milady," he said. "Even the ones he's grudgingly willing to admit are on the side of the angels. That's why he got shuffled off to the War Ministry where he doesn't have to deal with other politicians as much."

"I *wish*," Krietzmann muttered. Then he twitched a smile. "In fact, Samiha and I *are* getting along," he said more seriously. "She's not the worst sort, you know. I have to admit, I was a bit surprised when she resigned as the Spindle System President to take the Treasury Ministry. It seemed like an awfully big step down, prestige-wise. But she seems to be the right woman for the job, and unlike some of our other colleagues, she genuinely doesn't seem to mind working with an ex-factory hand from Dresden."

"Yes," Alquezar said, looking across at him. "I do know she isn't the worst sort. That's one reason I asked her to take Treasury. Unfortunately," he turned to Michelle, "she's off-world tonight, hosting a sort of local economic summit on Rembrandt."

"I imagine having all of your ministers here in Spindle at once is going to be the exception, not the rule, for at least the foreseeable future, Mr. Prime Minister," Michelle observed.

"That, unfortunately, is nothing but the truth," Alquezar agreed.

"Actually," Medusa said, "the entire process of creating the new government is going far more smoothly and efficiently than I think most of the people involved in doing the actual work realize. I have the advantage of a perspective none of the rest of you have, Joachim. Trust me, you're doing quite well."

"So far, at least," Van Dort murmured.

"Things can always change," Medusa acknowledged equably. "My distinct feeling at this moment, however, is that you're already past the most likely stumbling points, and the Quadrant's systems are showing a remarkable degree of mutual tolerance and internal cohesion. Don't forget how little a lot of these systems truly had in common—aside from astrographic location and the threat of OFS—before the annexation proposal came along. That was certainly a factor while the annexation was getting organized, as I expect all of us remember rather better than we'd like to. In fact, there's being far less infighting than I would ever have anticipated after watching the gladiatorial combat of the Convention!"

"You can thank the Sollies for that, I suspect," Alquezar said sourly.

"I probably could . . . if I were willing to thank them for *anything*," Krietzmann responded with cold, biting bitterness.

"There's quite a lot of truth to that, I think, though, Henri," Van Dort said quietly. "What happened in Monica—and what *was* happening on Montana and Kornati—reminded everyone OFS is still out there. And most of them think Verrochio and Hongbo would just love another shot at the Cluster."

"Do people really think that's likely, Minister?" Michelle asked.

" 'Bernardus,' please, Milady," he replied, then grimaced. "And in answer to your question, yes, there are quite a few people here in the Quadrant who think that's *very* likely, if Verrochio can figure out a new approach."

"Even after how badly he got his fingers burned this time . . . Bernardus?"

"Maybe even *especially* after getting his fingers burned." Van Dort shrugged. "First of all, we don't know how much—if any of this—is going to stick to him after Ambassador Corvisart gets done with her investigation in Monica. I'm not saying I don't think it *will* stick to him; I'm just saying we don't know how badly. Second, he's not exactly what someone might call a forgiving man. Even assuming he manages to squirm out without any official sanctions, he's undoubtedly been humiliated in front of the only people he really cares about—his peers in Frontier Security. I'm quite sure his position in the OFS hierarchy's taken some severe damage out of this, and he's going to be looking for a chance to recoup his status and power base. When you factor in his temper and the fact that he's going to want revenge, I think you can safely say that if he sees the opportunity to do us a disservice, he'll seize it with both hands."

"The view back home on Manticore is that he's most likely to pull in his horns and try to cut his losses," Michelle said.

"I'm not surprised." Van Dort shook his head. "That would be the smart thing for him to do, after all. After getting his fingers caught in the cookie jar this way, the last thing he needs is to shove his whole hand in while the entire galaxy is watching. That's obvious to everyone else, and one would hope it would be obvious to him, as well. In fact, it probably is. But never underestimate the ability of human nature to ignore the obvious once the emotions are fully engaged. Especially when the human being in question is a fundamentally stupid, superficially clever, and incredibly arrogant man like Lorcan Verrochio. A corner of his mind—such as it is, and what there is of it—must be thinking that if he can only get his hands on the Lynx Terminus after all, it would more than restore his pre-Monica position. After all, pulling that off after what looked like disaster would demonstrate his ability to adapt and overcome adversity, wouldn't it? As a matter of fact, I strongly suspect that if it weren't for Hongbo Junyan's ability to prevent him from throwing good money after bad, Verrochio might have responded to Aivars' attack on Monica by sending in a Frontier Fleet squadron with orders to do whatever it took to 'restore Monica's sovereignty.'"

"Which is why it's so important to keep that frontier strongly picketed," Baroness Medusa said. "I know you and Admiral Khumalo have already discussed that, Milady. And I know he and I are in fundamental agreement about the best use to make of our naval resources. But having both of you simultaneously here in Thimble, along with the Prime Minister and Mr. Krietzmann, presents entirely too good an opportunity to pass up. What I'd like for all of us to do is to kick around the basic strategic situation and get everyone's insight into what it is we're doing about it."

"I think that's an excellent idea, Madame Governor," Krietzmann said, sitting forward in his chair. "But part of our 'basic strategic situation' out here are the implications of the Old Star Kingdom's strategic situation closer to home. Specifically, I'm thinking about this summit meeting between Her Majesty and President Pritchart. How likely is that to lead to serious peace talks? And, short of serious peace talks, how long do we expect the cease-fire to last?"

"Those are two excellent questions, Mr. Krietzmann," Michelle said. "Unfortunately, the answer to the first one is that no one knows. Both sides have obvious reasons to want to stop shooting at one another, if we can. But, by the same token, both sides appear to have painted themselves into something of a corner where the question of 'war guilt' is concerned. I don't see how any sort of peace talks can succeed if we can't even agree on who falsified whose diplomatic correspondence before the war. The initiative came from the Havenites' side. If that means they're willing to make some genuine concessions, a serious effort towards establishing—and *admitting*—responsibility for the forgeries, then I think the chance of 'serious peace talks' is at least pretty good.

"Short of that, I'd guess the cease-fire is going to last for a minimum of several months. It's going to take that long just to get all of the messages setting it up sent back and forth. Then Beth—I mean, Her Majesty—and Pritchart are going to have to get to Torch for the actual summit. It's over a month's voyage for Pritchart, one way, and I doubt anyone is going to be willing to give up without spending at least a month or two proving to the other side—and to the galaxy at large—that however unreasonable the other fellows may be being, *we're* doing our dead level best to bring all this bloodshed to an end. And then you've got the voyage time home for Pritchart. Considering all of that, I'd say five T-months wouldn't be at all out of the question."

"That's about what Gregor I have been estimating from this end," Baroness Medusa said with a nod.

"And if it does last that long, what does it mean for us here in Talbott?" Krietzmann asked.

"The main thing it would mean, Henri," Khumalo said, "is that the majority of the emergency war program construction will have time to come into service. And that, in turn, means the Admiralty's plans to beef up our naval presence here in the Quadrant could proceed without worrying about diversions to meet unanticipated needs on the main front. Which means Vice Admiral Gold Peak's new fleet's order of battle would come forward more or less as scheduled, and that we ought to see the first light attack craft squadrons being deployed within the next month or so."

"Really?" Krietzmann looked as if he were more than half afraid to believe it. He obviously didn't think Khumalo was lying to him. It was more as if he found it difficult to believe the universe would allow things to go that smoothly.

"Really," Khumalo assured him. "In the long run, I think the LACs are going to be even more useful here in the Quadrant than Tenth Fleet. I doubt any Solly with Frontier Security or Frontier Fleet would consider them any sort of threat, so they aren't going to have any deterrence value for someone like Verrochio. That's what Tenth Fleet is for. But once we get two or three squadrons of them deployed to every one of the Quadrant's systems, we'll pretty much have knocked piracy on its head. And, to be honest, the LACs are going to be the best means for gradually integrating the personnel of the local system navies into the RMN."

"I certainly agree with that," Van Dort said firmly. "No pirate in his right mind is going to cross swords with a modern Manticoran LAC. Or, at least, not after the word gets around about what happens to the first couple of them to try it. And the LAC squadrons and their personnel are going to be seen by the locals as 'theirs' in a way hyper-capable ships aren't. They'll be the local police force, not the Navy that comes swinging through the vicinity to check on things every so often. And integrating local personnel into their complements is going to be the best way to start getting our people trained up on modern naval technology, as well."

"That's the Admiralty's thinking, Sir," Michelle agreed. "It won't be the same as running them all through basic training back home, but what they have in mind is more of an orientation mission. Each LAC detachment will have its own simulators for training, and running local personnel through them will give our people a chance to evaluate their general skill levels and basic competence, which aren't necessarily the same thing. Ultimately, BuPers is going to have to set up whatever remedial education is necessary in-house, since both the Admiralty and the PM have already made it clear that there *are* going to be Talbotters in the RMN and that they are *not* going to get stuck with some kind of second-class status. That means bringing their basic educational levels up to Manticoran standards, not trying to do some sort of rote training or 'enough to get by' training like the old Peep Navy used with its conscripts. That's going to require a lot out of them in terms of extra classroom studies, at least until we get the general education system out here up to Manticoran standards, but there's no way to avoid that, and I think the people who actually want to transfer to naval service will be willing to make the effort. In fact, that's probably going to be one of those Darwinian filters that help us recruit the cream of the crop.

"In the meantime, of course, the squadrons themselves will provide a defense in depth against the kind of . . . risk-averse scum who go into piracy as a career. And, frankly, there's another advantage to it from my perspective, given what you've just told me about Commissioner Verrochio. The quicker we can get the LACs up and running to deal with people like that, the quicker I can get my strength concentrated and pushed far enough forward to remind Mr. Verrochio to stay away from our cookies."

Michelle Henke finished toweling her hair vigorously, draped the towel around her neck, and settled into the chair in front of the terminal in her sleeping cabin. Her sadly worn-looking Academy sweats' fleecy lining was sinfully warm and sensual feeling against her just-showered skin, and she grinned as she looked down at her feet. Honor had given her her first pair of fluffy, violently purple treecat slippers as a joke several Christmases ago. Michelle had started wearing them as a joke of her own, but she'd *kept* wearing them because of how comfortable (if undignified) they were. The original pair had been lost with *Ajax*, but she'd insisted on finding time to buy a replacement pair before deploying with her new squadron, and they were finally getting properly broken in.

Chris Billingsley had left a carafe of hot coffee on a tray at her elbow, along with a single sugared doughnut, and she grimaced wryly at the sight. Unlike Honor, Michelle had discovered that it was distinctly necessary for her to keep an eye on her caloric intake. The majority of naval officers led relatively sedentary lives when they were aboard ship. Others—like Honor—verged on the fanatical when it came to physical fitness. Michelle was one of those who preferred to follow a middle-of-the-road path, with enough exercise to keep her *reasonably* fit, but without going overboard about it. And since every excess calorie seemed to go directly to her posterior, and since it was harder than ever for her to find the time for the amount of exercise she was prepared to tolerate, she had no choice but to watch what she was eating very carefully.

It had taken Billingsley a little while to realize that, but he'd caught on quickly. And Michelle was grateful to discover that as the immediacy of what had happened to *Ajax* receded into the past, the pain of losing Clarissa Arbuckle was easing. It would never go away, but like most naval officers of her generation, Michelle had acquired far too much experience in dealing with losses. In this case, the fact that Billingsley was so unlike Clarissa in so many ways actually helped, and she was glad it was so. He deserved to be taken on his own terms, without being measured against someone else's ghost. And, taken on his own terms, he was a gratifyingly competent force of nature who took no nonsense from *his* admiral where questions of her care and feeding were concerned. His style of bullying involved reproachful glances, deep sighs, and what Michelle privately thought of as "the Jewish mother" technique, which was very different from Clarissa's oh-so-polite insistence, but it was certainly . . . effective.

She chuckled at the thought, poured herself a cup of coffee, allowed herself a single (small) introductory bite of the doughnut, then brought the terminal on-line. She was just about to open the letter to her mother which she'd begun the evening before when something large, warm, and silky stroked luxuriously against her ankle. She looked down and found herself gazing directly into Dicey's large, green eyes. They blinked, then swivelled towards the doughnut before they tracked back to her face.

"Don't even think about it, you horrible creature," she told him severely. "*You* don't get enough exercise to be stacking up that kind of calories, either. Besides, I'm sure donuts are bad for cats."

Dicey looked up at her appealingly for several more seconds, doing his very best to look like a small, starving kitten. He wasn't noticeably successful, however, and she pointedly moved the plate farther away from him. Finally, he gave up with a mournful sigh, turned away, flipped his tail at her, and wandered off to see who else he might be able to mooch some desperately needed sustenance out of.

Michelle watched him go, then shook her head, finished opening the letter and ran forward through it, reviewing what she'd written previously while she sipped the rich, black coffee, savoring its touch of harshness after the doughnut's sweetness.

It was hard to believe the squadron had been here in Spindle for just over one T-week already. Despite the relentless schedule of training exercises and drills with which she and Victoria Armstrong had afflicted their personnel on the voyage here from the Lynx Terminus, those ten subjective days in transit looked positively soporific in retrospect. Or perhaps not. Perhaps that was only true for Michelle and her staff. The squadron's demanding training schedule hadn't relented—if anything, it had intensified—but while the rest of her people were grappling with that, Michelle, Cynthia Lecter, Augustus Khumalo, and Loretta Shoupe were engaged in an intensive analysis, along with Henri Krietzmann and his senior staffers, of the Quadrant's resources, as well as its needs, while they tried to formulate the most effective deployment plans.

So far, the main conclusion they'd been able to draw was that until more of Tenth Fleet's starships and the first of the LAC squadrons got forward, it was simply physically impossible for Michelle's ships to be everywhere they needed to be. Which was why she was due to leave Spindle the day after tomorrow and proceed with the squadron's first division to Tillerman. That would put her in position to pay a "courtesy call" on Monica about the time that *Hexapuma* and *Warlock* completed their repairs and O'Malley was withdrawing his Home Fleet battlecruisers from the system. At the same time, Commodore Onasis would split up her second division, and the individual ships would begin a sweep through the Quadrant's systems as visual reassurance of the Royal Navy's presence. Which, unfortunately, was about all Michelle could actually offer them until the rest of the Quadrant's assigned units put in their appearance.

*And, of course, we'll all go right on training,* she thought wryly. *No wonder all my people love me so much!*

She reached the end of her previous recording, which had covered Baroness Medusa's dinner party and the after dinner conversation, and straightened in her chair as she keyed the microphone.

"So I'm sure you and Honor are both going to sprain your elbows patting yourselves on the back and chanting 'We told you so!' in two-part harmony about my aversion for politics." She smiled and shook her head. "I knew I wouldn't be able to stay completely away from them once the Admiralty decided to send me out here, but I can't say I anticipated getting into them quite so deeply. At the same time, I have to admit it's actually pretty . . . exciting. These people are really fired up, Mom. Oh, there's still some opposition and unhappiness, but it looks to me like that's starting to fade. Nothing is going to convince someone like that maniac Nordbrandt to see reason, but I think anyone whose brain actually works has to realize everyone involved is doing her dead level best in a good-faith effort to work things out as quickly and equitably as possible. These people aren't saints, any more than our politicos back home are. Don't get me wrong about that. But I think most of them have a genuine sense that they're creating something greater than any of them. They know they're going into the history books, one way or the other, and I think most of them would prefer to get good reviews.

"I'm not too happy about what I'm hearing about New Tuscany, though." She grimaced. "Everyone warned me the New Tuscans were going to be a problem, but I'd really have preferred for them to be wrong about that. Unfortunately, I don't think they are. And, to be frank, I can't begin to get my head wrapped around wherever it is these people are coming from. They were the ones who decided to opt out of the Quadrant, but you wouldn't know that to listen to their trade representatives. Just yesterday one of them spent the entire afternoon in Minister Lababibi's office complaining about the fact that New Tuscany isn't going to be getting any of the tax incentives Beth is offering to people who invest in the Quadrant." Michelle shook her head. "Apparently, this guy was ranting and raving about how 'unfair' and 'discriminatory' that is! And if that's the way 'politics' work, Mom, I *still* don't want to get any deeper into them than I have to!

"On another front, though, I really wish you could try the cuisine out here. Thimble is right on the ocean, and the seafood they have here is incredible. They've got what they call 'lobsters,' even if they don't look anything like ours—or like Old Earth's, for that matter—and they broil them, then serve them with sauteed mushrooms and peppers, garnished with lemon juice and garlic butter, over a bed of one of their local grains. Delicious! And if I were only Honor, I could eat all of it I wanted to. Still—"

She broke off as a red light blinked on the corner of her terminal. She looked at it for a couple of heartbeats, then punched another key, and Bill Edwards' face appeared before her.

"Yes, Bill?"

"I'm sorry to disturb you, Ma'am, but there's an urgent priority call."

"From whom?" Michelle asked with a frown.

"It's a conference call, Ma'am—from Admiral Khumalo and Baroness Medusa."

Despite herself, Michelle's eyes widened. It was an hour or two after local midnight in Thimble, and Khumalo's staff coordinated its work schedule with the governor's. So what had both of them up at this hour talking to *her*?

*I don't think I'm going to like the answer to that question*, she thought.

"Have they requested visual?" she asked Edwards, running one hand across her short, still damp hair and wondering how her voice could sound so calm.

"No, Ma'am. In fact, the governor isn't visual herself, and she specifically said it would be satisfactory for you to attend audio-only, as well."

"Good." Michelle twitched a smile. "Chris would kill me if I let anyone see me sitting around in sweats for a conference with another flag officer and an imperial governor. Either that, or give me that terminally reproachful look of his! Go ahead and put it through, please, Bill."

"Yes, Ma'am."

Edwards disappeared, replaced almost instantly by a split screen. One quadrant showed Augustus Khumalo's face while the other displayed the wallpaper of Baroness Medusa's coat of arms. Khumalo was still in uniform, although he'd shed his tunic, and Michelle knew both of them were seeing the shield and crossed arrows of *Artemis'* wallpaper, overlaid with the two stars of her rank, instead of her.

"Good evening, Admiral. Good evening, Governor," she said.

"'Good morning,' you mean, don't you, Milady?" Khumalo responded with a tense smile.

"I suppose I do, actually. Although we're still on Manticoran time aboard ship." Michelle smiled back, then cleared her throat. "I do have to wonder why the two of you are screening me this late in your day, however, Sir."

"Technically, I don't suppose we really had to," Baroness Medusa's voice replied. "In fact, I suppose the reason we didn't wait until tomorrow is at least partly a case of misery loving company."

"That sounds ominous," Michelle said cautiously.

"A dispatch boat came in from the Lynx Terminus about twenty minutes ago, Milady," Khumalo said. "It carried an urgent dispatch. It would appear that three T-weeks ago, Admiral Webster was assassinated on Old Earth."

Michelle inhaled abruptly. For a moment, it felt as if Khumalo had reached out of the terminal and slapped her. The shock was that sharp, that totally unexpected. And, on the heels of the shock, came the grief. The Webster and Henke families were close—her father's sister had married the present Duke of New Texas—and James Bowie Webster had been an unofficial uncle of hers since she was a little girl. He was one of the ones who had actively encouraged her to make the Navy her career, and despite his monumental seniority, their relationship had remained close after her graduation from Saganami Island, although their different duties and assignments had forced them to stay in touch mostly by letter. And now—

She blinked burning eyes and shook her head sharply. She didn't have time to think about the personal aspects of it.

"How did it happen?" she asked flatly.

"That's still under investigation." Khumalo looked like a man with a mouth full of sour persimmons. "What has been definitely established so far, though, is that he was shot at close range on a public sidewalk—in front of the *Opera House*, in fact!—by none other than the personal driver of the Havenite ambassador to the League."

"My God!" Michelle stared at Khumalo's image.

"Indeed," Medusa's voice said. "Gregor and I are still going over the official dispatch and the reports which accompanied it. From what we've seen so far, I have to wonder if this is another application of whatever it was they used to try to kill Duchess Harrington."

"May I ask why, Governor?" Michelle's voice had sharpened with her memory of Tim Meares and his death.

"Because the assassin shot him right in front of half a dozen security cameras, at least two or three policemen, and Admiral Webster's own bodyguard. If that doesn't constitute a suicide attack, then I don't know what would."

"But why would the *Havenites* want to assassinate the admiral?" Michelle heard the plaintiveness in her own voice.

"I don't have a clue why they might have done it," Medusa said.

"Neither do I," Khumalo agreed, and Michelle sat back, thinking furiously.

James Webster had been one of the most popular officers in the Navy, both with his fellow service personnel and with the Manticoran public. An ex-First Space Lord, he'd been instrumental in breaking the criminally stupid, politically inspired policies which had almost gotten Honor Harrington killed on Basilisk Station years ago. And he'd commanded Home Fleet throughout the first Havenite War, as well. For the last couple of T-years, he'd been the Star Kingdom's ambassador to the Solarian League, and from everything Michelle had heard, he'd done that job just as well as he'd done everything else.

"This doesn't make sense," she said finally. "Admiral Webster's an *ambassador* these days, not a serving officer. And Old Earth is about as far away from Haven as someone could get."

"Agreed," Medusa said. "In fact, if I'd had to look for someone to blame this on—without the obvious Havenite connection, at least—*my* first choice would have been Manpower."

"Manpower?" Michelle's eyes narrowed.

"They'd have to be uncommonly stupid—or crazy—to try something like this right in the middle of Chicago," Khumalo objected. "But," he continued, almost unwillingly, "if there's anyone in the galaxy Webster was beating up on, it was Manpower. Well, Manpower, the Jessyk Combine, and Technodyne. He's been giving them hell in the League media over their attempts to spin what happened in Monica, and my impression is that things were only going from bad to worse for them in that regard. I suppose it's at least remotely possible they got tired of having him bust their chops and decided to do something about it. Still stupid, especially in the long run, but possible. And to be fair, God knows Manpower's done other stupid things on occasion—like that raid on Catherine Montaigne's mansion, or that whole operation on Old Earth, when they kidnaped Zilwicki's daughter."

"That's what I'm thinking," the governor agreed. "And you're right that killing him would be a really stupid thing for an outlaw bunch like Manpower to do. Unless, of course, they felt completely confident no one would ever be able to prove they'd had anything to do with it."

"But—" Michelle began, then cut herself off.

"But what, Milady?" Medusa asked.

"But it would be an equally stupid thing for Haven to do," Michelle pointed out. "Especially using their own ambassador's driver! Why would someone who had whatever it is they used to force Lieutenant Meares to try to kill Her Grace use it on their *own ambassador's* driver? What's the point in having a completely deniable assassination technique if you're going to hang a great big holo sign around your neck saying 'We did it!'?"

"That's one of those interesting questions, isn't it?" Medusa replied. "And, frankly, one of the reasons my own suspicion leans towards Manpower. Except, of course, for the fact that the only people who've demonstrated this particular capability are the Havenites."

"Maybe somebody did it just to drive us all crazy thinking and double-thinking the whole thing!" Khumalo rasped.

"No, Augustus. However crazy this looks, whoever did it had a reason," Medusa said. "A reason she thought justified taking all the risks inherent in assassinating an accredited ambassador in the middle of the Solarian League's capital city. From here, I can't imagine what that reason was, but it exists."

"Are there any theories about that 'reason' in the reports from home, Governor?" Michelle asked.

"As a matter of fact, there are," Medusa replied heavily. "Several of them, in fact—most of which are mutually incompatible. Personally, I don't find any of them especially convincing, but at the moment, I'm afraid, suspicion back home is focusing on Haven, not Manpower. And the superficial evidence against Haven *is* very damning. I have to admit that. Especially since, as I say, Haven has already demonstrated the ability to compel someone to carry out suicidal attacks, and that points directly at Nouveau Paris, too."

"And their motive is supposed to be what?"

"That's a matter of some dispute. I don't want to try to read too much between the lines here, not this far away from Landing. Officially, the Star Kingdom's position is that the assassination was arranged by 'parties unknown.' I have no idea how unanimously that position is supported within the Government, however. If I had to guess, based on what I've seen so far and what I know about the personalities involved, I'd guess that whatever the official position, there's a lot of suspicion that it was Haven. As to *why*, beyond the evidence the Solly police have been able to put together so far, I really couldn't say. Especially not on the very eve of the summit *Pritchart* suggested."

"Unless the entire objective was to prevent the summit from happening," Khumalo said slowly.

"I can't see that, Sir," Michelle said quickly. "Pritchart and Theisman both want this summit to go forward. I was there; I saw their faces. I'm sure of that much."

"Even assuming—which I'm perfectly willing to do—that your evaluation of them is accurate, Admiral," Medusa said, "the fact is that what you really know is that they *did* want the summit to go forward *at the time they spoke to you*. It's entirely possible that something we know nothing about has changed their thinking. In fact, derailing the summit is one of those 'theories' you asked about."

"But if that's all they wanted, why not simply withdraw their proposal?"

"Diplomacy is a game of perceptions," the governor replied. "There may be domestic or interstellar political considerations that make them unwilling to be the ones who kill the summit they originally proposed. This may be an effort to push *Manticore* into rejecting the summit. I don't say that makes a lot of sense from our perspective, but, unfortunately, we can't read Pritchart's mind from here, so we can't know what she may or may not have been thinking. Always assuming, of course, that Haven did carry out this assassination."

"Or assuming the *Pritchart Administration* carried it out, at least," Michelle said slowly.

"You think it may have been a rogue operation?" Khumalo said with a frown.

"I think it's possible," Michelle said, still slowly, her eyes slitted in thought. "I know the People's Republic was fond of assassinations." Her jaw tightened as she recalled the murder of her father and her brother. "And I know Pritchart was a resistance fighter who's supposed to have carried out several assassinations personally. But I don't think she would have wanted to do anything to jeopardize her meeting with Elizabeth. Not as seriously as she talked to me when she issued the invitation. Which doesn't mean someone else in the present Havenite government or covert agencies, maybe someone who's nostalgic for 'the good old days' and doesn't want the shooting to stop, couldn't have done this without Pritchart's approval."

"Actually," Medusa said thoughtfully, "that comes closer than anything that's occurred to *me* yet to making sense of any explanation for why Haven might have been behind this."

"Maybe." Khumalo clearly felt that "Because they're Peeps" was sufficient explanation for just about anything Haven might decide to do. Which, Michelle reflected, probably summed up the attitude of a *majority* of Manticorans. After so many years of war, after the forged diplomatic correspondence, after the "sneak attack" of Operation Thunderbolt, there must be very little the average woman-in-the-street would put past the Machiavellian and malevolent Peeps.

"At any rate," Khumalo continued, "it's obvious to me that this is going to have serious implications for our own deployment plans. Trying to figure out what those implications are, however, isn't going to be easy. The one thing I can say is that until this whole thing settles down, Milady, I want your squadron right here in Spindle. There's no telling which way we may have to jump if the wheels come off the Torch summit after all, and I don't want to be forced to send dispatch boats racing off in every direction to get you back here if that happens."

"I understand, Sir."

"Good." Khumalo's nostrils flared as he inhaled deeply, then gave himself a shake. "And on that note, Baroness, with your permission, I think we've probably discussed this as thoroughly as we can at this point. That being the case, suppose you and I see if we can't get at least a few hours of sleep before we have to get up and start worrying about it again?"

# Chapter Seventeen

"HI, HELGA," GERVAIS ARCHER said, and grinned from Helga Boltitz's com. There was more than a little worry in his green eyes, but the grin seemed remarkably genuine. "Got time for lunch?"

"Hello, Gwen. And how are you? Very well, thank you, Helga. And yourself?" Helga replied. "Fine, thank you, Gwen," she continued. "And to what do I owe the pleasure of this call? Well, Helga, I was wondering if you had lunch plans?" She paused, looking at him with one eyebrow raised. "Would it happen, Lieutenant Archer, that any of that sounded remotely familiar?"

"I suppose," he said unrepentantly, still grinning. "But the question still stands."

Helga sighed and shook her head.

"For someone from an effete, over-civilized Star Kingdom, you are sadly lacking in the social graces, Lieutenant," she said severely.

"Well, I understand that's a hallmark of the aristocracy," he informed her, elevating his nose ever so slightly. "We're so well born that those tiresome little rules that apply to everyone else have no relevance for us."

Helga laughed. Even now, she found it surprising that she could find anything about oligarchs—or, even worse, overt aristocrats— even remotely funny, especially with everything else that was going on. But the last ten days had significantly altered her opinion of a least one Manticoran aristocrat.

Gervais Archer had stood her concept of oligarchs on its head. Or perhaps that was being a little too optimistic, at least where oligarchs in general were concerned. It was going to take an awful lot of "show me" to convince Helga Boltitz and the rest of Dresden that all the protestations of selfless patriotism flowing around certain extremely well-off quarters here in Talbott—or, for that matter, back in Manticore—were sincere. Still, if Gervais hadn't inspired her to leap to a sudden awareness that she'd profoundly misjudged people like Paul Van Scheldt all her life, he *had* convinced her that at least some Manticoran aristocrats were nothing at all like Talbott Cluster oligarchs. Of course, she'd already been forced to admit that at least some Talbott Cluster *oligarchs* weren't like Talbott Cluster oligarchs, either, if she was going to be honest about it. Kicking and screaming the entire way, perhaps, but she'd still had to admit it, at least in the privacy of her own thoughts.

*The universe would be such a more comfortable place if only preconceptions could stay firmly in place,* she reflected.

Unfortunately—or perhaps fortunately—that couldn't always happen.

She'd already been forced to accept that people like Prime Minister Alquezar and Bernardus Van Dort were very different from people like that poisonous *Wurmfresser* Van Scheldt. Henri Krietzmann had been right about that. They still didn't really understand what someone like Helga or Krietzmann had experienced, but they did understand that they didn't, and at least they were trying to. And much as she'd wanted to cling to the belief that Van Dort's motivation for the original annexation campaign had been purely self-serving, she'd had no choice but to concede otherwise as she watched him working with Krietzmann and the other members of the newly elected Alquezar Government.

*Not that there aren't still plenty of Rembrandters who are just like Van Scheldt,* she reflected sourly. *And they've got plenty of soulmates in places like right here in Spindle.*

And then there was Lieutenant Gervais Winton Erwin Neville Archer. Despite his disclaimers, he really was a member of the Manticoran aristocracy. She knew he was, because she'd made it her business to look him up in *Clarke's Peerage.* The Archers were a very old Manticoran family, dating clear back to the original landing on Manticore, and Sir Roger Mackley Archer, Gervais' father, was not only ridiculously wealthy (by Dresdener standards, at least) in his own right, but stood fourth in line for the Barony of Eastwood, as well. Gervais was also a distant relative (Helga had found it almost impossible to decipher the complex genealogical charts involved in determining exactly *how* distant, although she suspected that the most applicable adverb was probably "very") of Queen Elizabeth of Manticore. As far as someone from the slums of Schulberg was concerned, that *definitely* qualified him for aristocrat status. And in the universe which had once been so comfortably her own, *he* ought to have been just as well aware of it as she was.

If he was, he concealed the fact remarkably well.

He was younger than she'd first estimated—only about four T-years older than she was—and she wondered sometimes whether or not some of the monumental aplomb he carried around with him was due to the fact that deep down inside he *was* aware of the intrinsic advantages of his birth. Mostly, though, she'd come to the conclusion that it was simply a case of his being exactly who he was. There was remarkably little pretense about him, and his lighthearted mockery of the aristocratic stereotypes appeared to be completely genuine.

*And unlike certain cretins named Van Scheldt, he also works his ass off.*

Her mouth tightened slightly at that thought.

"Should I assume there's an official reason for your question about lunch?" she asked him, and saw his own smile fade.

"I'm afraid so," he acknowledged. "Not—" he added with a resurgence of humor "—that I would ever have been gauche enough to admit any such thing without being forced." The flicker of amusement dimmed once more, and he shrugged. "Unfortunately, I'm afraid that what I really want to do is discuss some scheduling details with you for tomorrow. Since I know you're as busy as I am, and since I doubt very much that you've taken any breaks today, I thought we might do the discussing over a nice lunch at Sigourney's. My treat . . . unless, of course, you feel you can legitimately put it on the Ministry's tab and spare a poor flag lieutenant the grim necessity of justifying his expense vouchers."

"What kind of scheduling details?" she asked, eyes narrowing in thought. "Tomorrow's awfully tight already, Gwen. I don't think there's a lot of flex in the Minister's itinerary."

"That's why I'm afraid it might take us a while to figure out how to squeeze this in." His rueful tone was an acknowledgment that he'd already known how tightly scheduled Krietzmann was.

"And would that also be the reason you're having this discussion with me instead of Mr. Haftner?" she inquired shrewdly.

"Ouch!" He winced, raising both hands dramatically to his chest. "How could you possibly think anything of the sort?"

"Because otherwise, given how busy Mr. Krietzmann is and all the assorted varieties of hell breaking loose, your Captain Lecter would have brought a little extra firepower to bear by discussing this directly with Mr. Haftner instead of having you sneak around his flank. That *is* the way you military types describe this particular maneuver, isn't it? Sneaking around his flank?"

"*Us* military types, is it?" He snorted. "You don't do all that badly for a civilian sort, yourself. And," he shrugged, his expression darker and more serious, "I might as well admit that you've got a point. Captain Lecter doesn't think Mr. Haftner's going to be pleased by an official request to grab an hour or so of the Minister's time."

"An *hour*?" Helga's dismay wasn't in the least feigned.

"I know. I know!" Gervais shook his head. "It's an awful big chunk of time, and just to make it worse, we'd like it to be off the books. Frankly, that's another reason not to go through Haftner's office."

Helga sat back in her chair. Abednego Haftner was Henri Krietzmann's Spindle-born chief of staff at the War Ministry. He was a tall, narrowly built, dark-haired man with a strong nose and an even stronger sense of duty. He was also a workaholic, and in Helga's opinion, an empire-builder. As far as she could tell, it stemmed not from any sort of personal ambition but rather from his near-fanatical focus on efficiency. He was an extraordinarily able administrator in most ways, but he obviously found it difficult to delegate access to Krietzmann, and he wasn't about to let anything derail his own smoothly machined procedures.

In fact, that was his one true, undeniable weakness. He wasn't exactly flexible, and he didn't improvise well, which only reinforced his aversion to people who operated on an ad hoc basis. Under normal circumstances, that was more than offset by his incredible attention to detail, his encyclopedic grasp of everything going on within the Ministry, and his total personal integrity.

Unfortunately, circumstances weren't normal at the moment, and even in the radically changed circumstances following the Webster assassination, he persisted in his efforts to force order upon what he considered chaos.

That lack of flexibility had already brought him and Helga, as Krietzmann's personal aide, into conflict more than once, and she suspected that was going to happen more often for the immediately foreseeable future. It was less than two T-days since news of the Webster assassination had hit Spindle like a hammer, and the entire government—from Baroness Medusa and the Prime Minister on down—was still scrambling to adjust. So was the military, which probably had a little something to do with Gervais' request. Although his apparent desire to keep any meeting with Krietzmann off the War Ministry's official logs also rang more than a few distant alarm bells in the back of her brain.

"Can you at least tell me exactly what you want his time for?" she asked after several seconds.

"I'd really rather discuss that with you over lunch," he replied, his expression and his tone both totally serious. She looked at him for another moment, then sighed again.

"All right, Gwen," she conceded. "You win."


"Thank you for coming," Gervais said as he pulled out Helga's chair for her.

He waited till she was seated, then settled into his own chair on the other side of the small table and raised one finger to attract the attention of the nearest waiter. That worthy deigned to notice their presence and approached their table with stately grace.

"Yes, Lieutenant?" His tone was nicely modulated, with just the right combination of deference to someone from the Old Star Kingdom and the hauteur that was so much a part of Sigourney's stock in trade. "May I show you a menu?"

"Don't bother," Gervais said, glancing at Helga with a twinkling eye. "Just let us have a tossed salad—vinaigrette dressing—and the prime rib—extra rare for me; medium rare for the lady—with mashed potatoes, green beans, sautéed mushrooms, and a couple of draft *Kelsenbraus.*"

The waiter flinched visibly as Gervais cheerfully deep-sixed all of the elegant prose the restaurant had invested in its menus.

"If I might recommend the Cheviot '06," he began out of some spinal reflex effort to salvage something. "It's a very nice Pinot Noir. Or there's the Karakul 1894, a truly respectable Cabernet Sauvignon, if you'd prefer. Or—"

Gervais shook his head firmly.

"The *Kelsenbrau* will be just fine," he said earnestly. "I don't really *like* wine, actually."

The waiter closed his eyes briefly, then drew a deep breath.

"Of course, Lieutenant," he said, and tottered off toward the kitchens.

"You, Lieutenant Archer, are *not* a nice man," Helga told him. "He was so hoping to impress somebody from Manticore with this pile of bricks' sophistication."

"I know." Gervais shook his head with what might have been a touch of actual contrition. "I just couldn't help it. I guess I've spent too much time associating with the local riffraff."

"Oh?" She tilted her head to one side, gazing at him speculatively. "And I don't suppose you had any *particular* members of the 'local riffraff' in mind?"

"Perish the thought." He grinned. "Still, it was somebody from Dresden, I think, who introduced me to the place to start with. She said something about the food being pretty decent despite the monumental egos of the staff."

Helga chuckled and shook her head at him. Not that he was wrong. In fact, he'd picked up very quickly on the fact that she particularly enjoyed watching the oh-so-proper waitstaff's reaction to her buzz saw Dresden accent. Of course, the food *was* really excellent and, despite the waiter's reaction to Gervais' order, Sigourney's was one of the very few high-class restaurants here in Thimble which kept *Kelsenbrau* on tap. The dark, rich beer was a product of her own region of Dresden, and she'd been deeply (if discreetly) pleased by Gervais' enthusiastic response to it.

"Why do I think you chose this particular venue as a bribe?" she asked.

"You'd be at least partly right if you did," he admitted. "But only partly. The truth is, the admiral sent me dirt-side on several errands this morning. I've been a very busy and industrious little flag lieutenant since just after dawn, local time, and I figured I was about due a decent lunch, a nice glass of beer, and some pleasant company to share them with."

"I see."

Helga looked up with a faint sense of relief as a far more junior member of the waitstaff turned up with a pitcher of ice water. She watched the young man pour, murmured a word of thanks, then sipped from her own glass as he withdrew. She took her time before she set it down again and returned her attention to Gervais.

"Well, in that case, why don't we get whatever business we need to attend to out of the way while we wait for the salads?"

"Probably not a bad idea," he agreed, and glanced casually around the dining room.

There'd been another factor in his choice of restaurants, she realized. Although Sigourney's was completely public, it was also extraordinarily discreet. Several of its tables—like, coincidentally, the one at which they happened to be seated at this very moment—sat more than half enclosed in small, private alcoves against the rear wall. What with the lighting, the ambient noise, and the small, efficient, Manticoran-built portable anti-snooping device—disguised as a briefcase, which had kept her from immediately recognizing what it was—Gervais had unobtrusively parked between them and the open side of the alcove, it would be extraordinarily difficult for anyone to eavesdrop upon them.

*And if anyone's watching him, all he's doing is having a flashy lunch with an easily impressed little girl from Dresden,* she thought dryly.

"The thing is," he continued quietly, "that the admiral would like to invite Minister Krietzmann to a modest get together aboard her flagship. Purely a social event, you understand. My impression is that the guest list will include Admiral Khumalo, Gregor O'Shaughnessy, and Special Minister Van Dort. I believe Ms. Moorehead may well be able to attend, as well."

Despite her own previous suspicions, Helga inhaled in surprise. Gregor O'Shaughnessy was Baroness Medusa's senior intelligence officer and, effectively, her chief of staff, as well. And Sybil Moorehead was *Prime Minister Alquezar's* chief of staff. Which suggested all sorts of interesting things.

"A 'social event,'" she repeated very carefully after a moment.

"Yes." Gervais met her gaze levelly. Then his nostrils flared slightly, and he shrugged. "Basically," he continued in a slightly lower voice, "Admiral Gold Peak and Mr. O'Shaughnessy want to share some of the admiral's . . . personal insight into the Queen's probable reactions to what happened to Admiral Webster."

Helga's eyes widened. *Personal insight?* she repeated silently.

Part of her wasn't particularly surprised. Admiral Gold Peak seemed remarkably unaware of her own importance for someone who stood fifth in the royal—and now imperial—succession. It was painfully obvious that quite a few of the true sticklers of Spindalian society, especially here in Thimble, had been sadly disappointed by her low-key efficiency and easy approachability. Her businesslike, no-nonsense attitude towards her responsibilities, coupled with an almost casual, conversational personal style meant that even people from backgrounds like Helga's were remarkably comfortable with her. And the fact that she *was* fifth in the line of succession meant that not even the starchiest oligarch dared take open umbrage at her cheerful disregard for the ironclad rules of proper social behavior . . . or their own vast importance.

Setting up an informal "social event" as a cover for something considerably more important would be entirely like her. That was Helga's first thought. But her second thought was to wonder just what sort of "personal insight" the Queen's first cousin was likely to be offering and why it was necessary to go to such lengths to disguise the fact that she was?

*And O'Shaughnessy's presence, as well as Khumalo's, makes it even more interesting,* she thought. *If both of them are present—not to mention Van Dort and the Prime Minister's chief of staff—then this is going to be some sort of strategy session, as well. . . .*

"Where would this gathering take place? And what time did Lady Gold Peak have in mind?" she asked.

"She was thinking about offering everyone the courtesy of her flagship," Gervais replied. "Around nineteen hundred local, if Mr. Krietzmann could make it."

"That's not much lead time," Helga pointed out with massive understatement.

"I know. But"—Gervais looked directly into her eyes—"the admiral would *really* appreciate it if he could find time to join her."

"I see."

Helga gazed at him for several seconds, then looked up as their salads arrived, accompanied by their *Kelsenbraus*. The server's courteous interruption gave her time to think, and she waited until he'd withdrawn from the alcove. Then she picked up her beer glass, sipped, and set it back down.

"Obviously, I won't be able to make any promises until I've been able to get back to the office and check with the Minister. Having said that, though, I think he'll probably be happy to attend."

In point of fact, "happy" might well be the last thing Henri Krietzmann would be, she reflected. It all depended on exactly what sort of "insight" Lady Gold Peak proposed to share with him.

"Good. You'll screen me one way or the other when you've had a chance to talk to him about it?"

"Of course."

"Thank you," he said, smiling at her with quiet sincerity. "And as a reward for our having been such good little worker bees about organizing this, you and I are invited, as well. I'm sure there'll be enough 'go-for' work to keep us both busy, but we may be able to steal a few moments just to enjoy ourselves, as well."

"Really?" Helga smiled back at him. "I'd like that," she said with a sincerity which surprised her just a bit.

# Chapter Eighteen

"WELL, AT LEAST WORD DIDN'T get here in the middle of the night this time," Cindy Lecter observed sourly.

"That's straining awful hard to find a silver lining, Cindy," Michelle replied, and Lecter produced a wan smile.

"That's because it's awful hard *to* find one this time, Ma'am."

Cindy had that one right, Michelle reflected as she tipped back in her chair, closed her eyes, and squeezed the bridge of her nose wearily while she contemplated the dispatches which had occasioned this meeting. It was amazing how quickly—and drastically—things could change in barely three T-days. The memory of that first dinner party, of how *confidently* she and Admiral Khumalo and Governor Medusa and Prime Minister Alquezar had planned for the future, mocked her now, and she wondered what other surprises lay in store.

*At least there's a little element of "I told you so," isn't there, Michelle? Of course, you didn't see* this *one coming any more than anyone else did, but at least you get brownie points for warning everyone that Beth . . . wasn't likely to react well if anything else went wrong.*

She shook her head, remembering her "little get together" of the night before.

*If I were the superstitious sort, I'd be wondering if I hadn't somehow provoked this,* she reflected. *One of those "If I say it, it will happen" sorts of things. Except, of course, for the minor fact that it all actually happened the better part of a T-month ago.*

James Webster's assassination had been bad enough, but this latest news—the news of the attack on Queen Berry—had been worse, far worse. Just as, if not for the sacrificial gallantry and quick thinking of Berry's bodyguards, the death toll would have been immeasurably worse than it actually had been. Including Michelle's own cousin, Princess Ruth.

*And it has to have been another one of those programmed assassins,* she thought grimly. *It's the only possible answer. That poor son-of a bitch Tyler sure as hell didn't have any reason to try to kill Berry—or Ruth. And I can't think of anything more "suicidal" than using an aerosol neurotoxin in your own briefcase! How in* hell *are they getting these people to* do *this kind of thing? And* why?

Much as she hated to admit it, the attempt to murder Honor had made tactical and strategic sense. Honor was widely considered to be the Manticoran Alliance's best fleet commander, and the forces under her command had done, by any measure, the greatest damage to the Republic of Haven since the resumption of hostilities. For that matter, loathsome as Michelle found the technique of assassination—for, what she admitted, were some highly personal reasons—any military commander had to be considered a legitimate target by the other side. And if the technique the Republic had used had also inevitably led to the death of another young officer and half a dozen other bridge personnel in her vicinity, killing Honor's flagship to get at her would have resulted in thousands of additional deaths, not just a handful. So she supposed there was actually a moral argument *in favor* of assassination, if it allowed you to inflict possibly decisive damage on the other side with a minimum possible number of casualties.

But this—!

She released the bridge of her nose and opened her eyes, gazing up at the flag briefing room's overhead.

The thing that stuck in her mind most strongly, actually, wasn't the fact that Haven had come within an eyelash of murdering yet another member of her family. No, what stuck in her mind was that the Republic of Haven and the Star Kingdom of Manticore had always been the two star nations with the strongest record, outside that of Beowulf itself, for opposing Manpower and genetic slavery. Not only that, but the very existence of the Kingdom of Torch, and the only reason Queen Berry had been placed on its throne in the first place, with Ruth as her junior-spymaster-in-training, was that the Star Kingdom and the Republic had jointly sponsored the effort. In fact, support for Torch was the single foreign policy point they still had in common, the very reason Elizabeth had chosen that planet for the site of Pritchart's summit conference. So what could possibly have inspired the Republic of Haven to do its best to decapitate Torch *now*? It made absolutely no sense.

*Yes, it* does *make sense, girl,* a corner of her brain told her. *There's one way it makes sense, although why they'd want to do that is another question all of its own.*

The news of the deaths on Torch—and despite everything, there'd been almost three hundred dead—had reached Manticore barely two T-days after news of Webster's assassination. Which, allowing for the transit time, meant they'd happened on the same T-day. Somehow, she didn't think the fact that the attacks had been synchronized that tightly had been an accident, either, which did give significant point to the theory Elizabeth had embraced. Both attacks had been carried out using the same technique—the same still *unknown* technique—which, combined with their timing, certainly indicated that the same people had planned and executed them both. So far as Michelle could see, there were only two candidates when it came to propounding motives for the attackers.

As Baroness Medusa had pointed out in Webster's case, if it hadn't been for the similarity between the technique used against Honor and the technique used against him, Manpower would probably have been the first suspect on everyone's list, however stupid it might have been of them to carry out such an attack right in the middle of Chicago. And the same logic went double, or even triple, where an attack on Torch was concerned. No one else in the entire galaxy could have had a more logical motive to attempt to destabilize Torch. But Manpower, and to a lesser extent the other outlaw corporations based on Mesa and allied with Manpower, obviously had all the motives there were. The notion of an independent star system inhabited almost exclusively by ex-genetic slaves, its government heavily influenced (if not outright dominated) by the "reformed" terrorists of the anti-slavery Audubon Ballroom, could not be reassuring to Manpower or any corporate crony bedfellow. Add in the fact that the planet of Torch itself had been taken away from Manpower by force (and that several hundred of its more senior on-planet employees had been massacred, most of them in particularly hideous fashion, in the process), and Manpower's reasons for attempting to kill Berry—and Ruth, and anyone else on the planet they could get to—became screamingly obvious.

So one possible explanation was to assign both attacks to Manpower. Except, of course, for the unfortunate fact that the only people who had previously employed the same technique were *Havenites*. Whatever Pritchart might have said, no one else had any motive for that attack. Certainly Manpower hadn't had any reason to go after Honor at that time. For that matter, as far as Michelle could see, Manpower probably would have had every reason *not* to assassinate her. Manpower was at least as unfond of Manticore and Haven—separately and together—as they were of it, and the notion of eliminating someone who was doing that much damage to Haven could scarcely have appealed to Manpower's board of directors.

Which led, little though Michelle wanted to admit it, to Elizabeth's theory.

*Be fair*, she told herself. *It isn't just Beth's theory, and you know it. Yes, her temper's engaged, but Willie Alexander and a lot of other high-paid, high-powered types at the Foreign Ministry and in the intelligence services agree with her.*

What was scariest about that particular analysis, in Michelle's opinion, was the possibility that the Republic might actually have had an at least plausible motive for killing off their own conference. Given the dispute over how the current war had started, Pritchart and her advisers would scarcely be likely to reinitiate operations in a way that openly sabotaged a peace conference she'd initiated. So if some inkling of the Star Kingdom's accelerated building programs or—far worse—some hint of Apollo's existence had somehow leaked to Nouveau Paris only after Pritchart had suggested her meeting with Elizabeth, and if Pritchart and Theisman had concluded that the newly discovered threat left them no option but to seek a decisive military victory before those ships or those new weapons could be added to the balance against them, then it was entirely possible that they would have been delighted if they could get *Beth* to kill the conference for them.

And if that was what lay behind this operation, whoever had planned it had shown a devastating grasp of Beth's psychology. The timing, and the technique, could not possibly have been better selected to drive Elizabeth Winton into an incandescent fury.

Given the fact that the previous Havenite régime had already attempted to assassinate her and had succeeded in killing her uncle and cousin—who'd just happened to be Michelle's father and brother—and her beloved prime minister, expecting any other result would have been ludicrous. Not only that, but that assassination attempt had been planned and executed by Oscar Saint-Just for the express purpose of furthering a political strategy when he had no viable *military* strategy. So the theory that Pritchart—*or some rogue element in her security services*, Michelle reminded herself almost desperately—had deliberately chosen to use a variant on the same theme as a means to sabotage the summit meeting for some reason of their own was nowhere near as insane as Michelle would have preferred for it to be. In fact, she couldn't think of a single other hypothesis for why someone would have carried out those two particular assassinations in that particular fashion on the same damned day.

*And Beth and her advisers are also right about who knew about the summit,* she thought bleakly. *If someone was actually out to sabotage it, they had to* know *about it in the first place, and who could possibly have found out in time to put something like this together? Word would still have had to get to them somehow, and they would've had to get their assassination orders out in time, and Manpower is too far away for that. You simply can't get dispatch boats back and forth between Mesa and Torch—or Nouveau Paris, for that matter!—quickly enough for them to have found out what was happening, formulated a plan to stop it, and sent out the execution orders. Even if they're using the Junction and Trevor's Star under cover of some legitimate corporation or news organization or diplomatic boat, they're just plain too far outside the command and control loop to physically pass the needed orders. For that matter, everyone* is *outside the command and control loop . . . except, of course, for one of the two star nations setting the damned thing up in the first place! And even if you assume someone else did find out about it, and had time to set it up, what possible motive could that "someone else" have had for sabotaging a summit meeting like this one?*

Well, if that was what the mastermind behind the operation had wanted, he'd gotten it. The same dispatch boat which had brought news of the attack on Torch had brought with it a copy of Elizabeth's white-hot denunciatory note to Eloise Pritchart.

The note which had informed Pritchart that the Star Kingdom of Manticore would be resuming military operations immediately. And as a part of the shift in deployment stances that implied, Vice Admiral Blaine and Vice Admiral O'Malley had been ordered to concentrate all of their Home Fleet forces at the Lynx Terminus as quickly as possible.

Which was what had so thoroughly destabilized the preliminary plans she, Khumalo, Medusa, and Krietzmann had been working out.

At least they'd been in a position last night to discuss a few contingencies—like the Star Kingdom's potential withdrawal from the peace conference—without drawing official attention to them. Which meant that, little as any of them had cared for the possibility, she actually knew how the government and Vice Admiral Khumalo were likely to respond now.

"All right."

She let her chair come back upright, then swiveled it to face Lecter, Commodore Shulamit Onasis, and Captain Jerome Conner, the senior officer of BatCruDiv 106.1, the 106th's first division. Gervais Archer sat quietly to one side, taking notes, as always, and Onasis had brought her own chief of staff, Lieutenant Commander Dabney McIver, who was just as much a Gryphon highlander as Ron Larson, while Conner was accompanied by his executive officer, Commander Frazier Houseman.

Houseman had come as a considerable surprise to Michelle, and she looked forward to the first time he came face-to-face with Rear Admiral Oversteegen. Or, for that matter, with Honor! Houseman was a first cousin of *Reginald* Houseman, who was probably the single Manticoran political figure who most loathed Honor Harrington . . . and vice versa, since Pavel Young was dead. Of course, the competition for which politico most hated her would undoubtedly have been fierce, but Houseman had the unique distinction of being the only surviving member of the Manticoran political establishment who had been—literally—knocked on his wealthy, cowardly ass by Honor.

And of being loathed by the Navy in general almost as much as he was loathed by Honor.

His career and his influence alike had taken a powerful nosedive after that embarrassing little incident at Yeltsin's Star, although there were still members of his Liberal Party (such of it as survived, after its disastrous alliance with the Conservative Association in the High Ridge government) who continued to support him as a victim of "the Salamander's" notoriously brutal and vicious temperament. They were, however, noticeably thinner on the ground than they once had been. Perhaps that owed something to the fact that Houseman had accepted the position of Second Lord of Admiralty in the Janacek Admiralty. At the time, it had probably seemed like a good idea, since it had restored him to the first ranks of political power in the Star Kingdom and finally allowed him to do something about the "bloated and ridiculously over expensive" state of the Navy which he had decried for decades.

Unfortunately, it also meant he had been personally and directly responsible for planning and carrying out the Navy's deliberate build-down. Unlike Janacek, who had committed suicide when the enormity of his failure became obvious at the opening of the current war, Houseman had opted for the less drastic option of resigning his office in disgrace. And despite the investigation which had led directly to formal charges of corruption, malfeasance, bribery, and half a dozen other criminal activities on the part of Baron High Ridge, a dozen of his personal aides, eleven senior members of the Conservative Association in the House of Lords (including the current Earl of North Hollow), two Liberal Party peers, three *unaligned* peers, seventeen members of the Progressive Party's representation in the House of Commons, and over two dozen prominent members of the Manticoran business community, it appeared Houseman had at least not been guilty of any outright violations of the law.

Because of that, he had been able to retire into the safer, if far less prestigious (or remunerative), fields of academia. His sister, Jacqueline, had never been formally associated with the High Ridge Government, although her longtime position as one of Countess New Kiev's unofficial financial advisers had still managed to bring her into the outer radius of fallout when that government collapsed. Fortunately for New Kiev (and Jacqueline), New Kiev had probably been the only member of High Ridge's cabinet and inner circle who hadn't been personally party to any of his criminal activities.

Michelle found it difficult to believe the countess hadn't known *anything* about what was going on, however. Nor was she the only one. That very point had been raised quite broadly in the

Star Kingdom's newsfaxes, and it had undoubtedly contributed to her disintegrating Liberal Party's decision to "regretfully accept her resignation" as its leader with indecent haste. Whether she'd actually known or not, she damned well *ought* to have known, in Michelle's opinion, but it truly did appear that her main offense (legally speaking, at least) had been terminal political stupidity. And it *had* been terminal. Her retirement as the Liberal Party's official leader had been followed by her virtual retirement from the House of Lords, as well, and it seemed obvious her political career was over. For that matter, despite the speed with which it had dumped her and sought to disassociate itself from the High Ridge "excesses," New Kiev's Liberal Party, which had been dominated by its aristocratic wing from its very inception, was also deceased for all intents and purposes. The *new* Liberal Party which had emerged under the leadership of the Honorable Catherine Montaigne, the ex-Countess of the Tor, was a very different—and much brawnier and less couth—creature than anything with which New Kiev had ever been associated, and the majority of its strength came from Montaigne's bloc in the House of Commons.

Personally, Michelle far preferred Montaigne's "Liberals" to New Kiev's "Liberals," and she always had.

But Jacqueline Houseman's associations had all been with the aristocratic old guard, and the fall of that old guard had pretty much cut off her access to the Manticoran political establishment, as well. Which hadn't exactly broken Michelle Henke's heart.

But then there was *Frazier* Houseman, the only son of Reginald and Jacqueline's Uncle Jasper. Frazier, unfortunately, looked as much like Reginald Houseman as Michael Oversteegen looked like a younger edition of his uncle . . . Michael Janvier, also known as the Baron of High Ridge. The fact that Michael despised the uncle for whom he had been named and thought most of the Conservative Association's political leaders between them hadn't had the intelligence of a rutabaga, didn't mean he didn't share his family's conservative and aristocratic view of the universe. He was considerably *smarter* than most of the Conservative Association, and (in Michelle's opinion) possessed of vastly more integrity, not to mention a powerful sense of *noblesse oblige*, but that didn't precisely make him the champion of egalitarianism. And the fact that Frazier despised his cousin and had been known, upon occasion, to remark that if Reginald and Jacqueline's brains had been fissionable material, both of them in combination probably wouldn't have sufficed to blow a gnat's nose, didn't mean that *he* didn't share his family's *liberal* and aristocratic view of the universe. Which would undoubtedly make the two of them the proverbial oil and water in any political discussion.

Fortunately—and this was the cause of Michelle's surprise— Frazier Houseman gave every appearance of being just as capable as an officer in Her Majesty's Navy as Michael Oversteegen was. Whether or not their mutual competence could overcome the inevitable political antipathy between them was another question, of course.

*You have better things to do than think about Houseman's pedigree,* she scolded herself. *Besides, given the number of absolute idiots who have somehow ripened on* your *family tree over the centuries, you might want to be a little cautious about throwing first stones, even if you only do it inside your own head.*

"I don't think our initial deployment plan is going to work anymore, Shulamit," she said out loud.

"I wish I could disagree with you, Ma'am," Onassis replied sourly. The commodore was a short, not particularly heavy but opulently curved brunette with what would probably have been called a "Mediterranean complexion" back on Old Terra. She was also quite attractive, despite her present thoughtful and unhappy scowl.

"At the same time, though, Admiral," Conner pointed out, "Admiral O'Malley's recall gives even more point to the necessity of getting someone out in the region of Monica to replace him ASAP."

"Agreed, Jerome. Agreed," Michelle said, nodding. "In fact, I think you and I are going to have to expedite the First Division's departure. I'm thinking now that we need to pay a 'courtesy visit' to Monica as quickly as possible, and then establish ourselves—or at least a couple of our ships—permanently at Tillerman. Where the main change is going to be necessary is in our original plans for Shulamit."

She swivelled her eyes back to Onassis.

"Instead of splitting your division up and sending it out to touch base with the various systems here in the Quadrant, I think we're going to need to keep you right here at Spindle, concentrated."

"I won't be accomplishing very much parked here in orbit, Ma'am," Onassis pointed out.

"Maybe not. But whether you're *actively* accomplishing anything or not, you'll be doing something which has just become critical—keeping a powerful, concentrated force right here under Admiral Khumalo's hand. I need to be out there at Monica, just in case. At the same time, though, Admiral Khumalo needs a powerful naval element he can use as a fire brigade if something goes wrong while I'm away. And you, for your sins, are the squadron's second-ranking officer. That means you draw the short straw. Clear?"

"Clear, Ma'am." Onassis smiled briefly and sourly. "I said I wished I could disagree with you, and I do. Wish that, I mean. Unfortunately, I can't."

"I know you'd rather be doing something . . . more active," Michelle said sympathetically. "Unfortunately, they also serve who wait in orbit, and that's what you're going to have to do right now. Hopefully, once Rear Admiral Oversteegen comes forward, I can shuffle this off onto him. After all," she smiled a bit nastily, "he'll be *Tenth Fleet*'s second-ranking officer. Which will just happen to make him ideal for leaving here in a central position whenever I can find a good reason *I* have to be somewhere else, won't it?"

Onassis grinned, and Captain Lecter smothered a chuckle. But then Michelle's expression sobered.

"I'd really prefer not to have any additional surprises from back home while I'm away, Shulamit. That doesn't necessarily mean it isn't going to happen. If it does, I expect you to give Admiral Khumalo and Baroness Medusa the full benefit of your own views and insights. Is that understood, as well?"

"Yes, Ma'am." Onassis nodded, and Michelle carefully did not nod back. That was about as close as she could come to telling Onassis that, despite her growing respect for Augustus Khumalo, she continued to cherish a few doubts where his purely military insight was concerned. She more than half-expected those doubts to die a natural death in the not too distant future, but until they did, it was one of her responsibilities to be sure he had the very best advice she could provide for him, whether she did the providing in person or by proxy.

"Very well," she said, checking the time display. "It's about time for lunch. I've asked Vicki and the other skippers and their XOs to join us, and I intend to make it a working meal. I also intend to tell all of them how pleased I am with the readiness state we've managed to attain. We still have a ways to go, but we're in far better shape than we were, and I expect that improvement to continue. And I am well aware that I owe everyone in this compartment a matching vote of thanks for that happy state of affairs. So, all of you, consider yourselves patted on the back."

Her subordinates smiled at her, and she smiled back, then braced both hands flat on the tabletop as she pushed herself to her feet.

"And on that note, I think I hear a Cobb salad calling my name. And since I do, it would only be courteous if I went and let it find me."

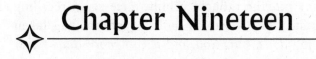

# Chapter Nineteen

AIVARS ALEKSOVITCH TEREKHOV swung out of his pinnace's personnel tube and into the boat bay of HMS *Black Rose* through the wailing twitter of the bosun's pipes. He released the grab bar, landed neatly outside the deck line, and saluted the boat bay officer of the deck as the bay sound system announced, "*Hexapuma*, arriving!"

"Permission to come aboard, Ma'am?" he said to the BBOD.

"Permission granted, Sir," the lieutenant replied, and Captain Vincenzo Terwilliger, *Black Rose*'s commanding officer, was waiting to clasp Terekhov's hand in greeting.

"Welcome aboard, Aivars."

"Thank you, Sir," Terekhov told his old friend, then reached out to take the hand of a short, slender man in the uniform of a Manticoran vice admiral.

"Captain Terekhov," Vice Admiral O'Malley said quietly.

"Admiral."

Terekhov released O'Malley's hand and looked around the battlecruiser's boat bay. He'd always thought "*Black Rose*" was an unusually poetic name for a Manticoran battlecruiser, but he'd always rather liked it, too. And the reason O'Malley's flagship wore that name was that it—like the name of Terekhov's own heavy cruiser—was listed on the RMN's List of Honor, one of the names to be kept permanently in commission. Perhaps that was one reason he'd decided to come aboard and take his leave of

O'Malley and Terwilliger face-to-face rather than simply bidding them—and the System of Monica—farewell over the com.

His mind ran back over the three months it had taken first Khumalo's repair ships and then the repair ships in O'Malley's support squadron, after the vice admiral had arrived and Khumalo had been able to head back to Spindle, to repair *Hexapuma* and *Warlock* at least well enough for them to make the voyage home to Manticore under their own power. Altogether, he'd been in Monica for four T-months, and it seemed like a lifetime.

*Actually, it* was *a lifetime for too many other people. Or the* end *of a lifetime, at any rate*, he thought grimly, once again recalling the horrendous casualties his scratch built "squadron" had taken here. *We got the job done, but, God, did it cost more than I ever dreamed it might! Even after Hyacinth.*

"So you're finally ready, Captain," O'Malley observed, pulling his brain back to the present, and he nodded.

"Yes, Sir."

"I imagine you'll be glad to get home."

"Yes, Sir," Terekhov repeated. "Very glad. *Ericsson* and the other repair ships have done a remarkable job, but she really needs a full-scale shipyard."

Which, he reflected, was nothing less than the truth. And at least, unlike the older and even more heavily damaged *Warlock*, *Hexapuma* would be getting that shipyard's services. He didn't like to think about how long it was going to take to return her to active service even with them, but at least she'd *be* returning. *Warlock*, on the other hand, almost certainly would not. It wasn't official yet—it wouldn't be until she'd been surveyed back home at one of the space stations—and she deserved far better after all she'd done and given here, but she was simply too old, too small and outmoded, to be worth the cost of repair.

"Well, Captain," the vice admiral said, holding out his hand once more, "I'm sure the yard will put her back to rights quickly. We need her—and you—back in service. Godspeed, Captain."

"Thank you, Sir."

Terekhov shook his hand, then stepped back and saluted. The pipes wailed once more, the side party came back to attention, and he swung back into the personnel tube.

He swam the tube quickly, nodded to the flight engineer, and settled into his seat as the umbilicals disengaged and the pinnace began backing out of the docking arms under nose thrusters. His mind ran back through his brief visit to the flagship, and he wondered again why he'd made that visit in person. He doubted that he'd ever really be able to answer that question, although his present sense of satisfaction—of closure—told him it had been the *right* decision.

He frowned thoughtfully, gazing out the viewport as the pinnace cleared the threat perimeter of its impeller wedge from *Black Rose* and accelerated rapidly towards the waiting *Hexapuma*. The two ships lay very close together in their parking orbits, separated by barely three times the width of the larger vessel's wedge. That was still too far apart for their relative size to be registered by the unassisted human eye, but Terekhov felt a familiar surge of pride as *Hexapuma* swelled steadily as the pinnace approached her. His ship might be "only" a heavy cruiser, but she was a *Saganami-C*-class. At 483,000 tons, she was almost half *Black Rose*'s size. Admittedly, she was far smaller compared to the RMN's more recent battlecruisers, but she was still a force to be reckoned with . . . as she'd demonstrated rather conclusively four months ago here in Monica.

Now, as he'd told O'Malley, it was time to take her home once more.

"Captain on the Bridge!" the quartermaster of the watch announced as Terekhov stepped onto *Hexapuma*'s command deck.

"As you were," Terekhov said as the bridge watch started to come to its collective feet, and made a note to have a word with the quartermaster in question. Or, better yet, to have the XO have that word with her, which would probably feel less threatening to her. After all, Petty Officer 1/c Cheryl Clifford was young for her rate, one of the people who'd been promoted in the wake of *Hexapuma*'s casualties. This was her first watch as bridge quartermaster, and it wouldn't do to step on her too hard . . . especially when her announcement was perfectly correct, according to The Book. It was not, however, Terekhov's preferred procedure. Like many of the younger captains in Manticoran service, he was normally less concerned about formalities on the bridge than he was about efficiency.

Ansten FitzGerald, however, continued to rise. He'd been sitting in the command chair at the center of the bridge, and Terekhov stepped across to him quickly.

It took a conscious effort on Terekhov's part not to reach out an assisting hand. Naomi Kaplan had been evacuated to Manticore aboard the high-speed medical transport which had departed along with Augustus Khumalo the day after O'Malley's arrival. Which, ironically, meant the tactical officer was almost certain to be returned to duty sooner than Fitzgerald. Although his wounds had been less serious, the medical technology available at Bassingford Medical Center, the huge (and, unfortunately, growing of late) hospital complex the Royal Manticoran Navy maintained just outside the City of Landing, was going to put Kaplan back on her feet much more quickly. "Less serious" than her massive skull trauma, however, didn't turn FitzGerald's injuries into "just a scratch," and the medical officers had . . . strongly suggested that he accompany her. But, as Terekhov had told Ginger Lewis, Ansten was a stubborn man. He'd been determined to return to Manticore with his ship, and Terekhov hadn't been able to bring himself to overrule his exec.

Acting Ensign Aikawa Kagiyama, currently standing his watch at Lieutenant Commander Nagchaudhuri's elbow as *Hexapuma*'s assistant communications officer, watched FitzGerald out of the corner of his eye. He had a distinct tendency to hover with what he obviously thought was unobtrusive worry where FitzGerald was concerned. It was rather touching, actually, Terekhov thought, although from the gleam in FitzGerald's eye, the XO found it at least equally amusing, as well.

"I have the ship, Mr. FitzGerald," Terekhov said formally, stepping past FitzGerald and seating himself in the command chair.

"You have the ship, Sir," FitzGerald acknowledged, and straightened his spine just a bit cautiously as he clasped his hands behind him.

"Anything from *Black Rose*, Communications?"

"Yes, Sir," Nagchaudhuri replied. "Vice Admiral O'Malley wishes us a quick—and uneventful—voyage."

"Well, that's certainly something I think we could all appreciate," Terekhov said dryly, and glanced across at Lieutenant Commander Tobias Wright, *Hexapuma*'s astrogator.

"May I assume, Toby, that with your customary efficiency you have already computed our course?"

"Unfortunately, Sir, in this case I haven't," Wright replied with a sorrowful expression. The astrogator was the youngest of Terekhov's senior officers, and normally the most reserved. It turned out that he'd always had a lively sense of humor behind that reserved façade, however, and it had bubbled to the surface after the Battle of Monica. Which probably said something interesting about his basic personality, Terekhov reflected.

"I'm afraid," Wright continued, "that this time we're all dependent on Enign Zilwicki's astrogation."

"Oh dear," Terekhov said. He looked at the sturdily built young woman sitting beside Wright and shook his head with a doubtful air. "Dare I hope, Ms. Zilwicki, that *this* time you've done your sums correctly?"

"I've certainly tried to, Sir," Helen replied earnestly.

"Then I suppose that will have to do."

Several people chuckled. Astrogation wasn't precisely Helen's favorite occupation, and everyone knew it. By now, in fact, Terekhov reflected, there was very little about anyone in *Hexapuma*'s company which "everyone" didn't know. Despite her impressive tonnage and firepower, the cruiser's total complement was little larger than a prewar destroyer's, and her ship's company had been through a lot together. They were all keel-plate owners, as well, and he knew that, like him, all of them already understood perfectly well that there would never be another ship like *Hexapuma*. Not for them, not ever.

His own awareness of that fact seemed to flow outward, settling across the entire bridge crew. Not oppressively, but almost . . . comfortingly. His subordinates' smiles didn't disappear; instead, they faded gradually into more serious expressions, as if their owners were soberly reflecting upon all they and their ship had endured and accomplished. Something very like love washed through Aivars Terekhov, and his nostrils flared as he inhaled deeply.

"All right, then, Astro," he said. "Let's go home."

"So what do you make of the Manties's latest little trick?" Albrecht Detweiler asked sourly.

He, Benjamin, and Daniel reclined on chaise lounges under the baking sun while turquoise waves and creamy surf piled on the eye-wateringly white beach, and despite the restfulness of their surroundings, his expression was as sour as his tone.

"You know, Father," Benjamin replied a bit obliquely with a slight smile, "you're a hard man to please, sometimes. We've got the Manties and the Havenites shooting at each other again. Wasn't that what you wanted?"

"I may be a hard man to please sometimes," Albrecht retorted, "but you're a disrespectful young whelp, sometimes, aren't you?"

"Isn't that one of my functions?" Benjamin's smile grew a bit broader. "You know, the lowly slave riding in the back of the chariot reminding Caesar he's only mortal while the crowd cheers."

"I wonder how many of those slaves actually survived the experience?" Albrecht wondered aloud.

"Odd how the history chips don't offer much information on that particular aspect of things," Benjamin agreed. Then his smile faded. "Seriously, though, Father, at this distance and this remove from Lovat it's hard to form any significant or meaningful opinion of what they've done this time."

Albrecht grunted in semi-irate acknowledgment of Benjamin's point. Even with streak-drive dispatch boats, there was a limit to how quickly information could get around. And to be honest, they were overusing the Beowulf conduit, as far as he was concerned. He knew there was nothing to distinguish a streak-drive equipped vessel from any other dispatch boat as far as any external exami-nation was concerned, but he didn't like sending them back and forth between Mesa and Manticore any more frequently than he had to. Beowulf had closed its terminus of the Manticore Wormhole Junction to all Mesan traffic from the day of its discovery, with Manticore's complete support and approval. None of the dispatch boats of the Beowulf conduit were Mesan-registered, of course, but there was always the unhappy possibility that Beowulfan or Manticoran intelligence might manage to penetrate that particu-lar deception. It was unlikely in the extreme, but the Alignment had developed a wary respect for both Beowulf's and Manticore's analysts over the decades.

*But there's not really any choice,* he told himself. *It's only sixty light-years from Beowulf to Mesa via the Visigoth Wormhole. That's only five days for a streak boat. We can't possibly justify not using that advantage at a time like this, so I guess I'll just have to hope the wheels don't come off.*

If he'd been the sort of man who believed in God, Albrecht Detweiler would have spent a few moments in fervent prayer that the wheels in question would remain firmly attached to the vehicle. Since he wasn't that sort of man, he only shook his head.

"One thing we do know is that Harrington just shot the shit out of another Havenite ambush attempt, though," he pointed out.

"Yes, we do," Benjamin agreed. "But we don't have any hard and fast numbers on the two sides' force levels, either. We *think* she was significantly outnumbered, but it's not exactly like the Manties' press releases are going to give out detailed strength reports on Eighth Fleet, now is it? And despite Collin's and Bardasano's best efforts, we still haven't been able to get anyone far enough inside the Manties' navy to give us that kind of information."

"That's all true enough, Ben," Daniel said. "On the other hand, there are a few straws in the wind. For example, it sounds like they've managed to improve the accuracy of their MDMs by a hell of a lot. And I'm inclined to think—mind you, I haven't had a chance yet for any sort of rigorous analysis of what information we do have—that the Havenites' missile defenses' effectiveness must've been reduced rather significantly, as well. Unless Harrington was reinforced a lot more powerfully than any of our admittedly limited sources have suggested, then the Manties' announced kills represent an awfully high ratio for the number of hulls they could have committed to the operation."

"I'd have to agree with that," Benjamin conceded. "Do you or your people have any idea about just how they might have accomplished that, though?"

Just as Everett Detweiler was the ultimate director of all of the Alignment's biosciences research and development, Daniel was the director of *non-bioscience* R&D, which meant he and Benjamin normally worked very closely together.

"I can only speculate," Daniel replied, looking at his brother, and Benjamin nodded in acknowledgment of the caveat. "Having said that, however," Daniel continued, "I'd have to say this sounds an awful lot like it's another example of their damned FTL capability."

He grimaced sourly. He felt fairly confident that his research people had finally figured out essentially what Manticore was doing, but duplicating the ability to create grav-pulses along the hyper-space alpha wall in anything but the crudest possible fashion wasn't a particularly simple proposition. It was going to take a lot of basic research to figure out how they were doing it, and even longer to duplicate their hardware, given that the Alignment, unlike the Republic of Haven, hadn't been able to lay its hands on any working examples of the technology.

*And even the frigging Havenites can't begin to do it as well as the Manties can . . . yet, at least,* he reminded himself once again.

"If I'm right about what they're doing, it's the next logical extension of what they've already accomplished, in a lot of ways," he said out loud. "We know they've got FTL-capable reconnaissance drones, so theoretically there isn't any reason they couldn't eventually cram the same capability into something the size of an MDM."

"Come on, Daniel!" Benjamin protested. "There's a hell of a size difference between a reconnaissance drone and even one of their big-assed missiles! And most missiles I know anything about are already crammed just about as full as they can be with other absolutely essential bits. Where would they put the damned thing?"

"I did say it was *theoretically* possible," Daniel pointed out mildly. "*We* couldn't do it, I'm pretty sure, even if we were certain how they were managing it in the first place. Not yet. But that's the significant point here, Ben—*not yet.* They've been using this thing for over twenty T-years, and they thought it up, in the first place. That means they know how to do it better than anyone else does, and it's obvious from the hardware they've deployed that they've been progressively downsizing the volume and mass constraints—and upsizing bandwidth—steadily. If I had to guess, I'd say that what they've probably done is to somehow squeeze an FTL receiver into a standard MDM. If they were to deploy one of their drones close enough to the target—and we know their stealth systems are probably as good as our own, if not better—then they'd have an effective FTL command and control loop. That would probably help to explain not only the increased accuracy, but also the apparent decrease in the effectiveness of the Havenites' defenses, as well. It would let the Manties manage their attack profiles and penetration EW on something a lot closer to a real-time basis than anyone has been able to manage since they started pushing missile ranges up in the first place."

"Does that sound reasonable to you, Ben?" Albrecht asked after a long, thoughtful moment, and Benjamin nodded. It was evident from his expression that he didn't much care for his brother's hypothesis, but he nodded.

"If Dan is right, though, then this constitutes a major—*another* major—shift in the balance of military capabilities, Father," he said. "Unless my staff's analysis of the two sides' overall relative ship strengths is way off, I don't think there's any way Haven is going to have enough of a numerical advantage to take Manticore out. Not if the Manties are able to get this thing into general deployment, at any rate. And once they *do* have it into general deployment, and their new construction programs start delivering, they're going to make what White Haven did to the Havenites in the last war look like a squabble at a kids' picnic."

"And even if Haven somehow manages to survive, it's only going to mean *both* of them are going to develop this capability—or at least its rough equivalent," Albrecht observed sourly.

"I'd say that follows logically, Father," Daniel agreed. "Haven comes closest to matching the Manties' capabilities already. Their education system sucks, but they're fixing that. In fact, let's be fair, the main thing that was wrong with it to begin with wasn't that they didn't have at least a core cadre of competent teachers and scientists. It was that the Legislaturalists had managed to hobble the general system with so much political indoctrination and water it down with so much 'feel-good' insistence on passing students regardless of their actual academic achievements, that the ratio of competent researchers to useless drones was so far lower than Manticore's. Research priorities tended to be assigned on the basis of who the researchers' patrons were, rather than any impartial analysis of potential benefits, too. And the fact that they'd made so little investment in basic infrastructure improvement meant even the competent researchers they had didn't have the resources or the sophisticated industrial platform Manticore had, either, regardless of who their patrons might've been. But they always had a bigger talent pool than most people would have thought looking at what they managed to accomplish, and whoever's running their R and D now is obviously making the best possible use of the pool they have.

"Not only that, but they're the only ones who really have access to firsthand sensor readouts and observational data, not to mention captured hardware to examine. And let's not forget the old saying about the man about to be hanged. They have a considerably more pressing motivation to figure out what the Manties are up to, or at least how to *counter* whatever they're up to, even than we do. So either they're going to figure out how to do this—or something like it—on their own, or else they're going to get plowed under, like Ben says. And if Manticore doesn't completely disarm them, then they're going to do exactly what they did after the last war and go away and think about it until they have figured out how to do it. We'd probably have at least a few more years before they managed that, under that scenario, but that would be about it."

"Don't you think the Manties *would* insist on their complete disarmament this time, given what happened last time?" Albrecht asked.

"I think I would, in their place," Benjamin said before Daniel could answer. "On the other hand, let's say they do make that demand. Do you really think even Manticore could ultimately keep Haven from managing a secret rearmament program somewhere? I'm not talking about the short term. But as time passed, I'm sure someone who's already figured out how to build a completely secret shipyard complex and R and D center once could figure out how to do it again. It would still be the best-case scenario from our perspective, though, since I don't think it's very likely Haven could manage to pull it off before we were ready. And I imagine Manticore would probably accept at least a modest build-down in its own active wallers once it had disarmed Haven."

"Against which, they'd have the countervailing pressure to maintain fleet strength if this expansion of theirs into Talbott and Silesia prospers," Albrecht observed.

"Probably." Benjamin shrugged. "The problem is that all we can do at this point is speculate, and we don't have enough information—or enough penetration, especially of the Manties, to *get* enough information—to base any sort of solid projections on."

"Assume Daniel's hypothesis is accurate," Albrecht said. "On that basis, does this represent a significant threat to Oyster Bay?"

"No," Benjamin said promptly. "It's not range or fire control that could hurt us where Oyster Bay itself is concerned, Father, and there's absolutely no evidence that anyone else anywhere, even the Manties, has remotely considered the possibility of the spider. If they don't know about it, then the odds of their ever even seeing Oyster Bay are virtually nil. If they do find out about the spider, though, and if they have time to develop some sort of countermeasure, then this could be a *major* problem for us in any period of sustained warfare."

"So our real best-case scenario would be to see the Manties finished off before they get it into general deployment," Albrecht mused.

"Yes, it would," Benjamin agreed, looking at him a bit warily.

"Could you expedite Oyster Bay?"

"Not significantly, Father." Benjamin shook his head with the expression of a man who'd heard pretty much what he'd been afraid he was going to hear. "The spider is an entirely new technology. Daniel and I *think* we've gotten all of the bugs out of it, but like I told you before, we're still prototyping. Technically, I suppose, the *Sharks* are warships, but their primary function's always been to serve as testbeds and training vessels, not strike units. I don't see any way we could produce enough of the new hardware to carry out Oyster Bay much sooner than we've already been projecting."

"I see." Albrecht's expression was enough like Benjamin's to make it obvious he'd expected that response, and it was his turn to shrug. "In that case, I think this whole Lovat business gives rather more point to the desirability of remounting the Monica operation, covered by an appropriately new lambskin, as soon as we can, doesn't it?"

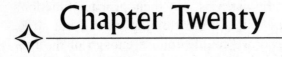

# Chapter Twenty

"YOU WANTED TO SEE ME, Albrecht?"

Albrecht Detweiler turned from his contemplation of the panorama of sugar-white beaches beyond his luxurious officer's windows as the dark-haired, boldly tattooed woman stepped through its door.

"Yes, I believe I did," he observed, and tilted one hand to indicate one of the chairs in front of his desk.

Isabel Bardasano obeyed the wordless command, sitting with a certain almost dangerous grace and crossing her legs as he walked back from the windows to his own chair. Her expression was attentive, and he reflected once again upon the lethality behind her . . . ornamented façade.

Bardasano belonged to one of Mesa's "young lodges," which explained the tattoos and the elaborate body piercings. The young lodges represented a "new generation" of the Mesan corporate hierarchy, one which had embraced a deliberately flamboyant lifestyle, flaunting its wealth and power under the nose of a virtuously disapproving galaxy. Very few members of any of the lodges had been admitted to the full truth of Mesa's plans, for several reasons. The largest one was that the wealth, sense of privilege, and arrogance which underlay their flamboyance had been deliberately encouraged as one more sign of Manpower and its fellow outlaw corporations' excesses and general degeneracy. It had been more necessary than ever to distract attention from the Alignment's activities now that the culminating moment was so rapidly approaching, and the "young lodges" had done that quite well. Of course, their members' lifestyles had also made them rather more vulnerable to the activities of the Audubon Ballroom's assassins. That was unfortunate, but all the genotypes in question had been conserved elsewhere, and it had been well worth the price tag in terms of misdirection. And if it also convinced the rest of the galaxy that Mesa at large was increasingly dominated by hedonistic sybarites and useless drones, so much the better.

But some of those "hedonistic sybarites" were anything but useless drones, and Bardasano was a prime example. In fact, she was *the* prime example. The Bardasano genotype had been notable for at least half a dozen generations for its intelligence and ruthless determination. There'd been a few unfortunate and unintended traits, as well, unhappily, and at one point there'd been serious consideration of simply culling the line's last several iterations and starting over again from a significantly earlier point. The positive traits had been so strong, however, that a remedial program had been instituted, instead, and Isabel was the current example of how successful it had been. It had been necessary to eliminate two of her immediate predecessors when their inherent ruthlessness had made them just a bit too ambitious for anyone else's good, but *intelligent* ambition, properly tempered, was always a useful thing, as Bardasano herself demonstrated. And if there was still a slight tendency towards sexual disorders and mildly sociopathic behaviors, neither of those posed any serious handicap, especially for someone whose area of expertise was covert operations. Of course, they'd have to be dealt with in the next generation or two if the Bardasano line was going to earn back permanent alpha status within the Alignment, which Isabel understood.

In the meantime, however, she was quite possibly the best covert ops specialist the Alignment had produced in at least the last T-century. It amused Detweiler that those outside the Alignment's innermost circle often cherished doubts about Bardasano's sanity, particularly when it came to her attitude towards him. The fact that it was well known within Mesa's star lines that the Bardasanos had almost been culled meant that her apparent insouciance with him only added to her reputation for . . . oddness, and provided a valuable extra level of protection when he or one of his sons called upon her services. As he gazed at her across the desk, he toyed once more with the notion of telling her that a cross between the Bardasano and Detweiler genotypes was even then being evaluated, but decided against it. For now, at least.

"Well," he said, tipping back slightly in his chair, "I'd have to say that so far, at least, removing Webster—and, of course, Operation Rat Poison—seems to be working out quite well. Aside from whatever new weapons goody the Manties seem to have come up with."

"So far," she agreed, but there was the merest hint of a reservation in her tone, and his eyebrows arched.

"Something about it concerns you?"

"Yes, and no," she replied.

He waggled his fingers in a silent command to continue, and she shrugged.

"So far, and in the short term, it's had exactly the effect we wanted," she said. "I'm not talking about whatever they did at Lovat, you understand. That's outside my area of expertise, and I'm sure Benjamin and Daniel already have their people working on that full time. If either of them needs my help, I'm sure they'll tell me so, as well. But leaving that aside, it does look like we got what we wanted out of the assassinations. The Manties—or, at least, a sufficient majority of them—are convinced Haven was behind it; the summit's been derailed; and it looks as if we've managed to deepen Elizabeth's distrust of Pritchart even further. I'm just not entirely happy with the fact that we had to mount both operations in such a relatively tight time frame. I don't like improvisation, Albrecht. Careful analysis and thorough preparation have served us entirely too well for entirely too long for me to be happy flying by the seat of my pants, whatever the others on the Strategy Council may think."

"Point taken," Detweiler acknowledged. "And it's a valid point, too. Benjamin, Collin, and I have been discussing very much the same considerations. Unfortunately, we've come to the conclusion that we're going to have to do more and more of it, not less, as we move into the end game phase. You know that's always been part of our projections."

"Of course. That doesn't make me any happier when it's forced upon us, though. And I really don't want us to get into a make-it-up-as-we-go-along mindset just *because* we're moving into the end game. The two laws I try hardest to bear in mind are the law of unintended consequences and Murphy's, Albrecht. And, let's face it, there are some fairly significant potential unintended consequences to eliminating Webster and attacking 'Queen Berry.'"

"There usually are at least some of those," Detweiler pointed out. "Are there specific concerns in this case?"

"Actually, there *are* a couple of things that worry me," she admitted, and his eyes narrowed. He'd learned, over the years, to trust Bardasano's internal radar. She was wrong sometimes, but at least whenever she had reservations she was willing to go out on a limb and admit it, rather than pretending she thought everything was just fine. And if she was sometimes wrong, she was *right* far more often.

"Tell me."

"First and foremost," she responded, "I'm still worried about someone's figuring out how we're doing it and tracing it back to us. I know no one's come close to finding the proverbial smoking gun yet . . . so far as we know, at any rate. But the Manties are a lot better at bioscience than the Andermani or Haven. Worse, they've got ready access to Beowulf."

Detweiler's jaw tightened in an involuntary, almost Pavlovian response to that name. The automatic spike of anger it provoked was the next best thing to instinctual, and he reminded himself yet again of the dangers of allowing it to affect his thinking.

"I doubt even Beowulf will be able to put it together quickly," he said after a moment. "I don't doubt they could eventually, with enough data. They certainly have the capability, at any rate, but given how quickly the nanites break down, it's extremely unlikely they're going to have access to any of the cadavers in a short enough timeframe to determine anything definitive. All of Everett's and Kyprianou's studies and simulations point in that direction. Obviously, it's a concern we have to bear in mind, but we can't allow that possibility to scare us into refusing to use a capability we need."

"I'm not saying we should, only pointing out a potential danger. And, to be frank, I'm less worried about some medical examiner's figuring it out forensically than I am about someone reaching the same conclusion—that it's a bioweapon and that we're the ones who developed it—by following up other avenues."

"What sort of 'other avenues'?" he asked, eyes narrowing once again.

"According to our current reports, Elizabeth herself and most of Grantville's government, not to mention the Manty in the street, are absolutely convinced it was Haven. Most of them seem to share Elizabeth's theory that for some unknown reason Pritchart decided her initial proposal for a summit had been a mistake. None of them have any convincing explanation for what that 'unknown reason' might have been, however. And some of them—particularly White Haven and Harrington—don't seem very convinced it was Haven at all. Since the High Ridge collapse, we no longer have enough penetration to absolutely confirm something like that, unfortunately, but the sources we still do have all point in that direction. Please bear in mind, of course, that it takes time for information from our best surviving sources to reach us. It's not like we can ask the newsies about these things the way we can clip stories about military operations like Lovat, for example. At this point, and even using dispatch boats with streak capability on the Beowulf conduit, we're still talking about very preliminary reports."

"Understood. Go on."

"What concerns me most," she continued with a slight shrug, "is that once Elizabeth's immediate response has had a little time to cool, White Haven and Harrington are still two of the people whose judgment she most trusts. I think both of them are too smart to push her too hard on this particular issue at this moment, but neither of them is especially susceptible to spouting the party line if they don't actually share it, either. And despite the way her political opponents sometimes caricature Elizabeth, she's a very smart woman in her own right. So if two people whose judgment she trusts are quietly but stubbornly convinced that there's more going on here than everyone else has assumed, she's just likely to be more open-minded where that possibility is concerned than even she realizes she is.

"What else concerns me is that there are two possible alternative scenarios for who was actually responsible for both attacks. One, of course, is that it was us—or, at least, Manpower. The second is that it was, in fact, a Havenite operation, but not one sanctioned by Pritchart or anyone in her administration. In other words, that it was mounted by a rogue element within the Republic which is opposed to ending the war.

"Of the two, the second is probably the more likely . . . and the less dangerous from our perspective. Mind you, it would be bad enough if someone could convince Elizabeth and Grantville that Pritchart's offer had been genuine and that sinister and evil elements—possibly throwbacks to the bad old days of State Security—decided to sabotage it. Even if that turned around Elizabeth's position on a summit, it wouldn't lead anyone directly to us, though. And it's not going to happen overnight, either. My best guess is that even if someone suggested that theory to Elizabeth today—for that matter, someone may already have done just that—it would still take weeks, probably months, for it to reach the point of changing her mind. And now that they've resumed operations, the momentum of fresh casualties and infrastructure damage is going to be strongly against any effort to resurrect the original summit agreement even if she does change her mind.

"The first possibility, however, worries me more, although I'll admit it would appear to be a lower order probability, so far, at least. At the moment, the fact that they're convinced they're looking at a Havenite assassination technique is diverting attention from us and all of the reasons we might have for killing Webster or Berry Zilwicki. But if someone manages to demonstrate that there has to be an undetectable bio-nanite component to how the assassins are managing these 'adjustments,' the immediate corollary to that is going to be a matching suspicion that even if Haven is *using* the technique, it didn't *develop* the technique. The Republic simply doesn't have the capability to put something like this together for itself, and no one as smart as Patricia Givens is going to believe for a moment that it does. And that, Albrecht, is going to get that same smart person started thinking about who *did* develop it. It could have come from any of several places, but as soon as anyone starts thinking in that direction, the two names that are going to pop to the top of their list are Mesa and Beowulf, and I don't think anyone is going to think those sanctimonious bastards on Beowulf would be making something like this available. In which case Manpower's reputation is likely to bite us on the ass. And the fact that both the Manties and the Havenites' intelligence services are aware of the fact that 'Manpower' has been recruiting ex-StateSec elements is likely to suggest the possibility of a connection between us and some *other* StateSec element, possibly hiding in the underbrush of the current Republic. Which is entirely too close to the truth to make me feel particularly happy.

"That could be bad enough. If they reach that point, however, they may very well be willing to go a step further. If we're supplying the technology to some rogue element in Haven, then what would keep us from using it ourselves? And if they ask themselves *that* question, then all of the motives we might have—all of the motives they already *know* about because of Manpower, even without the additional ones we actually do have—are going to spring to their attention."

Detweiler swung his chair gently from side to side for several seconds, considering what she'd said, then grimaced.

"I can't disagree with the downsides of either of your scenarios, Isabel. Still, I think it comes under the heading of what I said earlier—the fact that we can't allow worry about things which may never happen to prevent us from using necessary techniques where we have to. And as you've just pointed out, the probability of anyone deciding it was us—or, at least, that it was us acting for ourselves, rather than simply a case of Haven's contracting out the 'wet work' to a third-party—is low."

"Low isn't the same thing as nonexistent," Bardasano countered. "And something else that concerns me is that I have an unconfirmed report Zilwicki and Cachat visited Harrington aboard her flagship at Trevor's Star."

"Visited Harrington?" Detweiler said a bit more sharply, letting his chair come upright. "Why is this the first I'm hearing about this?"

"Because the report came in on the same streak boat that confirmed Elizabeth's cancellation of the summit," she said calmly. "I'm still working my way through everything that was downloaded from it, and the reason I requested this meeting, frankly, has to do with the possibility that the two of them actually did meet with her."

"At Trevor's Star?" Detweiler's tone was that of a man repeating what she'd said for emphasis, not dubiously or in denial, and she nodded.

"As I say, it's an unconfirmed report. I really don't know how much credibility to assign it at this point. But if it's accurate, Zilwicki took his frigate to Trevor's Star, with Cachat—a known Havenite spy, for God's sake!—on board, which would mean they were allowed transit through the wormhole—and into close proximity to Harrington's fleet units—despite the fact that the entire system's been declared a closed military area by Manticore, with 'Shoot on Sight' orders plastered all over the shipping channels and newsfaxes and nailed up on every flat surface of the Trevor's Star terminus' warehousing and service platforms. Not to mention the warning buoys posted all around the system perimeter for any through traffic stupid enough to head in-system from the terminus! And it would also appear that Harrington not only met with Cachat but allowed him to leave, afterward. Which suggests to me that she gave fairly strong credence to whatever it was they had to say to her. And, frankly, I can't think of anything the two of them might have to say to her that *we'd* like for her to hear."

Detweiler snorted harshly in agreement.

"You're right about that," he said. "On the other hand, I'm sure you have at least a theory about the specific reasons for their visit. So be a fly on her bulkhead and tell me what they probably said to her."

"My guess would be that the main point they wanted to make was that Cachat hadn't ordered Rat Poison. Or, at least, that neither he nor any of his operatives had carried it out. And if he was willing to confirm his own status as Trajan's man in Erewhon, the fact that he hadn't carried it out—assuming she believed him—would clearly be significant. And, unfortunately, there's every reason to think she *would* believe him if he spoke to her face to face."

Detweiler throttled another, possibly even sharper spike of anger. He knew what Bardasano was getting it. Wilhelm Trajan was Pritchart's handpicked director for the Republic's Foreign Intelligence Service. He didn't have the positive genius for improvisational covert operations that Kevin Usher possessed, but Pritchart had decided she needed Usher for the Federal Investigation Agency. And whatever else might have been true about Trajan, his loyalty to the Constitution and Eloise Pritchart—in that order—was absolute. He'd been relentless in his efforts to purge FIS of any lingering StateSec elements, and there was no way in the world *he* would have mounted a rogue operation outside channels. Which meant the only way Rat Poison could have been mounted without Cachat knowing all about it would have been as a rogue operation originating at a much lower level and using an entirely different set of resources.

That was bad enough, but the real spark for his anger was Bardasano's indirect reference to the never-to-be-sufficiently-damned treecats of Sphinx. For such small, fuzzy, outwardly lovable creatures, they had managed to thoroughly screw over altogether too many covert operations—Havenite and Mesan alike—over the years. Especially in partnership with that bitch Harrington. If Cachat had gotten into voice range of Harrington, that accursed treecat of hers would know whether or not he was telling the truth.

"When did this conversation take place, according to your 'unconfirmed report'?"

"About a T-week after Elizabeth fired off her note. The report about it came from one of our more carefully protected sources, though, which means there was even more delay than usual in getting it to us. One of the reasons it's still unconfirmed is that there was barely time for it to catch the regular intel drop."

"So there was time for Harrington to go and repeat whatever they told her to Elizabeth or Grantville even before she headed out for Lovat, without our knowing anything about it."

"Yes." Bardasano shrugged. "Frankly, I don't think there's very much chance of Elizabeth or Grantville buying Haven's innocence, no matter what Cachat may have told Harrington. All he can tell them is that as far as *he* knows Haven didn't do it, after all, and even if they accept that he was telling her the truth in so far as he knew it, that wouldn't mean he was right. Even if he's convinced Harrington he truly believes Haven didn't do it, that's only his personal opinion . . . and it's damned hard to prove a negative without at least some outside evidence to back it up. So I strongly doubt that anything they may have said to her, or that she may have repeated to anyone else, is going to sidetrack the resumption of operations. And, as I said before, now that blood's started getting shed again, the war is going to take on its own momentum all over again, as well.

"What worries me quite a bit more than what Zilwicki and Cachat may have told Harrington, frankly, is that we don't know where they went after they *left* her. We've always known they're both competent operators, and they've shown an impressive ability to analyze any information they get their hands on. Admittedly, that's hurt us worse tactically than strategically so far, and there's no evidence—yet—that they've actually begun peeling the onion. But if Cachat is combining Haven's sources with what Zilwicki is getting from the Ballroom, I'd say they're more likely than anyone else to start putting inconvenient bits and pieces together.

Especially after they start looking really closely at Rat Poison and how it could have happened if Haven didn't do it. Working on their own, they can't call on the organizational infrastructure Givens or Trajan have access to, but they've got plenty of ability, plenty of motivation, and entirely too many sources."

"And the last thing we need is for those Ballroom lunatics to realize we've been using them for the better part of a century and a half," Detweiler growled.

"I don't know if it's absolutely the *last* thing we need, but it would definitely be on my list of the top half-dozen or so things we'd really like not to happen," Bardasano said with a sour smile, and, despite himself, Detweiler chuckled harshly.

The gusto with which the Audubon Ballroom had gone after Manpower and all its works had been one more element, albeit an unknowing and involuntary one, in camouflaging the Alignment's true activities and objectives. The fact that at least some of Manpower's senior executives were members of at least the Alignment's outer circle meant one or two of the Ballroom's assassinations had hurt them fairly badly over the years. Most of those slaughtered by the vengeful ex-slaves, however, were little more than readily dispensed with red herrings, an outer layer of "the onion" no one would really miss, and the bloody warfare between the "outlaw corporation" and its "terrorist" opposition had helped focus attention on the general mayhem and divert it *away* from what was really going on.

Yet useful as that had been, it had also been a two-edged sword. Since all but a very tiny percentage of Manpower's organization was unaware of any deeper hidden purpose, the chance that the *Ballroom* would become aware of it was slight. But the possibility had always existed, and no one who had watched the Ballroom penetrate Manpower's security time and time again would ever underestimate just how dangerous people like Jeremy X and his murderous henchmen could prove if they ever figured out what was truly going on and decided to change their target selection criteria. And if Zilwicki and Cachat actually were moving towards putting things together . . .

"How likely do you really think it is that the two of them could pull enough together to compromise things at this stage?" he asked finally.

"I doubt anyone could possibly answer that question. Not in any meaningful way, at any rate," Bardasano admitted. "The possibility always exists, though, Albrecht. We've buried things as deeply as we can, we've put together cover organizations and fronts, and we've done everything we can to build in multiple layers of diversion. But the bottom line is that we've always relied most heavily on the fact that 'everyone knows' what Manpower is and what it wants. I'd have to say the odds are heavily against even Zilwicki and Cachat figuring out that what 'everyone knows' is a complete fabrication, especially after we've had so long to put everything in place. It *is* possible, however, and I think—as I've said—that if anyone *can* do it, the two of them would be the most likely to pull it off."

"And we don't know where they are at the moment?"

"It's a big galaxy," Bardasano pointed out. "We know where they *were* two T-weeks ago. I can mobilize our assets to look for them, and we could certainly use all of our Manpower sources for this one without rousing any particular suspicion. But you know as well as I do that what that really amounts to is waiting in place until they wander into our sights."

Detweiler grimaced again. Unfortunately, she was right, and he did know it.

"All right," he said, "I want them found. I recognize the limitations we're facing, but find them as quickly as you can. When you do, eliminate them."

"That's more easily said than done. As Manpower's attack on Montaigne's mansion demonstrates."

"That was Manpower, not us," Detweiler riposted, and it was Bardasano's turn to nod.

One of the problems with using Manpower as a mask was that too many of Manpower's executives had no more idea than the rest of the galaxy that anyone was using them. Which meant it was also necessary to give those same executives a loose rein in order to keep them unaware of that inconvenient little truth . . . which could produce operations like that fiasco in Chicago or the attack on Catherine Montaigne's mansion on Manticore. Fortunately, even operations which were utter disasters from Manpower's perspective seldom impinged directly on the *Alignment's* objectives. And the occasional Manpower catastrophe helped contribute to the galaxy at large's notion of Mesan clumsiness.

"If we find them, this time it won't be Manpower flailing around on its own," Detweiler continued grimly. "It will be us—*you*. And I want this given the highest priority, Isabel. In fact, the two of us need to sit down and discuss this with Benjamin. He's got at least a few spider units available now—he's been using them to train crews and conduct working up exercises and systems evaluations. Given what you've just said, I think it might be worthwhile to deploy one of them to Verdant Vista. The entire galaxy knows about that damned frigate of Zilwicki's. I think it might be time to arrange a little untraceable accident for it."

Bardasano's eyes widened slightly, and she seemed for a moment to hover on the brink of a protest. But then she visibly thought better of it. Not, Detweiler felt confident, because she was afraid to argue the point if she thought he was wrong or that he was running unjustifiable risks. One of the things that made her so valuable was the fact that she'd never been a yes-woman. If she did disagree with him, she'd get around to telling him so before the operation was mounted. But she'd also take time to think about it first, to be certain in her own mind of what she thought before she engaged her mouth. Which was *another* of the things that made her so valuable to him.

*And I don't doubt she'll talk it over with Benjamin, too*, he thought sardonically. *If she has any reservations, she'll want to run them past him to get a second viewpoint on them. And, of course, so the two of them can double-team me more effectively if it turns out they agree with one another.*

Which was just fine with Albrecht Detweiler, when all was said and done. The one thing he wasn't was convinced of his own infallibility, after all.

"All right," he said aloud, leaning back again with the air of a man shifting mental gears. "Something else I wanted to ask you about is Anisimovna."

"What about her?" Bardasano's tone might have turned just a tiny bit cautious, and she cocked her head to one side, watching Detweiler's expression intently.

"I'm not about to change my mind and have her eliminated, if that's what you're worrying about, Isabel," he said dryly.

"I wouldn't say I was exactly *worried* about it," she replied. "I do think doing that would be wasting a very useful asset, though, and as I said before, I don't think anything that happened in Talbott was her fault any more than it was mine. In fact, given the amount of information I had and she didn't, it was almost certainly *more* my fault than hers."

Bardasano, Detweiler reflected, was one of the very few people, even inside the Alignment's innermost circle, who would have made that last admission to him. Which was yet another of the things that made her so valuable.

"As I say, I'm not about to have her eliminated," he said. "What you've just said goes a fair way towards answering the question I was going to ask, though, I think. Which is—do you think it's time to bring her all the way inside? Is she a sufficiently 'useful asset' to be made a full member of the Alignment?"

"Um."

It wasn't often Detweiler saw Bardasano hesitate. Nor was that actually what he was seeing in this case, he realized. It wasn't so much hesitation as surprise.

"I think, maybe, yes," she said finally, slowly, her eyes narrowed in thought. "Her genome *is* an Alpha line, and she already knows more than most people who aren't full members. The only real concern I'd have about nominating her for full membership—and it's a minor one—would be that she's got a little more highly developed sense of superiority than I'd really like to see."

Detweiler arched an eyebrow, and she shrugged.

"It's not just her, Albrecht. In fact, I'd say I was a lot more concerned about someone like Sandusky than I am about Aldona. The thing is that quite a few of us—including some who are already full members—have a tendency, I think, to automatically assume their superiority in any matchup with *any* normal. That's dangerous, especially if the 'normal' is someone like Zilwicki or Cachat—or, for that matter, Harrington, although, given her pedigree on her father's side, I suppose she's not actually a normal herself, wherever her loyalties might lie. It's also something I have to guard against in myself, however, and in Aldona's case, I think it's probably exacerbated by the fact that she isn't already a full member . . . and she thinks she is. Based solely on what she and the other members of the Strategy Council who aren't full members know, or think they know, about the stakes we're really playing for, most of *her* sense of superiority would be survivable. And she's certainly smart enough to understand what's really going on—and why—if you decide to tell her. So, if she does come all the way inside, I think we could probably count on knocking most of that . . . smugness out of her in fairly short order. May I ask why the question's arisen at this particular time?"

"In light of the implications of what happened at Lovat, I'm thinking about trying to resurrect the Monica operation using a different proxy," Detweiler replied. "And given the way we got our fingers burned last time, I want whoever is in charge of it this time around to know what we're really trying to accomplish."

"*I* knew what we were really trying to accomplish last time," Bardasano pointed out.

"Yes, you did. But one of the things which is such a useful part of your cover is your relative lack of official seniority outside the Alignment itself. That's why Anisimovna had primary responsibility, as far as the Strategy Council was concerned, at least, last time. And it's also one reason I couldn't send *you* back out to handle this solo *this* time around. There are other reasons, however, including the fact that I want you close to home to monitor the situation between Manticore and Haven. And to deal with Cachat and Zilwicki, if we can locate them. I don't want you out of reach if I need you, and there's a limit to how much we can send streakers zipping around the galaxy without someone starting to notice that our mail seems to get delivered just a little quicker than anyone else's."

"I see."

Bardasano leaned back in her chair, obviously thinking hard, then drew a deep breath.

"On that basis, I would definitely recommend bringing Aldona fully inside. Although I also think it would be a good idea to think things over very carefully before we decide whether or not we want to 'resurrect' Monica. And to consider it in light of the concerns I've already expressed about flying by the seat of our pants."

"Granted," he agreed. "And I'm not saying I've firmly decided one way or the other. I'm still thinking about it. However, if we did decide to take this approach, it wouldn't be quite as improvisational as it might first appear, since we could use a lot of the spadework from the Monica operation. Oh," he waved one hand like a man swatting at a gnat, "not in Monica itself, obviously. But in Meyers, and with Crandall."

Bardasano frowned slightly, then nodded.

"Use Crandall to motivate Verrochio, you mean?"

"Use Crandall, yes. And Verrochio. But I'm thinking of Crandall more as . . . reassurance for Verrochio. The *motivation* we'll supply by way of Hongbo."

"You want to make an explicit approach to Hongbo?" Bardasano's tone was slightly dubious, and Detweiler snorted.

"We've already made an 'explicit approach' to Hongbo," he pointed out. "So far, he's done quite well out of us as our local manager for Commissioner Verrochio. It's not as if he should be particularly surprised if we 'request' his assistance once more."

"My impression is that he'd be . . . quite hesitant to try a variant on Monica this soon," she said. "He's smarter than Verrochio. I think he's probably a lot more aware of the potential consequences if they try something like this a second time and screw up. Oh, he's not worried about the Assembly or the courts. He's worried about what his and Verrochio's fellow OFS satraps will do to them if they get fresh egg on Frontier Security's face."

"I can see that," Detweiler conceded. "And, of course, he's not aware that if we succeed, his fellow Frontier Security commissioners are going to be the least of his worries. Be that as it may, though, I'm really hesitant to let all of our preparation go completely to waste. Especially since we'll have to eliminate Crandall and Filareta after this if we can't use them now."

"Sometimes it's better to just write an operation off, however much you've invested in it," Bardasano cautioned. "That old cliché about throwing good money after bad comes rather forcibly to mind. And so does the one about reinforcing failure."

"Agreed. And I fully intend to kick the entire notion around with Collin before we make any hard and fast decisions. I'll want you in on those conversations, as well, for that matter. But it's not just a case of pushing to recoup our investment. I'm genuinely concerned about the long term implications of whatever they used at Lovat. I think it's just become even more important to keep them under the maximum pressure and prune them back any way we can, and what's occurred to me is that with the summit off the table and the Manties going back to war with Haven, it shouldn't be too incredibly difficult to convince someone like Verrochio that they're under too much pressure from Haven to respond to a full bore threat from the Solarian League."

"A 'full bore threat'?" she repeated carefully.

"What I'm thinking is that with only a very little encouragement,

New Tuscany would probably make an even better cat's-paw than Monica did last time around. Frontier Fleet's already dispatched a reinforcing detachment to Meyers, which is probably enough to start bolstering Verrochio's nerve all by itself. And I just happen to know that the senior officer of that detachment doesn't much care for 'neobarbs.' In fact, he doesn't care for *Manties*. Something to do with getting his fingers rather severely burned in an incident with a Manticoran freighter when he was a much more junior officer. Franklin's contacts in the League meant we could get him assigned without ever having to approach him directly, so he doesn't know a thing about our involvement in this. Given his background, though, I'm sure he's already quite upset about the Manties' wild allegations about the complicity of major League business interests—and, of course, those nasty Mesans—in what happened in Monica. If he were properly approached by Hongbo and Verocchio, I'm fairly confident he'd be amenable to doing something about it, especially if the League's assistance was officially requested by someone with legitimate interests in the area. Like, oh, *New Tuscany*, perhaps. And one of Verrochio's outstanding characteristics has always been his temper. If Hongbo pumps a little hydrogen into the fire, instead of trying to put it out, Verrochio is going to be just itching for an opportunity to get even with Manticore for his current humiliation. And if he just happened to be aware—or to *become* aware—of the fact that our good friend Admiral Crandall is in his vicinity with an entire Battle Fleet task force of superdreadnoughts, it might stiffen his irate spine quite remarkably."

"And you want Aldona fully inside to handle New Tuscany and Hongbo," Bardasano said slowly. "Which means we aren't going to be able to fob her off with any nonsense about Technodyne getting hold of Manty technology, or about us only wanting to prevent them from annexing the Talbott Cluster because of its proximity to Mesa, this time around."

"That's pretty much it, yes." Detweiler shrugged. "Without Technodyne and Levakonic to front for us by providing Monica with battlecruisers anymore, she's going to have to be aware of our real knuckleduster. And that's going to suggest to someone as smart as she is that we're up to rather more than she knew about last time. Especially since it's going to become obvious to her that Crandall's task force wouldn't be where it is if we hadn't arranged for it before the two of you ever set out for Monica. She's going to wonder why we didn't tell her about it then, and I don't think it will take her very long to start making some reasonably accurate guesses about just how much *else* is happening that she doesn't know about. I'd far rather tell her everything that really is going on than have her guess just enough to make some serious mistake trying to adjust for what she *thinks* is going on."

"I think you really should discuss this with Collin," Bardasano said. "If you still think it's a good idea after that—and I'm not saying it isn't; I just don't know whether or not it is at this point—then I'd certainly recommend explaining everything to Aldona and putting her back in charge of it. But she's going to need something more persuasive than mere greed and bribery to get Hongbo solidly behind her on this one."

"In that case," Detweiler said with a thin, sharklike smile, "it's probably a very good thing we have all those bank records about the payoffs he's accepted over the years from those nasty Manpower genetic slavers, isn't it? I realize he might try to turn stubborn even so. I mean, after all, it's not like the League judiciary is likely to do any more than slap him on the wrist over it. If he does, though, Aldona could always point out that if that same information were to be unfortunately leaked to those Ballroom lunatics . . ."

He let his voice trail off and shrugged as he raised both hands shoulder-high, palms uppermost.

"I suppose that probably *would* motivate him suitably," Bardasano agreed with a smile of her own. "The Ballroom does come in handy from time to time, doesn't it?"

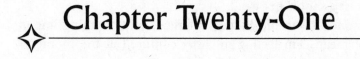

# Chapter Twenty-One

"WELL, WHAT DO *YOU* make of it?" Gregor O'Shaughnessy asked with a crooked smile.

"If you're asking for my professional opinion on how we pulled it off, I don't have a clue," Commander Ambrose Chandler, Augustus Khumalo's staff intelligence officer, replied.

He sat across a small table from his civilian counterpart on Baroness Medusa's staff, the two of them enjoying the afternoon sunlight of the city of Thimble, the improbably named planetary capital of the planet Flax. Spindle-A, the G0 primary component of the distant binary system in which Flax made its home, was warm on their shoulders, the tablecloth flapped gently on the iodine-scented breeze, and their terrace table above the seawall looked out across the Humboldt Ocean's tumbled blue and silver.

"Even if you could tell me how we did it, it probably wouldn't mean very much to *me*, Ambrose," O'Shaughnessy pointed out, and Chandler chuckled. O'Shaughnessy had come up through the civilian side of the Star Kingdom of Manticore's intelligence community. He neither truly understood how the military mind worked nor shared the military's perspective on quite a few problems. Fortunately, he was aware of that, and he tried—not always successfully—to make allowances for it when it was necessary to coordinate with his naval colleagues.

"I was more concerned with what I suppose you'd call the

strategic implications of it," O'Shaughnessy continued, and Chandler's smile faded.

"Militarily?" he asked.

"Militarily and politically." O'Shaughnessy shrugged. "I'm in a better position on the political side than on the military side, of course, but under the circumstances, any additional perspective I can get has to be worthwhile. I've got the oddest feeling that the entire Star Kingdom—excuse me, the Star Empire—is in the process of falling down that Old Earth rabbit hole."

"'Rabbit hole?'" Chandler repeated, looking at him oddly, and O'Shaughnessy shook his head.

"Never mind. It's an old literary reference, not anything important. It just means I'm feeling mightily confused at the moment."

"Well, you're hardly alone there," Chandler pointed out, then took another swallow of his beer and leaned back in his chair.

"Militarily," he said bluntly, "Haven is screwed *if*—and please do note the qualifier, Gregor—whatever Duchess Harrington used at Lovat can be gotten into general deployment. I'm guessing that it has to be some further development of the grav-pulse telemetry we're already using in Ghost Rider. Exactly how Admiral Hemphill's shop did it, and what sort of hardware is involved, is more than I could guess at this point. I'm a spook, not a tactical officer, and I'm actually probably better informed about *Peep* hardware than I am about ours. Something about knowing your enemy. But it's clear enough even from the preliminary reports that whatever Duchess Harrington did enormously increased her MDMs' long-range accuracy, and that's always been the biggest problem where they're concerned."

O'Shaughnessy nodded to show he was following Chandler's logic. Despite his own lack of military experience, he wouldn't have been Medusa's senior intelligence analyst if he hadn't managed to acquire at least some grasp of the navy's current capabilities.

The dispatches informing Khumalo and Baroness Medusa about the Battle of Lovat had reached Spindle only the evening before. He had no doubt Chandler was still in the midst of assimilating everything else that had come with them, much as he himself was. And he also had no doubt that Loretta Shoupe, who—unlike Chandler—*was* a tactical specialist, would have been a better source if he'd been interested in the nuts and bolts of whatever was going on. He liked Shoupe, and he did intend to discuss

Lovat's military aspects with her, but right now he needed the big picture more than the specifics. Besides, Chandler was a fellow analyst. He'd probably have a better feel for the sorts of details someone like O'Shaughnessy needed than Shoupe would.

"The MDM and the missile pod between them turned the balance between energy armaments and missile armaments on its head," Chandler continued, "but we've never been able to really take full advantage of the system because the range of the missiles has out-stripped the effective range of our fire control. If Admiral Hemphill really has found a way to effectively integrate FTL telemetry into the system, that's changed, though, and if we can do that and the Peeps can't, then they're going to find themselves as outclassed as they were when Earl White Haven kicked their asses the last time around. But to do that, Duchess Harrington is going to have to have enough ships with the capability to do whatever it is they're doing. If she doesn't, if the Peeps have enough hulls to soak up her hits and keep closing, then we're back to worrying about whether or not our quality is sufficient to overcome their quantity."

"Would we have used this thing in the first place if we didn't have it in general deployment?" O'Shaughnessy asked.

"I'd like to think we wouldn't have," Chandler said, rather more grimly, "but I'm a lot less confident of that than I'd like to be."

"Because of the collapse of the summit?"

"Exactly. Or, maybe to be more accurate, because of the *way* the summit collapsed. If I thought we'd backed away from it on the basis of a dispassionate analysis of our military advantages, I'd be a lot happier. But that isn't what happened, is it? *Political* considerations—political considerations that are driven at least as much by emotions as by analysis—dictated the Government's decision. Which means what we could be looking at here is a less than optimum military decision based on political necessity."

"Aren't all military decisions ultimately based on political necessities?" O'Shaughnessy asked just a bit challengingly, and Chandler snorted.

"You aren't going to get me involved in *that* discussion, Gregor! I don't have any problem at all with the notion that military policy and objectives have to be defined within a political context. And I'm an officer in the Queen's Navy, which means I fully accept the validity and necessity of civilian control of the military, which means the subordination of military decision making to the political leadership. All I'm saying in this instance is that the decision to resume active operations was essentially a political one. Admiral Caparelli and the Strategy Board are responsible for determining the best ways to carry out decisions like that, but they can only do that within the limitations of the tools available to them. So I'm saying they may have decided to use a weapon system that's not fully prepared for general deployment. Or, at least, to have used it at an earlier point in any deployment process than they would have under other circumstances."

"At least partly in an effort to bluff the Havenites into thinking it *is* ready for general deployment, you mean?"

"Maybe. And I could be worrying more about it than I ought to be, too," Chandler conceded. "After all, even if they're ready to go to general deployment tomorrow, they still have to use this thing for a first time *somewhere*."

"But you don't think they *are* ready for general deployment, do you?" O'Shaughnessy said shrewdly. "Why?"

"Because," Chandler replied, answering the blunt question with matching bluntness, "if we had this thing in general deployment already, we'd've gone straight for Nouveau Paris, not Lovat. Lovat's an important target, but not nearly as important as the Peeps' capital. And given the way everyone back home is feeling over Admiral Webster's assassination and that business on Torch, do you really think anyone at the Admiralty or the Palace wouldn't have gone for a knockout if they'd thought they had the capability?"

"Um." O'Shaughnessy frowned. He'd treasured a few reservations about the commander's imagination over the many months he and Chandler had worked together. There was nothing wrong with his imagination where that particular bit of analysis was concerned, however.

"Okay," the civilian continued after a moment. "Let's assume you're right. This new guidance system or whatever is limited right now to Eighth Fleet. Would you agree that we wouldn't have let Haven know we've got it unless we were at least getting ready to deploy it more broadly?"

He cocked an eyebrow at Chandler, who nodded.

"Good. So, assume we do get it into general deployment over the next few months. What happens then?"

"Assuming we *get* a few months in which to put it into deployment, the Peeps are history," Chandler replied. "It may take a few more months for the smoke to clear and the articles of surrender to get signed, but I can't see anything that would save them under those circumstances. And, frankly, I can't see any circumstances under which Her Majesty would settle for anything other than unconditional surrender this time around, can you?"

"Not hardly!" O'Shaughnessy snorted, but his expression was more worried than Chandler's. The commander looked a question at him, and he shrugged.

"I just wish we knew more about what the Sollies are going to do," he said. "I know it *looks* like they're going to fold their hand after what's happened at Monica, but I've just got this ... I don't know, this *itchy* feeling."

"Itchy," Chandler repeated thoughtfully.

"I know. I know! It's not the sort of technical terminology that contributes to the mystique of our profession, Ambrose. Unfortunately, I can't come up with a better adjective."

"Why not?"

"If I knew that, I'd be able to find the better adjective I wanted," O'Shaughnessy said tartly. Then he sighed. "I think it's just the fact that it looks like the entire Monica operation was set up by Manpower and Technodyne. Not by Frontier Security, or any of the Solly bureaucracies—by a pair of corporate entities. Right?"

"So far," Chandler acknowledged. "I think it's obvious they had to be pretty sure they had Frontier Security—or at least Verrochio—safely tucked away in their pocket before they tried it, but that's what it looks like."

"And that's what bothers me," O'Shaughnessy said. "First, the sheer scale and ... audacity of what they had in mind strikes me as being just a bit over the top even for one of the Mesa-based outfits. Second, look at the *expense* involved. I'm sure they'd have managed to recoup most of their investment one way or another if it had worked, but they invested literally hundreds of billions trying to bring this thing off. That's a pretty stiff risk exposure even for someone like Manpower or Technodyne. And, third, if I'd been Manpower, and if all I really wanted to do was to prevent the annexation of the Talbott Cluster, I could have found an approach that would have been a lot less expensive and risky ... and probably at least as effective."

"Really?"

"Sure." O'Shaughnessy shook his head. "This was a case of

using an awfully big, awfully expensive sledgehammer when a tack hammer would have done the job. Not only that, but they *had* the tack hammer they needed all along! Look at their return on Nordbrandt, alone. And if Terekhov and Van Dort hadn't literally stumbled across the Manpower connection—I'm not trying to downplay anything they accomplished, but they really did stumble across it, you know—then Westman would probably still be shooting at us in Montana, too. Investing a few hundred million in political action committees and funding and supplying other lunatics with guns and bombs would have let them keep the entire Cluster at the boil pretty much indefinitely, unless we wanted to resort to some sort of authoritarian repression. And it would have done that while simultaneously limiting Manpower's exposure, risk, and expense. They might not have been able to prevent the Constitutional Convention from voting out an acceptable constitution, although I'm not even sure of that. But even if the constitution had been voted out, they could probably have counted on keeping the political unrest going at a level which would have forced us to stay home and tend to our knitting instead of causing them problems in their own backyard. So why go for this sort of grandstanding operation? Why invest so much more money and risk the kind of beating they're taking in the Solly public opinion polls now that it's blown up in their faces?"

"I hadn't really considered it that way," Chandler admitted thoughtfully. "I guess I just assumed it was pure greed, as much as self-defense, from their perspective. Keeping us completely out of the Cluster and taking control of the Lynx Terminus would have to be the optimum solution from their viewpoint, after all."

"I don't disagree. I just think it's not the sort of solution Manpower would normally have reached for. With only a handful of exceptions—like Torch—the Mesan government's never shown any particular interest in playing the interstellar politics game. And virtually everything Manpower and the other Mesan *corporations* have done has been more . . . insidious. They've worked through acquiring influence, through bribery and coercion, at least where anyone who could potentially fight back might be concerned. This just isn't like them, and it makes me antsy when an established player suddenly starts changing. It leaves me with the feeling that there's something going on under the surface. Something we ought to figure out before it comes up out of the depths and bites us right square on the ass."

"You may have a point," Chandler acknowledged after several seconds. "On the other hand, whatever they had in mind this time around, it clearly didn't work."

"*This* time around," O'Shaughnessy agreed. "But we still don't know how the Sollies are going to react in the long haul. And if they've tried something like this once, who's to say they won't come up with something equally ... inventive for us in the future? That's one reason I hope you're right about what's going to happen to the Havenites' military position in light of Lovat. I may not be sure what they're up to, but I know I want us to be as free as possible from other distractions if they decide to have a second try at getting us into a war with the Solarian League!"

"Thank you for seeing me on such short notice, Junyan," Valery Ottweiler said as he stepped into the sun filled office and the door closed silently behind him.

"Your message indicated that it was rather urgent," Vice Commissioner Hongbo Junyan of the Office of Frontier Security replied, coming to his feet to shake Ottweiler's hand. "And on a personal level, it's always good to see you, Valery."

The vice commissioner didn't bother to lie very well in that last sentence, Ottweiler noted with a certain amusement. Given what had happened in Monica, he had to be one of the last people in the galaxy Hongbo Junyan actually wanted to see. Still, there were diplomatic niceties to be observed, even if the diplomats on both sides were fully aware of the total insincerity of the niceties in question. Unfortunately for Hongbo, he'd had no choice but to agree to this meeting. He'd been far too deep in Manpower's pocket for far too long to refuse to see a diplomatic representative of Manpower's home planet, since everyone knew the corporations of Mesa effectively were the government the Mesa System.

"What is it I can do for you this morning?" Hongbo continued, waving his visitor into one of the office's chairs. From his tone, it was apparent he didn't intend to do one single thing more for Mesa—or Manpower—than he absolutely had to. And since both of them were fully aware of that state of affairs, Ottweiler saw no point in beating about the bush.

*Especially since I'm probably going to have to twist his arm to the point of dislocation anyway before this is over*, he thought.

"Actually," he said out loud, "I've just received fresh instructions from home."

"You have?" Ottweiler wasn't particularly surprised that a certain wariness had crept into Hongbo's voice. The man was no fool, after all.

"Yes. It seems that several powerful interests in my government—and in the Mesan business community, as well, if we're going to be honest—aren't at all happy about how that business in Monica was finally resolved."

"Really? I can't imagine why." The sarcasm dripping from Hongbo's response was a mark of his own unhappiness with "that business." And also a pointed comment on just who *he* thought was to blame for its outcome.

"Please, Junyan." Ottweiler shook his head wearily. "Can we just take it as a given that no one involved in that entire operation is very happy about it? There was plenty of egg to go around for everyone's faces, I assure you."

He held Hongbo's eye for a moment until, finally, the Solarian nodded.

"Thank you," Ottweiler said, and sat back in his chair.

"Having said that, however," he continued, "the same considerations that inspired my government to become involved then continue to apply. A Manticoran presence in our area poses a significant threat not simply to our business community's commercial interests, but to the security of the Mesa System itself. I'm sure you can understand that the failure of our sponsorship of Monica has led to a certain reevaluation of our options and requirements back home."

"Yes, I can see that," Hongbo acknowledged. "On the other hand, I'm not sure I see what sort of 'options' you have left at the moment. They've ratified their precious constitution, the Star Kingdom has officially expanded itself into this 'Star Empire' of theirs, and the beating you people—and us—have taken in the press back home doesn't leave any of us very much room for maneuver, does it?"

"Yes... and no," Ottweiler replied, and Hongbo stiffened behind the desk. That was obviously the last response he'd wanted to hear, Ottweiler reflected.

"Before you go any further, Valery," the Solarian said, "let's be clear about one thing, shall we? I'm prepared to do a great many things to accommodate you and your 'government,' and so is Lorcan, but there are distinct limits to what we *can* do. Especially after what happened in Monica. And, not to put too fine a point on it, assassinating Webster didn't help any."

"That wasn't us," Ottweiler said mildly. "I thought everyone knew it was the Republic of Haven."

"Of course it was," Hongbo snorted. "But whoever it was, it's got the newsies all in a flutter back home, especially combined with what he was saying about you people's modest efforts out here in Talbott. When a mess is this big and gets this much play in the 'faxes, even our public starts to get interested. And when that happens, the Justice Department can't hush it up forever. The newsies demand show trials, so Justice has to give them exactly that. Hell, they've actually indicted half a dozen of Technodyne's top people!"

"Yes, that was unfortunate," Ottweiler said. "On the other hand, neither you nor I work for Technodyne, do we?"

"No, but Lorcan and I do work for the Office of Frontier Security," Hongbo said tartly, "and we're already hearing about this from the home office. So far, OFS has managed to stay out of the limelight, and that busybody Corvisart hasn't been all that interested in pulling us into it. So far," he repeated.

"Of course she hasn't." It was Ottweiler's turn to snort. "You think the Manties want to take on the League Navy? Especially now that this summit thing has collapsed and they've got Haven back on their backs again?"

"Of course they don't, but that's not really my point." Hongbo tilted back in his chair and tapped the desk blotter with one forefinger for emphasis. "While it would undoubtedly be very unfortunate for Manticore if they should find themselves in a direct shooting confrontation with the Navy, that could also be very unfortunate for whoever helped to . . . arrange that confrontation. Nobody in OFS wants to hand the newsies—or the Manties—even more ammunition to use against us. It's bad enough that we look incompetent enough to have let this happen under are very noses, as it were. After all, the Manties are hardly your typical neobarbs. They have far better connections on Old Terra than most people do, as you people—oh, excuse me, I meant *Haven*—clearly recognized when the decision was made to eliminate Webster. The truth is, Valery, Lorcan and I have been told in no uncertain terms to lay off Manticore. Which, to be perfectly blunt, is exactly what I would have decided on my own."

"I'm sorry to hear that," Ottweiler said calmly. "Unfortunately, my instructions are somewhat different."

"That's too bad, since there's nothing I can do about it."

"Oh, but there is."

"No," Hongbo disagreed flatly, "there *isn't*. You know as well as I do how OFS works, Valery. Yes, for the most part the commissioners have pretty much free rein to manage their own sectors. And everybody knows that means all of us have 'special friends' who get preferential treatment. But in the end, all of us are subject to the Ministry's control, and I'm telling you the word's gone out. No more bad press out of Talbott, at least until the current mess has had a chance to settle and recede in the public's memory. Given the fact that the public in question has the attention span of a fruit fly, that shouldn't impose too great a delay on whatever it is your superiors want to accomplish, but for right now, my hands are tied."

Ottweiler cocked his head to one side, his expression thoughtful as he presented the appearance of a man carefully considering what Hongbo had just said. From the Solarian's position, it made perfectly good sense, of course. When he spoke of "the Ministry's control," he wasn't talking about anything as unimportant or ephemeral as the current Solarian Minister for Foreign Affairs, whoever that might happen to be at the moment. What he was really talking about was the deeply entrenched bureaucracy which truly *ran* the Ministry of Foreign Affairs, just as similar bureaucracies ran every other aspect of the League's government and military. And although the bureaucrats in question were effectively free of any interference by their nominal political masters, the Solarian public's occasional outbursts of indignation over government corruption could be unpleasant for all concerned. That was the real reason Governor Barregos—who had somehow acquired a towering reputation for efficiency and honesty—hadn't been recalled from the Maya Sector long since. So it was hardly surprising that Hongbo's superiors and Verrochio's fellow commissioners and sector governors wanted this whole business to go away as quickly as possible so they could all climb back under their rocks and get on with business as usual.

"I'm sorry," he repeated aloud after several seconds, "but I'm afraid my superiors are rather insistent in this case, Junyan."

"Aren't you listening to me?" Hongbo was beginning to sound exasperated. "There isn't anything I can do!"

"But there is." Ottweiler allowed a little deliberate patience to creep into his own tone. "I wouldn't be sitting here talking to you if there weren't."

"Valery—"

"Just listen for a minute, Junyan," Ottweiler interrupted, and Hongbo's eyes narrowed at the peremptory note in his voice. It was not the sort of note he was accustomed to hearing from anyone in his own office, and there was no mistaking the flare of anger in those dark, narrow eyes. But he throttled the anger, tightened his jaw, and nodded curtly.

"All right," the Mesan said then. "Cards on the table time. The people I work for—and you know who they really are, as well as I do—aren't happy. In fact, they're very *unhappy*, and they intend to do something about it. That's why I'm sitting here, and to be honest, I'm more than a little astonished myself at the resources they have available. Just for starters, did you really think it was a coincidence Admiral Byng wound up in command of the Frontier Fleet detachment they sent out here to bolster your position after Monica? *Please!*" He rolled his eyes. "Byng is one of those sanctimonious Battle Fleet pricks. He wouldn't have wound up commanding a *Frontier Fleet* detachment without somebody making damned sure he did. And just who do you suppose that 'somebody' was?"

Hongbo's eyes were even narrower than they had been, but speculation was beginning to replace—or supplement, at least—the anger which had filled them.

"Then there's the little matter that Admiral Crandall has decided to conduct 'training exercises' at McIntosh."

"What?" Hongbo straightened in his chair. "What are you talking about? Nobody's told *us* anything about any exercises at McIntosh!"

"I'm afraid you may have failed to get the memo. Perhaps it has something to do with the fact that Crandall is Battle Fleet, not Frontier Fleet. Battle Fleet doesn't really talk to you Frontier Security peasants very much, does it?"

"Battle Fleet," Hongbo repeated. The depth of his surprise over that particular bit of information was obvious. It was even deep enough to distract him from the flick of Ottweiler's whip as he emphasized Battle Fleet's deep contempt for Frontier Fleet and Frontier Security.

"Yes," the Mesan said, then shook his head. "Frankly, I didn't know anything about it before Monica, but it would appear Admiral Crandall has selected McIntosh as the site for her latest fleet exercises." He shrugged. "I know it's a bit unusual for Battle Fleet to venture this far out into the Verge, but apparently Crandall wanted to exercise the Fleet Train, as well as the battle squadrons. According to my information, it's been over ninety T-years since Battle Fleet has deployed more than a single squadron all the way out to the frontier, and there's been some question as to whether or not it still has the logistics capacity to support its own operations outside the Old League's established system of bases."

"So am I supposed to infer that Admiral Crandall is exercising in greater strength than 'a single squadron,' then?" Hongbo asked slowly.

"As a matter of fact, I believe she has somewhere around a hundred of the wall," Ottweiler said in an offhand sort of way, and Hongbo sat suddenly back, deep in his chair.

"What's occurred to my superiors," Ottweiler continued, "is that with three full squadrons of Frontier Fleet battlecruisers, with screening elements, already attached to the Madras Sector to reinforce your own units, and with such a powerful Battle Fleet backup fortuitously so close at hand, it may be time for Commissioner Verrochio to repair the damage the League's prestige has suffered out of this entire ugly situation in Monica. I'm sure I hardly need to point out to you how unfortunate it could be if other Verge systems began to take Frontier Security lightly or got the mistaken notion that OFS won't take punitive measures if someone steps on your toes in public this way. And all of that exercised public opinion you're so concerned about back home could certainly use pointing towards another target, don't you think? A target like . . . oh, the proof that, whatever Manticore may have been saying, and however their mouthpieces back on Old Terra may have managed to spin events at Monica, the truth is that they're just as imperialistic and exploitive as *we've* always known they are."

"And we would accomplish this retargeting exactly how?" Hongbo asked.

"According to my latest information, the New Tuscany System Government is already experiencing severe problems with the Talbott Cluster's new management," Ottweiler replied. "Indeed, I expect it won't be very much longer before you and Commissioner Verrochio receive a request for a Frontier Security investigation of Manticore's systematic harassment of New Tuscany's merchant shipping."

Hongbo's expression was a curious mixture of anticipation and unhappiness. Although his disposition was far less naturally choleric than Verrochio's, he clearly hadn't enjoyed his own humiliation after Monica. And Ottweiler's point about the damage to Frontier Security's reputation had also been well taken. OFS had worked hard to make sure no Verge system wanted to risk pissing Frontier Security off at *it*, and letting Manticore get away with what it had pulled off at Monica wasn't the best way to shore up that perception. So, for a lot reasons, Hongbo obviously wanted some of his own back. But, equally obviously, he hadn't forgotten how foolproof the Monica operation had been supposed to be, and he was leery of sticking his foot back into the bear trap. And he was also smart enough to realize—just as Ottweiler himself had—that Byng and Crandall's involvement suggested that the interests in play were both much more powerful and even more ruthless than he'd first thought.

"I don't know, Valery." He shook his head slowly. "Everything you say may make perfectly good sense, and under normal circumstances, I'd be only too happy to help your superiors out. You know that. But the messages we've been getting through official channels have been what you might call brutally clear. Lorcan and I are supposed to sit here and behave like good little boys until the powers that be tell us differently. Besides, even if that weren't the case, Lorcan is almost as scared as he is pissed off. What the Manties did to Monica's battlecruisers shook him up badly."

"I don't blame him for that," Ottweiler said frankly. "On the other hand, you can always point out to him that they were manned by Monicans, not Sollies. And that they didn't have the entire SLN standing directly behind them. I'm sure the *Manties* are aware of those minor differences, at any rate, and with the resumption of operations against Haven, they aren't going to have a lot of combat power to be diverting this way even if they were stupid enough to take the SLN on directly. Certainly not enough to pose any sort of significant threat in the face of Crandall's presence."

"But if they don't know any more about Crandall's presence than *we* did before you told me about her, then it's not likely to exercise very much of a deterrent effect on their thinking, is it? Unless, of course, someone is going to make this minor fact known to them, as well."

He was watching Ottweiler's face very carefully, and the Mesan shrugged.

"I don't have any official information on that either way," he said. "On the other hand, it's my strong impression that no one's going to be going out of his way to tell the Manties a damned thing. Still, Commissioner Verrochio is a sector governor, himself. If he felt the need to request it, I'm sure Admiral Crandall would move her forces from McIntosh to Meyers. Purely as a precautionary measure, you understand."

Hongbo nodded slowly, his expression intent. Ottweiler could almost literally see the calculations working themselves out behind his eyes and wondered if the Solarian would reach the same conclusions he had.

"That all sounds very comforting," Hongbo said finally. "But the fact remains that Lorcan isn't going to want to do it. To be honest, that's at least partly my fault. I didn't have any idea something like this might be in the wind, so when we started getting word from the home office, I did my very best to sit on Lorcan's temper, and that took some pretty firm sitting. You know how he is. I'm afraid I may have sat on it too hard. He's swung from breathing fire and brimstone to worrying that he may give the Manty bogeyman another excuse to jump on him. It's going to take time to turn that around."

"Time is something we don't have very much of," Ottweiler said flatly. "Trust me, New Tuscany is going to be ready to start moving on this very soon."

"You're sure of that? New Tuscany's three hundred and sixty light-years from here. How can you be so confident they're going to play along when they're over a month away even for a dispatch boat?"

"Trust me," Ottweiler repeated. "The representative my superiors are sending to New Tuscany is very convincing, and what the New Tuscans stand to get out of this is going to be *very* attractive to them. They'll come through for us."

"Maybe you're right. Maybe I even believe you're right. But

Lorcan isn't going to jump for something like this until he's got confirmation of that. Even *with* that confirmation, he's not going to be happy about it. I expect him to dig his heels in every centimeter of the way."

"Then you're just going to have to be even more convincing than usual," Ottweiler told him. "Obviously, my superiors aren't going to forget what they owe the two of you for pulling this off, so I'm certain you can expect to be extremely well compensated for your efforts."

"I'm sure you're right about that much, at least. But that doesn't change the fact that I'm going to have to bring him around to this gradually."

"Our time window for this is too narrow for 'gradually,'" Ottweiler said. "Even though Crandall's set up for a lengthy deployment as part of her logistics test, she can't stay on station here forever. We've got to get this rolling while she's still around to back our play if it comes to that. That's what restricts our time frame so tightly, and I'm sure the commissioner is going to want to know she's around if he might need her. In any case, my instructions to get this all moving ASAP are about as firm as they get. So if you think you need a little more leverage with him, remind him of this. My superiors have records of all of their past transactions with him. And unlike him, they aren't citizens of the League and aren't subject to its laws."

Hongbo stiffened, and not just because of the icy chill which had invaded Ottweiler's voice. His eyes met the Mesan's, and their unspoken message was abundantly clear. If they had records of their transactions with Verrochio, then they just as certainly had records of their transactions with *him*. And if they were prepared to feed Verrochio to the wolves if he failed to follow instructions, then they were equally prepared to feed *him* to the same hungry fangs.

Hongbo Junyan had always recognized that Manpower and the other Mesan corporations could be dangerous benefactors. The chance of exposure was virtually nonexistent under normal circumstances, and everyone knew everyone else did exactly the same things. It was the way the system worked, how business was done. Even if some unfortunate personal arrangement should inadvertently intrude into the light, it could be expected to disappear quickly into the "business as usual," "everyone does it" basket. The rest of the system could be counted upon to make that happen smoothly and promptly.

But if Manpower chose to make his past dealings with them public knowledge, they could be counted upon to do it as loudly—and effectively—as possible. And after everything that had already gone wrong out here, the newsies would be just salivating for fresh, spectacular evidence of corruption and conspiracy. Which meant his fellows within the system would cheerfully throw both Verrochio and Hongbo to the howling mob. Indeed, his colleagues would probably lead the pack, shouting louder than anyone else as a way to prove their own innocence.

All of that was bad enough, but there was worse, because the Audubon Ballroom had made it abundantly clear over the years that bureaucrats and administrators who conspired and collaborated with Manpower when they were supposed to be working diligently to suppress the genetic slave trade were not among the Ballroom's favorite people. In fact, they'd made a point of coming up with especially inventive ways of demonstrating that fact. Ways that were usually punctuated with showers of body parts.

"I don't think the good commissioner is likely to prove too difficult if you bring that little point to his attention, do you, Junyan?" Valery Ottweiler asked softly.

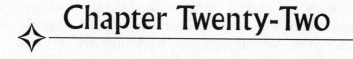

# Chapter Twenty-Two

ALDONA ANISIMOVNA HAD NEVER expected to be back in the Talbott Cluster this quickly, and for more than one reason.

The mere thought of how disastrously the Monica operation had failed was enough to send cold chills down anyone's spine—even that of a Mesan alpha line. She'd been more than a little astonished that she and Isabel Bardasano had survived the catastrophic unraveling of the Strategy Council's carefully crafted plans.

But even allowing for her unanticipated survival, she wouldn't have imagined she could make the trip back to the Cluster so quickly. Then again, she hadn't known about the top-secret "streak drive," either. She was going to have to remember that it had taken her much longer—officially, at least—to make the voyage than it actually had.

And she supposed she might as well go ahead and admit there was another reason for her surprise; she'd never imagined it might be possible to mount a replacement for the disastrous failure in Monica this quickly.

*It would have helped if Albrecht—and Isabel—had told me just what we'd really been supposed to achieve last time. Or how many resources were really available, for that matter,* she thought as she and her new bodyguard rode the luxurious, if old-fashioned, elevator towards the upcoming meeting. *Of course, I'm not sure exactly what else I could have done to make use*

*of them, even if I'd known they were there. And I don't sup-
pose they could tell me about them . . . not without telling me
everything else, at least.*

It was amazing how completely her galaxy had shifted with
Albrecht's explanation of what was really going on. A part of her
was absolutely stunned that the entire Mesan Strategy Council
and all of its deep laid plans and machinations had really been
only a part—and not the largest part—of the real strategy she'd
served, albeit unknowingly, for so many decades. Another part
of her was more than a little irked to discover just how much of
what she'd thought she knew, even in an operational sense, had
been less than complete or even deliberately falsified. Like the
"fact" that the Congo Wormhole hadn't been properly surveyed
before those Audubon Ballroom fanatics took the system away
from Mesa, for example, or who'd *really* been in charge of "her"
operation in Monica. Discovering that someone else could manage her puppet strings as well as she'd always prided herself on
managing *others'* strings hadn't been especially reassuring. But her
irritation over lack of complete information and need-to-know
compartmentalization of knowledge was as nothing compared to
the sheer shock of what was really happening. Aldona Anisimovna
was a hardy soul, yet she was both awed and more than a little
terrified by the grand, sweeping scope of the Mesan Alignment's
true objectives and resources.

*I thought it was just the usual dogfight over political power*, she
admitted to herself. *And, to be honest, I always thought the political aspects were purely self-defense, a way to protect our operations
and our economic power. I never dreamed anyone could be thinking
on such a . . . grand scale.*

*Or that so much of the groundwork could already have been
in place.*

The elevator stopped. Kyrillos Taliadoros—the newly assigned
bodyguard from the same gamma line which had produced
Albrecht Detweiler's bodyguard—stepped through the opening
doors first, glancing up and down the corridor. Taliadoros' physical senses had been sharply enhanced as part of his genotype's
modifications, and Anisimovna knew additional odd bits and
pieces of hardware had been surgically implanted to help suit him
for his present function. She'd discovered that even Detweiler's
bodyguard's fearsome reputation actually understated what he

was capable of, and the same was true of Taliadoros. Which, in some ways, was almost as frightening as it was comforting.

Then again, a lot of the things she'd had to wrap her mind around in the past couple of weeks were almost as frightening as they were comforting.

She pushed that thought aside and followed Taliadoros out of the elevator when his tiny gesture indicated his satisfaction with their immediate surroundings. He fell back into his properly deferential position at her heels as she led the way down the short corridor, and the ornate secretary seated behind the desk at its far end looked up with a professional smile at her approach.

*My, she's a pretty one*, Anisimovna thought appreciatively, taking in the young woman's flowing raven hair, striking blue eyes, and near-perfect complexion. *She'd almost do for one of the pleasure lines without any modification at all. Of course, there is that little mole. And I think her left eyebrow may be just a tad higher than the right. But in her case, that actually helps. I think she'd look . . . too perfect without those little flaws.*

"Aldona Anisimovna," she said aloud. "I believe President Boutin is expecting me."

"Of course, Ms. Anisimovna." The secretary's voice was exactly the right melodious contralto to match her striking appearance, Anisimovna thought appreciatively. "Just a moment."

She pressed a button on her panel.

"Ms. Anisimovna is here, Mr. President," she said, and listened to her earbug for a moment. "Yes, Sir," she said then, and looked back up at Anisimovna. "President Boutin is ready to see you now, Ma'am." She pressed another button and a rather splendidly decorated door slid open. "Right through that door, Ma'am."

"Thank you." Anisimovna smiled a bit more warmly than she normally smiled at servants, then nodded to Taliadoros and the two of them stepped through the open door.

"Excuse me a moment, Ma'am," a broad shouldered young man said as they entered the anteroom of the luxurious office suite.

"Yes?" Anisimovna gave him a rather cool glance, and he smiled with just a touch of apology.

"I'm afraid some of your bodyguard's implants have flashed several alarms on our security scans. I'm sorry, but security regulations prohibit allowing someone with unidentified implanted hardware into the President's presence."

"I see." Anisimovna considered him for a moment, then turned to Taliadoros.

"I'm afraid you're going to have to wait here for me, Kyrillos," she said.

"Ma'am, under the regulations, I'm not supposed—" he began, exactly as if they hadn't already rehearsed this moment.

"I realize it's against the rules," her own tone mingled patience with just a touch of brusqueness, "but at the moment, we're guests on someone else's planet. It's only polite of us to abide by *their* rules and customs."

"I know that, Ma'am, but—"

"This discussion is finished, Kyrillos," she said firmly, then smiled. "I'll take full responsibility, but this time good manners trump the regulations. Anyway, I'm sure the President's security team is up to the task of protecting me, right along with him, if it comes to that. And I really don't expect anyone to try to assassinate me in the middle of a meeting with him, anyway."

"Yes, Ma'am," Taliadoros said with manifest unwillingness, and Anisimovna turned back to the broad-shouldered young man.

"I believe that's settled," she said crisply.

"Yes, Ma'am. Thank you for being so understanding. If you'll follow me, please?"

Anisimovna followed him across the anteroom. She wasn't certain that little bit of theater had been necessary, but it wouldn't hurt to make her hosts aware of her own importance, especially since she was officially here as a private person. Of course, most private persons didn't travel in their personal hyper-capable yachts or come equipped with personal enhanced bodyguards. And Taliadoros' reference to "the regulations" should also neatly suggest that whether she was *supposed* to be a private person or not, she actually wasn't.

*Which is fair enough, since I'm not, even if everyone is about to spend the next few hours pretending I am.*

She stepped through yet another door into an absolutely magnificent office overlooking downtown Siena, the capital of the planet of New Tuscany. Several people were waiting for her.

President Alain Boutin, the official head of state of the New Tuscany System, stood in courteous greeting behind his shuttle-sized desk as she entered. System Prime Minister Maxime Vézien, the real head of government, turned from the floor-to-ceiling windows looking out over the capital city of Livorno with a smile of welcome of his own, and Alesta Cardot, the Minister of Foreign Affairs, and Nicholas Pélisard, the Minister of War, turned from their quiet side conversation with Honorine Huppé, the Minister of Trade. Damien Dusserre, the New Tuscan Minister of Security, stood by himself by the bookcases lining one wall of the office, and his smile was much cooler—and less professional—than Vézien's.

*I wish there'd been time for a little more research*, Anisimovna thought as she crossed the large room to the desk. There'd barely been time on the voyage here for her to fully absorb the in-depth briefing on New Tuscany's current state of affairs; there certainly hadn't been enough time for any sort of detailed historical study, and she had absolutely no idea, for example, why a planet named for a region of Old Terra's Italy should be inhabited by people with almost uniformly French names.

"Ms. Anisimovna!" Boutin offered his hand across the desk. When she took it, he raised her hand to his lips and brushed a kiss across its back, and she smiled at him.

"It was most gracious of you to agree to see me, Mr. President. And especially on such short notice."

"Mr. Metcalf made it clear your business was urgent," Boutin replied. "And, to be frank, that you . . . unofficially represent, shall we say, import interests on Mesa."

"Yes, I suppose I do," she said with a whimsical smile. She rather wished that Valery Ottweiler, the Mesan attaché who had been her official aide in Meyers when the Monica operation was first mounted, had been available here, as well. She'd found his competence both impressive and comforting. But he was still back in Meyers, where he had his own part to play, and Jansen Metcalf, the Mesan trade attaché who had been upgraded into a full ambassador when New Tuscany withdrew from the Spindle Constitutional Convention, was supposed to be a competent type, as well. He wouldn't be present today, however, of course. The fact that Mesa's official representative was absent—and that he had emphasized her own "unofficial" status ahead of time—were two more of the little clues that, in fact, she not only did speak for the true rulers of Mesa but that what she had to say was very important indeed.

"Please, allow me to introduce my colleagues," Boutin said,

and Anisimovna nodded pleasantly to each of the others in turn as the President murmured their names. Not that anyone in that room at that moment actually needed to be introduced to anyone else, she was quite certain.

Introductions completed, she settled into a comfortable chair, crossed her long legs, and leaned back. During her first visit to Roberto Tyler, Anisimovna had deliberately chosen a gown which emphasized the rich perfection of her own figure. Boutin and—even more importantly—Vézien were far less likely to be swayed by any physical charms, however provocatively displayed, and so she had chosen a severely tailored outfit in midnight blue. And, while she had no qualms about using whatever tactics—or attributes—would get the job done, she had to admit that she much preferred not feeling like a gussied up pleasure slave.

"And now, Ms. Anisimovna, may we know what it is that brings you to New Tuscany?"

"To be totally frank, Mr. President, I'm here in no small part because of the rather disastrous occurrences in Monica," she said, and hid a smile at the shock in the New Tuscans' faces.

*Didn't expect me to own right up to the fact that we were involved in that little catastrophe, did you?* she thought sardonically. *Well, I've got a few more surprises in store for you, as well.*

"I'm sure you're all well aware of what happened to the Union of Monica," she continued calmly. "That regrettable state of affairs was the result of a combination of coincidences no one could have predicted, coupled with a certain degree of botched execution on the Monicans' part."

"We *have* had reports on those . . . events," Boutin said slowly, his eyes flickering sideways to Dusserre. "May I ask exactly what about them has brought you to speak to us?"

"Frankly, Mr. President, we have no interest in seeing the Manties expanding their control and influence into this region of space," she replied with an air of total candor. "I'm sure all of you are very well aware of the long-standing hostility between the business community of Mesa and the Star Kingdom of Manticore. And as Manticore has demonstrated quite often in the past—and very recently, in Monica—the 'Star Kingdom' has never been shy about resorting to the use of naked force in the pursuit of its policy objectives. It seems very evident to us in the Mesa System that the establishment of a Manticoran bridgehead here in Talbott will almost inevitably lead to further harassment of Mesa and, quite possibly, to actual Manticoran military operations against Mesa in the not-too-distant future. That, to be completely honest, was the reason for our initial contacts with President Tyler.

"Unfortunately, as all of you are also aware, the Constitutional Convention in Spindle has ratified this new constitution, turning virtually the entire Cluster into another lobe of the Star Kingdom. Which means, of course, that what we hoped to prevent as a measure of self-defense by means of our support for President Tyler has become an established fact."

Several faces had tightened at her mention of the Constitutional Convention, and she concealed a mental smile of catlike satisfaction as she saw them. Frankly, she'd been flabbergasted—initially, at least—to learn that New Tuscany had, in fact, declined to ratify the new constitution. In their place, she would have been falling all over herself to get under the Manticoran security umbrella and share in the flood tide of commerce and investment which was likely to be coming the Cluster's way. Except, of course, for that other little problem they had. She'd already concluded, just in the short trip from the spaceport to this meeting, that Bardasano's analysis of the New Tuscan oligarchs and their motivations had been right on the money. In fact, the lid was screwed down even more tightly here on New Tuscany than she'd expected from Bardasano's briefings. Uniformed security forces had been a high-visibility part of the ground car drive from the shuttle pad, and she'd noticed an extraordinarily high number of extraordinarily obvious (for a planet with New Tuscany's tech base) security cameras on light standards and at intersections. No doubt there were other, far less obtrusive measures in place to monitor the situation without giving away their presence, but clearly the New Tuscan security forces wanted to do more than simply keep a close eye on things. They also wanted to make any potential troublemakers abundantly aware of the point that they *were* keeping that eye on things.

*Between the devil and the deep blue sea, weren't you, Mr. President?* Her mental tone was mocking, although she supposed it wasn't very funny from the New Tuscans' perspective. *If you didn't ratify the constitution, you got left out in the cold where all that lovely investment and capital flow were involved. But if you* did *ratify it, you'd've had the Manties swarming all over New Tuscany, and they wouldn't have approved of your 'security measures' at all, would they?*

Looked at from that perspective, she supposed the New Tuscan decision to opt out of the constitutional process when Manticore and their fellow Talbott delegates declined to give them the domestic security carte blanche they'd insisted upon actually made a degree of sense. The last thing any properly exploitative oligarchs could afford was for their social inferiors to get uppity notions, after all. Unfortunately for New Tuscany, the mere example of what was about to happen in the rest of the Cluster was virtually certain to contaminate their star system with those very notions. Their only real hope had been to siphon off enough of the increasing commerce and Manticoran investment to provide an at least modest but real improvement in the general New Tuscan standard of living. Frankly, the chance of their ever having been able to control the situation through any combination of carrot and stick had never been realistic, in Anisimovna's opinion, but it appeared to be the only one they'd been able to come up with.

*Not surprisingly, since the only other approach would have been to recognize when they were beaten and try to make the best terms they could with the people they've been systematically pissing on—and pissing off—for the last two or three generations,* she thought. *Somehow, I don't think they would have enjoyed the only terms they could get.*

"As you say, it would appear the organization of this 'Talbott Quadrant' is an accomplished fact, Ms. Anisimovna," Prime Minister Vézien said. His tone was sour, but she noticed he was regarding her shrewdly. "Yet somehow I can't avoid the suspicion that you wouldn't have come to call on us—or been so . . . forthcoming, shall we say?—about your involvement with Monica unless you thought that state of affairs could somehow still be . . . rectified."

"I see you're as perceptive as my briefings suggested you were, Mr. Prime Minister. Yes, we do believe the situation can be rectified, which I'm sure you here in New Tuscany would find almost as welcome as we would in Mesa. And, to anticipate your next question, yes, again. I have come here to discuss ways in which the two of us could assist one another in bringing that rectification about."

"Forgive me for pointing this out, Ms. Anisimovna," Alesta Cardot said, "but the last star system you recruited for this no doubt laudable objective doesn't seem to have fared very well."

"And there's also the little matter of certain collateral damage inflicted by your previous efforts, if you'll pardon me for saying so," Dusserre added. The Security Minister met Anisimovna's eyes very levelly, and she nodded slightly in acknowledgment of his point.

"Madam Minister," she said to Cardot, "you're absolutely correct about what happened to Monica. As I've already said, however, that was due to a completely unpredictable coincidence of circumstances—circumstances which are unlikely, at the very least, to ever repeat themselves. Moreover, even if they—or something like them—did repeat, they would have no significant impact on the strategy we have in mind this time. And, Mr. Dusserre," she said, turning to face the Security Minister squarely, "I'm afraid we must plead guilty to supplying Agnes Nordbrandt and her fellow lunatics with the wherewithal for their campaign against the Kornatian authorities. I'm sure that's made subsequent difficulties for you here on New Tuscany, and my own reading of events suggests that it helped Alquezar and his allies force through the constitutional provisions they favored all along. I regret that, but, in fairness, I ought to point out that at the time we decided to supply Nordbrandt, our objectives revolved around Monica, not anyone here in the Cluster itself. The consequences here on New Tuscany are unfortunate, but to be brutally honest, at that time New Tuscany was completely secondary to our calculations and concerns."

"Well, that's certainly frank enough, Ms. Anisimovna," Cardot said dryly.

"In this case, Madam Secretary," Anisimovna replied, "candor is clearly the best policy. And since that's the case, there's very little point in pretending that what I'm here to discuss is anything except a marriage of pragmatic self-interest. I'd be the first to admit you have a lovely planet here. Indeed, I quite enjoyed observing it from orbit and on the flight down, and the scenery around the spaceport is breathtaking. Nonetheless, it would be dishonest of me to pretend that Mesa has any intrinsic interest whatsoever in New Tuscany . . . aside from the fashion in which the two of us can assist one another in bringing about a state of affairs we both desire."

"I see." President Boutin folded his hands in front of him on his desk blotter and cocked his head to one side. "I think you're probably correct that there's no need for New Tuscany and Mesa to pretend they're bosom friends. At the same time, however, Alesta's point about what happened to Monica is entirely valid. I'm sure I speak for the rest of my colleagues when I say we have absolutely no interest in experiencing the same unfortunate consequences. And, to return candor for candor, Mesa's sheer distance from the Cluster, and your planet's habit of . . . acting from behind the scenes, shall we say, offers you quite a bit of protection which would not be available to *us* if we should arouse the Manties' ire. As you've already said, they have a pattern of using military force to achieve their policy ends, and please don't be offended, but I'd really prefer not to have the Royal Manticoran Navy do to us what it did to Monica."

"Mr. President, frankness is unlikely ever to offend me. And I entirely understand your feelings. However, I believe I can explain why what happened to Monica most definitely will not be happening to New Tuscany."

"Speaking for myself, as Minister of War, and, I'm sure, for all of us, I would be fascinated to hear that explanation," Nicholas Pélisard said, and his tone was even drier than Cardot's had been.

"The most important single difference between what we're envisioning this time around and the Monican operation is that we've decided our biggest mistake in Monica was attempting to maintain too great a degree of deniability. We stayed too far out of the loop—and relied too heavily on Monica to 'front' for us—when we arranged to supply President Tyler with the battlecruisers he required for his part of the operation."

"Which was?" Dusserre inquired mildly, and she looked at him. "We've heard several possible explanations. I was simply wondering which one—if any of them—was accurate?" the security minister added mildly, and he smiled.

It was cynical, that smile, but behind it she saw something else. Something not even his years of calculation and power could hide. Dusserre was a player, someone who gravitated as naturally to power—and to his own position as New Tuscany's chief policeman—as a moth gravitated towards an open flame, yet she wondered if he was truly aware of the fear she saw behind that smile. The sense that the entire power structure of his homeworld was sliding inexorably towards collapse . . .

*Albrecht and Isabel were right*, Anisimovna thought. *These people* are *desperate enough to save their little house of cards to be nicely receptive. What was it that Old Earth king said? Something about 'After me, the flood'? Well, these people already feel the water lapping around their ankles, don't they? That's good.*

"The objective," she said aloud, looking him straight in the eye, "was for Tyler to secure control of the Lynx Terminus of the Manticoran Wormhole Junction. Commissioner Verrochio, of the Office of Frontier Security, was prepared to support his actions—completely impartially, of course—while the League arranged for a new plebiscite, under OFS supervision, to determine the validity of the original plebiscite returns in favor of seeking annexation by Manticore. I'm afraid the commissioner anticipated discovering widespread fraud in the Manticoran plebiscite." She shook her head sadly. "If that had turned out to be the case, then obviously Frontier Security would have had no choice but to set those flawed results aside in favor of the results of its own plebiscite. Which would undoubtedly have led to the endorsement of a Cluster-wide government under the leadership and protection of the Monican Navy and recognized by the Solarian League as the legitimate government of the Cluster."

She had the satisfaction of seeing even Dusserre's eyes widen slightly as she admitted the breadth and scope of the original plan. She'd thought it was an audacious but workable plan herself, when she sold it to Roberto Tyler in the first place. Of course, she hadn't realized then what the Alignment's real objective was. And she had absolutely no intention of explaining that real objective to these people, either.

"I don't think New Tuscany would have liked that very much, Ms. Anisimovna," Honorine Huppé said after a moment, and Anisimovna chuckled.

"I don't imagine you would have, Madam Minister. Of course, that wasn't exactly foremost in our thinking when we formulated the plan. And, for that matter, New Tuscany's unhappiness would all have been a matter of perspective, wouldn't it?" She smiled winsomely as several of the New Tuscans bridled. "After all, the perspective is always different, depending upon who's on the bottom and who's on the top."

Boutin had been about to say something. Now the President paused, his expression arrested, and closed his mouth slowly.

"Are we to understand, Ms. Anisimovna," Cardot asked just a bit caustically, "that you now propose to take us to the mountaintop and show us the same vista you offered to President Tyler?"

"In general terms, yes," Anisimovna told the foreign minister calmly. "Except for a couple of minor changes."

"What sort of 'minor changes'?" Vézien asked.

"Instead of striking directly for the Lynx Terminus and using its disputed possession—plus, of course, the brutal repression of patriotic resistance groups spontaneously arising in reaction to the corrupt plebiscite—as the opening wedge for inviting Frontier Security to intervene to prevent additional bloodshed, we intend to demonstrate Manticoran vengefulness and arrogant imperialism to the galaxy at large," Anisimovna replied. "In particular, we're well aware of the fashion in which Baroness Medusa and Prime Minister Alquezar are already attempting to freeze New Tuscany out of the Cluster's new economic order. Alas, we have reason to believe this is only the first step in Manticore's attempt to punish New Tuscany for its principled stand against that bogus Constitutional Convention from which you withdrew your delegates. Worse, we feel confident, is still to come."

"What sort of 'worse'?" Huppé asked, her dark eyes narrow.

"Harassment of your shipping, violations of your territory, that sort of thing," Anisimovna replied with a sigh. "Indeed, I wouldn't be at all surprised to discover that they've already been harassing your merchant shipping, trying to squeeze you out of the Cluster's markets."

"And assuming we could provide you with documentation of such harassment, just what would you do with it?" Pélisard asked.

"Why, *we* wouldn't do anything with it." Anisimovna widened her eyes innocently. "I'm sure, however, that if you were to draw these weighty matters to the attention of Commissioner Verrochio, he would feel constrained to take them most seriously. Especially after the fashion in which Manticore brutally assaulted the Union of Monica in time of peace. Under the circumstances, I feel positive that he would dispatch a significant force here to New Tuscany to fully investigate matters. And, should it transpire that your allegations of harassment are justified, that same significant force would be under orders to protect you from further infringements of your territoriality."

"Forgive me for pointing this out," Pélisard said, "but the naval resources Commissioner Verrochio personally controls are quite limited. I'm afraid a handful of destroyers, or even a cruiser division or two, would scarcely constitute a significant deterrent to the Manticoran Navy."

"No, they wouldn't," Anisimovna agreed. "However, a full squadron or two of Frontier Fleet battlecruisers would, I suspect."

"A squadron *or two*?" Pélisard blinked.

"Or even three," she said calmly. "I just happen to know that a Frontier Fleet task force has been dispatched to the Madras Sector to reinforce Commissioner Verrochio's OFS naval detachment. It's under the command of an Admiral Byng, I understand. And it just happens I have a small file on him with me." She extracted a data chip folio from her slender purse and laid it on the corner of Boutin's desk. "It's fascinating viewing, actually. Or I think so, at least. Admiral Byng would appear to be the sort of League officer who recognizes Manticoran arrogance and imperialism for what they are. The sort of officer who would be naturally disposed to at least listen to the complaints of some single-system star nation which finds itself being bullied and harassed by the 'Star Kingdom.' If Commissioner Verrochio—or, for that matter, your own government—were to request him to send a detachment here to New Tuscany to investigate matters personally, I feel confident he would agree."

"And if it happened when he did that there was a . . . confrontation between him and the Manties . . ." Pélisard's voice trailed off, and Anisimovna nodded.

"Of course, by far the most likely outcome would be for the Manticorans to back down," she said. "They may have been willing enough to take on Solarian battlecruisers in Monican hands—after all, the Monican Navy had neither the experience to make full use of them nor the industrial power to replace them if they were damaged or destroyed—but I suspect they'd be far more leery of facing battlecruisers crewed by the *Solarian* Navy. And if they were foolish enough to do anything of the sort, I'm sure the SLN would make short work of them."

Pélisard looked less than confident of that last sentence's accuracy. On the other hand, Anisimovna thought, he had to be aware of the enormous imbalance between the Solarian League's resources and those of the Star Kingdom of Manticore. Ultimately, no other star nation had the wherewithal to resist the juggernaut might of the League. Which meant . . .

She could almost see the gears turning inside his head as he worked his way through the implications of what she'd just said. She could tell the exact moment when he reached the end of the process, because his eyes narrowed suddenly and he looked at her very intently.

"In some ways, it would almost be a pity if they did back down, wouldn't it?" he observed slowly.

"Well, it would mean the situation would remain . . . unresolved," Anisimovna agreed. "It's sometimes necessary to lance a boil to drain its poisons. It's seldom a pleasant experience, but that doesn't make it any less necessary in the long run. So, yes, it would be . . . suboptimal."

"But if their local commander chose to be imprudent," Pélisard said even more slowly, "and if there happened to be some sort of *shooting* incident, then this Admiral Byng you've mentioned would almost be forced to take steps."

"Not just a minute, Nicholas!" Dusserre said sharply. " 'Shooting incidents' are all very well, I suppose. But I'm not at all happy about the thought of having one of them right here in New Tuscany!"

"I don't blame you a bit, Mr. Dusserre," Anisimovna said calmly. "I wouldn't much care for the thought of having something like that happen in my star system, either. As I say, though, it would be unlikely for anything of the sort to happen if Admiral Byng were present in strength. I'm thinking—as I'm sure Mr. Pélisard was—more of an incident which occurs somewhere else. One that could be . . . suitably tweaked, shall we say, to demonstrate the ruthlessness and viciousness of the Manticorans. Say, one of your warships, badly damaged or even destroyed by an unprovoked Manty attack. The trick would be to time the incident properly. Ideally, we'd have Admiral Byng already in the vicinity when we complain about this atrocity to Commissioner Verrochio."

"At which point he would presumably move that detachment you referred to to New Tuscany immediately," Pélisard said. "With orders not to allow any further Manticoran aggression. In fact, he'd probably sail straight to Spindle to demand an explanation, wouldn't he?"

"Oh, I feel confident he would." Anisimovna smiled. "And I imagine the odds of an unfortunate confrontation between him and the Manties would be considerably enhanced when he did.

Oh, and I suppose I should also mention that my sources tell me a sizable force from *Battle Fleet* is also in this general neck of the galaxy. Carrying out training exercises in the McIntosh System, I believe."

It was very, very quiet in President Boutin's office. The McIntosh System was barely fifty light-years from Meyers, and Meyers was only a very little over three hundred light-years from New Tuscany. Which meant any task group carrying out exercises at McIntosh could reach New Tuscany in as little as thirty-two T-days.

"Given McIntosh's proximity to Meyers, I strongly suspect Commissioner Verrochio would send the Battle Fleet senior officer there a message, requesting her assistance, at the same time as he dispatched Admiral Byng—or one of the admiral's squadrons, at least—to New Tuscany to investigate your allegations. Which would mean, of course, that even if some Manticoran officer were foolish enough to fire upon New Tuscan units or anything of the sort, Admiral Byng would have ample forces in close proximity which he could call upon to . . . stabilize the situation once more."

The quiet was more intense than ever, and as Aldona Anisimovna listened to it, she knew she had their complete attention.

# Chapter Twenty-Three

JUST UNDER TWENTY-FIVE T-DAYS after leaving Spindle, Michelle Henke's flagship crossed the alpha wall into the star system of Monica. Michelle sat in her command chair on *Artemis'* flag deck, watching her displays and wondering what sort of reception she and her ships were likely to receive.

The dispatch boat with O'Malley's orders had sailed directly from the Lynx Terminus to Monica, without detouring by Spindle. That had saved it the better part of eleven days in transit, and the boat which had brought copies of his orders to Spindle had arrived there three days before Michelle had departed. Which meant, by her math, that O'Malley's task group had received its marching orders just under two T-weeks ago. Assuming *Hexapuma's* and *Warlock's* repairs had completed on schedule, they should have been ready to head home even before that, which would have freed O'Malley from any concerns for their security if he withdrew immediately in response to his orders. So, assuming everything had gone the way it was supposed to, there would be no Manticoran warship waiting here in Monica to greet her.

*And somehow I don't really think 'President Tyler' is going to be particularly happy to see me, either, even if we are "treaty partners" now,* she thought sardonically. *So maybe it wouldn't be a bad idea to sort of scout the area before I head in-system.*

The planet of Monica itself lay just over eleven light-minutes inside the G3 primary's 20.6-light-minute hyper limit, and Captain

Conner's division's closing speed was barely two thousand kilometers per second. At maximum military power with zero safety margin on her inertial compensator, *Artemis'* maximum acceleration was better than 6.5 KPS², which was a third again what any prewar ship of her tonnage could have turned out. Even at the eighty percent of maximum power which was the RMN's normal top acceleration, she could produce 5.3 KPS², which was still the next best thing to half a kilometer per second better than the old-style compensators could have produced running flat out. Given the present . . . delicate state of affairs with the Solarian League, the Admiralty had decided it might be wiser not to flaunt all of the Navy's current capabilities where Solly warships might see them. According to ONI's best current appreciations, the Solarians remained unaware of many of those capabilities. Some people—including Michelle—took that appreciation with a certain grain of salt, although she had to admit it wasn't as preposterous as it might have been if they'd been talking about any other navy in space.

It was obvious to anyone who'd ever had to deal with the Solarian League Navy that the SLN suffered from an extraordinarily severe case of professional myopia. The League's navy was divided into two primary components: Battle Fleet and Frontier Fleet. Of the two, Battle Fleet was the bigger and the more prestigious, but Frontier Fleet actually did the lion's share of the SLN's real work. Given the League's enormous size, population, and industrial power, it was scarcely surprising that the SLN was far and away the biggest fleet in human history. Unfortunately for the League, the SLN *knew* it was the biggest, most powerful, most advanced fleet in human history . . . and at least one—and possibly two—of those well known facts were no longer true.

The League's towering sense of superiority where any "neobarb" star nation was concerned, while scarcely one of its more endearing qualities, didn't normally constitute a direct threat to the League's security. When it's *navy* shared that same sense of superiority (and burnished it with the institutional arrogance of a service which had existed literally for centuries and never known defeat), that wasn't exactly the case, however. Despite the fact that several of the League's member planets had sent observers from their locally raised and maintained system-defense forces to both Manticore and Haven, the SLN itself, so far as Michelle was aware, never had. There was, after all, no reason for it to concern itself with what a couple of minor, neo-barbarian polities on the backside of beyond might be up to. Even assuming that Manticore and Haven hadn't been too busy killing each other (no doubt with the equivalent of clubs and flint hand-axes), both of them together couldn't possibly have built a fleet large enough to threaten the League, and the thought that two such insignificant so-called star nations could have appreciably improved upon the technology of the incomparable Solarian League Navy was ludicrous.

No one at ONI doubted for a moment that the SDF observers had offered their reports to the SLN. The majority opinion, however, was that the SLN's institutional blinkers were so solidly in place that those reports had been quietly filed and ignored . . . assuming they hadn't simply been tossed. The SDFs were only *local* defense forces, after all—the backup, second-string militia to the SLN's professional, first-string team. They were obviously going to be more parochial in their viewpoints, and, without the SLN's sound basis of training and vast experience, they were also likely to be unduly alarmist. Not to mention the fact that without the solid core of institutional and professional competence of the regular navy, their "observers" were far more prone to misunderstand—or even be deliberately misled by—what the neobarbs in question made sure they actually saw. Even if Solly naval intelligence was willing to grant their complete sincerity, the analytical methods already in place, relying upon tested and proven techniques, were bound to be more reliable than reports from what were little more than reservist observers who'd probably been steered to what the locals wanted them to see in the first place.

That, at any rate, was how ONI read the SLN's current attitudes and decision trees, and the Sollies' failure to deploy any significant improvements in their own military hardware certainly seemed to validate that interpretation, although Michelle, for one, preferred not to invest too much confidence in that particular assumption. The mere fact that no new hardware was being deployed didn't necessarily mean it wasn't being *developed*, after all, and for all its arrogance and condescension, the fact remained that the League had the greatest pool of human talent and wealth of any political unit in human history. If the SLN ever got its collective head out of its ass, that talent and wealth could almost certainly make it just as scary as it already thought it was.

Whether or not there was more R&D going on than anyone was mentioning, ONI's sources within the Solly navy all seemed pretty much in agreement that the vast majority of Solarian naval officers put very little credence in the obviously wildly exaggerated claims about Manticoran and Havenite military technology. Based on evidence from the Battle of Monica, the Sollies (or one of their major defense suppliers, at any rate) were at least experimenting with newer-generation missile pods, which was something they'd previously disdained, and their missiles' drives had proven surprisingly powerful and with greater endurance than anyone had really expected. But none of the missiles they'd fired—or, rather, supplied to Monica—had been MDMs, their pods hadn't had the new-generation grav-drivers which were so much a part of Manticore's designs, and there'd been no reports of increases in basic Solarian warship acceleration rates, which were incredibly low and inefficient compared to those of the Manticoran Alliance or even the Republic of Haven. After stirring all of that together and pondering it carefully, the Office of Naval Intelligence had come to the conclusion that at least some improvements could be anticipated out of the SLN, possibly as the result of privately sponsored in-house research and development by people like Technodyne, but that significant improvements were unlikely, at least in the short term.

Bearing that in mind, the Admiralty had instructed all of its captains not to exceed *seventy* percent of maximum military power in the presence of Solarian warships. The use of Ghost Rider and FTL coms was also to be minimized. And no MDM live-fire exercises were to be conducted in Solarian space.

All of which meant that *Artemis'* maximum allowable acceleration was only 4.7 $KPS^2$, and that it would take almost three and a half hours to reach a parking orbit around Monica. That was plenty of time for her to deploy recon drones to take a close look at the local real estate and report back, even using light-speed communications links.

"All right, Dominica," Michelle said, glancing at Commander Adenauer. "Confirm that the grav-pulse coms are shut down, then go ahead and fire them off."

"Aye, aye, Ma'am," the operations officer replied. She checked her own readouts carefully, then keyed in the command. "Drones away, Ma'am."

"Very good."

Michelle tipped back her command chair, waiting patiently as *Artemis* and the other ships of her first-division accelerated steadily—if slowly—towards Monica.

---

"Well, this is a fine kettle of fish," Michelle murmured an hour later as she gazed at the data codes on the master plot.

*Artemis'* combat information center had analyzed the (slowly) arriving sublight transmissions from the recon probes, and it was apparent that there had, indeed, been some changes since Vice Admiral Khumalo had received Vice Admiral O'Malley's latest update. The absence of any Manticoran units was scarcely a surprise, and while she couldn't precisely call the arrival of a visiting squadron of Frontier Fleet battlecruisers a *surprise*, the number of ships present was certainly unpleasant.

"CIC makes these eight their new *Nevada*-class, Ma'am," Dominica Adenauer said, highlighting the icons in question. "The other nine battlecruisers are *Indefatigables*. The IDs on the destroyers are a lot more tentative than that. CIC *thinks* they're all *Rampart*-class, but they can't guarantee it." She grimaced. "Frontier Fleet's modified and refitted so many of the *Ramparts* that no two of their emission signatures really match one another."

"I don't suppose the tin-cans really matter all that much," Michelle replied, still gazing at the icons. Then she turned and glanced at Edwards. "Still no communications from them, Bill?"

"No, Ma'am." Edwards' tone could not have been more respectful, but it was undeniably . . . patient, and a smile flitted across Michelle's lips.

*Guess I must be a little more nervous than I'm trying to pretend. If anybody over there had wanted to talk to us, Bill would have told me. Maybe I need to ask less obviously time-killing questions if I want to look suitably imperturbable during these little moments of stress?*

Still, she supposed she could forgive herself for feeling just a little tense, under the circumstances. Finding *seventeen* Solarian battlecruisers in orbit around the planet Monica constituted a rather significant escalation in potential threat levels. Whatever else might be happening, she had an unpleasant suspicion that their presence was evidence the Solarian League wasn't planning on pulling in its horns quietly after all.

*Don't borrow trouble,* she scolded herself. *It could be as simple as a reassuring gesture to a longtime "ally" like President Tyler. Frontier*

*Security wouldn't like the perception that it's prepared to abandon its stooges at the drop of a hat to get around, after all. For that matter, they could just be here to show the flag and shore up the League's prestige in the area after the hammering Monica took.*

The problem with both of those comforting theories was that it didn't really require two full squadrons of battlecruisers to make either of those points. And the fact that no one had taken the slightest notice of the arrival of her own four ships struck her as ominous. Either they really hadn't noticed her, which seemed . . . unlikely, or else they were deliberately ignoring her as if she were unworthy of their attention. Which was precisely the sort of dismissive arrogance all too many Manticoran officers had experienced from Sollies in the past.

*And if they* did *send these people out to make some kind of statement, and if the officer in command of them really is a typically arrogant, pompous twit, things could get messy*, she thought grimly.

"Do you want to open communications with them, Ma'am?" Cynthia Lecter asked quietly.

"Eventually, one of us is going to have to talk to the other one," Michelle replied wryly. "But while I don't really want to get into some sort of stare-the-other-fellow-down pissing contest about it, I'll be damned if we're going to be the whiny, nervous little kid begging the great big bully to take notice of us, either."

Lecter nodded, although Michelle thought she detected at least a faint shadow of concern behind the chief of staff's eyes. If so, she wasn't exactly surprised. One of the jobs of a good chief of staff was to worry about the mistakes her boss might be making rather than play yes-woman.

"We're still two and a half hours out of Monica orbit," Michelle observed, "and they're the people already in orbit. Besides, we're squawking our transponders, and technically this is still Monican space."

Lecter nodded again. The accepted interstellar convention was that the fleet in possession of a star system or a planet initiated contact with any newcomers. If contact wasn't initiated, if no challenge was offered, it indicated the fleet in possession wasn't planning on shooting at anyone who got too close. Besides, as Michelle had just pointed out, the Union of Monica was not a member system of the Solarian League, which made any Solarian units in Monican space at least as much visitors as the First

Division. No doubt everyone understood perfectly well that Monica's sovereignty—such as it was, and what there was of it—currently existed only on sufferance, but there were still appearances to maintain. Which meant that unless the Sollies had, in fact, occupied the star system, any contact—or challenges—should be coming from Monican traffic control, not from the Sollies.

Or, for that matter, from Manticore.

"Somehow, I think this is going to be an interesting port call, Ma'am," Lecter said quietly.

"Oh, I think you could safely put the odd thousand-dollar bet on that one, Cindy."

"We've been hailed by the Monicans, Ma'am," Captain Armstrong said from Michelle's com screen. "Finally."

Her voice was dust-dry, and Michelle chuckled as her flag captain added the final word.

"And they said?" she inquired.

"And they said we're welcome to Monica, Ma'am. Personally, I expect they're lying diplomatically through their teeth, given what happened the last time Queen's ships came calling here, but at least they're being polite."

"Did they happen to mention their Solarian visitors?"

"Not in so many words. They did instruct us to assume a parking orbit a minimum of eight thousand klicks clear of the closest Solly, though."

"Probably not a bad idea even if they hadn't made the suggestion official," Michelle said. "All right, Vicki. Go ahead and park us."

"Yes, Ma'am. Clear."

Armstrong nodded respectfully to Michelle, then disappeared from the display, and Michelle turned to Lecter, Edwards, and Adenauer, who stood in a loose semicircle around her command chair.

"So far, so good," she said. "And God knows I don't want to ruffle any Solly feathers any more than we have to. Nonetheless, Dominica, I think it would be a good idea to keep a very close eye on them. Let's make it passives only, but if a gnat breaks wind aboard one of those ships, I want to know about it. And inform all units that we'll maintain our own status at Readiness Two indefinitely."

"Yes, Ma'am."

Adenauer's expression was sober, and Michelle didn't blame her. Readiness Two was also known as "General Quarters." It meant that all of a ship's engineering and life-support systems were fully manned, of course, but it also meant her combat information center and tactical department were fully manned, as well. That her passive sensors were fully manned; that her active sensors were at immediate readiness; that her point defense laser clusters were active and enabled under computer control; that her counter-missile launchers had rounds in the tubes and backup rounds in the loading arms; that her passive defensive systems and EW were on-line, ready for instant activation; that her offensive missile tubes were prepped and loaded; and that the human backup crews for half her energy weapons were sealed into their armored capsules with the atmosphere in the surrounding spaces evacuated to protect them against the effects of blast. The *other* half of her energy weapons would be brought up and manned on a rotating basis to allow crew rest for the on-mount personnel, and twenty-five percent of her watch personnel from all other departments would be allowed rotating rest breaks, in order to allow her to remain at Readiness Two for extended periods.

In short, except for bringing up her wedge and sidewalls and running out her energy weapons, *Artemis* and every one of Michelle's other battlecruisers would be ready to respond almost instantly to any Solarian act of aggression.

*Of course, it's that "almost instantly" that's the killer,* Michelle reflected. *Especially at this piddling little range. They could reach us with their damned laser clusters, far less their broadside mounts! Keeping our wedges and sidewalls up in parking orbit would certainly be construed as a hostile act by the Sollies or the Monicans, and rightly so. But that means that if someone else decides to pull the trigger, they'll probably blow the ever-loving shit out of us before we can respond, anyway. Still, it's the thought that counts.*

"I don't want to do anything that could be construed as pro-vocative, Cindy," she continued aloud, switching her attention to the chief of staff.

It wasn't as if Lecter didn't already know that perfectly well, but Michelle had learned a long time ago that it was far better to make absolutely certain of something like that than it was to discover the hard way that someone hadn't in fact known some-thing "perfectly" . . . or, for that matter, at all.

"At the same time," Michelle went on as Lecter nodded, "I don't have any intention of letting these people 'Thunderbolt' us while we sit here fat, happy, and stupid. So I want you to help Dominica ride herd on CIC. If we pick up *any* status change aboard any of those Solly ships, I want to know about it before *they* do."

"Yes, Ma'am."

"Good. And now," Michelle drew a deep breath and turned her attention to Edwards, "I suppose it's time I did my duty and checked in with our hosts personally. And, of course," she smiled without any humor at all, "with our fellow visitors to this pleasant little corner of the universe. Please raise the Monican port admiral for me, Bill."

"Yes, Ma'am."

The conversation with Rear Admiral Jane Garcia, Monica Traffic Control's senior officer, went rather better than Michelle had anticipated.

Garcia didn't even attempt to pretend she was happy to see Michelle's battlecruisers, for which Michelle couldn't blame her. Having been a prisoner of war herself, she had a better appreciation than many Manticoran officers might have of just how bitter a pill it must have been to see the destruction of virtually Monica's entire navy. Undoubtedly a great many of Garcia's personal friends—quite probably family members, as well, given the way military service tended to run in families in most star nations—had been killed along the way. And however much Manticore might have regarded Monica as a corrupt, venal tool of Frontier Security, the Union was Garcia's star nation. Its ignominious surrender, and the fashion in which Manticore had dictated peace terms afterward, could only have made Garcia's anger worse.

Despite that, the other woman's demeanor had been crisp and professional. Although she hadn't welcomed Michelle to Monica, she'd been surprisingly courteous otherwise. Her lips might have tightened just a moment when Michelle asked her to pass her compliments to President Tyler, but she'd nodded almost naturally, then asked if Michelle had any pressing service requirements.

With that out of the way, unfortunately, Michelle no longer had any excuse for not contacting the *Solarian* senior officer. Fortunately, Garcia had volunteered the Solly's name.

"All right, Bill," Michelle sighed. "Go ahead and raise Admiral Byng's flagship. I suppose—"

"Just a minute, Ma'am," Cynthia Lecter interrupted respectfully.

Michelle paused and looked at her chief of staff, one eyebrow arched, and Lecter nodded towards the display in front of her at her own command station.

"I've just been looking at ONI's records, Ma'am," she said. "I punched in Admiral Byng's name, and it looks like I got a direct hit."

"Really?"

Both of Michelle's eyes rose in surprise. The Office of Naval Intelligence did its best to keep track of the senior personnel of other navies, but its records on the SLN were sparser than on, say, the Republic of Haven or the Andermani Empire. Despite the Manticoran merchant marine's deep penetration of the League's carrying trade, the Solarian Navy had been assigned a far lower priority than more local—and pressing—threats over the past half-century or so. And the fact that the SLN was so damned big didn't help. The same absolute number of officers represented a far smaller percentage of the total Solly officer corps, all of which helped to explain why it was actually unusual to find any given Solarian officer in the database.

"I think so, at any rate," Lecter replied. "It's always possible they have more than one Admiral Josef Byng, I suppose."

"Given the size of their damned navy?" Michelle snorted. "I'd say the odds were pretty good, actually." She shrugged. "Well, go ahead and shoot me whatever you've found."

"Yes, Ma'am."

The entry which appeared on Michelle's display a moment later was surprisingly long. For reasons which became depressingly clear as she skimmed through it.

The file imagery showed a tall, aristocratic-looking man with chestnut hair, just starting to go gray at the temples, and sharp blue eyes. He had a strong chin and sported a bristling mustache and a neatly trimmed goatee. Indeed, he looked every centimeter the complete professional naval officer in his immaculately tailored dress whites.

The biographical synopsis which went with that sharp, taut imagery, however, was . . . less aesthetically pleasing.

"It says here he's a Battle Fleet officer," Michelle said aloud, and even to herself, her tone sounded plaintive, like someone protesting that there *surely* had to be some sort of mistake.

"I know, Ma'am." Lecter looked profoundly unhappy.

"I hope—oh, *how* I hope—that either you've got the wrong

man or else this is just a very unhappy coincidence," Michelle said, and Lecter nodded.

In many ways, Josef Byng was a typical product of the SLN, according to the ONI file. He came from a family which had been providing senior officers to the League Navy for the better part of seven hundred T-years; he'd graduated from the naval academy on Old Terra; and he'd gone directly into Battle Fleet, which was far more prestigious than Frontier Fleet. He was a second-generation prolong recipient who was just over a T-century old, and he'd been an admiral for the last thirty-two T-years. Unlike the Royal Manticoran Navy, the SLN had not developed the habit of routinely rotating senior officers in and out of fleet command to keep them current both operationally and administratively, and it looked as if Byng (or his family) had possessed sufficient pull to keep him in what were at least technically space-going commands for virtually his entire flag career.

That didn't mean as much in Battle Fleet as it might have in other navies, given the huge percentage of Battle Fleet's wall which spent virtually all of its time in what the SLN euphemistically referred to as "Ready Reserve Status." It was quite possible for an admiral to spend several T-years in command of a squadron of superdreadnoughts, accruing the seniority—and drawing the pay—which went with that assignment, while the superdreadnoughts in question simply went right on floating around in their mothballed parking orbits without a single soul on board.

What was much more interesting to Michelle at the moment, however, was the fact that fifty-nine T-years ago, a young, up-and-coming *Captain* Josef Byng had been officially reprimanded—and moved back two hundred names on the seniority list—for harassing Manticoran shipping interests.

Her skimming eyes slowed down as she reread that particular portion of the entry again, and she grimaced. Despite the ONI analyst's dry, rather pedantic writing style, it was easy enough to read between the lines. Captain Byng had clearly been one of those Solly officers who regarded neobarbs—like Manticorans—as two or three steps below chimpanzees on the evolutionary tree. It also appeared that his wealthy and aristocratic family (although, of course, Old Terra didn't *have* an aristocracy . . . officially) was deeply involved in interstellar commerce.

It was common enough in Manticore for families involved in

the Star Kingdom's vast shipping industry to provide officers for the Navy, as well, and Michelle was perfectly well aware that more than one of those officers had used and abused her authority in her family's interest. When the RMN became aware of those instances of abuse, however, it usually took action. On those rare occasions—which no longer occurred with anything like the frequency they once had—when the officer involved had proved too well connected for the JAG to deal with the situation, she'd normally been eased out of any command which might give her the opportunity to repeat the offense.

That, unfortunately, was not the case in the Solarian League, where cronyism and the abuse of power were both common and accepted. Especially in the Shell and the Verge, officers with "comfortable" relationships with the local OFS structure routinely used their positions to feather their own nests or promote their own interests. Captain Byng had obviously seen no reason why he shouldn't do the same thing, but his harassment had been far more blatant than most. He'd gone so far as to impound three Manticoran freighters on trumped up smuggling charges, and the crew of one of them had spent almost two T-years in prison without ever even being given the opportunity to face a judge.

The Star Kingdom had attempted to deal with the problem locally, without raising it to the level of a major diplomatic incident, but Byng had flatly refused even to discuss the matter with the local Manticoran trade and legal attachés. The terms in which he had expressed his refusal had been . . . less than diplomatic, and the second time around, the legal attaché, without Byng's knowledge, had recorded the entire conversation. Which had then been presented formally to the Solarian Foreign Minister by the Manticoran ambassador to the Solarian League—who'd happened to be an admiral himself—with a polite but pointed request that the minister look into the problem. Soon.

Unfortunately for Captain Byng, the Star Kingdom of Manticore carried far more clout than the "neobarbs" he was accustomed to browbeating. Faced with the politely veiled suggestion that failure to return the impounded vessels—and to free the imprisoned crewmen, with apologies and reparations—might very well result in higher junction transit fees for all Solarian merchantmen, the League's bureaucracy had sprung ponderously into action. It had taken another six T-months, but eventually, the ships and the imprisoned crewmen had been released, the League had paid a sizable damages award, and Captain Byng had been required to apologize formally for "exceeding his authority." Despite that, he'd gotten off incredibly lightly for someone whose actions—and stupidity—had embarrassed an entire star nation, Michelle thought. He'd been allowed to make his apology in written form, rather than in person, and any Manticoran officer who'd acted in the same fashion would undoubtedly have been dismissed from the Queen's service. In Byng's case, however, there'd never really been any possibility of that outcome. In fact, it was astonishing he'd even been moved back on the promotion lists.

It would appear from his subsequent record that he held everyone but himself responsible for that outcome, however. It had undoubtedly delayed his promotion to flag rank by several T-years, and it seemed evident that he blamed Manticore for his misfortunes.

Michelle would have found all of that sufficiently unhappy reading under any circumstances, but the fact that he was out here commanding a *Frontier Fleet* task force—and what looked, despite the fact that it was far larger than one normally saw in the Verge, to be a rather small one, for an officer of his seniority—made her even more unhappy.

Battle Fleet and Frontier Fleet were not fond of one another. Battle Fleet, despite the fact that none of its capital ships had fired a shot in anger in over two T-centuries, received the lion's share of the SLN's funding and was by far the more prestigious of the two organizations. Its officer corps was populated almost exclusively with officers whose family backgrounds were similar to Byng's, making it virtually a closed caste. Whereas the RMN had a surprisingly high percentage of "mustangs"—officers who had risen from the enlisted ranks to obtain commissions—there were none at all of them in Battle Fleet. That helped contribute to an incredible (by Manticoran standards) narrowness of focus and interest on the part of the vast majority of Battle Fleet officers. Who not only tended to look down particularly long and snobbish noses at all non-Solarian navies—and even the planetary defense forces of major Solarian planets—but even looked down upon their Frontier Fleet counterparts as little more than jumped up policeman, customs agents and neobarb-bashers who obviously hadn't been able to make the cut for service in a *real* navy.

Frontier Fleet, for its part, regarded Battle Fleet officers as over-bred, under-brained drones whose obsolescent capital ships—as outmoded and useless as they were themselves—soaked up enormous amounts of funding Frontier Fleet desperately needed. Personally, Michelle would have been even more incensed by the fact that so much of the funding officially spent on those same capital ships actually disappeared into the pockets of various Battle Fleet officers and their friends and families, but she supposed it would have been unrealistic to expect Frontier Fleet to feel the same way. After all, graft and "family interest" were as deeply ingrained a part of Frontier Fleet's institutional culture as they were for Battle Fleet. And to be fair, Frontier Fleet was also dominated by its hereditary officer caste, which resented the hell out of the juicier opportunities for peculation which came the way of its Battle Fleet counterpart. Still, its commissioned ranks contained a significantly higher percentage of "outsiders," and even a relatively tiny handful of mustangs of its own.

Bearing all of that in mind, no Battle Fleet admiral would have been happy to find herself assigned to command a mere Frontier Fleet task force. And no Frontier Fleet task force would have been happy to find her assigned to command it, either. Under any circumstances Michelle could think of, a Battle Fleet officer of Byng's seniority would have to regard a command like this as a demotion, probably even a professional insult, and he damned well ought to have had the family connections to avoid it.

If, of course, he'd *wanted* to avoid it.

*Oh, I don't like this at all*, she thought. *This bastard must have "I hate Manticore" embroidered on his underwear, which means the situation out here just got one hell of a lot more... delicate. I wonder if it was all his idea? In fact, I hope it was. Because if it wasn't, if someone else pulled strings to get him assigned to this particular task force and he went along with it willingly, I think we can all be damned sure it's not going to be for a reason we're going to like. On the other hand, I doubt anything I could say to him is going to make him like us any better, so I suppose I can just go ahead and be my normal, infinitely tactful sort.*

"Well," she said finally, "I suppose I'd better go ahead and talk to him. Give me a minute to get my happy face put back on, Bill, then go on and hail him."

# Chapter Twenty-Four

"SIR, THE MANTY ADMIRAL is on the com," Captain Willard MaCuill said. "It's a Vice Admiral Gold Peak. She's asking to speak to you."

"Oh, she is, is she?" Admiral Josef Byng smiled sardonically as he turned his command chair to face his staff communications officer. "Took her long enough to get around to it, didn't it? I wonder why that was?"

"Probably took her that long to get back out of the head after she changed her underwear, Sir," Rear Admiral Karlotte Thimár, Byng's chief of staff, replied with a nasty chuckle. "Not quite like the last time one of their ships was here, after all."

"No, it isn't," Byng agreed, and glanced at the tactical display on SLNS *Jean Bart*'s flag bridge.

He didn't quite curl his lip as he considered the flag bridge's old-fashioned instrumentation and cramped size. He understood that Frontier Fleet had a lower priority for the Fleet 2000 upgrades, after all, so he'd also known from the beginning that it was unrealistic to expect better, but he didn't exactly attempt to conceal his feelings, either. There was no need, since all of his staff officers had come over with him from Battle Fleet. All of them shared his awareness of the step down they'd been forced to take for this particular mission, although they did do their best to conceal their feelings whenever any of their Frontier Fleet "brothers in arms" were present.

Not that anyone on either side of that particular division was actually likely to fool anyone very much, he supposed.

Still, even though they were only battlecruisers—and *Frontier Fleet* battlecruisers, at that—rather than the superdreadnought squadrons he should have had under command, Karlotte was undoubtedly correct about the Manties' reaction when they found *seventeen* Solarian League warships sitting here to greet them. Indeed, Byng's only real regret was that the Manty ships which had previously occupied the system had already withdrawn before his own command came over the hyper wall. He would've loved to see *their* reaction to his arrival. Or, for that matter, how they would respond when his *third* battlecruiser squadron arrived in a couple of T-weeks.

His eyes moved to the scarlet icons of the Manticoran ships, and this time his lip did curl ever so slightly as he considered CIC's data bars. Of course, it was a Frontier Fleet combat information center with a Frontier Fleet tactical crew, so one had to take its analyses with a grain of salt. Still, at this piddling little range, it was unlikely that even Frontier Fleet could get its sums wrong. Which meant the "battlecruisers" on his plot really did mass well over two million tons apiece.

*Just like them and their so-called "navy,"* he thought contemptuously. *No wonder the doomsayers have been whining and moaning about how "dangerous" Manty warships are all of a sudden. Hell, if we built "battlecruisers" twice the size of anyone else's, we could probably stick a lot of firepower into them, too! Sure, I'll bet they can take a lot of damage, too, but ONI's right. The real reason they're building them that damned big is the fact that they realize they couldn't go toe-to-toe with a real first-line navy without the tonnage advantage. And the biggest frigging "battlecruisers" in the galaxy won't help them if they ever come face to face with Battle Fleet!*

Before deploying to command Task Group 3021, Byng had dutifully read through all of the intelligence appreciations. Not surprisingly, those from Frontier Fleet's analysts had been much more alarmist than anyone else's. Frontier Fleet had always had a tendency to jump at shadows, in large part because viewing with alarm was one way to try to twist the accountants' arms into diverting additional funding to it. Then too, one had to consider the quality of the officers making those reports.

Still, even Frontier Fleet's reports had sounded almost rational and reasonable compared to the ludicrous claims being made by some of the system-defense forces. God only knew why any of them had bothered to send observers to watch two batches of neobarbs five hundred light-years from nowhere in particular butchering each other with muzzle-loading cannon and cutlasses in the first place. Perhaps that was part of the explanation for the wild exaggerations some of those observers had included in their reports? Not even an SDF admiral was going to send a *competent* officer that far out to the back of beyond. No, he was going to send someone whose services could be easily dispensed with . . . and who wouldn't be missed for the weeks or months he'd spend in transit.

Oh, there was no doubt the Manties and their Havenite dance partners had managed to fall into at least some innovations as they stumbled about the dance floor with one another. For example, they obviously had improved their compensator performance to at least some extent, although clearly not to the level some of those "observers" were claiming. And even though it irritated him to admit it, fair was fair; that improvement in their compensators had sparked Solarian R&D efforts in the same direction. Given the difference between the basic capabilities of their respective scientific communities, however, there was no doubt that the Manties' advantage—never as great as those exaggerated reports had asserted—had already been pared away. He only had to look at the acceleration rate of those outsized "battlecruisers" to know that!

*Oh, well,* he thought. *I suppose I'd better get this over with.*

"Very well, Willard," he said, turning back from the plot. "Go ahead and put her through."

*Well, so much for my hope that there were two Josef Byngs on the Solly officer list,* Michelle thought as the Solarian admiral's face appeared on her display.

It had taken him long enough to get around to taking her call, but that had scarcely been surprising. A lot of Solarian naval officers liked to keep their inferiors waiting as a not-so-subtle way of emphasizing that inferiority.

"I'm Admiral Josef Byng, Solarian League Navy," the white-uniformed man on her display said. "To whom do I have the pleasure of speaking?"

Michelle managed to keep her jaw from tightening. She'd never thought much of SLN officers' efficiency, but she rather suspected that Byng's subordinates had at least bothered to inform him of the identity of his caller. And she'd asked for him by name and rank, which made his self-introduction a deliberate and patronizing insult.

*I can already see how* this *is going to go*, she thought.

"Vice Admiral Gold Peak," she replied. "Royal Manticoran Navy," she added helpfully, just in case he hadn't recognized the uniform, and had the satisfaction of seeing his lips tighten ever so slightly.

"What can I do for you today . . . Admiral Gold Peak?" he inquired after a moment.

"I only screened to extend my respects. It's not often we see a full Frontier Fleet admiral this far out in the sticks."

From the look in Byng's eyes, he appreciated being called a Frontier Fleet officer even less than Michelle had expected him to. That was nice.

"Well, it's not often we have the sort of . . . incident which occurred here in Monica, either, Admiral Gold Peak," Byng replied after a moment. "Given the Union of Monica's long-standing and friendly relations with the League, I'm sure you can understand why it seemed like a good idea to send someone of our own out here for a firsthand impression of events."

"I certainly can," Michelle agreed. "We felt a need to do the same thing after the unfortunate events here in Monica." She shook her head. "I'm sure all of us regret what happened after Captain Terekhov attempted to ascertain exactly what President Tyler's intentions were. According to our own investigations, those battlecruisers provided to him for his projected attack on the Lynx Terminus were supplied by Technodyne. Have your people been able to turn up anything more about that, Admiral?"

"No." Byng showed his teeth in something a professional diplomat might have described as a smile. "No, we haven't. In fact, according to the briefings I received when I was dispatched, we still haven't managed to confirm where they came from."

"Aside from the fact that they obviously came from the SLN. Originally, I mean." Michelle smiled, adding the carefully timed qualifier as Byng appeared to swell visibly. "Obviously, once ships are listed for disposal and handed over to private hands for scrapping, the Navy's responsibility for them is pretty much at an end. And the paper trail can easily become . . . obscured, as we all know. Especially if some criminal—and civilian, of course—type is doing his best to *make* it obscure."

"No doubt. My own experience in those areas is somewhat limited, however. I'm sure our own investigation will be looking very carefully at the recordkeeping of our various suppliers. No doubt Technodyne will be included in that process."

Michelle toyed with the notion of telling him about the indictments which had already been handed down against several of Technodyne's senior executives. Given the Beowulf Terminus of the Manticoran Wormhole Junction, her own information loop from the Old League was far shorter than Byng's could possibly be. She strongly suspected that he must at least have known which way the wind was setting before he set out for Monica, and the possibility that she might be able to push his blood pressure up into stroke levels made the temptation to rub his nose in the evidence that Technodyne had been caught with its hand in the cookie jar clear to the elbow almost overwhelming.

*Down, girl,* she told herself, suppressing the desire right womanfully.

"I'm sure it will be," she said instead. "In the meantime, however, may I assume you're also here in something of the role of observer of the Talbott Quadrant's integration into the Star Empire?"

"Star Empire?" Byng repeated, raising his eyebrows in polite surprise. "Is that what you've decided to call it?" He gave her a small, almost apologetic wave of his hand. "I'm afraid I hadn't heard that before I was deployed."

His tone made his own opinion of the delusions of grandeur involved in calling something the size of Manticore's new star nation an "empire," and Michelle smiled sweetly at him.

"Well, we had to call it *something*, Admiral. And given the political arrangements the Talbotters came up with at their constitutional convention, the term sounded logical. Of course, it's early days yet, isn't it?"

"Yes, it is." Byng smiled back at her, but his smile was considerably colder than hers had been. "I'm sure it's going to be interesting to see how . . . successfully your experiment works out."

"So far, it seems to be going quite well," Michelle said.

"So far," he agreed, with another of those smiles. "In answer to your question, however, yes. I have been instructed to observe events out here in the Talbott area. I'm sure you're aware the public back home was deeply interested in events out here. Especially after that unfortunate business on Kornati began to make it into the newsfaxes." He shook his head sadly. "Personally, I'm confident the entire affair was grossly exaggerated—newsies do need to sell subscriptions, after all. Still, the Foreign Ministry does feel a certain responsibility to get a firsthand impression of events there, as well as throughout the Cluster. I'm sure you can understand why that would be the case."

"Oh, believe me," Michelle assured him with deadly affability, "I can understand exactly *why* that would be the case, Admiral Byng. And, speaking for Her Majesty and Her Majesty's government, I'm sure all of the Star Empire's new member systems will be prepared to extend every possible courtesy to you."

"That's very welcome news, Admiral."

"And, while you're here, Admiral, if there's any way Her Majesty's Navy can assist you—for example, if you would care to set up joint anti-piracy or anti-slavery patrols—I'm sure Admiral Khumalo would be as delighted as I would to coordinate our operations with you."

"That's very kind of you." Byng smiled again. "Of course, unlike your new Star Empire, the League has no direct territorial interests in this region. Aside from the security of our own allies in the area, that is. And, of course, the security—and territorial integrity—of those star systems which have been taken under the protection of the Office of Frontier Security. I believe we can see to those obligations out of our own resources. At least, it's difficult for me to conceive of a threat to those interests which we *couldn't* deal with out of our own resources."

"No doubt." Michelle smiled back at him. "Well, in that case, Admiral Byng, I won't keep you any longer. We won't be in Monica for very long. This was just in the nature of making certain our new allies here were secure, so I imagine we'll be on our way to Tillerman shortly. I need to pay a courtesy call on President Tyler first, however. Governor General Medusa has instructed me to inform him that the Star Empire is prepared to extend government-guaranteed loans to any of its citizens who might be interested in investing here." Her smile turned sweeter. "I believe Baroness Medusa—and Her Majesty—believe it's the least we can do to help Monica recover from the consequences of that unfortunate event."

"That's remarkably generous of your Star Empire," Byng said.

"As I said, I'm sure everyone regrets what happened here, Admiral Byng. And Manticore's experience has been that extending a helping hand to ex-enemies and treating them as equals is one of the better ways to see to it that there's no repetition of all that unpleasantness."

"I see." Byng nodded. "Well, since you seem to have quite a lot that still needs doing, Admiral Gold Peak, I'll bid you good day."

"Thank you, Admiral. I hope your mission here is a successful one. Henke, clear."

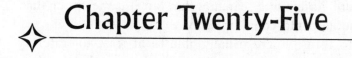

# Chapter Twenty-Five

"TAKE A SEAT, MATT," Commander Ursula Zeiss invited, pointing at one of the chairs in front of her desk as Lieutenant Maitland Askew stepped through her shipboard office door.

Askew obeyed the polite command, seating himself in the indicated chair, then watched as she punched the console button to close the door behind him.

Askew was twenty-eight T-years old, with sandy-brown hair, brown eyes, and a wiry build. He was slightly below average in height—in fact, the compactly but solidly built Zeiss was at least a centimeter taller than he was—and something about him gave an impression of continual bemusement. Zeiss was one of the people who knew better than to take that "bemusement" at face value. There was a brain behind those mild brown eyes, and it seldom truly shut down.

Which, of course, was part of her current problem, she thought, sitting back and contemplating him thoughtfully across her desk.

"You wanted to see me, Ma'am?" he observed after several moments of her silent scrutiny, and she snorted.

"Of course I wanted to see you. I *always* want to see you, don't I?"

Askew's lips twitched ever so slightly at her acerbic tone. Zeiss was SLNS *Jean Bart*'s tactical officer, and Askew had been her assistant tac officer for almost two T-years now. They'd worked well together over that time, but there was no denying that they had fundamentally different personalities. Zeiss was an excellent training officer, and her main interest—and strength—lay in recognizing the strengths and weaknesses of her human material and adjusting for them. Askew's personnel management skills, while adequate, were nowhere near as strong as hers were, and *his* main interest was in what he called the "nuts and bolts" of the tactical officer's trade. As a result, Zeiss tended to leave hardware issues in his hands while she got on with other things. As a rule, that worked well, but sometimes the difference in their emphases led to a certain amount of . . . friction, perhaps. That wasn't really the exact word Askew was searching for, but it came closer than anything else he could come up with.

"I'd like to think you're usually able to at least tolerate my presence, Ma'am," he said now. "On the other hand, I had the impression that there was something specific you wanted to discuss with me."

"You had the right impression, then," Zeiss said, straightening in her chair with a considerably more serious expression. She looked at him for another few moments, then waggled one hand in the air in front of her.

"Captain Mizawa had a little discussion with Captain Aberu yesterday," she said, "and it would appear your name came up."

"*My* name?" Askew repeated carefully, and frowned when Zeiss nodded.

Captain Warden Mizawa, *Jean Bart*'s CO, was one of the better officers Askew had ever served under. He was also career Frontier Fleet, like Askew—and, for that matter, Zeiss—and not particularly fond of Battle Fleet officers, like Ingeborg Aberu, Admiral Byng's staff operations officer. It wasn't likely the two of them had just gotten together for a friendly chat over a stein of beer. Coupled with Zeiss' expression, that lent a somewhat ominous aspect to the thought that his name might have come up in conversation between them.

"May I ask the context, Ma'am?" he inquired even more cautiously..

"It would appear, Matt, that Captain Aberu is not one of your greater admirers. Did you do something at some point that might have personally stepped on her toes? Something that might explain why she'd take a certain degree of dislike to you?"

"Ma'am," Askew said, "I don't even *know* Captain Aberu. Aside from the dinner party Captain Mizawa hosted when the admiral and his staff came aboard, I don't think I've ever even been introduced to her."

*Which*, he did not add aloud, *would* not *be the case if she were on the staff of a* Frontier Fleet *Admiral.*

There was remarkably little love lost between Battle Fleet and Frontier Fleet at the best of times, and Askew wasn't immune to that institutional lack of mutual admiration. All the same, Admiral Byng and his staff seemed to have taken the traditional rivalry between the two services to an all-time high. There'd been virtually no social interaction between them and Captain Mizawa's officers, despite the lengthy voyage involved in just getting to the Madras Sector. Obviously, they'd had better things to do with their time. And they'd made it abundantly—one might almost have said painfully—clear that the sole function of the none-too-bright ship's company of SLNS *Jean Bart* was to chauffeur them around the galaxy while they got on with the business of sorting out everything Frontier Security and the local Frontier Fleet detachment had managed to screw up beyond all repair here in the Madras Sector. Probably because none of them knew how to seal their flies after taking a leak.

So why, after totally ignoring *Jean Bart's* entire company ever since they'd come aboard, should Captain Aberu find herself "discussing" Maitland Askew with Captain Mizawa? Right offhand, he couldn't think of a single reason, and he doubted very much that he was going to like where this was headed.

"I didn't think you'd ever crossed swords with her," Zeiss said, "but apparently you've managed to really piss her off. I suspect *this* had a little something to do with it."

She reached into her drawer, withdrew a fairly thick sheaf of hard copy, and slid it across the deck to him. He picked it up, glanced at the header on the first page, then looked quickly back at her with his eyes full of questions.

"No," she answered the first of those questions, "I don't know how Aberu got hold of it. I suspect that neither the Captain, nor I, nor the Exec is going to be very happy if we ever manage to find out. The salient point in your case, however, is that the Admiral's operations officer has apparently read your little treatise and been singularly . . . unimpressed by it."

Askew looked back down at the header. "A Preliminary Appreciation of Potential Technology Advances of the Royal Manticoran

Navy," it said, and in the originating officer's name block it said "Askew, Maitland, LT."

"Ma'am, this is the report the captain asked me for," he began carefully, "and I never meant for it to—"

"I'm well aware that it was never intended for general circulation, Matt," Zeiss interrupted him. "That's why I said I don't expect to be particularly happy when I find out how it came to be in Aberu's hands. One thing I do know, though, is that it didn't get there by accident. So either someone from the ship's company gave it to her, or else . . ."

The tactical officer let her voice trail off, and Askew nodded. Bad enough if someone in their own company was passing potentially "interesting" information on to Admiral Byng's staff without authorization. But if it had come into Aberu's possession because Byng's people were hacked into the tactical department's information net—or, even worse, Captain Mizawa's personal internal com channels—it said even worse things about Task Force 3021's command structure.

*And in either case—whether she got it from a spy or through some illegal hack—the fact that Aberu decided to tell the captain she had the access isn't exactly a good sign either, now that I come to think about it.*

"Should I take it that she complained about my conclusions to the Captain, Ma'am?" he asked after a moment.

"She objected to your conclusions, your assumptions, your estimates, *and* your sources," Zeiss said almost dispassionately. "She characterized you as alarmist, credulous, ignorant, incompetent, and 'obviously not to be trusted with any significant independent analysis.' That last phrase is a direct quote, by the way. And she informed the Captain that if this represented the caliber of his officers' work and capabilities, the entire task force was obviously in deep and desperate trouble."

Askew swallowed. Naval service had run in his family for the last eight generations, but all of those generations had been spent in Frontier Fleet. That wouldn't cut a lot of ice with a Battle Fleet captain—or admiral—and he couldn't even begin to call upon the level of patronage and family alliances someone like Aberu could. If Byng or his staff decided an example had to be made of Maitland Askew, the destruction of his own naval career would become a virtual certainty.

"Ma'am—" he began, with absolutely no idea where he meant to take the sentence. Fortunately, Zeiss interrupted him again before he had to find out.

"You did exactly what the captain and I asked you to do, Matt," she said firmly. "I realize that may seem like cold comfort if someone like Aberu decides to set her sights on you, but neither of us have any intention of simply cutting your air line because she's a little miffed. Having said that, however, I have to admit that what she's chosen to be miffed over actually worries me more than the potential fate of one of my subordinates, however much I like and value him."

Askew couldn't pretend he was happy about that last sentence, but neither could he argue with her professional priorities.

Captain Mizawa had commissioned the report to which Aberu had taken such exception as part of his own background planning for their current mission. Askew had no idea how much of the report's content Mizawa was prepared to take at face value. For that matter, the assistant tactical officer wasn't really certain how much of it *he* was prepared to take at face value. Nonetheless, he was now convinced—and he knew Zeiss was, as well—that the official ONI estimates of the Manties' capabilities were badly flawed . . . to put it mildly.

Askew hadn't given much thought to the Royal Manticoran Navy himself before *Jean Bart* had been posted to the Madras Sector in the wake of the attack on the Republic of Monica. He knew the RMN was a lot bigger than most of the neobarb fleets floating around out in the Verge and beyond. It could hardly be otherwise, given the size of the Manticoran merchant marine, the need to protect it, and the fact that Manticore and the People's Republic of Haven had been at war with one another for the last twenty-odd T-years. That much he'd been prepared to admit, in a sort of offhand, casually incurious way, but his own assignments had kept him clear on the other side of the Solarian League's vast volume. He'd had rather more pressing concerns in his own area of operations. So even if he'd been vaguely aware of the Manty navy's sheer size, that awareness hadn't inspired him to think about it with any particular urgency. And if he'd thought about the ridiculous rumors about new "super weapons" coming out of the so-called Havenite Wars at all, it had mostly been to dismiss them as the sort of wildly exaggerated propaganda claims to be expected out of such a backward and distant corner of the explored galaxy. He certainly would have agreed that it was ludicrous to suggest that a single neobarb star system, be it ever so deeply involved in interstellar commerce, could have put together an R&D effort that could manage to outpace that of the Solarian League Navy!

Askew had found it extremely difficult to wrap his mind around the possibility that his initial estimate of the situation might have been seriously defective, but Captain Mizawa had asked him to keep an open mind when he undertook his appreciation of the Manticoran threat's severity. He'd done his dead level best to do exactly that, and the more he'd looked, the more . . . concerned Maitland Askew had become.

The actual hard data available to him was painfully limited. There'd never been much of it to begin with, and he'd decided at the outset that if he was going to come at his task with the "open mind" Captain Mizawa wanted, he'd have to start out by discarding the ONI reports which flatly dismissed the possibility of any threatening Manticoran breakthroughs. That left him gathering data on his own, and since they'd already been in hyper-space, on their way to their new duty station, there'd been precious little of that around until they reached the Meyers System, the Madras Sector's administrative center, and he was able to quietly talk things over with some of the officers of the Frontier Fleet detachment on permanent assignment to Commissioner Verrochio's office.

Commodore Thurgood, the senior officer in Meyers prior to Admiral Byng's arrival, had been more than willing to share all of the information, analysis, and speculation available to him. At first, Askew had been strongly inclined to dismiss Thurgood as an alarmist, but he'd dug into the commodore's documentation, anyway. And, as he'd dug, he'd begun to feel more than a little alarmed himself.

There was virtually no hard data from the actual attack on Monica. Any sensor data which had been available had either been destroyed along with Eroica Station's military components and the ships the Manticorans had engaged, or else swept up afterward by the Manticoran "investigation teams" which had swarmed over the Monican wreckage. Yet even though hard data was effectively impossible to come by, Thurgood had drawn certain very disturbing conclusions from the reports of as many Monican survivors as he'd been able to interview.

First, unlike a majority of Solarian Navy officers, Thurgood had declined to write off what had happened as due solely to Monican incompetence. He'd personally known the Monican flag officers involved—especially Isidor Hegedusic and Janko Horster, the two admirals who had actually engaged the Manticorans and gotten themselves killed for their pains. While the highest levels of the Republic of Monica's military had been as riddled by cronyism and political favoritism as any other Verge "star nation," Thurgood had respected the personal abilities of both Hegedusic and Horster, and he'd also informed Askew that the Monican Navy's basic level of competence had been surprisingly high.

Second, although he wasn't supposed to have been, Thurgood had been briefed on the missile pods Technodyne had made available to Monica. As a consequence, he'd been aware that the missiles in those pods had possessed a substantially higher rate of acceleration and drive endurance—and therefore a substantially greater effective range—than the standard missiles of the Solarian League Navy.

Third, ten Manticoran warships, four of them mere destroyers and only three of them as powerful as a heavy cruiser, had taken the combined fire of *all* of the pre-deployed missile pods and, although quite obviously surprised by the missiles' range and sheer numbers, not only survived as a fighting force but managed to destroy the entire military component of Eroica Station and nine of the fourteen modern battlecruisers Technodyne had provided to the Monicans. Not only that, but the six damaged Manticoran survivors of the engagement with Eroica Station had destroyed three *more* modern, fully functional battlecruisers in stand up combat. And they'd apparently managed to do that using nothing but their internal missile tubes, without any interference from pods at all.

Fourth, although there was no hard sensor data to explain exactly how they'd done it, it had been made abundantly clear—both during the engagement against Horster's three battlecruisers and afterward—that the Manticorans had managed to emplace what amounted to a system-wide surveillance system without being caught at it. And while Thurgood readily admitted that the supporting evidence and logic were much more speculative, the speed of the Manties' reaction to both Horster's attack and Admiral Bourmont's later maneuvers suggested that they might very well be capable of FTL communication with their recon platforms, after all.

There'd been more, but even Thurgood had conceded that a

lot of it—like the preposterous missile attack ranges some of the system-defense forces observers had been reporting from the main Manticore-Haven front and the ridiculously high acceleration rates attributed to Manticoran starships—sounded unlikely. On the other hand, he'd pointed out, he had absolutely no effective way of personally testing or evaluating those outrageous claims. He hadn't said so in so many words, but it had been evident to Askew that whether or not he could test or evaluate the claims in question himself, he was . . . strongly disinclined to reject them out of hand.

Askew had been taken aback by Thurgood's attitude. His original response had been strongly skeptical, but rather than simply reject the commodore's concerns, he'd painstakingly retraced Thurgood's logic, searching for the flaws he suspected had to be there. Unfortunately, he hadn't found them. In fact, as he'd dutifully searched for them, he'd come more and more firmly to the belief that Thurgood had a point. In fact, it looked as if he had *several* points.

And that was what he'd reported to Mizawa, Zeiss, and Commander Bourget, *Jean Bart*'s executive officer. He'd been a bit cautious about the *way* he'd reported it, of course. He was an SLN officer, after all, well versed in the ways of equivocation and careful word choices, and his own initial reaction to Thurgood had suggested how his superiors would probably respond to any wild-eyed, panicky warnings about Manticoran super weapons. Besides, even though the analysis had been requested only for Captain Mizawa's internal use, there'd always been the possibility that it might—as, indeed, appeared to be the case—have come into someone else's possession. If that happened, some other superior officer might prove rather less understanding than Captain Mizawa if young Lieutenant Askew came across as *too* alarmist.

*Apparently I wasn't cautious enough*, he reflected grimly.

"Should I assume, Ma'am, from what you said about Captain Aberu's response, that Admiral Byng feels the same way?" he asked.

"I don't have any idea how Admiral Byng feels," Zeiss told him. She shook her head and grimaced. "From the way Captain Mizawa described the 'conversation' to me, it sounds like Aberu was expressing her own opinions. From what I've seen of her so far, I'd guess she's one of those staffers who sees it as her duty to prevent obvious nonsense from cluttering up her admiral's desk. So I wouldn't be at all surprised to find out that she'd taken it upon herself to quash this sort of 'panicky defeatism' on her own, without ever discussing it with Admiral Byng at all. Unfortunately, Matt, we don't know that that's the case. It's equally possible that Admiral Byng sent her out to suggest rather firmly to the Captain that he leave the threat analysis business to the task force staff without the Admiral himself getting involved."

"I see, Ma'am." Askew gazed at her for several silent seconds, then cleared his throat. "May I ask what the captain intends to do about Captain Aberu's concerns?"

"He's not about to toss you out the nearest airlock, if that's what's worrying you." Zeiss actually produced a chuckle, but then her expression sobered again. "At the same time, though, he has to be a bit cautious about how he proceeds."

Askew nodded glumly. Captain Mizawa's family connections went quite a bit higher than Askew's own, but they still ended well short of the lofty sort of influence Byng could bring to bear. Given that, especially against the background of the traditional Battle Fleet-Frontier Fleet rivalry, Mizawa would have to pick his ground carefully for any quarrel with Byng. Coming to the impassioned defense of his assistant tactical officer probably wouldn't be the most career-enhancing move a flag captain could make.

*And it wouldn't solve the problem of Aberu's pigheadedness, either,* he thought.

"For the moment," Zeiss continued, "he wants you to lie as low as possible. Just go about your duties, and he and I—and the Exec—will keep you as far away from Flag Bridge and the Admiral's staff as we can. Bearing in mind that we don't know exactly how your report came into Captain Aberu's hands, it would probably be a good idea for you to keep your mouth shut about its contents, as well."

She looked at him levelly, and he nodded again. If they did have someone working as Byng's—or Aberu's—informant, talking about his and Thurgood's theories could very well get him charged with spreading defeatism.

"Yes, Ma'am," he said. Then, a bit more daringly, "And may I ask how the Captain reacted to my analysis?"

Zeiss rocked back in her chair, regarding him narrowly for several heartbeats, then shrugged.

"Captain Mizawa—like Commander Bourget and myself—is inclined to take your more alarming hypotheses with a sizable grain of salt. I think the Captain was as impressed as I was by the caliber of your work, but as you yourself point out, the supporting data is really pretty damned thin on the ground, Matt. You and Commodore Thurgood may very well be onto something, but I think we're all inclined to reserve judgment for the moment. I will say that your appreciation of the potential threat is likely to make all three of us approach the situation much more cautiously than we might have otherwise. It's just that until we've acquired some of that missing hard data we can't afford to get overly timid in our relations with the Manties." She gave him another of those hard, level looks, then added, "Or with anyone else."

"Yes, Ma'am. I understand."

Askew didn't try to keep his own worry—and not just for the possible implications for his naval career—out of his own voice, but he understood, all right.

"I thought you would, Matt," Zeiss said quietly. "I thought you would."

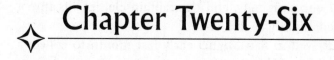

# Chapter Twenty-Six

"I UNDERSTAND YOU'RE NOT a professional reporter, Captain," the attractive brunette said in an almost soothing tone. "And I know it makes people a bit nervous the first time they have to go through an interview like this. But I promise you, I've done this hundreds of times, and none of my interviewees have ever died yet."

The man sitting across the small desk from her in the uniform of a merchant service deck officer grinned and chuckled just a bit nervously. Then he nodded.

"I'll, uh, try to bear that in mind, Ms. Brulé."

"Good. And remember, we don't have to get it perfect the first time. Just tell us what really happened, in your own words, and then we'll play it back and if you realize you've misspoken at some point, we can correct it. And if you realize you've left anything out, we can put it in at that point, too. The object is to get all of the information into the right people's hands, not to try to be perfect while we do it. Okay?"

"Yes, Ma'am."

"Good," the brunette repeated, then looked directly into the waiting pickup.

"This is a recorded interview with Captain Tanguy Carmouche, commander of the New Tuscany-registry freighter *Antelope*, concerning certain events which occurred in the San Miguel System. I am Anne-Louise Brulé, conducting this interview for the Foreign

Ministry, the Ministry of Trade, and the Treasury. This record is being made on July 7, 1921 Post Diaspora, on the planet of New Tuscany."

She finished the official tag, then turned back to Captain Carmouche.

"Very well, Captain Carmouche. Could you please explain to us, in your own words, exactly what happened?"

"In San Miguel, you mean?" Carmouche said, then grimaced in obvious embarrassment. "Sorry. I guess I really am a little nervous."

Brulé smiled encouragingly, and the captain cleared his throat and straightened slightly in his chair.

"Well, we'd arrived in San Miguel early last month to collect a cargo which had been chartered before this Constitutional Convention in Spindle voted out its 'constitution.' Now, San Miguel's always been part of the Rembrandt Trade Union, and the Union's always favored using its own bottoms instead of chartering foreign-registry ships, so there've been occasional problems for skippers who don't belong to the RTU, but generally, we've been able to work things out without too much trouble.

"This time, though, when *Antelope* made her parking orbit, we were boarded by a *Manticoran* customs party, not one from San Miguel or the Trade Union. That was unusual, but I just figured it was part of the new political set up, so I didn't worry about it too much. Until, that is, the Manties started tearing the ship apart looking for 'contraband.'"

Carmouche's face tightened in remembered anger, and he shrugged jerkily.

"I wasn't any too happy about that," he said. "I mean, I can understand wanting to keep a handle on smuggling, especially out here in the Verge. I don't have a problem with that. For that matter, I know our own customs people keep a close eye on ships entering New Tuscany, especially if they aren't regular visitors on this run. But there's courteous ways to go about it, and then there's ways that . . . aren't so courteous. Like the way these bas—"

He broke off, shook himself, and grimaced.

"Sorry," he said again. "I meant like the way these *people* did it. I don't necessarily expect anyone to bow down to me. I mean, I know I'm merchant service, not the Navy. But, by God, *Antelope* is my ship! *I'm* the one responsible to the owners, and even if

I'm only merchant service, there's a certain amount of respect any skipper has a right to expect out of visitors aboard his ship. I don't care who they are!

"But these people didn't waste any respect on *anyone* aboard *Antelope*. They were rude, insulting, and what I have to think was deliberately antagonistic. They didn't make requests; they *demanded* whatever it was they wanted. They insisted on bringing aboard all kinds of scanners and detection equipmet, too, and they went through every cargo space with a fine tooth comb. Took *hours*, given the size of our holds, but they insisted. Just like they insisted on checking every bill of lading individually against its cargo container—didn't matter whether or not the container's port-of-origin customs seals were intact, either. They even made us open a whole stack of containers so they could physically eyeball the contents! And they made it pretty clear that if we didn't do exactly what they wanted, they'd refuse us entry for the planet and prohibit any orbital cargo transshipment."

Carmouche leaned forward in his chair, his face and body language both more animated in an evident combination of anger and increasing confidence under Brulé's encouraging, gravely sympathetic expression.

"Well, I managed to put up with their 'customs inspection' without popping a blood vessel or slugging anyone, but it wasn't easy. We got them back off the ship—finally—and we got our clearances from them, but that was when we found out we were going to have to submit to a *medical* examination before we were allowed to take on or discharge cargo. We weren't *discharging* cargo, anyway, and they damned well knew it. And I've never been asked for a medical certification to *take on* cargo! At a port of entry, sure. Anyone wants to keep a close eye on anyone who might be bringing *in* some kind of contagion. But when there's not going to be any contact between any of my people or the planetary environment—for that matter, not even between any of my people and an orbital warehouse, for God's sake, since the cargo was coming aboard in *San Miguel* shuttles!—it didn't make any sense at all. For that matter, they'd checked our current medical records as part of their customs inspection!

"I didn't understand it then, but it started making sense later, when I realized it didn't have anything to do with medical precautions. Not really. No matter what we did, there was always another hoop waiting for us to jump through before we were going to be allowed to load our cargo. After the medical examination, they insisted on checking our engineering logs to make sure we weren't going to suffer some sort of catastrophic impeller casualty in heavily traveled volumes of the star system. And after *that*, they decided they had to inspect our enviro plant's waste recycling and disposal systems, since they didn't want us *littering* in their precious star system!"

He shook his head angrily.

"The only thing I could come up with, since every one of those 'inspections' of theirs was completely bogus, as far as I could tell, was that it was a systematic effort to make it very clear that *Antelope* wasn't welcome in San Miguel. The RTU's always been protective of its own interests, but I was under the impression from everything everyone was saying before the Constitutional Convention that the Manties supported free trade. Well, maybe they do, and maybe they don't, but I can tell you this—if they do think free trade is a good idea, they obviously don't think it's a good idea for *everyone*! And after I figured out what was going on, I asked around. There were a couple of other ships in orbit, but we were the only one from New Tuscany. And by the oddest coincidence, we were also the only one being subjected to all those 'inspections.' Which suggested to *me* that maybe what this was all about was the fact that we hadn't ratified their 'constitution,' and this was an example of payback. I don't know about that for sure, of course, but as soon as I got back to New Tuscany, I spoke to the Ministry of Trade about it, and I don't mind telling you I was just a bit hot when I did. Apparently, I'm not the only New Tuscan skipper this has happened to, either. Or that was my impression, anyway, when they asked me to make an official statement for the record."

He looked at Brulé and raised an eyebrow, but she shook her head with a commiserating smile.

"I'm afraid I don't really know about that, Captain Carmouche," she said, in the tone of voice someone used to add "and if I did know, I couldn't tell you," without ever saying so out loud.

"Well, whatever," Carmouche said after a moment, "that's about the size of it. Were there any specific questions you wanted to ask, Ma'am?"

"There were a few points where the ministries wanted a little more detail, Captain," Brulé said, keying a memo pad and glancing down at the display. "Let me see . . . All right, first, did you get the name and rank of the Manticoran officer in charge of the original customs inspection?"

"No," Carmouche replied with another grimace. "Never offered it. Suppose I should have insisted, but it's the first time I ever had a regular navy officer come aboard my ship and *not* give his name and rank. Personally, I think he didn't want me to have it in case I ended up lodging any formal protests. Of course, I didn't know then that I was going to be doing that, either. So, instead of asking, I—"

They were good, Aldona Anisimovna thought, watching approvingly from the studio's control room. In fact, the New Tuscan Information Ministry had shown a far more sophisticated touch where little things like propaganda and special effects were concerned than she would have expected out of someone with a Verge tech base. Of course, they'd probably *needed* a bit more sophistication than most, given their local proles' evident unhappiness.

She particularly liked the touch with the pre-interview conversation and Brulé's efforts to put Captain Carmouche more at his ease. They wouldn't be part of the formal report, of course . . . but they *would* "just happen" to have been left attached to the raw footage which would *accompany* the formal report. Where, of course, Commissioner Verrochio's people would "just happen" to discover them. They'd give a certain additional sense of veracity to the final report when it was presented to Verrochio as part of the evidence supporting claims of harassment. Of course, while there'd been no particular effort to hide the fact that Anne-Louise Brulé worked for the Ministry of Information, no one had bothered to mention the fact that 'Captain Carmouche' was actually being portrayed by one Oliver Ratté, who was also employed by the Ministry of Information. Unlike Brulé, whoever, who was a recognizable anchor from the New Tuscan news broadcasts, Ratté was effectively anonymous. Although he'd appeared in innumerable propaganda efforts, he'd never appeared under his own face. Instead, his job had been to provide the body language, voice, and facial expressions the computers transformed into someone else entirely.

It was still the best and simplest way to produce high-quality

CGI, especially for someone whose tech base might not have all of the latest bells and whistles. In fact, New Tuscany's computer technology was probably at least a couple of centuries behind that of the Solarian League in general. They'd demonstrated over the years just how much could be accomplished by substituting technique and practice for technology, however, and this time around, Ratté was appearing under his own face. There would be absolutely no computer chicanery with *this* little masterpiece, and the same held true for all the others the New Tuscans were working up. After all, it would never do for any of the Manties' contacts in the League to demonstrate that sort of fancy tricks by analyzing the recording.

*And by the time Dusserre and his little helpers over at the Security Ministry get done massaging the planetary database, there won't be any way to prove that Captain Carmouche and the good ship* Antelope *have never existed. In fact,* she thought with amused satisfaction, *there'll be all kinds of evidence that they* have *existed. Of course the Manties are going to* claim *that neither of them have ever visited San Miguel, but who is Frontier Security supposed to believe? The poor, harassed New Tuscans who are asking for their intervention, or the nasty Manties who are trying to come up with reasons why Frontier Security* shouldn't *investigate?*

It was a nice touch, although it was scarcely necessary. Not that she had any intention of telling the *New Tuscans* that. From their viewpoint, there was every reason to set up an invulnerable defense in depth, since they could anticipate the Manties' protestations of innocence. Especially given the fact that the Manties *were* innocent, she admitted. But what the Mesan Alignment in the person of one Aldona Anisimovna had seen no reason to worry New Tuscany over was that it really didn't matter at all. No one was going to be looking at any records on New Tuscany. The Solarian League wouldn't feel any particular need to do so; the Manties weren't going to be in a *position* to do so; and both sides were going to be far too busy with what the Alignment really wanted them to be doing to each other for it to matter one way or the other to anyone.

She watched Brulé and Ratté working their way smoothly through the well-written and carefully rehearsed script and wondered if the sense of almost godlike power she felt as she watched the entire New Tuscany System dancing to the *Alignment's* script was the same

sort of thing Albert Detweiler felt? And if so, was it as addictive for
him as she realized it could easily become for her? For that matter,
if it was, did he care?

I *understand what we're trying to accomplish and why—now, at
least*, she thought. *I wouldn't have understood before he and Isabel
explained it all to me, but I do now. But knowing only makes the
game even more intoxicating. It defines the scope, the scale, in a
way nothing else ever has before. But ambitious as it is, it's still
all . . . intellectual for me. The game is what's real. I wonder if it's
that way for Albrecht and the others? And if it is, what are they
going to do when we've finally pulled it off and there are no more
games to play?*

"He said what?"

Lieutenant Commander Lewis Denton frowned at Ensign Rachel
Monahan. The ensign sat just a little nervously in a chair across
the desk from him in his compact day cabin. Despite the fact that
Denton was only a lieutenant commander, and that HMS *Reprise*
was only a somewhat elderly and increasingly obsolescent destroyer,
he was still the captain of one of Her Majesty's starships, and at
the moment, Monahan seemed only too well aware of the fact
that she was the most junior officer aboard that same starship.

She was also conscientious and, although Denton had absolutely
no intention of saying so to a single living soul, remarkably easy
on the eye. She wasn't the very smartest junior officer he'd ever
encountered, but she had a generous helping of common sense,
and she was a long, long way from stupid. In fact, Denton was
one of those officers who preferred attention to duty and common sense to erratic or careless (or, even worse, *lazy*) intelligence,
and he'd been entirely satisfied with her performance since she'd
joined *Reprise*'s ship's company. That was one of the reasons he'd
been giving her progressively bigger opportunities to demonstrate
her competence and self-confidence, and, so far, she'd met all of
them quite handily.

Which was what had led directly to her request for this interview,
even if Denton didn't have a clue in Hell what was going on.

"He said he was going to formally complain about our 'harassment,' Sir," Monahan repeated now.

"*Your* harassment," Denton said in the tone of a man trying to
get some ridiculous concept straight in his own mind.

"Yes, Sir."

Monahan sounded more than a little anxious, and Denton could understand that well enough. A great many junior officers who'd screwed up would make it their first order of business to get their version of what had happened in front of their commanding officers before any inconvenient little truths could come along to make matters worse. In Monahan's case, though, that very notion was preposterous.

"About the harassing you obviously hadn't done, Rachel. Is that what he was implying?"

"Yes, Sir."

"Had you done anything that could have gotten him pissed off enough at you to fabricate some sort of complaint in an effort to make trouble for you?"

"Sir, I can't think of a single thing," she said, shaking her head. "I did everything exactly by The Book, the way I've done it every time before. But it was like . . . I don't know, exactly, Sir, but it was like he was *waiting* for me to do something he could complain about. And if I wasn't going to do it, then he was ready to claim I had, anyway! I've never seen anything like it, Sir."

She was obviously even more confused than she was worried, and Denton made another mental check mark of approval for her end-of-deployment evaluation. Despite her evident concern that he might wonder if she was trying to cover her posterior, she'd reported the entire episode to the XO as soon as she'd come back aboard ship. And the XO had been sufficiently perplexed—and concerned—to pass her report along to Denton before she'd even left his office. Which was the reason Monahan was now sitting in Denton's day cabin repeating her account of the customs inspection.

"So you went aboard, asked for his papers, checked them, and did a quick walk-through, right?"

"Yes, Sir."

"And he was giving you grief from the very beginning?"

"Yes, Sir. From the minute I cleared the personnel tube. It was like he was on some kind of hair trigger, ready to bite my head off over anything, no matter how polite my people and I were. Skipper, I think I could have complimented him on the color of the bulkheads and he would have managed to turn it into some sort of mortal insult!"

The young woman—she was only twenty-two T-years old—had clearly never experienced anything like it. Denton had, on the other hand, although it had usually been from a Solarian merchant spacer, not someone from New Tuscany. Some Sollies went out of their way to attempt to provoke a Manticoran officer into providing a basis for complaints and allegations of harassment. It was something Astro Control back in the home system encountered with depressing frequency from Solarian ships passing through the Manticoran Wormhole Junction, as well. Some Sollies simply resented the hell out of the fact that a single little out-system star nation dominated such a huge percentage of the League's total carrying trade. They went around with planet-sized chips on their shoulders where the Star Kingdom was concerned as a consequence.

But the Sollies who did that also knew they were representatives of the Solarian League. They were armed and armored with all of the arrogant Solly assurance that there was nothing any mere Manticoran could really do to punish them if they got out of line. That was one of the things Denton himself personally most hated about Solarians. And it was also what puzzled him about *this* incident, because New Tuscany was a single-system star nation, so poor it didn't have a pot to piss in. So what could possibly possess a *New Tuscan* merchant skipper to risk deliberately antagonizing the Royal Manticoran Navy here in a star system which had just become Manticoran territory?

"Sir?"

Denton shook himself back up out of his thoughts and looked back at Monahan.

"Sorry, Rachel." He gave her a quick smile. "Wool gathering, I'm afraid. You had something else you wanted to add?"

"Yes, Sir."

"Well, add away," he encouraged.

"Sir, it's just, well . . ." She seemed a bit hesitant, then visibly steeled herself for the plunge.

"Sir, it's just that I had this funny feeling that he wasn't really saying any of it for *my* benefit."

"What do you mean?" Denton's eyes narrowed.

"It was more like he was talking *about* me than *to* me," she said, sounding as if she were picking her words carefully, trying to find the ones to explain whatever it was she was groping towards. "Like . . . like somebody in one of the Academy's training holos, almost."

"Like he knew it was being *recorded*," Denton said slowly. "Is that what it felt like?"

"Maybe, Sir." Monahan looked more worried than ever. "And it wasn't just me he was complaining about, either."

"Meaning?" Denton tried to keep any note of tension out of his voice, but it was hard, given the mental alarm bells trying to ring somewhere deep down inside him.

"Meaning that he didn't say just 'you' when he was complaining about what a hard time I'd been giving him. He said that, but he also said things like 'you *people*,' too. Like there were dozens of me, all trying to give him and his friends trouble."

"I see."

Denton sat in thought for several more seconds, not particularly liking the speculations chasing around the inside of his brain like hamsters in an exercise wheel, then returned his attention to the ensign sitting before him.

"Rachel, I want you to know that you did exactly the right thing reporting this. And that neither the XO nor I believe for a minute that you did a single thing wrong aboard that ship. I don't know exactly what his problem was, but I'm sure you handled yourself just as well as you always have in the past."

"I tried to, Sir," she said, unable to hide her enormous relief at his firmly supportive tone. "The more it went on, though, the more I started wondering if I *had* done something to tick him off!"

"I doubt very much that you did anything at all," Denton said in that same firm tone of voice. "Unfortunately, you may well encounter the same thing again. God knows most of us have run into it a time or two, although it's usually from the Sollies, not from someone like the New Tuscans. I'm sorry it happened to you here, but it's probably just as well to get the first dose out of the way early in your career."

"Yes, Sir," she said, and he flashed her a smile of approval.

"All right," he said with an air of finality. "I think you've probably given me everything you've got, so there's no point our sitting here chewing it over any more or wondering what kind of wild hair might have inspired him to go off that way. I would like you to go ahead and record a formal report on this, though. If he does actually decide to complain to someone, I want to have your version of the encounter already on the record to help shoot him down."

"Yes, Sir," she said again.

"In that case, why don't you go ahead and get that taken care of right now, while events are still fresh in your mind?"

"Yes, Sir."

Monahan obviously recognized her dismissal, and she rose, braced briefly to attention, and left. Denton gazed at the closed door for several moments, then punched a combination into his com terminal.

"Bridge, XO speaking," a voice said. "What can I do for you, Skipper?"

"I've just finished talking with Rachel, Pete. I see why you sent her to see me."

"She did seem more than a little upset," Lieutenant Peter Koslov said. "But it was the nature of what that New Tuscan bastard said that really worried *me*."

"Agreed. I don't want to make a big thing out of this and worry her any more than she already is, especially not before she gets her formal report together for me. But, that said, I want you to have a word with the rest of her boarding party, especially Chief Fitzhugh. And have a quiet word with any of the other JOs who've been running the customs inspections. See if any of them may have heard some of the same kind of remarks and just not been as willing as Rachel to bring them to our attention. And if they have heard anything like that, I want details of time, place, and content."

"Yes, Sir."

Koslov sounded rather grimmer than he had a moment ago, Denton noticed.

"One other thing," the CO continued. "I want every party that goes aboard *anybody's* merchant shipping wired for sound and vision. I don't especially want you to mention it to anyone aboard ship, either, because I don't want anyone obviously playing to the camera from our side. So find someplace to put a parasite cam. I don't want to give away any image quality unless we have to, but I'm less worried about picture than I am about sound."

"Skipper, I don't think I like what I think you're thinking."

"Well, if you hadn't been thinking in the same direction yourself, you wouldn't have gotten Rachel in to see me quite this promptly, now would you?" Denton shot back.

"It was more an itch than any sort of full-blown suspicion, Sir."

"In that case, your instincts may just have been serving you entirely too well, I'm afraid," Denton said grimly. "I don't have any idea why this might be going on, and it may be that you and I are both just imagining things. But it may be that we aren't, either, and Admiral Khumalo made the point that he wanted us to keep our eyes and ears open when he sent us out. So go ahead and make those inquiries for me. And get those bugs planted. Maybe we can sneak them into the boarding officer's memo boards or something. I don't know, but I do know I want the best hard records we can get of every visit to a New Tuscan ship. And I want the same thing from our inspections of anyone else's shipping, as well, to serve as a base for comparison. Clear?"

"Clear, Skipper," Koslov replied. "I don't like where we seem to be going with this, but it's clear."

# Chapter Twenty-Seven

"NOT MUCH OF A PICKET, is it?" Michelle Henke commented quietly to Cynthia Lecter, twelve days after her conversation with Josef Byng, as HMS *Artemis* and the other three ships of the first division of Battlecruiser Squadron 106 decelerated towards a leisurely rendezvous with the ships Augustus Khumalo had detached to keep an eye on the Tillerman System when he returned to Spindle from Monica.

"No, Ma'am," Lecter agreed, equally quietly. "On the other hand, Admiral Khumalo didn't have a lot to work with. And I don't think anyone expected Vice Admiral O'Malley to be recalled quite so . . . precipitously."

"You do have a way with words, don't you, Cindy?" Michelle smiled without very much humor, but she had to admit that Lecter had made an excellent point. Two of them, in fact.

*Which leaves me with a not-so-minor problem of my own*, she thought dryly. *Nobody had a clue the Sollies were going to send such a big-assed task force straight out to Monica to wave in our face. But now we know they have . . . and that we are going back to war with Haven, too. So do I reinforce Tillerman by detaching a couple of battlecruisers, or do I leave Tillerman like it is and take everybody I've got back to Spindle to keep things concentrated?*

The question was, unfortunately, one she wouldn't be able to duck, much as she might have wished she could do exactly that. The mere notion of dividing her forces in the face of any potential threat from the Solarian League was calculated to inflict insomnia on any fleet commander. On the one hand, the three days she'd spent in Monica had convinced her that whatever else Josef Byng might be in the vicinity to accomplish, it wasn't to reassure one Michelle Henke of his friendly and pacific intent. So if she *didn't* reinforce the pair of over-aged light cruisers and the single destroyer Khumalo had been able to station here, she risked sending the entirely wrong signal not just to him but to everyone else in the Talbott Quadrant. She dared not give anyone—especially Byng—the impression that she would be unwilling to run serious risks, or even fight, to defend the territory and citizens of the newborn Star Empire of Manticore. For that matter, she had both a legal and a moral responsibility to do just that, regardless of the nature of the threat.

On the other hand, even a pair of *Nikes* might find themselves hard-pressed against all of Byng's battlecruisers at once. Despite the advantages in range and hitting power the Mark 16 and Mark 23 provided for the RMN, enough *effective* missile defense could go a long way towards blunting that advantage, and no one had any way to assess just how effective SLN missile-defense doctrine might actually be. Michelle strongly doubted that it would be enough to tip the odds in the Sollies' favor, but she couldn't be positive of that before the fact. Worse, even if it turned out after the fact that two *Nikes* were, indeed, a match for everything Byng had, *Byng* wouldn't know that ahead of time, either. For that matter, he'd never admit it—probably even to himself—no matter how much evidence anyone presented to him before the shooting started. Michelle had seen enough Manticoran officers who were capable of that sort of self-delusion when it suited their prejudices. Someone like Byng would be able to pull that off effortlessly.

*And if he doesn't recognize—or admit—the threat even exists, then the "threat" won't deter him for a moment, will it?* she thought bitingly. *Aside, of course, from the possibility that taking out our "outnumbered and outgunned" picket would be crossing a line he may have specific orders not to cross.*

*Yeah. Sure he does. If you're willing to bank on* that, *girl, don't be accepting any real estate deals that involve bridges or magic beans!*

She grimaced, then inhaled deeply and glanced over her shoulder at Lieutenant Commander Edwards.

"Contact *Devastation*, Bill. My compliments to Commander Cramer, and would it be convenient for him to join me for dinner here aboard *Artemis* at, say, eighteen-thirty hours?"

"Aye, aye, Ma'am," the com officer replied, and Michelle turned her attention to Gervais Archer.

"As for you, Gwen," she said with a smile, "you get to go tell Chris that Commander Cramer will be joining us for dinner. Make sure Captain Armstrong and Commander Dallas know they're invited, as well."

"Yes, Ma'am," Gervais replied gravely. He supposed some might argue that the admiral was being just a bit presumptuous to be organizing dinner parties when the guest of honor hadn't confirmed that he'd be present. On the other hand, it was just a bit difficult for Gervais to conceive of any commander who wouldn't somehow find it possible to fit an invitation from any admiral into his schedule, no matter how busy it might be.

"Oh, and, Bill," Michelle said, glancing back at Edwards. "While you're sending out the invitations, go ahead and invite Captain Conner and Commander Houseman, too."

Commander Wesley Cramer of Her Majesty's Starship *Devastation* was a hard-bitten looking officer, forty-one T-years old (which made him three T-months younger than his own cruiser), with dark hair and quartz-hard gray eyes. His neatly clipped mustache mostly hid a scar on his upper lip, one of several souvenirs of a bruising Saganami Island rugby career, and it didn't look as if he'd mellowed a great deal since leaving the Academy.

Which, Michelle reflected, suited her just fine, under the circumstances.

She examined him with carefully hidden intensity as Gervais Archer ushered him into the magnificent dining cabin BuShips had seen fit to provide for her. Despite the fact that he was both the commander of a Queen's ship and currently the senior officer assigned to Tillerman, he was also junior to every officer in the compartment except Archer himself. If he was particularly aware of that fact, however, it didn't seem to weigh too heavily upon him.

"Commander Cramer," Gervais murmured to her by way of formal introdmction, and she extended her right hand.

"Commander," she said.

"Milady," Cramer responded, gripping the offered hand firmly.

"Let me introduce you to everyone," she continued, turning to her other guests. "Captain Armstrong, of the *Artemis*, and her XO, Commander Dallas. Captain Conner, of the *Penelope*, and *his* XO, Commander Houseman."

Cramer was busy shaking hands as she spoke, and she gave him a moment to catch up before she turned to the members of her own staff who were present.

"Captain Lecter, my chief of staff; Commander Adenauer, my ops officer; and Lieutenant Commander Treacher, my logistics officer. And I believe you've already met Lieutenant Archer, my flag lieutenant."

It took Cramer a few more moments to shake all of the newly introduced hands, and then Michelle nodded towards the large table under its snow white tablecloth and burden of plates, crystal, and gleaming tableware.

"One of my own previous COs was firmly of the opinion that a good meal was often the basis for the most effective officers' conferences," she observed. "Which, in case any of you somehow failed to catch my subtle implication, was an invitation to eat."

It was fascinating to watch Admiral Gold Peak in action, Gervais Archer reflected some time later. Despite her lofty birth, there was an undeniable earthiness about her basic personality, and he'd come to wonder if she might not have developed that trait deliberately. He'd already seen ample evidence of her effortless mastery of the proper rules of etiquette and her ability to project the public persona appropriate to someone who stood only five heartbeats away from the Crown of Manticore. Very few people, watching her operate in that mode, would ever have grounds to suspect how much she clearly loved escaping from it, he thought, but anyone who'd worked with—or for—her for any length of time knew *exactly* how little she liked playing that particular role. And it wasn't as if she needed to remind anyone in the Navy that the Queen was her cousin. First, because however much she might have wished they didn't, everyone already knew. But second, and more importantly, because she needed no aristocratic airs to underscore her authority. She'd demonstrated her competence too many times, and even if she hadn't, five or ten minutes in her presence would have made that competence painfully clear to anyone, however "casual" or "earthy" she might choose to appear.

Now she leaned back in her chair at the head of the table, nursing a cup of coffee instead of one of the wineglasses several of her guests preferred, and favored Commander Cramer with a smile which held very little humor.

"Now that we've impressed you with my hospitality, Commander," she said dryly, "I suppose we probably ought to get down to business."

Cramer nodded politely in acknowledgment, and a trace of true amusement worked its way into her smile.

"I've read your reports," she continued, and Gervais knew she truly had *read* them, not simply skimmed them, after they'd been burst-transmitted to *Artemis*. "I'm very pleased with what you've managed to accomplish here," she went on. "On the other hand, there's not much point any of us pretending that you're in any position to hold off some sort of serious attack on Tillerman."

Cramer nodded again, and the admiral sipped from her coffee cup again.

"Under almost any other set of circumstances, Commander, I would be completely satisfied to leave Tillerman in your care. Given our recent encounter with so many Solarian battlecruisers at Monica, however, and given the proximity of both Meyers and Monica to Tillerman, I think we need something a bit more . . . impressive here in the system. Mind you, I'm not happy about the notion of spreading our forces out in penny packets. We're too thin on the ground—for the moment, at least—to go around diluting our combat power that way. Unfortunately, I don't see any real option here. At least for the foreseeable future, Tillerman's going to be our most advanced picket in an area where we've already crossed swords with a Solarian client state. Given that, it turns the entire region into a potential flashpoint that I believe requires a force which is not simply *more* powerful than yours but is *self-evidently* more powerful. Powerful enough to give any reasonable potential adversary pause. My judgment in that regard represents absolutely no reflection on you, any of your people, or the other ships under your command here."

She held his eyes levelly, letting him see the sincerity in her own, then twitched her head at Jerome Conner.

"I'll be returning to Spindle by way of Talbott, Scarlet, Marian,

Dresden, and Montana—I think this entire area needs a little reassurance, after what happened in Monica and Vice Admiral O'Malley's recall—but Captain Conner is going to be taking over as Tillerman's senior officer. I'm detaching his ship and Captain Ning's *Romulus*. Unless something changes, I'll be sending up additional destroyers as soon as some of them arrive from Manticore. In the meantime, I'll expect *Devastation*, *Inspired*, and *Victorious* to conduct anti-piracy patrols and generally show the flag in this vicinity while Captain Conner's battlecruisers stay home and mind the store. As soon as we can get some more modern destroyers, and possibly a few heavy cruisers, out here to replace you, I'll withdraw your ships to Spindle for a well deserved rest."

"I understand, Milady," Cramer replied, when she paused. It was, Gervais reflected, a rather tactful way for the admiral to describe pulling the older, less capable ships back for secondary duties elsewhere.

"Until we have the hulls in-quadrant to do that, however," she continued after a moment, "I'll expect you to make your own local knowledge and advice available to Captain Conner. It's clear to me from your reports that you haven't let any grass grow under your feet, Commander. The time you've spent making contacts with the local system government, emplacing the system surveillance platforms, and deploying missile pods for defensive use has been very well-used—a point I intend to make in my own report when I unreservedly endorse your actions and conduct here in Tillerman. You've done a great deal to make Captain Conner's job easier, and I'm confident that you'll be equally helpful during his settling-in period."

This time, there was an obvious flicker of appreciation in those hard gray eyes. Cramer was never going to be one of those officers who gushed effusively—especially to their superiors—Gervais thought. But it was clear he recognized genuine praise when he heard it . . . and that he realized when it was well deserved, as well.

"Jerome," the admiral went on, turning her attention to Captain Conner. "As I told the Commander, I'm not happy about leaving you and Kwo-Lai out here with only two battlecruisers. Unfortunately, for right now I don't see any option. I'll get you reinforced as quickly as I can, but in the meantime, you're going to be in what might charitably be called a somewhat exposed position. And, to be honest, after talking to that jackass Byng,

I'm even less happy about that state of affairs than I might have been otherwise."

"I can't say I'm delighted about all the aspects of my new, independent command, either, Admiral," Conner replied with a faint smile. "Not that I'm not grateful for the opportunity to distinguish myself, of course."

"Don't you mean to *further* distinguish yourself?" the admiral inquired, and a quiet laugh ran around the table. But then her expression sobered, and she sat forward, setting her coffee cup back on the table and folding her hands in front of her.

"Commander Cramer made a good start deploying pods from *Volcano* in strategic positions," she said very seriously. "On the other hand, he didn't begin to have the control links to take full advantage of them. *Penelope* and *Romulus*, on the other hand, both have Keyhole. They're going to be able to control a hell of a lot more pods than the Commander could have with a pair of light cruisers, and *Volcano*'s pods are loaded with all-up Mark 23s. I've had Jackson here"—she nodded at Lieutenant Commander Jackson Treacher, her logistics officer—"confer with Commander Badmachin. She tells him that Vice Admiral O'Malley topped off *Volcano*'s missile holds from his own fleet train before he headed back to the Lynx Terminus, so you've got plenty of pods. Which means you should be able to raise holy howling hell with anything that's likely to come at you out here."

She paused, waiting until Conner had nodded, then went on levelly.

"I'm fully aware that the Admiralty would prefer for us not to advertise all of our capabilities unless we have to. Nonetheless, I'm specifically authorizing you to use any weapon available to you—including the Mark 23s—to their full capabilities in defense of this star system . . . against anyone. If *anybody*, and I'm specifically including the Solarian League Navy in that 'anybody,' attacks this star system, you are to defend it as if it were the Manticore Home System itself. My formal written orders to you will emphasize those points, and they will further authorize you to use deadly force against anyone—once again, specifically including the Solarian League Navy—who violates the territorial sovereignty of this system."

She paused once more, and Gervais realized he was almost holding his breath. What she was doing was telling Conner he had carte blanche to do whatever he thought he had to do in the defense of Tillerman. It was obvious she wouldn't have done that if she hadn't trusted his judgment, but the fact remained that her orders would cover anything he did, including starting a shooting war with the Solarian League, and that the responsibility would be hers.

"I understand, Ma'am," the captain said quietly after a moment.

"I believe you do," she agreed, sitting back and reaching for her coffee cup once more. "On the other hand, I also want you to understand this. Defending this star system does *not* mean throwing away the ships under your command. I expect you to use all of the resources at your disposal, if necessary, to accomplish that mission. If it becomes evident, however, that you aren't going to be able to stop an attack, then I also expect you to pull your ships out. Kick as much hell out of the other side as you can, but get them out intact. Losing them, in addition to losing the system, won't help anyone, no matter how 'gloriously' you all die. Keeping them intact for when we come back to kick the Bad Guys back out of Tillerman on their asses, *will*. Strive to bear that in mind, please? I had the misfortune to make Elvis Santino's acquaintance too many years ago. The Royal Navy doesn't need another one of him."

"I understand, Ma'am," Conner repeated, and this time the admiral chuckled.

"I'm delighted to hear that. On the other hand, I'm not going to pull out and leave you here on your own tomorrow. Given the importance Tillerman looks like assuming, I think it would be a very good idea for me to make President Cummings' acquaintance and get to know as many senior members of the system government as I can. And it won't hurt for me to express my confidence in you in the proper quarters, either. So I'll probably be spending at least a couple of weeks in the vicinity before I go haring off."

"Yes, Ma'am. I understand. And I appreciate the thought, for that matter. I think it would have to help get us off on the right foot here."

"I'm glad you agree. I thought it was a rather clever notion myself."

She grinned at him, then drained her coffee cup and stood.

"And now that we have those details out of the way, I suggest that all of us adjourn to the flag bridge, where Commander Cramer will walk us all through his sensor platform deployment patterns. What I'd really like to do, Jerome, is to give you a day or so to look the situation over, then run a couple of simulations with *Penelope* and *Romulus* defending the system against several different levels of threat."

"Should I assume that *you* intend to be commanding the opposition force, Ma'am?" Conner asked just a bit warily.

"Me?" the admiral said innocently. "Oh, no, Jerome! I'm just going to be advising. Vicki here will be actually running the attack," she nodded to Captain Armstrong, who grinned challengingly at Conner. "And, I suppose that just to make it interesting, we ought to let Commander Cramer command a couple of units of that op force you were talking about." She smiled sweetly at Conner, then glanced at Cramer, who was obviously trying very hard not to smile himself. "You might want to bear that division of command responsibility in mind while you brief Captain Conner on your sensor deployments, Commander."

"Oh, thank you, Ma'am," Conner said. "Thank you *ever* so much!"

#  Chapter Twenty-Eight

"—SO THAT JUST ABOUT takes care of the domestic side," Joachim Alquezar said, looking across the conference table at Dame Estelle Matsuko, Baroness Medusa. "I'm not entirely happy about the situation at Marian, but I think it's mostly a tempest in a teapot. Someone in the local planetary government with too big an opinion of what he's due feels like he got his toes stepped on, and he's pissing and moaning about it. No one's going to let him get away with it long enough for it to become a real problem, but I'm afraid this is hardly going to be the only place something like this is going to come up before all's said and done. So it might not be a bad idea for Samiha to send someone from her ministry out to read them the riot act just to make sure his own people step on him hard enough."

Alquezar, Medusa was pleased to note, showed no signs—as yet—of developing the sort of formality-craving sense of self-importance she'd seen out of altogether too many political leaders over the decades. Of course, there was plenty of time for that, she supposed, reminding herself not to let her hopes get too high.

*After all, all of a pessimist's surprises are pleasant ones,* she thought drily. *Although I have to say, I think he's a lot less likely to go that way than some of the politicians I've seen back home! Than lots of the politicos I've seen back home, actually . . . or than that poisonous little twerp Van Scheldt would like him to be, for that matter.*

She wondered—again—why Alquezar didn't just go ahead and fire Van Scheldt. The man was certainly efficient, but if there was anyone in the entire Alquezar Government whom she trusted less in the dark...

"As you say, Mr. Prime Minister," she said out loud after a moment, "this is a domestic matter for the Talbott Quadrant. It doesn't really come under my umbrella as the Imperial Governor unless things get so out of hand I need to step in and squash someone. So far, this doesn't strike me as even beginning to reach that level. Would you concur, Madam Secretary?"

"Oh, I'd say that was definitely the case, Madam Governor," Samiha Lababibi replied with a smile. "Joachim is absolutely right about what's going on, except that in this case, I'm fairly sure it's not a 'he' who's doing the pissing and moaning. I've got a pretty good idea exactly who it is, as a matter of fact, and if I'm right, it's a 'she.' It's not really that she got her toes stepped on, either; it's that she was hoping for a little better opportunity to line her own pockets off of the investment credits program." Lababibi shook her head. "I'm afraid a few people are still having a bit of difficulty realizing it isn't going to go on being business as usual. As Joachim says, it's not the last time something like this is going to come up, either. I can think of some people right here in Spindle—and not *visitors* to my fair home world, either, I'm afraid—who feel exactly the same way and may actually be stupid enough to try to do something similar."

*And that's something pretty remarkable, too*, Medusa thought with a sense of profound satisfaction. *Back during the Constitutional Convention, it would never have occurred to Lababibi to say something like that. Not because she's ever been deliberately corrupt herself, but just because she's always been part of the topmost layer of the political and economic structures here in Spindle, with all of the insulation from everyone else's reality that comes with that. She might have sympathized intellectually with someone like Krietzmann, but she could never really have understood where Henri comes from. It was just too far outside her own experience. I wondered if putting her inside the Star Empire's fiscal policies as the Quadrant's treasurer would shake up her own comfortable little perceptions of the universe. I always knew she was* smart *enough for it to, at least, but smart doesn't necessarily equate to wise, and I'm glad to see it seems to be working out in this case, at least.*

"In this case, though," Lababibi continued, blissfully unaware of the governor's thoughts, "I believe I can . . . reason with the culprit. If I point out, speaking as the Quadrant's Treasury Secretary, that the investment credits are being offered solely on a private citizen basis and that both the Alquezar Government and Her Majesty would look with . . . profound displeasure, shall we say, on any effort by local governments to interfere with that, I think she'll get the message."

"Good." Medusa smiled, then sobered slightly. "As I say, this does strike me as an internal matter for the Quadrant, and you're quite right, Samiha. This entire credit program *is* being offered to private citizens, which means that, aside from the tax credit portion of it, it's not properly a matter for government control or intrusion at all. You might want to deliver your message in a fashion which makes it clear my office and I are being kept in the loop, however. Let me do a little ominous looming in the background, but don't make me any sort of explicit big stick. Let them draw any inferences they want, but not only is it not my place to be interfering in a matter like this unless you or Joachim request it, I want everyone to understand both that *I* know it isn't and that the Quadrant government is all grown up and able to make its own decisions and do any hammering you people think is required."

Lababibi nodded, and Medusa nodded back with another flicker of satisfaction at how well the former president of the Split System was working out handling Treasury matters for the Quadrant. And not, this time, simply because of the shift in her attitude away from the "way things are" view of oligarchical privilege. Her awareness of the need to find the right balance between local decision and policy making—and enforcement—and imperial authority was another huge plus in Medusa's opinion.

The entire situation was still something of a two-headed monster for everyone involved, of course. Under the new constitution, Alquezar, as the Quadrant's Prime Minister, was the legal head of government for the Quadrant. That gave him and the rest of the Quadrant an enormous degree of local autonomy . . . and the accountability that went with it. However, the entire Quadrant was responsible for accommodating itself to the policies of the Star Empire of Manticore, represented and enunciated in this case by one Baroness Medusa. While she could not normally overrule specific policy decisions or acts of local legislation, she had complete authority—and the power of the veto—when it came to making certain those decisions and pieces of legislation fitted smoothly into imperial guidelines in those areas where the Empress' authority was paramount. Despite the Quadrant Constitution's neatly delimited articles and sections, actually implementing its provisions remained a work in progress, and that wasn't going to change anytime soon. It was going to take some time for the lot of them to work out exactly how and where the pragmatic limits of specified authority and responsibility fell, but so far things seemed to be headed in the right direction. At least all of the members of the Alquezar Government seemed determined to see to it that they did.

The investment credits program and how Alquezar's Cabinet approached it provided a case in point, in Medusa's opinion.

Empress Elizabeth had decided, long before the Constitutional Convention had finally voted out the provisions of the Quadrant's new constitution, that her newer subjects were not going to be taken to the financial cleaners by her older ones. At the same time, it was clearly imperative—for a lot of reasons—to push investment in the Talbott Cluster as hard and fast as possible. The Quadrant had a lot of people and a lot of star systems, but its seriously backward technology base urgently required updating and expansion, and investment capital was hard to come by locally. So Elizabeth and Prime Minister Grantville had decided that for the first ten T-years of operation, any new startup endeavor in the Quadrant would enjoy a reduction in taxation equal to the percentage of ownership held by citizens of the Quadrant. After ten T-years, the tax break would reduce by five percent per T-year for another ten T-years, then terminate completely in the twenty-first T-year. That gave tremendous incentive for investors from the Old Star Kingdom to seek out local partners, and all government really had to do was to keep track of that percentage of local ownership and administer the tax breaks. It most emphatically did not have any role in creating the partnerships in question.

Some of the local oligarchs appeared unable (or unwilling) to grasp that point. They'd expected to control ownership of the new enterprises much as they had dominated the pre-annexation financial structures of the Talbott Cluster. The smarter of them, on the other hand, had recognized early on that there were going to be enormous changes. They'd realized that they'd better adjust to the realization that elements of their populations who previously had been insignificant blips as far as local financial markets were concerned were about to find themselves highly attractive to Manticoran investment partners.

Which was exactly the way things were working out, much to the satisfaction of Elizabeth Winton. Many of the Star Kingdom's investors were allowing their newfound Talbott partners to finance their share of ownership as a percentage of the tax credits, which had the effect of tremendously reducing the amount of startup capital the Talbotters required. That was allowing people from far outside the ranks of the traditional oligarchies to become significant players, which was about to both expand and strengthen the overall economy of the Quadrant while simultaneously severely curtailing the "old guard's" control over that economy. Joachim Alquezar, his Cabinet, and his Constitutional Union Party (which held an outright majority of over eighteen percent in the Quadrant's new Parliament), all understood that, and they were working hard to push the process along.

Which brought Medusa back to the situation in Marian. Apparently one of the local oligarchs—and, like Lababibi, Medusa thought she could make a fairly accurate guess as to exactly who the oligarch in question might be—had decided she ought to receive a "commission" for brokering and expediting the formation of partnerships between Manticoran investors and their Talbott colleagues. Words like extortion, graft, and bribery came to mind whenever Medusa thought about it, and she almost hoped the culprit would prove less amenable to sweet reason than Alquezar and Lababibi expected. She couldn't remember exactly who it was back on Old Terra who'd been in favor of shooting a few people "to encourage the others," but in this case, Estelle Matsuko was prepared to pay for the ammunition herself.

Figuratively speaking, of course.

"All right," Alquezar said now, looking around the conference table, "does anyone have anything else we need to deal with before adjourning?"

Another sign of how new things still were, Medusa reflected. It wouldn't be all that much longer, she was sure, before things like ironbound agendas for meetings like this would become the rule.

For now, things were still remarkably—and thankfully—flexible, however, and Alquezar looked in her direction when she cleared her throat.

"There is one matter Vice Admiral Khumalo tells me he'd like to bring to your attention, Mr. Prime Minister," she said. "I apologize for not having mentioned this to anyone ahead of this meeting, but the dispatch boat arrived only a few hours before we were scheduled to meet, and it took the admiral some time to digest the content of its messages and to share them with me."

"Of course, Madame Governor." Alquezar's voice didn't sharpen dramatically, but he'd obviously picked up on her own formality, and he raised one eyebrow at her slightly, before he turned his attention to the uniformed officer sitting to her right.

"Admiral?" he invited.

"Thank you, Mr. Prime Minister." Augustus Khumalo's voice was considerably deeper than Alquezar's. He nodded respectfully to the Prime Minister, then turned very slightly in his chair to glance around the rest of the conference table.

"What Baroness Medusa is referring to," he said, "is a dispatch from Lieutenant Commander Denton, the commanding officer of the destroyer *Reprise*."

"*Reprise*?" Henri Krietzmann repeated, cocking his head thoughtfully. Then his eyes sharpened. "She's the picket in the Pequod System, isn't she, Admiral?"

"She is, Mr. Secretary," Khumalo acknowledged.

"And the significance of Commander Denton's dispatch is?" Alquezar inquired, his own eyes narrowing.

"Apparently, there's being some friction with New Tuscany-registry merchantships, Mr. Prime Minister."

Khumalo seemed to be choosing words with some care, Alquezar observed.

"What sort of 'friction'?" the Prime Minister asked.

"Well, that's the peculiar thing about it, Sir," Khumalo replied. "We haven't received any formal communication about this from anyone aside from Denton at this point, but his report makes interesting reading. Apparently, there's been more New Tuscan traffic into Pequod of late then there ever was before the annexation. In a lot of ways, that isn't too surprising, given Pequod's relative proximity to New Tuscany. It's less than a T-week even for a merchie between the two systems, after all. But as we all know, Pequod is scarcely what anyone might call a major hub of commercial activity, and most of the shipping in and out of the system has been dominated by the RTU for a long time."

Alquezar nodded. His own home star system of San Miguel was under a hundred and thirty light-years from New Tuscany, and it had been the first non-Rembrandt star system to affiliate itself with the Rembrandt Trade Union. For that matter, Alquezar and his family controlled twelve percent of the RTU's voting shares. If anyone had a firm grasp of the realities of interstellar shipping and commerce throughout the Talbott Cluster, it was Joachim Alquezar.

"Now, I fully realize that the new political and financial relationships being worked out are going to result in a major reconfiguration of local shipping conditions, especially in concert with all of the additional traffic being attracted to the Lynx Terminus," Khumalo continued. "As such it probably makes sense for local shippers to be prospecting. There probably aren't going to be many local cargoes available on spec yet, but there may well be a few, and establishing contacts for future reference has just become a lot more important for a lot of reasons.

"Despite that, however, it seems to me we're seeing more New Tuscan ships in Pequod than the situation justifies. I wouldn't have worried about that—in fact, I doubt very much that anyone on my staff even would have noticed it—if not for Commander Denton's report about how the officers of some of those New Tuscan ships are conducting themselves."

"In what way, Admiral?" Bernardus Van Dort asked, his blue eyes intent.

"They seem to be exceptionally . . . prickly," Khumalo said. "They're quick to take offense. In fact, it seems to Commander Denton that they're actively looking for opportunities to do just that. Or even *manufacturing* such opportunities."

"Allow me to interrupt for a moment before Admiral Khumalo goes any further," Medusa said. Everyone looked at her, and she smiled without much humor. "I'm sure it's going to occur to many of us that Commander Denton might just be sending us observations to that effect because he's managed to give the New Tuscans legitimate *cause* to take offense. Neither Admiral Khumalo nor I believe that to be the case, however. I can't say I know Commander Denton personally. I believe I was introduced to him on at least one occasion, shortly after *Reprise* was first assigned to Admiral Khumalo's command, but, to be perfectly frank, I really don't remember him very well at all. But I have perused his personnel file since the Admiral shared his dispatches with me. From his record, he doesn't strike me as the sort of officer who would antagonize merchant service officers just for his own entertainment. And he *definitely* doesn't strike me as the sort who would try to falsely imply that the New Tuscans were being hyper-sensitive as a means to cover himself against any sort of reasonable complaints they might make because of his own actions."

"Governor Medusa's right about that," Khumalo rumbled. "I know Denton better than she does, of course, and I didn't deploy him to Pequod because he's stupid. He's not going to be going around stepping on anyone, and even if he'd been tempted to cover himself for some reason, he'd know any sort of deceptive reports would be bound to come unglued, which would only make things worse for him in the long run. In other words, I don't think he'd screw up in the first place, or be dumb enough to think he could cover it up if he had."

"If both you and the Governor feel that way, I'm certainly prepared to accept your judgment," Van Dort said. "Why does Commander Denton feel the New Tuscans are acting in this fashion?"

"If you're asking if he has any explanation for why they're being 'prickly,' as the Admiral put it," Medusa said, "he doesn't. But if you're asking what evidence of their prickliness he's presented, there's quite a bit of it, actually, Bernardus."

Van Dort's expression was an unspoken question, and Medusa gave Khumalo a small, inviting gesture.

"The Commander's attention was originally drawn to this matter by the report of one of his junior officers," the vice admiral told Van Dort. "After checking with others of his officers who have been conducting customs inspections and generally backstopping the Pequod System's local forces in managing the expansion of their traffic, he found that many of them acknowledged similar experiences, although most of them hadn't reported them at the time."

"And the Pequod System's customs agents," Alquezar said intently. "Do we have similar reports from them?"

"No, Mr. Prime Minister, we don't," Khumalo replied, his tone acknowledging the significance of Alquezar's question. "In fact, Commander Denton specifically inquired of his Pequod counterparts before he sent his dispatch to Spindle. They confirmed his own impression that New Tuscan traffic to Pequod is up very substantially, especially over the last few T-weeks before the Commander sent off his dispatch. None of them, however, have experienced the same degree of touchiness out of the New Tuscans."

Alquezar nodded slowly, his frown thoughtful.

"According to Commander Denton's inquiries, almost all of the New Tuscan ships which his personnel had boarded in the last ten local days prior to his dispatch had demonstrated the same pattern of behavior. The ships' officers were confrontational, acted as if they were highly suspicious of our personnel's motivations, cooperated as grudgingly as possible with requests for documentation and inspection, and generally appeared to be attempting to deliberately provoke naval personnel into some sort of open incident. Not only that, but Commander Denton suspects that in at least several of these cases the New Tuscans were using shipboard surveillance systems to record the entire episode.

"Because of those suspicions, he arranged to surreptitiously record several of our inspection visits himself. Obviously, I haven't had the time yet to view those records in their entirety myself. I have, however, viewed several clips which he included with his official report, and he sent the full recordings with them. At the moment, Commander Chandler and Captain Shoupe are viewing those records but, to be honest, I don't expect the result of their examination to change my own impression, which is that Commander Denton has accurately summarized the situation. There's very little question in my mind that the New Tuscans, for whatever reason, are deliberately pushing our personnel—and specifically our *naval* personnel—in what I can only construe as an effort to provoke some sort of incident."

"Forgive me, Admiral," Lababibi put in, "but if this had only been happening for less than two T-weeks before the Commander became aware of it, how many such visits could there have been? I mean, I don't question your observations, I'm simply wondering how large a base we have for drawing conclusions?"

"As a matter of fact, Madam Secretary," it was obvious Khumalo hadn't taken any sort of offense from Lababibi's question, "that's one of the reasons I think Commander Denton may have put his finger on something important here. In the ten local days before he sent his dispatch, six New Tuscan-registered merchant ships visited Pequod."

"*Six?*" Bernardus Van Dort sat suddenly upright in his chair, and Khumalo nodded.

"Is that number significant, Bernardus?" Lababibi asked, looking at her colleague, and Van Dort snorted harshly.

"You might say that, Samiha," he replied. "I know we're all still in the process of really coming to have a good feel for the other star systems in the Quadrant with us, but, believe me, Pequod is *not* Spindle. As the Secretary of the Treasury, I'm sure you're aware that it's nowhere near as poverty-stricken as Nuncio, but it's a much, much poorer star system than Spindle. In fact, if Henri will forgive me, Pequod is probably almost as poor as Dresden was thirty or forty T-years ago."

Lababibi nodded slowly, watching Van Dort carefully. While Joachim Alquezar was intimately familiar with the internal workings of the Rembrandt Trade Union, Bernardus Van Dort had virtually single-handedly *created* the Trade Union. In many ways, Lababibi had thought from the beginning that Van Dort would have made a far better treasury secretary than she herself had, since no one in the entire galaxy had a better feel for the economic realities of the Talbott Cluster. Unfortunately, he was still too polarizing a figure in too many eyes for him to have been handed that particular cabinet post. And, Lababibi admitted, not without a certain degree of reason. She herself trusted him completely, but the RTU had been too unpopular with too many of the Cluster's inhabitants for far too long for Bernardus Van Dort to have been acceptable as the Quadrant's chief treasury official.

"What you may not—yet—fully realize is what that means in terms of interstellar trade, though," Van Dort continued. "I'd have to check with our central records back on Rembrandt to confirm this, but I'd be surprised if Pequod ever saw more than a couple of freighters a T-month prior to the discovery of the Lynx Terminus. And if you glance at a star map, the system is hardly on a direct approach to Lynx. There's going to be a general upsurge in system visits by ships vectoring through the Terminus and looking for cargoes of opportunity, and Pequod will probably see at least some of it. But six ships from a single local star system in less than two T-weeks?" He shook his head. "No way. For that matter, the New Tuscan merchant marine isn't particularly huge. Six hyper-capable freighters represent a hefty percentage of their total merchant fleet, and probably two-thirds of its ships are registered elsewhere for tax purposes. That's what makes it significant that the Admiral mentioned New Tuscany-*registered* vessels, because there are only a relatively small handful of ships which are both owned and registered in New Tuscany. I can't conceive of any sound business reason that would send that many ships, out of such a limited pool, to a system like *Pequod*."

"I don't like the sound of that," Krietzmann half-muttered.

"You wouldn't like the sound of *anything* coming out of New Tuscany, Henri," Lababibi said rather tartly. But then she shook her own head. "On the other hand, in this case, I have to agree with you. Although I can't begin to offer any explanation of what's going on . . . or why."

"Neither can I," Baroness Medusa acknowledged. "I think, though, that given the . . . friction between the New Tuscan government and the Quadrant since New Tuscany's withdrawal from the Constitutional Convention, we have to approach this situation with a bit of caution."

"I can't disagree with that, either, Madam Governor," Lababibi said unhappily. "They're still pressing for a 'more equitable' distribution of Manticoran investment in the region, and at least some members of their delegation have made it clear that—as individuals, at least—they feel our refusal to give it to them represents economic retaliation against them for declining to ratify the Constitution as members of the Star Empire."

"Are you suggesting those delegation members and these merchant spacers miraculously appearing in such numbers in Pequod are part of some officially concerted effort?" Alquezar sounded even more unhappy than Lababibi, and she shrugged.

"I don't know," she admitted. "On the one hand, it's very tempting to conclude exactly that. But if I'm going to be honest, that's at least partly because of how thoroughly I detest New Tuscany on a personal basis. There's a part of me that would *like* to think that they're Up To Something. On the other hand, the timing of it seems to me to argue against it. If they were going to set up some sort of concerted effort, as you put it, Joachim, then why did they wait so long to begin sending ships to Pequod? Their delegation's been here in Spindle ever since the Constitutional Convention, and they've been whining and complaining about our 'unfair' efforts to restrict Manticoran investment in New Tuscany from the very beginning."

She looked at Khumalo.

"What's the dispatch boat flight time from Pequod to Spindle, Admiral?" she asked.

"Right on seventeen T-days, Madam Secretary."

"Well, if we take this spike in their merchant ships' appearances in Pequod and assume it extends back over only ten days before Commander Denton reported it to us, that's still less than a T-month," Lababibi pointed out. "It's been over *six* T-months since the Constitution was voted out, and the next best thing to five months since Parliament and Her Majesty ratified it. So why would they have waited so long and then crammed so many ships into Pequod in such a short timeframe that it had to create this kind of spike?"

"You're right." Alquezar nodded. "If it were a concerted effort of some sort, they would have started cycling their ships through Pequod sooner, wouldn't they? Done it in a way which wouldn't be obvious when we started looking at it?"

"Maybe, and maybe not," Van Dort said thoughtfully. The others looked at him, and he shrugged. "Without a better idea of what they're up to—or what they *may* be up to, at any rate—we don't have any solid basis for evaluating their tactics. And, frankly, at this point I don't have any idea of what it is they could hope to accomplish in the end. Aside from thoroughly pissing off the Star Empire, of course, which would appear to be something of a case of cutting off one's nose to spite one's face."

"I have to agree with that," Medusa said, "and that's the real reason I wanted to call this to the attention of the Quadrant's government. When I can't think of a reason for someone who I know doesn't like me very much to be doing something, it makes me nervous."

"I feel the same way," Alquezar agreed.

"And while we're all feeling nervous," Krietzmann pointed out, "think about this. I have to agree with Samiha's analysis that the original complaints from members of the New Tuscan trade delegation probably weren't designed as part of a coherent strategy. Or, at least, not of a coherent strategy directly connected to what's happening in Pequod right now. But the fact that they weren't part of that kind of strategy *then*, doesn't mean they aren't part of that kind of strategy *now*. Or that whoever's pulling the strings in Pequod didn't choose to incorporate what was originally a totally unconnected situation into an entirely new strategy. I know New Tuscany is only a single star system, and one that's not remotely in the Star Empire's—or even the Star *Kingdom's*—league. For that matter, they're a small enough fish they ought to be nervous about pissing off just the folks here in the Quadrant, if they're feeling rational about things. And I know I have a tendency to look under beds for plots by people like Andrieaux Yvernau, too. I admit it, and—no offense to anyone sitting around this table—I think Dresden's experience with people like him justifies that tendency. In this case, though, I really don't think it's just a matter of lower-class paranoia. I think the bastards really are up to something, and much as I hate them I don't really think they're stupid enough to be pissing in our soup just because they don't like us. If they *are* doing something, then there's a method to their madness *somewhere*, and given the general situation after the Battle of Monica and how early it is in the process of integrating the Quadrant into the Star Empire, I think we'd damned well better figure out what it is."

# Chapter Twenty-Nine

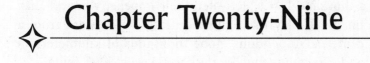

HMS *HEXAPUMA* AND HMS *WARLOCK* emerged from the central terminus of the Manticoran Wormhole Junction exactly one T-year from the day Midshipwoman Helen Zilwicki, Midshipman Aikawa Kagiyama, and Midshipwoman Ragnhild Pavletic had reported aboard her. Now Ensign Zilwicki tried to wrap her mind around how truly monumental the events of that year had been as she sat beside Lieutenant Senior Grade Abigail Hearns at Tactical. Abigail was undoubtedly too junior for permanent duty as a *Saganami-C*-class heavy cruiser's tactical officer, but Captain Terekhov had flatly refused to allow anyone to replace her before *Hexapuma*'s return to Manticore.

Helen was glad. And she was glad some other people were still aboard, as well.

She glanced over her shoulder and hid a broad mental smile as her eye met Paulo's. Ansten FitzGerald was still in obvious pain and more than a little shaky. That wasn't especially amusing to anyone who knew and respected the exec, but watching Aikawa Kagiyama hovering in the background while he kept an anxious eye on FitzGerald certainly was.

"Message from *Invictus*, Sir," Lieutenant Commander Nagchaudhuri announced from Communications.

"Yes?" Terekhov turned his command chair to face Nagchaudhuri. HMS *Invictus* was the flagship of Home Fleet, no doubt in orbit about the planet of Manticore.

"Message begins," Nagchaudhuri began, and something in his tone made Helen look at him sharply.

"'To Captain Aivars Terekhov and the men and women of HMS *Hexapuma* and HMS *Warlock*, from Admiral of the Green Sebastian D'Orville, Commanding Officer, Home Fleet. Well done.' Message ends."

Helen frowned, but before the message had time to sink in, the main tactical display changed abruptly. In one perfectly synchronized moment, forty-two superdreadnoughts, sixteen CLACs, twelve battlecruisers, thirty-six heavy and light cruisers, thirty-two destroyers, and over a thousand LACs, activated their impeller wedges. They appeared on the display like lightning flickering outward from a common center, a stupendous globe thousands of kilometers in diameter, and *Hexapuma* and *Warlock* were at its exact center.

Helen recognized that formation. She'd seen it before. Every man and woman in Navy uniform had seen it, once every year, on Coronation Day, when Home Fleet passed in review before the Queen . . . with its flagship in exactly the position *Hexapuma* and *Warlock* now held.

Even as she stared at the display, another icon appeared upon it. The crowned, golden icon of HMS *Duke of Cromarty*, the battlecruiser which had replaced the murdered HMS *Queen Adrienne* as the royal yacht, sitting just beyond the threshold of the Junction. A Junction, Helen sudden realized, which had been cleared of shipping—*all* shipping—except for Home Fleet itself.

The vast globe accelerated towards *Cromarty*, matching its acceleration rate exactly to *Hexapuma*'s, holding formation on the heavy cruiser and her single escort, and the raised wedge of every ship in that huge formation flashed off and then on again in the traditional underway salute to a fleet flagship.

"Additional message, Sir," Nagchaudhuri said. He stopped and cleared his throat, then continued, and despite his throat clearing, his voice seemed to waver about the edges.

"Message begins. 'Yours is the honor.'" He looked up from his display, meeting Aivars Terekhov's eyes.

"Message ends, Sir," he said softly.


"Hey, Helen!"

Helen Zilwicki looked up from the footlocker she was packing, and Paulo d'Arezzo waved at her, then pointed at the com unit on the outsized table in the commons area of HMS *Hexapuma's* Snotty Row.

"The Skipper wants to see you," he continued.

"Wants to see *me*?" Helen repeated carefully. "As in, 'I'd like to see you around sometime,' or as in 'Get your butt up here right now, Ms. Zilwicki'?"

"The latter," Paulo told her with a smile. "As in 'Mr. d'Arezzo, ask Ms. Zilwicki to come by my day cabin at her earliest convenience.'"

"Crap." Helen sat back on her heels, trying to think of anything she might have done to earn her a last-minute 'counseling interview' with Captain Terekhov. She couldn't come up with anything right off the top of her head, but that wasn't necessarily reassuring; it was the *unanticipated* reamings that smarted the most, she'd discovered. Of course, it was always possible he just wanted her to stop by because he'd heard a really good joke and wanted to share it with her, but somehow she didn't find that possibility extremely likely.

"I don't suppose he said anything about *why* he wants to see me?"

"Nope," Paulo said with what Helen privately considered to be appallingly callous cheerfulness.

"Great." She sighed, and stood up.

She looked down at the open locker for a second or two, then shrugged philosophically. She and Paulo were due to catch the regularly scheduled ferry flight from HMS *Hephaestus* to Saganami Island in order to clear the final Academy bits and pieces of paperwork required to formally graduate them and confirm their acting promotions to ensign. She'd been dreading it in some ways, since it would inevitably mean new assignments for both of them, and she was still working her way around the edges of turning her friendship with the stunningly handsome—and terminally standoffish—Mr. D'Arrezo into something deeper and more enduring. Given his hatred for the Manpower Incorporated genetic manipulation which was responsible for those looks of his, that wasn't the easiest job in the universe, and she didn't really like the thought of letting him get out of arm's reach before she was done working on him. At the same time, she was eager to see what new challenges the Navy was going to offer her. But if she didn't get done packing in the next twenty minutes, she was going to miss the ferry shuttle, and it seemed unlikely she could get up to the captain's day cabin, find out what he wanted, get back down here, and finish packing in that tight a time window.

*"Unlikely," ha! Try "no way in hell," honey*, she told herself sourly.

"Looks like I'll be catching the evening shuttle, instead," she told Paulo resignedly.

"Well, we won't be assigned a formal mess billet yet," he pointed out. "I'll save you a place in the cafeteria."

"Gee, thanks. Your generosity and thoughtfulness overwhelm me."

"I'm just a naturally generous and thoughtful kind of guy," he told her with a broad grin few other people had ever seen out of him. "A natural born philanthropist, too, now that I think about it. A veritable paragon. A giant among men, a—*ooph!*"

He broke off as the flying boot hit him in the region of his navel. Helen was an extraordinarily strong young woman, thanks to both natural aptitude and rigorous training, and she'd actually tossed the boot quite gently . . . for her. It seemed unlikely Paulo would have agreed with that particular adverb, and he sat down rather abruptly.

"And the strong silent type, too, I see," Helen observed sweetly, smiled at him, and headed out of the compartment.

"Ensign Zilwicki to see the Captain," Helen told the Marine sentry outside Captain Terekhov's quarters five minutes later.

"You're expected, Ma'am," the corporal told her, and reached back one hand to press the button for the admittance chime.

"Yes, Corporal Sanders?" Helen recognized the voice of Chief Steward Joanna Agnelli, Captain Terekhov's personal steward.

"Ms. Zilwicki is here," Sanders said.

"Thank you."

The hatch slid open a moment later, and Helen stepped through it . . . then paused in surprise. There were rather more people in the captain's day cabin than she'd anticipated.

Terekhov himself sat behind his desk, in the act of sipping from a cup of coffee. That much, at least, she'd expected. But Lieutenant Abigail Hearns sat in one of the comfortable armchairs facing his desk, and there were three other officers present, as well. One of them was Commander Kaplan, and Helen was both astonished and delighted to see how much better Kaplan looked than she had the last time Helen saw her, but the other two were a commander and a senior-grade captain Helen had never seen before in her life, and she braced quickly to attention.

"You wanted to see me, Captain?"

"At ease, Helen," Terekhov said, then smiled and waved his coffee cup at the chair beside Lieutenant Hearns. "And have a seat," he added.

"Thank you, Sir."

Helen obeyed his command and sat, hoping she sounded less mystified than she felt as she parked herself in the indicated chair. She sensed a presence at her shoulder and looked up to see Agnelli standing there with another cup and saucer in one hand and the coffee pot in the other. Helen was scarcely accustomed to sitting around sipping coffee with such astronomically superior officers, but she knew better than to decline the offer . . . which presumably indicated that this was at least marginally a social occasion. She took the saucer and held the cup while Agnelli filled it, then took a sip and nodded in appreciation before she turned her attention back to Terekhov.

"I realize this is a bit irregular," he said then, "but so is our situation. Abigail, I know you and Helen are both well acquainted with Commander Kaplan. However, you may not be aware—as I wasn't, up until about—" he glanced at the time display on the bulkhead "—fifty-seven minutes ago—that she is also the brand-new commanding officer of HMS *Tristram*."

Helen's eyes flipped to the petite, fine-boned blonde with the improbably dark complexion. Kaplan happened to be looking at her at the moment, and the commander smiled at Helen's obvious surprise. And her chagrin, for that matter, as she scolded herself for not noticing the white beret of a starship's CO tucked under Kaplan's epaulet.

"These other two gentlemen," Terekhov continued, pulling her attention back from Kaplan, "are Captain Frederick Carlson, the commanding officer of HMS *Quentin Saint-James*, and Commander Tom Pope . . . my new chief of staff."

This time both of Helen's eyebrows rose in astonishment. *Hexa-puma* had been back in home space for substantially less than two days. In fact, she'd only docked here at *Hephaestus* three hours ago. The captain hadn't even been off the ship yet—couldn't even have had so much as the opportunity to give his wife a hug! Things simply didn't change this quickly and drastically—not even in the Navy!

Not usually, at least.

"As I'm sure both of you were already aware, things have changed considerably since we first deployed to Talbott," Terekhov said, almost as if he'd heard her thoughts, and smiled thinly. "Quite a bit of that seems to be *our* fault, as far as the Admiralty is concerned, so they've decided we ought to do something about it.

"Obviously," he continued, "the Navy's deployment plans in general are in what we might charitably call a state of flux. The cancellation of the summit talks with Haven and the decision to resume active operations make it even more unlikely that the Admiralty is going to be able to free up wallers to reinforce Admiral Khumalo anytime soon. In addition, it's effectively anchored Admiral Blaine to the Lynx Terminus, where he can get home in a hurry if he has to. Which has lent added emphasis to the Admiralty's decision to reinforce Talbott primarily with lighter units.

"In addition to the ships Vice Admiral Gold Peak already has, an additional squadron of *Nikes* is in the process of forming. Admiral Oversteegen is its commander (designate), and as soon as all of its units have joined up, it—and he—will be transferred from Eighth Fleet to Tenth Fleet. In addition, however, the Admiralty is already prepared to deploy a full squadron of brand new *Saganami-Cs* and one of the new *Roland*-class destroyer squadrons to Talbott. *Tristram—*" he nodded at Kaplan "—is one of the *Rolands*. And I, to my considerable surprise, am the newly designated commodore of CruRon 94. Commander FitzGerald will take over *Hexapuma*, Commander Pope will be acting as my chief of staff, and Captain Carlson will be my flag captain."

Helen glanced at Lieutenant Hearns, who seemed remarkably composed, given how caught-in-the-slipstream *Helen* felt as the captain's—no, the *commodore's*—explanation rolled over her. She hoped she looked like she was at least managing to keep up with him, although she was at a loss to understand how he could be so calm about it all. He sounded as if things like this happened to him every day!

"I'm sure that by now both of you are wondering why I've dragged a pair of such relatively junior officers in to explain all of this to them. Well, I do have a reason. Two of them, in fact.

"With so many ships moving in so many directions in such a short period of time, the Admiralty is finding it just a *bit* difficult to meet everyone's manning requirements. For example,

Commander Pope didn't know until last week that he was going to be anyone's chief of staff, and the decision that he was going to be *my* chief of staff was actually made this morning. It looks as if we're going to be deploying at least one or two people short for the rest of the staff, as well, although BuPers has given me permission to poach additional officers from Admiral Khumalo when we get back to Spindle. Commodore Chatterjee, the senior officer of Commander Kaplan's destroyer squadron, is in rather better shape than that where his staff is concerned, but several of his units are undermanned.

"And the reason we've called the two of you in for this little conversation is that one of the slots I still need to fill is the flag lieutenant's billet, and *Tristram* needs a good tac officer.

"Helen," he looked directly at her, "you worked out very well as my liaison with Mr. Van Dort. I believe we have an established and efficient working relationship, and you're already very familiar—especially for an officer of your youthfulness—with the political and military realities of the Cluster. I mean, the *Quadrant*. Normally, the flag lieutenant's slot would be filled by someone rather more senior than you are at the moment, and I'm well aware that what you would really prefer at this point in your career is to move directly into a tactical department slot somewhere. I don't want you to feel pressured, and if you decide you want a tactical assignment, I will unreservedly recommend you for it. At the same time, the opportunity for this sort of experience, this early in your career, doesn't happen along every day. And, unfortunately, given the time constraints involved, I need your decision almost immediately—within the next twelve hours, at the latest. And I, also unfortunately, am about to leave for several hours of conferences at Admiralty House. Since I needed to speak to you personally about this, I had to cram it at you before I leave the ship, as it were.

"As for you, Abigail," he turned to the lieutenant, "Commander Kaplan has specifically requested you as *Tristram*'s tactical officer."

Helen's brain had been doing its best to imitate a chipmunk in the headlights as she tried to assimilate Captain—*No, damn it!* she told herself sharply—*Commodore* Terekhov's offer. Now, despite herself, her head snapped around towards Abigail.

At a hundred and eighty-nine thousand tons, the *Roland* was bigger than a pre-MDM light cruiser ... *and* she was armed with

Mark 16s, just like *Hexapuma*. She and her sisters were *the* plum assignments of the Navy's destroyer force, and they were offering a *Roland*'s tactical department to a brand new senior-grade lieutenant?

"I'm flattered, Sir, of course—" Abigail began, but Commander Kaplan interrupted her.

"With your permission, Sir?" she said to Commodore Terekhov. He nodded, and Kaplan turned to Abigail.

"Before you turn it down because you think you're too junior for the slot, or because you think it's time you moved back over to the GSN, let me explain a few things to you. First, you arguably have more tactical experience actually using the Mark 16 in combat than anyone else in the entire Navy—in fact, than anyone else in *either* of your two navies—given how quickly AuxCon—and I—got taken out of action in Monica. While there may be someone else whose overall experience with the Mark 16 matches yours, I can't think of any other officer of your rank who's been responsible for managing an entire squadron's—hell, an entire *light task group's*—fire in a furball like that one. So, yes, you are junior for the slot. But you've also demonstrated your competence under fire, which a lot of tactical officers senior to you haven't, and you bring with you a lot of very valuable experience with *Tristram*'s primary armament.

"And as far as moving back over to the GSN is concerned, this is the first squadron of *Rolands* to be formed. For a change, we're actually ahead of Grayson in deploying a new class, and High Admiral Matthews has specifically requested that Grayson personnel be assigned to it to help develop doctrine and accrue experience with the new class and its weapons. I'm thinking you'd be an extremely logical choice for that assignment. You're already fully experienced in how we Manties do things, and, let's face it, you're still the first Grayson-born female officer in the entire GSN. Getting your ticket punched as a full-fledged tactical officer, in command of your own department, is only going to bolster your authority when you finally return full-time to Grayson. And when you do, unless I very much miss my guess, High Admiral Matthews is probably planning to assign you to relatively light units, where your example will be most direct and where you're least likely to get shoved away into some admiral's convenient flagship pigeonhole just because he can't—or doesn't want to—figure out what to do with you. That being the case, adding demonstrated familiarity with the new destroyers and cruisers—and their main weapons systems—to your résumé strikes me as a very good idea."

"Ma'am, I *really* appreciate the offer," Abigail said. "And under other circumstances, I'd probably be willing to kill to get it. But if I run off with a prize like this, it's going to be a blatant case of string-pulling!"

"Of course it is!" Kaplan replied, and snorted at her expression. "Abigail, that's what happens with officers who demonstrate superior performance. Oh," she waved one hand in midair, "it happens for other reasons, too, and a lot of those other reasons suck, when you come right down to it. God knows we all know that! And I suppose there probably will be at least a few people who think you got this assignment because of who your father is. I rather doubt anyone who knows Steadholder Owens is going to think *he* pulled the string in question, but that's not going to keep some people from whining and bitching about the fact that you got it and they didn't. And most of those people who are going to be doing the whining and bitching aren't going to want to consider the possibility that you got it because you were *better* than they were, which is why—as far as they're concerned—it's *obviously* going to be a case of nepotism. Well, guess what? That happens, too. Or do you think there weren't plenty of officers who thought Duchess Harrington was being pushed up faster than she deserved, even after Basilisk Station, because of favoritism from people like Admiral Courvoissier and Earl White Haven?"

"I'm not Duchess Harrington!" Abigail protested. "I don't have anywhere near her record!"

"And *she* wasn't 'Duchess Harrington' at the time, either," Kaplan replied. "That's my point. She was given the opportunity to achieve what she achieved because of the ability she'd already demonstrated. I'm offering you this slot for the same reason. There's nothing wrong with pulling strings as long as the result is to put the right officer in the right billet at the right time, and if I didn't think that was what was happening here, I wouldn't have made the offer. You know that."

She held Abigail's eye firmly until the younger woman finally pulled away from her gaze to glance appealingly at Terekhov.

"I suppose that all sounds pretty embarrassing," the newly

promoted commodore told her with a crooked smile. "As it happens, though, I concur with Commander Kaplan's assessment of you and your capabilities. I think she's right about the reasons you'd be a perfect fit for this particular slot, too. And, to be honest, Abigail, I think you need to consider very carefully whether your reasons you should turn it down are anywhere near as good as her reasons why you should take it. Not just from the personal perspective of your own career, either. I think this is where the Navy—*all* of the Alliance's navies—will get the maximum benefit from your experience and your talents."

Abigail looked at him for several seconds, then looked back at Kaplan and managed a smile of her own.

"Am I on as tight a time schedule for making up my mind as Helen is, Ma'am?"

"Not quite." Kaplan smiled back, then twitched her head in Terekhov's direction. "I figured I might need the Skipper—I mean, the Commodore—to help twist your arm, so I asked him to play rabbi for this little discussion. Unlike Helen, you have, oh, *eighteen* hours before you have to decide, though."

"Gee, thanks." Abigail looked back and forth between her and Terekhov for another moment, then shrugged. "Actually, I don't need that long," she said. "I've just discovered that I'm neither sufficiently selfless nor concerned enough about whether or not people think I'm using 'influence' to turn something like *this* down. If you're really serious about wanting me, Ma'am, you've got me! And . . . thank you."

"Remember that sense of gratitude when I start working you till you drop." Kaplan's smile segued into a grin, and Abigail chuckled.

"Which brings us back to you, Helen," Terekhov said, and Helen's eyes popped back to him. "As I say, you have a few hours to think it over."

She stared at him, her mind racing as it dashed off down all the branching futures radiating from this moment.

He was right. She *had* been anticipating a stint as a very junior assistant tactical officer squirreled away aboard a battlecruiser or a superdreadnought somewhere. An assignment which would punch her ticket for the next stage of her desired career track. And, she admitted to herself, an assignment which would be unspeakably boring after *Hexapuma*'s deployment to Talbott. Then there were all the people she'd met in Talbott, the sense that she had a personal stake in making certain the Quadrant's integration into the Star Empire went smoothly, without still more bloodshed. Obviously, one lowly ensign—even if she was a commodore's flag lieutenant—was hardly going to be a maker and a shaker at that level of politics, but she found that she still wanted to be there.

Yet if she took this assignment, it would divert her from the tactical track. She'd lose ground on the other ensigns and junior-grade lieutenants who *were* putting in that boring time, laboring away in the bowels of some capital ship's tactical department.

*Oh, get real!* she scolded herself. *You're planning on making the Navy your* career! *You'll have plenty of time to make up for any ground you lose here. And Master Tye always did tell you you needed to cultivate more patience, didn't he? So if you're going to find an excuse, find a better one than* that!

Which brought her face-to-face with the real reason she was hesitating. A reason named Paulo d'Arezzo. He was almost certainly going to draw the same sort of assignment she'd expected—right here in Home Fleet, more likely than not—and she'd suddenly discovered that she really, really didn't want to be clear across the Talbott Quadrant from him.

*Oh, that's even better than the* last *excuse,* she thought sourly. *Or it's less logical, at least. You know damned well they'd assign the two of you to two different ships, don't you? Which means you'd see almost as little of each other even if you were both assigned to Home Fleet as you'd see with him here and you off in Talbott again.*

It seemed to her that it took forever for those thoughts to flow through her mind, even though she knew better. But, finally, they trickled to an end, and she drew a deep breath and looked up Terekhov again.

"It wasn't what I had in mind, Sir—obviously. But, like Abigail says, if you're serious about wanting me, you've got me."

# Chapter Thirty

*I WONDER IF THIS was really such a good idea, after all?* Helen Zilwicki asked herself wryly as she stepped into the lift car and punched in the proper combination.

She'd been half afraid the commodore might reconsider his choice of flag lieutenants once he discovered how unsuited to the position an officer as junior as she was truly was. She probably shouldn't have, since she'd had ample opportunity to observe just how decisive he was, but so far he actually seemed not even to have experienced any serious qualms. Which was more than *she* could say.

She grimaced at the thought, but there was at least some truth to it. Once upon a time, she'd thought the pressure a midshipwoman experienced on her snotty cruise was intense, and she supposed it was. She'd certainly felt more than sufficiently exhausted at the time, at any rate! But her present assignment had an intensity all its own.

*Oh, stop whining,* she told herself sternly. *"This, too, shall pass," as Master Tye was always so fond of telling you. You'll get your feet under yourself this time, too. After all, you've only* been *a flag lieutenant for four days!* Scant comfort as she went scurrying about the passages of HMS *Quentin Saint-James* on Commodore Terekhov's missions.

When she thought about it, she rather suspected that the commodore was running her harder than he actually had to.

For example, there was her present mission. There was absolutely no reason she could think of why the commodore couldn't have simply screened Commander Horace Lynch, *Quentin Saint-James'* tactical officer, for this particular message. In fact, it probably would have been more efficient. But, no; he'd decided Ensign Zilwicki should trot right on over to the TO's office and deliver it in person. Helen didn't mind the exercise, and the actual message was pretty interesting, but the fact remained that there had been other—and arguably much more efficient—ways for the commodore to deliver it.

*But this one keeps me busy*, she thought, watching the lift car's position indicator flicker across the display panel. *And he's been doing a lot of that ever since we found out about that assassination attempt on Torch.* Despite herself, she shivered at the thought of how close her sister had come to death. And she knew Berry entirely too well. She knew exactly how she must have taken the deaths of so many other people, especially as a consequence of an effort to murder *her*. And she could also understand why there'd been no message from her father about it. There probably was one chasing its way off towards Spindle, where he could expect it to be relayed to *Hexapuma*, but she had no doubt that he—*and probably that scary son-of-a-bitch Cachat, too, now that I think about it*—were off . . . looking into who had truly been responsible for it.

Unlike most subjects of the Star Kingdom of Manticore, Helen was less than convinced that Haven had orchestrated the attack on Torch. Of course, she had the unfair advantage of her sister's and her father's letters, which was why she knew Victor Cachat, that otherwise apparently unfeeling juggernaut of a Havenite secret agent, was madly in love with one Thandi Palane, who happened to be Berry's "unofficial big sister," as well as the commander-in-chief of the Torch armed forces. Not only would Cachat have refused to have anything to do with an assassination attempt which might so readily have caught Palane in its path, but he had to know how she would have reacted to his complicity in any attempt to kill Berry or Princess Ruth. And if he hadn't had anything to do with it, then it was for *damned* sure no other Havenite agent had. Not the way Cachat, the Audobon Ballroom—*and my own dear Daddy, of course*—were wired into the intelligence community.

Unfortunately, Helen Zilwicki was only one of the Royal Manticoran Navy's newest ensigns. The fact that she was convinced someone else had pulled the trigger wasn't going to cut very much ice with the powers that were. For that matter, she felt quite confident that one *Anton* Zilwicki had already reached as high up the intelligence food chain as he could in an effort to convince Manticore of that glaringly self-evident (in her own modest opinion) fact. If he hadn't been able to get anyone to listen to *him*, then no one was going to be listening to *her* anytime soon.

*And fair's fair,* she admitted grudgingly. *We Zilwickis have had just a bit more experience than most people with the sordid world of espionage and dirty tricks in general. And too much of that experience has been with the ladies and gentlemen of Manpower. I suppose we're as naturally predisposed to look for the Mesa connection as other people are to look for the Haven connection. But I do wish some of those people thinking* "Haven done it!" *would stop and think about the* weapon *they used. Sure, the* People's *Republic carried out plenty of assassinations, but so far as anyone on our side knows, they never used a sophisticated neurotoxin like that. They thought in terms of bombs and pulser darts and missiles. But* Manpower, *now . . . they* think in bioscience terms.

But there wasn't very much she could do about it, especially considering the fact that *Quentin Saint-James* (which had already come to be known as *Jimmy Boy* by her crew, despite the fact that she was less than three T-months old) was headed in exactly the wrong direction. And, since that was the case, she did her best to put it out of her mind once more and, as the lift car stopped and the doors slid open, turned her attention to the other reason she suspected Commodore Terekhov was keeping her so enthusiastically on the run.

She hadn't really thought about it when the commodore offered her the flag lieutenant's slot, but there were several very good reasons—two of which had presented themselves strongly to her over the last few days—why that particular position was never offered to someone who wasn't at least a lieutenant.

First, the reason a flag officer needed a personal aide to help keep him, his schedule, and his workload organized was fairly glaringly apparent. And, generally speaking, it took someone with rather more experience than any ensign could have accrued to do all that organizing. *Helen* had never actually realized—not in any emotional way, at least—just how much time a flag lieutenant spent making certain her flag officer's time was spent as efficiently and productively as possible.

When she'd discovered just how thoroughly she was supposed to be tapped into all of the squadron's departments, even her naturally hardy soul had quailed. The responsibility for learning what went on in the administration and coordination of all those various departments—plus operations *and* logistics—and their respective duties had come as something of a shock to Helen. And the fact that they still didn't have an operations officer, a staff astrogator, a staff communications officer, *or* a staff intelligence officer didn't help any, either. At the moment, Commander Lynch was holding down the operations department for Commodore Terekhov, and Lieutenant Commander Barnabé Johansen and Lieutenant Commander Iona Török, *Quentin Saint-James'* astrogator and com officer, respectively, were filling in as his astrogator and communications officers, but the whole arrangement had an undeniably temporary, makeshift feeling do it.

Helen suspected that everyone felt as off-balance in that regard as she did herself, but at least all of them were the heads of their own departments aboard the squadron flagship. That meant they had a far better understanding of what they were supposed to be doing than *she* did. Despite the fact that a midshipwoman on her snotty cruise was given experience working in every ship's department, Helen's perspective during her time aboard *Hexapuma* had always been that of a relative peon. Now she had to understand not simply *what* each department did, but how it did it in relationship to every *other* department, which was another kettle of fish entirely. Besides, even Lieutenant Ramón Morozov, Terekhov's logistics officer, was monumentally senior to her. Dealing with all of those other department heads on a "The-commodore-says-you-have-to-do-this-right-now!" basis could be . . . daunting, to say the least.

Even worse was the fear that she might drop some critical ball simply because of her own lack of experience. She knew she could count on Commodore Terekhov to keep an eye on her, but she'd also learned—the hard way, which, she often thought, was the way she tended to learn most things—that failure taught more than success. The commodore, unfortunately, was *also* aware of that minor fact, and she had no doubt at all that he was prepared to allow her to fail as part of the learning process. Which was probably all well and good from his perspective, but tended to suck vacuum from hers. Helen Zilwicki was unaccustomed to failing. She didn't like it when it happened, she didn't handle it well, and, she admitted to herself as she trotted down the ship's passage towards Lynch's office, she absolutely hated the thought of letting someone else down through her own ineptitude.

But that brought her to the other reason her present assignment was usually reserved for a full lieutenant. A flag lieutenant didn't exist simply because a flag officer needed an aide. She existed because an assignment as a flag lieutenant was a teaching experience, too. Well, in fairness, *every* naval assignment was a teaching experience—or it damned well *ought* to be, at any rate. But Manticoran flag lieutenants were far more than just aides and what were still called go-fors, and RMN flag lieutenacies were normally reserved for officers being carefully groomed for bigger and better things. The experience of managing a flag officer's schedule and sitting in on staff discussions and decision making processes other lieutenants never got to see was supposed to give a flag lieutenant a deeper insight into a flag officer's responsibilities. It was supposed to teach someone whose superiors felt she had already demonstrated the potential for eventual flag rank herself how the job was supposed to be done . . . and also how it *wasn't* supposed to be done.

So far, none of the senior officers she'd found herself working with seemed to resent the fact that she was a mere ensign. She didn't know how long that was going to last, though, and she had a sinking sensation that more than one *lieutenant* she ran into *was* going to resent it. Not to mention the fact that she could absolutely guarantee that at some point in her future career some officer to whom she'd just reported was going to have looked in her personnel jacket, examined her Form 210, noted her present assignment, and concluded she was receiving preferential treatment from Commodore Terekhov.

*Which, after all, is only the truth*, she admitted. It wasn't the first time that thought had crossed her mind, and she tried to banish it with the memory of Commander Kaplan's comments to Abigail. Which, of course, only made her wonder if she was reading too much into them in her own case . . . and if she was headed for what her father had always called a terminal case of infinitely expanding ego.

She reached her destination and pressed the admittance chime.

"Yes?" a velvety tenor inquired over the speaker above the button.

"Ensign Zilwicki, Commander," she said crisply. "Commodore Terekhov sent me."

The door opened, and she stepped through it.

Lynch's office was considerably larger than Helen's modest cubbyhole. In fact, it was larger than many an executive officer might have boasted aboard an older, more manpower-intensive ship. With a crew as small as a *Saganami-C* carried, there was room to give personnel a bit more cubage.

The commander was seated at his workstation in his uniform blouse, and the desktop around his terminal was mostly covered in neat stacks of data chips and sheaves of hardcopy. He was a man of moderate height, with sandy hair and deep set brown eyes, and he had a magnificent singing voice. He also appeared to be quite good at his job.

"And what can I do for the Commodore this morning, Ms. Zilwicki?" he asked.

"He asked me to bring you this, Sir," she said, placing a chip folio on the corner of his desk. "It's some thoughts he's been having about the new laser head modifications."

"I see." Lynch drew the folio closer to him, but he wasn't looking at it. Instead, he had cocked his head and those sharp brown eyes were studying *Helen*. "And would it happen that he discussed some of those thoughts with you before he sent you to see me?"

"As a matter of fact, he did say a little something about them," Helen acknowledged a bit cautiously.

"I rather thought he might have." Helen's eyes widened slightly, and Lynch chuckled, then pointed at a chair stacked high with what looked like tactical manuals of one sort or another. "Dump that stuff somewhere and have a seat, Ms. Zilwicki," he invited.

Helen obeyed, and Lynch tipped back his chair and gazed at her thoughtfully. She wondered what he was thinking, but the commander would have made an excellent poker player. His expression gave away virtually nothing, and she tried not to sit too nervously upright.

"Tell me, Ms. Zilwicki—Helen. What do you think of the new laser heads?"

"I think they're a great idea, Sir," she said after a moment, then grimaced. "Sorry, Sir. That sounded pretty stupid, didn't it? Of *course* they're a great idea."

Lynch's lips might have twitched ever so slightly, but if they had, he managed to suppress the smile quite handily.

"I think we might agree to consider that a prefatory remark," he said gravely. "But with that out of the way, what *do* you think of them?"

The faint twinkle Helen thought she might have seen in his eyes eased some of her tension, and she felt herself relax a bit in the chair.

"I think they're going to have a very significant tactical impact, Sir," she said. "The Mark 16 is a big enough advantage against other cruisers and battlecruisers as it stands, but with the new laser heads, they're actually going to be able to hurt genuine capital ships, as well." She shook her head. "I don't think the Havenites are going to like that one bit."

"No doubt," Lynch agreed. "Although I trust," he continued more dryly, "that what you've just said doesn't mean you think it's going to be a *good idea* for a heavy cruiser to take on a superdreadnought, even with the new laser heads?"

"No, Sir. Of course not," Helen said quickly. "I guess I was just thinking about Monica, Sir. If we'd had the new laser heads there, I don't think those battlecruisers would have gotten into their effective range of us in the first place. Or, at least, if they had, they would've had a lot more of the stuffing kicked out of them first."

"Now that, Ms. Zilwicki, is a very valid observation," Lynch said.

"I also think it's bound to have at least some implications for all-up MDMs," she continued. "I mean, I don't see any reason why the same engineering can't be applied to bigger laser heads, as well."

This time, Lynch simply nodded.

There was a reason it had taken so long for the laser head to replace the contact nuclear warhead as the deep-space long-ranged weapon of choice. The basic concept for a laser head was actually quite simple, dating back to pre-Diaspora days on Old Terra. In its most basic terms, a hair-thin, cylindrical rod of some suitable material (the Royal Manticoran Navy used a Hafnium medium) was subjected to the x-ray pulse of a nuclear detonation, causing it to lase in Gamma-rays until the thermal pulse of the detonation's core expansion reached the rod and destroyed it. The problem had always been that the process was inherently extraordinarily inefficient. Under normal conditions, only a few percent of the billions of megajoules released by a megaton-range nuclear warhead would actually end up in any single x-ray laser beam, mostly because—under normal conditions—a nuclear detonation propagated in a sphere, and each rod represented only a ridiculously tiny portion of the total spherical area of the explosion and so could be subjected to only a tiny percentage of the total pulse of any detonation. Which meant the overwhelming majority of the destructive effect was completely lost.

Given the toughness of warship armor, even two or three T-centuries ago, that was simply too little to have any appreciable effect, especially since the resultant laser still had to blast its way through not just a warship's sidewalls, but also its anti-radiation shielding, just to reach the armor in question. So even though the odds of achieving what was effectively a direct hit with a contact nuke were not exactly good, most navies had opted to go with a weapon which could at least hope to inflict some damage if it actually managed to hit the target. Indeed, pre-laser head missiles had been most destructive when they achieved skin-to-skin contact as purely kinetic projectiles. That, unfortunately, had been all but impossible to achieve, even with the best sidewall penetrators, so the proximity-fused nuclear missile had become primarily a sidewall-killer. Its function was less to inflict actual hull damage than to burn out sidewall generators.

Unfortunately from the missile-firer's perspective, active missile defenses had improved to such a degree that "not exactly good" odds of scoring a direct hit had turned into "not a chance in hell," which was the real reason capital ships had gone to such massive energy batteries. Missiles might still be effective against lighter combatants, but they'd been for all intents and purposes completely *ineffective* against the active and passive defenses of a capital ship, so the only way to fight a battle out had been to close to the sort of eyeball-to-eyeball range at which shipboard energy mounts could get the job done.

But then, little more than a century ago, things had begun to change when some clever individual had figured out how to create what was in effect a shaped nuclear charge. The possibility had been discussed in several of the galaxy's naval journals considerably longer than that, but the technology to make it work hadn't been available. Not until improvements in the gravitic pinch effect used in modern fusion plants had been shoehorned down into something that could be fitted into the nose of a capital missile.

A ring of gravity generators, arranged in a collar behind the warhead, had been designed. When the weapon fired, the generators spun up a few milliseconds before the warhead actually detonated, which was just long enough for the layered focal points of a gravitic lens to stabilize and reshape the blast from spherical to Gaussian, directing the radiological and thermal effects forward along the warhead's axis. The result was to capture far more of the blast's total effect and focus it into the area occupied by the lasing rods. By modern standards, the original laser heads had been fairly anemic, despite their vast improvement over anything which had been possible previously, and capital ship designers had responded by further thickening the already massive armor dreadnoughts and superdreadnoughts carried. But the ancient race between armor and the gun had resumed, and by fifty or sixty T-years ago, the laser head had become a genuine danger to even the most stoutly armored vessel.

There were other factors involved in the design of a successful laser head, of course. The length and diameter of a lasing rod determined its beam divergence, with obvious implications for the percentage of energy the laser delivered at any given range. Ship-mounted energy weapons, with their powerful grav lenses, could squeeze beam divergence in a way no laser head possibly could. There was simply no way to design those lenses into something as small as a laser head which, despite many refinements in design, remained essentially a simple, expendable rod which would have been easily recognizable by any pre-Diaspora physicist.

In the current Mark 23 warhead, the laser heads (the assemblies containing the actual lasing rods) were roughly five meters in length and forty centimeters in diameter, which carried the thread-thin lasing rods suspended in a gel-like medium. The laser heads also incorporated the wolter mirrors to amplify the beampath, reaction thrusters, *lots* of fuel, on-board power, telemetry, and sensors. They were carried in bays on either side of the weapons bus, which ejected them once the missile had steadied down on its final attack bearing. Each of the laser heads mounted its own thrust-vectoring reaction control system, which acquired the target on its own sensors, thrust to align itself with the target's bearing, and quickly maneuvered to a position a hundred and fifty meters ahead of the missile. At which point the gravity lens came up, the warhead detonated, and the target found itself out of luck.

The critical factors were laser head rod dimensions, the yield of the detonation, and—in many ways the most critical of all—the grav lens amplification available. Which was the main reason capital missiles were so much more destructive than the smaller missiles carried aboard cruisers and destroyers. There was still a minimum mass/volume constraint on the grav lens assembly itself, and a bigger missile could simply carry both a more powerful lens *and* the longer—and therefore more powerful—lasing rods which gave it a longer effective standoff range from its target. That was also the reason it had been such a challenge to squeeze a laser head capable of dealing even with LACs into the new Viper anti-LAC missile. The bay for the single lasing rod was almost two thirds the length of the entire missile body, and finding a place where it could be crammed in had presented all sorts of problems.

The general Manticoran technical advantage over the Republic of Haven had made itself felt in laser head design, as well. Manticoran missile gravity generators had always been more powerful on a volume-for-volume basis, and Manticoran sensors and targeting systems had been better, as well. The Star Kingdom had been able to rely upon smaller warheads and greater lens amplification to create laser heads powerful enough for its purposes, especially since it could count on scoring more hits because of its superior fire control and seeking systems. The Republic had been forced to adopt a more brute force approach, using substantially larger warheads and heavier lasing rods, which was one of the factors that explained why Havenite missiles had always been outsized compared to their Manticoran counterparts.

But now, thanks primarily to fallout from the Star Kingdom's ongoing emphasis on improving its grav-pulse FTL communications capability, BuWeaps had completed field testing and begun production of a new generation of substantially more powerful gravity generators for the cruiser-weight Mark 16. In fact, they'd almost doubled the grav lens amplification factor, and while they were at it, they'd increased the yield of the missile warhead, as well, which had actually required at least as much ingenuity as the new amplification generators, given the way warheads scaled. They'd had to shift quite a few of the original Mark 16's components around to find a way to shoehorn all of that in, which had included shifting several weapons bus components aft, but Helen didn't expect anyone to complain about the final result. With its fifteen megaton warhead, the Mark 16 had been capable of dealing with heavy cruiser or battlecruiser armor, although punching through to the interior of a battlecruiser had pushed it almost to the limit. Now, with the new Mod G's *forty* megaton warhead and improved grav lensing, the Mark 16 had very nearly as much punch as an all-up capital missile from as recently as five or six T-years ago.

Producing the Mod G had required what amounted to a complete redesign of the older Mark 16 weapons buses, however, and BuWeaps had decided that it neither wanted to discard all of the existing weapons nor forgo the improvements, so Admiral Hemphill's minions had come up with a kit to convert the previous Mod E to the Mod E-1. (Exactly what had become of the Mod *F* designation was more than Helen was prepared to guess. It was well known to every tactical officer that BuWeaps nomenclature worked in mysterious ways.) The Mod E-1 was basically the existing Mod E with its original gravity generators replaced by the new, improved model. That was the only change, which had required no adjustments to buses or shifting of internal components, and the new warheads could be fused seamlessly into the existing Mark 16 weapons queues and attack profiles. Of course, with its weaker, original warhead it would remain less effective than the Mod G, since its destructiveness was "only" doubled . . . while the Mod G laser heads' throughput had increased by a factor of over five.

*And,* she thought, *if they apply the same approach to the Mark 23—assuming the new grav lens scales—and then couple it with whatever it was Duchess Harrington's fire control used at Lovat . . .*

"And what else did the Commodore discuss with you about them, Ensign Zilwicki?" Lynch's question recalled her from her thoughts, and she gave herself a mental shake.

"Sir, it's all on the chips there," she said respectfully, indicating the folio she'd just delivered.

"I'm sure it is," Lynch agreed. "On the other hand, I've come to know the Commodore at least a little better since he came aboard, and I'm inclined to doubt that he 'just happened' to discuss this with you before he sent you off to deliver his memo to me. He doesn't strike me as the sort who 'just happens' to do much of anything without a specific purpose in mind. So why don't we just consider this an opportunity for a little hands-on tactical brainstorming session for just you and me?"

Helen felt a distinct sinking sensation and suppressed a powerful urge to swallow hard. Then, as Lynch tipped his chair further back, she saw the amusement in his eyes. Not the amusement at having put her on the spot she might have seen in some superior officers' eyes, but the amusement of watching her work through his reasoning and discover he was almost certainly right about what the Commodore had had in mind.

"All right, Sir," she replied with a smile, settling herself more comfortably in her own chair. "Where were you thinking we should begin?"

Her tone was respectful, but almost challenging, and he smiled back at her as he heard it.

"That's the spirit, Ensign Zilwicki! Let's see . . ."

He swung his chair gently back and forth for a few moments, then nodded to himself.

"You've already mentioned what happened at Monica," he said. "I've read the tac reports from the battle, and I know you were on the bridge during the engagement. In fact, you were acting as missile defense officer, correct?"

"Yes, Sir." Helen's eyes darkened slightly at the memories his question brought back. Memories of her, sitting at Abigail Hearns' side, managing the entire squadron's missile defenses while the Monican-crewed battlecruisers stormed steadily closer.

"In that case, why don't we start with your evaluation of how the availability of the Mod G—or, for that matter, the E-1—would have affected Commodore Terekhov's choice of tactics?"

Helen frowned thoughtfully, the darkness of memory fading as she concentrated on his question. She considered it carefully for several seconds, then gave her head a little toss.

"I think the main change in his tactics might have been that he'd have gone for early kills."

"Meaning what, exactly?" Lynch's tone was an invitation to explain her thinking, and she leaned slightly forward.

"The thing was, Sir, that I think we all knew the only way

we could realistically hope to stop those battlecruisers was with massed missile fire at relatively short range. Oh, we got one of them at extreme range, but that had to have been a Golden BB. No way did we manage to get deep enough to hit anything that *should* have blown her up that way!"

She shook her head again, her expression grim as she recalled the spectacular destruction of MNS *Typhoon* and her entire crew. Then she shook herself mentally and refocused on the present.

"Anyway, we knew we sure couldn't afford to let them into *energy* range of us, and because our laser heads were so much lighter, we knew we were going to have to concentrate a lot of hits, both in terms of location and time, if we were going to get through their armor. The *Kitty*—I mean, *Hexapuma*—was the only ship we had that was Mark 16-capable, and that meant we couldn't achieve that kind of concentration outside standard missile range. So what the captain was actually using our long-range fire for was to get the best possible feel for the Monicans' active defenses and EW capabilities. He was using the Mark 16s to force them to defend themselves so we could get a read on their defenses and pass it to the rest of the squadron to maximize our fire's effectiveness once they came into the range of the rest of our ships.

"But if we'd had *Mod Gs*, instead of the old Mod Es, we would have been able to get through battlecruiser armor even at extreme range and without the kind of concentration we had at the end of the battle. So, in that case, I think he still would have been probing for information, but at the same time—"

Helen Zilwicki leaned further forward in her chair, hands beginning to gesture enthusiastically as she forgot all about her qualms over her junior rank and lack of experience, and never even noticed the amused approval in Horace Lynch's eyes as she gave herself up to the discussion.

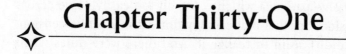

# Chapter Thirty-One

"YOU WANTED TO SEE ME, Milady?"

"Yes." Baroness Medusa looked up and waved for Gregor O'Shaughnessy to step fully into her office. "I was afraid you'd already left the Residence," she added as he obeyed the gesture and settled into his favorite chair.

"Ambrose screened to say he was hung up in some force analysis discussion. We've moved our meeting schedule back a couple of hours."

"It's just possible you won't be having that particular meeting at all." O'Shaughnessy's mental ears pricked up at the governor's tone, and she produced an expression which was more grimace than smile as his eyebrows rose.

"Should I assume there's been some new development, Milady?" he asked after a moment.

"More like a new wrinkle on a development we were already worrying about," she replied. "I've just received a formal communication from Alesta Cardot."

"Ah?" O'Shaughnessy frowned. "Does this have anything to do with what's been going on in Pequod, Milady?"

"That's what I've always liked about you, Gregor," Medusa said with a snort of genuine amusement. "You're quick."

"A natural talent, Milady." O'Shaughnessy smiled briefly, then sobered. "And just what did New Tuscany's Foreign Minister have to say about her obstreperous merchant spacers?"

"Interestingly enough, she didn't have a thing to say about her spacers. Had quite a bit to say about the conduct of *our* naval personnel, on the other hand."

"Why am I not surprised?" O'Shaughnessy murmured. Then he leaned back in his chair and stretched his forearms out along the armrests, fingertips drumming while he considered.

Medusa left him alone for several seconds. Gregor O'Shaughnessy could be infuriating when he truly put his mind to it. Despite his best efforts, his innate streak of intellectual arrogance got loose from time to time, and he'd been known to treat colleagues with a sort of dismissive patience which could all too easily come across as condescension. For that matter, sometimes it *was* condescension, although he didn't seem to realize it. And there were times when condescension turned into something considerably uglier and more dismissive if he decided the object of his ire was being particularly stupid by not grasping what he was saying. But he had impressive strengths to set against such minor character flaws. For one thing, he was ruthlessly intellectually honest. For another, he was always prepared to admit he'd made a mistake, if someone could demonstrate that he had, and however scathing he might have been during the debate which led up to that demonstration, he didn't hold the fact that someone else had been right against the other person afterwards. And he was also very, very smart.

"I take it Cardot's position is that Commander Denton and his people aren't just loose warheads?" he said after a moment.

"Oh, on the contrary," Medusa said dryly. "She's taken exactly the position that they *are* loose warheads. In fact, she's taken it so elaborately that no one could possibly miss the fact that she considers it a polite diplomatic fiction she's offering so that we can use it as a political fig leaf. From the tone of her note, it's obvious she intends to give us an out by repudiating and reprimanding Denton, thus proving we would never have authorized, far less *instigated*, such 'a pervasive pattern of Manticoran harassment of New Tuscan merchant shipping in the peaceful pursuit of legitimate commercial interests.'"

"She actually said that?" O'Shaughnessy said, then blinked as Medusa nodded. "My, whatever they're up to, they don't mind being a bit blatant about it, do they?"

"No, and that worries me," the governor admitted. She tipped back her own chair and pinched the bridge of her nose between her right thumb and forefinger. "This is about as subtle as heaving a brick through an office window during business hours. Oh," she released her nose to wave her hand, "all of the proper diplomatese is in place. In fact, in a lot of ways, it's quite a smoothly composed note. But I doubt any genuinely impartial observer could possibly miss the fact that she's systematically building a case designed to justify some unfriendly action on New Tuscany's part by disguising it as self-defense."

"How exactly did she present it, Milady?"

"Essentially, it's a formal protest alleging that Commander Denton—and apparently the entire ship's company of HMS *Reprise*—has systematically insulted, obstructed, and harassed New Tuscan merchant ships pursuing their lawful business in the Pequod System. She's enumerated all of the incidents Denton had reported to us, and added quite a few more. At least a couple of them occurred—according to her, at least—after Denton's dispatch to Admiral Khumalo, which presumably explains why we hadn't already heard about them. Others, though . . ." She shook her head. "Others, Gregor, have that 'manufactured out of whole cloth' feel to them. I've got the distinct feeling that they didn't really happen at all."

"Fictitious encounters tucked away in the underbrush of genuine ones, you mean?"

"That's exactly what I mean." Medusa's expression was grim. "It looks like they *were* recording all of our people's official shipboard visits, as well. According to them, they 'just happen' to have imagery available on a handful of inspections. No one was recording them on purpose, you understand. It was just a fortuitous coincidence that the internal systems of the ships in question were switched on at the critical moment. It's obvious they went through those recordings thoroughly before they very carefully picked the material Cardot included with her note, and I don't doubt for a moment that she's taken the remarks of our people even more carefully out of context, but they do have at least some imagery. Which is one reason I find the thought of fictitious incidents so disturbing. I mean, they have to know *we'll* realize they're lying about those . . . episodes, so who are they creating them to impress in the first place? It has to be a third party, and I think that also explains the imagery they're presenting, as well. You know how *any* imagery tends to substantiate even the most outrageous accusations for some people."

"Some people in this case being Frontier Security, do you think?"

"That's what I'm afraid of," she admitted. "And I'm even more afraid that they didn't hit on this notion, whatever it is, all on their own."

"You think Manpower could be behind it?" O'Shaughnessy asked as he recalled a certain seaside conversation with Ambrose Chandler, and Medusa shrugged unhappily.

"I don't know. If they are, though, they've been awfully damned quick off the mark. Even assuming New Tuscany was just sitting there like a ripe plum-apple, waiting to fall right into their hands, how the hell could they have gotten all of this up and running so quickly? And where in the name of God would even *Manpower* have gotten the chutzpah to try something like this after the hammering they took over Monica?" She shook her head. "What they *ought* to be doing is keeping their heads down and waiting for Monica to blow over, not playing with matches in something that could blow right up in their faces all over again. And even if they were too stupid to see that, I just don't see how they could have put it all together this rapidly. It's roughly three hundred and sixty-five light-years from Mesa to New Tuscany. Even for a dispatch boat, that's a forty-five-day trip, one way, and it's been barely three months since admiral Webster's assassination. For that matter, it's been barely *five* months since the Battle of Monica. With a three-month round-trip communications loop, how could they possibly have put something like this together this quickly?"

"Unless they were working the New Tuscany angle from the very beginning, Milady," O'Shaughnessy said slowly, his eyes thoughtful. "Do you think Andrieaux Yvernau might really have been trying to sabotage the Convention all along?"

"No." Medusa shook her head again, even more firmly. "I'm convinced Yvernau was just as big an idiot as he seemed at the time. Besides, I can't believe for a moment that someone like the New Tuscan oligarchs would be willing to work hand-in-glove with someone like Nordbrandt. Or even Westman, for that matter! They'd be far too terrified of the danger of Nordbrandt's example for their own domestic situation."

"They might have been being played," O'Shaughnessy pointed out. "You're right; there's no way they would have knowingly worked with someone like Nordbrandt. But if they didn't *know* they were working with Nordbrandt, the same way *Westman* didn't know, then all our analysis parameters shift."

"I suppose that's possible, in a remote sort of way." Medusa swung her chair gently from side to side, nibbling on her lower lip while she thought. "I still think it's unlikely, though. For one thing, I don't believe Yvernau is subtle enough—or *smart* enough, for that matter—to have deliberately presented a platform the most reactionary oligarchs of the Cluster were going to sign on for. And he did, you know. I think that if his real orders had been to sabotage the Convention, he would've been more confrontational from the beginning instead of trying to oil his way into controlling the way the final Constitution would have been drafted. And let's face it, his demands were considerably less extreme than Tonkovic's. If he'd really wanted to kill the Convention, why not go ahead and sign up under her banner? Why present what was actually a more moderate—and therefore more likely to be adopted—draft of his own?"

"I'm afraid you're right," O'Shaughnessy sighed. "He'd have to have been a lot smarter than we both know he really is to have tried to double-think his way into blowing up the Constitution that way. Unless someone else was pulling his puppet strings, at least."

"And there you come up against the time constraints again," Medusa pointed out. "You just can't move information across interstellar distances quickly enough to make something like that practical. Besides, if New Tuscany was in on the original plan, then why were they working so hard for a place at the feed trough? There's no question that the majority of the New Tuscan oligarchs wanted to get their own rice bowls out in front when the Star Kingdom started investing in the Cluster. That's why they supported the annexation in the first place, at least until they figured out how likely they were to lose control politically at home if it went through on Her Majesty's terms, instead of theirs."

"Then maybe they really are just pissed off enough over not getting their bowls filled that they're doing this on their own after all," O'Shaughnessy said with a shrug.

"No, Henri's right about that. Yvernau may be an idiot—he *is* an idiot—but there have to be at least some people on his planet and in his government who have IQs higher than a stewed prune's. By now, if nothing else, they'd have to realize Manpower had been playing them, as you put it. They'd be backing away from any kind of support for the people who turned Nordbrandt loose, I'd think. And especially with Nordbrandt's example to stir up their own underclass, they really, really wouldn't want to be ticking us off. Not unless they figured they had some powerful backing—backing powerful enough to keep us off their necks in retaliation *and* to help them keep their boots on the backs of their own underclass's necks—from somewhere."

"Somewhere closer than Mesa. That's what you're really suggesting, isn't it, Milady?"

"Yes," Medusa admitted with a grimace. "Meyers is closer to New Tuscany than Mesa is, and Frontier Security has a lot more in the way of resources than Manpower. It's got a depressing amount of experience in helping less-than-desirable régimes stay in power by repressing hell out of their domestic opposition, too, I'm afraid. That might just make it more attractive to New Tuscany than our own corrupting example. Not to mention the fact that Frontier Security was far better tapped into the star systems here in and around the Quadrant than anyone from Manpower was likely to be. Everything Ambassador Corvisart's turned up in Monica suggests that OFS brokered the deal between Manpower and the Jessyk Combine and people like Nordbrandt and President Tyler. I don't think there's any reason to assume Commissioner Verrochio wouldn't be thoroughly capable of brokering deals for himself if he decided to. And if there's anyone around who's probably more ticked off than Manpower by how Terekhov blew their Monica operation right out of space, it's got to be Lorcan Verrochio."

"That's a nasty thought," O'Shaughnessy acknowledged, pursing his lips thoughtfully. But then he shook his head. "It's a nasty thought, and it's possible you're onto something, Milady. But it occurs to me that a lot of the time constraints you've pointed out where Mesa is concerned would also apply to Verrochio. The transit time for a dispatch boat between Meyers and New Tuscany would only be about a T-week less than the time between Mesa and New Tuscany. That only saves them half a T-month on the round trip."

"Agreed. But I'm thinking that Manpower probably wouldn't have started sniffing around New Tuscany until after they'd assassinated Admiral Webster. Or no sooner than that, at any rate. In that case, they wouldn't have had enough time even to get the suggestion of an alliance to New Tuscany before the New Tuscans started manufacturing these 'incidents' of theirs. But if *Verrochio* started in on this the instant he found out how Monica had blown up in everyone's faces, they'd have had time for two complete two-way exchanges of communication before the first genuine incident in Pequod. Even assuming Manpower had started at exactly the same time, they could only have managed one and a *half* two-way exchanges in the same timeframe. In addition to which, Verrochio wouldn't have needed to invest still more time in coordinating with OFS, the way Manpower would. He *is* OFS in this neck of space."

"I agree with your logic," O'Shaughnessy said. "But with all due respect, Milady, both of us are just speculating at this point. We don't begin to have enough information for any kind of informed analysis, and it's one of the first principles of analysis that—"

"That if you start speculating too soon, with too little information, you predispose yourself to fit all later information into your initial hypotheses," Medusa interrupted, and gave him a remarkably urchinlike grin. "You see? I have been listening, Gregor."

"Yes, Milady, you have," he replied just the least bit repressively.

"I guess what I really wanted more than anything else was to get you brought up to speed with the information I've got and with the way my own thinking has been headed before we sit down with Khumalo and Chandler. I don't have any interest at all in double-teaming them into going along with my own brainstorms, but I figure it can't hurt to have that brain of yours already mulling over the info."

He nodded in understanding, and she glanced at the date-time readout in the corner of her desk display.

"And speaking about sitting down with Khumalo and Chandler, we're due to do that in about ninety minutes."

"All in all, Governor," Augustus Khumalo said the better part of three hours later, "I find myself substantially in agreement with you."

"Really?" Medusa smiled at him. "By this time, Augustus, I'm not sure what you're agreeing with!" She shook her head. "I've spun this around in my own mind so often that I'm half afraid I've forgotten my own theories!"

"Yes, I've noticed you can be easily distracted, Milady," Khumalo retorted with a level of comfort neither he nor Medusa would ever have predicted a few T-months earlier. "But allow me to summarize. Essentially, I think we're all in agreement that Minister of War Krietzmann's suspicions of New Tuscany would appear to have been soundly based in reality. I think we all also agree that they wouldn't have done this without some assurance of support to offset any retaliation we might be inclined to inflict on them. And that they wouldn't have gone to such pains to manufacture these so-called incidents of theirs if they weren't planning to use them as their 'evidence,' at least in the court of public opinion."

"And I think we should also add that our dispute with the Republic of Haven over the prewar correspondence is probably playing a part in the thinking of whatever mastermind's come up with all this," Amandine Corvisart put in.

Sir Anthony Langtry, the Foreign Secretary for the Star Kingdom of Manticore, had found himself occupying the same office for the Star *Empire* of Manticore, since foreign policy was one of the areas reserved for the imperial government, rather than being subject to local autonomy. Corvisart had been one of the Foreign Office's senior troubleshooters for years, which was how she'd come to be assigned to deal with the hot potato of Aivars Terekhov's completely unauthorized invasion of the Monica System. When the orders for Quentin O'Malley's battlecruisers to return to the Lynx Terminus had reached Monica, she'd received fresh instructions of her own from Langtry which had assigned her permanently to Baroness Medusa's staff. One of O'Malley's dispatch boats had diverted from the shortest possible flight home to Spindle just long enough to drop her off, and the imperial governor had been delighted to have her.

"That's a good point, Amandine," Medusa said now. "One that hadn't occurred to me, to be honest, though it should have. The accusations and counteraccusations flying back and forth between Landing and Nouveau Paris are going to resonate with any dispute between us and New Tuscany, aren't they?"

"They will for the Sollies, Milady," Corvisart agreed. "By this time, the diplomatic waters are awfully murky as far as any Solly observer is likely to be concerned. Why should they believe us instead of New Tuscany if we find ourselves involved in yet another diplomatic wrangle? Especially if the New Tuscans have what purports to be recorded imagery that proves their claims? I doubt anyone else is going to be particularly impressed by their 'evidence,' but that doesn't really matter. And look at it from Verrochio's perspective. If he can spin this thing properly, we suddenly become the heavies of the piece . . . which just happens to tie back into the Solly suspicions about our 'imperialist' leanings that Nordbrandt's atrocities were busy fanning. Not only that, but if he can spin things to make it look as if he's riding to the rescue on a white horse in *this* instance—which, as he'll make very sure the entire galaxy knows, is a totally separate incident with an obviously innocent third-party—then everything that came out of Monica becomes suspect by association."

"Which would let him rehabilitate himself in the Solly newsfaxes," O'Shaughnessy said, nodding slowly.

"While undoubtedly taking considerable pleasure out of planting one right square in our eye," Khumalo said sourly.

"Let's not get too carried away with conspiracy theories just yet," Medusa said bracingly. "As Gregor pointed out to me earlier today, we really don't have enough information at this point to justify drawing any firm conclusions."

"Well, if we can get the information, then I think we certainly should, Milady," Ambrose Chandler said with a lopsided smile.

"I agree with Commander Chandler," Corvisart said. "At the same time, I think we should bear in mind that if someone is trying to manipulate the situation—and us—so that we end up in a false position, the worst thing we could do in a lot of ways would probably be to try to get too proactive until we have that information. This looks to me like it's probably one of those cases where the best thing to do is nothing until we've got more pieces of the puzzle."

"You mean to do nothing in terms of officially responding to Cardot's note?" Khumalo asked with a moderately unhappy expression.

"Yes, Admiral. I don't mean to imply that we shouldn't do anything on other fronts—like trying to get Commander Chandler's additional information. I just think it would be a mistake to present New Tuscany with any sort of official response they could take out of context or twist."

"I think that makes excellent sense," Medusa agreed. "Which brings us to the point of deciding how to go about getting that additional information. Suggestions, anyone?"

"My first thought is that we should get someone senior to

Commander Denton into *Pequod*, Milady," Khumalo said after a moment. "Mind you, I'm not criticizing anything Denton's done. In fact, I think he's handled the situation remarkably well. But the fact is that he's only a commander, and *Reprise* is only a destroyer—and one who's getting pretty long in the tooth, at that. This isn't like the situation in Split when we sent in *Hexapuma*—" he gave Medusa a wry smile "—because we didn't have to worry about the Pequod system government's reaction, which meant we could afford to send in just enough ship to get the job done. In some ways, I'm starting to wish we'd given Pequod a higher priority when we started distributing the LACs, but Pequod's a lot less exposed than someplace like Nuncio or Howard, and, to be frank, the system is really capable of providing all of its own customs inspections, even with the legitimate increase in traffic in the area. *Reprise* is actually there more as a gesture of imperial support for the locals than anything else, when you come right down to it."

Medusa nodded. Despite the priority in getting LACs deployed into the Quadrant, it could only be done so quickly. The limiting factor was coming up with not just the CLACs to transport them to their new stations, but also the depot ships necessary to support them after they got there. The Admiralty was providing more depot conversions as quickly as possible, and the Hauptman Cartel had begun delivering the first modular depot bases, designed for independent deployment after being transported to their assigned stations in standard freighter holds and bolted together in place. But all of that was still taking time, and Khumalo and Krietzmann had chosen to cover their more exposed points first. Pequod was close enough to the Rembrandt Trade Union that the RTU's home systems could dispatch units of their own navies—which were considerably more powerful than those of any other Talbott star systems—to help cover it in an emergency, and that had given it a much lower priority under their original deployment plans.

"It would still be a good thing, though, I think," Khumalo continued, "to get at least a captain of the list into the system to take the heat off of Denton and with instructions to make it clear to New Tuscany that we know they're lying and don't intend to let them get away with it."

"I think I agree with you," Medusa said slowly. "But assuming we do that, who would you send, Admiral?"

"My current thought would be to send one of Commodore Onasis' *Nikes*," Khumalo replied. "I don't think I'd be in favor of sending Onasis herself. Not only would that mean depriving myself of her presence here in Spindle if something else comes up, but she'd be *too* senior, I think. We want to demonstrate resolution, not suggest that we're running scared."

Medusa nodded with a thoughtful frown. The events of the last seven months had clearly contributed to Khumalo's self-confidence. And she'd already decided that if she was going to be honest with herself, he'd always shown better instincts on the political and diplomatic side of his duties than she'd initially been prepared to recognize.

"Excuse me, Admiral, Governor," Captain Shoupe said in a careful tone of voice, and Medusa and Khumalo both looked at the admiral's chief of staff.

"Yes, Captain?" Medusa said.

"With all due respect, I'm not sure sending any of the Commodore's *Nikes* would be an . . . optimal response at this moment."

"Why not, Loretta?" Khumalo's question was genuine, not a dismissal *phrased* as a question, despite the fact that she'd just publicly indicated at least partial disagreement with one of her admiral's suggestions, Medusa realized.

"Two points occur to me, Sir," Shoupe replied. "First, I think sending a ship the size of a *Nike* to a small, poverty-stricken star system like Pequod, to act as a glorified customs cutter, is going to look like an overreaction. Your point about showing resolution without looking like we're afraid comes to mind. And, second, at the moment Commodore Onasis' division is the only real concentrated firepower at your immediate disposal. I don't think sending off twenty-five percent of it, before we at least hear back from Admiral Gold Peak about how things went when she visited Monica, would be an ideal solution."

"Um." Medusa scratched the tip of her nose for a moment, then nodded. "Both excellent points, Captain. But if we're not going to send a battlecruiser, what do we send?"

"Well," Shoupe said after glancing at Khumalo and getting his nod of approval for her to continue, "I'm inclined to suggest that we pretty much sit tight until we get that first squadron of *Rolands* out here, Milady. We still haven't actually seen any of them, of course, and I realize the deployment schedules we've gotten so far are still provisional and subject to revision. But a *Roland* is bigger than a lot of light cruisers, and I doubt the Admiralty is choosing their skippers by just pulling names out of a hat."

"That's not a bad idea at all, Loretta," Khumalo said approvingly. "She'd be big enough to make the point that we're serious, but she'd still officially be 'only' a destroyer. And as you say, Admiral Cortez is going to be handpicking their COs. I doubt we'll be lucky enough to get another Terekhov out of the deal, but whoever we do get is definitely going to be first-string."

"And delaying until we get additional units from home would make it clear we're moving deliberately, not rushing around in some sort of panic," Medusa agreed.

"Not to mention the fact that Admiral Gold Peak would probably appreciate it if we didn't start chopping up her squadron into penny-packets before she even gets back here so we can at least *discuss* it with her," Khumalo added with a chuckle. "Not without a real emergency to justify it, at any rate!"

Vice Admiral Jessup Blaine tried not to feel too bored as he worked his way through the routine reports and paperwork. It was nice to have his own task group to command, and to have two full squadrons of pod-laying ships of the wall at his beck and call, as it were. And it was nice that Quentin O'Malley's battlecruisers had returned to him from Monica.

It was also boring. There simply wasn't very much for a fleet commander to do, assuming he had a competent staff (and Blaine did), when he was tied down to picket duty, however large or important the picket in question might be. He certainly couldn't go looking for trouble, and there were only so many wargames, simulations, and exercises which he could contrive. Exercises against the fortresses protecting the Lynx Terminus, two-thirds of which were now fully on-line, were actually more interesting, and he'd been impressed by the fortresses' capabilities. Aside from that, though, all he really had to do was to hover in the background, like a watching, distant presence, while his staff and his squadron and starship commanders got on with the *interesting* bits of training and administering their commands.

*Oh, stop* whining, *Jessup!* he told himself severely. *When you were a captain, you thought the XO had all the real fun. And when you were an XO, you thought it was the department heads.*

*And when you were a department head, you thought it was the division officers. Which was probably pretty much true, now that I think about it.*

His lips twitched in a smile at the thought, and he scrawled his electronic signature and thumbprint across the signature block of yet another fascinating report on the status of his attached repair ships' inventories of spare emitter heads for laser clusters. Precisely why *he* had to sign off on that was one of life's little mysteries.

*I'll bet Admiral D'Orville doesn't sign off on parts inventories.* Blaine took a certain perverse satisfaction from the thought. *He's probably got some staff weenie hidden away down in the bowels of his flagship to take care of things like that. And well he should, too. In fact, I ought to take a look around and find someone I could dump it—*

His thoughts broke off as a lurid priority icon flashed suddenly and shockingly in the corner of his display. He stared at it for perhaps a heartbeat or two. In his entire naval career, he had never seen that particular icon outside a training exercise or a drill, a tiny corner of his brain reflected, and his hand flashed out to stand the acceptance key.

"Blaine!" he snapped the instant his flagship's communications officer of the watch appeared on the display. The officer looking out of it at him looked absurdly young to hold senior lieutenant's rank, and her youthful face was paper-white.

"I'm sorry to disturb you, Admiral," she said, speaking so rapidly the words blurred together at the edges. "We just received a priority message from the Admiralty. It's Code Zulu, Sir!"

For just a moment, Blaine felt the breath freeze in his chest. She had to be mistaken, a part of his mind tried to insist. Either that, or he must have misunderstood her. In naval use, Code Zulu had only one meaning: invasion imminent. But no one, not even the *Peeps*, could be crazy enough to take on the defenses of the Manticoran home system!

"Is there an enemy strength estimate attached, Lieutenant?"

Blaine was astounded by how calm his own voice sounded. It certainly wasn't because he *felt* particularly calm! In fact, he realized distantly, it was purely a reaction to the lieutenant's expression and the tension sputtering like a shorting power cable just under the surface of *her* voice.

"Yes, Sir, there is." The communications officer drew a deep breath, and despite everything, Blaine felt a flicker of amusement at her automatic response to the steadying influence of his own tone. But that amusement didn't last long.

"The Admiralty's initial assessment is a minimum of three hundred of the wall, Sir," she said. "Initial course projections indicate they're headed directly for Sphinx on a least-time approach."

Blaine felt as if someone had just slugged him in the belly. *Three hundred* of the wall? That was... that was *insane*. The one thing Thomas Theisman had persistently refused to do as the Republic of Haven's Secretary of War was to commit the men and women under his command to the sort of death-ride offensives the Committee of Public Safety had once demanded of them.

*But maybe it* isn't *a death ride,* Blaine thought around the icy wind blowing through the marrow of his bones. *Three hundred wallers... probably towing max pod loads... and with D'Orville forced to position himself to cover the Junction, as well...*

*Jesus Christ,* he realized suddenly, coldly. *This could actually work* for them! *And if it* does...

"Immediate signal to all squadron and divisional commanders," he heard his voice telling the lieutenant on his display.

"Yes, Sir." The young woman's relief as she found herself doing something comfortingly familiar was obvious. "Live mike, Sir," she said a moment later.

"People," Blaine told his pickup, "they need us back home. Activate Ops Plan Homecoming immediately. I want your impellers up and your ships moving in thirty minutes. Blaine, clear."

The lieutenant tapped a control, then looked back up at him.

"Clean copy, Sir," she confirmed.

"Attach the complete text of the Admiralty's dispatch," he instructed her.

"Yes, Sir!"

"Then get it sent, Lieutenant. Get it sent."

Blaine killed the connection, and as he started to punch in his chief of staff's com combination with the emergency priority code, his earlier thoughts about training exercises flickered through the back of his mind like summer sheet lightning on a distant horizon. At least they *had* exercised Plan Homecoming, the movement order for an emergency return to the home system. Not that anyone had ever truly expected to need it.

*Like my father always used to say, you never* do *really need something important . . . until you need it* bad. *Funny. I always thought he was being overly pessimistic.*

"Yes, Sir?" His chief of staff appeared on his display, dressed in a sweatsuit and mopping perspiration off his forehead and cheeks with a hand towel. Behind him, Blaine could just see a frozen basketball game.

"I'm afraid your game's just been canceled, Jack," Blaine told him. "It seems we have a little problem."

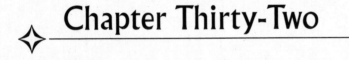

# Chapter Thirty-Two

"THAT WAS GOOD WORK picking up the contact, Pettigrew," Lieutenant Abigail Hearns said. "We need to be a little quicker on updating the ID on bogeys, though."

"Yes, My Lady," Sensor Tech First-Class Isaiah Pettigrew replied almost humbly, and Abigail managed not to grit her teeth.

The tall, lanky sensor tech's accent was just as soft, with just as much of a slight lilt, as her own. In many ways, hearing it was a deeply soothing reminder of who she was, since she'd been away from home for so long. In other ways, though, what she most wanted to do was to strangle Pettigrew—and a handful of other Graysons in HMS *Tristram*'s company—with her bare hands.

*It's not really his fault*, she told herself . . . again. *He's from Grayson. He can't forget that Daddy is Steadholder Owens, which makes me* Miss Owens, *not just Lieutenant Hearns. I suppose that's why he can't seem to remember the word "Ma'am" when he talks to me. And, irritating as that is, I could probably live with it, if he'd only stop looking like he wants to go down on one knee and kiss my hand whenever I* talk *to* him!

Somehow, of all the problems she'd envisioned facing on the day she returned to her birth world's navy, this one hadn't occurred to her, and it should have. She'd been too focused on Grayson's long-standing prohibition against seeing its wives and daughters serving in the military, worried too much about whether or not Grayson males would be prepared to accept a female *Grayson* voice of command as well as they had become accustomed to accepting female Manticoran voices from Steadholder Harrington and the other "loaners" from the RMN. She'd braced herself for dealing with subordinates who found it hard to believe any proper Grayson girl could be a "real officer," but she'd never considered how more traditional Grayson males might respond to the almost genetic-level social and religious programming of their birth society.

Pettigrew was the product of a *very* traditional Grayson rearing. He couldn't seem to get past the deference due to the daughter of any steadholder, which could be a real problem for Abigail, considering that she was the most junior of *Tristram*'s department heads. She already labored under the distinction of being the only member of the ship's company who was permanently assigned her own bodyguard, as Grayson law required. Mateo Gutierrez, her towering personal armsman, had fitted himself as neatly into *Tristram*'s small ship's company as he had into *Hexapuma*'s, but everyone knew he was there, and she suspected that some of her Manticoran-born fellows thought his presence was just the sort of pretension to be expected out of Neobarbs. And the sort of special consideration which was bound to give her a vastly inflated sense of her own importance. She didn't need any of the other lieutenants aboard who were senior to her deciding that the Grayson members of the crew accorded *her* greater respect and obedience than they did anyone else, either. Nor, for that matter, did Abigail like it very much, herself. One of the things she'd loved about her experience in the Royal Manticoran Navy was that as far as most Manties were concerned, she was only *Lieutenant Hearns*. No one wasted a lot of time kowtowing to her, or looking as desperately eager to please as puppies.

Even that, though, bothered her less in a lot of respects than the obvious conflict between Pettigrew's naval discipline and training, on the one hand, and the ingrained Grayson belief that women were to be protected at all costs. And not just from the physical dangers of the universe. Oh, no. They were to be protected from anything which might offend their delicate sensibilities, as well! Pettigrew had imbibed that notion with his mother's milk, and it showed.

*You've only been aboard ship for six days, Abigail,* she reminded herself. *It might be just a little bit early yet to be letting your frustration quotient rise so high, don't you think? Besides, at least thirty percent of the ship's company is Grayson.*

"I'm not saying you didn't do an excellent job over all, Pettigrew," she said out loud. "I'm just saying we need to move a bit more quickly working the contacts through to a positive identification, at least by class."

"Yes, My Lady. I understand."

Abigail bit her tongue before she reminded him—again—that she'd specifically told him, and all the other Graysons in her department, that she was a naval officer, to be addressed as such, and not as what was for all intents and purposes a Grayson princess.

*I do need to make that point to him again, but not right now,* she thought.

The tactical simulator was fully manned, and only three of the people in it, aside from Abigail herself, were Graysons. So far, most of her Manticoran personnel seemed to be taking their Grayson crewmates' peculiarities pretty much in stride. The fact that Manticore had its own aristocracy probably helped in that respect, although even now not all Manticorans seemed prepared to take Grayson titles quite seriously. But Abigail had decided at the outset that she couldn't accept one set of responses from Manticorans and another from Graysons. She'd seen enough evidence of what allowing cliques to form aboard a warship could do to its internal cohesiveness. *Her* department was going to be composed of people who were all members of the same ship's company, not internally divided into "us" and "them," Manticorans and Graysons. At the same time, she didn't want to hammer Pettigrew. For one thing, much as it irritated her, he hadn't really done anything to be hammered *for*. And, for another thing, reprimanding him for the way he addressed her would only draw attention to the very fault lines she was determined to eradicate in the first place.

"All right," she said instead, her tranquil tone revealing none of her internal thoughts as she turned to Missile Tech 1/c Naomi Kaneshiro and the next point of her post-simulation critique of the exercise Lieutenant (JG) Gladys Molyneux, *Tristram*'s most junior tactical officer had just conducted while Abigal monitored. "Kaneshiro, when Bogey Two started to swing wide of the wing escort and Lieutenant Molyneux designated her as *Tristram*'s primary target, your section was a bit slow to paint her properly."

Despite her rate and an almost unbroken string of "Excellent" and "Superior" evaluations from her instructors, Kaneshiro was very young, even younger than Helen Zilwicki. She was also fresh out of school, where she'd completed the testing for her first-class rate less than three weeks before reporting aboard *Tristram.* She'd borne up well under the burden of having the same first name as her commanding officer (for which, Abigail knew, she had been ribbed unmercifully for the first week or so) but it was evident to Abigail that Kaneshiro was also one of those people who took failure as an affront, rather than a challenge, and she watched the missile tech hovering on the brink of protesting her criticism. Abigail waited a moment or two to see if the other woman's obvious sense of ill use would actually spill over into disputing a superior officer's comments, but Kaneshiro rather visibly sat on her resentment.

"I realize you suffered a computer glitch," Abigail continued calmly when Kaneshiro kept her mouth shut. "In fact, that may be one of the reasons why I noticed it so specifically. I knew that glitch had been programmed into the sim, and I was watching to see how well we handled it. You responded quickly and well when you realized you were going to have to paint the target manually, but it took you longer to realize that than it ought to have. Longer than we might have in an actual combat situation. You need to be better prepared for the possibility of equipment failure. We all do. That's one of the points this simulation was intended to make. And the reason it was intended to make that point is that we all learn more from our mistakes than we do from our successes. Just between you and me, I'd prefer to do as much as possible of that kind of learning in a simulation instead of when missiles are flying for real."

"Yes, Ma'am." Kaneshiro' acknowledgment came out a bit stiffly but without that edge of personal resentment Abigail had initially detected.

"All right." Abigail checked that point off on her memo pad and turned to the next one. "This one is more in the nature of a general observation. I realize we haven't been together long, and we're still at an earlier point in shaking down the department and the ship than we really ought to be. Unfortunately, the time between here and Spindle is all the time we have before we're likely to find ourselves tasked for deployment somewhere in the

Quadrant. That doesn't give us very long to knock off our rough edges. I've discussed this with Captain Kaplan, and she's discussed it with Commodore Chatterjee, and the result is that we're going to be having a little competition."

She smiled slightly as a ripple of what might have been consternation or even apprehension flowed through the simulator.

"Starting the day after tomorrow," she continued, "we're going to begin a squadron-wide 'Top Gun' contest. Commodore Chatterjee and Commander DesMoines are going to design the problems and assign tasks. The first phase will be a direct competition between just the tactical departments of the squadron's ships, and we'll duke it out in a straight simulator-on simulator link. *But—*" she smiled again, much more thinly "—once we've made the first cut and winnowed it down to the best ship from each division, we'll go up against each other in real-time and real space. It'll be every department in the ship, then, people, not just us, but all the others are going to be relying on us to get our job done right. I wouldn't want anyone to feel particularly pressured, but I suppose I ought to point out that if we *don't* get our job done right and at least make the first cut, I'm going to be . . . unhappy. And, trust me, you really won't like me very much when I'm unhappy."

"Jesus," Lieutenant Wanda O'Reilly's voice was quiet but harsh as she leaned slightly across the table towards Lieutenant Vincenzo Fonzarelli in *Tristram*'s wardroom. "Who had *this* frigging brainstorm?"

Fonzarelli, *Tristram*'s chief engineer, took his time sipping from his beer mug while he considered O'Reilly thoughtfully. Like the rest of the destroyer's company, her officers were split between Manticorans and Graysons. *Unlike* the rest of *Tristram*'s company, they were split just about evenly, and O'Reilly was one of the Manticorans who seemed to have a bit of a problem with that.

*And with one of those Graysons in particular, I'd say*, Fonzarelli reflected. *The idiot.*

"As a matter of fact," the engineer said mildly, lowering his mug, "I believe the Skipper came up with the notion of making it a squadron-wide, winner-take-all competition. The original idea of having the ships exercise against each other, though, came from Lieutenant Hearns, I think."

"Well, *that* figures!" O'Reilly snorted.

"And just what exactly does that mean?" Fonzarelli asked, still in that mild tone of voice.

"You know," O'Reilly replied, waving one hand in the air between them and—Fonzarelli noticed—careful to keep her volume down.

"No, I don't," the engineer disagreed.

O'Reilly looked at him, eyes narrow, then smiled and shrugged.

"Oh, I guess it makes sense, sort of. It'd make *more* sense if we'd had more than two or three T-weeks to shake down our people first, though." She shook her head. "I mean, it's a great idea, in theory. But what's it really going to prove, this early? It's not like anyone really thinks this squadron's had time to train up properly, now is it?"

"I suppose not. Then again, I don't suppose a batch of pirates—or, even worse, a batch of *Sollies*, let's say—is going to check to see that we've had time to get ourselves properly together before they start shooting, either."

"Of course not." O'Reilly flushed slightly. "I just said I thought it was a good idea. But we're not going to have anyone shooting at anyone before we ever even get to Spindle, Vincenzo, and that won't be for another nine days yet. I'm just saying that I think it would make sense to wait another couple of days, maybe even another week, before something like this."

"Then maybe you should mention that to the Skipper," Fonzarelli suggested.

"Hah! Fat chance *that* would do any good!"

"Meaning?" Fonzarelli's voice was considerably sharper than it had been, although he hadn't raised it above a quiet conversational level . . . yet. O'Reilly's flush darkened, and her lips pressed firmly together, but the engineer held her gaze steadily.

"I mean I'm a com officer, not a tac officer," O'Reilly said finally, shaking her head. "And I haven't known the Skipper as long as Hearns has, either. Naturally her ideas are going to carry more weight than mine would at this point."

"I see."

Fonzarelli sat back, considering the communications officer even more thoughtfully. Then he cocked his head.

"Don't much care for Lieutenant Hearns, do you, Wanda?" he asked after a moment.

"What's not to care about?" O'Reilly responded with another of those shrugs. "I hardly even know her!"

"The very thought that had just crossed my own mind," Fonzarelli agreed. "But that wasn't really answering my question. So let me try phrasing it a bit more clearly. What's your problem with Hearns, Wanda?"

The engineer's voice hardened on the final sentence, and O'Reilly glowered at him. Unfortunately for the communications officer, while they were both senior-grade lieutenants, Fonzarelli was almost a full T-year senior to her. That didn't leave much wiggle room in the face of a specific question.

"I don't like her," she finally said, his expression almost defiant. "I don't like her, and I don't think she's really qualified for TO, either."

"I see." Fonzarelli smiled ever so slightly. It was not an extraordinarily pleasant expression. "Let me see if I've got it straight, though. You've known her for less than one week, and you've already decided you don't like her. And on the basis of that same lengthy acquaintance, you've decided she's not qualified as the ship's tactical officer, either. I am awed by the clarity and deliberate speed with which your extraordinary intellect comes to these carefully considered evaluations."

O'Reilly's face flushed more darkly than ever. Given her fair complexion, it was painfully obvious, too, and she knew it. Which only made her even angrier, Fonzarelli supposed.

"Look," the communications officer said rather more sharply, "I never claimed I know her well. You asked me what my problem with her was, and I told you."

"That's true enough," Fonzarelli agreed. "But you also said you don't think she's qualified for her position. That's a pretty serious accusation to be leveling at the ship's senior tactical officer."

"Maybe it is. But this wouldn't be the first time someone's family or connections got him moved up faster than his ability justified, and you know it. Christ, Vincenzo! Don't tell me you've never served with—or *under*—some idiot whose sole qualification for her position was whose *cousin* she was!"

"So you're thinking Hearns got where she is because she's a steadholder's daughter?"

"Well, what am I supposed to think? She's *three* frigging T-years out of the Academy, for God's sake! And she was a jay-gee barely a year ago—until her *last* skipper appointed her as an *acting* senior-grade. And when they get home from Talbott, the

Admiralty confirms her as a senior-grade lieutenant retroactive to Terekhov's appointment less than *three days* before they hand her a *Roland*-class's entire tactical department!"

She shook her head, looking as if she wanted to spit on the decksole in disgust.

"You tell me, Vincenzo. You *really* think all of that would have happened if she hadn't been a steadholder's daughter and one of 'the Salamander's' favorites at Saganami?"

Fonzarelli took another sip of beer to buy a little time before replying. He'd known O'Reilly resented Hearns, but he hadn't really recognized the true depth of that resentment until this moment.

In some ways, the engineer could understand where O'Reilly was coming from better than he really wanted to. As O'Reilly had just pointed out, Abigail Hearns had been a shiny new snotty barely three years ago. At that time, Vincenzo Fonzarelli had already been a jay-gee on the brink of promotion to senior-grade . . . and he'd been just over four years out of the Academy himself. Of course, the Janacek build-down which had set the stage so disastrously for the Peeps' Operation Thunderbolt had slowed everyone's promotions during that time period. The braking effect had been even more apparent given the speed with which promotions had come during the First Havenite War. The fleet's expansion and the opportunity to step into dead men's shoes had seen to that while the fighting had been going on, and the sudden deceleration when the peacetime Navy started downsizing so drastically under the High Ridge Government had come as an unpleasant surprise for everyone.

O'Reilly had left Saganami Island six T-months after Fonzarelli, just in time to run into that effect, and she'd spent considerably longer as an ensign than Fonzarelli had. On the other hand, she'd spent considerably *less* time as a jay-gee, since the need for officers was even more insatiable under the stress of this war than it had been during the last one. Still, there was no denying that Abigail Hearns' career bade fair to set some sort of all-time record for promotions.

"Let me stand your question on its head, Wanda," Fonzarelli said, finally lowering his beer again. "You really think that someone who took two squads of Marines down on to someone else's planet, without any outside support, on her *snotty* cruise, played tag with better than five hundred pirates for the better part of a full day, and killed damned near two hundred of them for the loss of only ten Marines, then turned around and as the acting tactical officer of a scratch built squadron that had already been hammered into scrap took out three Solly *battlecruisers*, wouldn't have been promoted, even if her father had been a sewer worker?"

O'Reilly's nostrils flared, but she didn't respond, and Fonzarelli shook his head.

"You just came mighty damned close to suggesting Commodore Terekhov and Captain Kaplan are playing favorites," he said. "You might want to think about that a little more carefully the next time. And you might want to think about who you express that opinion too, as well. I don't know the Skipper—not yet. Haven't had time to get to know her . . . any more than you have. But what I have seen of her, and what I've seen of—and heard about—Commodore Terekhov suggests to *me* that it's . . . unlikely they'd let favoritism run away with their better judgment. And that anyone who suggests they might is gonna find herself really, *really* wishing she hadn't if they should happen to find out about it. I'll grant you it can't possibly hurt Hearns' chances for promotion and eventual flag rank to be the daughter of a head of state. And having Duchess Harrington in her corner isn't going to hurt any, either. But the Salamander isn't the kind of woman who goes around allowing favoritism to overrule her judgment. I *know* that much, even if I can't be positive about that—yet—where the Skipper and the Commodore are concerned."

"Maybe not," O'Reilly said stubbornly. "And I'll grant you Harrington's got a reputation for not playing the favorites game. But I still say Hearns wouldn't be where she is today if her last name had been Smith."

"Or O'Reilly, maybe?" Fonzarelli asked softly.

"Maybe." O'Reilly's glower was unyielding. "And I'm not going to be the only one who thinks that, either."

"Well, allow me to suggest that you'd better let those others be the ones to badmouth her." Fonzarelli looked her up and down and shook his head. "The last thing any ship needs is some officer undercutting some other officer's authority. I believe you'll find the Regs frown on that sort of behavior. And I also believe you'll probably find the XO's boot so far up your backside you'll be tasting leather for a week or so."

O'Reilly's eyes narrowed, and Fonzarelli shook his head again.

"I don't have any intention of going to Commander Tallman about this, Wanda. And from what I've seen of her, neither will Hearns when it finally comes to her ears. And that *will* happen if you keep this up, as you and I both know perfectly well. I mean, that's one reason you're sharing it with me instead of discussing it directly with her, isn't it? To be sure the campaign gets nicely underway?"

His lip curled slightly, and O'Reilly's jaw muscles tightened angrily. Not that Fonzarelli seemed to notice her reaction particularly—or care about it if he did—as he continued levelly.

"I'd say Hearns is the kind of person who fights her own battles, and I think she's not going to want to go running to Commander Tallman to make the big, bad Manty lieutenant be nice to her and stop saying all those nasty things. Not that I think you're going to like what happens to you when she decides to handle you all on her own. And however *she* feels about involving the XO won't make one damned bit of difference, as far as you're concerned, if he hears about it on his own. Trust me on that one. Or don't." The engineer shrugged as O'Reilly almost visibly hunkered down and dug in her heels. "It's no skin off my nose which way you go with this. But I think it's gonna be quite a bit of skin off of another part of *your* anatomy if you piss off the Skipper and the XO."

"So what do you think about Abigail now?" Naomi Kaplan asked cheerfully, sipping after-dinner coffee as Chief Steward Brinkman removed the dishes.

"I beg your pardon?" Lieutenant Commander Alvin Tallman said guilelessly, eyebrows raised in question, and Kaplan chuckled. There was still a slight stiffness to her movements, but Bassingford had done its usual bangup job of putting someone back together again. And there was something remarkably feline about the skipper, Tallman thought. And not just about the way she moved, despite any lingering discomfort, either. There was that same sort of almost affable deadliness waiting for anyone foolish enough to trespass into *her* territory and a purring edge of sensuality, as well, he thought, and decided—again—that it was a pity the Articles of War forbade any sort of romantic relationship between officers in the same chain of command.

*Or maybe it* isn't *such a pity,* he reflected. *She'd probably chew me up and spit me out . . . in the nicest, most enjoyable sort of way, of course. Somehow, I don't think I'd be able to keep up with her long enough for it to work out any other way. And God knows there's a damned good reason the Regs frown on anyone sleeping with his—or her—exec! Still . . .*

"Oh don't give me that innocent look," Kaplan said, shaking an index finger in his general direction. "You know exactly what I'm asking."

"Yes, Ma'am. I guess I do," he acknowledged, his expression sobering, and reached for his own coffee cup. He sipped for a moment, then lowered the cup and shrugged.

"I never had any doubts about her *capability*, Ma'am," he said. "Obviously, I don't know her as well as you do, but just looking through her personnel jacket, it was pretty clear she's not the kind of person who panics and runs around in circles when the shit hits the fan. And I have to agree with you, however junior she may be, she's got as much or more experience with the Mark 16 than any other officer around. But if I'm going to be honest, I did cherish a few doubts about her age. She's so damned young I expect to hear her uniform squeaking when she walks by. And, let's face it, 'good when the shit hits the fan' doesn't automatically equate to someone who's a good officer all around. I guess a part of me just questioned whether or not anyone her age could possibly have enough experience on the administrative and training side to run an entire tactical department."

"And does that question still bother you?" Kaplan asked.

"No, Ma'am. Not really." Tallman shook his head. "I'll admit, I've been keeping a closer eye on her administrative and personnel management skills than those of anyone else on board. So far, she hasn't dropped a single stitch anywhere on the paperwork side. And my spies tell me she already knows every member of her department by name, along with the world he comes from, his hometown, whether or not he's married—or romantically involved with anyone—and apparently even who his favorite sports teams are."

"So you'd give her passing marks on that side?"

"Without turning a hair," Tallman agreed.

"And when it does come to training and exercising her department?"

"To be honest, I'm more impressed with her there than I am with her ability to manage paperwork. Oh, don't give me wrong. We've got so many damned rough edges—not just in Tactical, but in *every* department!—that I don't even know where to start counting them. Putting together a ship's company this quickly isn't what the recruiter promised me when I let him talk me into going to Saganami Island lo those many eons ago, Ma'am! But overall, I think we've got a good bunch, and Abigail is really tearing into her own problem areas. And this idea of hers to stage a competition between the ships is going to do nothing but help out every other tac officer in the squadron, as well."

"So you don't have any serious qualms about her?"

"Ma'am, if I'd had *serious* qualms about her, you'd already have heard about them," he said levelly.

"Good."

Kaplan's relief was evident, and Tallman quirked one eyebrow.

"Having you in her corner takes a certain load off my mind," she explained. "Because the fact is that even though every single thing I told her about her qualifications for the job is absolutely true, it's also true that if I were inclined to play favorites, I'd be playing the game hard on her behalf. In a way, actually, I *am* playing that game, and I know it."

"Yes, you are," Tallman agreed. "On the other hand, you're not alone about doing that in her case. Let me see . . . there's Commodore Terekhov, Duchess Harrington, Admiral Cortez . . ."

"And don't forget High Admiral Matthews," Kaplan reminded him with a quirky smile. "While we're thinking about her patrons, I mean."

"Oh, believe me, I won't, Ma'am."

"Good. But," she leaned back in her chair, "correct me if I'm wrong, but do I detect the merest hint of resentment on the part of some of her fellow officers?"

"Not on any sort of general scale," Tallman told her. "There are some people who feel their noses have been put out of joint, but to be honest, none of them would have been in the running for the tactical officer's slot even if Abigail had never come along at all. I wouldn't worry about it too much, Ma'am. We've got some cooler heads out there helping to sit on the ones with the problem, and she's turning out to be pretty damned good at doing that sort of thing herself. I think it probably has to do with growing up as a steadholder's daughter. She had to learn the basic people-managing skills early on. And if all else fails, you can always reach for your patented five-dollar special executive officer hammer. Not that I think you're going to need it any time especially soon."

"We can hope, anyway," Kaplan said. Then she gave herself a little shake.

"Well, since you've put my mind to rest on that little problem, let's look at the next one on the list," she suggested. "I've been thinking over what Fonzarelli was saying about the forward impeller rooms, and I think he's got a point. Given how cramped the access way is thanks to the chase armament and the launchers, getting everyone to battle stations is going to be a lot bigger pain in the ass than BuShips allowed for. We need to be looking at some revised flow patterns there, I think, if we want to avoid a major bottleneck when we can least afford it. I've been pushing some numbers around on the ship's schematic, and I think if we move the route for Point Defense Two's and Four's crews up one deck, and the crews for PD One and Three *down* a deck, we ought—"

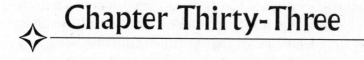

# Chapter Thirty-Three

ALBRECHT DETWEILER LOOKED OUT across the ranked seating of the palatial auditorium as he strode towards the lectern, and his expression was sober. The auditorium wasn't really all that large, despite its luxurious furnishings and absolutely state-of-the-art communications and briefing equipment. It was also buried under the next best thing to two hundred meters of solid earth and ceramacrete, making it impervious to any known snooping system, which was not a minor consideration on a day like this. And although its maximum seating capacity was under a thousand, there were no more than eight hundred people in its comfortable seats this afternoon. It was more than big enough for that, and he felt a sense of anticipation humming through his blood as he looked out at those eight hundred.

They represented the core leadership of the entire Mesan Alignment. A handful of people were missing, among them his sons Franklin and Gervais. He missed Franklin and Gervais more than most of the others, but their absence wasn't truly critical. Franklin was in charge of the Alignment's political penetration strategies, which meant most of his attention was focused on the Solarian League, and the Sollies were really at most a secondary concern today. Gervais, on the other hand, was effectively the Alignment's foreign secretary, the Alignment's primary contact with its out-system allies, which made his absence of greater significance than Franklin's this afternoon. Still, all of those allies already understood their parts in the overall plan, even if they didn't understand precisely how all of those parts fitted together or to what true end, and everyone had known for decades that when the time finally came to pull the trigger, there might well not be time to brief all of them first.

*Although I doubt any of them expected it to come at them with quite* this *little forewarning*, he thought wryly.

He watched the rustle of surprise running through the audience as he crossed the stage, for in a very real sense, today was the first time he'd ever really stepped out of the shadows. His own and his genotype's existence had been too important a secret for him to go gallavanting around openly, which, he had to admit, had always irked him more than a little. Oh, he'd been able to spend time in public, but always anonymously, without any activity or clue which might have led the Alignment's enemies to realize he existed, and even then only after the most stringent (if unobtrusive) security arrangements had been put into place ahead of time. That was why the majority of the people sitting out there had never actually met him . . . although he'd met several of them under the cover of carefully constructed false personae, especially when a firsthand evaluation had seemed necessary. Indeed, for many of these people, his very existence—and that of his sons—had been little more than a half-believed rumor until they received the emergency summons to this meeting, and even those among them who had received messages or com calls from him had never seen his natural face or heard his undisguised voice. But they recognized him now, and an electric shock seemed to fill the air as voices murmured in astonishment.

He stopped behind the lectern, looked out across their faces, and cleared his throat. The background hum of astonished speculation died almost instantly.

"I'm not going to bother with a lot of introductions this morning," he said, his amplified voice filling the auditorium while all of his sons who were physically present on Mesa filed onto the stage behind him. "The mere fact that I'm talking to all of you simultaneously—and directly—has no doubt already told you something important is going on, and it is. In fact, something *very* important is about to happen."

The silence intensified, and he gestured for Collin to join him at the lectern. Standing side-by-side, the physical resemblance between them was almost uncanny, despite the difference in their ages, and Albrecht took a half-step backwards, surrendering precedence to the younger man.

"Six days ago," Collin began without preamble, "the Republic of Haven attacked the Manticore home system."

A rustle of astonishment almost as great as that evoked by Albrecht's presence rushed around the auditorium, punctuated by more than a few exclamations of shock, and Albrecht smiled grimly. Their reaction didn't surprise him in the least, because no one had attacked the home star system of a major interstellar naval power literally in centuries, if ever.

"Havenite security was very tight, and we had absolutely no warning that this was in the works," Collin continued after a moment. "Thanks to the streak drive and the Beowulf conduit, we've been able to acquire at least preliminary estimates on the outcome of the attack, however. I'm not the best person to discuss the military implications of that outcome, so I'm going to ask Benjamin to address them. I'll be prepared to take any questions on the intelligence side after the main briefing when we break down into our initial task groups."

He stepped back from the lectern, and Benjamin Detweiler took his place.

"As Collin's just said, our estimates of exactly what happened are preliminary at this time. We don't have significant penetration of the Manticoran military, but the battle was fought inside the system hyper limit, for the most part, right under the Manticoran newsies' noses. Collin's estimate, with which I concur, is that the reports our agents in Manticore have been able to pick up from the media are essentially accurate, despite some possibility of exaggeration.

"Allowing for that exaggeration and rounding reported losses downward by twenty percent as a corrective, it would appear that the entire Manticoran Home Fleet has been destroyed."

A harsh sound, like a collective gasp, went through his audience. He seemed unaware of it as he continued speaking in the same, calm voice.

"Their Third Fleet would also appear to have been *effectively* destroyed. Preliminary estimates indicate that while a handful of its units may have survived, none of them are combat-capable at this time, and many of the survivors would appear to be damaged beyond a practical point of repair.

"On the Havenite side, our best estimate is that they committed between four hundred and five hundred ships of the wall to the attack. For all intents and purposes, that means they used at least ninety percent of their fully worked-up and trained wall of battle. According to the best information available to us, no more than twenty or thirty of their ships survived the engagement. The remainder were either destroyed outright or captured by the Manticorans."

There were no gasps this time. Genetically engineered for superiority or not, his audience was too stunned for that sort of expression.

"According to what our agents have been able to piece together, and what our analysts here at home have been able to do with their reports, it would appear the Havenites came within centimeters of succeeding in their objective. We're still trying to pull specific information on their tactics out of the reports we've received, but it looks like they used a two-pronged attack, bringing in a second force behind Third Fleet to ambush it when Admiral Kuzak came through from Trevor's Star in response to the initial attack. Unfortunately for the Havenites, it would appear that *Eighth Fleet* came through *after* Third Fleet, rather than in company with it, which allowed Harrington to ambush the ambushers, as it were. The result was to break the back of the Havenite attack, but every report available to us indicates that, for all intents and purposes, the Manticoran Navy's wall of battle has been pruned back to *only* Eighth Fleet and the odds and sods of wallers scattered around as pickets in places like the Lynx Terminus."

He paused and surveyed his audience levelly.

"What this means," he said flatly, "is that the combined walls of battle of Manticore and Haven have been effectively gutted. At this moment, the Manties' Eighth Fleet is probably the only organization on either side which actually deserves to be called a 'fleet' at all. I would be astonished to discover that they could have suffered fewer than a million and a half human casualties between them, which is bound to have its own impact in the not-too-distant future, but the critical point is that Haven no longer has an effective battle fleet at all, and that Eighth Fleet is going to be anchored to Manticore for the foreseeable future."

He stopped speaking and stepped back from the lectern, and Albrecht took his place there once more.

"Obviously," he said quietly, "there are still a great many things we don't know. But what we do know clearly indicates that, as Benjamin's just said, the combat power of both the Manticoran alliance and the Republic of Haven has been effectively—if temporarily—wiped out."

His smile would have done any Old Earth shark proud.

"In some ways, the timing on this is highly inconvenient for us. In others, it couldn't be better. And however we want to look at it, it represents an opportunity, an opening, and a warning we dare not ignore.

"What Harrington apparently managed to do to the Havenites is a warning that this new targeting system of theirs, whatever it is, is even more effective than we'd assumed from the original reports on it. I think we need to take it as a given that they'll be fitting the same technology into all of their new construction as it comes off the ways. That means Manticore is in a position to recover quickly from its losses, despite their severity, and that the Manticoran Navy will find itself in a totally dominating position once it does. According to all of our sources, Haven still has more ships under construction than Manticore does, but after the results of the Battle of Lovat and this new battle in Manticore, it's obvious that those ships are simply going to be targets for the Manties unless Haven somehow miraculously acquires the same technology for itself in the next few months. Which means Manticore is now in a position to score an outright military victory over the Republic of Haven—one so overwhelming they'll be able to dictate the terms of any peace they want to cram down Nouveau Paris' throat—within the next six to ten T-months. And if that happens, especially given their new targeting system and the fact that they'll be free to concentrate on something besides Haven, they will pose an extremely serious threat to our own strategy."

The auditorium was deathly silent when he paused. He let the silence linger for a moment, then continued.

"By the same token, however, neither Manticore nor Haven has been this vulnerable since their first war began. For all intents and purposes, Haven has no fleet, and Manticore's only existing fleet cannot uncover the Manticore System. That will change when—or *if*—the new wave of Manticoran construction starts coming out of their shipyards. All of our estimates are that that will begin happening quite soon, although it's highly probable that the need to incorporate this new technology into their new construction is going to push back their delivery dates somewhat. That gap between now and the delivery, manning, and training of their new wall of battle represents our window of opportunity.

"And, purely coincidentally, since none of us could possibly have seen this coming, our other operations have combined with this to present us with an opening, as well. Some of you are already aware of the operation we're currently pursuing in the Talbott Cluster. For those of you not yet aware of it, I'll simply say that we've set events in motion to bring about a direct, shooting confrontation between the Manties and more than seventy Solarian ships of the wall. I suspect that when the Manties realize what's coming at them in Talbott, it's going to rivet their attention fairly firmly in that direction.

"There are some downsides to that from our perspective. Prior to the Havenite attack on Manticore, we had every reason to project that the Manties would hammer the Sollies into drifting wreckage. That, of course, was what we wanted, given our own plans for the League. In light of the body blow the Manty Navy's just taken, they may not be able to hit the Sollies hard enough to fully accomplish our objectives for us in that respect. Our projections still indicate a significant chance that they would be able to, however, and even if that portion of our original plans achieves only partial success, it should still be adequate to set the stage for the next phase.

"Of course, the Manties are not alone at this time. In addition to the Royal Manticoran Navy itself, the Manticoran Alliance can count on the Grayson Navy and the Andermani. Indications are that the Andermani took significant damage themselves at Manticore, and previous reports have indicated that their general warfighting technology is still lagging behind the rest of the Alliance's. Moreover, the Andermani have always been . . . pragmatic. They signed on to the Alliance to fight *Haven*; none of our analysts believes they'd be willing to take on the *SLN*, especially if they'd be doing so effectively single-handedly. Which means that who we really have to worry about are the Manties and the Graysons. Given time, Haven would undoubtedly become a threat once more, as well, but once Manticore and Grayson go down, Haven won't *have* that time."

He smiled again, and this smile was even colder than the one before.

"A very few of you are aware that Benjamin has been working for quite some time now on an operation codenamed Oyster Bay. Those of you who know about it, also know we're still far short of all of our projected readiness dates for mounting it. However, Oyster Bay was originally intended to strike Manticore, Grayson, and all of the major Havenite building centers simultaneously. It would be impossible for us to launch an operation on that scale before the Manties' new construction comes out of the yards. But the fact that that new construction is still *in* the yards, concentrated in a limited volume of space where we can find it and get at it, and without the ability to defend itself, represents an enormous force multiplier for the Oyster Bay resources already available to us. In addition, we don't need to strike the Havenites at this moment. Their wall of battle has been effectively destroyed; their construction rates are still much slower than those of the Manties or the Graysons; and they don't have this new targeting system the Manties have deployed. In other words, we can deal with them later, using more conventional tactics if we have to.

"So, what it comes down to is this. The Manties' new technology is more dangerous than ever, but their combat strength has been cut back to no more than forty to sixty ships of the wall, and they have to be reeling strategically from the losses they've already taken. Despite their new tech, they're vulnerable in a way they've never been before. We have the means already in place in or approaching Talbott to cut off that entire lobe of this new 'Star Empire' of theirs, and get them into the shooting war with the League we've always wanted. And, after discussing our own readiness states with Benjamin and Daniel, I believe we're in a position to launch a modified, downscaled Oyster Bay, targeted on Manticore and Grayson only, within six T-months."

He paused once more, looking out across the motionless bodies filling the deathly still auditorium.

"I know that after so many centuries, recasting and reorganizing our plans on such short notice is enough to make anyone nervous. But let's face it, we've always known that when the time actually came, we were going to have to change planning and operational tempos. In many ways, I would prefer to continue with our original timetable. Unfortunately, the opposition hasn't chosen to cooperate with us in that respect. In my judgment, and especially in light of the outcome of the Battle of Manticore, the threat Manticore represents to our entire strategy has just increased exponentially. We cannot allow them to consolidate a clear-cut military victory over Haven, especially if they simultaneously manage to deploy four or five *hundred* podnoughts equipped with whatever it was they used to smash the attack on their home system. The odds of their having the strength to move directly against *us* under those circumstances if they realize what's really happening would be unacceptable, despite anything the Sollies might do.

"It's distinctly possible that our estimates of the completion times on their new construction are overly optimistic. In fact, we've been picking up some indications to that effect. Collin will be more than willing to discuss those indications with you shortly. At the moment, however, they are *only* indications, and, as I say, the need for the Manties to refit with their new targeting systems will probably slow them down.

"All of that is true, but even if we catch only half—or even less than that—of their new wallers still in the yards, it would be enormously advantageous for us. And, of course, that completely ignores the damage to their basic military building and support infrastructure. Not only that, but even if a sizable portion of their fleet escapes destruction in Oyster Bay, they'll still find themselves in an all-out war with the Solarian League. I know what we all hope will happen within the League as a consequence of that, but even if it does, it will take time for the realization to filter through such a huge dinosaur's nervous system.

"In other words," he said slowly and clearly, "for whatever combination of reasons, the moment is *now*. There are risks involved, but there have been risks involved at every step for the last six hundred T-years, and the nature of the opportunity and the scale of the threat if we do *not* act now, are overwhelming. Which is the reason I called all of you here today. Calling this many of us together in one place is always a security risk, but I think the time has come for us to realize that we have to step out of the shadows.

"I fully realize that many of you have ongoing projects of your own which are going to be thrown into significant disarray by stepping up the timetable on Oyster Bay. One of the things we'll be doing after this briefing is breaking up into task groups responsible for examining all of those operations and evaluating how Oyster Bay will affect them. In some cases, we'll need to accelerate your projects to coordinate with Oyster Bay. For example, I think we need to look very closely at expediting the neutralization and reconquest of Verdant Vista. We always intended to do that before kicking off the full-scale Oyster Bay, and even with the scaled-down version we're talking about now, having that extra avenue into the Manties' and Havenites' backyard would be extremely valuable.

"In other cases, some of you may find that accelerating Oyster Bay will prove fatal to your objectives. I recognize that, and I'm afraid it's simply going to have to be the price we pay. In other words, there will be no repercussions for anyone who does find his or her areas of responsibility severely damaged as a consequence.

"And whether that happens or not, my decision has been made. Although we still have to complete the detailed plans for a scaled-back Oyster Bay, our studies indicate that it will be completely feasible for us to do so. And on that basis, I have instructed Benjamin to plan for an execution date of a modified Oyster Bay strike no later than six T-months from today."

# Chapter Thirty-Four

"CONTACT!" ISAIAH PETTIGREW called out. "*Multiple* contacts, bearing zero-one-five, two-eight-eight, range three-point-eight-niner light-minutes, closing velocity six-zero-niner-one-six kilometers per second, accelerating at four-eight-seven-point-three gravities!"

"Acknowledged," Abigail Hearns said crisply. "Number of contacts?"

"Uncertain at this time, Ma'am," Pettigrew replied. His eyes never moved from his display's sidebars as he and *Tristram*'s Combat Information Center both worked the contacts, trying to pry more information out of them, and his voice was just as crisp, just as professional—and just as devoid of any excess "My Ladies"—as Abigail's.

"It looks like they just got close enough to the beta platforms for their impeller signatures to burn through stealth. Shall I go active on the platforms, Ma'am?"

Abigail considered for a moment, then nodded.

"Go active on the betas," she said, "but remain passive with the others."

"Aye, aye, Ma'am. Going active on the beta platforms only."

Pettigrew tapped in commands at his console, and the data codes on his display began to shift and change.

"CIC makes it three destroyer-range and three heavy cruiser or battlecruiser-range signatures," Pettigrew reported as the beta line of Ghost Rider reconnaissance platforms reported at FTL speeds. "Designate these targets Alpha One through Alpha Five."

"Understood." Abigail turned her head and looked at Lieutenant (JG) Gladys Molyneux. "Any IDs?"

"Negative, Ma'am," Molyneux replied. "CIC is still—Wait a minute." *Tristram*'s junior tactical officer peered at her own displays, then raised her head. "CIC has tentative class IDs on the heavies. Alpha One is a Solarian *Indefatigable*-class battlecruiser, and CIC's calling Alpha One and Alpha Two *Mikasa*-class heavy cruisers. No positive ID on the destroyer-range contacts at this time."

"Acknowledged."

Abigail gazed at her own display, thinking hard and fast. This particular simulation had been loaded to *Tristram*'s computers before the ship ever left Manticore. There were whole reams of similar sims tucked away in there, and she'd had no more idea than any of her subordinates had of what the computers were about to throw at them. They would hardly have constituted *learning* experiences if she'd known ahead of time what she was going to have to do in them, after all. Lieutenant Nicasio Xamar, *Tristram*'s assistant tactical officer, on the other hand, knew exactly what this particular simulation contained, since it had been his job to tweak the parameters just a little, just as Abigail did for *him* when it was his turn in the barrel. Fortunately, Xamar didn't seem to resent the fact that someone with over seven T-months less in grade than him had been assigned as his boss. On the other hand, he'd have been more than human if he hadn't taken advantage of the simulation to see what he could get past her.

*Okay*, she thought. *We've got these six coming at us from starboard and low, and they're headed almost directly for the convoy. That means they knew where we were long enough ago to build an intercept vector, and a pretty respectable one, too. So that means they've had us under observation, probably using their own remote platforms, for quite a while. Now, it's unlikely their passives are sensitive enough to track the Ghost Rider platforms, especially under these sensor conditions, but I don't know enough about Solly tech levels to be positive about that. They might have known exactly where we deployed our recon shells, and if they do, then that means they have to be pretty confident we'd manage to pick them up pretty soon now. Their stealth is pretty good for them to get this close without our seeing them, but even if we hadn't seen*

*them coming with the remotes, we'd start picking them up ourselves
on shipboard passives by the time they got down to a light-minute
and a half. So, assuming they have working brains over there, they'd
figure that we had to pick them up sometime in the next twelve
minutes or so . . . unless they dropped their acceleration a lot.*

She felt the pressure to start making decisions, but she resisted
it. Even at their present closing velocity and acceleration, it would
take eleven and a half minutes for anyone equipped with single-
drive missiles to get into their powered attack range, and they
weren't going to fire before that. Admittedly, they were going after
a convoy of merchantman, which meant any last-minute evasive
maneuvers by their targets were going to be sluggish, at best, but
even a merchie had a darned good chance of outmaneuvering
a missile which had gone ballistic. They couldn't get out of the
range basket of the attack bird's laser heads (unless the missile
in question had one almighty long ballistic component), but they
could maneuver to interpose their impeller wedges between those
laser heads and their own hulls, which would be just as good. So
there was still time for her to think things through.

*But not a lot of it,* she reminded herself grimly.

The problem was that she didn't know whether this particular
simulation had been set up with a smart and sneaky op force or
a sloppy one. With a sloppy one, the force Pettigrew and CIC had
picked up would be the only threat, and its commander could
probably be excused for thinking it was a pretty darned good one,
actually. A battlecruiser and two heavy cruisers packed a lot of
firepower, and the convoy's escort was only five destroyers. So a
head-on attack, disdaining subtlety in order to get into decisive
range as quickly as possible, would probably work. And if the bad
guys didn't know the defending destroyers were all *Rolands*, with
magazines full of Mark 16 dual-drive missiles, then they didn't
know *Tristram*'s powered missile envelope was three times their
own. Which, assuming the geometry remained unchanged, meant
*Tristram* and her consorts could open fire at over fifty-one million
kilometers. But if the bandits didn't realize that, then they were
probably anticipating a massive superiority in missile firepower
when they entered their own effective range.

*But missile superiority or not, they're still going to get hurt, at
least a little, and if they'd just reduced their impeller strength—or
even come in ballistic—they wouldn't have burned through their*

*stealth fields yet. They didn't* have *to let us know they were coming.
Not this soon, anyway. Not in h-space. So why . . . ?*

Her eyes narrowed suddenly as she realized that whoever had
designed this simulation—or tweaked it, she reminded herself,
thinking about Xamar—had assumed a very smart and sneaky
op force, indeed.

Detection ranges in hyper-space were far lower than in normal-
space, due to the higher particle density and general background
levels of radiation which obtained there. The attackers had caught
the convoy between gravity waves, where their impeller nodes were
configured to produce standard impeller wedges, rather than the
Warshawski sails necessary to navigate in the stressed and potentially
deadly volume of a grav wave. And where impeller-drive missiles
could be used. But that detection difficulty, coupled with the fact
that the attackers had obviously known where to wait for the convoy
and—especially—the intercept vector they'd managed to generate,
told her a lot. In particular, it told her they knew exactly where she
and every ship of her convoy was, and that there'd been absolutely
no need for them to come in this close under power at all.

The convoy consisted of merchantships with a maximum acceleration less than half that of the attackers. There was no way a
fat, wallowing herd of merchies could possibly evade them at this
point. So they could have killed their drives long ago and come
in ballistic without the betraying grav signature of their impeller wedges. Which, under these conditions, would probably have
allowed them to get all the way into their own powered missile
range before they were ever seen. For that matter, against someone
without the Ghost Rider platforms—*and without the platforms
deployed even in hyper,* she allowed herself to reflect with a certain complacency—they could very well have gotten into *energy*
range before anyone saw them coming.

So why hadn't they'd done that?

*Because they want me concentrating on* these *people,* she thought.
*They showed themselves to me on purpose, when they didn't have to.
Which means that sometime in the next five or six minutes . . .*

"Priority active and passive sensor sweep," she said sharply. "I
want *Galahad*'s and *Lancelot*'s alpha and beta platforms sweeping
astern. Have *Roland* sweep directly ahead of the convoy. *Ivanhoe*
is to continue to hold the known contacts on her platforms. And
I want *ours* to sweep *this* volume, right here."

She dropped a cursor into the master plot, using it to sketch an arc directly on the opposite side of the convoy from the known contacts.

Acknowledgments came back quickly. There were still rough spots in *Tristram*'s tactical crews, and they'd only come in second in the squadron's "top gun" competition. It had been a very *close* second, however, and they'd actually been edged out of first primarily because HMS *Gawain* had managed (somehow) to squirm around and block what *should* have been the fatal shot from *Tristram*'s broadside lasers with her wedge. That particular turn of events had scarcely been the tactical department's fault, and everyone in it knew that. In fact, in some ways, Abigail's people seemed to take a sort of perverse pride in being robbed of what they considered to have been their rightful victory by the intervention of the Demon Murphy. And the exercise had pulled them together as a group. They'd really buckled down since, and their rough spots were nowhere near as rough as they had been.

"New contacts!" Pettigrew announced suddenly. "I have *three* battlecruiser-range contacts on the alpha platform shell! Bearing one-niner-six, two-five-three, range one-point-eight-two light-minutes, closing velocity five-niner-three-three-zero kilometers per second. CIC designates them Beta One through Beta Three. No, I repeat, no impeller signatures!"

*My, aren't we clever?* Abigail thought, so intent on watching the three new scarlet icons blink into existence on the plot that she didn't even notice the looks she got from one or two of the simulator's occupants as they spotted the enemy exactly where Lieutenant Hearns had obviously *expected* to spot him. *The five we already knew about to keep us looking in that direction while these three come whooping in on almost an exactly reverse heading to pincer us. If we see the first five and turn away from them, we run directly into the others. And if we* don't *see them, if we concentrate on the ones we know about, then these people sneak in close and put daggers in our backs just about the time their buddies are starting to get into range.*

"Designate the new contacts the Beta group," she heard her own voice saying. "Prepare to flush the pods. Attack pattern Papa-Three and set for forty-six thousand gravities. We'll put all of them on the Beta targets and take the Alphas with internal tubes!"

"Aye, aye, Ma'am! Setting pods for Papa-Three on the Beta targets; drive setting four-six thousand gravities."

Abigail itched to enter the firing commands herself. If this had been a real combat situation, rather than a simulation, that was exactly what she would have been doing. But it *was* a simulation, and its purpose was not to have her doing things she knew perfectly well she could handle at need. It was to train the *rest* of her team to do those things . . . and her to *rely* upon them to do it.

"Beta targets designated and locked in, Ma'am," Lieutenant Molyneux reported barely twenty seconds later. "Missile drives set for four-six-thousand gravities acceleration."

"All units report pod separation and on-board fusion initiation," MT 1/c Kaneshiro announced at almost the same instant.

"Target acquisition!" Molyneux reported as the computers aboard the "flat pack" missile pods which had just fallen away from the destroyers' hulls and cleared their impeller wedges, turned on their on-board thrusters to align themselves with their designated targets.

"Launch!"

"Launching, aye!"

None of the destroyers had been carrying the maximum possible external load of pods. They couldn't without beginning to block shipboard sensor arcs or the firing arcs of their defensive laser clusters. But each of the five of them had carried fifteen of the pods, limpeted to their motherships' hulls with their internal tractors, and each of those pods contained ten Mark 23 MDMs.

Seven hundred and fifty capital missiles went shrieking away from the convoy, straight into the teeth of only three targets. Three targets which had continued closing at the next best thing to sixty thousand kilometers per second for just under thirty-two seconds since they'd been detected . . . and whose impeller wedges were still just starting to come up when the missiles launched. It took those missiles two hundred and sixty-one seconds to reach their destinations, and two hundred and fifty of them went slashing in on each of the battlecruisers.

The Solarian ships had clearly been prepared for the possibility that they might be detected on the way in. Their missile defense crews had obviously been waiting at maximum readiness, because their counter-missiles began launching almost instantly, and they were firing a lot of them. But Abigail had anticipated that anyone smart enough to set up something like this and actually pull it off wouldn't exactly be just sitting there with her hands in her lap. That was why she'd committed all of her pods to this attack. It was almost certainly going to be a case of overkill, but she wanted nothing threatening her back while she dealt with the more numerous but individually weaker Alpha bandits, and that meant putting the Beta targets out of action as quickly—and thoroughly—as possible.

The other side's counter-missiles were actually more effective than she'd expected, and she wondered if BuWeaps had updated their projected effectiveness on the basis of the captured Solly hardware the Navy had been able to examine after the Battle of Monica. They were certainly more effective than the Monicans' counter-missile fire had been then! On the other hand, those were supposed to be Solarian crews behind those launchers this time around, too, which could also explain why BuWeaps might have increased their kill probabilities.

She watched narrowly as the counter-missiles picked off almost three hundred of the attack birds. Manticoran defenses would have done considerably better than that, but, then, Manticoran defenses had been designed to survive against the volume of fire produced by pod-launched missiles, and the Sollies' defenses . . . hadn't been.

Despite everything the Solarian counter-missiles could do, four hundred and fifty-plus Manticoran missiles got through to the inner defensive zone, and laser clusters fired desperately. But those missiles were coming in at an effective velocity of sixty percent of light-speed. That didn't give very much engagement time, and to make matters far worse, the attack missiles had been liberally seeded with electronic warfare missiles specifically programmed to penetrate the inner boundary defenses. Dazzlers flared, beating holes in the Solarians' defensive coverage with massive spikes of interference, and in the same instant, the Dragon's Teeth platforms spun up, generating hundreds of false images to confuse any of the sensors which somehow managed to see past the Dazzlers.

Abigail couldn't tell exactly how many of her attack birds actually survived long enough to detonate, but it was obviously enough.

Beta One simply disappeared. Beta Two staggered, the impeller wedge which had just come up and stabilized fluctuating madly as x-ray lasers slammed into—and through—her sidewalls and armor. Then her forward impeller room went down completely, and she turned away, leaking atmosphere and water vapor in clear proof of massive penetrations of her core hull. Her active sensor emissions vanished almost completely in equally clear proof that her missile defenses and fire control had been hammered into wreckage.

Beta Three didn't seem to have been hammered quite as badly as Beta Two. Not at first. But then, ten seconds after Beta One, she suddenly broke in half. There was no stupendous explosion, no sudden, insane spike in her impeller wedge to explain it. She simply . . . broke up.

It was only a simulation, but even so, Abigail felt an icy chill blowing up and down her spine as she tried to picture the structural failure which could have produced that result. But then she shook herself. The Alpha bandits were still out there. They probably had no idea—yet—what had happened to the Beta bandits, given their limitation to light-speed transmissions from any recon platforms they might have deployed. But they were going to find out shortly.

Five minutes had elapsed since she gave the order to fire. Only five minutes, in which two battlecruisers had been totally destroyed and a third had been hulked. And during which the range to the Alpha bandits had fallen to 51,474,268 kilometers . . . which just happened to be 21,000 kilometers *inside* the range of a Mark 16 dual-drive missile against a target closing at 61,000 km per second. It would take the bandits another nine minutes to reach their own range of the convoy, however, and the Mark 16's new Mod G laser heads were going to make that just a bit *difficult* for them, she thought with a sharklike smile.

"Fire Plan Tango-Seven," she said.

"So, how do you *really* like her, Naomi?"

Aivars Terekhov grinned mischievously as Commander Naomi Kaplan gave him a very sharp glance, indeed. Her own *Tristram*, as well as Terekhov's heavy cruiser flagship and their various squadron mates were boring steadily through hyper-space under impeller drive, between gravity waves, and Terekhov had invited her aboard *Quentin Saint-James* for a private dinner. Joanna Agnelli had done her customary superb job with the meal, and the after-dinner wine was a vintage port from the O'Daley Vineyards, a Gryphon winery which had been established by Sinead O'Daley Terekhov's many-times-great-grandfather better than three hundred T-years ago. Kaplan didn't really understand why it had to be properly defined as a *Gryphon* vintage *porto*, but she suspected it had something to do with the ferocity with which wine-sticklers guarded the classifications of their favorite beverage. In this case, however, she had to admit that its rich, fruity flavor (whatever it was properly called) was a wonderful choice to accompany the wedges of cheese Agnelli had left on the table between her and Terekhov.

The dinner had been the first opportunity the two of them had had for any sort of relaxed, face-to-face meeting since Terekhov's return to Manticore and immediate departure back to the Talbott Quadrant. At the moment, despite his status as a relatively junior commodore, Terekhov found himself the senior officer commanding no less than sixteen ships—the eight cruisers of his own squadron and the eight destroyers of Commodore Chatterjee's squadron. Since not a single one of those vessels was more than four T-months old, and every single one of them mounted the Mark 16 dual-drive missile, it could probably be said with a fair degree of accuracy that it represented *the* plum command of any commodore in the Royal Manticoran Navy.

Which, Kaplan reflected, said quite a bit about how the Royal Navy regarded one Aivars Terekhov.

She also remembered the reserved, withdrawn captain who had joined HMS *Hexapuma's* company on effectively zero notice. There was still a lot of that captain in the commodore sitting across his dining cabin table from her, but now the humor and the warmth behind those arctic blue eyes found it far more difficult to hide from her. And this, she reminded herself, was a purely social occasion. He'd invited her to dinner as her ex-CO, not as her current squadron commander, and that gave a certain flexibility to the things she could discuss with him.

"Should I assume, Sir," she responded to his question primly, "that the 'her' in question refers to *Tristram*?"

"Yes, you should," Terekhov agreed. "I mean, I know any destroyer has to be seen as something of a step down from a heavy cruiser. And I certainly wouldn't care to suggest that a modicum of disappointment on receiving such a lowly command might not be understandable. Still, as destroyers go, she doesn't seem *that* bad. Of course, I understand from Commodore Chatterjee that she only came in *second* in the tactical competition. But I'm sure that if an officer of your caliber really buckles down and applies herself, most of those nagging little problems will speedily disappear."

He regarded her so earnestly across the table that she felt a very strong temptation, despite the difference in their ranks, to kick him smartly in the kneecap. Instead, she leaned back in her own chair, nursing her wineglass, and pursed her lips thoughtfully.

"I'm deeply touched by your concern for me, Sir," she told him. "And, I suppose I ought to admit, it was something of a wrench to leave the *Kitty*—although, to be honest, I don't actually remember *doing* that. Something to do with being unconscious at the time, I imagine. Still, when they offered me *Tristram*, I recognized the sort of challenge where my experience in rectifying more senior officers' errors could stand me in good stead. I feel we've made considerable progress, although we clearly still have some way to go to achieve the level of proficiency I'd truly like. Still, I'm confident we'll get there in the end. After all, I know exactly what *not* to do when bringing along a new ship's company."

She smiled sweetly at him, and he laughed.

"*Touché!*" He raised his own glass in salute and took a sip. Then his expression sobered a bit as he lowered the glass again.

"Seriously," he said, "is she as much fun as you expected her to be?"

"In some ways, yes," she replied, equally seriously. "In other ways, all joking aside, it's been even harder than I expected to knock off all the rough edges. I knew we were sailing with a green ship's company, but I don't think I'd let myself freely admit just *how* green some of them really were. And even though she doesn't have that big a crew, she's one *hell* of a first hyper-capable command, Sir!" She shook her head. "I hope I don't screw it up."

"If anybody at Admiralty House thought that was likely to happen, you wouldn't have her," Terekhov pointed out. "And as someone who's had the opportunity to watch you in action, *I* don't think it's likely to happen, either. Nobody can ever know what kind of circumstances may come along and bite someone on the ass—what happened to us on our last deployment is proof enough of that! But barring some sort of major disaster of someone else's making, I don't expect you to put any blots in your copy book, Commander."

"Thank you," she said quietly.

"No need to thank me for telling the truth," he said wryly. "And if you want to talk about the possibility of screwing up, don't forget who they decided to give a brand-new squadron to, either!" It was his turn to shake his head. "It's one thing to hijack a squadron nobody decided to give you in the first place. I've discovered that it's quite another to worry about disappointing people who *wanted* you to have it. And I suppose, if I'm going to be honest, that one reason I was teasing you about *Tristram* is how much I've discovered I miss the white beret."

"I can see how that would be." Kaplan's tone was thoughtful. "I've only had her for a few weeks, and I'm already beginning to suspect how much it's going to hurt when I have to hand her over to someone else. There's never another first starship, is there?"

"No," Terekhov agreed. "Unfortunately, Naomi, someday there *will* be a last starship. Enjoy her while you've got her."

"Oh, I intend to!" Kaplan replied with a fresh sparkle of humor. "And even though we've got a couple of potholes here and there, I think Alvin Tallman and I are on top of them. Not only that, but it's been amusing as hell watching Abigail deal with one of those potholes."

"Abigail?" Terekhov cocked one eyebrow, and Kaplan chuckled.

"It would appear Abigail's concern that some officers might feel she'd received an undeserved assignment wasn't totally without foundation. Lieutenant O'Reilly, my com officer, seems to have resented Abigail's elevation to *Tristram*'s tactical officer."

"Really?" Terekhov leaned back and crossed his legs.

"Really. O'Reilly was careful to keep it from coming to my ears, of course, but I've discovered that you were right when you told me how useful a captain's steward was for tapping into the grapevine. Of course, Clorinda hasn't been with me as long as Chief Agnelli's been with you, but it's remarkable how little goes on aboard ship that fails to come to her ears. And, of course, from her ears to my ears. So I knew when O'Reilly began voicing her opinion that Abigail might be less than totally qualified for her new position."

"From that gleam in your eye, I assume neither you nor Commander Tallman found it necessary to take a hand?"

"You assume correctly. As a matter of fact, it was pretty informative to see which of the other members of the wardroom stepped on her. My engineer was surprisingly effective, as a matter of fact. But what really did the trick was Abigail herself. Well, her and her people in Tactical."

"How?"

"She did it by being Abigail," Kaplan said simply. "Our last set of simulations, Tactical scored four hundred and ninety-eight out of a possible five hundred. That was the highest score in the entire ship, although she only beat out Engineering by two points. *Communications*, on the other hand, came in at barely three ninety-seven. I believe Alvin called Lieutenant O'Reilly in for a private conference in which he pointed out to her that her performance had been the weakest of any department and that it might behoove her to spend a bit more time drilling her personnel. And if she wanted any advice on how to do that, there were several of her fellow lieutenants who—judging by their own departments' performance—might be able to help her out. Like, oh, Lieutenant Hearns, let's say."

"Well, I bet *that* endeared Abigail to this O'Reilly," Terekhov observed dryly.

"Frankly, I don't think anything could 'endear' Abigail to O'Reilly," Kaplan said tartly. She looked at Terekhov steadily, and he knew she would never have voiced such a personal criticism of one of her officers to anyone else. But he wasn't "anyone else," and she continued. "She reminds me a lot of Freda MacIntyre, actually."

Terekhov managed not to grimace, but Kaplan's choice of examples conjured up a very precise image in his mind, given the rather scathing efficiency report he'd endorsed, on young Lieutenant (Junior Grade) MacIntyre of HMS *Hexapuma*'s Engineering Department. The actual report had been written by Ginger Lewis, who hadn't pulled any punches in her assessment of MacIntyre's capabilities, and he rather doubted it had done MacIntyre's career one bit of good, even in the manpower-starved RMN.

*Which is too damned bad . . . and still better than someone who treats her people like dirt deserves*, he thought grimly.

But choosing MacIntyre as her example had done more than give him a feel for O'Reilly's personality without ever meeting her. It also explained why Kaplan was almost certainly right about the inevitable antipathy between her and Abigail Hearns. Abigail was constitutionally incapable of giving less than a hundred and ten percent effort, and the officers Terekhov privately thought of as "sixty percenters" could never forgive people like her for the commitment they brought to any task.

*And every single one of them thinks the people they resent are getting unfair preference,* he reflected. *I suppose that's human nature. No one wants to admit he's being "overlooked" because he's an incompetent, lazy-assed timeserver. And now that I think about it, I'd really hate to be an officer like that aboard Naomi Kaplan's ship!*

That last thought gave him a certain glow of pleasure, and he shook his head mentally.

*Damn it, I am playing favorites,* he admitted cheerfully to himself. *Of course, unlike some people I've known, I try to make sure that the favorites I play deserve it. And, by God, if anyone deserves it, Abigail does! If she just manages to avoid getting herself killed in the next few years, that young lady's going to be one of the admirals who go into the history books. And when that happens, I'll be able to kick back, sniff my brandy, and say "Why, I knew her when she was only a JG, and let me tell you . . . !"*

That thought gave him even more pleasure, and he reached for his wine glass once more.

"Well, Captain Kaplan," he said, "I'm sure you have the situation well in hand."

"I feel pretty sure the commodore's offering something better than this to Commander Kaplan," Helen Zilwicki said wryly as she handed Abigail Hearns a chilled bottle of beer.

"More expensive, anyway," Abigail agreed. She took the beer, ignored the stein sitting on the table between them, and drank directly from the bottle.

"Oh, if your family could only see you now!" Helen shook her head, grinning hugely.

"My family might surprise you," Abigail replied, lowering the bottle with a satisfied sigh. "Formal occasions are one thing, but Daddy's always preferred beer to wine. In fact, I sometimes think it was Lady Harrington's introduction of Old Tilman to Grayson that *really* got him on the side of the reformers."

"Really?" Helen laughed. "Somehow that doesn't quite fit the image most Manticorans have about steadholders."

"I know." Abigail grimaced. "It's amazing to me how many people think all Graysons have to be dour, repressed, and just plain gloomy all the time." She snorted. "I guess I'd have to go along with 'repressed' in at least some ways, I suppose. But the rest of it—!"

"I think part of it is the way your armsmen spend so much time guarding your image, not just your skins," Helen suggested.

"You're probably right."

Abigail tipped back the chair in Helen's tiny cabin. It was so small that her senior mother Helen would have described it as having "too little room to swing a cat," but given the fact that it belonged to a mere ensign, it was downright palatial for any warship.

"You're probably right," she said again, thinking about her own personal armsman, Matteo Gutierrez. Gutierrez wasn't even a Grayson by birth, yet he'd somehow soaked up through his pores that guard dog protectiveness that seemed to infuse all personal armsmen. Fortunately, his background as a Royal Manticoran Marine also gave him a reasonable perspective on just how much "protecting" a mere lieutenant serving aboard one of Her Majesty's starships could survive. Which, now that she thought about it, a Grayson-born armsman might very well have lacked.

*You know, maybe Daddy put even more thought into picking Matteo as my keeper then I realized*, she reflected.

"I'm glad you were able to tag along with the commander," Helen said now, and Abigail's mental antenna pricked. There was something about Helen's voice, an almost hesitant note Abigail was unaccustomed to hearing from brash Ensign Zilwicki.

"Well, I didn't have the duty tonight," she pointed out. "I don't know whether I could have gotten pinnace time on my own, but since the skipper was headed over this way anyhow . . ."

She shrugged, and Helen nodded.

"That's kind of how I figured it would work when I invited you," she acknowledged, tipping back her own chair and propping her heels on her neatly made bunk.

"Why *did* you invite me?" Asked the wrong way, that question could have carried all sorts of sharp edges. The way Abigail actually did ask it, it came out oddly . . . sympathetic.

"I guess I'm just feeling a little . . . lonely," Helen said, looking away for a moment. Then she looked back at Abigail. "Don't get me wrong. Most of *Jimmy Boy*'s officers are just fine, and nobody seems to *resent* the fact that I'm only a lowly little ensign. But it's kind of hard, Abigail. I'm not really all that senior to Captain Carlson's snotties, but the commodore's flag lieutenant can hardly hobnob with them. In fact, there's not a single soul in this entire ship who's not astronomically senior to me that I could actually sit down and discuss what I do for the commodore with. I hadn't thought about that part of it."

"I hadn't thought about it either," Abigail said after a moment. She considered adding that it would never have occurred to her that it would have presented a problem to such a hardy and resilient soul as Helen Zilwicki. Which said more about her own lack of imagination than it did about any lack of confidence on Helen's part, she decided.

"It doesn't make any static where the job itself is concerned," Helen said quickly. "Nobody seems to resent the fact that I'm so junior. To be honest, that was what I was most afraid of, but they're a pretty good bunch. No, scratch that. They're a *damned* good bunch, and most all of them are ready to take time 'mentoring' the new kid. I think I'm actually getting the hang of things pretty well, too. It's just that, well, once we're off duty, they're all so damned *senior* to me again."

"I see." Abigail considered her for several seconds in silence, then smiled. "Tell me, Helen, how much of your 'loneliness' has to do with missing your fellow snotties from the *Kitty*?"

Helen twitched, and Abigail's smile grew broader at the confirmation that she'd scored a direct hit.

"I don't know what you're—" Helen began quickly, then stopped and actually blushed.

"I, uh, didn't think you knew about that," she said finally, and this time Abigail laughed out loud.

"Helen, there may have been some rating stuck down in Engineering somewhere—one of the ones that never gets out of the fusion room—who didn't figure it out. I don't think there could have been anyone else."

"Oh, damn," Helen muttered. Then she grinned just a bit sheepishly. "Actually, you know, there *was* at least one person on board who didn't figure it out."

"Paulo?" Abigail asked, her tone much more sympathetic, and Helen nodded.

"Yeah," she sighed. "He's too damned pretty—and too damned well aware of how he got that way. It's like . . . it's like trying to get too close to an Old Earth porcupine! I think he was finally starting to get the picture before I went haring back off to Talbott, but, Lord, the size of the clue stick it took!"

She shook her head, and Abigail used a quick swallow of beer to drown another laugh at birth. Helen obviously wasn't accustomed to having to work *that* hard to attract the attention of the male of the species, she thought.

"I don't think anyone could reasonably blame him for being a little gun shy," she pointed out once she was confident she had control of her voice again. "I mean, I'd probably feel a lot the same way if a bunch of genetic slavers had specifically designed me as—what? A 'pleasure slave'?"

"'Sex toy,' is the way he puts it." This time Helen's voice was harsh and hard with anger. "You know, I already hated those bastards—even before they tried to kill Berry. Hell, even before they tried to kill *me* back on Old Earth! But I never really understood what hate was before I realized not just what they've done to Paulo, but what they must have done to all the other 'pleasure slaves' they've sold like so much meat over the centuries. I mean, I *knew* what they were doing—even knew other people they'd done it *to*—but this time . . . well, I guess this time is different. It's finally *real*. And the truth is, I'm a little ashamed of that."

"Why?" Abigail asked softly.

"Because it shouldn't matter that they did it to *me*, to someone *I* care about. It should matter that they did it to *anyone*, anywhere, ever. It shouldn't have taken Paulo to make it real to me, not just some kind of intellectual awareness."

"Don't be too hard on yourself," Abigail said, and Helen looked at her quickly. "And don't be so sure you were really that blind to it before you met Paulo. Frankly, I don't think you were. I think your anger is different now, sure, but that's *natural*, Helen. It's not so much anger at what they did, but that they did it to someone *you* love. That doesn't make your anger 'real' in some way it wasn't before it—it only makes it *personal*."

Helen continued to look at her for several heartbeats, and then the younger woman's shoulders relaxed suddenly, and she drew a deep breath.

"Maybe that's what I've been trying to fumble my own way into figuring out," she said. "Thanks. I think, anyway. I wouldn't want you to be giving me a free pass when I don't really have one coming. Not that I think you are—or at least, probably not."

Abigail chuckled, but she only shook her head when Helen raised an eyebrow at her. Somehow, she didn't feel like explaining just how un-Helenish those last few sentences sounded. On the other hand, if there'd been any question in her own mind about the depths of Helen's feelings for Paulo d'Arezzo, the disappearance of the Zilwicki certainty would have laid it to rest.

"See, that's one of the things I can't discuss with anyone over here," Helen continued after a moment, clearly having decided not to ask Abigail what was so humorous. "Matter of fact," she added thoughtfully, "I don't know who I could have discussed *that* one with even aboard the *Kitty*!"

"Well, that's not because of anything to do with seniority," Abigail told her. "It has to do with *friendship*, Helen, and I don't suppose you've had the time to make a lot of new friends aboard the flagship anymore than I have aboard *Tristram*."

"Yeah, I guess it does," Helen said slowly. She took another swallow from her own beer bottle.

"It's okay," Abigail reassured her with a faint smile. "I'm not your training officer anymore, and you're not one of my snotties. For that matter, we're not even in the same chain of command, these days. So, despite my own lordly seniority, if I want to have a mere ensign for a friend, it's not against regs."

"Yeah, sure!" Helen laughed, but her eyes were curiously soft for a few moments. Then she shook herself.

"Well, as one friend to another," she continued, "what do I do about Paulo?"

"What? About catching him?"

"*Catching* him!" Helen shook her head. "I can't *believe* you said something like that!" she protested. "I'm shocked—*shocked*, I tell you!"

"Hey," Abigail shot back with a much broader smile, "*you* try living on a planet where women outnumber men three-to-one! Trust me, you Manties—both sexes of you—have it pretty darn good when it comes to stumbling into a relationship with Mr. or Ms. Right! Where *I* come from, women have to *work* at it . . . and the competition gets pretty darned cutthroat, too!"

Helen shook her head again, laughing, and Abigail glowered at her.

"See?" she growled. "There you go again. Another Manty thinking all Graysons are repressed. Probably that we're all *frigid*, for that matter!"

"I do not!" Helen protested.

"*Sure* you don't." Abigail rolled her eyes. "If you could've heard all the crap I had to put up with at the Academy—or in *Gauntlet*, for that matter—out of some of you 'enlightened' Manties...! Sometimes I couldn't decide who was worse. The guys who thought I must be starved for sex because there were so few men on my planet, or the women who were busy just oozing sympathy for the poor, repressed little foreign girl."

"Come on—we're not *all* that bad!"

"Actually, all of you aren't," Abigail admitted, satisfied that she'd loosened up any remaining reticence Helen might have harbored. "In fact, for a Manty, you're a fairly enlightened sort yourself, Ms. Zilwicki."

"Gee, thanks."

"You're welcome. And now, for that little question you raised a few minutes back. The one about catching Paulo."

"That's not exactly the way I phrased it," Helen replied with a certain dignity.

"No, but it's what you *meant*," Abigail said blithely. "And now that we have that out of the way, tell me what you've already tried." She smiled evilly. "I'm sure that between the two of us we can come up with... additional approaches, shall we say?"

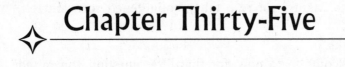

# Chapter Thirty-Five

HELEN ZILWICKI LOOKED OUT the pinnace viewport as the sleek, variable geometry craft settled gracefully onto the Thimble Spaceport landing pad. She still thought Thimble was a pretty silly name for a planet's capital city, although she had to admit that it at least offered more originality than "Landing," which was undoubtedly the most common name for capital cities in the entire galaxy.

*Well, maybe except for the ones that're named* First *Landing, anyway,* she amended with a silent chuckle. And whatever the citizens of the Spindle System might have chosen to name their capital, she was actually a bit surprised by how glad she was to be back here again.

It didn't hurt that Commodore Terekhov's little task group had made a huge amount of progress during the voyage to Spindle from the Lynx Terminus. Its various ships weren't anywhere near as well drilled and trained as *Hexapuma* had been when they went to Monica, but it would have been grossly unfair to compare them to the level of proficiency *Hexapuma*'s company had attained by that time. For a bunch of ships which had been more or less thrown together and sent off, mostly straight from their (highly abbreviated) builders' trials, less than three T-weeks before, they were actually *damned* good.

*Sure they are,* part of her brain thought mockingly. *And you, of course, are such a seasoned old vacuum-sucker that your highly experienced judgment of just how good they are is undoubtedly infallible, isn't it?*

*Shut up*, the rest of her brain commanded.

The pinnace touched down perfectly, and Helen stood, trying not to think about all the times Ragnhild Pavletic had piloted Captain Terekhov to one meeting or another. She gathered up Terekhov's briefcase and her own minicomp, then turned and led the way off the pinnace in obedience to the ironbound Manticoran tradition that required passengers to disembark in reverse order of seniority.

Vice Admiral Khumalo, Bernardus Van Dort, Captain Shoupe, Commander Chandler, and a small, dark-haired commodore almost as sturdily built as Helen herself, were waiting as she followed Commodore Terekhov, Commodore Chatterjee, Captain Carlson, and Commander Pope into the office. All of them rose in greeting, and Helen felt a flare of amusement as she saw the small, female commodore gazing up at her counterpart's towering centimeters. She was considerably shorter than Helen, while Chatterjee was one of the very few people Helen had ever met who could actually make Duchess Harrington look petite, which probably explained his nickname of "Bear." Despite her amusement, though, she was far more aware of her deep surge of pleasure as she saw Van Dort again. The special minister without portfolio smiled with obvious pleasure of his own and nodded to her as she trailed along in all the monumentally more senior officers' wake.

"Aivars! Welcome back." Khumalo reached across his desk, shaking Terekhov's hand with obvious pleasure and genuine warmth. Which, Helen reflected, was a noticeable—and welcome—change from the then-rear admiral's stiff-legged wariness when Aivars Terekhov had first arrived in the Talbott Cluster.

"I believe you know all of us," Khumalo continued, waving at the welcoming committee, "except, perhaps, for Commodore Onasis." He indicated the smallish woman Helen had noted, and Onasis stepped forward to offer her own hand in turn.

"Commodore Onasis," Terekhov murmured in greeting, then nodded to his own officers. "Commodore Chatterjee, commanding DesRon 301," he said, introducing Chatterjee first. "And this is Captain Carlson, my flag captain in *Quentin Saint-James*, and

Commander Pope, my chief of staff. And this, of course," he smiled very slightly, "is Ensign Zilwicki, my flag lieutenant."

More handshakes were exchanged, along with murmurs of greeting (although no one offered to shake her own lowly hand, Helen noticed with another flicker of amusement), and then all of them scattered, like uniformed birds accompanied by a single civilian-garbed crow, into the office's comfortable chairs. Helen waited until all those vastly senior officers had been seated, then found herself a perch to one side, pulled out her minicomp, and configured it to record mode.

"It really is good to see you back, Aivars," Khumalo said. "And to see more ships arriving with you."

"I'm glad you think so, Sir. And, frankly, I'm glad to be back, even though I could wish I'd had at least a day or so on Manticore, first. I'm sure I speak for Bear, as well," Terekhov said, nodding at Chatterjee. "On the other hand, I wouldn't want you to think we're fully up to snuff yet. For one thing, I still have to steal a few staff officers from you. And, for another, we've only really had the opportunity to start drilling as cohesive squadrons for the last two or three weeks. Our people are willing as hell, and I think they're individually about as good as it gets, but we're a long way from really shaking down the way we ought to have before we were ever deployed."

"There's been a lot of that going around lately," Shulamit Onasis observed with a tart smile.

"That's one way to put it," Khumalo agreed feelingly. "On the other hand, between you and Vice Admiral Gold Peak, we've already got a good twenty or thirty times as much combat power as we had in the Quadrant before Monica. I'm looking forward to still *more*, you understand, but adding eight more *Saganami-Cs* to the mix—not to mention Commodore Chatterjee's *Rolands*—is going to help me sleep a lot more soundly at night."

"All of us, I think," Onasis said, nodding firmly. Then she cocked her head at Frederick Carlson. "One thing I wanted to ask you, Captain Carlson. I thought there was already a *Quentin Saint-James* in the ship list?"

"There was," Carlson said. "In fact, she was one of the early *Saganami-As*. She was transferred to the Zanzibar Navy, though, as part of the program to try and rebuild their fleet after Tourville trashed it. Since *Quentin Saint-James* is on the List of Honor,

Zanzibar renamed her to release the name for my ship." He shook his head. "I'm flattered, of course, but it does give all of us a bit to live up to."

"Ah." Onasis nodded. "I *thought* I was remembering correctly. Still, with all the ships coming out of the yards, I don't suppose it's any wonder that some of the names are getting flipped around without warning."

"*Everything's* getting flipped around without warning, Shulamit." Khumalo's tone was considerably grimmer than it had been, Helen noticed. "Which probably means we should go ahead and get down to our own latest installment of what's-going-on-now, I suppose. Ambrose, would you care to take the floor and brief Commodore Terekhov and Commodore Chatterjee on all of our own recent fun and games?"

"...so that's about the sum of it, so far, at least," Ambrose Chandler finished up the better part of ninety minutes later.

"Thank you, Ambrose," Khumalo said, then looked at Terekhov. "As you can see, things are looking up over most of the Quadrant. In fact, when Minister Krietzmann gets back on-planet tonight, he and Loretta will be giving us a complete joint brief—not just for your benefit, Aivars; Baroness Medusa and Prime Minister Alquezar will be attending, too—on how well the local system-defense forces are integrating with the new LAC groups as we get them deployed forward. We're in pretty good shape on that front, according to our original schedule, but the LACs are still spreading out from the Lynx Terminus. It's going to be at least another month or so before we can get decent coverage around the northern periphery. And, frankly, our original deployment plans gave much lower priority to the areas around Pequod and New Tuscany because we figured the San Miguel and Rembrandt navies could handle security in the area. Now that the situation in Pequod is getting so...touchy, we really want to expedite the deployment of a LAC group to that system. Unfortunately, we're not going to have the transport platforms for that for at least two months, because the only CLACs available to us have already deposited their groups at their assigned destinations or are still in transit.

"Which still leaves us in a...less than ideal situation, shall we say?"

Khumalo's office was silent for several seconds after he finished speaking, and Helen glanced surreptitiously sideways at Terekhov's profile. His eyes were half-closed, his lips pursed in obvious thought, and she noticed the way both Khumalo and Van Dort were looking at him, both obviously waiting for him to surface with his own impression of Chandler's briefing. Van Dort's reaction didn't surprise her a bit, after the way he and Terekhov had worked together to stymie the entire Monica-based operation. Khumalo's still did, just a bit, although she was delighted to see it.

"I don't like the sound of this New Tuscany business at all, Sir," Terekhov said finally, eyes opening wide once again and focusing on Khumalo. "I didn't have the opportunity to actually visit New Tuscany in *Hexapuma*, but everything I've ever heard, seen, or read about the New Tuscans only makes me even unhappier about these latest shenanigans of theirs."

"So you agree that they're up to something we're not going to like very much, Aivars?" Van Dort asked with a quizzical smile, and Terekhov snorted.

"I can see how that razor-sharp brain of yours helped impel you to the top of the local financial heap, Bernardus," he said dryly. "Nothing much gets past *you*, does it?"

"One tries to keep up," Van Dort admitted modestly, and more than one of those present chuckled. But then expressions sobered again, and Van Dort leaned slightly forward. "What do *you* think we should do about it?"

Helen's eyes flicked sideways to Khumalo, wondering how he would react to having a *civilian* ask the opinion of one of his subordinates directly. But Khumalo only tipped his head slightly to one side, obviously listening for Terekhov's response as closely as Van Dort was.

"Give me a break, Bernardus!" Terekhov protested. "I just heard about this for the first time. What makes you think I've had long enough to formulate any kind of an opinion about it?"

"I'm not asking for an opinion. I want that first impression of yours."

"Well, my first impression is that we need more than just a LAC squadron or two in the system. More platforms would be good, of course, but if New Tuscany really is working to some concerted plan, I doubt that that alone would cause them to back off. In fact, my most pressing thought right this minute is that we ought to put someone senior to Commander Denton into Pequod. And that someone senior, whoever he is, should be authorized to kick any New Tuscan in the ass if that's what it takes to get them backed off."

Both Khumalo and Shoupe looked very much as if they agreed with the commodore, Helen decided. Not that agreeing with him was the same thing as being happy about the notion.

"That's pretty much the way we've been looking at it ourselves," Khumalo said, as if deliberately confirming Helen's impression. "The problem is that we can't help wondering if that's exactly the reaction they're hoping to draw. Mind you, none of us can think of how that would help them, but that's the problem, isn't it? Since we don't know what the *hell* it is they're trying to accomplish, we can't know how what *we* do is going to fit into their plans and objectives. Frankly," the vice admiral admitted, "one reason I haven't tried harder to divert one of the CLAC deliveries to Pequod is that ignorance."

"No, we can't know how any move on our part is going to affect their plans," Terekhov agreed thoughtfully. Then he shrugged slightly. "On the other hand, I don't think we can afford to allow our current ignorance to paralyze us, either. I'm certainly not recommending that we send someone in to play bull in the china shop, because if what we're looking at really is a deliberately orchestrated set of manufactured provocations, the last thing we want to do is actually give them the mother of all provocations. But by the same token, I don't see how anyone here in the region could possibly have guessed how much firepower the Admiralty is ready to begin transferring in this direction. I'm willing to bet that all of New Tuscany's calculations are based on the sort of shoestring force structure they gave you before Monica, Sir. In that case, I think it could be a very good idea to let them know there are going to be more and more modern ships out here in the Quadrant—and not just LACs. Let them see the kind of trouble they're going to be buying themselves if they push too far."

"I think there's quite a bit to that, Admiral," Van Dort said soberly.

"Agreed." Khumalo nodded. "And, to be frank, it's a thought that's occurred to my people, as well as to Minister Krietzmann and Baroness Medusa. I just hate the sense that somebody's getting ready to hit me right across the top of the head with the other shoe instead of just dropping it on the floor!"

"After what those Manpower and Monican bastards tried to do?" Terekhov showed his teeth briefly. "Admiral, I'm right with you on that one!"

"Now why," Khumalo asked almost whimsically, "does that fail to fill me with bubbling optimism, Commodore Terekhov?"

"Excuse me, Ensign Zilwicki."

Helen paused as the extraordinarily attractive blonde touched her elbow in the hallway outside Vice Admiral Khumalo's dirt-side office.

"Yes?" she replied courteously, wondering who the other woman was and how she happened to know who Helen was.

*Aside, of course, from the fact that I wear my name on the front of my tunic. D'oh.*

"I'm Helga Boltitz," the blonde said in a sharp-edged accent which reminded Helen somehow of Victor Cachat's. "Minister Krietzmann's personal assistant," she added as she clearly recognized the blank expression in Helen's eyes.

"Oh. I mean, of course," Helen said. She glanced down the hall, but Commodore Terekhov and Commodore Chatterjee were still engaged in some sort of last-minute personal conversation with Captain Shoupe, and she returned her attention to Ms. Boltitz. "Is there something I can do for you, Ma'am?"

"Well, as I explained to Admiral Gold Peak's flag lieutenant not so very long ago, you can start by not calling me 'Ma'am,'" Boltitz said with an impish grin. "It makes me feel incredibly old and entirely too respectable!"

"I'll try to remember that, Ma— Ms. Boltitz." Helen smiled back at her.

"Good. And, for that matter, given the fact that I do for the Minister basically what you do for the Commodore, I think it might actually be simpler if I call you Helen and you call me Helga. How's that?"

"As long as I still get to call you 'Ms. Boltitz' in public . . . Helga."

"I suppose I can live with that under those circumstances . . . Ensign."

"Well, in that case, let me rephrase. Is there something I can do for you, *Helga*?"

"As a matter of fact, there is," Helga said with a rather more serious air. "The Minister will, of course, be present with the

Prime Minister and the Governor General for the formal dinner before tonight's full-scale briefing. He's asked me to inform you that he's going to be bringing along a couple of guests—just for dinner, not for the briefing—who represent fairly important components of our local system-defense forces. One of them is from Montana, and he's requested what . . . well, what amounts to a photo op with Commodore Terekhov. My impression is that it has something to do with what Captain Terekhov—and your entire crew, of course—accomplished there. At any rate, Minister Krietzmann would greatly appreciate it if Commodore Terekhov could attend in mess dress uniform."

Helen managed to stifle a groan. It wasn't particularly easy. If there was one thing Aivars Terekhov hated, it was what he called the "fuss and feathers" side of his duties. Personally, Helen suspected it had something to do with all the years he'd spent in the Foreign Office's service, with their endless succession of formal dinners and political parties, before he returned to active naval duty.

*On the other hand*, she told herself rather hopefully, *that same Foreign Office experience means he'll* probably *understand the importance of Krietzmann's request. After he gets done pitching a fit, that is.*

"Is anyone else planning on attending in mess dress?" she asked after a moment. Helga quirked an eyebrow at her, and she shrugged. "He's not going to be happy about climbing into his 'monkey suit,' Helga. But if I can tell him he's not going to be alone . . ."

She allowed her voice to trail off hopefully, and Helga chuckled.

"Well, I doubt we could get *everyone* all dressed up," she said. "If it will help, though, I can go and have a word with at least a few of the others—Admiral Khumalo, Captain Shoupe, Commander Chandler, Captain Saunders—and suggest that the Minister would appreciate their attendance in mess dress, as well."

"Oh, good!" Helen made no particular effort to hide her relief. "If you can do that, I'll exaggerate a little myself and suggest that the Minister would appreciate it if Commodore Chatterjee and Captain Carlson came the same way. I mean, it wouldn't *exactly* be a lie. Minister Krietzmann *would* appreciate it, wouldn't he?"

"Oh, I'm sure he would," Helga agreed.

✧     ✧     ✧

Getting Aivars Terekhov into full scale mess dress had been almost as hard as Helen had been afraid it would. He'd started to dig his heels in the instant she opened her mouth, pointing out that nobody had mentioned anything about stupid mess dress uniforms to him in the original invitation. She'd headed that one off by reminding him that although the request *was* a late change, it was also one which had been made at the Quadrant's Minister of War's personal request for important political reasons. He'd glowered at that one, then brightened and pointed out that he didn't *have* a commodore's mess dress uniform . . . at which point Chief Steward Agnelli had silently opened his closet and extracted the *captain's* mess dress which she had thoughtfully had re-tailored for his new rank during the voyage out from Manticore.

Balked on that front by his underlings' infernal efficiency, he'd tried arguing that *Chatterjee* probably didn't have the right uniform, and he wouldn't want to embarrass the other officer. Helen and Agnelli had simply looked at him patiently, rather the way Helen supposed a nanny looked at a rambunctious child. He'd looked back at them for a moment or two, then heaved a deep sigh, and surrendered.

It was really a pity it took so much work to get him into the uniform, Helen reflected, since it could have been purposely designed to suit him. His height, blond hair, blue eyes, and erect, square-shouldered posture carried off even the archaic sword to perfection, and she saw eyes turning toward him as he followed her out of the official Navy air car on the landing stage of the downtown Thimble mansion that was the temporary Government House while the Governor General's permanent, formal residence was being built. There were quite a few air cars already there, or in the act of lifting off again after disgorging their passengers, and she saw Vice Admiral Khumalo—also in mess dress—waiting for them.

The vice admiral couldn't carry off his resplendent uniform—and sword—the way Terekhov could. Few could, after all, Helen thought just a tad complacently. But from his posture, it was obvious that he was quite accustomed to putting up with it, and Captain Shoupe, standing at his shoulder, looked almost as resplendent as Khumalo did as he extended his hand to Terekhov with a chuckle.

"I had a side bet with Bernardus that Ms. Zilwicki wouldn't manage to get you into mess dress!" he said.

"Well," Terekhov half-growled, glaring humorously at Helen, "you almost won. Unfortunately, she used to be *Bernardus'* aide. That's probably why he had a more realistic appreciation of her ability to . . . convince me than you did, Sir."

"He did say something about the Ensign's extraordinary persistence," Khumalo agreed with a smile. He glanced at Helen, but it was obvious even to her that at this particular moment, silence was the best policy.

"Well," Khumalo continued after a moment, "I suppose we should head on in. In some ways, you're the guest of honor tonight, Aivars, so they can't get this dog and pony show off the pad until you turn up."

"Wonderful." Terekhov sighed. Then he shook himself. "All right, I'm ready. I don't suppose it can be *much* worse than the Battle of Monica!"

The initial description of the evening as "an informal little supper with the Governor General and the Prime Minister" seemed to have been somewhat in error, Helen thought as she followed her commodore and Vice Admiral Khumalo down a broad hallway and into what was obviously the mansion's main ballroom. It was stupendous, and the tables which had been arranged in it filled it to capacity. There must have been at least three hundred chairs at those tables, probably more, and most of them were already filled.

Only someone who knew Aivars Terekhov well would have recognized the way his neck stiffened ever so slightly, the way his shoulders squared themselves that tiny bit further. He continued chatting with Vice Admiral Khumalo as the two of them headed for the head table, pausing occasionally for a brief aside with someone Terekhov had met on his original deployment to Talbott. From the vice admiral's expression, *he* wasn't surprised, Helen noticed, and began to wonder exactly what was going on.

As they finally approached the head table, she recognized three other commodores waiting for them. One of them—Commodore Lázló—she'd expected, as the senior officer of the Spindle Space Navy. The second startled her a bit, although she supposed that Commodore Lemuel Sackett, the uniformed commander of the Montana Space Navy, legitimately qualified as "a guest from Montana." How he'd happened to be there was something of a puzzlement, of course, but not as big a puzzle as the presence of Commodore Emil Karlberg, the senior officer of the Nuncio Space Force.

This time, Terekhov couldn't quite hide his surprise. Spindle was scarcely conveniently located for either of them—transit time between Spindle and their home systems was better measured in weeks than days; Montana, the closer of the two, lay eighty-three light-years from the Quadrant's capital system—but it would scarcely have been good manners to ask what they were doing here. Especially not when the two of them were so obviously delighted to see *him*.

*And they damned well* should *be*, Helen told herself. *The commodore and the* Kitty *cleaned those Peep "pirates" out of Nuncio when nothing Karlberg had could even have* found *them, much less fought them! And it's obvious Sackett isn't going to forget the way the commodore and Mr. Van Dort convinced Westman to hang up his guns in Montana, either. Still, I wonder why nobody mentioned they were going to be here?*

She was still wondering when a polite usher separated her from her astronomically superior officers and showed her to a much humbler table to one side. Helen was delighted to go with him and get her junior rank (and absurd youth) out of the spotlight of attention focusing on Terekhov and the others. The table to which he led her was close enough that she could keep an eye on him, in case he needed her, and the unobtrusive earbug in her left ear meant he could summon her anytime he wished to.

She was pleased to see Helga Boltitz seated at the same table, although Helga didn't seem quite as delighted by their location as Helen was. On the other hand, that might well owe something to her table companion. Well, Helen's, too, she supposed, since he was seated between the two of them. She didn't know who the dark-haired, brown-eyed man with the pencil mustache and the Rembrandt accent might be, but she recognized his bored, superior expression from too many of the political dinners she'd attended as Catherine Montaigne's adopted daughter. Some people, she thought dryly, didn't need cheering sections; they took their own with them wherever they went.

She was still reflecting on that point—and trying to decide if it would be cowardly of her to abandon Helga to the Rembrandter rather than trying to draw fire from the other woman—when a sharp, musical tone sang through the background rumble of side conversations. All heads turned toward it, and she saw Baroness Medusa standing in her place at the head of the master table still holding the table knife with which she had just struck a crystal pitcher.

The rumble of voices died almost instantly, and Medusa smiled.

"First," she said, "allow me to thank you all for coming. Some of you"—she glanced in Terekhov's direction—"were quite possibly under the impression that tonight's dinner would be a somewhat smaller and more humble affair. I apologize to anyone who received that mistaken impression. Actually, tonight represents a rare opportunity for all of us. As Her Majesty's personal representative here in the Quadrant, it is my privilege—as well as my pleasure—to welcome all of you on Her Majesty's behalf. We are fortunate tonight in having several of the Quadrant's senior naval officers present, and equally fortunate that they were able to take time away from the official conferences which brought them here to join us for dinner tonight. And, in addition, we are particularly fortunate to have with us tonight a man to whom the entire Quadrant owes a tremendous debt of gratitude. Ladies and Gentlemen, please join me in extending my heartfelt thanks to Commodore Aivars Terekhov!"

The stillness of the ballroom disappeared in a roar of applause. Vice Admiral Khumalo was probably the first person to come to his feet, applauding sharply, but if he was, it could only have been by half a heartbeat or so. Helen found herself standing, as well, clapping wildly, and it was all she could do to restrain a jubilant whistle as pandemonium erupted.

She hadn't realized until that moment how much she'd resented— on Terekhov's behalf, not her own—the way the rush to redeploy him had deprived him of the public recognition back home that he had so amply earned. Yet now that the moment was here, she realized how much more fitting it was for him to receive that recognition *here*, in the Cluster and from the people his moral courage had served so well.

The applause lasted quite some time, and Helen could see the heightened color in the commodore's face as the sound of all those clapping hands battered his ears. She didn't doubt that it embarrassed him, but she didn't really much care about that. He deserved it—deserved every decibel of it—and her smile felt as if it were going to break her face as she recognized how cunningly Khumalo and Medusa had arranged things so that he couldn't avoid it.

But the clapping died at last, people sat back down, and the Governor General waited for silence to fall once more. Then she cleared her throat.

"By now," she said, "I'm sure it's occurred to most of you that we got Commodore Terekhov here under what might be called false pretenses. Frankly, we were a little concerned that he might have bolted if he'd realized what we had in mind."

Laughter muttered across the room, and she smiled.

"I'm afraid, however," she continued then, "that we're not quite finished with the Commodore tonight."

She glanced at Terekhov, who looked back at her with an expression which could only have been described as wary.

"There is a phrase with which Queen's officers become altogether too familiar, ladies and gentlemen," she went on, her tone much more serious. "That phrase is 'the exigencies of the Service,' and what it means is that those men and women who have chosen to wear the Queen's uniform and to guard and protect all of us—you and me—frequently find their own lives being stepped upon by the demands of the service they have chosen to give. They do not simply risk life and limb for us, ladies and gentlemen. They also sacrifice the rest of their lives—sacrifice time as fathers and mothers, as wives and husbands. Commodore Terekhov was spared less than one T-week in Manticore before he was sent back to us. Less than one T-week, ladies and gentlemen, after all of the tremendous risks and dangers he and the men and women of HMS *Hexapuma* and the other ships of his squadron in Monica endured for all of us."

The huge ballroom was completely still, now. Completely hushed. Baroness Medusa's voice sounded clear and quiet against that backdrop of silence.

"There can be no true, adequate compensation for the sacrifices men and women in uniform make for the people they serve and protect. How does one set a price on the willingness to serve? How does one set a proper wage for the willingness to die to protect others? And how does one honor those who have honored their oaths, given the last true measure of devotion, in the service of their star nation and the belief in human dignity and human freedom?"

She paused in the silence, then shook her head.

"The truth is, that we cannot give them the compensation, the honor, they have so amply deserved of us. Yet whether what we can give them is what they deserve or not, we recognize our obligation to *try*. To try to show them, and everyone else, that we recognize the sacrifices they have made. That we understand how very much we owe them. And that they are to us pearls beyond price, men and women we cannot deserve yet must always thank God come to us anyway.

"Those were the men and women of HMS *Hexapuma*. Of HMS *Warlock*, HMS *Vigilant*, HMS *Gallant*, HMS *Audacious*, HMS *Aegis*, HMS *Javelin*, HMS *Janissary*, HMS *Rondeau*, HMS *Aria*, and HMS *Volcano*.

"We cannot individually honor those men and women. Too many of them are no longer here for us to honor, and most of those who survived are somewhere else this night, somewhere else in the Queen's uniform, serving her—and all of us—yet again as 'the exigencies of the Service' demand. But if we cannot individually honor each of them, we can honor *all* of them collectively in the person of the man who commanded them."

Aivars Terekhov looked straight before him, and it wasn't simple modesty. He was looking at something only he could see—the men and women of those ships. The faces no one would ever see again.

"Commodore Terekhov," Medusa said, turning to address him directly for the first time, "you were not aware that among the dispatches you carried when you returned to Spindle was a letter of instruction from Her Majesty to me. Please stand, Commodore."

Terekhov obeyed slowly.

"Come here, Commodore," she said quietly, and he walked across to her. As he did, Augustus Khumalo, Lemuel Sackett, and Emil Karlberg rose in turn and followed him. Sackett carried a small velvet case which had apparently been hidden under the table at his place. Karlberg carried a small cushion which had been similarly concealed.

The four of them came to a halt in front of Medusa, and Sackett presented the small case to her. She accepted it, but she also looked at Khumalo.

"Attention to orders!" the vice admiral's deep voice announced, and Helen felt herself coming to her feet in automatic response, accompanied by every other uniformed man and woman in that vast ballroom.

"Commodore Aivars Terekhov," Medusa said in a clear, carrying voice, "on the sixteenth day of February, 1921 Post Diaspora, units of the Royal Manticoran Navy under your command entered the Monica System, acting upon intelligence which you had developed consequent to your previous actions in the Split System and the Montana System. In the course of developing that intelligence, and of suppressing violent terrorist movements in both of those star systems, you had become aware of an additional, potentially disastrous threat to the citizens of those star systems then known as the Talbott Cluster and to the Star Kingdom of Manticore. Acting upon your own authority, you moved with the squadron under your command to Monica and there demanded the stand down of the ex-Solarian League Navy battlecruisers which had been delivered to the Union of Monica by parties hostile to the Star Kingdom who were determined to prevent the annexation of the star systems now known as the Talbott Quadrant by the Star Kingdom, for which the citizens of those star systems had freely and democratically petitioned.

"When the senior officer present of the Monican Navy refused to comply with your demand and opened fire upon your vessels, although surprised by the heavy volume, weight, range, and accuracy of that fire, and despite heavy damage and severe casualties, you and the units under your command successfully destroyed the military components of a massive industrial platform and nine of the battlecruisers in question, which were there moored. And, when subsequently attacked by three fully operational and modern battlecruisers, the six remaining units of your squadron engaged and destroyed all of their opponents.

"At the cost of sixty percent of the vessels and seventy-five percent of the personnel under your command, your squadron destroyed or neutralized *all* of the Solarian-built battlecruisers in the Monica System. Subsequently, although your surviving vessels were too severely damaged to withdraw from the system, you neutralized all remaining units of the Monican Navy, prevented the withdrawal or destruction of the two surviving Solarian battlecruisers, and maintained the status quo in the system for a full week, until relieved by friendly forces.

"It is now my duty, and my enormous honor, by the express direction of Her Majesty, Queen Elizabeth of Manticore, acting as Her Governor General for the Talbott Quadrant and Her personal representative, to present to you the Parliamentary Medal of Valor."

Helen inhaled sharply as Sackett opened the case and Medusa extracted the golden cross and starburst on its blue and white ribbon. Terekhov was much taller than she was, and she rose on tiptoe as he bowed to her so that she could slip the ribbon around his neck and adjust its fall. She positioned the gleaming medal carefully, then looked up at him and—in a gesture Helen was certain hadn't been formally choreographed—touched him very gently on the cheek.

"Her Majesty awards this medal to you, Commodore," she said, "both because you have so deeply and personally merited it, but also as a means of recognizing every man and woman who served with you in Monica. She asks you to wear this medal for them, as much as for yourself."

Terekhov nodded without speaking. Frankly, Helen doubted that he *could* have spoken at that moment. But Medusa wasn't done with him yet, and she nodded to Karlberg who stooped and placed his cushion on the floor.

"And now, Commodore, there's one more small matter of business which Her Majesty has requested that I take care of for her. Kneel, please."

Terekhov's nostrils flared as he inhaled sharply. Then he obeyed her, sinking to his knees on the cushion, and Augustus Khumalo drew his dress sword and extended it, hilt-first, to Baroness Medusa. She took it, looked at it for a moment, then looked down at the officer kneeling before her.

"By the authority vested in me as Her Majesty's Governor General for the Talbott Quadrant, and by Her express commission, acting for and in Her stead," her quiet voice carried with crystal clarity throughout the ballroom, "I bestow upon you the rank, title, prerogatives, and duties of Knight Companion of the Order of King Roger."

The gleaming steel touched his right shoulder, then his left, then went back to his right once more. She let it rest there for a moment, her eyes meeting his, then she smiled and stepped back, lowering the sword.

"Rise, Sir Aivars," she said softly in the hush before the cheers began, "and may your future actions as faithfully uphold the honor of the Queen as your past."

# Chapter Thirty-Six

"I HOPE WE KNOW what we're doing here, Junyan," Commissioner Lorcan Verrochio of the Office of Frontier Security said, giving his vice-commissioner a glance which was less than totally happy.

"So far everything's going exactly to plan," Hongbo Junyan pointed out.

"Refresh my memory, but wasn't everything 'going exactly to plan' *last* time right up until the very moment that son-of-a-bitch Terekhov—who'd somehow been left out of the plan—blew the entire Monica System straight to hell?" Verrochio inquired with a certain undeniable acerbity.

"Yes, it was." Hongbo tried very hard, and mostly successfully, to keep a note of over-tried patience out of his voice. "This time, however, instead of counting on a batch of battlecruisers manned by neobarbs who hadn't even managed to get more than three of them refitted and back into commission, much less trained up to any sort of real proficiency, we've got three *squadrons* of Frontier Fleet immediately on call. And then there's Admiral Crandall at McIntosh, as well. I'd say that's a significant difference in the balance of available forces, wouldn't you?"

Verrochio nodded, although it was evident he remained something short of completely enthralled by the current state of affairs.

It was odd, Hongbo reflected. He'd known Verrochio for more T-years than he really liked to contemplate, and the commissioner was hardly the most complex individual he'd ever met, yet the man could still surprise him upon occasion. He'd expected Verrochio to jump at the potential opportunity to pay Manticore back for the way the Star Kingdom had embarrassed him and damaged his powerbase among the only people who really mattered to him. And there was no doubt in Hongbo's mind that Verrochio did, indeed, want exactly that.

Yet Verrochio's initial ardor, the white-hot fury which had possessed him in the immediate wake of the Battle of Monica, had cooled noticeably. At the time, Hongbo had been entirely in favor of that change and had worked hard himself to encourage it. Unfortunately, his priorities had altered—or been altered— somewhat since, and he was finding it considerably more difficult than he had anticipated to switch the commissioner's choler back on once again. In no small part, he thought grumpily, due to Commodore Francis Thurgood.

Hongbo was no expert on naval matters, but he knew Verrochio's senior Frontier Fleet officer had spent days interviewing Monicans who'd survived the engagement and several weeks analyzing the sketchy data available on exactly what had happened. The amount of information available was extremely limited, of course. In fact, when Hongbo thought about it, he supposed the only real surprise—given how the Manties had blown the hell out of every military sensor platform in the system—was that there'd been any data for Thurgood to examine.

The disturbing conclusions Thurgood had come to based on what was available, however, had produced a chilling effect on Verrochio which all the official intelligence analyses from the SLN hierarchy hadn't quite served to dispel. Hongbo didn't know whether or not Thurgood had shared his own analysis with Admiral Byng's staff. He was a conscientious officer, surprisingly so, even for Frontier Fleet, so Hongbo suspected that he had . . . not that anyone in Task Group 3021 was likely to have listened to him. Given Byng's boundless contempt for all things Frontier Fleet, any warning from Thurgood would most likely have been counterproductive. In fact, it would probably have convinced *that* arrogant prick to believe exactly the opposite!

He'd definitely shared it with Verrochio, however, and as his report had pointed out, the Manties hadn't had a single ship bigger than a heavy cruiser, and they'd completely trashed Monica. In fact, Thurgood had suggested (although it was evident to Hongbo he hadn't much cared for his own conclusions), it was entirely possible that it wouldn't have mattered one bit whether Horster's battlecruisers had been manned by Monicans or Solarians.

Lorcan Verrochio hadn't liked the sound of *that* at all. For that matter, neither had Hongbo Junyan. In one sense, the vice-commissioner didn't really care how nasty the Manticoran navy might be. Even if every spacer in it was three meters tall, covered with long curly hair, immune to vacuum, and had to be killed with silver bullets, there couldn't possibly be enough of them to stand up to the Solarian League. Hongbo couldn't remember who it was back on Old Terra who'd said that "quantity has a quality all its own," but the cliché still held true, especially when the quantitative difference was as vast as it was in this case. So Hongbo nurtured no fears about what would eventually happen to the Star Kingdom of Manticore if it got itself into a shooting war with the League.

But there was that one word, "*eventually.*" That was why Thurgood's analysis worried him, as well as his nominal superior. "Eventually" wasn't going to do very much to save Lorcan Verrochio—or Hongbo Junyan—in the *short term* if it turned out Thurgood was right. And even if the Solarian League absorbed its losses and *eventually* squashed the "Star Empire of Manticore" like a bug, it wasn't going to forget who it was who'd managed to get the war in question started. Especially not if the war started with the sort of unmitigated disaster Thurgood was warning might well result.

*Still, Thurgood doesn't know about Admiral Crandall,* Hongbo told himself. *I don't care* how *nasty the Manties' heavy cruisers or battlecruisers are; they aren't going to stand up very well to sixty or seventy of the wall!*

"At any rate," Verrochio said, turning to look out his office windows at a panoramic view of the city of Pine Mountain as his voice pulled Hongbo back to the surface of his own thoughts, "at least it hasn't bitten us on the ass yet."

Hongbo didn't comment, since it was obvious Verrochio was actually speaking to himself.

Verrochio folded his hands behind him, gazing out across Pine Mountain. The city, the capital of the Kingdom of Meyers before the Office of Frontier Security had moved in and liberated the

Kingdom's subjects from its obviously tyrannical rulers (they were all tyrannical rulers, after all, weren't they?), was the central node of his personal satrapy. There were well over two million people in that city, which might make it little more than a pinprick on a map somewhere in one of the League's venerable old Core systems but was still a more than merely respectable population out here in the Verge. Like any OFS commissioner, Lorcan Verrochio was always ambitious when it came to improving his position, but at this particular moment he was actually more aware of all he had to *lose* if things turned out as badly as Thurgood's analysis suggested they just might.

*Oh, come on, Lorcan!* he told himself bracingly. *You know Thurgood is an old woman at heart. Do really think he'd still be just a* commodore *at his age if he had a clue about how things really work? They sent him out here to get* rid *of him, not because of his brilliance! And of course he's been running scared ever since Monica. Until Byng showed up, he was the one who'd have had to go up against the Manties, and the biggest thing he had under his command was a division of heavy cruisers. No wonder he didn't want to cross swords with the big, bad Manties!*

"I take it," he continued to Hongbo, never removing his eyes from the pastel towers of Pine Mountain, "that your good friend Mr. Ottweiler is satisfied so far?"

"So far," Hongbo replied, noticing that Ottweiler had suddenly become *his* "good friend," despite the fact that Verrochio had actually known him considerably longer than Hongbo had.

"Should we consider briefing Byng at this point, do you think?"

"I don't see any particular need to do that, Lorcan." The commissioner turned his head at last, looking over his shoulder at Hongbo with one eyebrow arched, and the vice-commissioner shrugged. "Byng doesn't need any prompting from us to be thoroughly pissed off with any Manty unfortunate enough to cross his path. That much is pretty obvious, wouldn't you say?"

Verrochio considered for a moment, then nodded.

"Well, my 'good friend' as you've just described him, hasn't asked us to explain exactly what's going on to Admiral Byng," Hongbo pointed out. "I don't think he sees any need to do that, and my thought is that if he's comfortable with that, then that's where we should leave it. If things work out for him and his superiors, then they work out for us, too. And if they don't work out, if it all goes south on us, then it's occurred to me that not having anything on record that could possibly be construed as our pushing Byng is probably a good idea. If he's prepared to take unilateral action against the Manties already, then let him. If it works out for us, good. If it doesn't, then it's the *Navy's* fault, not ours."

Verrochio obviously thought about that for a moment, then nodded. In fact, his expression became considerably more cheerful than it had been.

"In that case," he said, turning away from the desk to pick up the hard copy of the first formal request from New Tuscany for Solarian assistance against Manticore's systematic harassment, "I suppose we should just file this for right now. No sense running off half-cocked, after all."

"No, Sir. No sense at all," Hongbo agreed.

No one familiar with the customary workings of the Office of Frontier Security was going to be fooled after the fact, of course, but that didn't really matter. The reason no one was going to be fooled was because tried and true tactics were the best—and safest—ones. The New Tuscan note was the first step in a familiar dance, and it would never do for the vast and impartial might of the Office of Frontier Security to allow itself to be pushed into premature, ill-considered action. It was necessary to build up the proper groundwork, first. Let *several* notes and requests from the current OFS proxy accumulate, thus emphasizing the serious and long-standing nature of the problem once they were released (or leaked) to the newsies, before Frontier Security acted. Given a sufficiently fat file, Frontier Security's spinmeisters could turn almost anything into a noble and selfless response to an intolerable situation.

After all, look how much practice they'd had.

"All right, then," Verrochio said, flipping the hard copy across the desk towards Hongbo. "Go ahead and open a file. Somehow," he smiled thinly despite a lingering trace of uneasiness, "I don't think this will be the last entry in it."

"Good afternoon, Valery," Hongbo Junyan said a couple of days later as his secretary ushered Valery Ottweiler into his own office.

Hongbo's office was marginally smaller than Verrochio's, and without quite as good a view of Pine Mountain, but it was still luxurious, and he crossed the enormous room to shake Ottweiler's hand, then escorted him to a pleasant conversational nook arranged around a stone coffee table. An insulated carafe of coffee, a teapot, and a tray of fresh croissants sat ready on the table, and Hongbo gestured for his visitor to be seated.

"Thank you, Junyan," Ottweiler responded.

The Mesan settled into the indicated chair, waited while Hongbo personally poured him a cup of tea, then watched the vice-commissioner pour coffee into a second cup for himself. It was a homey, domestic little scene, Ottweiler thought, and most people might well have been fooled by Hongbo's calm demeanor. Ottweiler, however, knew the Solarian much better than "most people" did, and he recognized the other man's inner core of nervousness.

"I was a little surprised by your request for a meeting," Hongbo said a few minutes later, sitting back with his coffee. "We received the first note from New Tuscany day before yesterday, you know. Under the circumstances, I would've thought that perhaps a ... somewhat lower profile, perhaps, might have been indicated."

"I didn't exactly send any announcements to the 'faxes to tell them I was coming to visit you," Ottweiler pointed out with a slight smile. "And, let's be honest with one another here, Junyan—is anyone who really knows what's going on in the galaxy going to be fooled if I try to maintain a 'lower profile'? For that matter, even if I weren't up to Mesa's and Manpower's normal nefarious machinations, everyone would assume I was, anyway. That being the case, why go to all the inconvenience and inefficiency of trying to creep around in the dark?"

Hongbo wasn't amused by his guest's apparent levity, but he only shrugged and sipped more coffee. Then he lowered the cup.

"I'm not going to pretend I agree with you completely about that," he said levelly. "On the other hand, there probably is *something* to it. And, in any case, here you are. So, what can I do for you?"

"I've just received a somewhat lengthy dispatch from home," Ottweiler said in a much more serious tone. He put his teacup back on its saucer and set the saucer in his lap.

"What sort of dispatch?" Hongbo's eyes had narrowed, and he couldn't quite suppress the note of tension in his voice. Ottweiler arched one eyebrow, and the vice-commissioner snorted harshly. "You wouldn't be telling me about it unless it was likely to affect our . . . arrangement, Valery. And somehow I rather doubt it's going to tell me something I'll like hearing."

"Well, it does affect our 'arrangement,'" Ottweiler conceded. "And I won't pretend I was entirely delighted with it myself, when it arrived. "

"In that case, why don't you just go ahead and tell me about it rather than look for some way to candy-coat it?"

"All right. Without candy-coating, I've been instructed to tell you that we need to move the schedule up."

"What?" Hongbo looked at him with something approaching incredulity.

"We need to move the schedule up," Ottweiler repeated.

"Why? And what makes you think I can just turn some kind of switch and pull that off?"

"They didn't tell me exactly why." Ottweiler seemed remarkably immune to the scathing sarcasm of Hongbo's last question. "They just told me what they want to happen. And, exactly as they instructed me to, I've just told *you*."

Hongbo half-glared at him for a moment, then made himself draw a deep breath and step back from his instant flare of anger.

"Sorry," he said. "I know you're only the messenger. But that doesn't change the realities, Valery. There's only so quickly we can move on something like this. You know that."

"Under normal conditions, I'm sure I'd agree with you. In this instance, though, that doesn't really matter. I'm not trying to deliberately provoke you by saying that, but the truth is that I have my instructions, and there's not any leeway in them this time."

"Be reasonable, Valery! You *know* how hard I had to work to get Lorcan on board for this in the first place! That idiot Thurgood has him scared half to death with all those bogeyman stories about the Manties' new super weapons. He's terrified that Byng is going to take significant casualties if it comes to an actual exchange of fire. Which, coupled with what already happened at Monica, isn't exactly going to be conducive to his future career prospects. Or, for that matter, *mine*. Under the circumstances, it's more important than ever to have all of the requests for assistance safely on file before we move."

"I can understand that point of view completely," Ottweiler

said soothingly, but his expression was inflexible. "And I'm sure bringing Commissioner Verrochio around isn't going to be the easiest thing you've ever managed to pull off. But I'm afraid it has to be done."

"I don't think it *can* be!" Hongbo waved one hand in frustration. "Even if Lorcan were prepared to move on this tomorrow—which, I assure you, he *isn't*—Byng's split up his battlecruisers and sent them haring off all over the sector and to visit half a dozen independent systems outside this new Talbott Quadrant on flag-showing missions. He's only got one division here in Meyers. There's no way in the galaxy, I don't care how urgent it is, that I'm going to be able to convince Lorcan Verrochio to send a single division off to New Tuscany after all of the horror stories Thurgood's been pouring into his ears. Especially not now that we know the Manties have deployed at least some modern *battlecruisers* to the Quadrant. If he was worried about heavy cruisers, he's terrified thinking about battlecruisers! He's not going to sign off on facing that kind of firepower unless he's confident that Byng has a significant numerical advantage to offset it. It's just *not* going to happen, Valery!"

"I didn't say we need to send Byng off *today*," Ottweiler replied. "But we do need to accelerate our preparations."

"I can't do it," Hongbo said flatly. "Not without more time to bring Lorcan around."

"Well, then you're just going to have to change that," Ottweiler said, equally flatly. Their eyes locked for a moment, and the Mesan continued. "New instructions have been sent to our people in New Tuscany, as well, Junyan. They're going to be accelerating the schedule from their end, whatever happens at *your* end."

"Then somebody should have asked me about how much accelerating I can do first!" Hongbo half-snarled back.

"There wasn't time, obviously," Ottweiler said, as if explaining something to a small child. "I don't know everything that's going on back home. Hell, I don't know *half* of what's going on back home! But I do know they're taking it very seriously, and they're obviously responding to something I don't know about yet. And they aren't going to be very happy with anyone who screws up their plans."

"Meaning what?" Hongbo's eyes were narrow again, and Ottweiler shrugged.

"Meaning I'm going to pass along their instructions, whatever they are, and that anyone they wind up being unhappy with isn't going to be *me*."

Hongbo glared at him, but at the same time, the vice-commissioner knew Ottweiler had a point. It wasn't as if the other man had thought all this up on his own just to screw up Hongbo's week. Which, unfortunately, also meant Valery Ottweiler wasn't the person whose potential wrathful reaction he had to worry about if he didn't produce like an obedient little pawn. He remembered certain reports about Isabel Bardasano and her attitude towards those who failed to comply with her instructions. Then he thought about Ottweiler's not-so-veiled references to the Audubon Ballroom when this whole fresh round of lunacy began, and a distinct chill ran through the magma of his anger.

"There are going to be limits to what I can do," he said finally. "Not to what I'm *willing* to do, but to what I *can* do. I'm telling you right now, it doesn't matter what kind of leverage you have with me, if I tell Lorcan he *has* to change his schedule, he's going to freak out. And if he does *that*, then your entire operation's going to go straight into the crapper, Valery. It won't matter what other pieces you have in place, it won't matter what happens to me or to Lorcan after the fact. The operation will be blown out of space."

"I see."

Ottweiler sat back in his chair, regarding Hongbo with rather more respect than usual. The vice-commissioner was obviously unhappy and equally obviously frightened, but that only gave added point to his observation. And he was probably right, Ottweiler conceded. In Ottweiler's own opinion, Lorcan Verrochio had always been the most likely failure point in the entire plan. Unfortunately, he was also the one man they couldn't work around. Or could they?

"Suppose," he said slowly, "that something were to happen to Commissioner Verrochio. What would happen then?"

A considerably deeper and darker chill ran through Hongbo Junyan. He looked at the Mesan for a moment, then shook his head.

"Officially, if . . . something happened to Lorcan, I'd take over from him until the Ministry could get a replacement out here." He looked at Ottweiler, trying to conceal his icy tingle of dread at what the other man was obviously suggesting. "The problem is that everyone would know I was only a temporary replacement, and nobody would want to piss off whoever eventually wound up as the new commissioner. Which doesn't even mention the people who'd be opposed to what you want for reasons of their own. Thurgood, for example, would drag his heels just as hard as he could, and I don't begin to have Lorcan's personal contacts—not officially, at any rate—with the Gendarmerie and the intelligence community. I *might* be able to pull it off, but I'd say the odds were actually better that the wheels would come off completely."

Ottweiler eyed him thoughtfully, and Hongbo looked back as steadily as he could. What he'd just said was true, and he hoped Ottweiler was smart enough to accept that.

"All right," the Mesan said finally. "I can see that, I suppose. But in that case, we still have the problem of . . . properly motivating him. What would happen if I were to apply a little more *direct pressure*, shall we say?"

"I honestly don't know," Hongbo replied. There wasn't much doubt in the vice-commissioner's mind what Ottweiler meant. Especially not in light of the pressure which had been brought to bear upon *him* in the first place.

"So far," he continued, "he's done more or less what you wanted because I've been able to convince him it was in his own best interests and that, ultimately, he'd find it was more profitable to have Manpower owing him a favor than the reverse. If we start threatening him at this point, there's no telling how he'll respond, but there's at least a significant chance he'd panic and do something neither one of us would want to see."

"All right," Ottweiler said again, this time with a sigh. "You say there are limits. Tell me just what you can do in that case."

"The one thing I can't do is go to him and tell him we're changing the rules he thinks he knows about. In other words, I'm going to have to find a way to get him to do the things we need him to do without his realizing why I'm doing it."

"And you think you can actually pull this off?" Ottweiler looked skeptical, and Hongbo didn't blame him. Despite that, though, and despite his own serious misgivings, the vice-commissioner actually smiled.

"I've been managing him that way at need for a long time," he said. "I can't absolutely promise I can steer him into doing exactly what you want, but I think I can probably nudge him into doing *mostly* what you want."

"The biggest thing of all is that we have to be positioned as quickly as possible," Ottweiler said. "I know the original plan was to wait for at least a couple of more 'spontaneous complaints' from New Tuscany. Unfortunately, the timetable I got with my latest set of instructions is that the key incident is going to occur within less than one month."

"Less than one month?!" Hongbo stared at him. "What the hell happened to our *six-month* schedule?"

"I don't know. I told you I've been instructed to accelerate things, and that's all I *do* know. So, what do we do?"

"And we're still not going to tell Byng what's really going on?" Hongbo asked, watching Ottweiler's eyes very closely.

"No, we're not. My instructions are very clear on that point," the Mesan replied, and Hongbo nodded internally. Ottweiler's eyes said he was being honest with him—on this point, at least, and to the best of his own knowledge. Which meant . . .

"In that case, I think all we can do is to move Byng to New Tuscany ahead of schedule and hope his attitude towards Manties is as . . . unforgiving as you seem to think it is. I can probably convince Lorcan to send Byng out early as long as he's convinced we're still on that famous six-month timetable you gave me initially." Hongbo showed his teeth in a thin smile. "I'll sell it to him as an opportunity to get Byng's toes into the water in New Tuscany, as it were—establish Byng's contacts with the locals, that sort of thing. Lorcan will see it as more pump-priming."

"That might actually work," Ottweiler said slowly, his mind racing while he considered possibilities.

Byng's rabid anti-Manticore attitude was the reason he'd been maneuvered into his present assignment in the first place. If he were on-station when the critical incident occurred, he'd probably react the way Ottweiler's superiors wanted all on his own. He'd better, anyway, since there was no way Verrochio was going to explicitly tell him what was really going on or even give him the sort of firm "take no-nonsense" instructions the original plan called for. Not if the commissioner thought he still had months to go before anyone actually pushed the button.

"If we go ahead and send him out, though, we need to make sure he has enough of his task group available to bolster his confidence," the Mesan said, thinking out loud now. "I know what his *attitude* is going to be, but if he should actually find himself outnumbered, he might decide to back down after all."

"That's what I was thinking myself," Hongbo agreed. "Which means we can't send him out tomorrow. But we can still get him there a hell of a lot sooner than the original schedule called for. And, frankly, I think that's the best we can possibly hope for under the circumstances. So, tell me, Valery." He looked at Ottweiler very levelly. "Bearing in mind that practical limitation, do you have a *better* idea?"

# Chapter Thirty-Seven

"GOOD MORNING, MR. COMMISSIONER." Admiral Josef Byng bestowed his best gracious, depress-the-bureaucrat's-pretensions-without-stepping-on-him-*too*-hard smile on Lorcan Verrochio as he stepped into the Frontier Security commissioner's Meyers office. "How can the Navy be of assistance to you today?"

"Good morning, Admiral," Verrochio replied. "I appreciate your getting back to me so promptly."

Verrochio's smile was far less patronizing than Byng's, although not, perhaps, for the reasons the Battle Fleet admiral might have believed. That entrance was just like Byng, Verrochio thought. The man was a native of Old Earth herself, and like quite a few citizens of the ancient mother world, he gazed down from that lofty pinnacle upon all those smaller, inferior beings born of lesser planets as they clustered around his feet. And although Verrochio suspected Byng thought he was concealing it, the admiral's unmitigated Battle Fleet contempt for the bureaucratic plodders of OFS and the jumped up, bumptious policeman of Frontier Fleet followed him around like a second shadow.

But that was just fine with Lorcan Verrochio. In fact, the commissioner was delighted to see it, because he felt far more nervous about this entire arrangement than he'd let on to Hongbo Junyan.

He wanted his own back against Manticore—oh, *yes*, he wanted his own back! And he intended to have it. On the other hand,

492

he'd come to the conclusion that Commodore Thurgood's warnings about the efficiency and effectiveness of the Royal Manticoran Navy were probably justified. None of the evidence *he'd* seen from Monica argued against the Frontier Fleet officer's conclusions, at any rate, and Verrochio wished he'd had the benefit of Thurgood's insights before Hongbo had convinced him to sign on for a return match.

Unfortunately, Thurgood's report had arrived on the commissioner's desk only *after* he'd embraced Manpower's new designs. At which point it had inspired a bit of rethinking on Verrochio's part. The size and power of the Battle Fleet formations Manpower had managed to manipulate into position to support its new operation were still reassuring, but much less so than they'd been before the commodore's damned memo. And, Verrochio admitted to himself, they were almost equally frightening. He'd been aware for years of how Mesa's tentacles in general—and Manpower's in particular—extended into and permeated Frontier Security's upper reaches. He hadn't realized until now that Manpower also had the pull to actually manipulate the deployment of such powerful *Battle Fleet* formations.

*Oh, get a grip, Lorcan!* he scolded himself yet again. *Sure, it looks like a huge diversion of combat power to you, but that's because you're a Frontier Security commissioner, not a frigging admiral. You're used to seeing penny-packet squadrons of destroyers—a cruiser division or two, at most—from Frontier Fleet. All of Crandall and Byng's ships between them are hardly even a light task group for Battle Fleet!*

That was undoubtedly true, but it still didn't change the fact that Manpower had somehow managed to gather up more firepower than ninety-five percent of the galaxy's formal navies could have massed and get it deployed to an out-of-the-way corner like Lorcan Verrochio's. Which suggested to him (although he'd been very careful not to mention it to Valery Ottweiler or Ottweiler's buddy Hongbo) that it was past time for him to reevaluate just how deep into the League's bureaucratic and political structures the various Mesan corporations really could reach . . . and what that meant for *him.*

In the meantime, however, that recognition of Manpower's reach was one of the reasons Verrochio was secretly delighted by Byng's attitude. He'd come to the conclusion that disappointing

Manpower would be even less wise than he'd originally thought, which meant there was no going back on his quiet little agreement with them. And, to be honest, he didn't really want to. Or not as long as there was anyone else around to scapegoat if things went as badly as Thurgood's analysis suggested they might, at least. And that was where Verrochio's good friend Josef Byng came in.

Despite his own trepidation, Lorcan Verrochio sure as hell wasn't going to shed any tears if the Manties got reamed, and he wasn't going to lose any sleep over what happened to a Battle Fleet asshole like Josef Byng, either. In fact, in Verrochio's private best-case scenario, Byng would shoot up the Manties, providing the incident Manpower obviously wanted, and get his own ass shot off in the process. And the commissioner intended to be very careful about exactly what the official record indicated about just which fool had rushed in where the wiser and cooler-headed angels of Frontier Security and Frontier Fleet had declined to tread.

"Well, Mr. Commissioner," Byng said with another smile as Verrochio shook his hand and nodded welcomingly to Admiral Thimár, "your memo indicated you were concerned about something the Fleet might be able to assist with. So," he waved his free hand at his chief of staff, "here Admiral Thimár and I are."

"So I see, so I see."

Verrochio ushered his visitors to chairs which gave them an unimpeded view of Pine Mountain, then settled back down behind his desk once more and pressed the button to summon the servants who were primed and waiting. They appeared as if by magic with trays of coffee, tea, and snacks which they distributed with deft, courteous efficiency before they disappeared once more. Byng and Thimár ignored them as if they didn't even exist, of course.

"Vice-Commissioner Hongbo and I," Verrochio continued then, nodding to where Hongbo sat nursing his own cup of coffee, "have just been reviewing some rather . . . bothersome information, Admiral Byng. Information regarding a situation which may end up requiring action on the part of the League's official representatives in the region. We're not quite certain how best to proceed at this point, however, and we'd appreciate your input."

"Of course, Mr. Commissioner." Byng sipped tea a bit noisily, then patted his lips and mustache delicately with a linen napkin. "May I ask what sort of information is proving so bothersome?"

"Well," Verrochio replied with an air of troubled candor, "to be

honest, it concerns the New Tuscany System and the Manticorans."
Less experienced eyes might not have noticed the way Byng stiffened slightly in his chair, and the commissioner continued as if
*he* hadn't noticed it, either. "Part of my problem, I think, is that,
to be perfectly frank, I'm not really confident in my own mind
that I can consider anything that concerns Manticore without
prejudice at this point." He produced a crooked smile. "After what
happened in Monica, and after all of the wild accusations they've
been hurling about at everyone concerning that business in Split
and Montana, I feel a certain undeniable amount of . . . automatic
hostility, I suppose, where they're concerned."

He paused, his expression pensive, and Byng cleared his throat.

"Under the circumstances, Mr. Commissioner, I doubt anyone
could reasonably be surprised by that," the admiral said after a
moment. "Certainly *I* don't see how it could be any other way.
After my own visit to Monica, I'm convinced the people back
home who sent me out here—partly because of their concerns
over Manticoran imperialism, although I'm not really supposed
to admit that to just anyone—had a right to be concerned."

"Really?"

Verrochio put a carefully measured dose of worry into his
one-word response, tempered by exactly the right amount of
relief that someone whose opinion he respected didn't think he
was jumping at shadows. He gazed at Byng for a second or two,
just long enough for his expression to register, then twitched his
shoulders in a small shrug.

"I've tried to put some of that same view before my own
superiors, Admiral," he admitted. "I don't believe I've succeeded
very well, however. In fact, given the replies and instructions I've
received, I've had the impression more than once that the Ministry feels I'm jumping at shadows. In fact, that impression's been
persistent enough for me to come to doubt my own evaluation
of the situation, to some extent, at least. But if the *Navy* feels
that way, perhaps I haven't been as alarmist as my own superiors
appear to believe."

Hongbo Junyan took another sip from his own coffee cup to
hide an involuntary smile. It was truly remarkable, he reflected.
He'd made at least a third of his own career out of manipulating
and steering Lorcan Verrochio, yet Verrochio himself was one
of the most consummate manipulators Hongbo had ever seen

in operation. Which, the vice-commissioner reminded himself, shouldn't really have come as that much of a surprise, perhaps. No one could rise to Verrochio's rank in Frontier Security without having learned how to play the seduction and manipulation game with the best of them. Unfortunately for someone like Lorcan Verrochio, guile and intelligence weren't necessarily the same thing. He'd acquired what was still called (for some reason Hongbo had never managed to pin down) the "apparatchik" skill set, but no one had been able to give him an infusion of brains to go with it. Which was how he'd wound up with the Madras Sector instead of something juicier.

Yet Hongbo was coming to the conclusion that Byng was even stupider than Verrochio. In fact, he seemed a *lot* stupider, which took some doing.

"Well, we in the Navy have had to endure more Manticoran arrogance and meddling in areas far outside their legitimate spheres of interest than most people," Byng responded to Verrochio, and his thin smile was considerably uglier than either of the Frontier Security bureaucrats suspected he thought it was. "That's probably given us a rather more . . . realistic appreciation for what they're really like than other people are in a position to gain."

*He* is *stupider than Lorcan*, Hongbo thought, then grimaced mentally at his own ability to leap to hasty judgments. *Maybe not actually* stupider, he thought. *It doesn't seem to be a lack of native intelligence, at any rate. It's more like a mental blind spot that's so profound, so much a part of him, he doesn't even realize it's there. It's not that he* couldn't *think about it rationally if he wanted to. It's that it never even occurs to him to think about it at all, isn't it?*

But whatever the reason for it, it was apparent to Hongbo that Josef Byng was almost eager to snap up the bait Lorcan Verrochio was trolling before him.

"You may have a point, Admiral," Verrochio said earnestly, as if he'd if read Hongbo's thoughts and decided it was time to set the hook. "And what you've just said—about what the Navy's seen out of the Manticorans over the years—gives added point to my own current concerns, I'm afraid."

"How so, Mr. Commissioner?"

"As I say, we've been receiving information about the New Tuscans' situation vis-à-vis this new 'Star Empire of Manticore' business,"

Verrochio said. "I'm not at liberty to disclose all of our sources—the Gendarmerie has its own rules about need-to-know, I'm afraid, and even *I* don't know where some of Brigadier Yucel's information comes from—but some of the reports causing me concern are based on communication directly from New Tuscany. It would appear to me after looking at all of those reports that Manticore has decided to retaliate against New Tuscany for its refusal to ratify the so-called constitution their 'convention' in Spindle voted out."

"In what way?" Byng's eyes had narrowed, and he leaned forward ever so slightly in his chair.

"The reports aren't really as comprehensive as I'd like, you understand," Verrochio cautioned with the air of a man trying to make certain his audience would bear in mind that there were still holes in his information. "From what we do have, however, Manticore started out by deliberately excluding New Tuscany from any access to the Manticoran investment starting to flow into the Cluster. Of course, if we're speaking government-funded investment, the Star Kingdom—excuse me, I meant the Star *Empire*—has every right to determine where to place its funds. No one could possibly dispute that. But my understanding is that this investment is primarily private in nature, and Manticore hasn't officially prohibited private investment in New Tuscany. Nor, for that matter, has it officially prohibited private New Tuscan investment in the Cluster. Not officially. Yet there seems little doubt that the Manticoran government is *unofficially* blocking any New Tuscan involvement.

"On a personal level, I would find that both regrettable and more than somewhat reprehensible," the commissioner continued a bit mournfully, clearly dismayed by the depths to which human pettiness could descend in the pursuit of vengeance, "but it would scarcely amount to a violation of New Tuscany's sovereignty or inherent rights as an independent star nation. Nor would it constitute any sort of unjustifiable or retaliatory barrier to trade. I think, though, that it's a clear indication of the way Manticore's policymakers—and policy enforcers—are thinking in New Tuscany's case. And that, Admiral, causes me considerable concern over reports that Manticoran warships are beginning to systematically harass New Tuscan merchant shipping."

*Well*, that *was a bull's-eye*, Hongbo thought from his position on the sidelines as Byng's mustache and goatee seemed to bristle suddenly. So far, at least, Ottweiler's private briefing on one Josef

Byng and his attitude towards Manticore had clearly been right on the money.

"Harassing their merchant shipping," the admiral repeated. He sounded like a man trying very hard to project a much greater calm than he felt. "How . . . Mr. Commissioner?" he asked, remembering the title belatedly.

"Accounts are sketchy so far," Verrochio replied, "but it seems clear that they've been imposing additional 'inspections' and 'customs visits' targeted solely and specifically at New Tuscan freighters. Confidentially, I've received at least one official note from Foreign Minister Cardot on behalf of Prime Minister Vézien's government about this matter. I'm not at liberty to tell you its specific contents, but coupled with other things we've been hearing, I'm very much afraid we're looking at an escalating pattern of incidents. They seem to be becoming both more frequent and more serious, which leads me to believe the Manticorans are gradually turning up the heat in a concerted campaign to push New Tuscany entirely out of the Talbott Cluster's internal markets."

He shook his head sadly again.

"I wish I could be positive in my own mind that I'm not reading more into this than I ought to. But, you know, that kind of manipulation and exclusionary control of the local economy was exactly the sort of thing this 'Rembrandt Trade Union' was doing well before Manticore ever started meddling—I mean, before Manticore became involved in Talbott's affairs. And it was the Trade Union that was really the moving force behind the initial annexation plebiscite. I've always had a few reservations about the legitimacy of that plebiscite, and I'm afraid my distrust for the Trade Union and its practices was a large part of the reason for those reservations. Now it looks to me as if Manticore is either allowing its policies to be manipulated by the Rembrandters, or—even worse—is simply picking up where Rembrandt left off."

"Mr. Commissioner," Hongbo said quietly, obediently picking up his own cue, "even if you're right about that—and, frankly, I think there's an excellent chance you are—there's not very much we can do about it." All of the others looked at him, and he gave an eloquently unhappy shrug. "Believe me, Sir, it doesn't make me any happier to mention that than it makes you to hear it, but the Ministry's policy guides are clear on this matter."

"The *League's* policy is to support the free and unimpeded flow of trade, Mr. Hongbo," Byng pointed out just a bit coldly, and Hongbo nodded. After all, that *was* the Solarian League's official policy . . . except where any soul with sufficient temerity to compete with its own major corporations was concerned, of course.

"Yes, Sir. Of course it is," he acknowledged. "But the Ministry's position has always been—and rightly so, I think—that the Office of Frontier Security isn't supposed to be making foreign policy or trade policy on its own. Unless someone with a legitimate interest in a region requests our assistance, there really isn't anything we can do."

"Has New Tuscany requested assistance, Mr. Commissioner?" Rear Admiral Thimár asked, speaking up for the first time, and Verrochio didn't even smile, although Hongbo could hear his mental "*Gotcha!*" quite clearly.

"Well, *technically*—" he drew the word out "—no. Not *yet*." He twitched his shoulders again. "Foreign Minister Cardot's note expresses Prime Minister Vézien's concerns frankly, and I think from what she's said that he hopes we'll send an observer of our own to look into these matters. For that matter, I wouldn't be at all surprised if we were to find ourselves asked to launch an official investigation sometime in the next several T-months, but no one in New Tuscany's gone quite that far at this time." The commissioner smiled with a certain sad cynicism. "I think the Prime Minister is hoping—how realistically I couldn't say, of course—that if he's just patient, this will all blow over."

"Not bloody likely," Byng muttered, then shook himself.

"Excuse me, Mr. Commissioner," he said more clearly. "That was quite rude of me. I'm afraid I was simply . . . thinking out loud."

"And not reaching any conclusions I don't share, I'm afraid," Verrochio said heavily.

"Mr. Commissioner," Thimár said after a quick glance at her superior's profile, "may I ask exactly why you've shared this information with us?" Verrochio looked at her, and she smiled dryly. "I don't doubt that you genuinely wanted a second viewpoint, Sir," she said. "On the other hand, I *do* doubt that that's all you wanted, if you'll pardon my saying so."

"Guilty as charged, I'm afraid," Hongbo admitted. "What I'm really looking for, I think, is a way that we could encourage and reassure New Tuscany while simultaneously communicating our unhappiness to Manticore without violating the official limitations placed on what Frontier Security can legitimately do in a case like this."

"I see." Byng nodded, and smiled again himself. It was a noticeably colder smile than Thimár's, Hongbo noticed. "Admiral Thimár and I don't work for Frontier Security, however, do we?"

"Well, that's rather a gray area in your case, I suppose, Admiral." There was a conspiratorial gleam in Verrochio's eye. "You command a *Frontier Fleet* task group, and out here in the marches, Frontier Fleet does—nominally, at least—work for—or *with*, at any rate—Frontier Security. You, however, as a *Battle Fleet* officer, are outside the normal Frontier Fleet chain of command. I think that would give you a valuable difference of perspective in a case like this, but it does create a certain ambiguity when it comes to the notion of my giving you any sort of formal instructions."

*What a crock*, Hongbo thought rather admiringly. *It doesn't matter where Byng comes from—not legally. He's commanding a Frontier Fleet task group, and the table of organization when he was sent out here clearly tasked him to support us in any way possible. If that's not tantamount to putting him under our orders, then I don't know what would be! But that's not the point, either. The point is that if Lorcan can maneuver him into suggesting that he isn't under our orders and get it into this meeting's official recording . . .*

"I suppose that's true, Mr. Commissioner," Byng said. "On the other hand, whether you have the power to give me binding orders or not, my own superiors clearly wanted me to be aware of your concerns and to act to support you in any way I can. Perhaps I could make a suggestion?"

"By all means, Admiral. Please."

"Well, as you've just pointed out, as a Battle Fleet officer, I stand outside the normal Frontier Fleet chains of command, and I believe it would be entirely feasible for Battle Fleet to take a somewhat more . . . proactive stance than the Ministry's instructions might permit *you* to take."

"That sounds just a bit potentially . . . risky to me, Admiral," Verrochio said, allowing his tone to show a trace of cautious hesitancy now that he was completely confident the hook had been well and truly set.

"Oh, I don't really think so, Mr. Commissioner." Byng waved one hand. "It's not as if I were proposing any sort of preemptive military action like that Manticoran business in Monica, after all." He smiled thinly. "No, what I had in mind was more of a simple—and quite unexceptionable—flag-showing visit designed to demonstrate to both New Tuscany and Manticore that we consider amicable relations with independent star nations in this region important to the Solarian League's official foreign policy."

"A flag-showing visit?" Verrochio repeated without a trace of triumph.

"Yes, Sir. I'm sure no one could possibly construe a simple port visit as any sort of unwarranted provocation, especially if the decision to make it originated with Battle Fleet, rather than anyone in your office. If, in the course of such a visit, I were to pass any private messages from you to Prime Minister Vézien, I'm sure that would be quite unobjectionable, as well. But a visit by a division or two of Solarian battlecruisers is likely to have a bracing effect on New Tuscany. At the least, it should convince the New Tuscan people that they don't stand alone in the face of Manticoran retaliation against them. And if the Manticorans should learn of it, I can hardly see how it could fail to have at least some moderating impact on their ambitions."

"I'm not sure 'a division or two' would be sufficient, Admiral," Verrochio said. Byng looked at him with an unmistakable edge of incredulity, and the OFS commissioner grimaced. "Oh, I don't doubt that it *ought* to be sufficient, Admiral. Don't mistake me about that! But we've got the example of Monica in front of us, and I've reviewed that 'conversation' between you and that Manticoran Admiral—Henke, or Gold Peak, or whoever she is." He grimaced. "They *are* impressed with their own jumped up little aristocracy, aren't they? But reading between the lines of what *she* said—and how she said it, for that matter—and the reports which have reached me from Old Terra since their attack on Monica, it's apparent to me that the Manticorans are just as impressed with their own accomplishments as they are with their titles of 'nobility.' I've had some locally generated reports about the possibility that they've increased their combat effectiveness, as well, although that's scarcely my own area of expertise. Obviously, your judgment would be superior to my own where something like that is concerned. But my main concern is more with the way the *Manticorans* might be thinking, and we know they've sent at least some reinforcements to Talbott since the 'annexation' went through."

"And your point is, Mr. Commissioner?" Byng's voice was just a bit frosty, and Verrochio sighed.

"Admiral, I want the situation resolved, and I want New Tuscany's legitimate interests protected, both for New Tuscany's sake and to demonstrate to the local star nations that the Solarian League, at least, is a good neighbor. But we've already had recent and painful experience of what Manticoran high-handedness and readiness to resort to brute force can mean. I don't want *anyone* killed, not even Manticorans, and I'm simply concerned that they could get . . . carried away again, the way they did in Monica, unless it's painfully obvious even to them that the consequences would be disastrous *for* them."

"I believe the commissioner is suggesting that it would be better to arrange a somewhat greater show of force, Admiral Byng," Hongbo said almost apologetically. "Something powerful enough that not even a Manticoran could misread the odds badly enough—or be stupid enough—to try a repeat performance of something like Monica."

"Against the Solarian Navy?" Byng seemed to find it difficult to believe anyone could take such an absurd concept seriously.

"No one is suggesting that it would be particularly wise—or rational—of them to do anything of the sort, Admiral," Hongbo said earnestly. "The commissioner is simply suggesting that it's incumbent upon the League to go the extra kilometer and do everything in its power to prevent such a tragic . . . miscalculation, shall we say, on anyone's part from leading to a repeat of Monica."

"Any such 'miscalculation' would have a radically different outcome for Manticore than the 'Battle of Monica' did," Byng said coldly. "On the other hand, I suppose there's quite a bit of validity to your concern, Mr. Commissioner." He looked directly at Verrochio. "Mind you, it would take a particularly stupid neobarb to make that sort of 'miscalculation,' but that doesn't mean it couldn't happen. We are talking about Manticorans, after all."

The admiral pursed his lips and thought for several seconds, then looked at Thimár.

"How long would it take to reassemble the entire task group here in Meyers, Karlotte? A month?"

"More like six T-weeks, Sir," Thimár said so promptly that it was apparent she'd been running the same calculations in her own mind. "Maybe even seven."

"Too long," Byng objected—an objection with which Hongbo earnestly agreed, given his own conversation with Valery Ottweiler.

"We could recall Sigbee's and Chang's squadrons sooner than that," Thimár replied. "In fact, we could probably get both of them reassembled here in less than your original one-month estimate. And we have at least half a dozen tin-cans available as a screen. For that matter, we could tap Thurgood, as well."

Verrochio started to open his mouth to protest. The last thing he wanted was for a naval force which was clearly and unambiguously under his command—and whose senior officer had reported such reservations about Manticoran capabilities—involved in something like this. Byng beat him to it, though.

"I scarcely think *that's* going to be necessary, Karlotte," he half-sneered. Then he seemed to remember where he was and who Thurgood currently worked for, and he glanced at Verrochio. "What I mean, Mr. Commissioner," he said just a bit hastily, "is that adding Commodore Thurgood's forces to the one Admiral Thimár is already talking about would scarcely constitute a significant increase in its combat power. In addition, of course, if I were to take the Commodore or any significant portion of his order of battle with me, it would leave *you* with no quick response force ready to hand if something should come up while I was away."

"I see." Verrochio looked at him for a moment, then shrugged. "That's certainly sounds logical to me, Admiral. And, as I've said before, this is scarcely my area of expertise. I believe you're a much better judge of these matters than I am. By all means, make whatever arrangements seen best to you. I'll leave all of this in your capable hands."

Michelle Henke felt a wave of profound satisfaction as HMS *Artemis* and HMS *Horatius* made their alpha translations just outside the Spindle System's hyper limit the better part of four T-months after departing for Monica. Although she'd hated being gone so long, and dumping so much responsibility on Shulamit Onasis while she was away, she hadn't exactly been sitting on her own hands all that time, and she also savored a sense of solid achievement. She'd completed her visit to Monica, placed that insufferable twit Byng on notice (in the most pleasant possible way, of course), gotten the new picket station at Tillerman up and running to her own satisfaction—well, as close to her satisfaction as she could, under the circumstances—and made port visits to Talbott, Scarlet, Marian, Dresden (where she'd discovered that Khumalo, at Henri Krietzmann's suggestion, had diverted one of the newly arrived LAC wings to Tillerman), and Montana on her way back to Spindle.

*By now, those LACs are already in Tillerman, setting up house to support Conner*, she thought cheerfully, leaning back in her command chair. *That ought to come as quite a surprise to any pirates who haven't gotten the word yet. And it should go a long way towards beefing up his missile defenses if Byng really is stupid enough to try something, too. Which, unfortunately, he probably is, at least under the wrong circumstances. In fact, he's the only really* unpleasant *surprise of the entire trip. Why couldn't even* Battle Fleet *have sent us an admiral with an IQ higher than his hat size? They have to have at least* one *flag officer with a functional brain! Don't they?*

She shook her head at the thought, comforting herself with the reflection that even though Byng might be an idiot, she'd at least been able to quietly brief the system presidents in the vicinity—and their senior military officers—about him. And most of those presidents and officers had seemed reassuringly competent and tough-minded too. She'd been particularly impressed by the Montanans, and she'd also been glad of the opportunity to meet the formidable and reformed (if that was the proper word for it) Stephen Westman.

*Thank goodness Terekhov and Van Dort got him on our side, at least,* she thought, then looked across the flag bridge to Dominica Adenauer's station and the tallish, brown-haired lieutenant commander sitting at her side. Maxwell Tersteeg had been waiting at Dresden along with the dispatches informing Michelle about the LAC deployment to Tillerman. Augustus Khumalo had sent him forward as a candidate to fill the electronic warfare officer's hole on her staff, and so far he appeared to be working out quite well. Most importantly, he was good at his job, but he also got along well with both Adenauer and Edwards, and he was a good "fit" for the staff's chemistry. He had a sly, quiet sense of humor and his pleasantly plain face was remarkably mobile and expressive . . . when he chose for it to be. In fact, when he wanted to, those brown eyes could effortlessly project a soulful "Aren't I pitiful?" air as good (and apparently guileless) as Dicey's food mooching expression at its best.

*I think he's going to do just fine*, she thought. *And he pretty much fills all the gaps . . . aside from an intelligence officer.* She grimaced mentally at the thought. *Still, Cindy's doing well with that. It's not fair to dump it on top of her along with everything else she already has on her plate, but I haven't heard any complaints out of her. In fact, I think she* likes *the duty. And I know she's enjoyed "mentoring" Gwen. By now, she's got him trained up as a pretty fair deputy, really.*

Michelle sometimes found herself suspecting that she'd worked hard to convince herself that Lecter was satisfied with the situation because things seemed to be working out so well. "If it ain't broke, don't fix it" was one of the more fundamental aspects of her professional philosophy, after all. And all justifications on her own part aside, it wasn't hurting young Lieutenant Archer one bit to have his own professional resume extended.

She glanced over her shoulder at the thought, to where Archer stood attentively just behind her command chair, hands clasped lightly behind him, gazing into the main plot.

*Well, however stupid* Byng *may be, at least* Gwen's *been one of the more pleasant surprises of this entire deployment, and not just because of how well he's "subbing" for Cindy on the intelligence front,* she thought, turning her own attention back to the plot. Honor had been entirely correct about his basic ability when she'd recommended him, and although Michelle still sometimes caught the shadow of a ghost behind those green eyes, it was obvious he'd come to grips with the memories and doubts which had afflicted him the day they first met. Not that those memories or doubts had ever been permitted to affect the apparently effortless efficiency with which he performed his duties. Nor was he particularly shy about prodding his admiral—ever so respectfully, of course—when she needed prodding. As a matter of fact, he and Chris Billingsley got along with one another remarkably well for two people with such disparate backgrounds . . . and Michelle had discovered early on that they were prepared to double-team her unscrupulously. As long, of course, as whatever they wanted was for her own good.

*Honor told me she was going to be looking for good nannies for Raoul. If she doesn't mind corrupting influences—and the fact that she puts up with Nimitz clearly proves that she doesn't—I know where she could find* two *of them!*

She chuckled at the thought, and Gervais raised one eyebrow. "Ma'am?"

"Oh, nothing really important, Gwen," she told him. "I was just thinking." She started to wave one hand dismissively, but then she paused, arrested, as the imp of her evil side whispered in her ear.

"Thinking about what, Ma'am?" Gervais asked when she clearly stopped in mid-thought, and she smiled wickedly at him.

"I was just thinking about the fact that we're going to be reporting in to Admiral Khumalo and Minister Krietzmann shortly," she said. "I hope you and Ms. Boltitz are prepared to be your usual . . . efficient selves in organizing our meetings. We all really appreciated the long, hard hours you two put in, even outside regular business hours, slaving away to make our conferences a success, you know."

*You know, Gwen,* she thought, watching his admirably grave expression, *one of the things I really love about your complexion is how easily you color up when I score a direct hit. You may be able to keep a straight face, but . . .*

"I mean, I understand that you actually subjected yourselves to the hardship of dining at Sigourney's just so you could set up that 'dinner party' of mine." Her eyes radiated soulful gratitude as she gazed at him. "I do hope that we're not going to be forced to demand any equally painful sacrifices out of you this time around."

"I—" Gervais began, then stopped, his color brighter than ever, and shrugged.

"You got me, Ma'am," he acknowledged. "Direct hit, center of mass. What can I say?"

"Nothing at all, Gwen." Michelle reached out a repentant hand and patted his forearm. "I shouldn't be teasing you about it, really."

"Is it really that obvious, Ma'am?"

"Probably not to someone who doesn't see as much of you as I do," she said reassuringly.

"I'm not sure it's obvious to *her* yet." He shook his head, his expression wry. "She's just the least little bit skittish where people from 'aristocratic' backgrounds are concerned."

"Hard to blame her, I suppose," Michelle said. "Dresden's no Garden of Eden, you know. And it's still awfully early in the day for any of the Talbotters to have a real feel for how the Star Kingdom differs from their local landlords."

"Calling Dresden 'no Garden of Eden' is one hell of an understatement, if you'll pardon my saying so, Ma'am." Gervais' expression was suddenly darker, his voice grim. "I'm glad I got to see it firsthand. There've been times I thought Helga must have been exaggerating conditions there. Now I know better."

"Welcome to Frontier Security's 'benign neglect,' Lieutenant," Michelle half-growled. "If those useless bastards would spend a *tenth* of the budget they spend on fur-lined toilet seats for their commissioners' heads on the Verge planets they're supposed to be looking out for—"

She cut herself off with a quick, curt headshake.

"Let's not get me started on that one," she said in a more conversational tone, and smiled at him again. "In the meantime, I hope your campaign with Ms. Boltitz succeeds, Gwen. If, ah, you should require any . . . senior support to communicate the honorable nature of your intentions to her, shall we say—?"

She allowed her voice to trail off suggestively, and Gervais felt his face heating again.

"That's quite all right, Ma'am," he said with the utmost sincerity, eyes steadfastly locked once again upon the main plot. "Really."

"We're picking up additional transponders, Ma'am," Dominica Adenauer reported.

"Really?" Michelle turned her chair towards the operations officer. She'd expected more ships to have arrived during her absence, but it was nice to find that her expectations had been realized. "What kind of transponders?"

"It looks like a full squadron of *Saganami-Cs*, Ma'am. And a squadron of *Rolands*, as well."

"Outstanding!" Michelle smiled hugely. "I assume one of the *Saganami-Cs* is squawking a flagship code?"

"Yes, Ma'am. She's the *Quentin Saint-James*."

"Really?" Michelle quirked one eyebrow in surprise at the name. *I wonder what happened to the* last *one of those*, she wondered, then turned to Lieutenant Commander Edwards.

"Bill," she turned to Lieutenant Commander Edwards, "see if you can raise *Quentin Saint-James*. I'd like to speak to the squadron commander . . . whoever he turns out to be!"

"Yes, Ma'am," her com officer replied with a smile of his own, and began entering commands. Given the way dispatches tended to chase fleet detachments around without ever quite catching up, little uncertainties like that were far from uncommon. And the

Star Empire's current scramble to reallocate its Navy in response to events here in the Quadrant were only making that even worse, Michelle reminded herself.

*As my own recent perambulations handily illustrate,* she reflected, feeling her sense of accomplishment fade just a bit. *It all needed doing, but I wish to hell I could've done it faster!*

She heard the soft mutter of Edwards' voice, as well, transmitting her own communications request to *Quentin Saint-James,* but at the moment, *Artemis* was still a good nine light-minutes from the heavy cruiser, and even the grav-pulse com wasn't really instantaneous. Faster than light, yes; instantaneous, no. There was a delay of almost seventeen and a half seconds built into any two-way conversation at this distance, and it took a few minutes for Edwards to get through to his counterpart in the heavy cruiser squadron.

"Ma'am," he said then, "I have that connection you asked for."

"Really?" Michelle said again, raising one eyebrow at what sounded suspiciously like a note of pleasure in Edwards' voice.

"Yes, Ma'am. I have the senior officer of CruRon Ninety-Four on the com. A . . . Commodore Terekhov, I believe."

Michelle's eyes widened, and then she smiled even more hugely than before.

*Jesus,* she thought, *they must have stuck an impeller node up his . . . um,* backside *and fired him back out our way before* Hexapuma *ever got as far in-system as* Hephaestus! *Poor bastard probably didn't even have time to kiss his wife first! But they couldn't have found anyone better to give the squadron to.*

"Switch it to my display, Bill," she directed.

"Yes, Ma'am."

Aivars Terekhov's face appeared on the com display deployed from her command chair just at knee level, and she smiled down at it.

"*Commodore* Terekhov!" she said. "It's good to see you . . . and to hear about your promotion. No one told me that was in the works when they sent me off to Talbott, but everything I saw at Monica tells me it was well-deserved. And, to be honest, having your squadron here is at least equally welcome."

Michelle waited the seventeen seconds it took for the transmission to make the round-trip, and then Terekhov smiled.

"Thank you, Milady," he said. "I won't pretend I wouldn't have preferred a little bit more time at home, but the promotion is nice, and they gave me a brand-new squadron to play with to go with it. And I have to admit that I feel a certain proprietary interest in the Quadrant that makes it feel good to be back."

Michelle's eyes narrowed. The words—as words—were just fine, almost exactly what she would have expected. But something about the tone, and about the quality of that smile . . .

*Strain*, she thought. *He's worried—even frightened—about something and trying like hell not to show it.*

Her sudden, irrational suspicion was ridiculous, and she knew it. But she also knew that she couldn't shake it, and an icy wind seemed to blow through her bones at the thought. She knew exactly what this man had done, and not just in Monica. Anything that could frighten *him* . . .

"Commodore," she said slowly, "is there something I ought to know?"

Seventeen more seconds passed, and then the arctic blue eyes on her com display widened ever so slightly, as if in surprise. Then they narrowed again, and he nodded.

"Yes, Milady, I suppose there is," he said quietly. "I'd rather assumed you'd have received Admiral Khumalo's dispatches about it, though. I suppose they must have passed you in transit."

He paused, clearly suggesting that perhaps the vice admiral would prefer to tell her about whatever it was in person, and Michelle snorted. If he thought she was going to sit around on her posterior waiting for the penny to drop after an introduction like that, he had another think coming!

"I'm sure Admiral Khumalo and I will be discussing a lot of things, Commodore," she said just a bit tartly. "In the meantime, however, why don't you go ahead and tell me about it?"

"Yes, Milady," he said again, seventeen seconds later, and drew a visible breath and squared his shoulders ever so slightly. "I'm afraid we received dispatches from the home system just over three T-weeks ago. The news isn't good. According to Admiral Caparelli, the Havenites attacked in overwhelming strength. From all appearances, Theisman and Pritchart must have decided to put everything on one throw of the dice after what happened to the Havenites at Lovett and go for an outright knockout blow before we could get Apollo into full deployment. We stopped them, but we got—*both* sides got—hit really hard. According to the follow-up reports we've received since, it looks like—"

# Chapter Thirty-Eight

"I'M NOT HAPPY ABOUT THIS, Maxime," Damien Dusserre said. "I'm not happy about it at all."

"I don't think you see me doing handsprings of joy about it, either, do you?" Prime Minister Maxime Vézien shot back tartly.

"Damn it, I knew this whole thing looked too good to be true from the very beginning," Dusserre grumbled.

Vézien felt a powerful urge to punch the security minister squarely in the nose, but he suppressed it easily enough. First, because the younger, larger, stronger, and physically much tougher Dusserre would probably have proceeded to remove the Prime Minister's limbs one at a time, with the maximum possible amount of discomfort. But secondly, and even more to the point, because Dusserre was, indeed, the one member of the Vézien Government who had consistently voiced his reservations about the entire operation.

*Which didn't keep him from going ahead and signing off on it, anyway,* Vézien thought rather snappishly. *Maybe he didn't like it, but I didn't see him coming up with any better ideas!*

Actually, as Vézien was well aware in his calmer moments, one of the reasons he was so easily pissed off with his Security Minister these days was that Damien Dusserre was Andrieaux Yvernau's brother-in-law. It was Yvernau's brilliant strategy at the Constitutional Convention which had gotten the entire New Tuscany System into the Star Empire of Manticore's black books

510

in the first place, and Vézien couldn't quite suppress the ignoble urge to vent his frustration on Yvernau's relatives. And he could at least tell himself there was some justification in it, given the fact that it was Yvernau's family connections which had gotten him named to head the delegation to Spindle in the first place.

*Yes, there is,* he reflected. *But the truth is, as you're perfectly well aware, Max, whether you want to admit it, that even though Yvernau is an idiot, not even a genius could have come up with a good strategy once those parliamentary bastards back in Manticore got up on their high horse and started bleating about "repressive local régimes" here in the Cluster. And having that bitch Medusa in the driver's seat didn't help one damned thing, either. If we'd only realized where all of this was going to go when that son-of-a-bitch Van Dort came around selling us on what a gold mine that whole damned annexation idea was going to be for everyone involved . . . !*

"I know you've had reservations, Damien," he said out loud instead of the considerably more cutting (and satisfying) responses which flickered through his head. "Unfortunately, reservations or no, we're where we are, not where we might want to be. So why don't we both just go ahead and admit that neither of us is happy about the situation and then do what we can to make the best of it?"

Dusserre gave him a sour look, but then the Security Minister drew a deep breath and nodded.

"You're right," he acknowledged.

"Good."

Vézien tilted back in his comfortable chair and gazed up through the office's huge skylight. That skylight was one of the Prime Minister's favorite perks, one that offered refreshment and energy whenever the weight of his high political office crushed down upon him. It wasn't a view screen, wasn't an artificial image gathered from remote cameras. It was an actual, honest to God *skylight*, almost three meters on a side. Its thermal-barrier smart glass panes automatically configured themselves to filter sunlight, and then, under other conditions, seemed almost to disappear entirely. When it rained, the sound of the raindrops—from a gentle patter to a hard, driving rhythm—filled the office with a soothing sense of natural energy. When lightning rumbled about the heavens, he could watch God's artillery flashing in mist-walled valleys among cloudy mountains. And when it was night, he could look up through it to moon-struck cloud chasms or the clear, awesome vista of the distant stars burning so far above him.

At the moment, unfortunately, the sight of those stars was much less soothing than usual.

"Do you have the feeling, Damien," he asked slowly after several seconds, "that Ms. Anisimovna is privy to information the rest of us haven't received yet?"

"I've *always* felt she was working to an agenda and a set of instructions we didn't know anything about—and that she wasn't about to *tell* us anything about, either." Dusserre sounded almost surprised by the question, as if its answer was so painfully self-evident he couldn't quite believe the Prime Minister had asked it.

"That's not what I asked." Vézien lowered his eyes from the skylight to gaze at the other man instead of the stars. "Of course we don't know what her real instructions are, and, of course, she's not going to tell us. We wouldn't tell her everything if our positions were reversed, either, would we? But what bothers me at the moment is that I have the oddest feeling that she knows more about a *lot* of things than we do." He frowned, seeking the words to more clearly explain what he was getting at. "I mean about things the rest of the galaxy is going to find out about in due time but doesn't know about *yet*," he said. "Things—news stories, events—that no one here on New Tuscany's even heard about yet that she's already factoring into her plans."

Dusserre looked back at him for several seconds, then snorted.

"I'll grant you the woman is fiendishly clever, Max. And I'll also point out that she's receiving regular messages via private dispatch boats from Mesa and God knows where else, whereas we're basically dependent on the news services—which don't exactly see us as one of their red-hot bureau depots—to find out what's going on anywhere else in the galaxy. So, yes, she probably does know quite a few things we haven't found out about yet. But let's not talk ourselves into thinking she's some kind of sorceress, all right? It's bad enough that we don't have much choice but to dance with her and let her lead without our deciding she somehow magically controls the orchestra's choice of music, as well!"

Vézien grimaced, but he also let the point drop. His initial question had been at least partly whimsical, after all. Still, though . . . Try as he might, he couldn't quite shake that feeling—that . . . intuition, perhaps—that Aldona Anisimovna was always at least a couple of jumps ahead of anyone else in the New Tuscany System, and he didn't much care for the sensation.

"Well, anyway," he said, waving aside his own question, "I suppose what really matters is whether or not we have the assets in place to actually do what she wants as quickly as she wants it done."

"That and the question of whether or not doing what she wants on this revised schedule of hers is also going to accomplish what *we* want," Dusserre replied. "And, while I'm perfectly ready to concede that you're right and we don't have much choice but to continue with this strategy, the timing on it really worries me, Max."

The security minister's tone was cold, sober, and—most worrisome of all—sincere, Vézien thought. And, as usual, he had a damnably good point.

"We weren't supposed to be doing this for *months* yet," Dusserre continued, "and I damned well wish I hadn't told Anisimovna we'd been able to complete our arrangements for it this early."

"It wouldn't have made that much difference in the end," Vézien said, offering what comfort he could. "The message turnaround time to Pequod is too short. Even if we hadn't done a single thing to get ready for it already, it wouldn't have taken more than a week or two to set it all up from scratch. And, frankly, a week or two either way isn't going to make that much difference."

"I know," Dusserre muttered, then puffed his cheeks out and sighed. "I know," he repeated more distinctly. "I suppose I'm just still looking for things to kick myself over because I'm scared enough to piss on my own shoes."

Despite himself, Vézien felt himself warming at least briefly towards the security minister as Dusserre admitted to the same trepidation Vézien felt.

"I know the Solly battlecruisers were supposed to already be here before we kicked off this phase of the operation," he said almost gently. "But we do have confirmation from other sources that Byng is in the Madras Sector. She's not lying to us about that. And hard as I've tried, I can't come up with any scenario where it would help Manpower in any conceivable way for her to have come clear out here and set us up to fall flat on our asses just so her people can get egg on their faces in all the Solly 'faxes all over again. There may *be* one, but I sure as hell can't figure out what it might be! And assuming she'd prefer for us all to succeed,

I can't see why she'd lie to us about Manpower and Mesa's ability to bring Verrochio up to scratch and get Byng moving ahead of schedule. So we're just going to have to take her word that they can do that and act accordingly."

"Wonderful." Dusserre inhaled deeply. "Well, in that case we really need to be talking to Nicholas and Guédon. I know my people did most of the organizing and operational planning, and picking the merchant ship wasn't as difficult as I'd been afraid it would be. We've got all of that in place, but we didn't have the resources outside the home system to set something like this up at the other end, as well. We had to rely on the Navy for that, and we're pretty much completely outside the pipeline in that regard. We had to let them put it into place, and we're going to need their resources to actually pull the trigger, as well."

Vézien nodded. He was right, of course, and it wouldn't be all that hard to get hold of Admiral Josette Guédon, the New Tuscan Navy's chief of naval operations. Getting hold of the Minister of War was going to be a bit tougher, though, since Nicholas Pélisard had chosen this particularly inconvenient moment for a vacation trip to visit family in the Selkirk System. He wouldn't be back for at least another week, and his Deputy Minister of War hadn't been briefed in on the operation. There'd seemed no particular need to do that—or, rather, it had seemed they had plenty of time to do it, just as Pélisard should've had plenty of time to complete his vacation trip. Besides, his deputy was a . . . less than stellar choice for the coordination of any covert operation.

"I don't want to bring Challon in on this, not without discussing it with Nicholas first, at least," the Prime Minister said after moment. "I'm not confident enough in his ability to keep a secret to feel comfortable doing that. But Guédon already knows what's supposed to happen, right?"

"I discussed it with her myself," Dusserre agreed. "I left it up to Nicholas to organize the nuts and bolts and get the ship properly rigged. He's the one with the connections for that side of things, after all. But I do know that he personally spoke to her directly about it, so she has to have been in the loop. In fact, knowing her, she probably wouldn't have trusted anyone outside her own office to arrange it."

"All right, then I'll take care of bringing her up to speed on the changes," Vézien decided. "One of the nice things about being

Prime Minister is that I can talk to anyone I need to just about any time I want to, and with Nicholas out of the system, I don't imagine anyone will be particularly surprised if I need to talk to the CNO directly."

"Which still brings you back to deciding what to do about Challon, doesn't it?" Dusserre asked. Vézien glanced at him, and the security minister grimaced sourly. "I'm not that fond of Challon, Max. I'll admit it. But if I do, then *you* have to admit he's given me ample reason to be *unfond* of him. If he finds out you've been talking to Guédon without involving him when he's at least temporarily perched on the top of his own dung heap during Nicholas' absence, his vanity is going to demand that he figure out whatever secret you were obviously trying to keep from him. And, unfortunately, he's not a *complete* idiot. There's a damned good chance he'll be able to dig up enough to present a real problem if he starts blathering about it. And he *will* blab about it if he figures it out. Probably to a newsy he figures could make him look good, although God knows *that's* a challenge few mortals would care to embrace!"

That, unfortunately, was an all too likely scenario, Vézien thought. Armand Challon was actually quite a bright fellow, in a lot of ways. In fact, he was very good at his job, which was one reason (if not the most important one) he was the Deputy Minister of War. But he had a shrewish, nastily vindictive nature and an inveterate need to bask in the admiration of others. It was important to him that he be *perceived* as important, and he had a penchant for dropping bits and pieces—what he fondly thought were "mysterious" hints—about all of the important things he was up to. They made for good gossip material at the sorts of parties he graced with his presence . . . and the newsies had learned ages ago to hover around him with suitably admiring expressions. Which was the very reason he was normally kept as far away as possible from any secret that was genuinely important.

Unfortunately, he was also the son of *Victor* Challon, and Victor controlled about twenty percent of the delegates to the System Parliament's upper chamber. Which was the most important reason Armand had been named Deputy War Minister in the first place.

*There are times*, Vézien reflected, *when I think it would actually be simpler—easier, at least—to let the Mob take over than it* is to go on wading through this bottomless sea of cousins, in-laws, families, friends, and relations. Let them drain the pond and then shoot the fish flapping around in the mud. There'd have to be at least some gain in efficiency, wouldn't there?

"If I have to, I'll talk to Victor about it," he said out loud. "I don't want to, but at least he's smart enough to realize why we have to keep this completely black. And if he has to sit on Armand to keep his mouth shut, he'll do it. But let's not borrow any more trouble than we have to. Hopefully, that's one fire we won't have to put out in the first place."

"Hopefully," Dusserre agreed just a bit sourly.

"At any rate, I'll talk to Guédon tomorrow. Like you, I don't see how Nicholas could have set it up without involving her. If it turns out she's not directly hands-on with it, then I'll get back to you and we'll have to see about reorganizing things. At least the timing doesn't seem to be absolutely critical. We can hit a few days off in either direction without making Ms. Anisimovna unhappy."

"Oh, by all means," Dusserre said, and this time his tone was sour enough to curdle milk, "let's not do anything to make *Ms. Anisimovna* unhappy!"

Captain Gabrielle Séguin did her best to look completely calm and poised as she tucked her uniform cap under her left arm and followed the youthful lieutenant into the chief of naval operations' private office.

The fact that there'd been absolutely no warning of this meeting until the order to report to Admiral Guédon's office arrived approximately fifty-three standard minutes ago was not calculated to make Séguin confident. Admittedly, the light cruiser *Camille* was one of the New Tuscan Navy's most powerful and most modern units, and Séguin would probably be looking at her own rear admiral's star at the end of this commission. It wasn't as if she were some junior lieutenant being called into the captain's day cabin to be reamed a new one, she told herself.

*No*, a stubborn part of her replied, *it's got the potential to be a lot worse than that, and you know it.*

That cheerful thought carried her through the door and through the ritual handshake of greeting. Then the lieutenant disappeared, and Séguin was alone with Guédon.

Guédon was an older woman, a first-generation prolong recipient whose once-dark hair had gone gunmetal gray and whose face had developed well-defined lines. But she was still a tall, imposing figure, one who kept herself an excellent physical condition, and the stiff rings of golden braid on her uniform sleeves reached almost all the way from cuff to elbow.

"Sit down, Captain." Guédon's voice had a harsh edge, a slight rasp that wasn't exactly unpleasant but gave it a certain snap of command. Séguin had always wondered whether that was her natural voice or if she'd carefully cultivated that whiff of harshness.

"Thank you, Ma'am." Séguin obeyed the instruction, and Guédon came around to stand in front of her desk, folding her gold-braided arms in front of her while she leaned back against the edge of the desk.

"I realize you don't have a clue why I wanted to see you, Captain," Guédon said, coming to the point with all of her customary bluntness. "Well, I'm about to explain that to you. And when I'm finished, you're going to go back to your ship, and your ship is going to Pequod, and when you get to Pequod you're going to carry out a highly classified mission which the President and Cabinet have determined is vital to the interests and security of our star nation. You will *not* discuss this mission, its parameters, or its particulars, with anyone—*ever*—without my specific and personal authorization. You will not even *think* about this mission without my specific and personal authorization. But you *will* carry it out flawlessly, Captain, because, if you don't, there may not be a New Tuscany very much longer."

Séguin felt herself turning into stone in the comfortable chair, and Guédon smiled thinly.

"Now that I presume I have your attention, Captain," she said, "here's what you're going to do . . ."

# Chapter Thirty-Nine

"YES, MA'AM? YOU WANTED to see me?" Lieutenant Askew said just a bit nervously as he entered Commander Bourget's office aboard SLNS *Jean Bart*.

"Yes, Matt, I do," Bourget said, leaning back in her chair. The commander was a petite brunette, with hazel eyes and what would have been called a "pug nose" on someone of less towering authority than the executive officer of one of the Solarian League's battlecruisers. As a general rule, Askew liked Bourget, who reminded him rather strongly of one of his favorite grammar school teachers, but the summons to her office had been as unexpected as it had been abrupt.

"You may recall a conversation you had with Commander Zeiss a couple of months ago," the XO said now in a straight-to-the-point tone which set all of Askew's mental hackles quivering.

"Yes, Ma'am. I do," he confirmed cautiously when she paused and cocked an expectant eyebrow at him.

"Well, correct me if I'm wrong, but didn't she say something to you about 'lying low'?"

"Well, yes, Ma'am, but—"

"But me no buts, Lieutenant Askew," Bourget interrupted in a rather colder tone. "I thought Commander Zeiss had made herself quite clear at that time. And I suppose I should add that she did so at my specific instructions, on behalf of the Captain."

"Yes, Ma'am. But—"

"When I want to hear interruptions, Lieutenant, I'll let you know," Bourget said flatly, and Askew closed his mouth.

"Better," the exec said with a frosty smile. She swung her chair gently from side to side for several seconds, regarding him with cold hazel eyes, then drew a deep breath.

"In case you haven't already figured it out," she said, "I'm more than just a little bit pissed with you at this particular moment. Damn it, Matt—what did you think you were *doing*?"

This time, despite the fact that it was obviously a question, Askew found himself much more hesitant about replying. Unfortunately, he didn't have much choice.

"Ma'am, I didn't mean to make any waves. It's just that . . . just that I haven't been able to turn my brain off, and the more I looked at Thurgood's analysis, and the more I've looked at our own intelligence reports, the more convinced I am that we've well and truly underestimated the Manties' capabilities."

"It may surprise you to discover this," Bourget voice was somewhat gentler yet still carried an unmistakable note of asperity, "but the Captain and I already entertain some modest suspicions in that direction ourselves. Suspicions which, unlike certain lieutenants I might name, we've kept rather quietly to ourselves."

Askew started to open his mouth again quickly. Then he stopped, and his momentary flash of anger dissipated as he looked into Bourget's eyes.

"I didn't know that, Ma'am," he said more quietly after a moment.

"No," Boucher sighed. "No, I don't suppose you did. And I guess that's my fault. For that matter, it's probably the reason I'm so pissed at you. People tend to be that way when someone else makes a mistake because they didn't warn her not to." She rubbed her forehead. "I should've called you in for a heart-to-heart myself instead of delegating it to Ursula. But, to be completely honest about it, given that we didn't—and still don't—know exactly how your original report came into Aberu's hands in the first place, I figured having her handle it as a purely intradepartmental matter might keep the entire conversation below Aberu's radar. Not drawing any more attention to you seemed like a good idea. And, frankly, so did distancing myself and the Captain from any appearance of . . . over enthusiastically endorsing your conclusions."

Askew nodded slowly. He found himself wishing rather passionately that the exec had been willing to explain the situation to him more aggressively from the outset, but he understood her logic. It was the sort of convoluted thinking that too often turned out to be the price of survival in the SLN's Byzantine internal maneuvering.

"Now, however," Boucher continued a bit more briskly, "you appear to have well and truly loomed above the radar horizon, Matt. Apparently your latest literary effort got squeezed right through the same rathole—whatever it is—into Aberu's in-basket. And if she was less than amused with your first memo, that was nothing compared to the way she reacted to *this* one."

Askew swallowed. He'd taken every precaution he could, short of writing the entire report in longhand on old-fashioned paper and hand-delivering it to the captain, to keep it secure. Obviously, he'd failed. That suggested among other things that it had to be some sort of unauthorized, illegal hack from someone on Admiral Byng's staff. It couldn't have come to them through what the ONI sorts called a "human intelligence source," since he hadn't opened his mouth and verbally discussed his conclusions and concerns with a solitary living soul. The only question that remained in Askew's mind was whether the hacker in question had penetrated only his own security or that of his report's single addressee: Captain Mizawa.

"Ma'am," he said finally, "I'm not going to pretend I'm happy hearing about any of this. Just between the two of us, I'm especially concerned about how Captain Aberu got access to a confidential report addressed solely to the Captain."

Even here, in Bourget's office, with no other human ear actually present, that was as close as he cared to come to suggesting that someone on Byng's staff had actually violated half a dozen regulations and at least two federal laws to acquire that "access." The two of them looked into one another's eyes for a second or two, sharing the same thought, before he went on.

"Having said that, however, I wrote that memo for two reasons. One was because I really had collected some additional evidence in support of Commodore Thurgood's analysis and wanted to make the Captain aware of it. But the second was expressly to give him something he could use in any discussions with Admiral Byng and his staff." He held Bourget's eyes unflinchingly. "Something he could throw out as a worst-case set of assumptions from a junior officer too inexperienced to realize how absurd they were . . . who might still have managed to stumble across something that needed to be considered."

"I thought that was probably what you had in mind," Bourget said softly, and those hard hazel eyes warmed with approval.

"Don't get me wrong, Ma'am." Askew produced a tight smile. "If the Captain didn't think he *needed* it, I hoped to hell that no one else—especially Captain Aberu—would ever even see it! I just wanted him to . . . have that warhead in his ammo locker if he did need it."

"I appreciate that, Matt. And so does the Captain. But I'm very much afraid that it's actually had something of the reverse effect."

"Ma'am?" Askew twitched in surprise, and Bourget's eyes hardened once more—though not at him, this time—and she snorted harshly.

"However Aberu got hold of it, and whether Admiral Byng ever saw your initial memo or not, she sure as hell showed *this* one to him. I'm not absolutely positive about this, and under normal circumstances I wouldn't even be suggesting the possibility to you, for a lot of reasons, but I'm inclined to think at this point that Aberu deliberately chose her moment carefully for sharing it with the Admiral." Askew's eyes widened, and the exec shook her head. "As I say, normally I wouldn't even suggest such a thing to you. In this case, though, to be honest, the shit you're in is deep enough that I think you need to know exactly who the players are and what they may be up to."

"Ma'am, it sounds to me like we're getting into things here that are *way* above my pay grade," Askew said nervously, and Bourget's laugh was even harsher than her snort had been.

"I'll keep it simple. Ingeborg Aberu and Admiral Thimár both have close personal and family links to . . . various industrial interests in the defense sector, shall we say? Both of them have spent their entire careers in the tactical track, and both of them have established firm reputations—in Battle Fleet, at least—as being on the cutting edge. Admiral Thimár, in particular, was one of the senior staffers when the Navy Ministry put together the 'Fleet 2000' initiative. As a matter of fact, she was the lead author on the final report."

Askew couldn't quite keep himself from grimacing at that. The Fleet 2000 Program had been the brainchild of Battle Fleet, although it had since spread and found adherents in Frontier Fleet, as well. Essentially, it combined good, old-fashioned pro-Navy propaganda with a more-or-less hardware response to some of the more extreme rumors coming out of the Manticore-Haven wars.

Funding within the gargantuan Solarian League was far more a bureaucratic than a legislative function, and had been for centuries.

Nonetheless, public opinion often played a not insignificant role in deciding how funds were split up between *competing* bureaucracies, and so Fleet 2000 had been initiated. At its most basic level, it could arguably have been described as a "public education" effort designed to inform a largely ignorant Solarian public about the valuable services the Navy provided as humanity entered the twentieth century of interstellar flight. As such, it had included HD features on "Our Fighting Navy" and "The Men and Women of the Fleet," both of which had focused primarily on Battle Fleet, which had then been plastered across the entertainment channels.

Frontier Fleet hadn't had any objection to the notion of additional funding going to the Navy, but it had objected—strenuously—to the notion of that funding going to the white elephants of Battle Fleet's superdreadnoughts rather than Frontier Fleet battlecruisers, or even *destroyers*, which might actually do something useful. As a consequence, Frontier Fleet's Public Information Office had gotten into the act, as well, producing such features as "On the Frontiers of Freedom" and "First to Respond."

"First to Respond" had been particularly effective, concentrating as it did on the many instances of disaster relief, deep-space rescue, and other humanitarian missions Frontier Fleet routinely carried out.

The other prong of "Fleet 2000," however, had been a deliberate effort to impress the public with the value—and effectiveness—it was receiving in response to its lavish funding. As a tactical officer himself, Askew had looked askance (to put it mildly) at that aspect of the program. Oh, there'd been some genuine advances, and some recognition of shifting threat levels where things like missiles were concerned, but nowhere near as much of it as the PIO releases suggested. In fact, a much greater degree of effort had been invested in what amounted to window dressing with the express purpose of making the Navy's ships and their equipment look even more impressive on HD.

Consoles had been redesigned, bridges and command decks had been rearranged, and the parts of the ships the public was ever likely to see had been generally opened up so that they looked more like something out of an HD adventure flick than a real warship. There'd actually been some improvements along the way—for example, those sleek new consoles not only looked "sexier" but actually provided better information and control interfaces. And although nothing much had been done to actually upgrade most of the fleet's tactical hardware, more recent construction had been redesigned to reflect a modular concept. It would appear that someone was at least willing to admit the possibility that improvements and upgrades might be forthcoming—someday—and the Office of Ship Design had been instructed to design for the possibility of plugging in new components. That was one of the major differences between the older *Indefatigable*-class ships and the newer *Nevadas*, like *Jean Bart*.

Yet despite the impression which had been deliberately created for the Solarian public, and despite all the money which had been spent in pursuit of Fleet 2000, very little in the way of actually improving the SLN's combat power had been achieved. After all, the Solarian Navy was already the most powerful and advanced fleet in space, wasn't it?

To be fair, Askew had partaken of that same confidence in the SLN's qualitative edge until very recently. Now, however, he'd been forced to confront the mounting evidence that his confidence—and everyone else's—had been misplaced. Which meant that whether or not anyone had intended them as such, the Fleet 2000 public relations claims amounted to . . . untruths. In fact, if it turned out Askew's fears were justified and it really did hit the fan out here, the public was going to see them as outright lies. And if Aberu and Thimár had direct family connections to the people who'd put the entire program together . . .

"Obviously, I can't be sure about this," Bourget said now, "but I don't think I'd be particularly surprised to discover that Captain Aberu and Admiral Thimár both had . . . vested interests in quashing any 'panicky fears' about 'impossible Manticoran super weapons,' especially if those 'panicky fears' suggest that our hardware might really need some minor improvements. And if that's the case, they wouldn't be very happy to have anyone rocking their boat."

Askew nodded more than a bit sickly, and she gave him a sympathetic smile.

"Captain Mizawa never meant to put you into a possible crossfire, Matt. That initial report he asked you for was something he *needed*—needed for his own information—mainly because he'd already figured out that ONI's official reports on what the hell was going on out here were crap. He trusts your judgment and your integrity, and I think he figured you were junior enough no one would notice what you were up to if he sent you out to talk to people like Thurgood. And I *know* he didn't expect your memo to fall into Aberu's hands any more than I did.

"I also think her initial 'discussion' with the captain was her own idea. Or, possibly, hers and Thimár's. But when she got her hands on your second effort—which, let's face it, really does sound a lot more 'alarmist' than your first memo did—I think she picked a moment when Admiral Byng was already feeling . . . frustrated over the delay in getting the task force reconcentrated here at Meyers and shared it with him."

The bottom seemed to fall straight out of Maitland Askew's stomach. He stared at Bourget, and she nodded slowly.

"That's right. This time around, the Admiral—through Admiral Thimár, not Captain Aberu—has expressed his personal displeasure with your 'obvious defeatism, credulity, panic-mongering, and at best marginal competence.'"

She said it quickly, a numb part of Askew's brain noted, with a sort of surgical brutality that was its own kindness.

"He also stated—through Admiral Thimár," Bourget continued with obvious distaste "—that since the 'defeatist officer' in question was a Frontier Fleet officer, rather than a Battle Fleet officer, he would leave the 'suitable disposition' of your case in Captain Mizawa's hands. There wasn't much doubt from the way Admiral Thimár delivered his message about what he had in mind, however."

Askew only looked at her. It was all he could do as he felt the total destruction of his career rushing towards him.

"Aside from the personal repercussions in your own case," Bourget said, "it's pretty obvious where Admiral Byng has decided to come down on the question of Manticoran capabilities. And, unfortunately, your second memo—which, by the way, both the Captain and I feel was very cogently reasoned—is now irrevocably tainted in his eyes. In fact, if the Captain tries to dispute Aberu's or Thimár's views, Admiral Byng will probably automatically reject anything he says because, as far as he's concerned, it's going to be coming from your report and just thinking about it is going to piss him off all over again. From what we've already seen of him, it's pretty apparent that when his temper is engaged, it tends to *disengage* his brain, and that's what's going to happen any time he even suspects the Captain is waving your report in his direction. Which, unless I am considerably mistaken, is exactly what Aberu and Thimár had in mind."

"Ma'am, I'm *sorry*," Askew half-whispered. "I was trying to *help*. I never thought that—"

"Matt, neither Captain Mizawa nor I think that you're anything other than an intelligent, talented, conscientious young officer doing his dead level best to do his duty under extraordinarily difficult circumstances. If either of us has any personal regrets, it's that we inadvertently stranded you in the middle of this minefield."

Askew closed his mouth again and nodded once more, hoping he didn't look as sick as he felt.

"I've explained all of this to you for a specific reason," Bourget told him. "Normally, I would never have suggested to an officer of your relatively junior status that I cherished suspicions about Captain Aberu's and Admiral Thimár's motives. Nor, for that matter, would I have discussed with you the . . . shortcomings of Admiral Byng's own attitude towards Frontier Fleet *or* Manticoran capabilities. In this instance, however, you need to be aware of the fact that you've potentially made some very highly placed, and probably highly vindictive, enemies. I can't begin to estimate all of the potential professional repercussions, and I wish there were some way to deflect them from you if any of those three decide to make 'punishing' you a personal project. But at least now you know.

"That wasn't my main reason for explaining it to you at such length, though. What I especially want you to understand, Matt, is why Captain Mizawa has taken the action he's taken in regard to you."

"What . . . what action, Ma'am?" Askew managed to ask.

"You are relieved as *Jean Bart*'s assistant tactical officer, effective immediately," Bourget said flatly. "Your new assignment will be as Admiral Sigbee's assistant public information officer aboard *Restitution*."

Askew felt as if he'd just been punched in the gut, and his face tightened painfully.

"Let me finish before you say anything," Bourget said quickly, holding up her index finger. Her eyes met his, and after a moment, he managed to nod yet again.

"I realize exactly how this looks to you at this moment," the exec continued then in a quietly compassionate voice. "Hopefully, it will also look like that to Aberu and Thimár—and, for that matter, Admiral Byng. As far as they'll be concerned, Captain

Mizawa got the message and shit-canned your entire career. And getting you aboard *Restitution* will also get you out of *Jean Bart* and hopefully out of their field of vision, as well.

"In this case, however, appearances are a little deceiving. First, Admiral Sigbee is an old friend of the Captain's. He's discussed this situation with her—I don't know in exactly how much detail—and she's agreed to make a place on her staff for you, despite the potential for pissing off Admiral Byng. Second, whatever Aberu and Thimár may conclude, the Captain—and I, and Commander Zeiss—will all be endorsing your efficiency report in the most positive terms. Third, there's been no *official* communication between Admiral Byng or any member of his staff and Captain Mizawa about the Admiral's concerns about your 'defeatism.' Because of that, no mention of it will appear in your file."

She paused at last, and Askew inhaled deeply.

He understood what Captain Mizawa was trying to do, and he deeply, deeply appreciated it—especially considering the distinct possibility that if Admiral Byng or his staffers did decide to personally oversee the "shit-canning" of his career, they, too, would recognize what the captain was up to. But it wasn't going to be pleasant, whatever happened. When the number two officer in a battlecruiser's tactical department suddenly found himself assigned as an *assistant* public information officer, people were going to assume—usually with reason—that he had royally screwed up somehow. The efficiency reports from Captain Mizawa and Commander Bourget would probably counter that assumption in front of some theoretical future promotions board, but they weren't going to do a thing about how his new shipmates were going to regard him when he arrived aboard *Restitution*. Nor was there any assurance that Aberu and/or the others, would be prepared to settle for his obvious current disgrace.

Which didn't mean it wasn't absolutely the best Captain Mizawa could do for him.

"I . . . understand, Ma'am," he said finally, very quietly. "Thank you. And please thank the Captain for me, too."

"I will, of course," she replied. "Not that there's any need to. The only thing I regret—and I'm sure I speak for the Captain, as well—is that you got caught up in all this crap and that this is the best we can do to protect you from the consequences of doing your job." She shook her head. "I know it doesn't seem that

STORM FROM THE SHADOWS


way at the moment, but sometimes, the good guys really do win, Matt. Try to remember that."

Lieutenant Commander Denton frowned unhappily as he contemplated the events of the last couple of days.

He appreciated Admiral Khumalo's official approval of his actions here in Pequod, but he hadn't needed the dispatches from the admiral and Captain Shoupe to warn him to watch his back. In fact, there were more dispatches from *him* already en route to Spindle, with the details of fresh confrontations with New Tuscan skippers. Now the New Tuscan trade attaché was getting into the mix, as well, registering "formal protests" over the "increasing high-handedness" of HMS *Reprise* and her personnel. And, to make things even worse, there were being genuine incidents and confrontations now. The New Tuscans were being increasingly sullen, insulting, and rude during routine inspections and ship visits, and even their non-officers were starting to push the limits. Denton suspected that a lot of what they were seeing out of the regular spacers was the result of their having been fed stories about Manty insults and bullying aboard other ships by their own officers. By now, most of them seemed to believe all of those alleged incidents had actually occurred, and none of them were in particularly conciliating moods. Which meant—since Denton and his people had jobs to do—that every New Tuscan ship was a smouldering powder keg just waiting for a spark, and there'd been some genuinely ugly confrontations as a result.

His people were trying hard to avoid pumping any hydrogen into the fire . . . for all the good it seemed to be doing. The entire ship's company knew about the stream of complaints and protests by now, but they still had their duties to discharge. And, like their captain, they'd come to the conclusion that all of this had to be orchestrated by some central authority and that it had to be headed towards some specific climax. And, once again like their captain, every damned one of them wished he or she had some clue—*any* clue—what that climax might be . . . and how it might be avoided.

Unfortunately, no one had been able to come up with that clue.

*Oh, how I wish the Admiral would hurry up and get someone senior out here,* Denton thought fervently. *I don't care if it would be an escalation. I'm delighted that everyone is so damned pleased with how well I've done so far, but I'm getting awful tired of waiting for that other shoe. And I'm damned certain that whenever it finally comes down, I'm gonna find myself ass-deep in a shitstorm that's way the hell and gone above my pay grade!*

He knew why his nerves were even tighter than they had been, and his eyes slid across the tactical display to the data code of NTNS *Camille*. The New Tuscan light cruiser was about thirty percent larger than *Reprise*, and the NTN had a decent tech level for a Verge star system. It wasn't as good as the Rembrandt Navy, or the San Miguel Navy, perhaps, but it was two or three cuts above the average hardscrabble, hand-to-mouth, third- or fourth-tier "navies" one normally saw out in this neck of the woods.

Despite that, and despite the fact that *Reprise* was no spring treekitten, Denton wasn't at all intimidated by the larger ship's firepower. The truth, as he felt quite confident *Camille*'s captain realized as well as he did, was that the cruiser wouldn't stand a chance against the smaller Manticoran destroyer.

*Unfortunately, it's not as simple as deciding who can blow who out of space,* he reflected grimly.

*Camille* had arrived in Pequod almost five local days ago, and Captain Séguin had immediately informed the Pequod system authorities that New Tuscany had decided it would be both useful and advisable to permanently station one of its warships in Pequod as a formal observer. It was not, she had hastened to assure everyone in sight, viewed or intended by New Tuscany as a hostile act or as an affront to Pequod's sovereignty. Indeed, it was New Tuscany's hope, as the formal notes she'd delivered on behalf of Foreign Minister Cardot and Prime Minister Vézien made clear, that having an official New Tuscan presence in the system would help to cool things down, rather than heat them up.

*Sure* it was. Denton shook his head. If he hadn't been convinced all of the "incidents" New Tuscan merchant skippers were complaining about had been deliberately concocted on orders from their home government, he might have been willing to at least entertain the possibility that Séguin was telling the truth. Unhappily, he was convinced that if the New Tuscan government had been serious about bringing an end to the tension, all it really had to do was tell its captains to stop doing what it had them doing. Which meant *Camille* was obviously here for something else, and that "something else" wasn't going to turn out to be something Denton wanted to know anything about. That much, at least, he was sure he could count on.

His mouth twitched in a humorless smile as he watched Ensign Monahan's pinnace heading for another vessel. He tapped an inquiry into his plot, and his smile disappeared as the name NTNS *Hélène Blondeau* appeared.

*Not another of those damned New Tuscan freighters!* he thought. *Dammit, they must be cycling their entire frigging* merchant marine *through Pequod! Don't they have a single ship still in—*

His thoughts broke off as the *Hélène Blondeau's* icon was abruptly replaced with the flashing crimson symbol that indicated a spreading sphere of wreckage, flying outward from the point in space at which a ship had just blown up.

"—so after completing my debrief of Ensign Monahan and each member of her crew separately, it is my conclusion that their reports—singly and as a group—are an accurate account of what actually happened during their approach to *Hélène Blondeau*," Lewis Denton told his terminal's recording pickup fourteen hours later.

His voice was more than a little hoarse, exhaustion-roughened around the edges, and he knew it, just as he knew the report he was recording would show his weary eyes and the dark, bruised-looking bags which had formed below them. There wasn't much he could do about that, though. He had to get this report off, and the sooner the better. It was the better part of seventeen days from Pequod to Spindle by dispatch boat, but it was less than *six* days from Pequod to New Tuscany. He didn't really think anyone in New Tuscany would be insane enough to launch some sort of punitive expedition against *Reprise* or Pequod, but he was nowhere near as confident of that as he would have liked to be. Not after the most recent episode.

"Despite Captain Séguin's assertions to the contrary, there is absolutely no evidence that Ensign Monahan or her pinnace played any part in *Hélène Blondeau's* destruction," he continued. "I am, of course, appending *Reprise's* sensor and tactical recordings for the entire time period, beginning one full standard hour before *Hélène Blondeau* blew up and ending one full standard hour after the ship's destruction. I am also appending a copy of the pinnace's flight log and a complete inventory of my ship's magazines, which accounts for every small craft and shipboard missile issued to us. Based upon those records, I will state unequivocally and for the record that I am absolutely convinced no one aboard Ms. Monahan's pinnace or aboard *Reprise* fired a single shot of any sort or for any reason.

"Indeed, I must reiterate that I have been able to find no evidence anywhere in any of our records or sensor data that indicates *any* external cause for *Hélène Blondeau*'s destruction. There is no indication of missile fire, energy fire, or collision. The only tentative conclusion I have been able to arrive at is that the ship and—apparently—her entire company were lost to an *internal* explosion. Neither I nor any of my officers, specifically including my engineering and tactical officers, have been able to suggest any normally occurring cause for such an explosion. The vessel was so completely destroyed that little short of a catastrophic and completely unanticipated failure of her fusion bottle would appear to be a remotely reasonable explanation. I find that explanation completely implausible, however, given the observed nature of the explosion. In fact, from the admittedly partial sensor data we have of the vessel's destruction and our analysis of the wreckage's scatter patterns, it appears to me and to my tactical officer that she was destroyed not by a single explosion, nor even by a single primary explosion and a series of secondary explosions, but rather as the result of a virtually simultaneous chain of at least seven *distinct* explosions."

He paused, his exhausted face gaunt and bleak, and his nostrils flared. Then he continued, speaking slowly and distinctly.

"I fully realize the seriousness of what I am about to say, and I very much hope that a more thorough and complete analysis of the limited data I have been able to include with this report will prove that my suspicions are in error. However, it is my considered opinion that the destruction of *Hélène Blondeau* was the result of a careful, skillfully planned, and well executed act of sabotage. I can think of no other explanation for the observed pattern of destruction. I am not prepared at this time in a formal report to speculate upon who might have been responsible for that act of sabotage. I am not a trained investigator, and I do not believe it would be proper for me to make any formal charges or allegations before a more detailed analysis can be performed. However, if, in fact, this was an act of sabotage, whoever may have been responsible for it clearly does not have the best interests of the Star Empire at heart. Given that Captain Séguin, *Camille*, and all other New Tuscan shipping in the system have been withdrawn, I believe the potential for some sort of additional and unfortunate incident is high. I must, therefore, respectfully request that this star system be promptly and strongly reinforced."

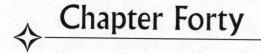

# Chapter Forty

"THEY'RE GONE."

Valery Ottweiler looked up from the report he'd been reading and quirked one eyebrow at the man standing in his office doorway. Damien Harahap, late of the Solarian League Gendarmerie, was an eminently forgettable-looking man—a quality of which had served him well during his time with his former employer—but Ottweiler had discovered that there was an extremely capable brain behind that unremarkable façade.

There was also someone who had an inordinate amount of good luck. Everything taken together, Harahap was extraordinarily fortunate to be alive, but Ottweiler knew he'd proved very useful to Aldona Anisimovna and Isabel Bardasano. Despite how spectacularly the Monica operation had crashed and burned, Harahap had performed his role in it almost flawlessly, and he'd been as ruthlessly honest in critiquing his own performance as he had when critiquing that of anyone else. He wasn't Mesan, but operatives of his professionalism and ability—and intelligence—were rare, and Bardasano, who had never had any prejudices against employing "outside talent" if it proved itself valuable and reliable, had hired him away from the Gendarmerie almost before the wreckage in Monica had finished glowing.

The fact that Harahap knew where all the bodies in the Madras Sector were buried had suggested he might be of particular value to Ottweiler, which was how he'd come to be a member

of Ottweiler's staff here in Meyers. Of course, there were a few
downsides to having him openly working for Ottweiler here on
the capital world of his old stomping grounds. In fact, Hongbo
Junyan had looked just a little askance at the relationship, but
Ottweiler had already demonstrated who was in charge in that
particular relationship, and any objections the vice-commissioner
might have cherished had remained unspoken.

"I take it you're referring to the departure of the intrepid
Admiral Byng?" Ottweiler said now, and Harahap nodded.

"Just translated out for New Tuscany," he said.

"And about time, too," Ottweiler muttered. Harahap didn't
seem to notice, which was fresh proof of both his intelligence
and his discretion, Ottweiler thought. Then the Mesan inhaled
deeply and shrugged.

"Thank you, Damien," he said.

"Is there anything else you need me to do this afternoon?"
Harahap asked.

"No, thank you. Well, not here, anyway. But, on second thought,
it would probably be a good idea if you went and hit your Gendarmerie contacts again. Try to get a read on how the Sollies see
what's going on in New Tuscany."

"Not a problem," Harahap replied, then left, closing the door
quietly behind him.

Ottweiler gazed at that closed door for a moment, thinking of the
man who had just passed through it and all he represented.

Damien Harahap had been one of the best field men the Solarian Gendarmerie had ever recruited and trained, but he'd never
felt any intrinsic loyalty to the League. Born in the Verge himself,
he'd managed to claw his way off of one of the planets Frontier
Security had handed over to one of its multi-stellar corporate
patrons to be squeezed and exploited. He'd done it by taking
service with the very people who had stripped his home world
of its freedom and its dignity, and Ottweiler suspected that that
still ate at him at times. If so, it hadn't kept him from doing his
job superlatively, but that stemmed more from his own pride of
workmanship and refusal to perform at less than his best than
from any vestige of devotion to his employers. He'd always seen
himself—with good reason, in Ottweiler's opinion—much more
as a foreign mercenary than as a citizen of the League.

And that was ultimately going to prove the Solarian League's

Achilles' heel, Valery Ottweiler suspected. Too many of the people doing what had to be done to keep the machine up and running were like Damien Harahap. Skilled, capable, ambitious, often ruthless . . . and with no sense of loyalty to the League at all. They were simply playing the best game available to them, and if someone came along and offered to change the rules . . .

Ottweiler looked back at the report he'd been reading, but he didn't really see it. His mind was too busy with other things.

He was glad Byng had finally gotten underway, even if it had taken almost an entire T-month. That was longer than his instructions had specified as the maximum acceptable interval, but only by a day or two. Unless the people who'd written those instructions were far stupider than Ottweiler expected, they would have allowed for some slippage even in their "maximum acceptable" timing delays. And whether they had or not, it was the best Ottweiler had been able to do without coming a lot further into the open and squeezing Lorcan Verrochio a lot harder—and a lot more obviously—than his instructions from Isabel Bardasano permitted.

And he was also relieved that Byng had, indeed, settled for taking only two of his three battlecruiser squadrons with him.

He tipped back in his chair, lips pursed while he whistled tunelessly. He wasn't supposed to know what was really going on. That much was obvious from the way his instructions had been written, the way Bardasano's directives had been phrased. But, like Damien Harahap, it was Valery Ottweiler's intelligence which made him so useful to his own employers. And that intelligence had been suggesting things lately which he had been very careful to keep discreetly to himself. Things which had given added point to his thoughts about the fundamental loyalty of people like Harahap.

And his own.

Nobody had told him exactly what was supposed to happen in New Tuscany, but it didn't take a hyper physicist to figure out that it wasn't what the *New Tuscans*—or Admiral Byng—were expecting to happen. Especially after what had happened in Monica, and what that had demonstrated about Manticoran military capabilities, the only possibility Ottweiler could see was that someone wanted to reprise the Battle of Monica, but with Josef Byng in the role of the Monican Navy. No one as smart as Isabel Bardasano or Aldona Anisimovna could expect any other outcome, which meant that was the one they wanted. Which led inevitably to the question of *why* they wanted it.

Ottweiler had asked himself that very question, and as he'd pondered it, a very disturbing thought had come to him. One which made him look at the actions of someone like Governor Barregos in the Maya Sector quite differently. One which made him wonder how someone as bright as he was could have missed the signs he saw so clearly now.

Which made him consider exactly what it was to which he'd truly given his own loyalty all these years and how much further it might turn out that the ambitions of his own employers extended than he'd ever guessed before.

And one which made him wonder how the Solarian League was going to react when it discovered the true disadvantage to hiring mercenaries to protect its life.

"You know, Father, when you first came up this brainstorm of yours, I actually found myself wondering about your contact with reality. In fact, I started to say just that, actually. But now . . . "

Benjamin Detweiler shook his head as he stood beside his father in the salon of a luxuriously furnished private yacht, gazing at the needle-sharp view screen.

"Really?" Albrecht gave his son a humorous glance. "Changed your mind, did you? You do remember that one of your responsibilities is to warn me if you think I'm going off the deep end, don't you?"

"Oh, certainly." Benjamin chuckled. "The problem is that no one else really knows all of the labyrinthine—not to say Machiavellian—details rolling around inside your brain. Sometimes it's sort of hard for those of us on the outside to tell the difference between strokes of genius and wild hairs."

"Your filial respect overwhelms me," Albrecht said dryly, and Benjamin chuckled again. Although, Albrecht reflected, there was at least a tiny kernel of truth buried in his son's comments. There usually was, where Benjamin was concerned. Out of all of his "sons," Benjamin probably was the most likely to tell him if he thought he was going off at a dangerous tangent.

*Probably because Benjamin's the most like me, when you come right down to it,* Albrecht thought. *Which is why I picked him to run the military side of things, after all. And*—Albrecht's eyes refocused on the view screen—*so far, he's done us all proud. Well, he and Daniel and Daniel's little shop of wonders.*

Truth to tell, the view screen's images weren't all that exciting ... unless, of course, one realized what one was seeing. There was no pressing need for Albrecht to be out here aboard Benjamin's yacht, watching it from such short range, either. He could have viewed exactly the same imagery from the security of his own office. But Albrecht *did* realize what he was seeing, and six hundred T-years of planning and effort, of sweat and toil, of enormous investment and even more enormous patience on the part of entire generations who couldn't be here with him, were rumbling through the marrow of his bones as he watched. He couldn't possibly have stayed away. He needed to be as physically close to the units of Oyster Bay as he could possibly be, and if that was illogical, he didn't really much care.

He watched the stupendous freighters getting underway. They weren't the largest freighters in the galaxy, by any stretch of the imagination, but they were still big, solid ships, all of them of at least four million tons, and they'd been carefully modified for their current role. Their cargo doors were considerably larger than usual, and the cargo holds behind those doors had been configured to provide secure nests for the roughly frigate-sized *Ghost*-class scout ships they concealed.

They were something entirely new in the annals of interstellar warfare, those scout ships, and he wished they had more of them—hundreds of them. But they didn't. Their total inventory of the new spider-drive ships was extremely limited, and he'd committed virtually all of them to this operation. If they'd only had a few more months—another T-year or two—to prepare, he would have been much happier.

*But we've got enough of them for this*, he told himself almost fiercely, and let his eyes sweep across to the other half of Oyster Bay.

The *Shark*-class strike ships were much larger than Commodore Østby's and Commodore Sung's scouts. Any pod-layer had to be, although these were still essentially prototype units in many ways, and they had only twenty-eight of them, divided between Admiral Topolev's Task Force One and Admiral Colenso's much smaller Task Force Two. Substantially larger units with far more magazine space were on the drawing board, designs based in no small part on the experience Benjamin and his crews had acquired working with the ships currently under Topolev's and Colenso's command. Some of those larger units were already entering the first phases of construction, for that matter. And, again, Albrecht wished they'd been able to wait until those larger ships were available in greater numbers. But the key to everything was timing, and the two admirals had enough combat power for their assigned mission.

Albrecht wasn't the military specialist Benjamin was, but even he could tell the *Sharks* looked subtly wrong. They were too far away for the naked eye to see, but the view screen's magnification brought them to what seemed like arm's-length and made it obvious that all of them lacked the traditional "hammerhead" design of a military starship. Indeed, the lines of their hulls were *all* wrong, in one way or another, as if their designers had been working to a completely different set of constraints from anyone else in the galaxy.

Which was precisely what they *had* been doing.

The strike ships turned slowly, and then, as one unit, they went loping away into the trackless depths of space. And that, too, was wrong. The light-warping power of a starship's impeller drive made the ship within it impossible to see, except from exactly the right angle. But there was no gravitic distortion around these ships, nothing to bend and blur light waves, because they didn't *use* impeller wedges.

*And isn't that going to come as a nasty surprise for the Manties and their friends?* Albrecht thought fiercely.

He watched for several more moments, then shook himself and inhaled deeply.

"Well," he said, "that's that. I'm proud of you, Ben." He reached out to squeeze his son's shoulder. "I sometimes think I forget to tell you—and the other boys, for that matter—that as often as I ought to, but it's true. I know how much pressure I put on you when I decided to move Oyster Bay up this way. But I also knew that if anyone could get it organized and moving in that time frame, you were the one."

"Flattery will get you everywhere, Father," Benjamin said with a grin, but Albrecht could tell that his son recognized the sincerity behind his words. He gave the shoulder under his hand another squeeze, then shook his head.

"And now, I'd better get back to the house. I'm sure something else has crawled out of my in-basket while I was away, and your mom has something special planned for dinner tonight. She didn't tell me what, and I didn't ask. Sometimes I am a little afraid to ask her, actually. I'd hate to think she was getting her cookbooks mixed up with her lab notebooks!"

This time, Benjamin laughed out loud. Evelina Detweiler was one of the Mesan Alignment's top biosciences researchers, with a special expertise in bioweapons, working closely with Benjamin's brother Everett and Renzo Kyprianou. And unlike her husband, who was always sharply focused on the task in hand, Evelina was all too often the epitome of the "absent minded professor."

"Whatever it is she's planning on feeding me, though, *you'd* better be there too," Albrecht said now, glaring at the laughing Benjamin. "It's a special dinner to celebrate launching Oyster Bay, and I understand it's going to include seafood, somehow or other. So be there. Nineteen-thirty sharp—and no excuses, young man!"

"Yes, Sir," Benjamin said meekly.


"Well," Augustus Khumalo said gloomily, "I could wish we'd been wrong at least this once."

"If it makes you feel better to be wrong, Augustus," Baroness Medusa said with a crooked smile, "don't get too worried. I'm sure we'll be able to make enough mistakes to satisfy you while we try to figure out what to *do* about it!"

"I know what I'd *like* to do about it," Henri Krietzmann muttered just loud enough to be heard, and Joachim Alquezar gave him a reproving glance.

"While direct action has a certain primitive appeal, especially at moments like this, it isn't always the best course of action, Henri. Besides, there's a little thing called the Eridani Edict to worry about, so a nice saturation kinetic bombardment of New Tuscany is *probably* out of the question."

"Spoken like a true effete aristocrat," Krietzmann shot back with a twinkle, despite the tension of the moment, and Alquezar chuckled. But his momentary humor disappeared quickly, and he shook his head and looked at Medusa.

"I have to admit that I'm at a loss to even suggest what it is this was supposed to accomplish," he said, running one fingertip across the hardcopy printout of the diplomatic note lying on the conference table in front of him beside his copy of Commander Denton's report.

"I think at least part of it is fairly obvious, Mr. Prime Minister," Gregor O'Shaughnessy said. "I realize New Tuscany is actually five days closer to Spindle than Pequod is, but the fact that Vézien's nastygram got here less than twenty-four hours after Commander Denton's report still says quite a lot. Even if this Captain Séguin let the merchies make the trip on their own and went ahead of them in her light cruiser, she still burned the better part of five and a half days just getting home to New Tuscany. Which means they conducted this entire 'investigation' of Vézien's, discussed how to respond, and got his damned note off to us in less than one T-day. How many governments do *you* know of that could have done that from a standing start?"

"None," Alquezar said grimly. "Or not at least if there really was any sort of an investigation involved."

"I think we can take it as a given that there was no need for any investigations," Michelle Henke put in from her place to Khumalo's right, and her husky contralto was far grimmer than usual.

Medusa glanced at her, and the baroness didn't exactly like what she saw. Michelle had been back in Spindle for less than a T-month, and it was obvious to Medusa that the horrendous casualties the Navy had suffered in the Battle of Manticore had hit her especially hard.

*Well, of course they did!* Medusa scolded herself. *How many of those people did she know personally? How many close friends were killed? And even leaving all of that out of the equation, she's an officer in the Queen's Navy. The Navy that was supposed to keep anyone from ever doing something like that to the home system.*

And even if none of the rest of that had been true, the baroness reflected, Michelle Henke was Tenth Fleet's commanding officer. That organization had been officially activated following the arrival of Aivars Terekhov—*Sir* Aivars Terekhov, she reminded herself—and his cruiser squadron at Spindle, and as Tenth Fleet's CO, Vice Admiral Gold Peak was only too well aware of how the savage losses the Royal Manticoran Navy had suffered were going to affect force availability here in Talbott, as well. It was entirely possible—indeed, almost inevitable—that many of the ships she'd been scheduled to receive were going to be delayed or even permanently diverted to other duties as the Admiralty tried frantically to fill all the holes the Battle of Manticore had blasted into its order of battle.

All of which made the timing on the New Tuscans' little operation, whatever it was, even more . . . inconvenient.

"It's almost like they already knew about what happened in Manticore, isn't it?" Terekhov mused out loud, like an eerie echo of Medusa's thoughts. He sat in a comfortable armchair at one corner of her desk, the new, blue-and-white ribbon of the POV heading the "fruit salad" on the breast of his tunic.

"Let's not get carried away giving them credit for arcane powers, Aivars," Michelle said.

"Oh, I'm not, Ma'am." Terekhov smiled briefly. "It's just particularly frustrating to have this happening right now."

"Now that's what I'd call a masterful piece of understatement, Sir Aivars," Bernardus Van Dort put in wryly.

"Put it down to my years of Foreign Office experience," Terekhov replied. "But while you're doing that, those same years of Foreign Office experience are ringing all kinds of alarm bells over this one. As Gregor just pointed out, this whole thing stinks to high heaven. It's got 'Put-Up Job!' painted all over it in great big, glowing letters, and I don't like any of the reasons I've been able to come up with for why that is. You and Joachim know these people a lot better than I do, Bernardus. Are they stupid enough to think we wouldn't even *notice* the timing involved in their ability to get their note to us this damned quickly?"

"Well, obviously they were stupid enough to send Andrieaux Yvernau to the Constitutional Convention, which has to raise at least some questions, don't you think?" Van Dort pointed out. "If they really expected to get a constitution out of it, then that wasn't exactly what anyone would consider an inspired choice. But in answer to the question you're really asking, no, none of them—except probably Yvernau—is *that* stupid. They have to realize there's no way in the galaxy we're going to miss the timing on this. Which means they frankly don't care about that. The entire note isn't for our benefit at all; it's for someone else's."

"Exactly," Terekhov said, and his blue eyes swept the table for a moment before coming back to Joachim Alquezar and Baroness Medusa.

"It's Monica all over again," he said flatly. "I don't know exactly how all the pieces are supposed to fit together this time, but New Tuscany's the door knocker for someone else, exactly the same way Monica was. And as Bernardus says, the way these incidents are being stage-managed is for someone else. Does anyone in this room doubt who that someone else is?"

"Of course it's the Sollies, Commodore," Alquezar said. "Whatever else they have in mind, the New Tuscans are obviously planning on calling in some 'impartial outside power' to . . . mediate in the crisis which the Star Empire has clearly provoked for sinister reasons of its own."

"I'm beginning to wish now that we'd gone ahead and sent Chatterjee out to relieve Denton as soon as he got here with his *Rolands*," Khumalo said frankly, running the fingers of his right hand through his hair in an uncharacteristic, harassed gesture.

"I don't think it would have made any difference, Sir," Terekhov said.

Khumalo looked at him, and Terekhov raised one hand and made a little throwing away gesture with it.

"First of all, Sir, I don't see where you and Admiral Gold Peak had any choice but to freeze ship movements and deployments, at the very least until Admiral Gold Peak got back to Spindle, until you got a better feel for how what happened in Manticore is going to affect your force availabilities out here in the Quadrant. Even with the benefit of hindsight, I don't think any other decision was possible. But, secondly, whatever it is these people are up to, it's obvious they've been working to a detailed game plan from the very beginning. I really don't see them doing anything different just because Commodore Chatterjee was sitting there with half a dozen *Rolands* instead of Commander Denton with a single over-the-hill tin-can."

"Unless having half a dozen *Rolands* sitting there would have convinced them of the unwisdom of their actions," Michelle pointed out.

"With all due respect, Ma'am," Terekhov said, "if they can count to twenty without taking their shoes off, they already know the New Tuscan Navy in all its glory does *not* want to piss off the RMN. Putting more destroyers in Pequod wouldn't have changed any perceptions of the real balance of force in New Tuscany."

Michelle nodded slowly. He was right, of course, and the fact that he was only made her even happier to have him and his judgment back here in the Quadrant. Not that she felt particularly "happy" about anything else at the moment.

"All right." Medusa looked around the conference table as her quietly firm tone gathered up everyone else's attention. "What I'm hearing is a consensus that New Tuscany is acting as a front man for some party or parties unknown, although I suspect we could all put a name on at least one of the aforementioned parties if we really tried. And I think we're all also in agreement that at the moment they have the advantage of knowing what the hell it is they're trying to do while we don't have a clue. Unfortunately, I see no option but to respond rather firmly to what they've already done."

"I'd like to insert a word of caution, Milady," O'Shaughnessy said. She nodded for him to go on, and he continued. "I can't disagree with anything you've just said, but I think we need to bear in mind that responding forcefully may be exactly what they want us to do."

"It may be," Medusa agreed. "On the other hand, I see no other choice. We certainly can't ignore it, when their prime minister is sending us formal notes accusing one of our pinnaces of having deliberately fired upon and destroyed a New Tuscan merchant ship with all hands—and, by implication, accusing us of lying about it rather than admitting Commander Denton's responsibility. It's obvious from our analysis of the records that nothing of the sort happened, but nobody aside from us and the New Tuscans has any evidence to look at at all. Much as I hate it, that means this is going to be a battle for credibility, not something that can be resolved through the presentation of evidence in some sort of insterstellar court. And if that's the case, the last thing we can afford is to allow them to get their version of the facts established, unchallenged."

All of the naval officers at the table nodded soberly. They'd run the sensor data Commander Denton had sent along with his report through their tactical computers and simulators, and those computers and simulators had been far more capable than anything aboard *Reprise*. Unfortunately, there were still limits. As Denton had warned, there was less of that data than they could have wished. *Reprise* was a single destroyer whose sensor platforms had been keeping an eye on an entire star system. Nothing had warned her that she needed to be keeping a closer watch over *Hélène Blondeau*, and none of her platforms had been looking in the right direction at the right moment. What they had was almost entirely from her shipboard sensors, and they hadn't been focusing their attention on the New Tuscan merchant ship, either.

Despite all of those disadvantages, however, it had become glaringly evident to the analysts that Denton had been correct. *Hélène Blondeau* had been destroyed by an internal explosion. Or, to be more precise, the freighter had been destroyed by a single explosive event consisting of eight—not the seven Denton had identified—simultaneous detonations equidistantly spaced throughout her volume. It hadn't been a *sequence* of explosions spreading, however rapidly, from a single initial site, which would have been the case with almost any conceivable "natural" catastrophe . . . and would definitely have been the case if they had been the result of energy fire or a missile strike impacting on the hull. The only way that so many detonations could have occurred simultaneously throughout the volume of a ship that size was as the result of very carefully placed scuttling charges. There was no question in the analysts' minds; the New Tuscans had blown up their own ship.

"I'm not about to go to the newsies and hand them our analysis," Medusa continued. "I have every confidence that it's accurate, but saying 'They did it themselves' isn't going to play well with the 'faxes. It's the kind of 'He said; she said' defense that sounds weak at the best of times, especially when it's based on the disputed analysis of sketchy information or data. And, frankly, whoever thought this up obviously realizes how our diplomatic squabbles with Haven—which haven't gotten any better, now that we're accusing them of sabotaging the summit and they're denying they had anything to do with any assassination attempts—is going to make that particularly true in our case.

"Nonetheless, it's equally imperative that we clearly and unequivocally maintain that we were not in any way responsible for what happened. We can certainly provide our own sensor data, as well as the results of our own internal inquiry, to support our own innocence without necessarily making any allegations of guilt on anyone else's part. We need to do just that, to be sure our side of the story is presented as clearly and as forcefully as their version of events. And we also have to proceed in the way any innocent star nation acting in good faith would proceed. Which means we must respond directly to Vézien's note."

"In what way, Milady?" Alquezar asked.

"By presenting a note to them in reply. One which makes it very clear that we reject their accusations, and one which describes—in detail, using Commander Denton's recordings as corroboration of our description—what's really been going on in Pequod and demands an explanation for their increasingly provocative behavior."

"Are you thinking about sending it through normal diplomatic channels, Milady?" Michelle asked, and Medusa gave her a distinctly sharklike smile.

"They sent their official government dispatch boat all the way here to Spindle to make sure we got our mail, Admiral. The least we can do is to make sure they get our reply equally promptly. I think Amandine Corvisart would make an excellent representative, and I think Commodore Chatterjee would make an impressive postman."

"That *could* be viewed as a provocative action, Milady," O'Shaughnessy pointed out. Medusa looked at him, and he shrugged. "They sent a single unarmed dispatch boat. If we send an entire destroyer squadron, or even a single destroyer division, to deliver our response, it could easily be construed as some sort of 'gunboat diplomacy.'"

"A threat that they'd better shut up if they don't want us to blow their miserable little star system to pieces around their ears, Mr. O'Shaughnessy?" Khumalo said just a touch frostily. "Is that what you mean?"

"As a matter of fact, yes, Admiral," O'Shaughnessy replied unflinchingly. "I'm not slamming the Navy when I say that, either. As a matter of fact, I think gunboats or the occasional cruiser—or even the occasional battlecruiser squadron," he added, smiling crookedly at Michelle "—are legitimate diplomatic tools. I'm simply pointing out that in this particular case, we're looking at someone who's already obviously trying to provoke us. Someone who's presenting the destruction of one of their freighters as a consequence of our actions. If we appear to be overtly threatening them, we could be playing into their hands."

"I considered that, Gregor," Medusa said before Khumalo could respond, "and you may well have a point. On the other hand, I think this is one of those occasions when a small show of force is indicated. I'm sure Commodore Chatterjee will be professional and nonconfrontational, and I *know* Amandine will be firm without descending into overt threats. But there's no way we or any other genuine interstellar power wouldn't accompany the delivery of this sort of note with at least a modest show of force. However we choose to phrase it, we're accusing them of deliberately provoking an incident between our star nations, and if they seriously claim we destroyed their freighter and killed its entire crew, *they're* accusing *us* of an overt act of war against New Tuscany. If we don't respond with enough force to warn them there's a line they'd better not cross, then we're stepping outside those normal—and accepted—parameters of a major power's response in a case like this."

"And if their 'game plan,' as Commodore Terekhov described it, was designed on the assumption that we'd react *within* those normal and accepted parameters, Milady?"

"I can't read their minds, Gregor," the imperial governor said. "So if I'm not simply going to sit here and let myself be paralyzed by double-think and triple-think, I'm just going to have to do the best we can. And as long as we're operating within those normal and accepted parameters, without waving great big clubs around, on the one hand, or letting ourselves look like we're running scared, on the other, we'll be in the best position we can be in if and when this thing finally goes to the court of public opinion. That may not be much, but to be brutally honest, it's about the best we can do. If they're determined to go on pushing this, we can't stop them. And if it comes to some kind of *genuine* violent incident as a result, then it's going to come to some kind of violent incident, and we'd best all accept that now. In the meantime, we'll conduct ourselves as a civilized star nation dealing with a preposterous allegation. It certainly can't hurt anything, and, who knows, it *might* even help."

"I think you're right, Milady," Michelle said, and her expression hardened. "I don't want any kind of 'violent incident' with New Tuscany, and God knows the last thing we need is some sort of replay of Monica!" She quirked a taut smile at Terekhov and Khumalo. "I think the two of you did remarkably well at Monica—don't get me wrong about that. But I think all of us also know how ugly things would have gotten if a Frontier Fleet task force had come translating into Monica with blood in its eye. That would have been bad enough before Haven hit the home system. Now, when we're so completely off-balance strategically, the term 'disastrous' comes to mind.

"Despite that, though, or maybe even because of it, I think we need to make it very clear to the New Tuscans that, as the governor says, there's a line they don't want to step over. It might not be a bad idea to remind them that no matter how badly a 'second Monica' might work out for us in the long term, it would work out one hell of a lot *worse* for them in the short term! And I think it's equally important that we make it clear to the Sollies that we intend to be the mistress of our own house. Let's not forget that all of these incidents they're accusing us of fomenting are taking place in Pequod, and Pequod is part of the Star Empire of Manticore, the last time I looked. They inserted one of their warships into sovereign Manticoran territory, and they're informing us of the conclusions of a *New Tuscan* court of inquiry held on events occurring in a *Manticoran* star system, and one at which none of our witnesses or investigators were even present. That's a clear infringement of our sovereignty, on several levels, and I don't believe we can let that stand. Especially if whoever is orchestrating this thing has Frontier Security lurking in the background."

"I think those are both very good points, Admiral," Medusa said. "Of course, that may be because they'd already occurred to me! At any rate, that's how I want to proceed. I'll leave it up to you and Admiral Khumalo to structure Commodore Chatterjee's orders. That's your area of expertise, not mine. I *would* like a briefing on his instructions before he departs for New Tuscany, however. In the meantime, I'll sit down with Amandine. I don't intend to be overtly confrontational in my note to Vézien, but I do intend to make the point—firmly—that New Tuscany is dealing with the Star Empire of Manticore, not with the independent star system of Pequod, and not with some problematical political entity which may come into existence at some point in the future. He's dealing with something that already exists, and something he really, *really* doesn't want to turn into an overt enemy."

# Chapter Forty-One

ABIGAIL HEARNS SAT AT her station on HMS *Tristram*'s bridge and concentrated on radiating a sense of calm. It wasn't easy.

Abigail had never put much faith in the notion of some sort of intuition or "second sight." Not where *she* was concerned, at least; she'd seen and heard enough about Steadholder Harrington not to discount it in the Steadholder's case. Some other officers she'd served with, like Captain Oversteegen, had seemed to possess something very like those reputed psychic powers, as well, but Abigail Hearns' psychic antennae had always been absolutely devoid of any sort of warning signals. Which was why she felt particularly nervous today, because *something* was definitely twisting her nerves into a solid, singing knot of tension.

She didn't know why, couldn't have explained it to a soul, but it was true. And she wasn't the only one who felt it, either. She'd seen it in several of her fellow officers, both on the bridge and off it, and she knew all of them were trying to project the same calm she was . . . and wondering how well they were doing it.

She glanced away from her own displays for a moment, checking the master astrogation plot, and the internal tension she was working so hard to conceal ratcheted up another notch or two. It wouldn't be long now, she thought.

*No, it won't, and thank the Intercessor we've had the extra time to drill,* she told herself. *I don't imagine I'm the only person aboard who wishes we'd gotten a handle on the situation with New Tuscany sooner, but I can't honestly say the time's been wasted.*

*Tristram*'s tactical department still wasn't as well-oiled and proficient as *Hexapuma*'s had been on the eve of the Battle of Monica, but it was immeasurably better than it had been. In fact, she thought it was as good as the Nasty Kitty's had been at Nuncio, and she felt a warm glow of solid accomplishment as she contemplated that improvement and knew it for her own handiwork. Yet there was also something else to keep that satisfied glow company; a dangerous something she'd seen in many of the better tactical officers she'd served with and had discovered lived deep inside *her*, as well. Abigail Hearns had killed enough people in her youthful existence to feel no pressing need to kill still more of them, and yet she could not deny that faint, predatory stirring. That awareness of the lethality of the weapon lying ready to her hand, like a steadholder's blade. She didn't actually *want* to use it, and yet . . . and yet . . .

*There's always that "yet," isn't there, Abigail?* she thought, remembering a conversation in Nuncio with Ragnhild Pavletic. *There's always that hunger to* test *yourself, to prove you're just that little bit better than the next person. Or—let's be honest here—than* anyone *else*.

She glanced at the captain's chair, where Naomi Kaplan sat looking even calmer than any of her subordinates. Unlike anyone else on *Tristram*'s bridge, however, Abigail had seen Commander Kaplan sitting in the tactical officer's chair. She'd seen Kaplan's pre-battle face before, and she knew what she was seeing now.

"Excuse me, Skipper," Lieutenant O'Reilly said. "We have a com request from the flagship. It's the Commodore for you, Ma'am."

"Put it on my display, Wanda," Kaplan responded. There was an almost infinitesimal delay, and then she smiled down at her small private com screen.

"Good afternoon, Commodore. What can I do for you?"

Commodore Ray Chatterjee, commanding officer, Destroyer Squadron 301, smiled back at her from the flag bridge of his flagship, HMS *Roland*. His smile might have been a little more tense than hers, but, then again, he was responsible for all four ships of his first division (Captain Jacob Zavala and Chatterjee's *second* division had been sent straight to Pequod to relieve *Reprise* when Lieutenant Commander Denton returned to Spindle to give

Admiral Khumalo and Admiral Gold Peak his firsthand impressions of the situation in Pequod), whereas Kaplan had to worry about only *Tristram*.

"I've been thinking, Naomi," the commodore said, "and while that's always a somewhat risky occupation in my case, I think I may have hit on something this time. Specifically, I've just as soon keep at least one or two of our cards tucked firmly up my sleeve. Just as a precaution, you know."

"Sir, given what's been going on in Pequod, I'd be in favor of keeping a *pulser* or two tucked firmly up our sleeves. And preferably one in each boot, as well!"

"Well, *that* might be a little overkill," Chatterjee observed mildly. "After all, this is supposed to be a diplomatic mission. But I've been going over everything we have on New Tuscany, and one thing that struck me is that they don't really have any deep-space sensor arrays worth mentioning."

Kaplan nodded. Any moderately prosperous star nation—or, at least, any moderately prosperous star nation which was concerned about military shenanigans in its vicinity—maintained deep-space sensor arrays. In the case of a star system like Manticore, those arrays could be literally thousands of kilometers across, with an exquisite sensitivity capable of picking up things like hyperfootprints and often even impeller signatures light-months out from the system primary, vastly beyond the range possible for any shipboard sensor.

But New Tuscany wasn't "moderately prosperous" by Manticoran standards. In fact, despite its oligarchs' often lavish lifestyles, New Tuscany was little more than a pocket of wretched poverty by the Old Star Kingdom's meter stick, and it didn't have anything remotely like modern deep-space arrays.

"These people are the next best thing to blind outside the hyper limit," Chatterjee pointed out. "I won't say they couldn't possibly see anything beyond that range, but the odds wouldn't be very good for them, and their resolution has to suck once you get out beyond twenty or twenty-five light-minutes from the primary."

"That's about what I'd estimate, yes, Sir," Kaplan agreed, yet there was an almost wary note in her voice, and he smiled again, thinly, as he realized she'd already guessed where he was headed. Well, in that case he supposed he might as well go ahead and confirm her suspicion.

"What I intend to do," he continued, "is to shift our formation to close *Tristram* up a little closer behind *Roland* and see if we can't use her footprint to screen yours. We'll make our translation at twenty-two light-minutes—if they want to think our astrogation is shaky, that's all right with me, but that gives us an extra light-minute and a half to play with. As soon as we make our alpha translation, though, I want you to go to full stealth."

"Sir, with all due respect—"

"'With all due respect yada-yada-yada,'" Chatterjee interrupted with something that was much closer to a grin. "How did I know you were going to say that?"

Kaplan clamped her jaw tightly, although the gleam in her eyes communicated her unspoken thought quite well.

"Better," Chatterjee approved. Then his expression sobered.

"I'm not coming up with this brainstorm just to make your life hard, Naomi, I assure you. The problem is that nobody has a clue what the New Tuscans think they're going to accomplish, but we do know they've been fabricating incidents. In fact, we know they're willing to blow up one of their own freighters—which I hope to hell didn't *really* have a crew on board at the time—and blame it on us. I don't think they would've done that unless they felt they'd been able to cobble up at least some sort of 'sensor data' to support their claims, and Commander Denton, unfortunately, wasn't able to give us really conclusive counter evidence.

"I'm inclined to doubt that they're going to try anything with three Manticoran destroyers sitting right here, watching them like hawks, but I'm also not inclined to bet the farm on that. So what we're going to do is to use *Roland*, *Lancelot*, and *Galahad* to drop Ghost Rider platforms on our way in. We'll launch a few active platforms of our own to sweep ahead of us, but the others will be completely passive, won't even bring their drives up, and you'll be monitoring all of them from out beyond the hyper limit, using light-speed links so there aren't any unexplained grav pulses floating around the system. The New Tuscans won't know we're basically watching their entire star system and recording everything we see. If they try sneaking anything around outside our known sensor range, the covert platforms ought to nail them at it, which would probably strengthen Ambassador Crovisart's hand a lot if they are up to something and try to get shirty with her. So, in a way, I'd almost like for them to go ahead and try something if it let us catch them with their hand in the cookie jar. And you're the one who's going to be watching the cookies for us."

Kaplan was silent for a moment or two, and then she gave a barely perceptible sigh.

"Very well, Sir. I don't like it, but I understand the logic, and I guess somebody has to draw the duty. But the next time you come up with something like this, couldn't we cut cards, or shoot dice, or flip coins, or something to see who gets to play grandma rocking on the porch while the rest of the kids run out to play?"

"Goodness, Commander! I hadn't realized you had such a gift for imagery. But I suppose I can at least take your suggestion under advisement."

Chatterjee frowned thoughtfully for a moment, then grinned.

"Personally, I've always preferred paper, rock, scissors when it comes to *serious* command decisions, though."

"They've arrived, Ms. Anisimovna."

Aldona Anisimovna sat up quickly on the chaise lounge on the terrace of her temporary townhouse in Livorno. She'd been luxuriating in the warmth of New Tuscany's G3 primary like a big, blonde cat for almost an hour, and it took a moment or two for her sunsodden brain to catch up with Kyrillos Taliadoros' announcement.

"The Manties?" she said, and he nodded in confirmation.

"According to our contacts, they turned up in a bit greater strength than we'd expected, Ma'am."

"How much greater?"

"Three of their new *Roland*-class destroyers," Taliadoros replied. "And according to their initial messages, they've sent no less than Amandine Corvisart to deliver their response to the Prime Minister's note."

"Really?" Anisimovna smiled nastily. Given the demolition job Corvisart had done at Monica, the opportunity to repay her for her efforts was an unanticipated bonus. She felt herself wanting to purr like a hunting lioness at the thought, yet even as she did, she felt her pulse beginning to speed. Not even a scion of a Mesan alpha line was immune to the effect of old-fashioned adrenaline. Or dread, she admitted, her smile fading just a bit. Or, for that matter, to a slight churning in her stomach as she contemplated the little detail she'd added to the plan without mentioning it to any of her allies here in New Tuscany.

*Stop that!* she told herself firmly. *It's the first move in a damned war, you silly bitch! Of course it's going to be . . . messy. But it's going to* work, *too, and that's a hell of a lot more important!*

"You said this was according to our contacts," she said out loud. "Should I assume from that that no one from Vézien's office has passed us the official word yet?"

"No, Ma'am. But that doesn't necessarily mean anything." Taliadoros allowed himself a faint smile of complacency. "I'd be very surprised if our communications lines to the NTN—and his own office, for that matter—aren't actually shorter—or at least faster—than his are."

"Let's not let ourselves get overly confident here, Kyrillos," Anisimovna said just a bit quellingly, and her bodyguard's smile disappeared as he nodded in sober acknowledgment.

Not that he didn't have a point, Anisimovna conceded in the privacy of her own mind. Upon his arrival on New Tuscany, Jansen Metcalf had done what Mesan attachés and ambassadors always did. Even before he'd finished unpacking, he'd gone about establishing "contacts" throughout the local political and economic structure. It was always easier on planets like New Tuscany, where graft, patronage, and corruption were accepted, everyday facts of life. Anisimovna sometimes wondered if it was the relative absence of that trinity of tools which explained Bardasano's failure to penetrate someplace like Manticore—or, for that matter, Thesiman's and Pritchart's new Republic—the way she'd managed to penetrate so many other star nations.

Whatever might have been true in Manticore's case, however, New Tuscany had offered fertile soil for the standard Mesan techniques, and until Manticore had become involved in the Talbott Cluster, Metcalf hadn't had anything more important to do than to polish his network. Which meant Taliadoros was almost certainly correct—Anisimovna probably *was* better informed about what was happening throughout the New Tuscany System than Prime Minister Vézien. Quite possibly even better informed than Damien Dusserre, for that matter, although she'd have been less willing to wager on that possibility.

"You're probably right, though," she continued out loud. "It's more likely that Vézien is doublechecking his information before passing it on than it is that he's deliberately trying to keep us in the dark."

Taliadoros nodded again, and Anisimovna flowed to her feet. She padded barefoot to the terrace wall, gazing out across New Tuscany's capital for a few more moments of thought. Then she turned back to her bodyguard.

"I think it's time that I be very carefully sitting here doing absolutely nothing suspicious," she said. "And if I'm here, you have to be here. I think it would probably be a good idea to close down any private communications channels we might have open. I trust Lieutenant Rochefort has already received his instructions?"

"Yes, Ma'am. And Ambassador Metcalf has doublechecked the communications relay. Even if anyone detected it, there's no way it could be traced back to us."

"I like a positive mindset, Kyrillos, but my own recent experience leaves me disinclined to take anything for granted."

"Of course, Ma'am."

"All right, then," she said. "Go and make sure we aren't talking to anyone Mr. Dusserre's eavesdroppers can't listen in on. Wouldn't want him getting any nasty suspicions about why we might be trying to evade him, after all. And while you're doing that," she smiled, "I think I'll go have a shower and a pre-supper martini."

"I don't *believe* this shit," Commodore Ray Chatterjee muttered as he studied the icons on the plot being driven by the recon platforms he'd sent in-system ahead of himself. "How the hell did these people get here, and what the hell are they *doing* here?"

"I don't know, Sir," Lieutenant Commander Lori Olson, his operations officer, said quietly. "Right off the top of my head, though, I doubt it's anything we'd be happy about if we *did* know."

"You've got that right," Chatterjee agreed grimly.

He sat back in his command chair, his expression even grimmer than his tone had been, and thought hard.

When he and Ambassador Corvisart had been sent off to New Tuscany, no one had counted on *this*. So just what were the two of them supposed to do when they found seventeen Solarian battlecruisers and five of their destroyers parked in orbit around the planet?

*This stinks to high heaven*, he thought. *The only question is whether or not the Sollies know they're part of whatever the New Tuscans are up to . . . and I've got a bad feeling about that. I suppose it's at least remotely possible the Sollies don't* know, *but they'd have to be dumber than rocks not to realize the New Tuscans were trying to play them. Not that I haven't known a few Sollies who were dumber than rocks. Strange how that's not a very comforting reflection at the moment.*

"Contact the Ambassador, Jason," he said to Commander Jason Wright, his chief of staff. "Ask her to join us in my briefing room. Then get hold of Captain DesMoines and ask him to join you, me, and the Ambassador."

"Yes, Sir."

"Yes, Mr. Prime Minister?" Anisimovna said pleasantly, raising one eyebrow at the view screen while she swirled ice gently in her martini glass. "To what do I owe the pleasure?"

"I thought you'd like to know that we've just been notified that three Manticoran destroyers or light cruisers have entered the system. They're headed for New Tuscany right now. We expect them to reach parking orbit within the next three hours."

"Indeed?" Anisimovna allowed her eyes to narrow with exactly the correct degree of sudden speculation as she leaned forward to set her glass on the edge of the coffee table in front of her. "I hardly expected them so soon, Mr. Prime Minister. Are all of our . . . special assets in place?"

"We're getting plenty of emissions and other data off them from the new platforms," Vézien assured her, although she suspected he was rather less confident than he chose to appear. "Minister of War Pélisard is in contact with Admiral Guédon right now. She says she's confident of capturing enough data for us to . . . massage however we have to for the Sollies' consumption. My only concern is having Byng right here in-system already." He shook his head and allowed a hint of concern to creep into his expression. "I wish he hadn't been in such a tearing hurry to get here!"

"I understand, Mr. Prime Minister." Anisimovna gave him a wry smile. "I never expected Commissioner Verrochio to respond so promptly to our first note, either. After all, Sollies *never* do things in a hurry—that's one of the things the rest of us dislike about them so much. Does Admiral Guédon expect to be able to work around them?"

"Probably." Vézien puffed his cheeks for a moment. "Nicholas—I mean, Minister Pélisard—seems to feel fairly confident of that, at any rate. But if the Sollies make a close comparison between the data their own sensors are undoubtedly recording right this minute and the 'incidents' we're going to be sending them shortly, they could very well spot the stuff *we're* recording right now when they see it again later."

"Oh, I wouldn't worry too much about that, Mr. Prime Minister." Anisimovna's smile turned wolflike. "Admiral Byng is sufficiently unfond of the Manties to overlook any inconvenient little problems, and Commissioner Verrochio and his staff are already primed to do exactly that, as well. All we need is something that's remotely plausible for anyone who *doesn't* have access to the data you're capturing at the moment."

"What do you make of them, Ingeborg?" Josef Byng asked, standing with his hands clasped behind him as he studied the enormous master plot on SLNS *Jean Bart's* flag bridge.

"Preliminary reports are still coming in, Sir," Captain Ingeborg Aberu, Byng's operations officer, replied. She looked up from her own console for a moment and grimaced as her eyes met Byng's, as if to ask what else could be expected from a combat information center manned by Frontier Fleet personnel.

"From what we have so far, though," she continued, "it looks like three light cruisers. They're headed in-system. We believe they've already burst-transmitted to the local government, but they haven't squawked their transponders, so we don't have any definitive IDs just yet. Under the circumstances, though, I don't think there's much doubt who they belong to, Sir."

"Ballsy of them, Admiral," Karlotte Thimár observed. Byng looked at her, and the chief of staff shrugged. "I mean bringing it straight to New Tuscany this way. That's a bit of an escalation from harassing the New Tuscans' shipping in someplace like this Pequod System."

"From 'harassing,' maybe, Karlotte," Byng replied. "But from firing on and destroying an unarmed merchantship going about her lawful business?" His jaw muscles tightened. No one in Meyers before his departure for New Tuscany, not even he, had dreamed the situation could have escalated that rapidly out here, or that even the Manties would be that blatant about their behavior, and he felt a fresh wave of righteous anger go through him. "I think what we're seeing here is a direct progression of the kind of crap they've been pulling all along," he continued. "I think they've decided to come turn the screws on the New Tuscan government in its own backyard!"

"Well, if that's what they're thinking, Sir," Commander Lennox Wysoki, Byng's intelligence officer, said with an evil chuckle, "they'll probably be *really* unhappy when they finally realize *we're* sitting right here in orbit!"

"I agree that it's unfortunate, Commodore," Amandine Corvisart said. "And I won't pretend I'm happy about it, either—for a lot of reasons. But I don't see how we can allow it to interfere with our mission. We certainly can't just turn around and go home as if the mere presence of Solarian warships scared us off!"

"I think the Ambassador's right, Sir," Commander John Des-Moines, *Roland*'s CO and Chatterjee's flag captain, said somberly, and Chatterjee snorted.

"Of course she is, Jack! First, because she's the Ambassador and we're the people who are supposed to be supporting *her* mission, which makes it her call. And, second, because I happen to agree with her. What I'm trying to do is to get a feel for how we want to handle it. Do we just ignore the Sollies? Pretend they aren't even here unless *they* decide to talk to *us*? Or do we treat this as a normal port call and follow the protocols for exchanges between friendly powers meeting in a neutral port?"

"I don't think there's any point being too disingenuous about it," Corvisart said after a moment. Chatterjee waggled one hand in a gesture which invited her to continue, and she shrugged. "There's no way this many Solarian warships would just happen to be parked in an out-of-the-way star system like New Tuscany unless they'd been invited. And the only thing that could have gotten them all the way here from the Madras Sector would have been a fairly urgent invitation. Something accompanied by a note about all of those nasty Manticoran depredations against innocent New Tuscan merchantships, for example. So I think we have to assume the Sollies aren't here by accident, that they're predisposed to be hostile to us, and that we'll have to put up with quite a bit of unpleasantness from them while we're here."

"Well, at least *that* won't be anything we don't have experience with!" Lori Olson's muttered comment was just low-voiced enough for Chatterjee to pretend he hadn't heard it. Not that he didn't agree with it wholeheartedly.

"On the other hand," Corvisart continued, "they're still at least technically neutral and impartial bystanders. Our business is with the New Tuscan government, not with the Solarian League Navy, and that's the way we ought to approach it. If the senior Solarian officer chooses to insert himself into the process, I'll have to deal with it as it occurs. But until and unless that happens, *I'm* going to ignore them completely—after all, I'm a civilian here to deal with other civilians—while you and your staff make the normal courtesies of one navy to another."

"My," Chatterjee said dryly. "Won't *that* be fun."

Several hours later, Commodore Chatterjee found himself still on *Roland*'s flag bridge.

There were really two reasons for the *Rolands*' huge size compared to other destroyers. One was the fact that they were the only destroyers in the galaxy equipped to fire the Mark 16 dual-drive missile. Squeezing in that capability—and giving them twelve tubes—had required a substantial modification to the Mod 9-c launcher mounted in the *Saganami-C* class. The *Rolands*' Mod 9-e was essentially the tube from the 9-c, but stripped of the support equipment normally associated with a standalone missile tube. Instead, a sextet of the new launchers were shoehorned together, combining the necessary supports for all six tubes in the cluster. *Roland* mounted one cluster each in her fore and aft hammerheads, the traditional locations for a ship's chase energy weapons. Given the Manticoran ability to fire off-bore, all twelve tubes could be brought to bear on any target, but it did make the class's weapons more vulnerable. A single hit could take out half of her total missile armament, which was scarcely something Chatterjee liked to think about. But destroyers had never been intended to take the kind of hammering wallers could take, anyway, and he was willing to accept *Roland*'s vulnerabilities in return for her overwhelming advantage in missile combat.

The other reason for her size (aside from the need to squeeze in magazine space for her launchers) was that every member of the class had been fitted with flagship capability. The Royal Manticoran Navy had been caught short of suitable flagships for cruiser and destroyer service during the First Havenite War, and the *Rolands* were also an attempt to address that shortage. Big enough and tough enough to serve with light cruisers, and with a substantial long-range punch of their own, they were also supposed to be produced in sufficient numbers to provide plenty of flag decks this time around. They weren't anywhere near as big or opulently equipped as those of a battlecruiser or a waller, but they were big enough for the job and, even more important, they'd be there when they were needed.

Which was why Ray Chatterjee came to have such spacious comfort in which to sit while he stewed.

*I didn't really expect this to go smoothly,* he thought. *I didn't expect it to be quite* this *complicated, either, though.*

He could hardly say he was surprised the New Tuscans were stonewalling to avoid making any sort of meaningful response to the note Ambassador Corvisart had delivered. They could scarcely acknowledge the note's accuracy, after all, so he supposed simply refusing to accept it was their best move at the moment, although he was a little surprised they hadn't already appealed to the Sollies to intervene on their side, at least as a friendly neutral.

*Probably means they don't have all of their falsified data in place yet,* the commodore reflected. *Even a prick like this Byng probably wouldn't be very amused if they handed him something* too *crude. I wonder if they even knew he was coming this soon?*

Whatever the New Tuscans' attitude towards Amandine Corvisart might be, though, there was no question about Admiral Josef Byng's attitude towards the Star Empire of Manticore. The New Tuscans' senior traffic control officer had looked and sounded as if someone had inserted a broom handle into a certain orifice, in Chatterjee's opinion. He'd been just barely on the stiffly correct side of outright incivility, although Chatterjee hadn't been able to decide whether that was because he knew exactly what was going on and was part of it, or whether it was because he *didn't* know what was going on and genuinely believed his own government's horror stories about vicious Manticoran harassment. There hadn't been much doubt about what *Byng* believed, though.

"So long as the New Tuscan system government is prepared to tolerate your presence, 'Commodore,'" Byng had said, biting off each word is if it had been a shard of ice, "then so shall I. I will also do you the courtesy—for now, at least—of assuming that you, personally, have not been party to the gross abuse of New Tuscan neutral rights here in the Cluster. The Solarian League, however, does not look kindly upon the infringement of those neutral rights, and especially not upon the destruction of unarmed merchant vessels and their entire crews. I have no doubt you are under orders not to *discuss* these matters with me, 'Commodore,' and I will not press you on them at this time. Eventually, however, what's been happening out here will be . . . sufficiently clarified, shall we say, for my government to take an official position on it. I look forward to that day, at which time, perhaps, we will have that *discussion* after all. Good day, 'Commodore.'"

It had not been an exchange—if the icy, one-way tirade could be called an "exchange"—designed to set Chatterjee's mind at ease. Nor was his mind particularly comforted by the Solarian battlecruisers' actions. None of them had their wedges or side-walls up, but close visual observation—and at a range of under five thousand kilometers it was possible to make a *very* close visual inspection, even without resorting to deployable reconnais-sance platforms—made it evident that their energy batteries were manned. Sensors detected active radar and lidar, as well, which CIC identified as missile-defense fire control systems. Technically, that meant they were defensive systems, not offensive ones, but that was a meaningless distinction at this piddling range. Those battlecruisers knew exactly where every one of Chatterjee's ships were, and at this distance, it would have been extraordinarily difficult for them to miss.

*Stop that,* he told himself sternly. *Byng is an asshole, but he's not a* crazy *asshole . . . I hope. And only someone who was* crazy *would start a war just because he's feeling pissed off. Corvisart is going to finish her discussions with Vézien and Cardot one way or the other within the next day or so, at which point we can get the hell out of here. In the meantime, all we really need is for everyone on our side to stay cool. That's all we need.*

He told himself that very firmly, and the reasoning part of his brain knew it was a logical, convincing analysis of the situation.

Still, he was just as happy he'd left Naomi Kaplan and *Tristram* to watch his back.

"I'm liking this less and less by the minute, Skipper," Lieutenant Commander Alvin Tallman murmured.

"I suppose that's because you have a functional brain, Alvin," Naomi Kaplan replied, looking up at her executive officer. "I can't think of any *other* reason you wouldn't like it, at any rate."

Tallman's lips twitched in a brief smile, but it never touched his eyes, and Kaplan understood perfectly. The tension must be bad enough aboard the other three ships of the division, but in its own way, the tension aboard *Tristram* was even worse, because Kaplan's ship was over ten light-minutes from New Tuscany. Thanks to the Ghost Rider platforms, they could see exactly what was happening—or, at the moment, *not* happening—in the volume immediately around the planet, even if the data and imagery was ten minutes old when they got it. Even with Mark 16s, though, there wasn't anything they could *do* about whatever might happen that far away, and their own safely insulating distance from the Solarian ships only made them feel perversely guilty over their helpless inviolability.

Kaplan glanced around her bridge, considering her watch officers thoughtfully. She'd had time to get to know them by now, although she still knew Abigail better than any of the others—including Tallman, for that matter. That was changing, though, and she'd become aware of their strengths and weaknesses, aware of the way those qualities must be blended together so that strength was reinforced and weakness was compensated for.

For example, there was O'Reilly's continuing, festering resentment of Abigail's position. She'd managed to keep it sufficiently in check that Kaplan and Tallman hadn't been forced to take official notice—or, at any rate, any *additional* official notice—of it, but she wasn't convinced things were going to stay that way. At the same time, she'd found that despite O'Reilly's unpleasant personality, she was actually quite good in her own specialty. It might have taken Tallman's kick in the pants to get her off her ass to *prove* it, but she'd turned the com department around quite nicely since. In fact, it irritated Kaplan that the lieutenant had managed it, although she recognized that it was rather foolish of her to want the other woman to be *bad* at her job just because she couldn't warm to her.

And then there were the others. Lieutenant Hosea Simpkins, her Grayson-born astrogator. Lieutenant Sherilyn Jeffers, her electronic warfare officer, as Manticoran and secular as anyone was ever likely to get who nonetheless had formed a smoothly functioning partnership with Abigail . . . unlike O'Reilly. Lieutenant Fonzarelli in Engineering, Chief Warrant Officer Zagorski, her logistics officer . . . They were like the strands of steel layered through one of those swords a Grayson swordsmith hammered out so patiently. They weren't perfect. In fact, they remained far short of that forever unattainable goal. But they were good, one of the best groups of ship's officers she'd ever served with. If she managed to screw up, it would be *her* fault, not theirs.

*Now there's a cheerful way to look at things, Naomi,* she told herself tartly. *Any more doom and gloom you'd like to rain on yourself this afternoon?*

Her lips hovered briefly on the brink of a smile for a moment, but then she drew a deep breath and returned her attention to the silent, glittering data codes on her plot.

Lieutenant Léopold Rochefort checked his chrono unobtrusively for no more than the five hundredth time since receiving the activation code and wished his palms didn't feel quite so damp.

This had all seemed very simple when it was first described to him. After all, Rochefort was one of the small handful of New Tuscan officers who knew what was actually going on, since his older brother was Admiral Guédon's senior communications officer. So he knew, whether he was supposed to or not, that what he'd been asked to do was only another facet of the master plan. The fact that someone was prepared to pay him so handsomely to do something which could only contribute to his own government's objectives was merely icing on the cake.

That was how it had seemed when he was originally recruited, at any rate. He'd discovered, however, that now that the moment was here, it no longer seemed quite so simple. He was operating outside the normal naval chain of command, after all, which meant there would be no official cover for him if he managed to screw this up. On the other hand, he *was* acting under the direct authority of Minister of Security Dusserre. That ought to give him at least some protection it things went wrong.

*But they aren't* going *to go wrong,* he told himself firmly . . . again. *After all, how badly* can *I screw this up?*

Remembering certain events in his career as a junior officer, he decided it would probably be better if he didn't dwell too deeply on that last question.

He looked away from his chrono, glancing around the compartment. Rochefort was an assistant communications officer aboard the space station *Giselle*, the primary communications and traffic control platform of the New Tuscany System, as well as a major industrial node in her own right. As the inspector from Security had explained to him, that meant *Giselle* was the logical place from which to insert the "Manticoran" worm into the system's astrogation computers. Rochefort had wondered why they'd chosen to use the com section rather than someone actually inside traffic control, but the nameless, anonymous inspector had explained it willingly enough. Obviously, for the Manties to be responsible for the attack on the computers, it had to come from outside. It had to be inserted into the system through a com channel, since the Manties would have had no physical access to the computers. So what would happen would be that Rochefort would send it from his station to a com satellite near the Manties' position and parking orbit, and the satellite would relay it back to Traffic Control, where it would faithfully attack the computers.

From Rochefort's perspective, it seemed like an unlikely thing for the Manties to do. Fortunately, perhaps, it wasn't his job to critique the strategy he'd been ordered to execute, and presumably those who were in charge of that strategy had come up with some way to make it seem like a logical move on the Manties' part.

And speaking of the Manties...

It was time, he realized, and reached out to punch the function key he'd set up weeks ago.

Unfortunately for Lieutenant Rochefort, he had never actually been approached by a member of the Ministry of Security. Or, rather, not by a *current* member of the Ministry of Security. The man who had passed himself off as a Security inspector *had* been an employee of Dusserre's ministry some years ago, but he'd been far better paid by Ambassador Metcalf and his new Mesan employers for the last couple of T-years.

Like Lieutenant Rochefort, the bogus inspector had wondered just how Manpower was going to convince anyone to accept that the Star Empire of Manticore had wasted its time trying to insert a worm into the traffic control computers of a third-rank star system like New Tuscany. Also like Lieutenant Rochefort, however, he had decided the answer to that particular question lay at a level well beyond even his current pay grade. So he'd passed on his instructions and provided the lieutenant with the necessary prerecorded transmission and the activation code which would tell him it was time for him to do his bit for New Tuscany's national interests.

Promptly after which, he had met with a fatal accident named Kyrillos Taliadoros and quietly and completely disappeared.

That meant there was no one who could possibly have tied Lieutenant Rochefort to Manpower or Mesa before he pressed that function key.

And no one could possibly tie the lieutenant to anyone *after* that, since the message he transmitted was actually the detonation command for the two-hundred-kiloton device hidden inside a cargo container a Jessyk Combine freighter had transshipped to *Giselle* a month before . . . and which was now stored in a cargo bay approximately one hundred and twelve meters forward and three hundred meters down from Lieutenant Rochefort's compartment.

Ray Chatterjee was sipping from a coffee mug when he heard an odd sound. It took him a moment to realize it was the sound of someone sucking in air for an explosive grunt of surprise, and he was turning towards the sound, his brain still trying to identify it, when he realized it had come from Lieutenant Commander Olson. Then her head came up, and she turned towards him.

"Sir! The space station—*Giselle*—it's just blown up!"

"*What?*"

Despite his own earlier thoughts, for just an instant, it completely failed to register and he simply stared at the ops officer. He'd been focused on the Solarian ships, worrying about the future, trying to figure out the past. . . . None of that had prepared his mind for the possibility that a space station the better part of ten kilometers in length should just suddenly *blow up*.

His eyes whipped around to the visual display, and he froze as he saw the awesome spectacle. Sheer shock and disbelief held him there, staring at it, trying to wrap his mind around the unexpected enormity of it all. It was more than he could do as the seconds dragged past, but then, suddenly—

"Communications!" he snapped. "Raise Admiral Byng immediately!"

"What the—!"

Josef Byng was watching the visual display, not the tactical plot, at the moment *Giselle* blew up. The sudden eruption of light and fury that wiped away the forty-two thousand men and women aboard the space station took him totally by surprise. The view screen polarized instantly, protecting his eyes from the blinding flash, but it was so close, so powerful that he flinched back from it involuntarily.

"*Sir!*" Captain Aberu half-shouted. "Sir! The New Tuscan space station's just blown up!"

"The Manties!" Byng snapped, and whipped around to punch a priority key on his com. Captain Warden Mizawa, *Jean Bart's* commanding officer, appeared on his display almost instantly.

"Case Yellow, Captain! The Manties have just—"

"Sir, I know the station's been destroyed," the captain said, speaking quickly and urgently, "but it was definitely a nuclear explosion—a *contact* explosion; CIC sets the yield at at least two hundred kilotons—and *not* an energy weapon. But we didn't pick up any missile trace, so—"

"Goddamn it, I just gave you a fucking order, *Captain!*" Byng snarled, absolutely infuriated that a mere Frontier Fleet captain would dare to interrupt him with *arguments* at a moment like this. "I don't *care* what you did or didn't pick up! We're sitting here bare-assed naked, without even sidewalls, and just who the hell *else* d'you think would have done something like this?"

"But, Sir, it *couldn't've* been a missile if we didn't detec—"

"Don't you fucking *argue* with me!" Byng bellowed while panic pulsed through him. However the Manties had done it, they couldn't afford any witnesses, and with their wedges down even friggng *destroyers* could—

"But, Sir, if they'd—"

"Shut the hell up and execute your goddamned orders, Captain, or I swear to *God* I'll have you shot this very afternoon!"

For one fleeting moment, Warden Mizawa hovered on the brink of defiance. But then the moment passed.

"Yes, Sir," he grated. "Case Yellow, you said." He gave Byng one last, searing look, then turned away from the com to his own tactical officer.

"Open fire," he told Commander Ursula Zeiss harshly.

# Chapter Forty-Two

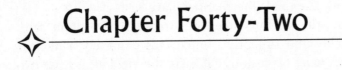

HELEN ZILWICKI WAS STILL getting accustomed to the notion that, as Commodore Terekhov's flag lieutenant, her duty station when the ship went to battle stations was no longer on the bridge or manning a weapons console somewhere. Instead, it was on *Quentin Saint-James'* flag bridge, with the commodore. It was a strange sensation, and one she didn't care for very much . . . probably because she didn't really have anything to *do*. Oh, she helped to maintain and update the log, or went to "run and find out" through the ship's data system if he needed some odd bit of fact one of his staff officers didn't already have at her fingertips, and she was always available if the commodore decided he needed to send her somewhere, but that wasn't the same thing at all. Nor was it supposed to be. It was another of those on-the-job-training aspects of her position, putting her inside the flag officer decision-making loop like an observant little fly on the bulkhead, and she had to admit she found that part of her flag lieutenant assignment fascinating. It was just that she felt as if she ought to be *doing* something, contributing something other than her mere presence when her ship needed her.

At least they'd finally managed to fill the holes in the commodore's staff, so the flag bridge didn't seem quite so *empty* anymore. Helen suspected that the commodore had actually picked out the officers he planned to "requisition" when he got to Spindle long before the squadron ever departed from Manticore. He'd seemed to know exactly who he wanted after they arrived, at any rate, and given his new relationship with Admiral Khumalo, it probably wasn't surprising that he'd gotten his choices, although not everyone had been delighted at the prospect of surrendering them to him.

They were a good bunch, Helen thought, and they'd shaken down well with the commodore and *Quentin Saint-James'* officers. She particularly liked Commander Stillwell Lewis, the new ops officer, who rejoiced in the nickname of "Stilt," and Lieutenant Commander Mateuz Ødegaard, the staff intelligence officer. Commander Lewis was a tall, rangy redhead—from Gryphon, like Helen herself—who got along well with Commander Lynch, and Ødegaard reminded Helen in some ways of her father. Physically, the slightly built, fair-haired Ødegaard couldn't have been less like Anton Zilwicki, but both of them had the same implacably patient, unremitting, logical concentration on the task in hand. Both of them seemed to know that in the battle between stone and water, water always won.

The other newcomers were Lieutenant Commander Mazal Inbari, the astrogator, and Lieutenant Atalante Montella, the communications officer. Both of them were far more than merely competent, and Helen liked both of them, but she hadn't yet warmed to them the way she had to Stillwell and Ødegaard.

At the moment, however, that thought was far from foremost in her mind as she sat very quietly at her own terminal and watched the master plot at the forward end of the flag bridge. It wasn't configured for tactical or astrographic mode at the moment. Instead, it was configured as a view screen, and Vice Admiral Michelle Henke looked back out of it at Helen.

In point of fact, Helen knew, Admiral Gold Peak's image was on every view screen aboard every ship of Tenth Fleet as it swept through hyper-space towards the system of New Tuscany at an apparent velocity three thousand times that of light.

"Attention all hands," the voice of Lieutenant Commander Edwards, the admiral's staff com officer said quietly. It was probably the most unnecessary announcement in the history of the Royal Manticoran Navy, a corner of Helen's mind thought, but ninety-nine percent of her attention was focused on Gold Peak's stony expression.

"People," the admiral said without further preamble, "by this time, I'm sure, all of you have a fairly accurate idea of the content of *Tristram*'s report. For any of you who are still wondering, I can confirm that *Roland*, *Lancelot*, and *Galahad* have been destroyed by Frontier Fleet units of the Solarian League navy under the command of Admiral Josef Byng. *Tristram* had been detached to observe events in New Tuscany through her remote platforms, and we have detailed records of the destruction of all three vessels. They were attacked without warning or challenge, without wedges and with no time to raise sidewalls, at pointblank range, by the massed energy fire of seventeen Solarian battlecruisers and eight destroyers. At this time, we have no evidence of any survivors. We will continue to hope, and the recovery of any of our people will be our highest priority. It is highly unlikely, based on *Tristram*'s data, however, that there will be anyone to recover."

She paused, and Helen felt her jaw muscles tighten as she pictured what it must've been like aboard Commodore Chatterjee's destroyers. Unlike almost anyone else in *Quentin Saint-James*' company, Helen had been aboard a vessel after it had been taken totally unawares by heavy energy fire at point-blank range. In fact, she'd been there twice, little more than a T-year ago. She didn't need to imagine the carnage as men and women suddenly found their ships ripped open to space without warning, without any time to prepare before the howling tornado of escaping atmosphere plunged them into the deathly embrace of vacuum. She knew exactly what it must have been like as the destroyers' crewmen were torn apart by splinters and fragments of their own ships' hulls, as they had fleeting instants to realize no one was going to reach a life pod in time.

There might have been a handful of survivors, people who'd found themselves trapped in pockets of life-sustaining atmosphere behind blast doors or emergency hatches, but there couldn't have been many. Not aboard ships murdered as Commodore Chatterjee's destroyers had been.

"At this moment," Vice Admiral Gold Peak continued in that same level, unflinching voice, "we have no idea what we will find in New Tuscany when we arrive. To the best of our knowledge, neither the New Tuscans nor the Solarians even realize *Tristram* was there, far less that we have detailed knowledge of everything that happened. Since they presumably don't know *Tristram* got away to tell us about it, it seems entirely possible that they won't be expecting this prompt a response from us. That, in fact, is the reason for all the rush to get underway. If they don't expect us, we want to arrive while they're still sitting there fat, dumb, and happy with their thumbs up their asses."

For the first time, the admiral showed some expression—a thin, hungry, somehow feral smile.

"We know *what* happened in the sense of what was destroyed and who actually fired at whom," she went on. "What we do not know is the *why*. There had been no communication between the Solarian battlecruisers and our destroyers for well over two hours before Admiral Byng opened fire. According to the take from *Tristram's* ELINT platforms, *Roland* was in the act of opening a communications link with one of the battlecruisers at the time she was destroyed. It does not appear the link was ever established or that the two vessels were in communication at the moment the Solarians opened fire.

"According to the analysts, there is at least a possibility that the Solarians were responding to a perceived attack."

Helen could physically feel the wave of incredulity which swept through the flag bridge's occupants at that statement, and she shared fully. Three destroyers attacking *seventeen battlecruisers* plus their screen? The very idea was absurd!

"I'm not suggesting that any *competent* fleet commander would fall prey to such a . . . misperception," Gold Peak continued as if she'd heard Helen's very thoughts. "We know, however, that one of the New Tuscans' major space stations was completely destroyed immediately before the Solarians opened fire. That destruction was the result of a nuclear explosion. Analysis of its emissions signature makes it very clear that the explosion resulted from a relatively low yield nuclear warhead, probably in the vicinity of two hundred kilotons. It was *not* some bizarre sort of 'industrial accident,' but rather a deliberate action on someone's part. It is conceivable that, given the state of tension between the Star Empire and New Tuscany, Admiral Byng leapt to the conclusion that Commodore Chatterjee was responsible for the station's destruction."

She let her listeners digest that for a few moments, let them work through the implications.

*If it wasn't us—and I know damned well it wasn't*, Helen thought— *then it had to be someone else. And if the Sollies thought it was* us, *then it obviously wasn't* them. *Which only leaves . . .*

"Our best estimate is that the New Tuscan death toll from this disaster was somewhere between forty and fifty thousand," Gold Peak said softly. "We can't be positive whether or not there was any crew aboard the *Hélène Blondeau* when she mysteriously blew up in Pequod, but we know positively that the space station in New Tuscany was fully manned and in normal operation at the time of its destruction. Which means whoever was responsible *deliberately* killed all of those people.

"Our intelligence people believe there is a distinct possibility that someone is attempting to maneuver the Solarian League into a shooting war with the Star Empire. I'm sure I need not remind any of you about last year's efforts in Split, Montana, and Monica. This may—I stress, *may*—be more of the same.

"Despite that, there is one enormously significant difference between the events leading up to Commodore Terekhov's visit to Monica and our own visit to New Tuscany. This time, Manticoran warships—*Queen's* ships—have been destroyed, ruthlessly and without warning, and the finger that pushed the button—for whatever reason—was Solarian. What this means, People, is that we are now effectively at war with the Solarian League Navy."

The marrow of Helen's bones seemed to freeze, and for the first time since she'd been a thirteen-year-old trapped in the lightless tunnels under Old Chicago, she felt like a small, furry creature fleeing from a hexapuma's claws. The mere thought of the League's enormous size, of the literally endless fleets it could build and man, was enough to strike terror into the hardiest soul.

"Special Minister Bernardus Van Dort is with me here on the flagship as the direct personal representative of Prime Minister Alquezar, Baroness Medusa, and Her Majesty," Gold Peak resumed after another brief pause, "and a special diplomatic mission has been dispatched to the Meyers System with *Tristram's* sensor records to demand an explanation from the Office of Frontier Security. Obviously, we continue to hope it may be possible to nip this confrontation with the League in the bud, but for that to happen the situation here in the Quadrant must be prevented from getting further out of hand, all evidence must be preserved, there must be a thorough investigation into these events, and there must be *accountability*.

"Because of those considerations, our instructions—*my* instructions—are to proceed to New Tuscany. When we reach that star system, I have been instructed to demand that Admiral

Byng stand down his ships, that the New Tuscan System government stand down its defenses, and that both of them cooperate fully with our investigation until such time as a Manticoran court of inquiry has determined what actually transpired in New Tuscany eleven days ago. Mr. Van Dort will represent the Star Empire, and it will be he who presents our demands to the New Tuscan government, but it is Her Majesty's Navy which will see to it that those demands are complied with."

She paused again, her dark-skinned face boulder-hard, gazing levelly out of the scores of view screens aboard the ships of her command for what seemed to be endless seconds. Then she continued in a voice of measured, inflexible steel.

"To be honest, I am far from confident that Admiral Byng will willingly accede to our demands. I will attempt to give him every opportunity to do so, but I'm sure many of you have had your own personal experience of how Solarians are likely to react to such demands from 'neobarbs.' Make no mistake about this, however, People—if he does not willingly comply with our demands, then we *will* compel him to do so. It is one thing to be reasonable; it is another thing entirely to be *weak*, and we must know what happened in New Tuscany—and who was responsible for it—if we are to have any hope at all of controlling this situation. Neither Baroness Medusa, nor Admiral Khumalo, nor Prime Minister Alquezar, nor Mr. Van Dort, nor I want a war against the Solarian League. But unless we can stop it here, stop it now, the first shots in that war have already been fired, and our orders are to act accordingly."

"We've just received another dispatch from New Tuscany, Valery," Hongbo Junyan said. "Something about a ship blowing up in Pequod."

"Really?" Valery Ottweiler's expression of courteous surprise could not have been bettered by the most experienced professional actor, and he raised one eyebrow as he gazed at the com display. "And when did this event take place?"

"Almost exactly six T-weeks ago," Hongbo replied, his own eyes narrow.

"I did tell you my dispatches from home indicated that fresh instructions have been sent to New Tuscany, as well," Ottweiler pointed out.

"Yes, you did," Hongbo acknowledged slowly. There were aspects of Manpower's apparent ability to coordinate message traffic over long distances that were beginning to puzzle the vice-commissioner. At the moment, however, he had other things to worry about.

"Lorcan is going to want a recommendation from me," he pointed out, and Ottweiler shrugged.

"I think it's fairly obvious that the situation is getting steadily uglier," he said. "If I were Commissioner Verrochio, I think I'd want to be certain I had an adequate force available if something untoward should happen while Admiral Byng is away."

"And you think you might find this 'adequate force' someplace like, say, McIntosh?"

"Actually, under the circumstances, I think that's exactly where I'd look first, Junyan," Ottweiler agreed. "Although it would probably be better to move it even closer sometime soon."

"I thought that might be your view." Hongbo smiled thinly. "Well, as always, it's been a pleasure talking to you, Valery. Thanks for the advice."

"Anytime, Junyan," Ottweiler said, reaching for the button to terminate the conversation. "Anytime at all."

"So they still don't have any better explanation at all, Karlotte?"

Admiral Josef Byng never turned away from the old-fashioned armorplast viewport on *Jean Bart*'s observation deck. His hands were clasped behind him as he gazed out into the volume of space which had once contained a space station named *Giselle* . . . and three Manticoran destroyers.

"No, Sir," Rear Admiral Thimár admitted, looking at the admiral's back and wondering what thoughts were going through his mind.

"And may I assume Captain Mizawa remains his uncooperative self?"

"Well, as to that, Sir, I—"

"Please, Karlotte!" Byng shook his head, still gazing out into space. "I doubt there are any bugs or listening devices here. So, let me ask it more directly. May I assume Captain Mizawa continues to deny access to the originals of his bridge logs?"

"Yes, Sir," Thimár admitted unhappily. "He's made it clear he's willing to provide us with certified copies of the logs, but not the originals."

"I see."

Byng's mind worked busily as he continued his study of the silent stars. He felt certain there was no more doubt in Thimár's mind than in his own that Captain Mizawa was doing more than simply covering his own ass in time-honored fashion. Despite the astronomical difference in their ranks, and despite the fact that Mizawa was only Frontier Fleet, while Byng was Battle Fleet, the captain wasn't even bothering to disguise his contempt. And in addition to the bridge logs, there was also the matter of those memos by that gutless little Lieutenant . . . Askew, was that the name? If Captain Mizawa was actually building up a file to be used against Byng, he probably saw those as additional logs on the fire. They were nonsense, of course, as both Karlotte and Ingeborg had amply demonstrated, but the fact that Byng had dismissed them so summarily as a classic example of GIGO might be construed as additional evidence of . . . hastiness on his part. Of a certain tendency to dismiss other viewpoints and advice, even from his flag captain, out of hand. Possibly even as evidence that he routinely acted before thinking.

Given what had happened here in New Tuscany—and how—that could be unfortunate, in many ways . . . unless it ended up being even more unfortunate for Captain Mizawa first, of course. That was one of the things friends in high places were good for.

Unfortunately, there was the matter of those bridge logs, and Byng cursed his own impetuousness. He *had* reacted too quickly this time—he admitted it, privately, at least—and Mizawa intended to hang him for it. The captain actually had the recording of his own voice telling Byng they'd detected no missile trace. Unless something happened to that recording—and according to Ingeborg, the captain clearly recognized that his ship's information systems were . . . less secure than he'd once thought and taken precautions accordingly—that was going to be a difficult point to tidy up in the report by the inevitable board of inquiry. Under the circumstances, given the mounting tension between New Tuscany and the Star Empire of Manticore, no reasonable board of experienced naval officers could possibly question Byng's overriding responsibility to ensure the security of his own command by neutralizing the threat those three Manticoran light cruisers had represented. The sudden, total destruction of a major space station, obviously as a consequence of hostile attack, had left him no choice but to act as he had. Any board would recognize that!

Unless some bleeding heart, or some Manty apologist, got his hands on a recording of Byng's own flag captain questioning whether or not it had been the consequence of a hostile attack at all before the order to fire was ever given.

*I never should have kept him on after they gave me the task force,* Byng thought darkly. *I should've beached him, gotten myself a reliable Battle Fleet captain to take his place. Someone whose competence—and loyalty—I could have relied on. The bastard's resented having someone from Battle Fleet brought in from the very beginning. He's been waiting to stick a dagger in my back all along—that's what those damned memos by what's-his-name were really all about—and now the frigging Manties and the New Tuscans have handed him the knife!*

He realized his jaw muscles were squeezing too tightly when his teeth began to ache again, and he forced himself to relax. Or to come as close to it as he could, at any rate. And, as he did, he wondered yet again just what the hell really had happened. He'd already written the rough draft of his official report, explaining what *had* to have happened, but that wasn't the same thing as what had *actually* happened.

Much as he'd come to hate Warden Mizawa, he'd been forced to admit that the flag captain had made at least one valid point. Whatever had happened to *Giselle*, the damage hadn't been inflicted by a warship's broadside energy weapons, nor had it been inflicted by a laser head. It had been an old-fashioned, contact nuke, and there was absolutely no indication of how it had been delivered to the station.

Mizawa, Byng knew, inclined to the theory that it had been an act of sabotage. The reason, according to him, that no one had been able to detect or track the delivery vector was that it had probably been hidden in a cargo container somewhere and smuggled aboard for either timed or command detonation.

Byng could follow his reasoning, but even Mizawa had no explanation for who might have done the smuggling, or why. Byng had no doubt that the New Tuscans might well have exaggerated the provocation the Manties had been offering. If *he'd* had to deal with those arrogant, neobarb pricks the way the New Tuscans had, he wouldn't exactly have wasted any effort trying to find the fairest possible light in which to view their actions when he reported them to someone else, either. But exaggerating things was a far cry from blowing things up, and he simply couldn't conceive of a planetary government which would be willing to murder forty-two thousand of its own citizens just to blacken the reputation of the other side in a *trade* war. He'd seen some cold, calculating cynicism in his time, but that was too much.

Yet if it hadn't been the New Tuscans themselves, who *had* it been? That was the question he couldn't answer . . . unless, of course, it had been the Manties all along. There was no reason why they couldn't have chosen to smuggle the warhead aboard. For that matter, the space station had been a completely non-evading target, with neither sidewalls nor an impeller wedge to protect it. They could have launched a small, purely ballistic missile at any point during their approach to the planet. If it had come in without power, with no impeller signature to give it away, it could easily have struck the space station without anyone—including the oh-so-perfect Captain Mizawa's ham-fisted sensor techs—picking it up at all. For that matter, anyone in the entire star system could have done the same thing!

Assuming they had a motive, at any rate.

He shook himself. This was accomplishing nothing, and he couldn't afford to accomplish nothing. If he wanted to preserve his own career—and to get to the bottom of what had really happened, while he was at it—he was going to have to figure out some way to turn the screws on Mizawa. Either that, or at least convince the New Tuscans to give him whatever domestic terrorist group might have been responsible for smuggling a weapon aboard the space station or launching his hypothetical ballistic missile.

Personally, he preferred the notion of squeezing Mizawa. An intense, mutual, and profound hatred would have been reason enough, he supposed, but there was also the precedent to be considered. Frontier Fleet captains could not be encouraged to go around screwing over Battle Fleet admirals. Even more importantly, however, if not for that whole inconvenient business about the failure to detect missile traces or weapons fire from the Manties, there was no doubt in his mind about how the conclusions of the board of inquiry would have been shaped. The best interests of the service would have played a part, of course, as would the natural desire of a panel of senior flag officers to protect the reputation and good name of a brother officer against undeserved slander and accusations. But most importantly of all, even if the

Manties hadn't actually fired the missile or planted the smuggled nuke, all of this was still their fault. They were the ones who'd been systematically harassing the New Tuscans after extending their infernal, meddling interference with free trade into yet another volume of space where they had no legitimate business. If it hadn't been for the confrontation between their so-called Star Empire and New Tuscany, Commissioner Verrochio would never have suggested Byng's visit to New Tuscany, which would have deprived the perpetrators of this heinous act (whoever they were) of the charged circumstances which had led Byng to engage the Manticorans. So, ultimately, *they* were the ones to blame for what had happened to them.

He simply had to find a way to make that self-evident fact clear to people who hadn't been here at the time.

"All right, Karlotte," he said, still looking out through the viewport, "I think we may have to take the offensive with Prime Minister Vézien and Mr. Dusserre. I don't want to make it an official confrontation or sound like I'm issuing any ultimatums, so what I want you to do is to contact Mr. Dusserre. Do it yourself. And when you do, tell him—as one chief of staff to another, as it were—that you think I'm getting impatient. Remind them of how important to New Tuscany the Navy's and OFS' friendship really is, and then ask them if they don't have some local batch of dissidents who might have deliberately set out to provoke what happened by sabotaging the space station."

"Yes, Sir," Thimár said, but her unhappiness was evident, and Byng snorted.

"I don't say it's the ideal solution, Karlotte. And we need to go on working on Mizawa, as well. I'm sure we can finally find a suitable crowbar if we just keep looking long enough. But if it turns out that we can't get him to see the light, we're going to need a fallback position."

"Understood, Sir," Rear Admiral Thimár said.

Maitland Askew sat in his cramped, cubbyhole of a cabin aboard SLNS *Restitution* and worried. He'd been doing a lot of that over the last two or three weeks.

His exile to *Restitution* had been just as unpleasant as he'd anticipated. Admiral Sigbee had been distantly kind to him, although she'd also managed to make it clear (without saying so in so many words) that while she was prepared to do an old friend like Captain Mizawa a favor, she had no desire to get caught in the crossfire of any disputes between Mizawa and a Battle Fleet admiral. Askew wasn't even certain if she'd seen either of the memos he'd produced. He rather doubted that she would have told him, even if she had.

As far as the other officers on her staff—or assigned to *Restitution*'s ship's company—were concerned, he must have screwed up in some truly monumental fashion to have been so summarily reassigned to his present duties. Captain Breshnikov, *Restitution*'s CO, appeared to share that view of things, as well. That hurt, since Askew was aware that Adolf Breshnikov and Captain Mizawa had been friends for many years. Although Breshnikov hadn't gone out of his way to personally step on Askew, it was apparent that he took a particularly dim view of an officer who could so thoroughly have pissed off someone like Mizawa as to be kicked off of Mizawa's ship.

Yet bad as all that was, it wasn't the worst. No, the *worst* was the fact that he was the only person aboard *Restitution* who knew that the idiot wearing an admiral's uniform—the one who'd murdered the entire companies of three Manticoran destroyers in a fit of unreasoning panic—not only *didn't* know but didn't *want* to know just how nasty a surprise the Manties might have for him when they came sailing over the hyper limit with blood in their eyes.

"I'm telling you, Max, it was that crazy bitch Anisimovna!"

"Calm down, Damien!" Prime Minister Vézien said sharply.

"'Calm *down*?'" Damien Dusserre repeated incredulously. "I'm telling you that our so-called good friend and ally killed forty-two thousand-plus of our citizens, including President Boutin's second cousin, and you're telling me to 'calm down'?"

"Yes," Vézien said flatly. "And stop pacing around like some kind of wild animal and sit down, too," he added.

Dusserre stared at him for a moment, then obeyed, settling into an armchair. Actually, he settled *onto* it, and he seemed to be crouched there, ready to launch himself back to his feet on an instant's notice.

"Now," Vézien said, "take a deep breath, count to fifty, and tell me if you really want me to inform Admiral Byng that the Manpower operative we've been using to maneuver the Solarian

League into attacking the Manticorans—which, I might add, he's just finished doing—was responsible for blowing up *Giselle* and getting him to do it in the first place?"

Dusserre glowered and opened his mouth, but then he closed it again, and the Prime Minister nodded.

"That's what I thought."

"Maybe telling Byng about Anisimovna isn't the best idea in the entire galaxy," Dusserre said stubbornly, "but sooner or later we're going to have to tell him and the newsies *something*, Max."

"Of course we are . . . sooner or later. But in the meantime, there are a couple of things I'd like you to consider. First, are you any closer to demonstrating *how* Anisimovna—or anyone else—might have done it?"

"No," Dusserre growled. "We're still looking, but however she did it, and whatever conduit she used for it, it's buried deep. Really deep. To be honest, given that we haven't found anything more than we have in the first ten days, I don't think we'll ever be able to *prove* any of it."

"All right, that brings me to my second point. Can you think of anyone *besides* Anisimovna who might have done it?"

"No," Dusserre said again, but there was less certainty in his tone this time, and Vézien chuckled harshly.

"No?" the Prime Minister shook his head. "Weren't you the one in here just a few months ago presenting that beautifully detailed briefing on our home grown 'liberation fronts' and general insurrectionary lunatics?"

"Yes, but—"

"Ah-ah!" Vézien waved an admonishing index finger. "I'm simply making the point that there are possible suspects other than Ms. Anisimovna. And, to be honest, the fact that you had all of her communications links tapped both before and during the Manties' visit actually gives her a better alibi."

"Maybe it does, but that still doesn't change the fact that I'm positive, and so are a solid majority of my top analysts, that she and Manpower did it to force exactly the response she actually got out of that idiot Byng."

"To be completely honest with you, I'm inclined to the same conclusion," Vézien admitted finally, his expression bleak.

"What?" Dusserre blinked at him, then shook himself angrily. "If that's what you think, then why the hell have you been putting me through this whole dog and pony show for the last three weeks?!"

"Because it doesn't matter," Vézien said heavily. Dusserre looked at him in disbelief, and the Prime Minister shrugged.

"Look, Damien," he said. "We can't bring back the people who are dead, and we can't undo the destruction of those three Manty warships. Those are the two ugly points we're stuck with and can't change, however hard we try. So whatever we do from this point on, it has to take those two things as givens.

"Now, we can push for a big, fancy investigation if we want to. In the end, it's going to have to conclude one of two things, though. Either *Giselle* was blown up by 'parties unknown,' who we still haven't been able to identify, or else it was blown up on Anisimovna's orders. If we name some domestic group as the culprits, then we're also admitting a bunch of our home grown lunatics managed to blow up an entire space station and kill the next best thing to fifty thousand New Tuscans. Do you really want to give the lunatic fringe that kind of encouragement? Personally, I'd just as soon not have our own Nordbrandt running around blowing the planet up.

"But if we conclude it was Anisimovna, and if we go public with that, then we have to explain just why she might have wanted to do such a thing. I don't think we'd have a lot of success painting her as some sort of psychotic serial mass murderer who simply picked New Tuscany at random as the place to slaughter her next few thousand victims. In fact, the most likely scenario I can come up with would be that we wind up blowing the whistle on ourselves, expose all the sordid little details of our agreement with her and with Manpower, and end up becoming at least indirectly responsible for all of those deaths in the public's eye. And in Manticore's eyes, as well. Somehow, I don't think that would be conducive to domestic tranquility, either, and you know as well as I do what the standard Manty response to attacks on Manticoran warships has been for the last T-century. I don't think a visit from a squadron or two of Manty wallers would do a whole lot to help our system infrastructure recover from *Giselle*'s loss, and it for *damned* sure wouldn't do anything for your career, or mine."

"So what are you suggesting, instead?" Dusserre was watching the Prime Minister very closely. He was pretty sure he already knew exactly where Vézien was going with this, but some things had to be explicitly spoken.

"I'm suggesting that from our perspective the best possible explanation is still that the Manties did it. We take the readings we got from the sensor platforms on their way in, and we go ahead and massage them to show a possible missile trace from one of the Manties to the station. We were already planning something along those lines, anyway; now we've got no choice but to go ahead and do it right here. You can be pissed off at Anisimovna all you want. In fact, I'll *help* you be pissed off at her, and if the opportunity should arise a few years down the road, I'd be entirely in favor of your Ministry terminating her with as much prejudice as humanly possible. At the moment, though, she's got the only life pod in sight. We've got Byng sitting right here in the system, and he's got a strong vested interest in the Manties' having been responsible for what happened to *Giselle*, as well. We work on him—subtly, of course—to make sure we're all still on the same page and he's ready to sign off on our Manty missile trace, and then we announce our findings that the Manties were, in fact, responsible. At that point, the entire plan is back on schedule."

Dusserre looked like a man who'd bitten into one of his favorite fruits, only to discover half a worm. He opened his mouth, obviously to protest, then closed it again.

"And if Manpower screws us over again somewhere down the road?" he asked sourly.

"Then we get screwed again. But at least this time we'll be looking for it, and I don't know about you, but considering the alternatives, my willingness to consider possible screwings by our Mesan friends just got enormously expanded. On the other hand, if we get Byng on board and the League comes in like it's supposed to, gives them what they've wanted out of this all along, I honestly don't see any reason for them to shaft us again."

Dusserre sat and chewed on that for a while, and the Prime Minister found himself wondering how much of the Security Minister's frustrated anger stemmed from the fact that they'd been out-thought (or at least out-betrayed) by Manpower, and how much stemmed from the massive loss of life aboard *Giselle*.

Personally, Vézien wanted nothing more than to strangle Anisimovna with his bare hands. He'd never signed on to have his own citizens slaughtered for mere political window dressing or to force the Sollies' hand, and he'd been dead serious about having her killed later. Indeed, he was rather looking forward to it as a simple act of justice. Yet at the moment, she had them well and truly over the proverbial barrel. They were almost certain they knew who'd done it, yet they couldn't charge her with the mass murder without disastrous political and military consequences, both domestic and foreign.

"I don't like it," Dusserre said finally, almost conversationally, admitting defeat, and Vézien barked a laugh.

"*You* don't like it? How d'you think *I* feel about it? If you'll recall, Nicholas and I were Anisimovna's strongest supporters in the Cabinet when she first brought this idea to us. I'll bet you she was thinking about doing something like this if it seemed advisable from the very beginning, and I never even noticed. Trust me, there's nothing I'd like better than to shoot the bitch myself, or just 'disappear' her into one of the reeducation camps up north and let her rot there for a decade or three. But we can't. Right this minute, she's got us by the short and curlies, and there's nothing we can do about it without making matters even worse."

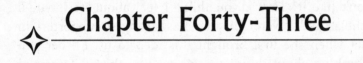

# Chapter Forty-Three

ALDONA ANISIMOVNA RECLINED IN a comfortable chair, eyes closed, while haunting strains of music filled the small, luxuriously appointed compartment. She didn't simply listen to the music; she *absorbed* it, as if all the skin on her body were one enormous receptor.

It was odd, a corner of her mind reflected dreamily. Of all the composers in the entire galaxy, it was a Manticoran who was her favorite. A Sphinxian, in fact. She'd never really understood why Hammerwell's skeins of melody spoke to her so strongly, yet they did, and there were times she needed that. Needed to let herself simply float upon the music, to empty herself of thoughts, of schemes and plans.

Of guilt.

*Don't be silly*, the part of her which hadn't been filled with woodwinds and the subtle interplay of brasses and strings scolded yet again. *You're here as part of a strategy to provoke a war that's going to kill millions—probably* billions*—and you're agonizing over killing forty thousand people? You're coming a little late to that particular party, aren't you, Aldona? It certainly didn't seem to bother you very much during the planning stages.*

No, it hadn't. But that had been when she was considering it as an abstract strategy, part of a carefully crafted piece of superlative manipulation, of the grand design which was going to have the greatest, most powerful political entity in the history of mankind

dancing to the Mesan Alignment's piping. From that perspective, it had been . . . exciting. Enthralling. The sheer intoxication
of playing the Great Game at such stratospheric heights and for
such unimaginable stakes was like some powerful drug. There was
a compulsion to it, a sense of reaching out near-godlike hands
to take the entire universe by the throat and *force* it to do her
bidding.

*No wonder Albrecht is so fascinated with ancient mythology,* she
thought. *I know he says it's to remind him of how many blunders
all those ancient gods made because they were so convinced of their
own power and so jealous of their own prerogatives. So petty and
capricious. So unwilling to work together. Given what we're trying
to accomplish, I suppose he's right, we really do need to remember
the dangers of convincing ourselves that we're gods. I'm sure all of
that's true . . . but it's really about Prometheus for him. About daring
to steal the forbidden fire, to raise his hand—our hand—against all
the established power of the galaxy and* make *it change.*

Seen on that scale, the men, women, and children who had
died aboard *Giselle* were literally insignificant. Such a small casualty total would be lost to the simple rounding process when
the statisticians began counting up the cost of the Alignment's
magnificent vision.

But that would only be after the Alignment had won, and this
was now. This was when those deaths were fresh and immediate . . . and hers. Not a consequence of one of her strategies at
a dozen removes, but deaths which she had personally ordered,
personally contrived. It wasn't a Nordbrandt being provided with
weapons through deniable cutouts and conduits. It was Aldona
Anisimovna personally giving the order.

She'd get over it. She already knew that, although a part of her
wanted to pretend she didn't. Pretend there truly was some inner
core of innocence that would resist the next time something like
this came along. But she knew herself too well to fool herself for
long, and so she didn't even try. She simply sat back in her chair
aboard the palatially furnished, streak drive-equipped "yacht" which
had delivered her to New Tuscany, and let the music fill her.

"This just keeps getting better and better," Lorcan Verrochio
said moodily.

He sat with his elbows on the balcony table, looking out across

Pine Mountain. A half-drained beer stein sat in front of him, accompanied by the remnants of a Reuben sandwich, an order of fries, and a tossed salad. Hongbo Junyan had just arrived, but he'd already eaten lunch, and he sat nursing a glass of iced tea.

"It's not exactly as if this should be coming as a great surprise, Lorcan," the vice-commissioner pointed out. "Something like this happening at a . . . convenient moment's been an inherent under-pinning of everything we've done so far."

Verrochio gave him a moderately dirty look, but Hongbo only shrugged. Discussing something like this on an open balcony, without the protection of the anti-snooping systems installed in Verrochio's office, might constitute a moderate security risk. Unless the wheels came off, though, that wouldn't matter; and if the wheels *did* come off, there was already so much incriminating crap lying around in various files for any moderately competent investigator to dig up that any recordings of this conversation weren't going to matter.

Verrochio continued to eye him disapprovingly for several seconds, then seemed to think better of it himself, and reached for his beer. He took another healthy swallow, set the stein back on the table, and regarded Hongbo a touch less sourly.

"How much of this exploding freighter do you think is real?" he asked.

"About as much as *you* do," Hongbo returned with a humor-less grin.

"That's what I thought you thought." Verrochio grimaced. "You know, this all seemed like a much better idea when this kind of crap was still somewhere off in the future."

"Whatever happens from here on out, our hands are clean." Hongbo gestured with his glass of tea. "Byng is off safely in some-one *else's* hands, and all we have to do at this point is respond to whatever requests he makes. After all, he's the man on the scene now, isn't he? And he's a full admiral in Battle Fleet, as well. Given his attitude, I don't think Anisimovna will find it particularly dif-ficult to manipulate him into committing the actions and making the reinforcement requests she wants. All we have to do is give him what he asks for, then stand back while the Manties take the fall."

"So you think it's Anisimovna out in New Tuscany?"

"No one's specifically said so," Hongbo admitted, "but I imagine it is. She certainly seemed more than enough hands-on where

Monica was concerned, and if I were looking for someone to send, I'd probably pick someone who was reasonably familiar with the Cluster."

"Your friend Ottweiler hasn't said one way or the other?"

"You know him as well as I do, Lorcan," Hongbo said mildly, if not entirely accurately. "And I already said no one has specifically confirmed that she's handling the other end of this. I'd just be surprised if she wasn't. Although I suppose it could be Bardasano."

"And aren't *they* a pair," Verrochio muttered, then managed a rather off-center smile. "They played me like a violin before Monica. I guess I should go ahead and admit that much. So if one of them—or even *both* of them, God help us all!—*is* the other end of this operation, I imagine you're right about Byng's doing whatever they want him to. Which means we ought to be thinking about what *we're* likely to need to do, I guess."

"I've already been thinking about that, as a matter of fact," Hongbo said, without mentioning the fact that a lot of his thoughts on the subject had centered around Valery Ottweiler's directives. "It seems to me that the most reasonable thing for us to do, from all perspectives, is to pass this message along to McIntosh for Admiral Crandall's information. She's not remotely under your command, of course, but given the fact that Admiral Byng has already headed off for New Tuscany—on his own authority, of course, although as the local Frontier Security governor you obviously agreed that we ought to defer to his judgment—it would be only prudent and courteous of you to inform another Battle Fleet officer who just happens to be in the vicinity about his movements and the continuing deterioration of Manticoran-New Tuscan relations."

"And what do you think she'll do when we pass along this little tidbit?"

"That depends on her, I suppose," Hongbo said. *And on what her instructions from Manpower might be*, he very carefully did *not* say out loud. "It's remotely possible she might head off immediately for New Tuscany herself, although I don't really see it as at all likely. You want my best guess?"

"That's the reason I asked the question," Verrochio said just a bit sarcastically.

"Well, I think her most likely course of action would be to move her command from McIntosh to Meyers. We don't have the facilities to support her task force here, but we're no worse off in that regard than McIntosh is, and the whole reason for her deployment is supposed to be a test of the Navy's ability to sustain itself without local support. And this is our administrative hub for the area, so she could rely on the best communications here. This is where any fresh messages from Byng would be directed, and it's where Admiral Nelson is supposed to hold the rest of Byng's battlecruisers. Bearing all of that in mind, I can't really see any other logical location for her."

"Wonderful." Verrochio drank some more beer, then twitched his shoulders. "I'm beginning to feel decidedly excess to requirements, but I suppose you're right. Go ahead and have the communications center relay the information to her."

"Any last-minute thoughts, anyone?" Michelle Henke asked quietly, looking around the cool, quiet, dimly lit expanse of HMS *Artemis'* flag deck. "Any last-minute suggestions?"

Cynthia Lecter did her own once-over examination of the rest of the staff, one eyebrow raised, then turned back to Michelle and shook her head.

"No, Ma'am," she said for all of them, and Michelle nodded.

She hadn't really expected any, although that hadn't kept her from spending last night fretting and worrying on her own. She'd often wondered how Honor could appear so calm just before some enormously important operation kicked off. Michelle had done her own worrying before each of Eighth Fleet's rear-area attacks, but she'd always been one of the subordinate commanders. And that, she realized now, was another of the reasons she'd resisted playing the patronage game to reach flag rank sooner. Her hatred for that sort of nepotism really had been the major component of her resistance, but she knew now that there'd been another factor, as well. One that was almost—but not quite—its own form of cowardice.

Michelle Henke admired Honor Harrington enormously, but she wasn't Honor, and she knew it. She knew hers was in many ways a less complex personality, and she'd never been plagued by the soul-searching that was so much a part of Honor. When it came down to it, she'd always been more . . . direct. More black-and-white, less inclined to empathize *with* an enemy or agonize over the consequences *to* an enemy. She was comfortable with the notion of "us" and "them," and she didn't like ambiguities that could cloud and confuse her decisions.

As a captain, or even a junior flag officer, that had worked just fine for her. She'd been concerned only with the part her ship or her squadron was supposed to play in an operation planned by, coordinated by, and the ultimate responsibility of someone else. But that wasn't true this time. No, *this* time that ultimate responsibility was hers and hers alone, and this time, despite the relatively small size of the forces involved, the stakes were probably—no, certainly—as high as any for which Honor had ever played.

*Be honest, girl*, she told herself tartly. *That's what's really scaring the crap out of you. You're not afraid of getting killed. Well, not* terrified *of it, at any rate. What you're* really *afraid of is that you personally—you, Michelle Henke, not just the Royal Navy—are going to screw this one up. That this isn't really the right job for a woman who'd rather kill them all and let God sort them out, no matter how much an asshole like Byng deserves it. That the Star Kingdom is going to find itself fighting for its life against the Solarian League because the wrong woman was in the wrong spot and* you *screwed the pooch.*

*Yes, that's* exactly *what I'm scared of*, she replied to herself, *and no wonder! I signed on to chase pirates, to fight battles, to defend my star nation. I never expected to have something like* this *dumped on my shoulders!*

*Well, you've got it now*, the first voice told her, even more tartly. *Last time I looked, it came with that black beret sitting on your head. So unless you want to admit this is all to much for itty-bitty you and give the nice hat back, I guess all you can really do is suck it up and get to it. And while you're at it, let's at least* try *to keep the body count within limits, shall we?*

"Well, in that case, seeing as how no one seems to have spotted any t's we've left uncrossed or any i's we've left undotted," the Countess of Gold Peak said calmly, "I suppose we'd best be about it."

For the first time in his naval career, Josef Byng made his appearance on his flag bridge without his uniform tunic. He felt acutely out of place in just his shirt sleeves, but that thought was distant and unimportant as he came through the flag deck door at something just short of a run and slid to a halt, staring at the master plot.

Karlotte Thimár and Ingeborg Aberu were bent over the more detailed information CIC was channeling to the operations officer's console. The rest of Byng's staff was also present, aside from Captain Vladislava Jenkins, his logistics officer. Jenkins was aboard SLNS *Resourceful*, where she'd gone to confer with Captain Sharon Yang about some problems with the battlecruiser's spares.

"What do we have on them?" he asked, eyes locked to the icons sweeping inward from the system's hyper limit.

"Not very much yet, Sir," Aberu acknowledged more than a bit unhappily, straightening and turning to face him. "All we really know is that we've got nineteen point sources. It looks like five of them are considerably smaller than the others—probably destroyers or light cruisers. We're tracking their impeller signatures now, Sir, and I'm assuming that the larger contacts are probably battlecruisers. Under the circumstances, I think we have to assume they're Manties."

Byng nodded almost absently, but Aberu wasn't quite through. She cleared her throat quietly to attract his attention.

"Their current velocity relative to the primary is approximately six thousand KPS, Sir," she said when she knew she had his attention. "But their acceleration is right on six KPS squared."

"*What* was that acceleration?" he asked sharply.

"Six KPS squared, Sir," Aberu said even more unhappily. "That's one-point-three KPS more than they showed us at Monica. Call it a twenty-eight percent difference."

"They must be running at maximum military power, Sir," Thimár said, and Byng turned sharply to look at her. "That's over six hundred gravities," the chief of staff continued. "They've *got* to be redlining their compensators to crank that much accel!"

Byng only looked at her for several seconds, then he nodded. She had to be right. He couldn't think of any reason for the Manties to have gone to their maximum possible acceleration, with the attendant risk of someone's suffering compensator failure and the death of every man and woman aboard the ship involved. But a Solarian ship of that tonnage would have a maximum acceleration of less than four hundred and fifty gravities. For that matter, his own ships' maximum acceleration was less than four hundred and ninety gravities, despite the fact that they were less than half as massive. And if the Manties *hadn't* maxed out their compensators, if they had still *more* acceleration in reserve . . .

The ghost of that insufferable little lieutenant's ridiculous memos flickered through the back of his mind for just an instant, but he shook it off irritably to concentrate on the concrete details that mattered.

"Well, it seems they're a little faster than we thought," he observed as calmly as possible, and returned his attention to Aberu. "And what travel agenda do you project for our speedy friends, Ingeborg?"

"On their current heading and at that acceleration rate, assuming a zero-zero intercept with New Tuscany, they'll be here in about two hours and fifty-five minutes, Sir. That's about all we've got."

"I see." Byng nodded again, commanding his expression to be merely thoughtful, then glanced at his communications officer.

"How long until we could hear something from them, Willard?"

"They made translation just over six minutes ago, Sir," Captain MaCuill replied. "Current range is ten-point-six light-minutes, so it's going to be another three or four minutes, minimum."

"I see."

Byng folded his hands behind him and made himself take a deep, calming breath. Like Aberu, there wasn't much question in his mind as to who those icons belonged to, although he couldn't imagine what they were doing here this quickly. And, he admitted very privately, the acceleration they were displaying was . . . worrisome. It implied that they truly could have other surprises in store, and he didn't care for that possibility at all.

*Especially*, a tiny voice whispered, *not if it gives Mizawa any more ammunition.*

He shoved that thought aside, although it wasn't as easy as he would have liked it to be, and refocused his attention on the problem at hand. Even if they were Manties, there was no reason for all this unseemly haste on his own part, he told himself severely, suffused by a sense of chagrin as he realized just how thoroughly his rush to the bridge had underscored his own tension.

"Have someone drop by my quarters and collect my tunic from my steward, please, Karlotte." He made his voice come out drolly, as if amused by his own precipitousness, and he gave the chief of staff a smile. "If we've got a few minutes before we can talk to them anyway, I suppose I should be certain I'm properly dressed for the occasion."

✦ ✦ ✦

"Oh, *shit*," Maxime Vézien said with soft, heartfelt intensity as he stared at Nicholas Pélisard's com image. He'd anticipated a forceful reaction out of Manticore, but he'd never expected a force the size of the one which had just been detected. Nor had anyone in New Tuscany expected that it could possibly arrive so promptly.

"How the hell did they get here so *quickly*?" Alesta Cardot demanded. "For that matter, why are they here at *all*? It's been barely three weeks, and no one's left the system except a couple of merchantships, not *dispatch* boats. So how could they even know anything happened here?"

Vézien's eyes slipped to the foreign minister's quadrant of the conference call display as she put his own question into words. Then he looked back at Pélisard.

"That's an excellent question, Nicholas," he pointed out. "Does anyone at the War Ministry have any suggestions about that?"

Pélisard's face tightened. He started to answer quickly, defensively—and angrily, Vézien suspected. But then he stopped and visibly got a grip on himself.

"Judging by the elapsed time," he said flatly, "their Commodore Chatterjee must have deployed at least one more ship. Obviously, we didn't pick up an extra hyper footprint when they translated into normal-space, or we would have mentioned it by now. As you may recall, I've been saying for some time that our system arrays need upgrading."

He paused for just an instant, and Vézien managed not to grimace. He supposed that a certain degree of ass-covering was inevitable, even at a moment like this one, and so he simply nodded in acknowledgment of Pélisard's point, and the Minister of War continued.

"Having said that, I think it's the only explanation. They know exactly what happened, and they must have turned this task force around from Spindle the instant they found out."

*Which*, Maxime Vézien reflected unhappily, *doesn't suggest they're here just to say hello. You don't kick a force this size loose that quickly unless you're ready to go to the mat. And if that's the way the Manties are thinking . . .*

His eyes flicked to Damien Dusserre's quadrant of the display. The Security Minister hadn't said a single word, but Vézien knew exactly what he was thinking.

*And he's right*, the Prime Minister thought. *It's a* damned *good thing we still haven't gotten around to faking up that "missile trace" for Byng's consumption. The Manties are going to be unhappy enough with us already, but if they decide we're that deeply in bed with the Sollies . . .*

"I think you're probably right about that," he said out loud, returning his attention to Pélisard. "And I also think that whatever the Manties may have to say to the Sollies, *we're* staying out of it. I want you to immediately stand down every military unit we have, Nicholas. Do it on my authority, and do it now. I'll get the official presidential directive to you from Alain ASAP, but let's not do anything to even suggest to the Manties that they should consider *us* a target."

Pélisard nodded, his expression an inextricable mix of agreement, chagrin, anger, fear, and humiliation at the helplessness of his own utterly outclassed ships and personnel in the face of such an impending clash of titans.

"And while Nicholas is doing that, Alesta," Vézien continued, turning to the Foreign Minister, "I think you'd better be thinking about the best possible way for us to reassure the Manties that all *we* want to do is get to the bottom of what happened here. And how to make it very, *very* clear to them that we didn't have one damned thing to do with that idiot Byng's decision to open fire!"

"What do we have, Dominica?" Michelle asked. "Anything?"

"As a matter of fact, Ma'am, we do," Commander Adenauer replied with a smile, and twitched her head at the lieutenant commander sitting at the console beside hers. "Max here is actually picking up the platforms Commander Kaplan left behind."

"Outstanding." Michelle smiled back at the operations officer, then turned to Maxwell Tersteeg. "So tell me what you know, Max," she said.

"Yes, Ma'am."

The EWO input a string of commands, and a detailed schematic of the New Tuscany System's inner planets and the space about them appeared on the master plot. The schematic swelled dramatically as he zoomed in on the planet of New Tuscany itself. The planet's two moons dominated the space about it, but that same volume was dotted with the icons of merchant ships in parking orbits, industrial shuttles plying back and forth between orbiting space stations, and the bright icons of warships, color-coded by class and all circled by the blood-red rings that indicated hostiles.

"Basically, Ma'am," Tersteeg continued, "there's been no change. We have these three destroyers here"—a green sighting ring enclosed three of the icons—"that have shifted orbits. They're about eleven hundred klicks outside and well ahead of the rest of their formation. It looks like they were probably moved out towards where Commodore Chatterjee's ships were destroyed, maybe for search-and-rescue. Aside from that, they haven't moved as far as I can tell."

"Do you have Byng's flagship IDed?"

"Yes, Ma'am. I got a good read on her emissions signature at Monica. Unless he's shifted his flag to another ship, this is her, right here."

A green carat indicated the gold-edged orange icon of a battlecruiser. There was a total of three matching symbols, each indicating an identified battlecruiser flagship, but Tersteeg's confidence that he'd picked out the right one was obvious.

"Good." Michelle nodded. "What about the status of their impellers?"

"Hard to be absolutely certain about that, Ma'am," Tersteeg admitted. "Commander Kaplan didn't want to get the platforms too close when she left them behind, so we're a bit far out for definitive readings. From what I can see, though, they aren't hot."

"Good," Michelle repeated, and patted him on the shoulder. "Keep me advised of any changes."

"Of course, Ma'am."

Michelle nodded and walked slowly across to her own command chair and settled into it. Naomi Kaplan's decision to leave the stealthy Ghost Rider platforms behind had just been amply justified, although Michelle had felt a certain undeniable concern over that decision when she'd first learned of it. Ghost Rider was one of the RMN's greatest advantages, and the thought of the Solarian League getting its hands on one of the platforms and figuring out how to reverse-engineer the technology hadn't been particularly comforting. But even then, she'd felt Kaplan's decision had been the right one. They were designed with every self-destruct device and security fail-safe R&D could figure out how to build into them, which *probably* meant the Navy in general, and one Michelle Henke in particular, worried more than they had to about their being compromised by simple capture, and even if that hadn't been true, the things had been designed to be used. Right off the top of her head, Michelle hadn't been able to think of a more important place to have used them, and the chances of anyone's managing to localize one of them, far less snag it for study without its on-board suicide charge destroying it first, had been minuscule. So any concern she had felt had been far too small a thing to prevent her from firmly endorsing Kaplan's decision in her own pre-departure dispatches to the Admiralty.

And as it happened, that decision was turning out to have been just as good as Michelle had thought it was. In powered-down passive mode, the way Kaplan had left them, their endurance had been good for far longer than the twenty-three T-days since the destruction of Commodore Chatterjee's destroyers. Now, in response to the properly authenticated command codes, they were fully awake once more, faithfully reporting everything they'd seen over those three T-weeks via grav-pulse, which amounted to real-time reporting at this range.

*So I know where you are, Admiral Byng,* she thought coldly. *That's nice. If I have to kill people anyway, I'd like to make sure the idiot asshole responsible for it is on my little list when I do.*

"What do you make of it, Ma'am?" Gladys Molyneux asked very quietly, and Abigail Hearns glanced at her. The junior-grade lieutenant's battle station was missile-defense, which put her at Abigail's elbow. Despite the quiet, waiting hush of *Tristram*'s bridge, Abigail doubted anyone could possibly have overheard the nervous question.

"It's a little too early to be making anything of it, Gladys," she replied, equally quietly but with a slight smile. She saw confidence seeping back into Molyneux as the smile registered, then shook her head.

"The one thing I *can* tell you," she continued, "is that if those people over there"—a flick of her head indicated the icons of the orbiting Solarian battlecruisers—"have even a clue about what this task force can do, then they're a lot more nervous than *we* are right this moment."

She smiled again, and this time it was a cold, cruel smile.

*Mother Church says vengeance is the Tester's,* she reminded herself, *and I believe that. But I also believe He can use anyone He wants as the instrument of His vengeance. And right this minute, I'm not feeling very forgiving, Gladys.*

✧     ✧     ✧

"Sir, Captain Mizawa would like to speak to you."

Josef Byng paused in the act of slipping into the tunic some-one had fetched for him and looked at the bridge communications rating who'd spoken. He managed not to scowl, although it wasn't easy.

"Did the Captain say why?" he asked, sliding the tunic the rest of the way on and sealing it.

"No, Sir," the rating replied. His careful tone only emphasized the fact that everyone aboard *Jean Bart* knew all about the hostility between Byng and his flag captain.

"Very well." Byng tried to keep his own voice coolly professional as he acknowledged the rating's message, then took the two steps to his command chair. Rather than seat himself, he swiveled the com display around to face him and punched the acceptance key.

"Captain Mizawa," he said as the Frontier Fleet officer's face appeared.

"Admiral," Mizawa replied.

"I'm just a trifle busy at the moment, Captain," Byng said as pleasantly as he could. "What can I do for you?"

"Sir, I don't know if CIC has reported it to you, but Commander Zeiss is picking up a sudden cascade of gravitic pulses."

"Gravitic pulses?" Byng repeated just a bit blankly.

"Sir, according to the latest intelligence reports, the Manties have an effective FTL communications ability over relatively short ranges. One that's based on grav pulses."

"I'm aware of that fact, Captain." A hint of frost crept into Byng's tone in response to the patience edging Mizawa's voice, as if the Frontier Fleet officer were trying to explain Newtonian physics to a village idiot. Especially since those never-to-be-sufficiently-damned memos had touched upon the same point.

*Now the bastard's going to pretend that he personally warned me all about it, isn't he?* the admiral thought bitterly.

"Yes, Sir. I'm sure you are," the flag captain agreed. "But what concerns me are the reports that they've built the same capability into their reconnaissance drones. I think that's what Commander Zeiss is picking up."

"*Reconnaissance* drones," Byng repeated carefully.

"Yes, Sir. I think the Manty destroyers probably deployed them on their way in. Now these new Manties have tapped into them, and they're receiving real-time reconnaissance reports on us."

"I see."

Byng couldn't quite keep his incredulity out of his expression, although he managed to keep it out of his voice. But really! He was willing to concede that the Manties had at least some sort of ship-to-ship FTL communications ability—ONI had tentatively confirmed that much—but to build the same capability into something the size of a *recon* drone? Not even that stupid lieutenant of Mizawa's had suggested that! Or, at least, Byng didn't think he had, and he suddenly found himself wondering if perhaps he ought to have read those memos for himself rather than simply accepting Thimár's summary of their content.

He brushed that thought firmly aside. There'd be time enough to worry about it later; right now he needed to concentrate on the matter at hand, and he tried—really tried—to consider Mizawa's preposterous notion dispassionately. But no matter how hard he tried, it remained just that: preposterous.

R&D was beginning to experiment with the same FTL technology back home, and unlike many of his fellows, Byng had made it a point to follow at least the unclassified aspects of their efforts. According to them, just the power storage any grav-pulse installation would have required would have been impossible to fit into any drone-sized platform. And that completely ignored the fact that actually generating the pulse in the first place took the equivalent of an all-up impeller node, many times the size of any recon drone ever built!

"I appreciate the warning, Captain," he said after a few moments, choosing his words with some care as he spoke for the benefit of the flag bridge recorders, "but I strongly suspect that the reports about faster-than-light recon drone transmissions have . . . grown in the telling, let's say. As you may know, our own research people"—by which, of course, he meant *Battle Fleet's* researchers—"have been looking into this alleged capability of the Manties. Our own R and D indicates that it probably is possible, at least on the level of gross communication, but the sort of bandwidth which would be required for any useful reports from something like a recon drone is highly unlikely. And even if it were possible, the energy budget and the sheer mass of the hardware would almost certainly limit it to something the size of a starship."

"Sir, I haven't had access to the reports you have on the research side," Mizawa said, "but I have had access to other reports, including . . . Commodore Thurgood's. According to them, the Manties *do* have that capability."

White-hot anger flashed through Byng at Mizawa's obvious reference to his lieutenant's memos. He started to snap back quickly, but then he made himself pause. This had to be handled cautiously, and his chose his words with care.

"I'm familiar with the reports to which you refer, Captain." He allowed his voice to get a bit crisper, a bit more brisk. "I'm convinced that they're exaggerated, at the very least."

He and his flag captain locked eyes on the com, and he saw Mizawa's jaw muscles tighten briefly. Then the captain's nostrils flared, and he shook his head.

"I'm aware that many people feel those reports are exaggerated, Sir," he said then. "As a matter of fact, that was my own opinion before we were ordered to New Tuscany. But that was my opinion where the acceleration rates ascribed to Manty warships were concerned, as well." He looked at Byng levelly, challenging the admiral, but Byng said nothing, and the captain continued. "Whether the reports about their FTL capability are exaggerated or not, Sir, *something* is producing the pulses Commander Zeiss is picking up, and whatever it is, it's stealthy enough that we can't find it, even with the pulses giving us an exact bearing to it. To me, that spells a very capable reconnaissance platform."

"Your concerns are noted, Captain. Thank you for calling them to my attention. Now, if you'll excuse me, I believe I'm needed elsewhere. Byng, out."

The admiral cut the circuit before his temper betrayed him into giving Mizawa the tongue-lashing his irritating insistence deserved. Reconnaissance drones! Granted, the Manties' acceleration rates were a little higher than Intelligence had believed. And granted that they might have a few other minor tricks up their sleeves, but even so—! The Solarian League was the most technically advanced star nation in the history of mankind. Did Mizawa honestly believe that a pinhead-sized "star kingdom" consisting of only a single star system up until only a very few years before could produce an R&D establishment that could actually outperform the *League's*? God only knew what the man was going to come up with to worry about next! Invasions of brain-devouring hordes from Andromeda, perhaps? Or possibly a deadly revolt by the galaxy's cocker spaniels, intent on devouring their masters one toe at a time?

Byng grimaced at his own thought, but, really, what else could he expect out of a Frontier Fleet captain? Especially one who already knew he'd made a mortal enemy of a Battle Fleet *admiral*? In fact, Mizawa probably *didn't* believe his own doom-saying predictions, but whether he believed them or not was really beside the point, in many ways, wasn't it? The captain was going to do anything he could at this point—including predicting disaster—to rattle Byng into mishandling the situation. Making the admiral look bad would be one of the most effective ways of making the captain look *good*, after all! Unfortunately for Mizawa, Byng knew all about playing *that* game.

"You know, Sir," Aberu spoke slowly, as if she didn't much care for what she heard herself saying, "it's just possible Mizawa is onto something."

"Good God, Ingeborg!" Byng looked at her in disbelief. "Are you going to climb onto the same paranoid bandwagon?"

"No, Sir," Aberu said quickly. "But CIC's relayed the same grav-pulse detection to me." A tip of her head indicated her console. "I agree with you that the idea of putting some kind of FTL transmitter into something the size of a drone is ridiculous, but we are picking up pulses from something, and we can't seem to find whatever it is, however hard we look for it. That's what I meant when I said Mizawa might be onto something."

"Well, whatever it is, it isn't any 'reconnaissance drone,'" Byng retorted testily. "Even assuming for the moment that they'd managed to come up with a way to meet the energy requirements, and then that they'd managed to develop something that could produce a worthwhile bandwidth, and *then* that they'd managed to squeeze it down into something that could be crammed into a drone's body, where the hell would the things have *come* from? Those Manty destroyers wouldn't have had any need to deploy them this close to us, and they sure as hell didn't have time to deploy any after we opened fire on them! And *these* Manties have been in-system for less than ten minutes! Whatever kind of transmitter technology they might have, they couldn't possibly have gotten reconnaissance drones this close to us this quickly. Not without producing some kind of FTL *drive* technology, as well, anyway, and I'd like to know what kind of stealth systems could hide *that* kind of energy signature at this short a range!"

"No, Sir. Of course not," Aberu said, and returned her attention to her own station.

✧          ✧          ✧

"They should be receiving your initial transmission just about now, Ma'am," Commander Edwards told Michelle.

"Thank you, Bill," she replied, looking up from a quiet conversation with Lecter and Adenauer. She smiled at the com officer, then returned her attention to the chief of staff and ops officer.

"Uh, Admiral, we've . . . received a burst transmission from the bogeys. It's addressed to you, Sir."

"By name?" Byng asked.

"Yes, Sir." Captain MaCuill confirmed.

The communications officer didn't sound any happier than Byng felt, and the admiral glanced across at Thimár . . . whose expression was as troubled as his own. There was no way the Manticorans could possibly know he was in New Tuscany. For that matter, there was no way they could know *any* Solarian unit was in New Tuscany. Unless . . .

A sudden chill touched his heart as the logic chain Nicholas Pélisard had already followed flowed through his own brain.

There was only one way the Manties could have put together a force this size and sent it to New Tuscany this soon after the destruction of their destroyers, especially a force which knew to ask specifically for him when it arrived. There hadn't been three Manty ships that day; there'd been *four*. That was the only possible explanation. There'd been just enough time for another ship, probably another destroyer, to make the trip to their central base at Spindle and for this force to have been dispatched to New Tuscany in response. Even so, the Manty authorities must have made the decision within hours of receiving their surviving unit's report, and for anyone accustomed to the glacial pace with which the Solarian League formulated policy, that speed of decision was almost as frightening as anything else.

*And maybe Mizawa and Ingeborg have a point after all,* he thought icily. *I still don't see how anybody could have squeezed something like that into a reconnaissance drone. It just doesn't seem possible . . . unless they're using some sort of dispersed architecture? Multiple platforms, each containing only a small portion of the total system? Could that be it? But even if it is, how the hell are they powering the things?*

His mind raced, trying to consider the possibilities, but it didn't really matter *how* they'd done it. What mattered was that they actually *could* have done it, in which case any drones out there wouldn't have been deployed by these newcomers. No, they would have been there all along. In fact, they'd have been deployed by Commodore Chatterjee on his way in. And if they had a standard light-speed communications link as a backup for their FTL systems, then they could have been reporting every single thing that happened via laser to that fourth ship, hiding out there in the dark, without anyone in-system suspecting or detecting a thing. Which would mean the Manties knew precisely what had happened three weeks ago....

"Well, Willard," he told MaCuill, keeping his tone as light as possible, "I suppose I'd better view the message, hadn't I?"

This time he did seat himself in his command chair. He let it adjust comfortably under him, then nodded to MaCuill.

"Go ahead, Willard."

"Yes, Sir."

The communications officer pressed a button, and a face appeared on Byng's display. It was a face he'd seen before, and his lips tightened as he recognized Vice Admiral Gold Peak from their exchange at Monica.

"Good morning, Admiral Byng," she said coldly from his display. "I'm sure you remember me, but for the official record, I am Vice Admiral Gold Peak, Royal Manticoran Navy, commanding officer Tenth Fleet, and I am here in response to your unprovoked attack upon units of the Royal Navy in this star system on October twenty-fifth. Specifically, I am referring to your destruction of the destroyers *Roland*, *Lancelot*, and *Galahad*, under the overall command of Commodore Ray Chatterjee, which had been sent to New Tuscany for the express purpose of conveying a diplomatic note from my Queen's government to that of New Tuscany. We have detailed sensor records of the event. As such, Admiral, we know our vessels were not even at battle readiness. Their impeller wedges were down, their side walls were inactive, and their broadside weapons had not been cleared away. In short, they posed absolutely no threat whatsoever to your command, and their personnel weren't even in skinsuits, at the moment you cold-bloodedly opened fire on them and completely destroyed them.

"This, as I'm sure you must be aware, constitutes not merely a cowardly act of murder, but also an act of war."

That cold, precise voice paused, and Byng felt his facial muscles congeal. If they truly did have sensor records showing what Gold Peak claimed, then they'd be able to make a damnably good argument—at least to anyone who hadn't been here, who didn't have the experience to set events into a proper context—that his response had been . . . unjustified. But for any so-called flag officer of a pissant little neobarb navy to accuse the *Solarian League Navy* of committing an act of war—!

"Neither Prime Minister Alquezar nor Governor General Medusa desire additional bloodshed," Gold Peak continued. "However, they would be derelict in their duties and in their responsibilities to my Queen if they did not take the strongest measures to clearly establish responsibility for these actions, and if they did not demand accountability of those who are, in fact, responsible for them. Accordingly, I am instructed to require you to stand down your vessels. I am not demanding their permanent surrender to the Royal Manticoran Navy. I am, however, informing you that you will stand them down; you will make arrangements with the New Tuscan government to transfer all but a skeleton anchor watch of your personnel to the surface of the planet; you will stand by to be boarded by parties of Royal Marines and Royal Navy personnel, who will take temporary possession of your vessels and custody of your tactical data; and you will *not* delete any tactical information relevant to this incident from your computers. Your vessels will remain in this star system, under Manticoran control, until a Manticoran board of inquiry has determined precisely what happened here and who bears the responsibility for the deaths of hundreds of Manticoran personnel."

Despite himself, Byng felt his eyes flaring impossibly wide in disbelief as Gold Peak rolled out that litany of arrogant, intolerable demands.

"Special Minister Bernardus Van Dort is here aboard my flagship as the direct representative of the the Talbott Quadrant's Prime Minister, Governor, and Cabinet. He will present a formal note to you, recapitulating the points I've just made. He will also present a similar note to the New Tuscan government, informing them that the Star Empire of Manticore requires its cooperation in this investigation, that none of our requirements are negotiable, and that, should New Tuscany prove wholly or partially responsible for what happened here, it, too, will be held to account by the Star Empire."

She paused once more, her eyes as unyielding as her face, and her voice was harder still when she continued.

"I will reach New Tuscany orbit approximately one hour and thirty-five minutes after your receipt of this message. I require a response from you, accepting my requirements, within the half-hour. Should you choose to *reject* my government's requirements, I am authorized to use deadly force to compel you to change your mind. I have no more desire to kill Solarian personnel than anyone else, Admiral Byng, but Manticoran personnel have already been killed in this star system. I will not hesitate, should you choose to resist, to employ whatever force is necessary and inflict whatever casualties are required to compel your compliance. I will expect to hear from you within thirty standard minutes of now.

"Gold Peak, clear."

"Oh, *fuck!*"

"My own thoughts exactly," Alesta Cardot told Maxime Vézien tartly, despite the fact that the foreign minister, who was something of a bluenose, would normally have found his language offensive. At the moment, however, she had other things on her mind, and she'd just finished playing Bernardus Van Dort's transmission—which had been remarkably like Michelle Henke's message to Admiral Byng, aside from one small variation—for the Prime Minister.

"They know we're fronting for Manpower," Vézien said bitterly.

"That isn't exactly what they said, Max," Cardot disagreed. "What they *said* is that they know Manpower was behind what happened last year, and that it was using Monica as a front. The implication is certainly that they believe we're doing the same thing, but they didn't say they *know* we are."

Vézien's expression must have betrayed his opinion of such semantic hairsplitting, but Cardot shook her head.

"Think about it, Max. They were very specific about what they know about what happened here three weeks ago. They told us they have sensor data, they told us they know the Sollies fired on them, and they told us the exact status of their own ships at the moment they were destroyed. Those are facts, and they presented them as facts. If they had solid evidence that we were in Manpower's back pocket, they would have said so."

"All right, so they don't *know*—yet," Vézien said. "But they obviously suspect very strongly. And if we give in to these demands of theirs, any investigation is probably going to come up with the proof you've just said they don't have. In which case, we're fucked."

It was a sign of her own tension that Cardot didn't even turn a hair at his choice of verbs. What she did do was to shake her head again.

"Look, you told me to be thinking about ways to convince the Manties we didn't have anything to do with Byng's decision to kill their destroyers, right? Well, I think this is probably the best shot at that we're going to have."

"And *I* think it's the best way to hand them the proof that we damned well helped set it up, whether we meant to or not!" Vézien shot back.

"You're probably right about their finding the proof," Cardot acknowledged. "But I think you may be missing the most critical point of their linking us with Monica."

"Which is?" Vézien asked skeptically.

"Which is that given everything that happened in the Cluster and at Monica, they were actually very restrained in the terms they imposed on Monica. Had the Monicans surrendered those Solly battlecruisers to Terekhov when he initially demanded that, I doubt a shot would have been fired. I doubt Tyler would've been allowed to *keep* his battlecruisers, but nobody would have been killed on either side, and his navy wouldn't have been totally demolished. I think one of the points of this message from Van Dort is to signal us that they aren't interested in kicking us any harder than they have to. I don't think they *like* us very much, and I don't think we'll be getting out of this without some serious repercussions, and probably some painful reparations, but I doubt very much that they want to impose destructive sanctions against us if they can avoid it. If nothing else, I don't think they want to be responsible for what's likely to happen on this planet if they punch us so hard the government collapses. And I *know* they don't want to be seen as the imperialistic conquerors of New Tuscany—not after how hard they've worked on demonstrating to the galaxy that the annexation was the result of a voluntary, spontaneous request from within the Cluster. And you just put your finger on the most critical point of all a moment ago."

"I did?" He looked at her blankly, and she shrugged.

"You said that we've helped to set up what happened here 'whether we meant to or not.' I submit that the best we can possibly hope for at this point is to prove that we *didn't* mean for that to happen. Whether we admit it, or they find proof of it, or not, they already know we were fronting for Manpower. That's a *given*, Max, and they're eventually going to take action against us on that basis, whether we cooperate right now or not. If we want to have any control over what they do to us, we'd better start distancing ourselves from any intentional shedding of Manticoran blood just as fast as we possibly can. However restrained they may want to be, for whatever reasons, if we can't distance ourselves from that, they won't have any choice but to up the ante all around."

"So you're suggesting we should tell them we intend to accept their conditions? Is that what you're saying?"

"I'm giving you what I believe would be the *consequences* of our accepting them," Cardot replied. "Whether or not those consequences are acceptable isn't my decision. You're Prime Minister. I think this falls into your lap, not mine."

"Oh, dear," Aldona Anisimovna murmured as she finished replaying the two messages her taps into the New Tuscan communications system had relayed to her yacht. "This *is* looking unpleasant, isn't it?"

The excitement of playing the Great Game was upon her once more, and her eyes gleamed with malicious satisfaction as she contemplated the Manticoran demands. This wasn't working out exactly according to her playbook, but then, things seldom did. And even if it wasn't perfect, she was confident it was close enough to get the job done.

Her own analysis of the players suggested there was a better than even chance the New Tuscans would choose to comply with the demands levied against them. That was unfortunate, but the speed of the Manticoran response made it much more probable than she really cared to admit. On the other hand, it didn't come as a total surprise, either. She'd hoped to have more time in hand, more time to work at binding New Tuscany firmly enough into the Alignment's web to make it impossible for Vézien to bolt. But the space station's destruction had put the New Tuscans' backs up more than the mission planners had hoped, and she'd always estimated that the Manties were going to respond more quickly than either the New Tuscans or Byng anticipated. Unlike either of them, she'd assumed from the beginning that the Manties would be intelligent enough to leave a watchdog out near the hyper limit, and the fact that no one in New Tuscany had detected any such watchdog hadn't shaken that assumption.

That was one reason she'd moved out to her yacht this early. Keeping herself safely out of the New Tuscan authorities' reach in the event of a premature Manticoran arrival (and any messy little details associated therewith) had seemed only prudent. And she'd always intended to be safely aboard when the Manties really did arrive, since it was no part of her plan to be stuck in New Tuscany when Manticore finished kicking Byng's ass and took possession of the system.

The only real question in her mind at this point was whether or not Byng was going to have his posterior kicked as soundly as the Alignment hoped before he surrendered to Gold Peak's demands. The idiot clearly still had no idea of what he was up against. Given his disposition and his attitude towards Manties in general, that meant he was unlikely to give in until he'd been properly . . . convinced. Which she felt quite confident Gold Peak would be simply *delighted* to do.

"I think it's time to go, Kyrillos," she told her bodyguard.

"Yes, Ma'am," Taliadoros replied. "I'll tell the captain immediately."

"Thank you," Anisimovna said, and leaned back, contemplating the possibilities once again.

Her yacht was scarcely the only vessel departing New Tuscany orbit. The word had already gone out over the public information channels, and no civilian vessel wanted to be anywhere in the vicinity if it was possible warships were going to be firing missiles at each other. In fact, New Tuscan traffic control had actually ordered all civilians to clear the volume of space around the planet as a precautionary measure. That was another reason Anisimovna had made certain she was already aboard ship. And it was why the "yacht's" impeller nodes had been kept permanently hot. It meant they could get underway immediately yet be safely hidden in the underbrush of the other evacuees, which was precisely what she intended to do.

*I wonder if we'll still be in our sensor range of the planet when the first missile flies?* she thought. *In a way, I'll be sorry to miss it if we're not. But I don't suppose anyone can have everything.*

# Chapter Forty-Four

THE SILENCE IN THE conference room deep inside Mount Royal Palace was profound as the report from Augustus Khumalo and Estelle Matsuko ended and the holo display blanked. Simultaneity normally had very little meaning over interstellar distances, especially given how long it took simply to send dispatch boats back and forth, but this time that concept had a very *real* meaning. Given the distances involved, all of the watchers knew, Michelle Henke and Aivars Terekhov must even then be preparing for their alpha translation back into normal-space just outside the New Tuscany hyper limit. And that meant that even as they sat here, the Star Empire of Manticore might be firing its very first shots in the war no sane star nation could ever want to fight.

No one said anything for several seconds, and then, predictably, Queen Elizabeth III cleared her throat.

"You know," she said almost whimsically, "when you and the Admiralty sent Mike off to Talbott, Hamish, I thought we might be sending her to a relatively quiet little corner of the galaxy while she recuperated."

Hamish Alexander-Harrington, the Earl of White Haven and First Lord of Admiralty, produced a rather sour chuckle.

"We never said it was going to be a 'quiet little corner,'" he told his Queen. "On the other hand, given the way people seemed to be pulling in their horns after Monica, I never thought it was going to get quite this . . . interesting, either."

"No?" White Haven's younger brother, William Alexander, Baron Grantville and Prime Minister of the Star Kingdom of Manticore, clearly wasn't going to be producing any chuckles, sour or otherwise. His expression was profoundly unhappy, and he shook his head. "'Interesting' isn't the word I'd choose, Ham. It doesn't even come close to what this little vest pocket nuke is going to do to us!"

"No, it doesn't, Willie," Honor Alexander-Harrington told her brother-in-law, and her expression was almost as unhappy as his. She reached up to stroke the ears of the cream and gray treecat stretched across the back of her chair. "In fact, I've got a really bad feeling about all this."

"Other than the fact that we've just lost three destroyers and their entire crews, you mean, I take it, Honor?" Elizabeth asked.

"That's exactly what I mean." Honor's mouth tightened, and she made a small throwing-away gesture with her right hand. "Don't take this wrongly, but after what happened to us—and to the Havenites—in the Battle of Manticore, the loss of life is of less concern to me than the future implications. I don't like saying that, and when I do, I'm not speaking as someone named Honor Alexander-Harrington; I'm speaking as *Admiral* Alexander-Harrington, the officer in command of Home Fleet."

"I understand," the Queen said, reaching out to lay one hand on Honor's left wrist. "And, to be honest, I agree with you one hundred percent. I think that may be one reason I'm making weak witticisms as a way to keep from looking at it squarely. But I suppose that's exactly what we need to do, isn't it?"

"To put it mildly," Grantville agreed.

He gazed at the backs of the hands folded on the tabletop in front of him for a second or two, then looked up at the other three people seated at the table. Sir Thomas Caparelli, the First Space Lord, sat to White Haven's right. Honor sat to her husband's left, between him and the Queen, and Second Space Lord Patricia Givens sat just to Grantville's immediate left, between him and Caparelli. Sir Anthony Langtry, the Star Kingdom's Foreign Secretary, completed the gathering, sitting between Grantville and the Queen.

"Anything new on that business in Torch, Pat?" the Prime Minister asked Givens, whose duties included command of the Office of Naval Intelligence.

"No, not really," she admitted. "All we know for certain at this point is that what looks like it must have been most of the StateSec 'refugee fleet' that had taken service with Manpower was committed to the attack. Rear Admiral Rozsak intercepted it, and it looks like he and Barregos got even more tech transfer from Erewhon than we'd thought. Or got the new stuff into production faster, at any rate. I'm sure that came as a really nasty surprise to the other side, but he still got hammered hard. Frankly, quite a few of my analysts—and I was one of them, for that matter—were surprised when he waded into them that way. I think it's the clearest evidence we've had to date that he and Governor Barregos take their treaty obligations seriously."

"But there's not much question Manpower was behind it?"

"No question at all, really," Givens agreed. "We've been aware ever since Terekhov took out *Anhur* in Nuncio that Manpower's been picking up every StateSec refugee it could. We never expected it to use them for something like this, but everything we already knew and interrogation of survivors all says Manpower was the mastermind behind the attack."

"I see where you're going with this, Willie," Honor said. "You're wondering if the timing is a coincidence or not, aren't you?"

"Yes, I am." Grantville snorted and shook his head at his sister-in-law. "Mind you, I'm not sure I'm not succumbing to terminal paranoia, but after what happened in the Quadrant and at Monica, having obvious Manpower proxies suddenly busy in our own backyard just at the same time things seem to be going to hell in New Tuscany strikes me as a particularly ominous coincidence."

"Are you seriously suggesting that Manpower's deliberately set out to embroil us in an all-out war with the Solarian League, Willie? That *that's* what they were really after in Monica?" Langtry asked, and Grantville shrugged.

"I don't know, Tony. For that matter, Manpower might simply have stumbled into all this. They may not have had any concerted plan from the get-go. For all I know, they've been improvising as they go along, and everything that's happening could be pure serendipity from their perspective. But whether they're behind what happened in New Tuscany or not—and the similarity to what happened at Monica *does* appear to be rather striking, doesn't it?—we're still faced with the consequences. I don't think anyone sitting at this table is likely to criticize Mike, Baroness

Medusa, or Admiral Khumalo for their response to the destruction of Commodore Chatterjee's ships. I certainly don't, and I know Her Majesty doesn't. Under these circumstances, they're absolutely right; when that idiot Byng opened fire, it was an act of war."

He paused, letting that last sentence sink fully home, then shrugged.

"I know none of us really want to think about all the implications of that, but Mike, Medusa, and Khumalo had to do just that. And, frankly, I'm of the opinion that they've made the right call."

He glanced at the queen, who nodded her own agreement. She didn't look happy, but it was a very firm nod.

"Everything they've proposed is in strict accordance with our own existing, clearly enunciated policies and positions. More than that, it's all in strict accordance with interstellar law, as well. I'm quite sure that no one in the Solarian League ever thought for a moment that some 'neobarb navy' would ever have the sheer temerity to even contemplate applying that particular body of law to *it*, but that doesn't change the fact that the people responsible for deciding what to do about it have made the right choice. I suppose it's always possible that even Sollies will be able to recognize that, and, obviously, all of us hope the Solarian units in New Tuscany—assuming they're still there when our ships arrive—will comply with Mike's demands without any further loss of life. Unfortunately, we can't count on that.

"Even if they do, there are going to be plenty of Sollies who don't give a single solitary damn about what happened to *our* destroyers first," Langtry pointed out. "And for those people, whether any more shots are fired or not is going to be completely beside the point. We'll still be the 'neobarb navy' you were just talking about, Willie, and our 'arrogance' in daring to issue *demands* to them will constitute an act of war on *our* part, even if not a single one of their ships even has its paint scraped! After all, they're the *Solarian League!* They're *important!* Why, if the omnipotence of their Navy was ever challenged, it would be the end of civilized life as we know it! Assuming, of course, that the sheer impiety of anyone's having the audacity to even suggest that *they* should be held accountable for a minor thing like mass murder would probably bring about the end of the universe itself, given the fact that God is obviously a Solarian, too!"

There were times when it was easier than at others to remember that Sir Anthony Langtry had been an officer in the Royal Marines before he ever became a diplomat, Grantville reflected. The Foreign Secretary's sheer anger was bad enough, but the savage irony of his tone could have withered a Sphinxian picketwood forest. Which didn't change the fact that it was a masterful summation of exactly what the Solarian League's attitude was likely to be.

"You're right, of course," he conceded aloud. "And that means we're going to have to be careful exactly how we handle our protest to the League."

"At least we can get our diplomatic note in the first," his brother pointed out. "The message turnaround time from New Tuscany to Old Terra is only about twenty-five days by way of Manticore and the Junction. It's a lot longer for anyone trying to work around the outside of our communication loop. New Tuscany to Meyers is over five T-weeks for a dispatch boat, and it's over *six* T-weeks even for a message direct from New Tuscany to Mesa." White Haven grimaced, as if the system name physically tasted bad. "From there, it's another thirteen T-days or so to Old Terra by way of the Visigoth Junction and Beowulf. If they waste time following protocol and report to Meyers first, it'll take them right on eighty-six days—damned close to three T-months—just to get their first report back to Sol. Of course, assuming that we're right about Manpower's involvement, they probably will send dispatches directly by way of Mesa and Visigoth and get them there in only sixty-seven days or so, but even on that basis, our note will be there in less than half the time."

"I know," Grantville agreed. "But that leaves us with an interesting quandary."

"How public we want to go," Langtry said, and the Prime Minister nodded.

"Exactly. At this point, nobody else has a clue what's going on out there. Well, that *something* is going on out there, at any rate. I don't think any of us are really prepared to say exactly *what's* going on." He smiled thinly. "So do we make this a very quiet note to the Solly Foreign Ministry, or do we hand *Tristram's* sensor data directly over to the newsies?"

"What a wonderful set of options," Elizabeth said sourly, and her Prime Minister shrugged.

"I'm not incredibly happy about them myself, Your Majesty.

Unfortunately, they're really the only two we've got. So do we try
to handle this as quietly as we can in the faint hope that refrain-
ing from splashing egg all over the League's face will inspire the
Solly powers-that-be to actually work *with* us, or do we go for
maximum publicity? Launch our own offensive in the League's
newsfaxes in hopes of *pressuring* them into being reasonable?"

No one said anything for several thoughtful seconds. Then
Honor inhaled deeply and shook her head.

"Given how divorced the real decision-makers in the League are
from anything remotely resembling the electoral process, I doubt
that any sort of propaganda offensive is going to have much effect
in the short term. At the same time, though, if we go public with
it, we start backing those same decision-makers into a corner. Or
that's how they're likely to see it, at any rate.

"As Hamish just pointed out, it's going to take a lot longer
for any of their dispatches to get to Old Terra, unless Byng is
smart enough to stand down and sends his own message traffic through the Junction. So I don't think there'd be any point
in expecting the League to reach any final decisions on how it's
going to respond very quickly even if it wanted to. And, frankly,
I don't think it *is* going to want to. Sheer arrogance would take
care of that, but as Tony's already suggested, they're also going
to be thinking in terms of precedents. Of what's going to happen if they 'let us get away with this' sort of response. If we go
ahead and start inflaming public opinion, that's only going to
make them even stubborner about admitting for an instant that
their man screwed up."

"All true," Elizabeth said. "On the other hand, I don't think
anyone in this room really expects them to be anything *but* stubborn about admitting that they're at fault."

"No," Langtry said. "But that doesn't mean we shouldn't appear
as reasonable as possible, Your Majesty."

He grimaced, obviously unhappy at the thought of playing the
part of a moderating influence. Unfortunately, that responsibility
came with his present job, and he buckled down to it.

"The fact that we're demanding the at least temporary surrender of their warships—and that our commander on the spot is
authorized to use deadly force if they refuse—is going to infuriate them," he continued. "There's no way around that. The fact
that we're *willing* to infuriate them, though—that we're willing

to go eyeball-to-eyeball with them over this, which no one else has been gutsy or crazy enough to do literally for centuries—is going to make a pretty firm statement about how seriously *we* take this. I think we could probably afford to handle it in a way that suggests we don't want to publicly humiliate the League without looking irresolute."

"I think Tony and Honor have both made valid points, Your Majesty," Grantville said after a moment. "I'm inclined to recommend that we *not* go public at this point. In fact, I think we should specifically point out to them that we haven't handed the story over to the media when we draft our note to Foreign Minister Roelas y Valiente."

Elizabeth thought for a moment, then nodded.

"I think that makes sense," she said. "At the same time, though, I don't think we can afford to sit on it for too long, for several reasons."

"Which reasons are you thinking about?" Grantville asked just a little bit warily.

"The most important one to me personally is that we have a responsibility to inform our own citizens," the queen replied. "And that's not just coming from any moral sense of responsibility, either, Willie," she added a bit pointedly. "Sooner or later we're going to have to go public with this, and if we delay too long, people are going to wonder why we didn't tell them about it sooner, since it happens to involve the minor matter of the possibility of our ending up at war with the most powerful navy in the galaxy while we're *already* at war with the Republic of Haven. I think it's important that they understand *why* we're running this sort of risk, and exactly how important the principles involved really are."

Grantville winced slightly. Although he'd been Chancellor of the Exchequer in the the Duke of Cromarty's cabinet, he'd never fully agreed with Cromarty's news policies during the First Havenite War. Cromarty's position had been that things could be kept secret only so long, however hard people in positions of authority tried. Since unfortunate news items were going to leak anyway, he'd reasoned, a policy of openness and honesty would be the best way to increase the public's confidence in official statements when they did. Grantville—although he'd been only the Honorable William Alexander at the time—hadn't disagreed with either of those points. His problem had been his intense dislike (actually, he was prepared to admit without any particular apology, *hatred* would have been a better choice of noun) for the official news establishment of the Solarian League. Anything reported in Manticore would be reported on Old Terra within the week, and the Solly newsies had not, in his opinion, wasted very much effort trying to report it factually and without bias.

There'd been a time, before the initial Peep attacks at places like Hancock Station and Yeltsin's Star, when the Solarian press had covered the looming confrontation between the Star Kingdom of Manticore and the People's Republic with something approaching evenhandedness. In fact, a segment of the Solly news establishment had covered it from a pro-Manticore position, and the Star Kingdom's government and its well-established public relations organs in places like Beowulf, the Sol System, and Far Corners had deliberately played to the "plucky little Manticore" view of that portion of the press.

But the Solarian resentment of the Star Kingdom's dominant position in interstellar commerce had always been there in the background, and once the actual shooting began, it had started coming to the fore. "Plucky little Manticore" had been seen in quite a different light when the Royal Manticoran Navy was winning battle after battle after battle. The fact that it was winning those battles against heavy numerical odds only seemed to make many Solarians more inclined to see the Star Kingdom as the militarily superior side, and it was only a short hop (for many of them) to somehow transforming Manticore ("I never liked those pushy Manties, anyway. Always too greedy and sure of themselves for a bunch of neobarbs, if you ask *me!* If *I* were Haven, I wouldn't much care for 'em either!") into the aggressor. And the Cromarty Government's success in getting the League to embargo tech transfers to the People's Republic had only irritated that traditional Solarian resentment.

Under those circumstances, it hadn't taken the Solarian media very long to switch to what Grantville, at least, had always regarded as a revoltingly pro-Peep stance. Even the least anti-Solly Manticoran had to concede that there'd been a definite bias against the Star Kingdom, and quite a few of them would have agreed with Grantville that there was an orchestrated anti-Manticore lobby within the Solarian press corps. Yet Cromarty had stuck to his policy of openness and agreed to modify it only on a case-by-case basis and only in the face of pressing operational requirements.

That didn't mean Cromarty had been blind to the realities of news coverage in the Solarian League. Indeed, in many ways he'd been just as bitter about slanted Solarian newsfaxes as Grantville himself. But Cromarty's policy had reflected his concern with the *Alliance's* media. He'd accepted that the Star Kingdom was going to get hammered in the *League's* reportage, whatever it did, and under his premiership, the Star Kingdom's PR had concentrated primarily on making sure that a contrarian view was also presented and the accurate information from both sides was at least available to Solarians in general. Manticore hadn't exactly tried to understate StateSec's brutality in the information it fed the League through its own conduits. Nor, for that matter, had Manticoran journalists and commentators been at all shy about pointing out the fact that whereas the Star Kingdom did *not* censor reporters, the People's Republic *did* . . . and that Solarian correspondents assigned to Haven never mentioned it because doing so would get them expelled from the People's Republic.

Which, in many ways, had only made the self-appointed masters and mistresses of the Solarian Establishment even more bitterly anti-Manticore. They'd resented the Star Kingdom's and its surrogates' efforts to debunk their more outrageous misrepresentations, and the constant reminders that they uncritically repeated the Committee of Public Safety's propaganda rather than condemn PubIn's censorship had infuriated them . . . especially since they knew it was true. The fact that the Havenite propaganda had suited their own dislike of Manticore so much better than the truth, combined with their vindictive fury that anyone would dare to challenge *their* version of reality, had produced inevitable consequences, of course. Given the way their version of events played to stereotypical Solarian biases, the Star Kingdom's efforts had all been uphill, especially in light of the powerful vested interests in both the League's bureaucracy and its economic establishment with their own strong motives for blackening Manticore's image.

And then, of course, along had come the High Ridge Government, which couldn't have been more effective at reinforcing the most negative possible Solarian view of the Star Kingdom if it had been purposely designed for it. The demise of the People's Republic; the resurrection of the old Havenite Constitution; the resucitation of a functioning Havenite democracy; the High Ridge refusal to negotiate seriously (or to reduce the "wartime emergency" increases in transit fees on Solarian shipping); and the fact that neither High Ridge nor his Foreign Secretary, Elaine Descroix, had seen any need to "pander" to Solarian public opinion had produced predictably catastrophic results where the Solarian media's coverage of the Star Kingdom was concerned. Which was why one of Grantville's first priorities as Prime Minister had been to authorize heavy investments in rebuilding the PR organization High Ridge and Descroix had allowed to atrophy.

Unfortunately, the sudden fresh outbreak of fighting between the Republic and the Star Kingdom had made his rebuilding task much more difficult. And, he was forced to admit, the way in which the Star Kingdom had divided the Silesian Confederacy with the Andermani Empire, had given its Solarian press critics altogether too much fresh grist for its "Manticore As the Evil Empire" mill. Which had undoubtedly been a factor in the thinking of whoever had set out to destabilize the annexation of the Talbott Quadrant in the first place.

"Your Majesty," he said carefully, "I understand what you're saying, and I don't disagree with you. But Honor's point about not making the League's leadership feel we're trying to back it into a corner has a lot of merit. And, frankly, you know about the beating we've been taking in the Solarian media ever since Operation Thunderbolt." He paused, then snorted. "Excuse me, ever since that idiot High Ridge formed a government, I mean."

"I realize that, Willie." Elizabeth's tone was, in its way, as careful as Grantville's. Unlike her current Prime Minister, she'd always been firmly in agreement with the Duke of Cromarty's media policies. "And I don't disagree with Honor or with the point you and I both know you're making. But be that as it may, I'm still convinced that we need to avoid any appearance that we're trying to keep bad news hidden from our own people. In fact, I'm even more inclined to feel that way in the wake of the Battle of Manticore than I was before it. And I'm also firmly of the opinion that if we sit on this too long, we're likely to suggest to a bunch as arrogant as the Sollies that we're afraid to 'out them' for their actions. Not only that, but we give those bastards at Education and Information more time to decide how they're going to spin the news when it finally breaks."

Grantville had started to open his mouth. Now he closed it again, and nodded, almost against his will. The Solarian League's Department of Education and Information had very little to do with education and a very great deal to do with "information" these days. The bureaucratic structure which actually ran Education and Information (along with the *rest* of the League) had turned it into an extremely effective propaganda ministry.

"Those are both very valid points, your Majesty," he admitted. "I'd still really prefer to sit on this at least until the Sollies have had time to receive our note and respond to it. And at the same time, I think, we need to do some preliminary spadework of our own. I think we need to spend some time deciding exactly how we'll respond if the news leaks before we're ready to officially release it—the last thing we need is to get caught off balance, without having done our homework, when or if that happens—and also of deciding how we want to break it on our own terms, if that seems like the best policy. So could I suggest a compromise? We hold the news for the moment, but we quietly contact some of our own newspeople. We brief them in on what's happening in Talbott on a confidential basis in return for their agreement to sit on the story until we release it. And to sweeten the pot, as it were, we offer them official access in Spindle. We send their reporters out to talk to Khumalo, Medusa—even Mike, after she gets back—on the record, and we promise them as much freedom of access to all our information as operational security allows."

Elizabeth thought about it for several seconds, and then it was her turn to nod.

"All right," she said. "I think that makes sense. And it's not as if our own newsies aren't already accustomed to putting holds on specific stories because of those operational security concerns of yours. I don't want to hold this one any longer than we have to, though, Willie. The reason our newspeople respect the holds we do request is because they know we haven't abused the practice."

"I understand, Your Majesty," Grantville said, and glanced at Langtry. "How soon do you think you can have a draft of our note, Tony?"

"I can have a first draft by this afternoon. I imagine we'll want to kick it around between your office and mine—and Her Majesty, of course—through several iterations before we finally turn it loose."

"I'm sure you're right about that," Grantville agreed. "But while I'm willing to admit that you and Honor are probably on the right track, or as close to the 'right track' as anyone could be in a mess like this, let's not fool ourselves here. This is a situation which can slide totally out of control in the blink of an eye. In fact, depending on how stupid this Admiral Byng really is, it could very well be sliding totally out of control at New Tuscany before we finish this meeting."

He paused, and let the silence hiding in the corners of the conference room whisper to all of them, then turned his eyes to his brother.

"A few months ago, Hamish," the Prime Minister of Manticore said, "you gave us your evaluation of what would happen if we found ourselves in a shooting war with the Solarian League. Has that evaluation changed?"

"In the longer term, no." White Haven's prompt response—and grim expression—made it evident he'd been thinking about exactly the same question. "I'll want to look at the technical appendices of Khumalo's dispatches—just as I'm sure Tom and Pat will want to do—in case they tell us anything interesting, but everything BuWeaps has turned up from its examination of the Monica prizes has only strengthened my conviction that the SLN is several generations behind us in terms of applied military hardware. Obviously, there's no way of knowing exactly where they are in terms of research and development, and God only knows what they might have in the procurement pipeline, but even for the League, putting such fundamentally new weapons technologies into mass production and fitting them into an existing fleet structure is going to take time. *Lots* of time. God knows it took *us* long enough, and we had a life-or-death incentive to make the move. The League doesn't, and its political and military bureaucracies suffer from a lot more inherent inertia than ours ever did. In fact, I'll be very surprised if the bureaucratic bottlenecks and simple ingrained resistance to change and 'not invented here' prejudices don't double or triple the time requirement the purely physical constraints would impose.

"Assuming we do have the sort of technological edge BuWeaps is currently projecting, we'll rip the ass off of any Solarian force we run into, if you'll pardon my language, at least in the immediate future. Eventually, though, assuming they have the stomach for the kinds of casualty totals we can inflict on them, they'll suck up whatever we can do to them, develop the same weapons, and run right over us. Either that, or we'll hit some sort of 'negotiated peace,' and they'll go home and pull a Theisman on us. We'll wake up one fine morning and discover that the Solarian League Navy has a wall of battle just like ours only lots, *lots* bigger ... at which point, we're toast."

"For that matter, they've got another option, Hamish," Honor pointed out. "One that actually worries me more, in some ways."

"What option?" Elizabeth asked.

"They could just refuse to declare war at all," Honor said bleakly. Elizabeth looked confused, and Honor shrugged.

"If we get into a shooting war with the League and we're going to have any chance of achieving a military victory—or, for that matter, of inflicting the kind of casualty totals Hamish was just talking about, so that they settle for a negotiated peace—we're going to have to take the war to them. We're going to have to demonstrate everything we've learned about deep-area raids instead of system-by-system advances. We're going to have to go after their military infrastructure. Take out their more modern and larger system defense force components. Rip up their rear areas, wipe out their existing, obsolete fleet and its trained personnel, take out the shipyards they'd use to build new ships. In other words, we're going to have to go after them with everything we have, using every trick we've learned fighting Haven, and demonstrate that we can hurt them so badly that they have no choice but to sue for peace."

Elizabeth's face had hardened with understanding, and her brown eyes were grim as they met Honor's.

"But even that won't be enough," Honor continued. "We can blow up Solarian fleets every Tuesday for the next twenty years without delivering a genuine knockout blow to something the size of the League. The only way to actually defeat it—and to make sure that we've put a stake through its heart and it doesn't just go away, build a new fleet, and then come back for vengeance a few years down the road—is to *destroy* it."

Elizabeth's hard eyes widened in surprise, and Sir Anthony Langtry stiffened in his chair. Even White Haven looked shocked, and Honor shrugged again.

"Let's not fool ourselves here," she said flatly. "Destroying the

League would be the only way for the Star Empire to survive in the long haul. And frankly, I, for one, think that might actually be a practical objective, under the right circumstances."

"Honor, with all due respect," Langtry said, "we're talking about the *Solarian League*."

"A point of which I'm well aware, Tony." Her smile was as bleak as her tone. "And I realize we're all accustomed to thinking of the League as the biggest, wealthiest, most powerful, most advanced, most anything-you-want-to-mention political unit in the history of humanity. Which means that right along with that, we think of it as some sort of indestructible juggernaut. But *nothing* is truly indestructible. Crack any history book, if you don't believe me. And I'm seeing quite a few signs that the League is at or very near—if, in fact, it isn't already past—the tipping point. It's too decadent, too corrupt, too totally assured of its invincibility and supremacy. Its internal decision-making is too unaccountable, too divorced from what the League's citizens really want—or, for that matter, think they're actually *getting*! We were just talking about Governor Barregos and Admiral Roszak. Hasn't it occurred to any of you that what's really happening in the Maya Sector is only the first leaf of autumn? That there are other sectors—not only in the Verge, but in the Shell, and even in the Old League itself—that are likely to entertain thoughts of breaking away if the League's veneer of inevitability ever cracks?"

They were all looking at her now, most of them with less shock and more speculation, and she shook her head.

"So if we get into an all-out war with the League, our strategy is going to have to have a very definite political element. We'll have to make it clear that the war wasn't our idea. We'll have to drive home the notion that we're not after any sort of punitive peace, that we're not trying to annex any additional territory, that we have no desire to conduct reprisals against people who don't want to fight us. We need to tell them, every step of the way, that what we really want is a negotiated settlement . . . and at the same time, we have to hit the League as a whole so hard that the fracture lines already there under the surface open right up. We have to split the League into separate sectors, into *successor states*, none of which have the sheer size and concentrated industrial power and manpower of the present league. Successor states that are our own size, or smaller. And we have to negotiate bilateral peace treaties with each of those successor states as they declare their willingness to opt out of the general conflict to get us to stop beating on *their* heads. And once we have those peace treaties, we have to not only honor them, but step *beyond* them. We need to use trade incentives, mutual defense pacts, educational assistance, every single thing we can think of to show them that we are—and to really *be*, not just *pretend* to be—the sort of neighbor and ally they'll want around. In other words, once we break the League militarily, once we splinter it into multiple, mutually independent star nations, we have to see to it that none of those star nations have any motive to fuse themselves back together and gang up on us all over again."

She paused, and there was a new and different silence in the conference room. All of them, with the probable exception of Hamish Alexander-Harrington, were gazing at her in astonishment. Elizabeth looked less surprised than most of the others, but there was an edge almost of wonder in her expression.

Not a man or woman at that table would have questioned Duchess Harrington's military insight, or tactical or strategic ability . . . in the purely military arena. Yet most of them still tended to think of her as a fleet commander. Manticore's *best* fleet commander, perhaps, but still a fleet commander. As they'd listened to her, they'd come to realize how silly that was—and how foolish they'd been not to recognize their own silliness much earlier. In their defense, most of the insight she'd previously shown in the field of political strategy and analysis had focused on domestic concerns, or on the internal workings of the Manticoran Alliance. It hadn't occurred to them that she might have already focused that formidable ability on the Solarian League as the Star Empire's next great challenge, and that had been remarkably blind of them.

"I think you're right," Elizabeth said finally, and managed a half-humorous grimace. "I suppose I've been so fixated on how much I don't want to fight the League, how terrifying an opponent it would be, that I've been much more aware of our own weaknesses and disadvantages than I have of any weaknesses *it* might suffer from."

"You're not the only one who's been guilty of that, Your Majesty," Sir Thomas Caparelli said. "Over at Admiralty House, the Strategy Board has been aware for quite some time of the need to launch all-out operations against the League in the event of open hostilities. But we'd never been able to take our planning beyond the point of somehow beating the League to its knees, taking out its military infrastructure, and then committing the Star Empire to a multigeneration occupation policy. There's no way we could possibly hope to garrison or physically occupy every system of the League, or even just the more important industrial nodes. But what we could do is to *picket* the major systems. To require the League to renounce a large, modern navy after defeating its existing navy militarily, and then to post observers in all of the systems where a navy like that could be rebuilt in order to keep an eye on the shipyards and call in our own heavy units at the first sign of treaty violations in the form of new warship construction.

"But the problem with that kind of strategy is that it virtually assures that at some point someone in the League is going to emerge with a revanchist policy and the muscle to back it up. They're going to figure out a way to do a Thomas Theisman on us, and they're going to be able to build a fleet big enough to at least force us to pull our pickets out of the occupied systems to deal with it. At which point *other* systems that won't like us very much will join the fray and then, as Hamish so succinctly put it, we're toast.

"But if Honor is right—and, actually, I think there's a very good chance she is—about the probability of the League's being much more fragile than anyone is accustomed to believing, then there's another option. *Her* option. Instead of occupying the League for generations, we accept that it's already moribund, break it up, and make its successors our allies and trade partners, not our enemies."

" 'I destroy my enemy when I make him my friend,' " White Haven quoted softly.

"What?" His brother blinked at him, and the earl smiled.

"A quote from an Old Earth politician Honor's gotten me interested in, Willie. I think it has to do with her views on genetic slavery."

"What politician?" Grantville still looked puzzled.

"A president of the ancient United States of America named Abraham Lincoln said that," White Haven said. "And if I'm remembering correctly, he also said 'If you would win a man to your cause, first convince him that you are his sincere friend.' "

He smiled again, this time at his wife, much more broadly. "I can see I haven't read him as carefully as Honor has, but you ought to take a look at him, too, now that I think about it. He was in a pretty sticky military situation himself."

"Well, maybe I've got a point, and maybe I don't," Honor said a bit more briskly, and her expression had turned bleak once again. "But assuming I do, then the most dangerous thing *I* can see the League doing is simply refusing to declare war on us and conducting whatever operations are going on in and around the Talbott Quadrant as a 'police action.' If they refuse to extend their operations beyond that area, no matter how intensive their operations are *within* that area, and if they consistently take the position that they're reacting *defensively*, then we can't expand the fighting into the other areas where we would need to take the war to them before they manage to duplicate our hardware advantages without becoming the aggressor in the eyes of all the rest of the League. And if we do *that*, our chances of breaking the League and 'destroying our enemy by making him our friend' probably go right out the airlock. Which means they get the time they need to build the steamroller they need to roll right over us."

"Wonderful," Elizabeth sighed.

"I'll admit it's worrisome." Despite his words, White Haven sounded quite a bit more cheerful than his wife had, "but I'm also inclined to think it's very unlikely the League's real leadership in the bureaucracies is truly going to recognize its danger soon enough to adopt a sensible policy like that. I realize that predicting what your enemy will do and then betting everything you have on the probability that your prediction is accurate is a really, really stupid thing to do. I'm not suggesting we do anything of the sort, either. But at the same time, I think there's a very real probability, not just a *possibility*, that as soon as OFS and the SLN realize just what sort of sausage machine they've shoved their fingers into, they're going to start screaming for all the help they can get. Whether they paint us as savage aggressors or themselves as liberators, they're going to take this a lot further than any mere 'police action.'"

"And they wouldn't be the only decision-makers involved in the process, either." Sir Anthony Langtry sounded much more thoughtful than he had a few moments before. "Whatever position they take, we'll always be able to edge at least a little further around their flank, push them a little more in the direction we want to go, without turning ourselves into Attila the Hun in starships in the eyes of the rest of the League. We'll have to be careful, but we've had plenty of experience dancing around the League in the past. As long as we coordinate our PR and diplomatic and military efforts carefully, I think we'll be able to shape the political and diplomatic side of the battleground much more effectively than you may have been allowing for, Honor. And it's not like we're not going to have allies inside the League, either—especially if Manpower's role in all of this becomes public knowledge. Beowulf carries a hell of a lot of prestige, and every one of her daughter colonies is going to follow her lead where anything having to do with genetic slavery is involved. I think we can count—no, I *know* we can count—on a powerful Solarian lobby on our side in any Mesa-engineered confrontation."

"And there's still another side to all of this, Your Majesty," Patricia Givens pointed out. "Thanks to the wormhole network, we have an enormous degree of penetration into the League. If they try to shut the network down to cut off our trade, they'll cripple themselves just as badly—possibly even worse—by effectively destroying the carrying trade they rely on. For that matter, until they do manage to overcome the advantages of our hardware—for the foreseeable future, in other words—we should be able to keep all of the critical termini open with fairly light forces. All of which means we'll continue to have a lot of contact with the League and that we're actually likely to have considerably more economic clout with quite a few of the League's sectors than the League bureaucracy itself does. Which would mean one hell of a lot more clout than anything as ephemeral as an elected League politician could hope for. If we use that clout while bearing in mind the need to make our enemies into friends, rather than letting ourselves turn predatory in the short-term interests of survival, I think we could probably pry quite a few of the League's citizens loose from it."

There was silence again, and then Elizabeth inhaled deeply.

"Honor, I have to say you've pointed my mind in a direction that makes me feel much less pessimistic about the future. Mind you, there's still a huge difference between 'less pessimistic' and anything I'd call remotely '*optimistic*,' but I think you've got me headed in the right direction."

She smiled at the other woman, but then her smile faded.

"In the short term, though, we have to think in terms of our immediate survival. And wherever we wind up going in the end, I think we're all in agreement that first we've got to accomplish Hamish's predictions about beating the crap out of them. Which brings me to another point, Sir Thomas." She looked at Caparelli. "What's the status on our new construction?"

"We're well ahead of projections." Caparelli shook himself. Despite the strategic insight Honor had just laid before him, his eyes were still weary looking. But if there was any defeat in those eyes, Elizabeth couldn't see it. "We've got the next best thing to two hundred brand new wallers either out of the yards or leaving them in the next month to six weeks," he continued, "and all of them have been fitted with Keyhole-Two, which makes them Apollo-capable. Coupled with what Honor has in Home Fleet, the new construction that's come forward from the Andermani, and what the Graysons have made available, that's going to give us somewhere in excess of three hundred and eighty ships-of-the-wall—almost all of them Apollo-capable—by the third week of February."

The Star Kingdom of Manticore officially ran on the Manticoran calendar, but Caparelli—like many people throughout the galaxy (and most in the Manticore Binary System)—thought in terms of T-years and the ancient calendar of Old Terra, despite the fact that all three of the home system's planetary days varied considerably in length from the standard T-day. It made things simpler than translating back and forth between multiple calendars, and given the fact that each of the Star Kingdom's three original planets had different years of different lengths, as well as days, Manticorans were more accustomed even than most to using the standard calendar. And the habit was undoubtedly going to get still more pronounced for the citizens of the new Star *Empire* of Manticore, given the numbers of planets—and the plethora of local calendars—which would be involved. By Manticoran reckoning, Caparelli was talking about Ninth Month of the year 294 After Landing. By the standard reckoning of the galaxy at large, he was talking about the month of February of the year 1922 Post Diaspora. And if he had been speaking to someone from before mankind had departed for the stars, he would have been talking about the year 4024 CE.

But all his listeners really needed to know was that he was talking about a period seventy or so T-days in the future.

"How long for them to work up to combat readiness?" Grantville hadn't been the brother of one of the Royal Navy's more senior officers for so long without learning a few hard-won realities along the way.

"That's more debatable," Caparelli acknowledged. "The Andies and Graysons should have finished working up by the time they get here, so we don't need to worry about that. And most of the new construction's going to be out of the yards by the end of January, so they'll be at least a couple of weeks into their training cycles by the time the Andies and Graysons show up. But I'd be lying if I didn't say that it's going to take longer for us to get our *own* people up to speed than anyone is going to like. We took a really heavy hit when the Havenites took out Home Fleet and Third Fleet. We already had cadres assigned to almost all of the new construction, and we had pretty close to complete crews assigned to the sixty or seventy ships closest to completion. All of those are out of the yard by now, and beginning to work up in Trevor's Star. Unfortunately, an awful lot of them are having the same 'teething problems' we've been seeing in the lighter units. We got them through the construction process in record time, but not without hitting more glitches than we'd like. Still, none of the problems we've identified so far are really critical, and I expect to have most of them ready for service within another thirty T-days. Call it the middle of January.

"After that, things get more difficult. We were expecting to find a lot of the personnel we're going to need from the old-style wallers assigned to Home Fleet. Obviously, that's not going to happen now."

His jaw tightened briefly and involuntarily as he remembered the carnage of the Battle of Manticore. Then his nostrils flared briefly, and he continued.

"As I say, that's not going to happen, but despite that, Lucian and BuPers have managed to come up with most of the warm bodies we need. A lot of them are short on training and experience, of course, and that hits us hardest when it comes to officers and senior enlisted. We're looking at accelerating a lot of noncoms' promotions to fill the gaps there, and we're planning on cutting the current class at the Academy six months short and sending the midshipmen straight off to the fleet, without the traditional snotty cruise. We're probably looking at accelerating the next class the same way, and we've been forced to pull back on our LAC program simply because we need the officers we would have been sending off to command LACs. That's also why we're setting up quickie OCS courses—expanding on the ones we've always had outside the Academy for 'mustangs.' We expect a substantial return on that, as well, although it's going to cost us more of those senior enlisted when we 'suggest' that they become officers, instead. A couple of years down the road, we should be pretty much past this particular bottleneck. For that matter, once we've had a chance to run them through the appropriate remedial education, I imagine we'll be able to find a lot of enlisted and officers coming out of the Talbott Quadrant. That's going to take a while, though, and in the meantime, I have no doubt that any skipper unfortunate enough to go in for extensive yard work or overhaul is going to find his command structure picked clean by Lucian's vultures.

"By robbing Peter *and* Paul, though, Lucian's actually managing to fill most of the slots aboard most of the new ships as they come out of the yards. Frankly, I don't have any idea how he's doing it, and I'm afraid to ask. I also don't know how long he's going to be able to go *on* doing it, although the first flight of mass recalls of reservists from the merchant marine should be offering us at least some relief in the next couple of months. Even that has its downside, though. It's going to take time to run them through the necessary refresher courses, especially to update them on the new hardware. And just as bad, maybe, the merchant fleet needs them, too, and *we* need the merchant fleet to maintain our revenue flows."

Grantville nodded, and Caparelli shrugged.

"The bottom line is that with the lower manpower requirements of the new designs, there's no reason we shouldn't be able to support the manning requirements for the fleet we're talking about. Unfortunately, that's what we were doing when Tourville came along and destroyed something like half the entire Navy. It's going to take us time to recruit and recover from the huge hole that made, so I don't think we're going to be manning any more enormous expansion waves any time soon. In the shorter run, it means we've got the bodies we need—barely—but working up periods are simply going to have to be expanded. The prewar rule of thumb was that it took three to four months for a brand new waller's crew to shake down to a satisfactory, combat-ready level. During the First Havenite War, with experienced officers who'd been there and done that, we got it down to somewhere around two and half months. But with the situation we're in now, frankly, I'll be surprised if we can do it in less than four, and I *won't* be surprised if it takes as much as *five* months, given the fact that we're going to be correcting so many minor construction faults along the way. So for the immediate future, you'd better count on basically what Honor has now—here in Home Fleet and working up in Trevor's Star—plus, say, another sixty Apollo-capable podnoughts still in the yards. And the Andies' new construction and refits, of course . . . except for the fact that we don't know if Gustav will be willing to back us if we go up against the League."

"Is that going to be enough to stop whatever the Sollies can do to us during that same time period, Hamish?"

"Probably . . . if we could aim it all at them," Grantville's brother replied. He glanced at Caparelli, one eyebrow raised, and the First Space Lord nodded in agreement with his assessment.

"To be brutally honest," White Haven continued, "and at the risk of sounding a little complacent, the main problem we're probably going to face in any early engagements against the Sollies is going to be our ammunition supply. But for at least five or six months, assuming either that we fight close to home and our industrial base or that we have a decent logistics train to keep us supplied with missiles, we should be able to hold anything they can throw at us with that many podnoughts, even without the Andies. Unfortunately, we've still got that minor problem of the war with Haven to worry about."

"Maybe yes, and maybe no," Grantville said grimly, and swiveled his eyes to Langtry. "Her Majesty and I already discussed this briefly a couple of days ago, Tony," he said, "but we were only brainstorming at the time. Now it looks like we may have to put our brainstorm into practice."

"Why does that fill me with a sudden feeling of dread?" Langtry murmured.

"Experience, probably," Grantville replied with a brief, tight smile. The smile vanished as quickly as it had come, and the Prime Minister leaned intently towards the Foreign Minister.

"Given the strength estimate Sir Thomas has just presented, we probably have the capacity to punch out the Haven System itself," he said flatly. "To do to them what they tried to do to us. But we've got Apollo, and they don't, which means we don't have to enter their effective range at all. And that we could go right *on* doing it to every one of their systems with a single naval shipyard. We could pound every major developed system of the Republic back to the Stone Age."

It was very quiet around the conference table once more, and this time the quiet was tense, almost brittle.

"To be perfectly honest," Grantville continued, "that's precisely what I'd *like* to do, and I doubt I'm exactly alone in that sentiment. There's probably not a single family here in the home system who didn't lose someone in the Battle of Manticore, and that doesn't even consider all the deaths that came before that. So, yes, there's a part of me that would love to hammer the Peeps into rubble.

"But now we've got this situation with the Solarian League, and even if we didn't, brute vengeance, however tempting in the short term, is the worst possible basis for any sort of lasting peace. We're not Rome, and we can't plow Carthage up and sow the ground with salt. So, riddle me this, Mr. Foreign Secretary. If we demonstrate that we can blow the Peeps' Capital Fleet out of space, destroy the entire orbital infrastructure of Eloise Pritchart's capital system, and then tell her we're prepared to blow up however many *additional* systems it requires for her to see reason, what do you think she'll say?"

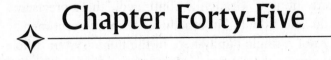
# Chapter Forty-Five

"I TAKE IT WE haven't heard back from Admiral Byng, Bill?"

"No, Ma'am," Commander Edwards agreed.

"Somehow, I rather thought you would have mentioned it if we had," Michelle said with a faint smile. Then she turned back to Adenauer and Tersteeg. "What's the status on their impellers?"

The ops officer and the EWO had maneuvered the Ghost Rider platforms closer to the Solarian ships to keep an eye on them. Now Adenauer looked up in response to Michelle's question, and her expression was unhappy.

"We were trying to get close enough to get a read off their nodes, Ma'am, but I don't think we needed to bother. We just picked up first-stage initiation on their wedges, and they're already turning on attitude thrusters. They're headed out."

"Frigging idiots," Michelle muttered under her breath, once again feeling the temptation to let God handle the sorting chore.

"All right, Bill," she sighed aloud. "I suppose we have to give these dumbasses one more try. Prepare to record."

"Yes, Ma'am."

Michelle glanced up at the master plot while she waited. Her force had been headed in-system for forty-three minutes now, accelerating towards the planet at a steady six hundred and three gravities, which left the *Nikes* with seventy gravities in reserve. Their closing velocity was up to 21,271 KPS, and they'd reduced the range from just over one hundred and ninety-two million kilometers to just under a hundred and fifty-six million. Given that geometry, the effective powered envelope of the Mark 23s in the pods riding the outsides of her ships' hulls was well over seventy-two million kilometers against a stationary target, and the effective range against Byng and his ships would only increase as he accelerated towards them and increased their closing velocity.

"Live mike, Ma'am," Edwards told her, and she nodded to him and turned back from the plot to face the pickup.

"Your time limit has expired, Admiral Byng," she said coldly, without preamble. "I can only assume from your current heading and the fact that your impellers are about to come on-line that you intend to engage me. I caution you against doing so. Be advised that I have the capacity to destroy your ships from far beyond any range at which you can possibly threaten us. Be further advised that if you do not immediately cease your attempt to close with my ships or flee the system rather than accept my government's requirements and standing down, I will demonstrate that capability to you in a fashion which not even you can ignore. Gold Peak, clear."

"Clean recording, Ma'am," Edwards confirmed after a moment.

"Then send it," Michelle said flatly.

"Aye, aye, Ma'am."

Eight minutes and forty-three seconds after it had been transmitted, Michelle's message reached SLNS *Jean Bart*, and Josef Byng's face darkened with fury as Willard MaCuill directed the message to his com.

*That arrogant little* bitch! *Who the* hell *does she think she* is, *talking to me—talking to the* Solarian League—*that way?*

He felt his jaw muscles aching from the effort of restraining his snarl, and his nostrils flared wide as he sucked in a deep, angry breath. There was dead silence on the flag bridge for several seconds, then MaCuill cleared his throat.

"Will there be any response, Sir?" the communications officer asked in a painfully neutral voice.

"Oh, yes," Byng grated. "There'll be a *response*, all right, Willard! But not with any com transmissions!"

"Yes, Sir."

MaCuill turned back to his own displays, his shoulders tight, and Byng felt a fresh spasm of anger. Was his own staff starting to buy into the ridiculous claims about the Manties' "invincible weaponry?" He started to snarl something at MaCuill, then made himself stifle the urge. The last thing he needed was to begin sounding like some hysterical old woman himself!

"Sir," Karlotte Thimár said in a very careful tone, "Captain Mizawa would like to speak with you."

"Oh, I bet he does," Byng growled. "I don't suppose he's screening to apologize for reading mail that wasn't addressed to him?" he added, twitching his head towards his now-blank com.

"I'm sorry, Sir," MaCuill said, "but the Manties' last message wasn't addressed specifically to you. It carried a general heading . . . to all ships, Sir."

Byng's face took on a dangerously mottled coloration, and he glared at the communications officer.

"And why the hell didn't you mention that little fact to me before?" he snarled.

"I'm sorry, Sir," MaCuill repeated, "but the address block was displayed in the message header. I . . . assumed you'd seen it."

Byng bit back an even more furious response, then closed his eyes, clenched his folded hands tightly behind him, and tried to suppress the anger boiling inside him. After several moments, he opened his eyes once again and smiled tightly at Thimár.

"Well, I suppose that if the good captain wants to speak to me, the least I can do is take his call," he told the chief of staff, and slid back into his command chair once more. He paused for one more second, then tapped the acceptance key.

"Yes, Captain?" He kept his voice as neutral as possible, although he knew it was still giving away more of his inner fury than he wanted it to.

"Admiral." It was obvious Mizawa was working hard at keeping his own voice nonconfrontational, which only made Byng perversely more angry as the flag captain continued. "I realize you and I haven't exactly seen eye-to-eye on several matters of late, but I strongly urge you to consider the possibility that this Admiral Gold Peak really has the capability she's talking about."

"Captain, that's ridiculous," Byng replied. "I know about the rumors of impossible range on Manty missiles. Good God, I *did* read the ONI appreciations before I headed out here, you know! And I know the missiles Technodyne deployed in Monica had enhanced drive systems to increase their range. For that matter I know that R and D back home has been looking into adopting the same concept for some time now. But I also know how *big* the Technodyne missiles were, and so should you, if you've read the same reports. That's the main reason we haven't pursued the same concept ourselves, you know. We simply don't have the magazine capacity, or shipboard launchers big enough, to accommodate anything with drives the size of the ones Technodyne used in Monica . . . and neither does anyone *else*! We saw the launch tubes on these damned big-assed 'battlecruisers' of theirs at Monica, if you'll recall. There's no way in the galaxy they could fire a missile that size out of those launchers! I'll grant you that their *wallers* might—conceivably—have the tubes for them, but no way in hell does one of *these* ships have them! And we've got *Javelins* in the magazines, not those crap Pilums Technodyne supplied to Monica. Not to mention the fact that none of the Monicans had Halo, either."

"Sir, I realize all of that's true," Mizawa said. "But the Javelin is still a single-drive missile. A damned good one, yes, but only single-drive. If the reports about the Manties' cruisers at Monica having *multi*-drive weapons are accurate, then these people certainly have them, too."

Byng forced himself not to roll his eyes in exasperation. As he'd just pointed out, the system defense missiles Technodyne had supplied to Monica had been too big for any shipboard launcher, and they'd been *single*-drive missiles. Now he wanted to put something big enough to mount *multiple* drives through a launch tube? Good God! The man wasn't just paranoid, he was a frigging idiot! Even a Frontier Fleet officer should have been bright enough to figure out that something the size of a cruiser-range missile tube couldn't possibly fire something even bigger than those Technodyne birds!

He'd obviously given away at least some of his reaction, despite his best efforts not to, because Mizawa's expression tightened even further.

"I'm aware of the size argument against the idea, Sir. But, with all due respect, look at that last message of theirs. It was sent before we'd actually brought our wedges up, but they knew exactly what we were doing. That means they *do* have FTL recon capability, and they're using it. In my judgment, especially coupled with their observed acceleration rates, that demonstrates that at least a sizable chunk of the reports about Manty capabilities which ONI has been discounting are actually accurate."

His eyes burned into Byng's. He'd very carefully refrained from mentioning Askew's memos, but they were there, between them, and his voice turned harder, harsher.

"Given that evidence—the *proof* that ONI's been wrong in at least some of its assessments—I think we have to take the possibility of the sort of missile ranges they're talking about seriously."

"Well that makes *one* of us, Captain," Byng said sarcastically, before he could restrain himself. Mizawa flushed, and Byng shook his head. "I apologize for that last remark," he made himself say. "There's enough going on to make anyone tense, but that's no reason for me to take it out on you."

From Mizawa's expression, it was obvious he knew Byng's apology was strictly *pro forma*, but he gave a jerky nod, and Byng forced himself to smile.

"I've noted your concerns, Captain. On the other hand, we have twenty-two ships, seventeen of them battlecruisers, to only nineteen, total, Manties. Admittedly, their 'battlecruisers' are bigger than ours—probably tougher, too, for that matter—but each of ours has as many missile launchers as one of theirs, and they only have six, and their heavy cruisers only have *twenty*-tube broadsides! That gives us a significant advantage in tubes and an even bigger one in throw weight. And, with all due respect, I'm not prepared to discount intelligence appreciations formulated by analysts with access to all the information coming to us on the basis of appreciations generated independently, with partial information, by officers who—justifiably, I might add—have every reason to adopt pessimistic assumptions in order to avoid underestimating a potential enemy's capabilities. Granted, their acceleration rates are higher than Intelligence predicted, but that single point aside, there is absolutely no evidence, aside from apocryphal accounts, that the Manties have the capabilities you're ascribing to them, and I cannot in good conscience permit a third-rate neobarb navy with delusions of grandeur to even attempt to dictate terms to the Solarian League Navy. The precedent would be disastrous from any foreign policy perspective, and the insult to the honor of the Fleet would be intolerable."

"Sir, I'm not suggesting you cave in to their demands. I'm simply suggesting that it may be time to try negotiating a stand down on *both* sides. They say they've sent a diplomatic note to Meyers. All right, what if we were to refuse to surrender our ships to them but agreed to return to orbit and maintain the status quo here in New Tuscany while *we* sent a dispatch boat back to Meyers to seek

Commissioner Verrochio's instructions? If they accept, then the decision of how we respond to their demands legitimately becomes a political decision to be made by the highest local political authority. And if this Gold Peak accepts, it would also give Commissioner Verrochio an opportunity to dispatch reinforcements in the event that—as would almost certainly be the case—he decides that we are correct to *reject* her demands. At the very least, it would allow us to play for time while—"

"Any negotiations such as you're suggesting would immediately be seen as a sign of weakness by Gold Peak," Byng interrupted. "In my opinion, she's running a colossal bluff—in fact, that's probably the reason she's accelerating so hard; to convince us that *all* the wild stories about Manticore's 'technical superiority' are true—and I'm not going to encourage her to believe it's working. For that matter, even assuming for a moment that they have the weapons capability you're worrying about, she'd have to be not simply a lunatic but stupid beyond belief to pull the trigger on us! I don't care what kind of magic bullets they've got over there, Captain. Hell, they could have every single thing in Commodore Thurgood's most pessimistic assessment! That doesn't change the fact that it's the *Solarian League* they're fucking around with, and if they fire on Solarian battlecruisers in neutral space, they really *will* have an act of war on their hands. Do you seriously think any bunch of neobarbs is going to deliberately create that kind of situation? Especially when they're already at war with *another* bunch of neobarbs who can't wait to wipe them out?"

"I didn't say it would be smart of them, Sir. I only said they may have the capability to *do* it. And, respectfully, Sir, if we give them what they initially demanded, it will be an act of war against the League, anyway. It could—and should—be construed that way, at any rate. They're obviously willing to risk *that*, so what makes you assume they aren't willing to risk a *different* act of war?"

"Captain," Byng said frostily, "it's obvious you and I are not in agreement. Accordingly, I have to ask you whether or not our *dis*agreement runs deep enough that you are unwilling to execute my orders?"

"Admiral," Mizawa said, his voice equally frigid, "I am prepared to execute any lawful order I may receive. With respect, however, one of my functions as your flag captain is to offer my best judgment and advice."

"I realize that. If, however, you are sufficiently . . . uncomfortable with my proposed course of action, then I will relieve you—without prejudice, of course—of your present duties."

Their eyes locked through the electronic medium of the ship's communications system. Tension hummed and vibrated between them for several seconds, but then Mizawa shook his head. It was a jerky gesture, hard with his own suppressed anger.

"Admiral, if you choose to relieve me, that's clearly your privilege. I do not, however, request relief."

"Very good, Captain. But in that case, I have other matters which require my attention. Byng, clear."

"Still no sign of sanity breaking out over there, I see," Michelle murmured to Captain Lecter.

Twenty-five minutes had passed since her second message to Byng, and the Solarian battlecruisers' velocity had increased to 7,192 KPS. Her own ships' velocity was up to over thirty thousand kilometers per second, giving them a closing velocity of better than thirty-seven thousand KPS, and the range was down to a little over one hundred and thirteen million kilometers.

"Not so anyone would notice, at any rate," her chief of staff agreed equally quietly. The two of them stood before the master plot, gazing into its depths. Around them, *Artemis'* flag deck was quiet, almost hushed, as the men and women manning their stations concentrated on their duties.

"You know," Lecter continued, "I've studied our dossier on Byng until my eyes ache, and I still can't figure out how much of him is bluster, how much is raw arrogance, and how much of it is simply sheer stupidity." She shook her head. "Do you think he really *wants* to fight, or is he just going to play chicken with us while he tries to break past and hyper out?"

"I don't know, and it doesn't matter," Michelle said grimly. "Our orders are clear enough, and so are the alternatives I spelled out to him. And I don't have any intention of waiting until he fires first."

"Excuse me, Ma'am," Dominica Adenauer said, and Michelle turned towards her, eyebrows raised.

"CIC's just picked up a status change," the operations officer said. "The Sollies have deployed some sort of passive defensive system."

"Such as?" Michelle asked, crossing to Adenauer's console and gazing down at the ops officer's displays.

"Hard to say, really, Ma'am. Whatever it is, Max and I don't think they've brought it fully on-line yet. What it *looks* like is a variation on the tethered decoy concept. From what the recon platforms can tell us, each of their ships has just deployed a half-dozen or so captive platforms on either flank. They have to have a defensive function, and I don't think they're big enough to carry the sort of on-board point defense stations our Keyhole platforms do. I don't want to get too overconfident, but it looks to me like they've got to be decoys, and we already know Solly stealth technology is pretty damned good. If their decoys are equally good, this is probably going to degrade our accuracy considerably, especially at extended ranges."

"Where *is* Apollo when you need it?" Michelle asked half-whimsically.

"When you say 'degrade our accuracy considerably,' do you have any sort of guesstimate for just *how* considerably we're talking about?" Lecter asked.

"Not really, Ma'am," Tersteeg replied for both of them. "Until we've seen it in action—and confirmed that it actually is a decoy system, for that matter—there's no way we could give you any real estimate."

Lecter grimaced, although the response was hardly a surprise, and looked at Michelle.

"Do you want to let the range drop a little lower than we'd originally planned, Ma'am?"

"I don't know." Michelle frowned and tugged at the lobe of her right ear as she considered Lecter's question.

ONI and BuWeaps had evaluated the weapons aboard the Solarian-built battlecruisers captured intact at Monica. The energy weapons, although individually smaller and lighter than was current Manticoran practice, had been quite good. The passive defensive systems had been good, as well, although not up to Manticoran standards, but the missiles—and counter-missiles—had been another story entirely, and the software support for the ships' sensors had been sadly out of date by those same standards. For that matter, the sensors themselves were little, if any, better than the hardware the RMN had deployed at the beginning of the *First* Havenite War, twenty-odd T-years before.

There was some division of opinion among the analysts as to whether or not the prize ships' electronics reflected the best the

Sollies had. The standard Solarian policy for supplying military vessels to allies and dependencies had always been to provide them with downgraded, "export versions" of critical weapons technologies, which suggested the same thing had been done with the battlecruisers intended for Roberto Tyler. Except, of course, that *those* battlecruisers had come from recent service with Frontier Fleet, which should have meant they carried close to first-line, current-generation technology, and a bunch of outlaws like the ones at Technodyne probably wouldn't have gone to the expense of replacing that technology with less capable versions for what was already a thoroughly illegal transaction.

For the moment, BuWeaps had decided to split the difference and assume that everything they'd seen from Monica represented a minimum benchmark. The existence of the defensive system Adenauer and Tersteeg had just described—assuming their analysis was accurate—suggested that that decision had been wise, since none of the ships at Monica had been equipped with anything like it. But that also suggested it would probably be *unwise* to rely too heavily on the demonstrated range and acceleration rates of the anti-ship missiles those battlecruisers had carried, as well.

Those missiles' powered range envelope from rest generated a maximum range of just over 5,900,000 km, with a terminal velocity of 66,285 KPS. Given their current closing velocity, that equated to a range at launch of a shade better than 12,680,000 kilometers, whereas the Mark 23 had a range at launch of 85,930,000 given the same geometry. Even the Mark 16 had a range at launch of well over 42 million kilometers under current conditions. So even if she assumed Byng's battlecruisers carried missiles twice as capable as those captured at Monica, she still had better than three times his maximum powered range on her Mark 16s, much less her Mark 23s.

"What will our closing velocity be at forty million klicks?" she asked Adenauer, and the ops officer punched numbers.

"Approximately five-four-point-seven thousand KPS, Ma'am. We'll be there in roughly twenty-six minutes."

"Um."

Michelle pulled harder on her ear lobe while she did the math. At that velocity, the Sollies would cross through her Mark 16s' range to her ships in about thirteen minutes. At one launch every eighteen seconds her shipboard launchers could fire forty-three missiles each in that timeframe, and she had six hundred and twenty tubes aboard her *Nikes* and *Saganami-Cs*, alone. That worked out to better than twenty-six thousand missiles, which she suspected—decoys or no—would be a fairly significant case of overkill.

On the other hand, the Mark 23s from the pods limpeted to the exterior of her ships' hulls would have a powered envelope at launch of well over ninety-six million kilometers, assuming the target's acceleration held constant, which would let her she could open fire with almost fifty million kilometers sooner. Her accuracy would be lower, but . . .

"What will our closing velocity be at eighty million klicks?"

"Four-six-point-zero-five thousand KPS," Adenauer replied. "We'll reach that range in almost exactly thirteen minutes."

"Given that geometry, what do our Mark 23 envelopes look like?"

"Assuming constant target acceleration, a two-drive burn would give us . . ." Adenauer punched numbers ". . . just over four-six-point-one million klicks at launch. An all-up burn would make it about nine-one-four million."

"Thank you."

Michelle folded her hands behind her and walked slowly back across to the main plot to stand gazing into its depths. Lecter followed her, standing quietly at her right shoulder, waiting while she thought. After what seemed like hours but probably wasn't actually more than a handful of seconds, Michelle turned her head to look at Lecter.

"We'll send Byng one more message," she said. "That's it. If he doesn't stop this horse shit after that, we'll go with William Tell at forty-five million klicks."

For a moment, it looked as if Lecter were going to say something, but then she simply nodded and contented herself with a simple, "Yes, Ma'am," and Michelle smiled faintly.

*It is sort of a balancing act, isn't it, Cindy?* she thought dryly. *Unless I'm prepared to go ahead and kill all of them, anyway—which, while tempting, would probably upset Beth just a smidgen, given the foreign policy implications and all—firing at that range is going to tell the Sollies a lot about our capabilities, and that could very well come under the heading of a Bad Thing. If this situation turns as nasty as I expect it to, given the fact that Byng is obviously even stupider than I thought, I'm sure the Admiralty would prefer to keep them ignorant of the Mark 23's real reach for as long as we can. But I'll still be holding over twenty million klicks of range in reserve, and the best way to keep this situation from going completely south on everyone is to finish up with the lowest possible casualties here in New Tuscany.*

In her more pessimistic moments, she was certain the situation was already beyond retrieval, but she wasn't ready to simply go ahead and surrender to the inevitable despite the fact that, in many ways, the wholesale massacre of Byng's entire force would actually be a far simpler proposition. Instead, she was faced with the problem of convincing the idiots to surrender before she *had* to kill them, and that was far trickier. If she could ever break through the typically Solarian assumption of inevitable superiority, then Byng—or his successor in command, at least—might prove more amenable. That was the real reason she'd come in at such a high rate of acceleration. She wanted them thinking about that, wondering what other technological advantages she might have tucked up her sleeve. And if she had to fire on them at all, then the greater the range at which she did so, the more likely they were to recognize how outclassed they were before it was too late . . . for them.

*And there's always the other factor*, she thought grimly. *If we open fire at sixty million and they don't begin decelerating immediately, it would take over twelve hours for us to match velocities with them. And they'd be across the hyper limit and into hyper in an hour and forty minutes. So if we can't convince them to stop and begin immediately decelerating themselves, I'll have no choice but to take them* all *out before they pull out of range.*

She glanced at the time display, considering when to send her next—and final—message to Josef Byng.

"Admiral Byng," the face of the woman on the com display might have been chipped from obsidian, and her voice was harder still, "I have warned you twice of the consequences of failing to comply with my requirements. If you do not immediately reverse your heading at maximum deceleration, preparatory to reentering New Tuscany orbit, as per my directions, I will open fire. You have five minutes from the receipt of this message. There will be no additional warnings."

Byng glared at the display, but he was through talking to the impertinent bitch. Maybe she did have better missiles than he did, but they couldn't be *enough* better to back up her preposterous threats, and with Halo and the other recent upgrades in his anti-missile defenses, the odds were overwhelming that most of his ships would survive to break past her, no matter what she did. She simply didn't have enough tubes for any other outcome. And once his task force was across the hyper limit, running free and clear, her days—and the days of her wretched little "Star Kingdom"—would be numbered. There could be only one response from the Solarian League Navy for something like this, and Manticore couldn't possibly stave off the vengeful avalanche headed its way.

"Deploy the pods," Michelle said quietly, watching the time display tick down towards Byng's deadline.

"Aye, aye, Ma'am. Deploying pods now," Dominica Adenauer replied, and the task group's acceleration rate dropped as the pods which had been tractored tight against its ships' hulls moved beyond the perimeter of their impeller wedges.

The battlecruisers' Keyhole platforms were already deployed, but the Keyholes' mass was low enough that the *Nikes'* acceleration curves hadn't been significantly affected. Deploying the missile pods, still tractored to their motherships but clear of those motherships' sidewalls (and wedges), was another matter entirely, and the task group's acceleration dropped from six hundred and three gravities to only five hundred and eighty.

"Flip us, Sterling," Michelle told Commander Casterlin.

"Aye, aye, Ma'am. Reversing heading now."

The entire task group flipped, putting its sterns towards Byng's battlecruisers and beginning to decelerate. Even with the pods deployed, Michelle's command had an advantage of almost a hundred gravities, and the rate of closure began to slow.

"Execute William Tell on the tick, Dominica."

"Aye, aye, Ma'am." Commander Adenauer depressed a key, locking in the firing commands and sequence, then sat back. "William Tell enabled and locked, Ma'am."

"Very good," Michelle said, and leaned back in her command chair, watching the last few seconds speed into eternity.

Josef Byng sat in his own command chair, watching another time display count down towards zero, and his belly was a knotted lump of tension.

Captain Mizawa had tried one last time to convince him to lie down, like a dog rolling belly-up to show its submission. Now they were no longer speaking, for there was nothing to speak about.

It was easy for Mizawa to put forward his arguments, Byng thought resentfully. Mizawa wouldn't be the one censored for cowardice. Mizawa wouldn't be the first Solarian flag officer in history to surrender to an enemy force. *Mizawa* wouldn't be known as the officer who'd rolled over for a batch of neobarbs without firing even a single shot.

*It's not just "easy" for him,* a voice said in Byng's brain. *It's also his way of making sure I'll never be in a position to hammer him like the disloyal, traitorous bastard he is. Well, it's not going to happen,* Captain—*trust me! It's not going to be* that *simple for you.*

Despite his fury at Mizawa, he'd come to the conclusion that there probably was at least a little something to the flag captain's arguments. Oh, there was no way the Manties had the magic missiles Mizawa was yammering about, but they could have substantially *better* missiles than Intelligence had suggested. If they did, it was entirely likely he was going to lose at least a few ships on his way out of the system. That would be regrettable, of course, but with the recent upgrades in the SLN missile defense and so many targets to spread their fire between, it was extremely unlikely that the Manties could get through with enough missiles to cripple more than a handful—half a dozen at the most. And they were only Frontier Fleet units. They could be replaced relatively easily, and once the survivors were past the Manties, the decisiveness of Byng's actions would be obvious. As the admiral who'd cut his way past the Manties to carry home word of their unprovoked attack on the Solarian League, he'd be immunized against the sort of wild allegations Mizawa had threatened to make about events in New Tuscany. In fact, he'd be well positioned to crush Mizawa, after all, and he couldn't deny that he'd take a sweetly savage satisfaction when the time came.

Of course—

"Missile separation!" Ingeborg Aberu announced suddenly. "*Multiple* missile separations! Range, forty-five million kilometers. Missile acceleration four-six-thousand KPS$^2$! Estimated flight time at constant acceleration, five-point-seven minutes."

"Missile Defense Aegis Five!" Byng's snapped command was automatic, a response which never had to consult his forebrain at all . . . which was fortunate, since his forebrain wasn't working very well at the moment.

*My God, she actually* did *it! She actually* launched missiles *at the* Solarian Navy! *I didn't think anyone could be that crazy! Doesn't she know where this has to end?*

Yet even as that thought ripped through him, there was another, one that was darker and more terrifying by far. Gold Peak wouldn't have launched from that far out unless she genuinely had the range to score on his ships, and that meant Mizawa's concerns hadn't been so much blathering nonsense after all.

The range at launch was over two and a half light-minutes, but with a closing velocity of 53,696 KPS, the geometry meant the Mark 23's maximum powered envelope was well over ninety-five million kilometers. Even a Mark 16, with only a pair of drive systems, would have had a powered envelope of almost forty-nine million kilometers . . . which meant her Mark 23s could reach their targets without ever activating their *third* drive system and still have the necessary endurance for final attack maneuvers. That was the real reason Michelle Henke had closed to that range before firing. It would give her ample opportunity to make her point, but she could do so while concealing a full third of the MDMs' powered endurance. At the same time, she wanted to finish this without using her broadside launchers at all, if she could. No doubt the Solarian survivors—*If there* are *any,* her mind supplied grimly—would figure out that she'd used pod-launched missiles, and that was the way she preferred it. If the hammer was really coming down, she wanted the Mark 16's existence to come as a complete surprise to the first Solarian officer unfortunate enough to face it in combat.

"Sir, CIC estimates that these things were launched from pods, not tubes." Ingeborg Aberu's voice was harsh, tight with fear and also with something else. Something plaintive, almost petulant. An anger stoked by the sudden realization that the Star Kingdom of Manticore really *could* produce technology well in advance of anything the Solarian League had even considered deploying. "They must have had them tractored inside their wedges. That's why their acceleration dropped just before they launched; they had to deploy them clear of the wedge perimeter."

"Understood," Byng replied tersely.

*At least I was right about* that *much,* he thought bitterly. *They* can't *launch things this big from the broadside tubes we saw at*

*Monica . . . not that that's going to make things any better. Unless they don't have very many of the damned pods available.*

"Sir," Aberu said a moment later, her voice flatter than it had been, "CIC is projecting that all their missiles have been targeted on a single unit." She turned her head to look at him.

"On *us*," she said.

Warden Mizawa swore viciously as Ursula Zeiss reported the same conclusion to him.

*That fucking idiot! That stupid, arrogant, Battle Fleet prick! Now he's going to get all of us killed, and for absolutely nothing!*

"Time to impact five minutes," Zeiss said harshly.

"Stand by missile defense," Mizawa said, and glanced into the display which showed him the face of Hildegard Bourget, in Command Beta. From her tight, bitter expression, she'd obviously guessed exactly the same thing he had.

*Looks like getting you off the ship worked out even better than I'd expected, Maitland,* a corner of his brain thought even now. *Sorry I never told you personally what a job you did for me, but I guess I'm not going to have the chance to make up for it. Good luck, boy—and watch your ass! The Navy's going to need you, I think.*

*God, I wish I'd been wrong,* Maitland Askew thought sickly, his face white and clenched as he watched the master tactical plot on Admiral Sigbee's flag bridge and thought of all the men and women he knew aboard Josef Byng's flagship. *God, why couldn't I have been wrong?!*

Despite all of the simulations BuWeaps and BuTrain had been able to put together after examining the hardware captured at Monica, Michelle and Dominica Adenauer were only too well aware that their knowledge of actual Solarian capabilities was limited, to say the least. They had no real meter stick for the toughness of the Sollies' missile defenses, so they'd decided to err on the side of caution. Each of their *Nikes* had eighty "flat pack" pods limpeted to her hull, and each of the *Saganami-Cs* had forty. That gave Michelle a total of nine hundred and sixty pods, or the next best thing to ten thousand missiles. Operating on her assumption that the Sollies' actual defensive capability was twice that of the captured vessels examined at Monica, Michelle had decided that two hundred and fifty of those missiles ought to do the trick. They might not destroy their target outright, but that was fine with her. In fact, she would really *prefer* that outcome. She wasn't the sort of homicidal maniac who *enjoyed* killing people, after all. She'd be more than willing to settle for demonstrating that she *could* destroy their vessels . . . and she'd be *delighted* if that convinced them to throw in the towel before she actually had to.

The Solarian League Navy had been the premier navy of the explored galaxy for centuries. Indeed, no one could remember a time when it hadn't been acknowledged as the most powerful fleet in existence. But that very preeminence had worked to undermine its efficiency. There was, quite simply, no enemy for it to take seriously, no peer against which to measure itself, no Darwinian incentive to identify weaknesses and correct them.

The nature of the Solarian League itself, dominated by the permanent bureaucrats who actually ran it rather than the political leadership which had long since lost any power to rein in those bureaucrats, was another factor. As with the civilian bureaucracies, the naval bureaucracy had become immovably entrenched, and the internecine warfare between competing departments for limited funding had been both intense and brutal. Funding decisions were fought out on the basis of who had the most clout, not the greatest need, and owed very little indeed to any impartial analysis of actual operational requirements. So it probably wasn't very surprising that the fundamental assumption of Solarian technological supremacy in all things meant R&D's budget was the smallest of all. After all, since the SLN's technology was already better than anyone else's, why waste money on that when it could more profitably be spent on prestigious things like additional superdreadnoughts . . . or quietly eased into the private banking accounts of Navy procurement officials?

All of which helped to explain why the SLN had also been one of the galaxy's most conservative navies. With thousands of ships in commission, and more thousands mothballed in reserve, its margin of superiority over any conceivable opponent had been utterly decisive. Which meant getting money even to build new ships, or to radically overhaul and modernize existing ones, had always been a difficult exercise. As one consequence, the SLN had been slow to recognize the potential of the laser head, and even slower to adopt it. And because no one had ever used similar weapons *against* it, its evaluation of the threat the new weapon presented—and of the doctrinal changes necessary to *defeat* it—had lagged behind even its own hardware.

That lag was about to have serious repercussions for SLNS *Jean Bart*.

"Those platforms are definitely decoys, Ma'am," Sherilyn Jeffers said flatly as she watched her displays. "They've spun up now, and Ghost Rider's giving us good data on them."

"What do they look like?" Naomi Kaplan asked.

"It looks as if the system as a whole is pretty good, Ma'am." The electronics warfare officer tapped a few keys, her eyes intent as she absorbed CIC's analysis of the reconnaissance platforms' datastream. "I'd say the individual platforms probably aren't quite as capable as what we've been seeing out of the Havenites lately, but their *combined* capability is actually better."

"Enough better that we should've used more missiles, do you think, Guns?" Kaplan asked.

"Oh, no, Ma'am." Abigail never looked up from her own displays and telemetry, and her smile could have frozen a star's heart. "Not that much better. In fact, I'd say their hardware is better than their doctrine. Either that, or their helmsmen are a little shaky. The interval between their units is at least three times anything the Havenites would accept, and that means the other ships' decoys are too far from the target to give it much cover. Our attack birds are going up against just its own platforms, and they aren't good enough to hack it against that much fire without a lot more support."

"Launching counter-missiles," Ursula Zeiss announced tersely, and Mizawa gave a jerky nod of acknowledgment.

He wasn't certain how much good the counter-missiles were going to do. The LIM-16F was a third again as capable as its predecessor, but even so, there wouldn't be time for a proper, layered defense. By the time they reached *Jean Bart*, the Manticoran missiles' closing velocity would be up to seventy-nine percent of the speed of light. The LIM-16's drive simply didn't have the endurance to hit the monsters the Manties had launched far enough out for an effective second launch at the same targets before they zipped right through the entire defensive envelope.

*That's going to be a bitch for the laser clusters, too,* he thought harshly. *And they obviously know where that asshole Byng's been talking to them from. I can hardly fault them for wanting to kill his* worthless ass, *but I'd just as soon they hadn't decided to kill mine* at the same time!

Despite everything—despite his own fear, despite his desperate concern for his ship and his crew, despite even his incandescent fury at Josef Byng—he actually smiled as the last sentence ran through his brain.

Aboard the attacking MDMs, computers consulted their pre-launch instructions, and suddenly jammers and decoys began to blossom. The Solarian counter-missiles were basically sound pieces of technology, but despite the SLN's belated awareness that *something* peculiar had happened to missile combat out in the Haven Sector, it was only beginning any sort of serious attempt to upgrade its active anti-missile defenses. Worse, neither the hardware nor the officers groping towards some new defense doctrine had profited from the last two decades of savage combat which had refined their Manticoran and Havenite counterparts. Their counter-missiles' software wasn't as good, the doctrine for their use was purely theoretical, without the harsh Darwinian input of survival, and the officers doing their best—not just aboard *Jean Bart,* but aboard all of Byng's battlecruisers—had no true concept of the threat environment into which they had intruded.

For all of its towering reputation, all of its size, all of the wealth and industrial power which stood behind it, the Solarian League Navy was simply outclassed. Even Frontier Fleet was accustomed only to dealing with pirates, the occasional slaver, or the privateer gone rogue. No one had *destroyed* a Solarian warship in combat in almost three centuries, and the complacency that had engendered had produced fatal consequences. Despite its preeminent position, the SLN was a second-rate power, inferior even to many of the Solarian system-defense forces it had derided as "amateurs" for so many decades. Far, far worse, the men and women of its officer corps didn't even recognize their own inferiority . . . and Josef Byng's ships found themselves matched against what was by almost any measure the most experienced, battle hardened, and technologically advanced fleet in space.

✧    ✧    ✧

Byng stared at the master plot in disbelief as the Manticoran missiles suddenly and magically reproduced. There were no longer hundreds of incoming missiles—there were *thousands*, and the counter-missiles trying to kill them went berserk. Scores of them targeted the same false images, went after the same decoys, and then the EW platforms the Manticorans called Dazzlers spun up, radiating with impossible power. No one in the Solarian League had realized that the RMN had managed to put actual fusion plants aboard their missiles, so no one had even considered what jammers or decoys could do with that sort of energy budget. And, unfortunately for *Jean Bart*, it was far too late to start thinking about that sort of thing as the hell-bright bubbles of multi-megaton nuclear explosions spawned x-ray lasers.

Despite the Manticoran penetration aides, despite weaknesses in doctrine, despite surprise and the disastrous underestimation of the threat, the Solarian League Navy managed to stop seventy-three of the incoming missiles. Another thirty of the Mark 23s had carried nothing but penetration EW, which left "only" one hundred and forty-seven actual shipkillers. One hundred and forty-seven missiles, each of which carried six individual laser heads designed to blast through superdreadnought armor.

A hungry, wordless sound flowed across HMS *Tristram*'s bridge as rapiers of focused x-rays stabbed deep into *Jean Bart*.

*No, not "rapiers,"* Abigail Hearns thought from behind the hard, cold anger of her eyes as the fury of the bomb-pumped lasers ripped huge splinters and mangled chunks from the battlecruiser's hull. *That's too neat, too precise. Those are* axes. *Or chainsaws.*

The Mark 23 was designed to kill superdreadnoughts, ships with incredibly tough armor that was literally meters thick. Ships which were intricately compartmentalized, honeycombed with blast doors, internal bulkheads, and cofferdams—all designed to contain damage. To channel it away from vital areas. To absorb almost inconceivable hammerings and remain in action.

But SLNS *Jean Bart* was no superdreadnought.

Her wedge stopped dozens—scores—of lasers. Her decoys attracted still others away from her hull. But more dozens of them were neither stopped nor decoyed, and they blasted through her battlecruiser sidewalls and battlecruiser armor with contemptuous ease. They ripped at her vitals like the talons of some huge demon. And then, abruptly, she simply . . . came apart.

Abigail Hearns watched the next best thing to a million tons of starship disintegrate, and her stony eyes never even flickered. Deep within her, there was a sense of horror, of terrible regret, for the thousands of human beings who had just died. Most of them had been guilty of nothing worse than obeying the orders of a criminally stupid and arrogant superior. She knew that, and that inner part of her mourned for their deaths, but not even that could dim her sense of triumph. Of justice done for her ship's murdered squadron mates.

*"Behold, I will make you a new threshing sledge with sharp teeth; you shall thresh the mountains and beat them small, and make the hills like chaff,"* her mind recited the old, old words coldly as the wreckage began to spread on her tactical plot. *"You shall winnow them, the wind shall carry them away, and the whirlwind shall scatter them."*

But all she said aloud was—

"Target destroyed, Ma'am."

*Well,* that *was a case of overkill after all,* Michelle thought, gazing at the spreading cloud of debris and gas which had once been a Solarian battlecruiser, but the thought was muted, almost hushed. Even for her, even after all the death and destruction she'd seen in two decades of warfare, there was something dreadful about *Jean Bart's* execution. And "execution" was exactly the right word for what had happened, she reflected. She'd expected the Sollies to be fat, happy, and soft, *expected* to kill the ship with her single salvo, but her wildest estimates had fallen far short of just how great an edge the Royal Manticoran Navy currently enjoyed.

*But that's the rub, isn't it, girl? That word "currently." Well, that and the fact that the Sollies have probably got at least four times as many superdreadnoughts as we have* destroyers! *But done is done, and maybe* somebody *on their side will be smart enough to realize just how many of their spacers are going to get killed before that size advantage of theirs lets them carry through against us. I'd really like to think sanity could break out* somewhere, *at any rate.*

No trace of her thoughts touched her expression as she turned to look at Commander Edwards.

"All right, Bill," she told the communications officer calmly. "Let's see if the *next* link in their chain of command is prepared to see reason now."

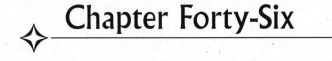

# Chapter Forty-Six

"YOU KNOW, I'D REALLY like to meet this Anisimovna one day," Michelle Henke said as she accepted a fresh cup of steaming black coffee from Chris Billingsley. She gave the steward a quick smile of thanks, and he continued around the table to her two guests with his coffee pot, refilling and topping off, then withdrew from the day cabin.

"I don't imagine you're alone in that, Ma'am," Aivars Terekhov said grimly. "I know *I'd* like an hour or two alone with her."

"She does seem to get around, doesn't she?" Bernardus Van Dort agreed. "Assuming this really is the same person Tyler claims to've met with."

"Same name, same description," Michelle pointed out. She sipped from her cup, then set it back down and leaned back in her chair. "I realize there are a lot of women in the galaxy, Bernardus, but how many gorgeous, man-eating blondes with Mesan accents, Manpower credit chips, Solly task groups in their back pockets, and a taste for slumming in the vicinity of the Talbott Cluster so they can arrange operations designed to break our kneecaps are there?"

"I admit, the evidence suggests she's the same person," Van Dort replied with unflappable calm. "Assuming she went all the way home to Mesa after Monica blew up in her face, though, she certainly got back out here in what must be close to record time. In fact, I'm inclined to wonder if they had the entire New

646

Tuscany operation in mind from the very beginning, as well, if only as a backup. She can hardly have spent very much time at home on Mesa conferring or coming up with new strategies before they sent her back out."

"They did recover quickly, didn't they?" Michelle agreed thoughtfully, and Terekhov snorted.

"I don't think they so much 'recovered' as just 'reloaded,'" he said. "And I *really* don't like what Vézien and the others had to say about how the late, unlamented Admiral Byng came to be in a position to pull something this incredibly stupid in the first place."

His remark was met by a brief silence as the other two thought about all of the implications of Prime Minister Vézien's testimony. Then Michelle looked at Van Dort.

"Do you really think Baroness Medusa and Prime Minister Alquezar are going to sign off on your agreement with Vézien, Bernardus?"

"I think yes . . . probably." Van Dort smiled tightly. "I didn't really promise him all that much, you know. Basically just that the Royal Navy isn't going to come and dismantle his star system's entire orbital infrastructure as a reprisal."

"That and that New Tuscany wouldn't really be excluded from all Quadrant markets," Terekhov said in a chidingly correcting tone. Van Dort raised an eyebrow at him, and Terekhov snorted again. "That's a hell of a lot more than *I* would have given him, Bernardus! And, frankly, after what they tried to pull this time, I'm not sure it's a justifiable security risk, either."

He started to say something more, then broke off with a sound suspiciously like an "*Oof!*" as several kilos of cat launched themselves into his lap with absolutely no warning. Terekhov was one of Dicey's favorite people. Not only did his long legs give him a comfortably large lap, but Dicey's radar had an uncanny ability to differentiate the cat-lovers from those who merely tolerated a feline presence. Now he sat up, bumping his broad, scarred head against Terekhov's chin, and purred loudly to remind his admirer of what human hands had really been invented to do.

Michelle shook her head at the intrusion, but before she could call Billingsley to remove his thoroughly illegal pet, Terekhov's hands began obediently stroking the outsized beast, and she closed her mouth, instead. There was something irresistibly appealing about seeing the tough-as-nails victor of Monica firmly under the paw of a much battered and bedamned feline.

"As far as security risks go," she said after a moment, "they aren't going to risk pissing us off a second time anytime soon, Aivars, I don't think those issues are going to be a deal breaker, but I think the lack of reprisals could be. For that matter, I'm inclined to think it *should* be."

"Which is why we specifically left open the question of the amount of the reparations to be assessed," Van Dort pointed out. "Both sides know it's coming and that the price tag's going to be stiff, and if you'll notice, I specifically didn't rule out the possibility of reprisals against the New Tuscan industrial establishment if we can't come to a meeting of minds on that particular topic."

"I'm not too sure it's a meeting with *their* minds I'm concerned about," Michelle said with a wry smile. "I know the Queen a bit better than most people do, and I don't think she's going to be very happy with New Tuscany. It must've been bad enough when the initial report about what happened to Bear and his ships hit her desk a week or so ago. When she gets the one on what happened to Byng here in New Tsucany, it's going to be even worse. And when she gets our follow-up, including everything Vézien and the others had to say about Ms. Anisimovna, I think she's going to be just a bit *peeved* with them."

"I don't doubt it for a moment," Van Dort acknowledged, "and I'm not saying they should get off scot-free. But look at the way it worked out from their side for a moment. I don't have any great store of sympathy for Vézien, Boutin, and the others, and I'm not going to shed any tears if they get kicked out on their blood-sucking, power-mongering, oligarchical asses. But New Tuscany as a star nation's already lost in the vicinity of forty-three thousand lives. That's a pretty hefty price to pay, and I'd say the Vézien Government is just as furious at Manpower as it says it is. I'm sure that in time, he and his cabinet members will get over their current spasm of sanity and revert to type, but in the meantime why kick them any harder than we need to? We've got enough problems already without nurturing any ill will we don't absolutely have to."

"Well, *that's* certainly true," Michelle agreed glumly. "For the admiral who just handed the Solarian League Navy its first ever task group-level defeat, I'm not feeling all warm and fuzzy inside over my accomplishment."

Terekhov looked up from Dicey and chuckled with very little humor, and Michelle gave him a crooked smile.

After the destruction of *Jean Bart*, Rear Admiral Evelyn Sigbee, commanding the 112th Battlecruiser Squadron, had seen reason very quickly indeed. The fact that Michelle had made it clear she knew which ship was Sigbee's flagship might well have contributed to that, but it was obvious the woman was also considerably smarter—or at least willing to actually *use* whatever intelligence she had—than Byng had been. Michelle wondered how much of that was because she was Frontier Fleet, not Battle Fleet.

There'd been no survivors from *Jean Bart*, and the other ships of the Solarian task group had returned very promptly to their parking orbit around New Tuscany. Sigbee had been a little stickier about meekly transporting her personnel down to the planetary surface and handing her ships over to Michelle's boarding parties with their computers intact, but Michelle had held her battlecruisers and heavy cruisers well outside the Solarians' effective missile range while she sent just the destroyers in to be sure Sigbee was complying with her instructions. As she'd hoped, the memory of what had just happened to *Jean Bart*—and her obvious willingness to repeat the demonstration—had carried the day.

The anchor watches who'd been left aboard had been no more cooperative than they had to be, but they'd displayed no overt resistance, either. Again, not too surprisingly, given the heavily armed Marines who'd accompanied the naval boarding parties. And once those boarding parties were aboard, it had quickly become evident that the Sollies' computer security was far inferior to that of Manticore. On the other hand, it was also inferior to some of the civilian-market Solarian software the navy computer techs had seen, so that didn't necessarily prove anything about the tech base *available* to the SLN; only about the tech base of which it had actually availed itself.

Once through the fences and into the data banks, it hadn't taken very long to determine that the Sollies own tactical recordings clearly demonstrated that Commodore Chatterjee's ships hadn't had a thing to do with the destruction of the New Tuscan space station. How much good that was going to do after more recent events in the star system was debatable, but Michelle's technicians had made complete copies of the original files.

For that matter, they had some of the actual computers in which those files had been stored, since she'd also chosen to take the battlecruisers *Resourceful* and *Impudent* home with her. *Resourceful* was one of the *Indefatigable* class, like the ships captured in Monica, and she felt certain BuShips and BuWeaps would want to compare her electronics and weapons loadouts with that of the ships Technodyne had provided to President Tyler. *Impudent*, despite the letter with which her name began, was one of the new *Nevada*-class ships. As such, she represented the very latest in deployed SLN technology, and Michelle *knew* how eagerly the engineers and analysts back home would greet her arrival.

Aside from those two units, she'd left the rest of Byng's ships in New Tuscany with Sigbee. She'd seen no reason to try to take any more of them with her, for several reasons, including the fact that the newer Manticoran designs didn't provide a lot of redundant personnel to make up passage crews for prize vessels. Besides that, she'd quickly come to the conclusion that there was no particular point in trying to refit them for Manticoran use. They were clearly inferior do anything presently in Alliance service, and the expense and effort to bring such manpower-intensive designs up to something like current standards could be far more profitably applied to other ends.

She'd considered scuttling them, and under accepted interstellar law, she would have been entirely within her rights to do so. In the end, though, she'd decided that actually scuttling them might be a case of pouring unnecessary salt into a wound. Nothing she could do was going to make the SLN happy with her, but sailing off into the sunset with every one of their ships, or blowing them up in orbit, was only likely to piss them off even worse. Not that she was any too sure that what she'd ended up doing would make them any happier. Eighty percent of their ships and ninety-five percent of their personnel were still there, and both ships and people were pretty much physically intact, but before leaving, Michelle's boarding parties had deliberately triggered those ships' internal security charges . . . which had reduced all of the surviving battlecruisers' central computer nets to so much slagged molecular circuitry, as inert and useless as a solid block of granite. No one would be reprogramming *those* computers; it was going to take physical replacement if the Sollies ever wanted one of those ships to get underway under her own power again. That wouldn't necessarily take them permanently out of service, but it would take months to get a suitably equipped repair fleet all the way out to New Tuscany. In fact, it might actually be cheaper and faster in the long run to send out a fleet of tugs and tow them back to a Solarian shipyard.

*And if they're not permanently out of service, at least they aren't going to be available to the other side any time soon,* she reflected grimly. *If this goes as far south as it could, that's not exactly anything to sneer at, I suppose.*

"I wish we had a better feel for how the Sollies are going to react to all of this," Van Dort said, as if he'd been reading her mind. Not that it would have taken a genius to figure out what she was thinking.

"I wish the same thing," she said. "But what I wish even more was that we had some idea how any transstellar—even one the size of Manpower—comes up with the juice to manipulate the SLN on this level. Battle Fleet admirals who just happen to hate all Manties in charge of Frontier Fleet task groups? Entire *task forces* of Battle Fleet superdreadnoughts on call, assuming Anisimovna wasn't just blowing smoke to the New Tuscans? I'd say this goes at least a little beyond most corporations' definition of 'business as usual.'"

*Which,* she added silently, *is the reason I also handed complete copies of the depositions Vézien, Dusserre, Cardot, and Pélisard gave us over to Sigbee for her to pass on to their ONI. I doubt it's likely to make them any less pissed off with* us, *but I don't have any problem at all with getting the League simultaneously pissed off enough at* Manpower *to finally do something about it!*

"You think Vézien is right about Byng?" Terekhov asked.

"I don't know," Michelle said slowly. "If he is, I'm even more nervous than I was, I think. Bernardus, you know people out here better than Aivars and I do. Who do you think was closer to right, Vézien or Dusserre?"

"Dusserre," Van Dort said promptly. "I don't like him, you understand, but for somebody stuck in a fundamentally unworkable position, he's probably the smartest of the lot. Vézien may think Byng knew what was going on, but I don't. Your own intelligence dossier on him indicates that he's never been exactly the sharpest stylus in the box, and his prejudices against Manticore are glaringly obvious. I'd say they were obvious to Manpower, as well. And assuming Anisimovna really was responsible for *Giselle's* destruction, it looks to me as if they planned all along on putting him in a position where his anti-Manticore attitude would trigger a spinal-reflex reaction. I don't know if they anticipated that he'd go quite so far, give them such a blatant *causis belli*, but they probably figured they could count on him to open fire on at least one Manticoran ship, somewhere along the way."

"I have trouble believing anyone could be that good a puppeteer," Terekhov objected. Van Dort looked at him, and the commodore shrugged.

"Your basic analysis sounds good, Bernardus, but I find it difficult to believe that anybody competent enough to put all of this together would rely on somehow maneuvering our ships close to Byng's right in the middle of the New Tuscany System, then blowing up a space station to get him to open fire. That's so far outside the KISS principle it isn't even funny!"

"I don't think that's what they did at all," Van Dort replied. "I think the 'puppeteers' relied on the fact that Anisimovna is an extremely talented and—obviously—extraordinarily ruthless operative. I think they told her what they wanted to happen, gave her the best tools for the job they could, and then sent her out to manipulate the situation however seemed best to her. From everything Vézien and his crowd had to say, she obviously had them right in her pocket. And it must have been obvious—to her, at least—that even if we hadn't responded by sending Chatterjee to New Tuscany, we'd eventually have responded by doing *something* that would have put our ships in close proximity with Byng's. Either that, or she and the New Tuscans would have managed to manufacture an 'incident' sufficiently serious to send Byng looking for *us* with blood in his eye. What's that saying from Old Terra about Muhammad going to the mountain?"

"I think you're right about that," Michelle said, "and, to be honest, that troubles me almost as much as anything else that's happened."

The others looked at her, and she waved her coffee cup in the air and grimaced. Then she set the cup down in front of her, folded her forearms on the edge of the table, and leaned forward over them, her expression serious.

"Look, we've always known Manpower hated the Star Kingdom's guts. Well, that's fair enough, because we've reciprocated. But we've also always thought of Manpower as a bunch of arrogant, money hungry, amoral bastards. They don't care about anything except money, and their arrogance leads them to do things like that business in Old Chicago when they kidnapped young Zilwicki. Or that idiotic attack on Catherine Montaigne's townhouse. Or the blatant stupidity of using *slave labor*, of all damned things, on Torch before the Ballroom took it away from them. Ruthless, yes. And rich, and unscrupulous as hell, but not really all that smart. Not . . . sophisticated."

"I might quibble with some of your terminology, Ma'am," Terekhov said thoughtfully. "I never really thought of them as stupid, but I guess I'd have to admit that the quality I associated with them was more . . . *cunning*, let's say, than intelligence."

"And their operations in the past—or the ones we've known about, at least—have all been related to the bottom-line somehow," Michelle pointed out. "Sometimes the connection's seemed a little strained, but it's always been there if we looked close enough. And they've never used major military forces—their own, or anyone else's. Even when they tried for Montaigne, they used mercenaries. And that business of yours in Nuncio, Aivars—that was using orphaned StateSec units, which was effectively just another batch of mercenaries. But this time, neither of those things is true."

She shook her head, her eyes unwontedly worried.

"Arguably, I suppose, you could say both the Monicans and the New Tuscans were more 'mercenaries,' whether they realized it or not, but what about Byng? What about the connections it took to get *him* assigned to a Frontier Fleet command and then sent out here? And what about this Battle Fleet task force Anisimovna claimed was stationed at McIntosh? That's a huge escalation in force levels from anything we've *ever* seen out of them in the past. I suppose Battle Fleet's corrupt enough that they could conceivably have managed it with only a few people in key spots in their pockets, but even so, it shows a degree of hubris that strikes me as almost insane. And look at the timing on it. They *had* to have the McIntosh deployment and Byng's appointment already in the pipeline *before* you hit Monica, Aivars. They literally couldn't have gotten the ships out here so quickly, if they hadn't already arranged for it. So either they really were already looking at New Tuscany—or something like it—or else they'd decided to arrange it all as a second string to their bow if Monica failed. Either way, that's a sort of multilayered strategy I don't think any of us would have expected out of them. And if we're going to talk about escalations, think of everything else they've risked here. They're headquartered on an independent planet which isn't even part of the League, but they're deeply involved in the League's economy. They *depend* on that involvement, and they've always relied on their connections in the League's bureaucracy and Assembly to deter any Solarian action against them. But now they start throwing Battle Fleet admirals and task forces around? Even the League is going to react—and react *hard*—if it figures out a single outlaw corporation—a *foreign* outlaw corporation—is sending entire *fleets* of its wallers around the galaxy!

"And even leaving that risk aside, look at the financial side of it. They have to have lost a fortune on that fiasco in Monica, but they didn't even slow down. Instead, they switched right over to this New Tuscany operation, and I'll guarantee you *it* didn't come cheap, either. I'll concede that they've got every reason in the world to keep us as far away from the Mesa System as they can, but after taking the hit to the bank account Monica must've represented, shouldn't simple financial pain have made them at least a little slower out of the launch tube for New Tuscany? And after such an obvious failure, and all the bad PR it's gotten them from the League newsies, I'd have expected them to keep a low profile, at least for a little while. Which, obviously, they didn't do, if they're actually manipulating major SLN command appointments and fleet movements. And to top it all off, the person they sent out to coordinate it is also the person who coordinated the Monica operation, and before Monica, we'd never even heard of her. Which wouldn't worry me as much as it does if she didn't seem to be so damned *capable*. If they've had her tucked away in their forward magazine all this time, why haven't we seen her—or her handiwork, at least—before? Where did this rogue corporation suddenly come up with an operative of her caliber? And why is it acting like it thinks it's a *star nation*, not just a criminal business enterprise?"

The other two looked back at her, and no one said another word for quite a long time.

# Chapter Forty-Seven

"THANK YOU FOR FINDING room in your schedule so promptly, Minister," Sir Lyman Carmichael said as Foreign Minister Marcelito Lorenzo Roelas y Valiente's private secretary ushered him into the stupendous office.

That office offered enough square meters for a basketball game, Carmichael thought more than a tad sourly . . . and with very little exaggeration. Which, given that property values in the city of Old Chicago, the capital of the Solarian League, were almost certainly the highest in the explored galaxy, made the office's size an even more ostentatious statement of its inhabitant's status.

*Of course,* he reflected, *status and* power *aren't always exactly the same thing, are they? Especially here in the League.*

"Well," Roelas y Valiente replied, standing behind his desk—which was no larger than a standard air car—and extending his hand, "your message sounded fairly urgent, Mr. Ambassador."

"Yes, I'm afraid it is. Rather urgent, I mean," Carmichael said, shaking the foreign minister's hand.

Roelas y Valiente allowed his well-trained expression to show at least a trace of concern, and indicated one of the two armchairs on Carmichael's side of his desk.

"In that case, please make yourself comfortable and tell me about it," the Foreign Minister invited.

"Thank you, Minister."

Carmichael's voice was a bit warmer than it might have been

in the presence of another senior member of the Gyulay Government.

Roelas y Valiente was the youngest member of Prime Minister Shona Gyulay's cabinet—not even out of his sixties yet, which made him the next best thing to thirty T-years younger than Carmichael himself—and unlike most of his fellows, he obviously felt a sense of responsibility for the proper discharge of his office. That was a pleasant and unexpected surprise here in the Solarian League. He also appeared to be at least reasonably competent, which (in Sir Lyman Carmichael's considered opinion) was an even greater surprise in such a senior League politician.

It was unfortunate that someone who possessed both of those virtues was as much a prisoner of his office's limitations as the stupidest and most corrupt demagogue could have been. There were times when Carmichael, as a bureaucrat (or call it a "career civil servant," if it sounded better) himself, felt a certain envy for his Solarian counterparts. At least they didn't have to worry about the possibility of some unqualified buffoon (like, for example, one Baron High Ridge and his cronies) managing to delude enough voters into sharing his own fantasies of competence so that they gave him actual decision-making power. Some things were more likely than others, but the possibility of any mere elected official exercising genuine power in the Solarian League at the federal level were about as likely as water suddenly deciding to flow uphill without benefit of counter-gravity.

And that, despite any occasional whimsical fantasies Carmichael might entertain, was the true reason someone like a Josef Byng could rise to flag rank, or someone like a Lorcan Verrochio could become a commissioner in something like the Office of Frontier Security. When no "unqualified buffoon" could be given effective power by the electorate, neither could anyone else. And when those who exercised true power were unaccountable to voters, they could not be *removed* from power, either. The consequences of that were unbridled empire building, corruption, and lack of accountability, all of them as inevitable as sunrise, and bureaucrat himself or not, Sir Lyman Carmichael knew which type of system he preferred.

Unfortunately, that wasn't the type of system the Solarian Constitution had created . . . a fact of which, he never doubted, Roelas y Valiente was even more aware than *he* was. The authors of the

Solarian League's Constitution had represented literally scores of already inhabited, thoroughly settled star systems. Some of those star systems had been colonized a thousand years before the League's creation. All of them had seen the advantages of regulating interstellar trade, of creating a single interstellar currency, of crafting effective regulatory agencies to keep an eye on interstellar finance and investment, of combining their efforts to extradite interstellar criminals, suppress piracy, and enforce things like the Eridani Edict and the Deneb Accords. But they'd also had an entire millennium of self-government, an entire millennium of developing their own planetwide and systemwide senses of identity. Their primary loyalties had been to their *own* worlds, their *own* governments, not to some new galaxy-wide super government, and none of them had been willing to surrender their hard-earned sovereignty and individual identities to *anyone*—not even to the mother-world of all humanity—just to create a more effective regulatory climate. And so they had carefully crafted a constitution designed to deprive the League's central government of any coercive power. They had eviscerated the federal government's political power by granting every single full member of the League veto power; *any* star system had the legal power to kill *any* legislative act of which it disapproved, which had turned the League Assembly into nothing more than a debating society. And the same constitution had prohibited the League from imposing *any* direct taxation upon its citizens.

The intent had been to provide the member star systems with the ability to protect themselves from any sort of despotic central authority, on the one hand, and to systematically starve the potentially coercive arms of that central authority of the sort of funding which might have allowed them to encroach upon the rights of the League's citizens, on the other.

Unfortunately, the law of unintended consequences had refused to be evaded. The universal right of veto had, indeed, eviscerated the political powers of the League, but that very success had created a dangerous vacuum. For the League simply to survive, far less provide the services which its founders had envisioned, there had to be some central power to manage the necessary bureaucracy. It was really a very simple choice, Carmichael reflected. Either some central power emerged, or the League simply ceased to function. So, since the Solarians had systematically precluded the possibility of running the League by statute, they were forced to turn to bureaucratic regulation, instead.

And it worked. In effect, the bureaucracies became self-directed, and for a while—a century or two—they functioned not simply effectively, but well and even more or less honestly. Unfortunately, the people running those bureaucracies had discovered an interesting omission in the Constitution. Acts of the Assembly could be vetoed by any full member system, which meant there was no probability of a *statutory* despotism, but there was no provision for the veto or repeal of *regulations*. That would have required the statutory creation of someone or something with the power to repeal or reform the regulations, and the bureaucrats had cultivated far too many friends and cozy "special relationships" for that ever to happen. And while the federal government could enact no direct taxation measures, there'd been no constitutional prohibition of regulatory fees or indirect taxes—imposed by regulation, not statute—on businesses or interstellar commerce. To be sure, all of the League's federal funds combined represented an absurdly small percentage of the Sollies' Gross Interstellar Product, but given the staggering size of the League's GIP, even a tiny percentage represented a stupendous absolute cash flow.

There'd been actual attempts at political reform, but the bureaucrats who wrote the League's regulations, who managed its appointments and the distribution of its expenditures, had always been able to find someone willing to exercise his veto authority to strangle those efforts in the cradle. And always out of sheer, selfless, disinterested statesmanship, of course.

Still, there were appearances to maintain, here in the kabuki theater that passed for the Solarian League's government. Carmichael knew that, yet he felt an undeniable sensation of regret for what he knew he was about to inflict on this particular Solarian.

"Forgive me," Roelas y Valiente said as Carmichael laid the traditional and thoroughly anachronistic briefcase in his lap. "I completely forgot to ask if I could offer you some refreshment, Mr. Ambassador."

"No, thank you, Minister."

Carmichael shook his head with a smile of appreciation for the Foreign Minister's offer. Quite a few of his fellow ministers, Carmichael suspected, would have "forgotten" to make any such offer to a neobarb ambassador, regardless of the wealth and commercial power of the star nation he represented. In Roelas y Valiente's case, however, that forgetfulness had been completely genuine. It was rather refreshing, really, to deal with a senior Solly politician who didn't seem compelled to look for ways to put "neobarbs" in their proper place. Which only lent added point to Carmichael's regret this morning.

Now, as Roelas y Valiente nodded acknowledgment of his polite refusal and sat back in his own chair, Carmichael opened the briefcase and extracted its contents: a computer-chip folio and a single envelope of thick, cream-yellow parchment bearing the Star Kingdom of Manticore's arms and the archaic wax seal tradition required. He held them both in his hands for a moment, gazing down at them. The envelope was heavier than the folio, even though it contained no more than three sheets of paper, and he found himself wondering why in the galaxy high-level diplomacy continued to insist upon the physical exchange of hardcopy documents. Since the content of those hardcopy documents was always transmitted electronically at the same time, and since no one ever bothered to actually read the paper copies (except, perhaps, at the highest levels when they were initially handed over, and it was deplorably gauche for a foreign minister to just rip a note open and read it in the ambassador's presence, anyway), why were the damned things sent in the first place?

That was a question he'd asked himself more than once over the half T-century and more of his service in the Manticoran diplomatic corps. It was also one which had become rather more relevant to his own activities in the seven T-months since Admiral James Webster's assassination had made him the Manticoran ambassador to the League. There'd been more than enough exchanges of diplomatic correspondence (although, to be fair, most of it had been exchanged at a level considerably lower than this) since the Battle of Monica. Especially once the Manticorans' discoveries about the involvement of Manpower and Technodyne in the Talbott Quadrant had come to light. No doubt Roelas y Valiente expected this to be more of the same, and despite his pleasantly attentive expression, he couldn't possibly have been looking forward to receiving it. Yet Carmichael devoutly wished that "more of the same" was all he was about to hand the foreign minister. Unfortunately . . .

"I'm afraid that I've come to call on you concerning a very grave matter, Minister," he said in a much more formal tone. "There's been an incident—an extremely *serious* incident—between Her Majesty's armed forces and the Solarian League Navy."

Roelas y Valiente's polite expression transformed itself almost instantly into an impenetrable mask, but not instantly enough for someone with Carmichael's experience to miss the shock—and astonishment—that flared in his eyes first.

"This," Carmichael continued, indicating the chip folio, "contains complete sensor records of what occurred. At Foreign Secretary Langtry's instructions, I've reviewed them personally, with the assistance of Captain Deangelo, my naval attaché. While I'm obviously less qualified in these matters than Admiral Webster was—or, for that matter, than Captain Deangelo *is*—I believe they clearly demonstrate the background circumstances, the sequence of events, and their outcome."

He paused for just a moment, letting what he'd already said settle in, then drew a deep breath.

"Minister," he said slowly, "I'm afraid we find ourselves facing the very real probability of a direct military confrontation between the Solarian League and the Star Empire of Manticore. In fact, it would be more accurate to say that we've already had one."

Despite Roelas y Valiente's best efforts, his facial muscles twitched and his nostrils flared. Aside from that, however, there might have been a marble statue seated in his chair.

"Just under one month ago, on October twenty-first," Carmichael continued, "in the system of New Tuscany, three Manticoran destroyers—"

"Jesus Christ," Innokentiy Arsenovich Kolokoltsov muttered, suppressing an urge to crumple his own copy of the official Manticoran note in his fist. "What was that goddammed idiot *thinking?*"

"Which one?" Nathan MacArtney asked dryly. "Byng? Prime Minister Vézien? That Manticoran klutz—what's-his-name . . . Chatterjee, or whatever? Or one of the other assorted Manticoran idiots involved in handing us something like this?"

"Any of them—*all* of them!" Kolokoltsov snarled. He glared down at the note for a few more incandescent seconds, then flipped it angrily—and contemptuously—onto the deck of the third member of their little group.

"I admit none of them seem to have exactly covered themselves with glory," Omosupe Quartermain observed with a grimace, picking up the discarded note as if he'd deposited a small, several-days-dead rodent in the middle of her blotter, "but I wouldn't have believed even *Manties* could be stupid enough to hand us something like *this!*"

"And why not?" Malachai Abruzzi demanded with an even more disgusted grimace. "They've been getting progressively more uppity for years now—ever since they managed to extort that frigging 'technology embargo' against Haven out of *your* people, Omosupe."

Quartermain gave him a moderately scathing look, but she didn't deny his analysis. None of them did, and Kolokoltsov forced himself to step back and consider the present situation as dispassionately as he could.

None of the four people in Quartermain's office had ever stood for election in his or her life, yet they represented the true government of the Solarian League, and they knew it. Kolokoltsov was the permanent senior undersecretary for foreign affairs. McCartney was the permanent senior undersecretary of the interior; Quartermain was the permanent senior undersecretary of commerce; and Abruzzi was the permanent senior undersecretary of information. The only missing member of the quintet which dominated the Solarian League's sprawling bureaucracy was Agatá Wodoslawski, the permanent senior undersecretary of the treasury, who was out-system at the moment, representing the League at a conference on Beowulf. No doubt she would have expressed her own disgust as vehemently as her colleagues if she'd been present, and equally no doubt, she was going to be more than moderately pissed off at having missed this meeting, Kolokoltsov reflected.

Unfortunately, she was just going to have to live with whatever her four colleagues decided in her absence. And they were going to have to decide *something*, he thought sourly. It came with the territory, since—as every true insider thoroughly understood—it was the five of them who actually ran the Solarian League . . . whatever the majority of the Solarian electorate might fondly imagine. Politicians came and went, changing in an ever shifting shadow play whose sole function was to disguise the fact that the voters' impact on the League's policies ranged somewhere from minute to totally nonexistent.

There were moments, although they were extraordinarily infrequent, when Kolokoltsov almost—*almost*—regretted that fact. It would have been extremely inconvenient for the lifestyle to which he had become accustomed, of course, and the consequences for his personal and family wealth would have been severe. Still, it would have been nice to be part of a governing structure that wielded direct, overt authority rather than skulking about in the shadows. Even if they were extraordinarily lucrative and luxurious shadows.

"All right," he said out loud, and twitched his shoulders in something that wasn't quite a shrug. "We're all agreed they're idiots. The question is what we do about it."

"Shouldn't we have Rajampet—or at least Kingsford—in here for this?" MacArtney asked.

"Rajampet's not available," Kolokoltsov replied. "Or, not for a face-to-face meeting, at any rate. And do you really want to be discussing this with anyone electronically, Nathan?"

"No," MacArtney said after a moment, his expression thoughtful. "No, I don't believe I do, Innokentiy."

"That's what I thought." Kolokoltsov smiled thinly. "We probably could get Kingsford in here if we really wanted to. But given how close all of those 'First Families of Battle Fleet' are, he's not likely to be what you might call a disinterested expert, now is he? Besides, what do you really think he could offer at this point that we don't already have from the damned Manties?"

MacArtney grimaced in understanding. So did the others, although Quartermain's sour expression was even more disgruntled than than anyone else's. She'd spent twenty T-years with the Kalokainos Line before she'd entered the ranks of the federal bureaucracy. The others had spent their professional lives dealing with the often arthritic flow of information over interstellar distances, and all of them had amassed far too much experience of the need to wait for reports and the dispatches to make their lengthy, snaillike way to the League's capital planet. But there was more to it for Quartermain, especially this time around. Her earlier private-sector experience—not to mention her current public-sector responsibilities—had all too often brought her nose-to-nose with the Star Kingdom of Manticore's dominance of the wormhole network that moved both data and commerce about the galaxy. She was more accustomed than the others to dealing with the consequences of how that dominance put Manticore inside the loop of the League's communications and carrying trade, and she didn't like it a bit.

In this instance, however, *all* of them were unpleasantly aware that it was going to take much longer for any message traffic from the League's own representatives in the vicinity of the Talbott Sector to reach them. Which meant that at the moment all they had to go on was the content of the Manticorans' "note" and the sensor data they had provided.

"And how much credence do we want to place in anything the Manties have to say?" Quartermain demanded sourly, as if she'd been following Kolokoltsov's thoughts right along with him.

"Let's not get too paranoid, Omosupe," Abruzzi said dryly. She glowered at him, and he shrugged. "I'm not saying I'd put it past them to . . . tweak the information, let's say. But they're not really idiots, you know. Lunatics, maybe, yes, if they actually mean what they've said in this note, but not idiots. Sooner or later we're going to have access to Byng's version of the data. You know that, and so do they. Do you really think they'd falsify the data they've already given us knowing that eventually we'll be able to check it with our own sources?"

"Sure they would," Quartermain retorted, her dark-complexioned face tight with intense dislike. "Hell, I shouldn't have to tell *you* that, Malachai! You know better than anyone else how much the successful manipulation of a political situation depends on manipulating the public version of information."

"Yes, I do," he agreed. His position made him effectively the League's chief propagandist, and he'd manipulated more than a little information of his own in his time. "But so do the Manties, unless you want to suggest that they haven't built themselves a very effective public relations position right here on Old Terra? And let's not even get into the contacts they have on Beowulf!"

"So?" Quartermain demanded.

"So they're not stupid enough to hand us information that's demonstrably falsified," he said with exaggerated patience. "It's easy enough to produce *selective* data, especially for a PR campaign, and I'm sure they're very well aware of that. But from what Innokentiy's been telling us, they seem to have given us the entire sensor files, from beginning to end, and the complete log of Byng's original communication with the Manties when they arrived in New

Tuscany. They wouldn't have done that if they hadn't known our own people's sensor records and com logs were eventually going to confirm the same information. Not when there's any possibility that the information's going to leak to the newsies."

"Probably not," MacArtney said. "On the other hand, that's one of the things about this entire situation that most bothers me, Malachai."

"What is?" Abruzzi frowned.

"The fact that they haven't already handed this to the newsies," MacArtney explained. "It's obvious from their note that they're pissed off as hell, and, frankly, if the data's accurate, I would be, too, in their place. So why not go straight to the media and try to turn up the pressure on us?"

"Actually," Kolokoltsov said, "I think the fact that they didn't do that may be the one slightly hopeful sign in this entire damned mess. However angry their note may *sound*, they're obviously bending over backward to avoid inflaming the situation any farther."

"You're probably right," Abruzzi said. "Of course, the question is why they might be trying to avoid that."

"Hah!" Quartermain snorted harshly. "I think that's probably simple enough, Malachai. They're accusing an SLN admiral of destroying three of their ships, and they're demanding explanations, 'accountability,' and—by implication, at least—reparations. They're not going to want to go public with something like *that*."

"For someone who doesn't 'want to go public' they seem to be perfectly willing to push things," MacArtney pointed out. "Or did you miss the bit about this admiral of theirs they're sending off to New Tuscany?"

"No, I didn't *miss* it, Nathan." Quartermain and MacArtney had never really cared for each other at the best of times, and the smile she gave him was thin enough to sever his windpipe. "But I also observed that they're sending only six of their own battlecruisers, whereas Byng has *thirteen*. Do you honestly believe they're stupid enough to think a *Solarian* flag officer is going to tamely surrender to a force he outnumbers two-to-one?"

She snorted again, more harshly than before, and MacArtney shook his head.

"I don't know if they are or not, Omosupe. But I do know that the mere fact that they're sending one of their own admirals off to issue what are clearly *demands*, not requests, to a Solarian task force is going to raise the stakes all around. If Byng's already fired on their warships, and if they send still more warships into the area to press demands against him, then they're clearly willing to escalate. Or to risk escalation, at least. And as they've pointed out in their note, what Byng's already done can certainly be construed as an act of war. If they're already making that point to us, and if they're ready to risk escalation, then I'd have to say that I don't see any reason to assume they're not prepared to see all this hit the 'faxes eventually."

His expression was unwontedly serious, Kolokoltsov realized. Then again, he might well be feeling a little excessively gun-shy at the moment. In fact, Kolokoltsov took just a bit of vindictive satisfaction from the thought that MacArtney might be feeling a certain degree of . . . anxiety. As far as Kolokoltsov was concerned, the Office of Frontier Security clearly ought to have come under the authority of the Foreign Ministry, since it spent so much time dealing with star systems which weren't officially part of the League just yet. Unfortunately, the Foreign Ministry had lost that particular fight long, long ago, and OFS was officially part of the Interior Ministry. He could see the logic, even if he didn't much care for it, since like the Gendarmerie—which was also part of the Interior Ministry—Frontier Security was effectively an internal security agency of the League.

And at this particular moment, that wasn't necessarily such a bad thing in Innokentiy Kolokoltsov's considered opinion, either, given the hullabaloo over that business in Monica. Which, now that he thought about it, probably also helped to explain why Quartermain was even more pissed than usual where Manticore was concerned. The revelations about Technodyne and its collusion with Mesa had quite a few of her colleagues over at Commerce all hot and bothered. Attorney General Brangwen Ronayne had actually had to indict several people, and that was always messy. After all, one never knew when one of those under indictment was going to turn out to have embarrassing connections to one's self or other members of one's ministry. The folks over at Justice would do what they could, of course, but Ronayne wasn't really the sharpest stylus in the box. There was always the distinct possibility that something might slip past her, or even evade Abruzzi and make its way into the public datanets, with potentially . . . unpleasant consequences even for a permanent senior undersecretary.

Still, those occasional teapot tempests were a fact of life in the League. They were *going* to happen from time to time, and MacArtney and Quartermain were just going to have to suck it up and get on with business.

"As I say," he said just a bit loudly, retaking control of the conversation, "the fact that they haven't said anything to the newsies yet probably indicates one of two things. Either, as Omosupe says, they're trying to avoid pumping any hydrogen into the fire because of its potential for blowing up in their faces, or else they're trying to avoid pumping any hydrogen into the fire because what they really want is to get this whole thing resolved before the public ever finds out about it. In fact, those two possibilities aren't necessarily mutually exclusive, now are they?"

"Not so far, at any rate," MacArtney replied. "But if there's another exchange of fire, or if Byng tells this Admiral Gold Peak to kiss his arse, that could change."

"Oh, come on, Nathan!" Abruzzi snorted. "You know Omosupe and I don't always see eye-to-eye, but let's be realistic here. It's obvious Byng is an idiot, all right? Let's be honest among ourselves. Anyone who fires on warships just sitting there in a parking orbit without even having their wedges on line is clearly a nut job, although I'm sure that if our good friend Admiral Kingsford were here he'd find some way to explain this whole thing away as a completely reasonable action. Obviously it couldn't *possibly* have been the fault of one of his Battle Fleet friends or relations, could it?"

He rolled his eyes expressively. Malachai Abruzzi was not among the Navy's greatest admirers.

"But unlike Kingsford or Rajampet, *we're* not handicapped by having to defend Byng's actions, so why don't we go ahead and acknowledge, just among ourselves, that he overreacted and killed a bunch of Manties he didn't have to kill?"

He looked around at the others' faces for a moment, then shrugged.

"All right, so the Manties are pissed off. Well, that's probably not all that unreasonable of them, either. But however pissed off they may be, they aren't really going to open fire on a Solarian task force which, as Omosupe's just pointed out, outnumbers them two-to-one. So what they're actually doing is basically running a bluff. Or, more likely, posturing. They may be prepared to 'demand' that Byng stand down and submit to some sort of *Manty* investigation, but they know damned well they aren't going to get anything remotely like that. So what they're really hoping for is that Byng will settle for effectively flipping them off, then pull out of New Tuscany and let them claim that they 'ran him out of town' for his high-handed actions."

"And the reason they'll do that is exactly what, Malachai?" MacArtney inquired.

"Because they need to do it for domestic consumption." Abruzzi shrugged again. "Trust me, I know how this sort of thing works. They've got three dead destroyers, they've been fighting a war for twenty-odd T-years, and they've just finished getting their asses kicked when the Havenites hit their home star system. They know as well as we do that even if they hadn't taken any losses at all from the 'Battle of Manticore,' they couldn't possibly take on the *Solarian League Navy*. But they also know their domestic morale has just been shot right in the head . . . and that the loss of three more destroyers—especially if it looks like the opening step in getting the *League* added to their enemies—is only going to hit it again. So they issue these incredibly unrealistic demands to us here in Chicago, and to Byng at New Tuscany, in order to show their own domestic newsies what big brass balls they've got. And then, when Byng basically ignores them and sails back to Meyers in his own good time, they trumpet that the big, bad Sollies have backed down. They tell their own public that the League's cut and run and that, purely in a spirit of magnanimity, Queen Elizabeth has decided to exercise moderation and settle for a diplomatic conclusion to the entire affair."

He shrugged.

"To be honest, they almost certainly realize that they've got enough economic clout that we'll decide to offer reparations—pay them off out of petty cash so they'll go away and leave us alone—just so we can get on with moving our commerce through their wormhole network. The bottom line is that it's no skin off our noses if we *offer* reparations as long as we make it clear that it's totally voluntary on our part and that we completely reject their right to press any *demands* against us. They get a settlement they can wave under their public's nose to prove how resolute they were, and *we* avoid establishing any actual diplomatic or military precedents that might come home to bite us on the arse later."

Kolokoltsov looked at him with a thoughtful frown. It was entirely possible that Abruzzi was on to something, he reflected. That particular explanation of what the Manties were up to hadn't occurred to him, of course. Not immediately, at least. But looked at logically, especially in light of the hammering they'd reportedly taken from the Havenites barely four months ago, there was absolutely no way they could really be seeking some sort of eyeball-to-eyeball confrontation with the *SLN*. He should have seen that for himself, but unlike Abruzzi, he wasn't accustomed to thinking in terms of massaging public opinion or how to shore up what had to be a badly battered civilian morale.

"I'm not so sure about that," MacArtney said with a mulish grimace. "They didn't exactly avoid an incident at Monica, now did they?"

"Maybe not," Abruzzi conceded. "On the other hand, that was *before* the Battle of Manticore, wasn't it? And that captain of theirs—what's-his-name . . . Terekhov—is obviously as big a lunatic as Byng! The fact that he dragged them into what *could* have been a direct confrontation with the League doesn't mean they're stupid enough to *want* to go there. For that matter, they've got to be aware that they just finished dodging that particular pulser dart. Which is going to make them even less eager to run straight back into our line of fire."

"All of this is very interesting," Quartermain said. "But it doesn't change the fact that we've got to decide what to do about this note of theirs."

"No, it doesn't," Kolokoltsov agreed. "But it does suggest that there's no reason we have to fall all over ourselves responding to it. In fact, it may just suggest that there are some very valid reasons for us to to deal with this in a leisurely, orderly fashion. And, of course, spend a little effort depressing any pretensions of grandeur on their part along the way."

Quartermain looked noticeably more cheerful at that, he noticed, and suppressed a temptation to smile at her sheer predictability.

"As a matter of fact," he continued, "this may turn out to be useful to us." Abruzzi and MacArtney both looked a bit puzzled, and this time he let a little of his smile show. "I think our friends in Manticore have been getting just a little too full of themselves," he went on. "They got away with demanding that technology embargo against the Havenites. They've gotten away with raising their Junction fees across the board to help pay for their damned war. They've just finished dividing the Silesian Confederacy right down the middle with the Andermani. And they've just finished annexing the entire Talbott Sector *and* shooting up the entire Monican Navy, not to mention turning the League into the villain of the piece in Monica and the Talbott Sector. They must feel like they've been on a roll, and I think it may be time for us to remind them that they're actually only a very tiny fish in a really big pond."

"And that we're the shark in the deep end," Quartermain agreed with an unpleasant smile of her own.

"More or less." Kolokoltsov nodded. "It's bad enough that the accidents of astrophysics give such a pissant little 'Star Kingdom' so much economic clout. We don't need them deciding they've got enough *military* clout that they can rattle their battle fleet under our nose and expect us to automatically cave in to whatever they decide to demand from us next time."

"Don't you think it might be a good idea to talk to Rajampet before we make our minds up to tell them to pound sand?" MacArtney inquired mildly.

"Oh, I think it's a very good idea to talk to Rajampet," Kolokoltsov agreed. "And I'm not suggesting that we tell them to 'pound sand,' although I must admit the idea has a certain attractiveness." MacArtney cocked an eyebrow at him, and he shrugged. "All I'm suggesting at this point is that we refuse to fall all over ourselves responding to them. We may even decide to give them a little bit of what they want, in the end, exactly the way Malachai's been suggesting. But, in the long run, I think it's more important that we make it clear to them who the big dog really is. We'll get around to handling this on *our* timetable, not theirs. And if they don't like it . . ."

He let his voice trail off, and shrugged.

"Ah, there you are, Innokentiy!" Marcelito Roelas y Valiente's smile was a bit more restrained than usual, Kolokoltsov noticed as he stepped into the Foreign Minister's office.

"I'm sorry I didn't get back to you sooner, Minister," he said gravely, crossing to Roelas y Valiente's desk. He seated himself without invitation, in the same chair Carmichael had occupied earlier that morning, and Roelas y Valiente leaned back in his own chair.

"As I told you I expected it to earlier, Sir," Kolokoltsov continued, "it took a little time to consult with my colleagues in the other ministries. Obviously, we needed to consider this matter very carefully before we could feel comfortable that we were in a position to make any useful policy recommendations. Especially in the case of an incident with so much potential for setting what could be extraordinarily unfortunate precedents."

"Of course," Roelas y Valiente agreed with a sober smile.

That smile didn't fool Kolokoltsov any more than it fooled Roelas y Valiente himself.

Kolokoltsov would literally have found it difficult to remember (impossible, really, without consulting the archives) how many foreign ministers had come and gone during his own tenure. Given the number of political factions and "parties" in the Assembly, it was extraordinarily difficult for any politician to forge a lasting majority at the federal level. The fact that everyone knew that any government could have only the appearance of actual power meant there was really very little reason to form lasting political alliances. It wasn't as if the continuity of political officeholders was going to have any real effect on the League's policies, yet everyone wanted his own shot at holding federal office. Status wasn't necessarily the same thing as power, and a stint as a League cabinet minister was considered a valuable resume entry when one returned to one's home system and ran for an office that really possessed actual power.

All of that combined to explain why most premierships lasted less than a single T-year before the current prime minister was turned out and replaced by someone else—who, of course, had to dole out cabinet positions all over again. Which was why Kolokoltsov had so much trouble remembering the faces of all the men and women who'd officially headed his ministry over the years. All of them—including Roelas y Valiente—had understood who truly made the League's policy, just as all of them—including Roelas y Valiente—had understood why that was and how the game was played. But Roelas y Valiente resented it more than most of the others had.

*Which doesn't mean he thinks there's any way to change the rule book,* Kolokoltsov thought, and felt a moment of something almost like regret. But *he* wasn't the one who'd deliberately created a constitution, all those centuries ago, which had precluded the real possibility of any strong central government. *He* wasn't the one who'd created a system in which the permanent bureaucracies had been forced to assume the roles (and the power which went with them) of policy-setters and decision-makers if the Solarian League was going to have any sort of administrative continuity.

*But at least we can give him an illusion of authority*, the permanent senior undersecretary bought almost compassionately. *As long as he's willing to* admit *that it* is *an illusion, anyway.*

"We've considered at some length, Sir," he said, "and it's our opinion that this is a time to exercise restraint and calm. What we'd recommend, Minister, is that—"

# Chapter Forty-Eight

"YOU'RE PUTTING ME ON," Admiral Karl-Heinz Thimár said.

"No, Karl-Heinz, I'm not," Fleet Admiral Winston Kingsford replied, sitting back in his chair and frowning at the commanding officer of the Solarian League Navy's Office of Naval Intelligence.

"You're *serious*," Thimár said almost wonderingly, as if he found that difficult to credit, and Kingsford's frown deepened.

"I'm sorry if you find this humorous," he said. "Under the circumstances, though, I'd appreciate it if you could find the time to give at least a little personal attention to the problem."

Thimár's face stiffened, and a slight flush stained his cheekbones. Anger flickered at the backs of his eyes, and his jaw muscles tightened, but he sat back in his own chair and nodded.

It was a bit jerky, that nod, but Kingsford decided to let that pass. He'd made his point, after all, and there was no need to rub the other man's nose in it. Especially because despite the fact of his own seniority as the commanding officer of Battle Fleet, Kingsford wasn't blind to how high Thimár's family connections reached in the Byzantine world of the Solarian League Navy's command structure.

"Thank you," he said rather more warmly, and produced a wry smile. "And, believe me, Karl-Heinz, I found it just about as hard to believe as you did when they first sprang it on me, too."

"Yes, Sir." Thimár nodded again, and this time his expression was thoughtful.

"All right." Kingsford let his chair come back upright with an air of briskness. "I haven't had an opportunity to thoroughly review the data myself, but I've skimmed the summary and read the 'note' that came along with it, and I find myself pretty much in agreement with our civilian 'colleagues' . . . even if the assholes *didn't* even do us the courtesy of mentioning it to us before they settled on 'our' response."

He grimaced.

"I don't think the Manties would have given this to us in the first place if it wasn't going to show what their note already says happened," he continued. "Kolokoltsov and the others want us to analyze it thoroughly, anyway, of course—give them our independent assessment of its reliability and implications—but I don't think they expect us to find any real surprises. For that matter, *I* don't expect us to find any. But it's also our best chance to figure out what the hell Josef thinks he's doing out there, and it's always possible the Manties have slipped up and let something useful get past them."

Thimár started to say something, then visibly stopped himself, and nodded once again.

"To be honest," Kingsford continued, "what I'm most concerned about is the potential for setting an unfortunate precedent. I don't think the Navy wants to find itself with pissant neobarb navies thinking they can get into the habit of popping out of the underbrush to make 'demands' on us. If this looks likely to head anywhere in *that* direction, we may just need to step on it—hard. In that respect, at least, I think Kolokoltsov has an excellent point. And so does Rajani."

Thimár nodded again, recognizing an oblique instruction when he heard it.

Fleet Admiral Rajampet Kaushal Rajani was the Solarian League Navy's chief of naval operations. In theory, that made him merely the uniformed commander of both Battle Fleet and Frontier Fleet, as Minister of Defense Taketomo Kunimichi's deputy. In fact, however, Taketomo's real command authority was sharply circumscribed (despite the fact that he himself was a retired admiral), and since Battle Fleet was the senior of the SLN's two branches, Rajampet was the *de facto* Defense Minister.

On the other hand, even Rajampet's actual, direct authority

over Battle Fleet and Frontier Fleet was, itself, largely illusory. In no small part, that was because his time was too occupied with the day-to-day affairs of keeping the entire Ministry of Defense running to act as any sort of genuine commander in chief. In addition, however, there was the minor fact that over the centuries Battle Fleet and Frontier Fleet had each become its own separate empire, currently ruled over by Kingsford and Fleet Admiral Engracia Alonso y Yáñez, the CO of Frontier Fleet, respectively. Both of them were much too jealous of their own prerogatives to surrender any of them—or any true authority—to Rajampet. Especially not if giving up any of those prerogatives might reduce their own commands' slices of the funding pie.

Some navies' CNOs might have resented that attitude on the part of their uniformed subordinates. Some might even have attempted to do something about it. But the force of precedent had set iron hard over the centuries, and Rajampet had always been more of an administrator than a fleet commander, anyway. He was a hundred and twenty-three T-years old, one of the very first wave of first-generation prolong recipients, and he hadn't held a space-going command in over fifty years, so it was entirely possible—even likely—that he didn't resent it at all. But that didn't mean he was completely out of the loop. Thimár knew that . . . just as he knew that Kingsford's last remark had been deliberately intended to remind him of it.

"You know," he said after a moment, "I never have really understood why Josef accepted that command in the first place. I mean, *Frontier Fleet?*" He shook his head. "That's just so *wrong*, somehow."

Kingsford snorted in amused agreement, but he also shrugged.

"Don't ask me," he said. "As far as I know, that was Rajani's idea. For that matter, it could actually have come from Takemoto, himself. You'd probably have a better chance of finding out by asking Karlotte."

Thimár looked at him for a second or so, then decided Kingsford was telling him the truth. Which only made the entire question even more perplexing, and—particularly as ONI's commanding officer—he found that irritating as hell. He supposed Kingsford was right. It would take months for him to get any letters back from his cousin, but Karlotte's position as Byng's chief of staff probably did put her in the best position to answer his question.

*And maybe, while she's at it, she can explain to me just what the* hell *Josef thought he was doing blowing three Manty destroyers out of space*, he thought rather more grimly. *Not that the irritating bastards didn't have it coming, likely as not. But still . . .*

He hid a mental grimace. Without any way to ask Karlotte—or Byng—what the hell had really happened, all they could do was look at the Manties' so-called data. Not that it was particularly probable that the Manties would have handed it over to Roelas y Valiente in the first place if they'd thought it was likely to give them any *useful* information. Still, forewarned was forearmed, and all that. And they might need all of the forewarning they could get to tidy *this* one up before it splashed all over everyone.

"Anyway," Kingsford said, flipping the chip folio across his desk, "here it is. Go analyze away. I'd like to hear something back in a day or two."

"So, Irene, what do *you* make of all this?" Captain Daud ibn Mamoun al-Fanudahi asked casually as he seated himself beside Captain Irene Teague in the Anchor Lounge, the Navy Building's 0-6 dining room, and Teague glanced at him sharply.

The Anchor Lounge was reserved solely for Navy captains, although the occasional, particularly audacious Marine colonel might occasionally invade its sacred precincts, and it was a very nice dining room, indeed. Far short of the sybaritic luxury of the flag officers' dining room, of course, but much more magnificent than mere commanders or lieutenants (or Marine majors) were likely ever to see. And, because it was located in the Navy Building, it was much less uncommon to see Battle Fleet and Frontier Fleet officers rubbing elbows here, as it were. Officially, it was even encouraged, since they were all members of the same Navy. Unofficially, it was extraordinarily rare, even here, for officers in the Solarian League Navy's competing branches to actually seek out one another. It simply wasn't done.

Al-Fanudahi and Teague were something of a special case, however. Although he came from an old and well respected Battle Fleet family while Teague was equally well connected in *Frontier Fleet*, they both worked (theoretically together) under Admiral Cheng Hai-shwun in the Office of Operational Analysis. Of course, the majority of the SLN's officers still wouldn't have socialized with someone from the wrong side of the Battle Fleet-Frontier Fleet dividing line, and Teague found herself rather wishing that al-Fanudahi hadn't quite so obviously sought her out in such a public venue.

*The man really is completely tone deaf,* she thought. *Not enough he has to put his own career at risk, now he's got to do the same thing for me!*

She gave him an exasperated look, yet her heart wasn't fully in it. Although *she* (unlike him) was far too politically astute to openly contest official wisdom in some sort of quixotic quest, she rather respected al-Fanudahi's apparent indifference to official displeasure. Of course, he was still only a captain, despite the fact that he was twenty T-years older than she was—and Battle Fleet, at that. So while she was prepared to respect him, she really had very little desire to *emulate* him.

Even though she did find herself quite often in agreement with at least some of his less outrageous theories.

"What do I make of what, Daud?" she asked after a moment.

"Of our latest little tidbit," al-Fanudahi said. "You know, the one from our friends in Manticore."

"I'm not sure this is the best place to be discussing it," she responded a bit pointedly. "This isn't exactly the most secure—"

She broke off as one of the uniformed stewards arrived with her soup course. The steward placed it before her, made sure both her water glass and her glass of iced tea were full, and took al-Fanudahi's order, and Teague found herself hoping that the interruption would distract her politically inept colleague from his current self-destructive hobbyhorse.

Not that she really expected it to happen, of course.

"Oh, come on," he said, confirming the accuracy of her expectations almost before the steward was out of earshot. "You don't really think the entire content of the Manties' note hasn't already hit the grapevine running, do you? I mean, *security,* Irene?"

He snorted and rolled his eyes. Teague glared at him, but then her glare faded just a bit as she recognized the glint of amusement in those same eyes. The rotten bastard was actually *enjoying* himself!

She started to say something tart and pithy, then stopped herself. First, because it was only likely to amuse him even more, given his obviously twisted sense of humor. And, second, because he was right. She had no doubt at all that the information the two of them had been ordered to keep "Most Secret" was all over the Navy Building by now.

*I really ought to shut him up anyway, because I just* know *he's going to say something I don't want anyone thinking I might agree with. On the other hand, he's way senior to me—in fact, he's probably the most senior captain in the entire damned Navy, given how many times he's been passed over for promotion by now. There's no way anybody's going to be able to blame a wet-behind-the-ears young sprout like me just because one of the old sweats she works with decides to bend her ear over lunch.*

*For that matter,* her lips twitched in what could have turned into a smile, *if I let him run on and just nod politely here and there, I can probably convince anybody who's watching us that I wish he'd just take his ridiculous theories and go away.*

"All right." She sighed, dipping her spoon into the lobster bisque in front of her. "Go ahead. I'm not going to be able to stop you, anyway, am I?"

"Probably not," he agreed cheerfully. "So, to repeat my original question, what *do* you make of all this?"

His voice remained as amused as ever, but his eyes had narrowed intently, and she realized he was serious. She gazed at him for a second or two, then swallowed a spoonful of the rich, thick soup and looked back up at him.

"With all due respect, Captain," she said, "one of the things I make of it is that a certain Battle Fleet admiral doesn't have the brains God gave a cockroach."

It was not, she realized, the most respectful possible comment a mere captain might have made about a senior admiral, but she wasn't too worried about that. Given traditional attitudes on both sides of the divide, people probably would have been more surprised if she *hadn't* been disrespectful. Besides, Byng obviously *was* an idiot . . . even if his chief of staff was related to her (and al-Fanudahi's) ultimate boss at ONI.

"I might not have expressed myself quite that, um . . . frankly," al-Fanudahi said with a grin. "Not that I don't think the sentiment was entirely appropriate, of course. But I believe we can both take Byng's less than stellar intellect as a given. I'm more interested in your impressions of the data itself."

"The data itself?" Teague's eyebrows furrowed in genuine surprise. He only nodded, and she considered the question for several seconds, then shrugged.

"It seems fairly straightforward to me, actually," she said finally.

"Something—or some*one*, rather—blew up the New Tuscans' space station, Admiral Byng clearly pani—"

She paused, deciding there were some verbs a Frontier Fleet Captain shouldn't be using about an admiral even if he was a Battle Fleet officer.

"Admiral Byng clearly concluded that the Manties had been responsible for it," she said instead, "and responded to the perceived threat. I wasn't there, of course, but my initial impression is that he responded too quickly and . . . too forcefully, but that's not really my call."

Al-Fanudahi cocked his head, his expression skeptical, and Teague felt the tips of her ears heat. While she was undoubtedly correct that it wasn't her place to make any final judgments on Byng's actions, providing the analysis on which those judgments would be based was *supposed* to be one of Operational Analysis' primary functions. The fact that its analysis was more likely to be used to whitewash someone than to nail actual cases of obvious incompetence was one of those little secrets polite people didn't talk about in public. On the other hand, failing in its responsibility to report unpalatable truths was hardly OpAn's only fault. They were also supposed to be the office which identified and analyzed potential foreign threats or new developments which might require modifications of the SLN's operational doctrine, and they didn't do very much of that, either. In fact, OpAn did a lot less of either of those things than al-Fanudahi—and Teague—thought it ought to be doing, although Teague (unlike al-Fanudahi) wasn't prepared to make her views in that regard officially explicit.

*Not unless I want to spend the next twenty or thirty years as a captain, too, at any rate.*

"That's not what I was talking about, either," the Battle Fleet officer said after a moment. "Or, not directly, anyway."

"Then just what *are* you talking about, Daud?" she demanded.

"They provided us with really good sensor resolution, don't you think?" he responded—rather obliquely, she thought.

"So?"

"I mean, it was *really* good resolution," he pointed out.

Teague sat back in her chair, wondering where he thought he was going with this, and it was his turn to sigh.

"Didn't it occur to you to wonder how they happened to be able to provide us with that kind of data?" he asked.

"No, it didn't." She shrugged. "After all, what diff—"

She broke off abruptly, her eyes widening, and al-Fanudahi nodded. There were very few traces of his earlier humor in his expression now, she noticed.

"I've put their data through the computers half a dozen times," he said, "and it keeps coming out the same way. That's shipboard-quality data. Actually, it's pretty damned good even for first-line shipboard sensors. Better than anything smaller than a battlecruiser—or *maybe* a heavy cruiser—should have been pulling in. So where did they get it?"

Teague said nothing for several seconds, then shook herself and swallowed a couple of more spoonfuls of her rapidly cooling bisque. She was only buying time, and she knew he knew it, but he waited patiently, anyway.

"I don't know," she admitted finally. "Are you thinking that maybe it's *too* good? That the quality of the data is evidence it's actually a fake?"

"No, it's not a fake," he said flatly. "No way. They'd have to know we're going to get our own ships' data in the end. If they'd faked it, we'd find out eventually, and I don't think we'd be particularly amused by their little hoax."

"Then . . ." she said slowly.

"Then I only see four real possibilities, Irene." He held up his left hand, counting his points off on its fingers as he made them. "First, the Manties have somehow developed a shipboard sensor that can get this kind of resolution from outside missile range of our ships. Second, the Manties have some sort of recon platform whose stealth is so good that none of our sensor crews noticed it was there even at what must have been point-blank range. Third, they've managed to come up with some kind of stealth so good that they got an entire *starship* that close without anyone noticing. Or, fourth, Admiral Byng opted to blow *three* Manticoran destroyers out of space without warning while allowing a fourth ship that must also have been well inside his missile range to sail merrily on its way. Now, which of those do you think is most likely?"

She felt a distinct sinking sensation as she gazed at him.

"It had to be a recon platform," she said.

"My own conclusion, exactly." He nodded. "But that leads us to another interesting little question. I'm not familiar with any recon platform in our inventory that would have pulled in data this good even if it had been inside *energy* range, must less missile range. Are you?"

"No," she said unhappily.

"I'm trying to remind myself that we still don't have anything from Byng," al-Fanudahi said. "Maybe he did pick up something and then went ahead and fired anyway, but I find that difficult to believe even of him. And here's another interesting little point to consider. Even if it was a remote platform, there had to be someone out there monitoring its take. I'm inclined to wonder if even Josef Byng—and, by the way, I think you were doing cockroaches a disservice there a minute ago—would be stupid enough to kill three destroyers and their entire crews while he knew he was on camera!"

"Which suggests the Manties do have shipboard stealth capability good enough that he never realized this Chatterjee had deployed at least one trailer on his way in," she said even more unhappily.

"That's exactly what it suggests to *me*, at any rate," he agreed.

"Crap," she said very, very softly, looking down at her lobster bisque and suddenly not feeling very hungry after all.

"Listen, Irene," he said equally quietly, "I know you've been being careful to keep your mouth shut, but I also know you have a working brain, unlike altogether too many of our esteemed colleagues. You've had your own suspicions about all of those 'ridiculous' reports from the SDF observers, haven't you?"

She looked back at him, unwilling to confirm his suspicions even now, but she knew he saw the truth in her eyes, and he nodded.

"What I thought," he said. Then he smiled crookedly. "Don't worry. I'm not about to invite you to commit professional suicide by suddenly announcing that you, too, believe that every spacer in the Manticoran Navy is three meters tall, impervious to pulser fire, and able to snatch speeding missiles out of space in his bare teeth. I've had a little experience myself with the consequences of being 'overly credulous' and 'alarmist.' In fact, Admiral Thimár himself saw fit to 'counsel me' on my obviously distorted pet theories. But look at this data. No, it's not a smoking gun, not conclusive proof, but the implications are there, aren't they? The Manties have to have a significantly more capable level of technology than anyone here on Old Terra is willing to even consider. For that matter, I'm coming to the suspicion that at least some of their toys aren't just better than most people think they have but actually are better than *ours* are, as well. When you couple that with some of the reports about their missile ranges at Monica, or the ridiculous salvo sizes some of the system-defense force observers say they can generate . . ."

He shook his head, and his eyes were dark. Worried.

"They can't *all* be true," she protested quietly. "The rumors, I mean. Manticore's only one tiny little star system, Daud! All right, so it's a *rich* little star system, and it's got a hell of a lot bigger navy than anybody else its size. But it's still *one* star system, however many other systems it may be in the process of annexing. Are you seriously suggesting that they've managed somehow to put together a better, more effective R and D establishment than the entire *Solarian League*?"

"They don't have to have done that," he said flatly. "The *League* could be ahead of them clear across the board, but that doesn't mean the *Navy* is. These people have been fighting a war for better than twenty T-years, and they started their military buildup way the hell before that. You think maybe they could have been working really hard on weapons R and D in the process? That maybe, unlike us, they've been looking at real combat reports, instead of analyses of training simulations where the 'secret details' get leaked to all the senior participants before they even begin the exercise? That, unlike us, the people building *their* weapons and evaluating *their* combat doctrines might once have heard of a gentleman named Charles Darwin? Compared to someone who's been fighting for his life for two decades, we're *soft*, Irene—soft, underprepared, and complacent."

"And even assuming you're right, just what the hell do you expect *me* to do about it?" she demanded, her voice suddenly harsh with mingled anger, frustration, and fear. Not just fear for the consequences to her career, either. Not anymore.

"At this particular moment?" He looked at her levelly for a heart-beat or two, then his nostrils flared. "At this particular moment, I don't expect you to do anything except what you've been doing. Hell, for that matter *I* don't propose to make the full extent of my 'alarmist conclusions' part of my official report. Even if I did, it would never get past Cheng. And if it miraculously got past *him* somehow, you know damned well that *Thimár* would kill it. Or

Kingsford himself, for that matter. It's too far outside the received wisdom. I'm going to go ahead and raise the question of exactly what sort of platform could have gathered the data, but I'm not going to offer any conclusions about it. If someone decides to ask me about it, I'll tell them what I think, but, frankly, I hope they won't. Because without a lot more to go on than the inferences I've been able to draw, I'll never convince the powers that be that I'm not crazy. And if they decide I'm crazy, they'll shit-can my arse so fast my head will spin, which means I'll be able to accomplish exactly nothing if the wheels do come off.

"But what I *do* want you to do is to keep your eyes and your mind open. I've got a strong suspicion that there are even more of those system-defense observer reports out there than ever made it to us in the first place. Unless I'm mistaken, they've been being tossed as 'obvious nonsense' somewhere between their originators and us. But if you and I both start very quietly looking around, maybe we'll be able to turn some of them up. And maybe, if we manage that, we'll be able to start drawing at least some of the conclusions we're going to need if the shitstorm hits."

"Surely the Manties aren't that stupid," she said softly, in the tone of someone trying to convince herself. "I mean, no matter how many technological advantages they may have, they have to know they can't fight the entire Solarian League and win. Not in the long term. They're just plain not big enough—not even if they make this annexation of Talbott stand up!"

"Maybe they are that stupid, and maybe they aren't," al-Fanudahi replied. "Frankly, though, if they really did send this Admiral Gold Peak off to New Tuscany to press the demands they say they did, I'm not so sure they *aren't* ready to go nose-to-nose with us, however stupid that might be. And even if you're right, even if they can't possibly win in the end—and I'm inclined to think you *are* right about that—God only knows how many thousands of our own people are going to get killed before they lose. Somehow, I don't think that either you or I will sleep too soundly at night if we just sit back and watch it happen. Nobody's going to take any warnings from me seriously at this point, but you and I need to start pulling the truth together now, because if this blows up in our faces, *somebody* is going to need the closest thing to accurate information we can give them. And, who knows? Whoever that 'somebody' is, he may even *realize* he does."

✧   ✧   ✧

"We're coming up on the deployment point now, Commodore."

"Thank you, Captain Jacobi," Commodore Karol Østby replied, nodding to the woman on his com display.

Captain Rachel Jacobi looked like any other merchant service officer, although she might have been just a little young for her current rank. Appearances could be deceiving, however, and not just because of prolong. Rachel Jacobi was even younger for her actual rank than she seemed, not to mention an officer in a navy the rest of the galaxy didn't even know existed . . . yet.

"Bay doors are opening, Sir," another voice said, and Østby turned from his com to look across the cramped bridge at Captain Eric Masters. If Jacobi looked young for her rank, then Masters looked far too senior to be commanding a ship little larger than an old-fashioned frigate, but, again, appearances could be deceiving. Despite her tiny size (she had no flag bridge, and Østby couldn't even fit all of his abbreviated staff onto her command deck) MANS *Chameleon*, Østby's flagship, was something entirely new in the history of galactic warfare. Whether or not she was going to live up to her name and the expectations invested in her remained to be seen . . . and was going to depend very heavily on the actions of Østby and Masters and the rest of *Chameleon*'s small crew.

"My panel shows doors fully open, Commodore," Jacobi said. "Do you confirm?"

"Confirm, Sir," Masters said, and Østby nodded, then looked back at Jacobi.

"We confirm doors fully open, Captain," he said formally.

"In that case, Sir, good hunting."

"Thank you, Captain Jacobi."

Østby nodded to her once more, then turned his command chair to face Masters.

"Anytime you're ready, Captain Masters."

"Yes, Sir." Masters looked at his astrogator and helmsman. "Take us out," he said simply, and *Chameleon* twitched ever so gently as the web of tractor and pressor beams which had held her exactly centered in the freighter *Wallaby*'s cavernous Number Two hold were switched off at last.

A gentle puff of compressed air from the specially modified

thruster packs strapped to her bow sent her drifting backward, without the pyrotechnics of her normal fusion-powered thrusters. That would have been . . . contraindicated inside a ship, Østby thought dryly while he watched the visual display as the hold's bulkheads went sliding by.

It was the first time they'd made an actual combat deployment, but Østby's captains and crews had practiced this same maneuver dozens of times before ever leaving the Mesa System. He had no concern at all about this part of the mission, and his mind strayed ahead to the *rest* of the mission.

*No point worrying about any of that yet*, he told himself firmly. *Not even if you and Topolev did draw the harder target. But at least you didn't have quite as far to go as Colenso and Sung just to get to your objective. Sung won't even be deploying for another week!*

The deployment maneuver took quite a while, but no one was in a tearing hurry, and no one wanted to risk a last-minute, potentially catastrophic accident. *Wallaby* had made her alpha translation thirty minutes ago, and she was still several hours away from the wormhole junction she'd ostensibly come here to transit. At this range, even a fully conventional ship *Chameleon's* size would almost certainly have been invisible even to Manticoran sensor arrays (assuming its skipper was smart enough not to bring up his wedge, at any rate). Not that anyone intended to take any chances.

*Chameleon* slid completely free of *Wallaby*, like an Old Earth shark sliding tail-first from its mother's womb, and the modified packs fell away as the jettisoning charges blew. They disappeared quickly into the Stygian gloom—this far out from the system primary, even the star gleam on *Chameleon's* own flanks was scarcely visible—and Østby continued to watch the visual display as the running light constellations bejeweling the clifflike immensity of the freighter's mammoth hull drew steadily away from them.

"Confirm clean separation, Sir," Masters' astrogator announced.

"Very good. Communications, do we have contact with the rest of the squadron?"

"Yes, Sir. *Ghost* just plugged into the net. Telemetry is up and nominal."

"Very good," Masters repeated, and looked at his executive officer. "Take us into stealth and bring up the spider, Chris," he said.

"Aye, aye, Sir." Commander Christopher Delvecchio punched in a string of commands, then nodded to the astrogator. "Stealth is up and operating. The ship is yours, Astro."

"Aye, aye, Sir. I have the ship," the astrogator responded, and MANS *Chameleon* and her consorts reoriented themselves and began to slowly accelerate, invisible within the concealing cocoon of their stealth fields, towards the primary component of the star system known as Manticore.

# Chapter Forty-Nine

"WELL, IT WOULD APPEAR that our good friends in Chicago aren't in any tearing hurry after all, wouldn't it?"

Elizabeth Winton's tone was caustic enough to make an excellent substitute for lye, Baron Grantville thought.

Not that she didn't have an excellent point.

"They've only had our note for about ten days, Your Majesty," Sir Anthony Langtry pointed out.

He and Grantville sat in comfortable armchairs in Elizabeth's personal office, flanking her deck. They'd both eaten earlier, although each of them had a coffee cup, but the remains of Elizabeth's lunch had just been removed, and she continued to nurse a tankard of beer.

"Sure they have, Tony," she agreed, waving her tankard. "And just how long would it have taken *us* to respond to an official note alleging that we'd killed somebody's spacers with absolutely no provocation? Especially if they'd sent along detailed sensor data of the event . . . and informed us that they were sending a major naval force to find out what the hell happened?"

"Point taken, Your Majesty." Langtry sighed, and Grantville grimaced.

The Queen did have a point. In fact, she had a damned *good* one, he thought glumly. Assuming the League had decided to respond immediately, they could have had a reply back to Manticore at least four T-days ago. And even if they hadn't wanted to make a formal response that quickly, at the very least they could have acknowledged receipt of the note! The Foreign Office had Lyman Carmichael's confirmation of his meeting with Roelas y Valiente, and a memo summarizing the essentially meaningless verbal exchange which had accompanied it. But that was all they had. So far, the Solarian League's government had simply ignored the communication entirely. That could be construed—no doubt with total accuracy, in this case—as a deliberate insult.

"Obviously they're trying to tell us something by their silence," he said, his tone almost as acid as Elizabeth's had been. "Let me see now, what could it possibly be . . . ? That we're too insignificant for them to take seriously? That they'll get around to us in their own good time? That we shouldn't get our hopes up about any willingness on their part to acknowledge Byng's culpability? That it'll be a cold day in hell before *they* admit to any wrongdoing?"

"Try 'all of the above,'" Langtry suggested sourly.

"Well, it's stupid of them, but we can't exactly pretend it's unexpected, can we?" Elizabeth asked.

"No," Grantville sighed.

"Then I think it's probably time we thought about turning up the wick," Elizabeth told him just a bit grimly. He looked at her, and she shrugged. "Don't get me wrong, Willie. This isn't just the famous Winton temper talking, and I'm not eager to be sending them any fresh notes until we've heard back from Mike again. The last thing we need to do is sound like anxious little kids pestering an adult for a response! Besides, I've got a pretty strong suspicion that when we *do* hear from Mike, we're going to have all the justification in the world for sending them an even stiffer follow-up note. But it might just be time to consider going public with this."

"I think Her Majesty has a point, Willie," Langtry said quietly. Grantville switched his gaze to the Foreign Secretary, and Langtry snorted. "I'm no more eager to 'inflame public opinion' than the next man, Willie, but let's face it. As you just said yourself, four days is too long for a simple 'delayed in the mail' explanation. What it is is a calculated insult, for whatever reason they decided to deliver it, and you know how big a part perceptions play in any effective diplomacy." He shook his head. "We can't allow something like this to pass unanswered without convincing them they were right in their obvious belief that they can ignore us until they get around to bullying us into accepting *their* resolution of the problem."

"Agreed," Grantville said after a moment or two of silence. "At the same time, I'm still more than a little anxious over how the Solly media is going to react when they find out about this. Especially if they find out about it as 'unconfirmed allegations' from a bunch of neobarbs they already despise."

"That's going to happen in the end, anyway, Willie," Elizabeth pointed out.

"I know."

Grantville sipped coffee, then put his cup back on the saucer and rubbed an eyebrow in thought. Elizabeth was certainly right about that, he reflected. The first Manticoran reporters had been briefed by the Foreign Office and the Admiralty after they and their editors had agreed to abide by the government's confidentiality request. Legally, Grantville could have invoked the Defense of the Kingdom Act and slapped them with a formal order to keep silent until he told them differently, but that particular clause of the DKA hadn't been invoked by any prime minister in the last sixty T-years. It hadn't had to be, because the Star Kingdom's press knew it had been official policy over almost all of those T-years to be as open as possible in return for reasonable self-restraint on the 'faxes' part. He had no intention of squandering that tradition of goodwill without a damned good reason.

And, so far, the members of the media here in the Star Kingdom who knew anything about it were clearly living up to their end of the bargain. In the meantime, the first of their correspondents would have reached Spindle yesterday aboard an Admiralty dispatch boat. In another couple of weeks, those correspondents' reports would be coming back through the Junction to their editors, and it would be both pointless and wrong to expect their 'faxes not to publish at that point. So . . .

"You're both right," he acknowledged. "I'd like to hold off for a little longer, though. For two reasons. One is that they may actually have sent us a response that just hasn't gotten here yet. But the other, to be frank, has more to do with whacking them harder when we do turn it loose."

"Really?" Elizabeth cocked an eyebrow, and Ariel raised his head on his perch behind her chair. "I think I'm in favor of that," the Queen admitted after a moment, "but I'm not sure I see exactly how we're going to do it."

"I was thinking about that passage from St. Paul, but instead of doing good unto them in order to 'heap coals of fire upon their heads,' I'm in favor of using obvious restraint," Grantville said with a nasty smile. "What I suggest is that we hold off for another four days. That will just happen to have given the Sollies exactly twice as long as they really needed to acknowledge the receipt of our note, and we make exactly that point in our official news release. We explain that we'd delayed making the news public both to give us time to notify the next of kin of Commodore Chatterjee's personnel and to be sure that the Solarian League government had been given ample time to respond to our concerns. Now that they've had twice as long as needed for that, however, we feel no further point can be served by failing to make the news public."

"And waiting that long makes the point that we had a specific delay interval in mind all along," Langtry mused. "We're not just going ahead and calling in the newsies because we're getting nervous about the Sollies' failure to respond."

"Exactly." Grantville nodded with a nasty smile. "Not to mention the fact that, as the real adults of the piece, we gave the petulant, spoiled *children* of the piece extra time before we blew the whistle on them. But, equally as the real adults of the piece, we are not going to allow the spoiled brats to hunker down forever in the corner with their lips poked out while they sulk."

"I like it," Elizabeth said after considering for a moment or two, and her answering smile was even nastier than Grantville's had been.

She sat for a moment longer, then took another sip from her tankard and tipped her chair back.

"All right. Now that we've got that out of the way, what do we want to do about Cathy Montaigne's suggestion that we beef up Torch's security? To be honest, I think there's a lot of merit to the idea, and not just because Barregos and Rozsak got hammered so hard. There're some good PR possibilities here, not to mention the possibility of easing into a closer relationship with the Maya Sector's navy, and it can't hurt where Erewhon's concerned, either. So—"

"I can't say your report is very cheerful reading, Michelle," Augustus Khumalo said heavily. "On the other hand, I completely endorse all of your actions."

"I'm glad to hear that, Sir," Michelle Henke said sincerely. She and Khumalo sat facing one another in comfortable armchairs in his day cabin aboard *Hercules*, nursing large snifters of excellent brandy. At the moment, Michelle was far more grateful than usual for the way the brandy's comforting warmth slid down her throat like thick, honeyed fire.

*And I damned well deserve it, too*, she thought, allowing herself another sip. *Maybe not for what happened at New Tuscany, but definitely for putting up with Baroness Medusa's tame newsies!*

Actually, she knew, the newsies in question—Marguerite Attunga of the Manticoran News Service, Incorporated; Efron Imbar of Star Kingdom News; and Consuela Redondo of the Sphinx News Association—had been remarkably gentle with her. None of them had been gauche enough to say so, but it was obvious to her that they and their editors back home had been very carefully briefed before they were allowed in on what promised to be one of the biggest news stories in the Star Kingdom's history.

Especially now that things had just finished going so badly south in New Tuscany.

Unfortunately, they were still newsies, they still had their job to do, however nonadversarial about it they'd been this time, and she still hated sitting in front of their cameras and knowing that the entire Star Kingdom would be seeing and hearing her responses to their questions. It wasn't *nervousness*—or she didn't think it was, at least. Or maybe it was, just not on a personal level. What really worried her, she admitted finally, was that she'd say or do something wrong, and the combination of her naval rank and her proximity to the throne would elevate whatever mistake she made to the level of catastrophe.

"I agree that there's nothing particularly cheerful about the situation, Sir," she continued out loud after a moment, shaking off—mostly—her reflections about potential media disasters with her name on them. "In fact, I'm beginning to wonder if it was such a good idea to send *Reprise* off to Meyers before we knew exactly what was going to happen at New Tuscany. Especially since I didn't manage to keep the Sollies from getting a dispatch boat out."

"That decision was Baroness Medusa's . . . and mine," Khumalo told her. "As I recall, you were against it at the time, too."

"Yes, Sir, but not for exactly the same reasons I'm regretting it now. I didn't want to telegraph anything to Frontier Security and Frontier Fleet. I wasn't worried about one of our ships sailing into a broadside of missiles the instant she showed her face!"

"Commander Denton is a competent, conscientious officer, and no fool," Khumalo pointed out. "I think he demonstrated that pretty clearly in Pequod, and he'll follow the established protocols. Before *Reprise* ever gets into range of any Solarian ship, Mr. O'Shaughnessy will have delivered Baroness Medusa's note via com. And Commander Denton will also, by my specific instruction, carry out a Ghost Rider sweep of the system before *Reprise* even squawks her transponder. I authorized him to use his discretion if he happened to spot anything of concern, and he is specifically directed to remain outside weapons range of any Solarian unit until and unless Commissioner Verrochio has guaranteed our envoy's safety as per the relevant interstellar law."

"I know, Sir." Michelle's expression was grim. "What concerns me is that Verrochio might *give* that guarantee, then have *Reprise* blown out of space, anyway."

Despite everything that had already happened, Khumalo looked shocked, and Michelle smiled tightly at him.

"Mr. Van Dort and Commodore Terekhov and I have discussed this situation at some length, Sir. It's evident to us from what Vézien and his people had to say that we're looking at a very complex, very expensive, and extremely far-reaching operation. I'd call it a conspiracy, except that it looks very much to us—to me—as if some outside party is pulling all the strings and most of the people actually carrying out the dirty work don't have any clue what the ultimate objective is. They may be *conspirators*, but they're not part of the *same* conspiracy as the puppeteer behind them, if you see what I mean."

"And all three of you believe the 'puppeteer' is Manpower?"

"We do, Sir."

"Well, so do Baroness Medusa and I," Khumalo told her, and smiled faintly at her surprised expression. "As I say, we've both read your report already, and we find ourselves in fundamental agreement with your conclusions. And, like you, we're deeply concerned about the apparent scope of Manpower's intentions and ambitions. It's completely outside anything we would have expected out of them, even after the business with Monica and Nordbrandt. And I find the degree of reach and influence required to position Byng as disturbing as you do. I think you're absolutely right; they *are* acting as if they thought they were a star nation in their own right."

"What's even more worrisome to me, especially where *Reprise* is concerned," Michelle said, "is that they'd managed to maneuver an officer like Byng—one who would pull the trigger without even blinking when they presented the right scenario—into a critical position in New Tuscany. If they've done the same thing in Meyers, and if there's another Anisimovna placed to provide the right stimulus at the right moment, some 'out-of-control' Solly officer may go ahead and blow Denton away whatever guarantees Verrochio may have given. After all, they've already got two incidents. Why shouldn't they go for three?"

"Now *that* is an unpleasant thought," Khumalo said slowly. "Do you think Verrochio would be in on it?"

"I genuinely don't have a clue what to think about that particular aspect, Sir." Michelle shook her head. "We know he was more or less in their pocket last time around, so I don't see any reason to assume he's going to be pure as the driven snow *this* time. By the same token, though, they had Vézien at least as firmly in their pocket this time around, and they obviously cut him entirely out of the loop when they punched Byng's buttons. I'd say they've shown a remarkably good grasp of what they could reasonably—and I use the term loosely—convince one of their tools to do. If they need something they're pretty sure she won't be willing to do, then they manipulate the situation without warning her until they get it. That's what happened to Vézien. I don't doubt that he was entirely prepared for an incident between one or more of Byng's ships and our vessels, and I don't think he would have shed any tears about getting quite a few of our people killed. But there was no way he expected the incident to happen right there in the middle of New Tuscany, and he certainly never counted on having *Giselle* blown up to provide the necessary spark! Besides, he knows what the Star Kingdom's policy has always been when someone fires on one of our ships without provocation. Trust me, he didn't plan on doing the firing himself, and he *sure* as hell didn't plan on its happening right on his doorstep. So I don't see any reason to assume Verrochio would have to know what's supposed to happen if they really have arranged a Byng Mark Two in Meyers."

"Wonderful," Khumalo sighed.

"I'm afraid it gets even better, Sir. All they managed to give Byng was battlecruisers. This Admiral Crandall they were telling Vézien about apparently has a lot more than that under her command."

"Do you think 'Admiral Crandall' really even exists?"

"That's a good question," Michelle admitted. "Anisimovna told Vézien and the other New Tuscans about Crandall, but no one on the planet ever actually saw her or any of her ships. Given what happened to *Giselle*, it's pretty evident Anisimovna wouldn't have suffered any qualms of conscience over lying to them about a little thing like fifty or sixty superdreadnoughts. And I'd really like to think that it's one thing to get a Battle Fleet admiral with a pathological hatred for all things Manticoran assigned to a Frontier Fleet command but another thing entirely to get an entire fleet of Battle Fleet ships of the wall maneuvered this far out into the boonies. If Manpower has *that* kind of reach, if it can really move task groups and battle fleets around like chessmen or checkers, we've obviously been underestimating the hell out of them for a long, long time. And if that's true, who knows what *else* the bastards are up to?"

The two of them looked at one another unhappily for several silent minutes, then Khumalo sighed again, heavily. He took a generous sip of brandy, shook his head, and gave her a crooked smile.

"You and Aivars do have a way of brightening up my days, don't you, Milady?"

"I wouldn't say we do it on *purpose*, Sir," Michelle replied with an answering smile.

"I realize that. In fact, that's part of what makes it so . . . ironic." Michelle cocked an eyebrow at him, and he chuckled and a bit sourly. "For quite some time, I was convinced I'd been sent out here—and left here—because the Cluster was absolutely the lowest possible priority for the Admiralty. In fact, to be honest, I still cherish rather strong suspicions in that direction."

He smiled more warmly at her, and she hoped she'd managed to conceal her surprise at hearing him say that. The fact that it accorded well with her own view of the situation made it even more remarkable that he'd brought it up. And especially that he'd done it with so little evident bitterness.

"In fairness," he continued, "I'm relatively sure the Janacek Admiralty sent me out here because of my connections with the Conservative Association and the fact that I'm related, although rather more distantly than you are, to the Queen. It put someone they considered 'safe' out here, and my connection to the Dynasty didn't hurt any in terms of local prestige. But they never showed any interest in providing Talbott Station with the ships required to provide any sort of real security in such a large volume of space. It was one of those 'file and forget' sorts of situations.

"Then the new Government came in, and I wondered how long I'd stay here until I got yanked back home. Politics being politics, I really didn't expect to be left out here for long, and it got more than a little unpleasant waiting for the ax to fall. But it became pretty evident that the Grantville Government had assigned a lower priority to Talbott than to Silesia, and, again, I couldn't really argue on any logical basis. So, here I sat in a humdrum, secondary—or even tertiary—assignment out in the back of beyond, with the firm expectation that the most exciting thing likely to happen was the chance to chase down an occasional pirate, while I waited to be relieved and banished to half-pay.

"Obviously," he said dryly, "that's changed."

"I think we might both safely agree that that's an accurate statement, Sir," Michelle said. "And, if you'll forgive me, and since you've been so frank and open with me, I'd like to apologize to you."

He quirked an eyebrow, and she shrugged.

"I'm afraid my evaluation of why you were out here was pretty close to your own, Sir," she admitted. "That's what I want to apologize for, because even if the logic that got you out here in the first place was exactly what you've just described, I believe you've amply demonstrated that it was a damned good thing you were here."

She held his eyes, letting him see the sincerity in her own, and, after a moment, he nodded.

"Thank you," he said. "And there was no need to apologize. Not when I'm pretty sure you were right all along."

There was another moment of silence, then he shook himself.

"Getting back to the matter of the hypothetical Admiral Crandall," he said in a determinedly lighter tone, "I have to say I'm rather relieved by one of the dispatches I received day before yesterday."

"May I ask which dispatch that may have been, Sir?"

"Yes, you may. That, after all,"—this time the smile he gave her was suspiciously like a grin—"was the reason I casually worked mention of it into the conversation, Admiral Gold Peak."

"Indeed, Admiral Khumalo?" she responded, raising her brandy snifter in a small salute.

"Indeed," he replied. Then he sobered a bit. "The dispatch in question informed me that, despite whatever is or isn't going on closer to home, Admiral Oversteegen and his squadron will still be arriving here in Spindle. In fact, I expect him within the next twelve to fifteen T-days."

"Thank God!" Michelle said with quietly intense sincerity.

"I agree. It's taken some time for them to feel comfortable enough back home after the Battle of Manticore to go ahead and release him, and I still don't have an *exact* projected arrival date, but he's definitely in the pipeline. I understand he'll be bringing another squadron of *Saganami-Cs* with him, as well, and I'm sure we'll all be relieved to see them."

"Based on the Sollies' performance at New Tuscany, and what my people were able to see of their hardware on the prize ships, I'd say that with Michael and another squadron of the *Charlies* we ought to be able to handle just about anything below the wall they're likely to throw our way."

"I'm sure you would," Khumalo said even more soberly. "But I'm afraid that's sort of the point, isn't it? *I'm* not too worried about anything *below* the wall, either."

"What do you think happened at New Tuscany?" Lieutenant Aphrodite Jackson, HMS *Reprise*'s electronic warfare officer, asked quietly.

Lieutenant Heather McGill, the destroyer's tactical officer, looked up from her book reader. She and Jackson were off duty, seated in *Reprise*'s wardroom. At the moment, the EWO's hands were busy building a sandwich out of the ingredients she'd collected from the mid-rats laid out as a buffet, and Heather smiled slightly. Promotions came quick in the electronics warfare specialty these days. That tendency was probably going to become only more pronounced as the new construction began to commission in Manticore, and Jackson had actually been a JG when she arrived aboard *Reprise*. In fact, her current rank was still technically "acting" (although everyone was certain it would be confirmed in due time). Which meant that although McGill was still short of her own thirty-fifth birthday (standard reckoning), Jackson was a good nine T-years younger than she was.

Yet there were times when Heather felt a lot more than nine years older than Jackson. The younger woman often seemed to suffer from the perpetual, ravenous hunger which afflicted all midshipmen, and there was a new-puppy eagerness about her. Maybe that was part of the reason Heather had more or less taken the electronics warfare officer under her wing off duty, as well as on.

"I don't know, Aphrodite," she replied after a moment. "I know what probably happened if that idiot Byng didn't do exactly what he was told to do, though."

Jackson' blue eyes looked up from her plate and darkened. Unlike Heather, she'd never personally experienced combat, and what had happened to Commodore Chatterjee's destroyers had hit her hard.

Well, Heather couldn't fault her for that. In a lot of ways, she supposed, she'd been lucky that she'd been far too busy during her own first taste of violence to think about it very much. Not that she'd felt particularly "lucky" at the time. Still, at least she'd been too . . . preoccupied during Esther McQueen's Operation Icarus to dwell on the horrors about her. She'd been on her snotty cruise at the time, almost ten T-years earlier, and there'd been very little time to think about anything besides doing her job—and hopefully surviving—as the sullen chain of Peep superdreadnoughts came over the hyper wall, missile batteries firing. The entire universe had seemed to go insane all about her as x-ray lasers chewed viciously into her ship and three of her fellow middies were torn apart less than fifteen meters from her own duty station.

But Aphrodite Jackson had never faced combat herself. And Commander Denton had quietly informed Heather that Lieutenant Thor Jackson had been Commander DesMoines' astrogator aboard HMS *Roland*, Commodore Chatterjee's flagship at New Tuscany. She hadn't seen the sights and smelled the smells Heather had, yet she obviously had an excellent imagination, and like every other member of *Reprise*'s company, she'd seen the detailed tactical and visual imagery of the savage attack *Tristram*'s platforms had recorded with such merciless accuracy. Even at second hand, the blinding speed with which those three destroyers—and her big brother—had been wiped away was its own sort of brutality, and Heather saw the ghosts of it behind her eyes even now.

"I . . . still can't really believe they're all gone, sometimes," Jackson said, speaking even more softly, and Heather smiled sadly.

"I know. And don't think it's something you'll 'get over.' Idiots tell you that, sometimes, you know, but what happened stays with you. And it doesn't get any easier the *next* time it happens, either—not emotionally, anyway. You just have to figure out how to deal with the memories and keep going. And that's not very easy, either."

"How do *you* do it?"

"I don't really know," Heather admitted. "I suppose a big part of it is family tradition, actually, in my case." She smiled just a bit sadly. "There've been McGills in the Navy as long as there have been Saganamis, when you come right down to it. A lot of them have gotten themselves killed along the way, so we've had a lot of practice—as a family, I mean—dealing with that kind of loss. My mom and dad are both serving officers, too. Well, Mom's detached from Bassingford right now—she's a psychologist, and the Navy has her working with Dr. Arif and her commission on treecats—but Dad's a senior-grade captain, and according to his last letter, he's in line for one of the new *Saganami-Cs*. Between the two of them, they make a pretty good sounding board. And," her eyes darkened, "we all had to figure out how to cope when my brother Tom was killed at Grendelsbane."

"I didn't know that—about your brother, I mean," Jackson said softly, and Heather shrugged.

"No reason you should have."

"I guess not."

Jackson looked down long enough to finish constructing her sandwich, then picked it up as if to take a bite out of it, only to lay it back down again, unbitten. Heather looked at her a bit quizzically, cocking her head to one side, and the EWO snorted softly.

"I'm dithering," she said.

"I wouldn't go quite that far," Heather disagreed. "You do seem to have something on your mind, though. So why don't you just go ahead and tell me what it is?"

"It's just—" Jackson began, only to break off. She looked down

again, staring at her own hands as her fingers methodically shred-
ded the crust away from her sandwich's bread. Then she inhaled
deeply and looked back up, meeting Heather's eyes squarely, and
her own gaze was no longer hesitant. This time, it *burned*.

"It's just that I know I shouldn't, but what I really want is for
Admiral Gold Peak to blow every one of those fucking bastards
right out of space!" she said fiercely. "I know it's wrong to feel
that way. I know most of the people aboard those ships didn't
have any voice at all in what happened. I even know that the
last thing we need is a war with the Solarian League. But still,
I think about what happened to Thor—to all those people—for
absolutely no good reason at all, and I don't want the 'right
response.' I want one that kills the people who killed my brother
and his friends!"

She stopped speaking abruptly, and her lips thinned as she
closed her mouth tightly. She looked away for a moment, then
made herself smile. It was a tight, hard expression—more of a
grimace than a smile, really—but at least she was trying, Heather
thought.

"Sorry about that," Jackson said.

"About what?" Heather looked at her quizzically. "Sorry because
you want them dead? Don't be ridiculous—of *course* you want
them dead! They killed someone you love, and you're a naval
officer. One who chose a combat specialty. So should it really
surprise you when your instincts and your emotions want the
people who killed your brother to pay for it?"

"But it's not professional," Jackson half-protested. Heather quirked
an eyebrow, and the EWO made an impatient, frustrated gesture.
"I mean, I ought to be able to stand back and recognize that
the best thing all around would be for us to settle this without
anyone else getting hurt."

"Oh, don't be so silly!" Heather shook her head. "You *do*
recognize that, that's the reason you're upset with yourself for
wanting something else! And if you want me to tell you you're
right to be upset with yourself for that, I'm not going to. Now, if
you were in a position to dictate the outcome, and you let your
emotions push you into a massacre that could have been avoided,
*then* you'd have a problem. But you're not, and I suspect that if
you were, you'd still do that 'right thing' you really don't want
to happen. In the meantime, I'm sure a young, attractive, female

officer of your precocious bent can go out and find all sorts of better things to spend your time regretting!"

"Coming up on the hyper wall, Sir," Lieutenant Bruner announced.

"Very well," Lewis Denton told his astrogator, and glanced at the quartermaster of the watch. "Pass the word, PO."

"Aye, aye, Sir," the quartermaster said, and pressed a button. "All hands," he announced over the ship's com system, "stand by for translation into normal-space."

Thirty-two seconds later, HMS *Reprise*'s crew experienced the familiar but never really describable queasiness of an alpha translation as their ship crossed the hyper wall and the G0 star called Meyers blazed twenty-two light minutes ahead of her. She'd come out almost exactly on the hyper limit, in a piece of virtuoso hyper navigation, and Denton smiled at Bruner.

"Well done!" he said, and the lieutenant smiled back at him as *Reprise* altered heading slightly, aligning her prow on the spot in space the planet Meyers would occupy in two hours and fifty-three minutes, and went to five hundred gravities of acceleration. Then Denton's smile faded and he turned his attention to Heather McGill.

"Deploy the platforms, Guns," he said.

"Aye, aye, Sir. Deploying the alpha platforms now."

Heather nodded to Jackson, who gave her readouts one last check, then pressed the key. Heather watched red lights flash to green and watched her own panel carefully.

"Alpha patterns have cleared the wedge, Sir," she announced a few moments later. "Stealth is active and deployment appears nominal." She glanced at a time display. "Beta platforms prepped for launch in . . . ten minutes and thirty-one seconds."

"Very good," Denton said again, and as he leaned back in his chair, his earlier smile was not even a memory. His imagination pictured the Ghost Rider platforms speeding outwards, peering at the emptiness around them, and his eyes were hard with the memory of the last Solarian-occupied star system a Manticoran destroyer force had entered.

*Not* this *time, you bastards,* he thought coldly. *Not this time.*

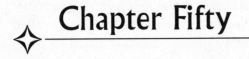

# Chapter Fifty

"HYPER FOOTPRINT, LIEUTENANT," the sensor tech announced, and Lieutenant Oliver Bristow raised an eyebrow and bent over the tech's shoulder to eyeball the display himself.

Despite its status as the administrative center of the Madras Sector, the Meyers System was scarcely a bustling hive of interstellar commerce. In fact, it was a rare day that saw more than two or three hyper translations, and it was scarcely unheard of for days or even weeks to go by with no new arrivals at all.

Traffic had been a bit more brisk since the fiasco in the Monica System, but most of the "special investigators" and representatives of the Inspector General's office had already come and gone. Most of them hadn't even bothered to unpack, as far as Bristow could tell. The fact that they'd come all the way out to Meyers was sufficient proof of their devotion to duty, and there was no point actually investigating anything, since most of them had been informed of their reports' conclusions before they were dispatched in the first place.

But business had been picking up again for Meyers Astro Control lately. The arrival of Admiral Crandall's task force three weeks earlier had been as much excitement as Bristow had ever seen here in Meyers. Admiral Byng's battlecruiser squadrons had represented more firepower than any system out in the Verge was ever likely to see, but they were dwarfed by Task Force 496. Bristow couldn't think of the last time he'd seen even one actual ship of the wall all the way out here, far less an entire task force of them with appropriate screening elements! He wasn't sure what Admiral Crandall was doing out here, but he was fairly confident she hadn't made the trip just for her health, and that made every unexpected arrival interesting. One never knew which of them might be whatever the hell it was Crandall was waiting for.

"What do you make of it, Coker?" he asked.

"Hard to say from this range, Sir."

Petty Officer 2/c Alan Coker, like Bristow, was Frontier Fleet, and the lieutenant suspected that a Battle Fleet officer like the ones on Byng's staff or aboard Crandall's superdreadnoughts would have found the petty officer's tone lamentably unprofessional. Bristow didn't. Which probably had a little to do with the fact that he assumed that, unlike most Battle Fleet officers he could name, Petty Officer Coker could actually find his own posterior if he got to use both hands.

"We've been telling them for months that we need to replace the arrays covering that sector," the petty officer continued more than a little sourly, "and resolution's not anything I'd care to screen home about. If I had to guess, though, I'd say it's probably a destroyer from the impeller signature. *Might* be a light cruiser—some of the piss pot 'navies' out here still have some awfully small 'cruisers' in inventory—but I don't think it's anything bigger than that, anyway."

"A light cruiser?" Bristow straightened slowly, scratching one eyebrow.

"Maybe, Sir. Like I say, though, it's more likely a destroyer," Coker replied, and Bristow nodded.

"Keep an eye on it. Let me know as soon as it squawks its transponder."

"Yes, Sir."

Bristow patted him absently on the shoulder, folded his hands behind himself, and began to pace slowly and thoughtfully back and forth across the limited width of the compartment. Coker was right about the condition of the arrays in question, but the petty officer was also a past master at getting balky equipment to do his bidding, and he had a good eye for ship IDs. So if he said that was a destroyer, it probably *was* a destroyer. Which was interesting, since so far as Bristow knew, the only *Solarian* destroyers in the sector were all either off with Admiral Byng or already right here in-system.

✧     ✧     ✧

"Permission to enter the bridge, Captain?"

Gregor O'Shaughnessy might have had his odd moments of disagreement with the Star Kingdom's military, but it was clear he'd learned the rudiments of naval courtesy along the way, and he was always careful to observe protocol aboard ship. It wasn't what Denton had expected out of someone with his prickly reputation, and the commander had found himself wondering if perhaps O'Shaughnessy was so careful because of that history of his. Whether that was the case or not, though, he'd gone out of his way—successfully—to be a pleasant passenger on the almost six-week voyage from Spindle to Meyers.

"Permission granted, Mr. O'Shaughnessy," Denton said now, and pointed at the chair at Heather McGill's left elbow. It would have been occupied by Ensign Varislav, the junior assistant tactical officer, at battle stations, but it was empty at the moment.

"Have a seat," he invited.

"Thank you, Captain."

O'Shaughnessy crossed to the indicated bridge chair and settled into it, careful to keep his hands well away from the console in front of it or the chair arm keypads. Heather turned her head to smile at him, and he smiled back. The ATO's place was where Commander Denton normally parked him when he visited the bridge, and Heather had gotten to know the analyst rather better than she'd ever expected to.

She'd also locked out the control pads he was so carefully avoiding, though she had no intention of telling him so. First, because she didn't want to risk rubbing in any perceived distrust in his ability to keep his hands out of trouble, and, second, because there was something rather touching—almost endearing—about how cautious he actually was.

She turned back to her own displays, watching the expanding hemisphere covered by her Ghost Rider platforms. As *Reprise* proceeded deeper into the system and the platforms closed in astern of her, watching her back, that hemisphere would become a complete sphere, but at the moment, CIC's attention—and Heather's—was focused on the leading edge of the surveillance zone.

*Reprise*'s hyper translation lay thirty-five minutes in the past. The destroyer's closing velocity relative to the system primary had risen to 20,296 KPS, and she'd traveled just under thirty-two million kilometers farther in-system. In that same interval, the Ghost Rider platforms, loping along at the low (for them) acceleration of only five thousand gravities in order to stay stealthy, had already moved three minutes past their turnover time. They were over sixty million kilometers ahead of the destroyer, with their velocity back down to a mere 85,413 KPS, which also meant they were only seventy-three million kilometers from Meyers, and four light-minutes was close enough for their passive instrumentation to begin picking up more detailed information.

She waited patiently, since Commander Denton had decided they would rely on directed lasers rather than the platforms' FTL capability. As a result, anything Heather saw would be just over four minutes old by the time it reached her. Not that she expected the delay to have any significant consequences, and it wasn't as if anyone—

An unanticipated icon blinked suddenly into existence on her display. Another one followed, and another, and the data sidebar began to flicker and change.

"Captain," she heard her own voice say calmly, "I'm picking up some unexpected readings. A lot of them."

"You're confident about this, Captain?"

"Yes, Mr. O'Shaughnessy, I am," Lewis Denton said, speaking rather more coolly to Baroness Medusa's personal representative than was his wont.

"I'm sorry," O'Shaughnessy said quickly. "I didn't mean to sound as if I were challenging the competency of any of your personnel, and particularly not Lieutenant McGill's. It's just that I'm having trouble wrapping my own mind around the implications. I guess it comes under the heading of asking redundant questions while I spar for time to get my brain working again."

"No apology necessary," Denton said in a more normal tone. "And I don't blame you. I never expected to see something like this out in the Verge, either. And just between you and me, I'm not very happy to be seeing it now."

"Amazing how we're thinking the same thing, isn't it?" O'Shaughnessy replied, and Denton snorted harshly, then turned back to the updated tactical plot.

*Reprise* had stopped accelerating and started coasting ballistically twenty-six minutes earlier. During that interval, her recon platforms had reached their destinations, spreading out to englobe the planet Meyers at a range of barely fifteen light-seconds. At that distance, there could be no mistake. There really were seventy-one Solarian superdreadnoughts, accompanied by sixteen battlecruisers, twelve heavy cruisers, twenty-three light cruisers, and eighteen destroyers orbiting the planet.

*Not to mention three repair ships, what have to be a couple of dozen stores ships, and what looks like a pair of straight ammunition carriers. It would appear New Tuscany isn't the only star system out this way benefitting from Battle Fleet's attention of late,* he thought ironically.

"May I ask a question, Mr. O'Shaughnessy?" he said.

"Captain, you can ask anything you like." The analyst turned to face him, his expression serious. "Believe me, you're cleared for anything you think you need to know in a situation like this one."

"Thank you, Sir. I appreciate that. What I was wondering was whether or not any one's come up with a better theory for how a Battle Fleet admiral ended up in command of a Frontier Fleet task group?"

"Given what we know about Byng, it didn't just happen by the luck of the draw," O'Shaughnessy said grimly. "Byng hates Frontier Fleet. Not as much as he hates *us*, maybe, but badly enough. He's got the connections to avoid an assignment like this one without even raising a sweat, too. And that completely ignores the fact that Frontier Fleet must've screamed bloody murder when it found out it was expected to hand a command like that over to anyone from Battle Fleet, far less Byng. Somebody with a lot of influence had to get him nominated for the command, and he had to want to accept it."

"That's pretty much the way I figured it already," Denton said. "The reason I asked is that I have to find myself doubting that these people"—he pointed at the display with his chin—"just happen to be here by the luck of the draw, either. I think there's a connection between them and Byng. In fact, the evidence seems to be screaming pretty loudly that we're looking at a setup."

"I'm very much afraid I agree with you," O'Shaughnessy said heavily. "I wish to God I didn't, and I suppose there *might* be some other explanation for it,. But if there is, I haven't been able to think of what it might be yet, either."

"I don't think Byng fired on Commodore Chatterjee by accident or in a panic." Denton's voice was hard, harsh-edged. "Not anymore. I don't know who's behind it, although I'd be willing to hazard a few guesses based on what's already happened here in the Quadrant, but someone wants us in a war with the League. And these people"—another quick, angry jut of his chin at the master plot—"are the hammer that's supposed to make sure it's a short, *nasty* war."

"We probably don't want to wed ourselves too immovably to that conclusion, Captain. I say that purely as a professional analyst who's gone a bit too far out on a limb upon occasion only to see it sawed off behind him. Having cast my professional sheet anchor to windward, however, I think you're absolutely right. But unlike you, I don't have any idea of just how bad the military odds really are, given these people's presence, and I'd like to get one."

"Against what we've got in the Quadrant right now?" Denton raised an eyebrow at him, and he nodded. "Not good," the commander said. "In fact, that's understating the situation fairly significantly. In technical terms, I believe the phrase would be 'We're screwed.'"

"I was afraid that was what you were going to say."

"Don't get me wrong, Mr. O'Shaughnessy. We could hurt them, probably even pretty badly, but no way in the galaxy could we *stop* them if they're prepared to keep coming. The battlecruisers and the small fry—*phffft!*" Denton snapped his fingers. "But those big bastards are something else entirely. We could probably rip hell out of them as long as the Mark 23 pods hold out, but it would take a lot of hits—even with the Mark 23—to kill one of them, and we don't have an unlimited supply of the pods. Worse than that, we don't have *any* podnoughts. That means we can only carry and deploy pods externally, which makes them a lot more vulnerable and tactically less flexible. They'd be at their most effective in a purely defensive deployment, with lots of shipboard control links to manage them, but to make that work, we'd have to figure out where we needed them far enough in advance to get them—and enough ships to control them in worthwhile salvos—there before the Sollies came calling, and that wouldn't exactly be a trivial challenge.

"It's more likely we'd find ourselves having to face up to them without a powerful pod reserve—especially if we decide we have to insure the security of Spindle and dump most of the pods there. If that happens, we'll have to use mobile units to cover the Quadrant's other systems, and that means nothing heavier than a *Nike* or a *Saganami-C*. And *that* means using primarily whatever we can fire from our internal tubes... which sure as hell *doesn't* mean Mark 23s.

"From what I've heard about the new Mark 16 warhead mods, we could probably get in some good licks even against wallers, once the pods are gone, but I don't think we could do enough to knock them out. Certainly not in large enough numbers to do us any good. And that's assuming they didn't just decide to split up into smaller task units and go after each of the Quadrant's star systems individually—which, by the way, would require us to parcel out everything we've got, not just the Mark 23 pods—on a penny-packet basis if we wanted to try to give some cover to the Quadrant as a whole. But our only real chance of inflicting significant damage on wallers would be to stay concentrated and hammer them with everything we've got from outside their effective powered envelope. Splitting up into smaller units to defend multiple targets would hurt us more than it would hurt them."

"What about the Lynx Terminus?"

"That's probably another story, Sir. For one thing, most of the forts are on-line now, and each of them is a hell of a lot tougher than any piece-of-crap Solly superdreadnought ever built. And for another thing, Home Fleet is right on the other side of the terminus. Trust me. If these people want to dance with Duchess Harrington after what she did to the Peeps at Manticore, they're toast."

"What do you think they'll do?"

"I'm only a destroyer skipper, Mr. O'Shaughnessy. One with a nasty suspicious streak, maybe, but only a destroyer skipper. That kind of strategic assessment is *way* above my pay grade."

"I realize that. And I'm not going to hold you to anything. But I'd really like to hear your thoughts."

"Well, if it was me, and if we really are looking at some kind of orchestrated plan, a setup designed to get us out of the Quadrant once and for all, I'd start by taking out the administrative center of the Quadrant."

"You'd go for Spindle?"

"In a skinny minute, Sir," Denton said flatly. "I'd head straight there on the assumption that if the Manties tried to fight me, they'd have to come to me, well away from the terminus, on my terms. I'd figure I was going to take some nasty lumps, but that the Admiralty would never allow any really heavy force to get too far away from the Lynx Terminus, given the situation back home. So all I'd really have to take on would be whatever Admiral Gold Peak had under her command. And if she *didn't* try to fight me, the Star Empire would effectively concede possession of the entire Talbott Cluster, which would let me gather up all the other systems at my leisure. I might not get to kill as many Manty starships, but I'd have taken what would probably be my primary objectives for minimal losses. Not to mention the morale damage I would have inflicted on all those people who'd just voted to join the Star Empire if the Navy cuts and runs instead of trying to defend them."

He spoke coldly, confidently, but then he visibly paused and took a step back.

"I said that's what I'd do if it was my call, and I think it's what anyone on the other side would do . . . if he were capable of finding his ass with both hands and *if* he had a realistic appreciation for the actual balance of military capabilities. From what we've seen of the Sollies, though, it's entirely possible they don't have that realistic appreciation. In which case, they might just decide to head direct for the Terminus, after all. The logic would be pretty compelling, given that kind of misestimate of the relative balance of combat effectiveness. Seize and hold the Terminus, cut us off from any relief from the home system, then steamroller the forces isolated out here in the Quadrant. So I guess the bottom line is that without any clearer idea of how accurately they've assessed our capabilities, it's really impossible to say which way they're going to jump. Except, of course, that I think we can be fairly confident it will be a way we won't like."

"As I said earlier, it's amazing how we seem to be thinking the same thing," O'Shaughnessy said.

"Well, with all due respect, Sir, I think it's time we aborted your diplomatic mission. Somehow, I don't think protesting Byng's actions or presenting a note explaining our response is going to do much good. And given what happened the last time some of our destroyers got too close to Solarian *battlecruisers*, I'd just as soon not get any closer than this to Solarian ships of the wall!"

"Captain, for what it's worth, I concur entirely."

✧    ✧    ✧

"There it is again, Lieutenant," PO Coker said.

"Where?"

Bristow looked over the petty officer's shoulder again, frowning. The impeller signature of the elusive destroyer, assuming that was what it was, had disappeared a half-hour earlier. Now it was back again, but where it had been accelerating in-system at five hundred gravities, it was now *decelerating* at well over six hundred. Clearly, it had changed its mind about its destination.

"Never did squawk their transponder, Sir," Coker observed.

"No, I noticed that myself, PO," Bristow replied with a touch of irony, and Coker chuckled.

"Suppose they saw something they didn't much care for, Sir?"

"That's exactly what I think," Bristow said slowly, "and that's what bothers me."

"Sir?"

"Just how the hell did they see anything to make them nervous from way the hell and gone out there?" Bristow asked, and the petty officer frowned. It wasn't a particularly happy frown, and Bristow nodded slowly. "That's what I thought, myself. Of course, whether or not we can convince Admiral Crandall of it is something else entirely, isn't it?"

Fleet Admiral Sandra Crandall was a solidly built woman with mahogany-colored hair and hard brown eyes. She was always immaculately groomed and uniformed, perfectly tailored, and yet it seemed to Hongbo Junyan that some subliminal whiff of decay followed her around like rancid incense.

On the plus side, she seemed to be smarter than Josef Byng. On the negative side, she was even stubborner and at least as thoroughly imbued with Battle Fleet arrogance as he was.

Or as he'd *been*, rather, Hongbo corrected himself. The Navy dispatch boat from New Tuscany which had arrived just over two hours ago had announced the change in its late commanding admiral's corporeal status. Personally, Hongbo would have considered that change a positive step even if it hadn't pushed events exactly where his Manpower ... patrons wanted them to go. Not everyone shared that view of the universe, however, and it had upset Admiral Crandall just a tad.

Which was rather the point of this afternoon's meeting.

"I don't *care* what their frigging 'warning messages' to Josef said!" Crandall snarled, glaring across the conference table at Lorcan Verrochio as if *he* were a Manty. "And I don't give a good goddamn what happened to *their* damned destroyers! The bastards fired on and destroyed a *Solarian League Navy* battlecruiser with all hands!"

"But only after Admiral Byng had—" Verrochio began.

"I don't give a flying fuck what Byng may or may not have done!" Crandall interrupted furiously, her expression livid. "First, because the only evidence we have is what they've seen fit to provide us, and I don't trust it as far as I can damned well spit. But second, and even more importantly, because it damned well doesn't *matter*! The Solarian League can't accept something like this—not out of some frigging little pissant navy out beyond the Verge—no matter what kind of provocation they may think they have! If we let them get away with this, God only knows who's going to try something stupid next!"

"But the Manticorans aren't a typical—"

"*Don't* tell me about their super weapons again, Mr. Commissioner," Crandall snapped. "I'll grant you that they obviously have much longer ranged missiles than we'd appreciated. That may actually make some sense of the preposterous stories we've been hearing about their damned war with the Havenites. But what they could do against a dozen Frontier Fleet battlecruisers won't help them very much against modern, integrated missile defense from nine squadrons of the wall, plus screen. Trust me, they'll need something more than a few fancy tricks with missiles to stop *my* task force! And I don't intend to stand here with my thumb up my ass while they get themselves organized."

"What do you mean, 'organized,' Admiral?" Hongbo asked in a carefully unprovocative tone.

"I mean they obviously didn't have any idea my task force was anywhere in the vicinity, or they wouldn't have tried this shit in the first place. But they damned well know now. Or they know more than they did, at any rate. Just who the hell do you think that mysterious hyper footprint yesterday morning was, Mr. Hongbo? I don't know what it was doing here, but I know damned well it was a Manty, and whoever it was, she's on her way straight back to tell her superiors about my wall of battle. Well now that they know, I don't intend to give them time to send wallers of their own through from Manticore!"

"Admiral," Verrochio said as forcefully as he could (speaking for the recorders, of course), "I cannot authorize any sort of action or reprisal against the Manticorans without approval from higher authority within the Ministry!" He raised one hand like a stop sign and continued quickly as Crandall seemed to swell visibly. "I'm not saying you aren't totally justified in your feelings. And assuming the information available to us at this time is accurate, I think it's extremely likely Ministry approval would be forthcoming. As you say, allowing something like this to go unchallenged, to set some sort of precedent for other neobarb navies, could be disastrous. But making a decision which would amount to going to war with a multi-system stellar power, especially one so deeply involved in the League's carrying trade, is well beyond the scope of my authority as a Frontier Security governor."

Hongbo felt an unusual glow of admiration for his nominal superior's footwork. If Verrochio had shown the ability to play Byng like a violin, he was playing Crandall like an entire string quartet! This was working out even better than either of them had hoped, at least from the perspective of evading responsibility. From the perspective of what was about to happen to other people, it was something else entirely, he supposed. But there wasn't much he could do about that, and from a purely selfish viewpoint, it could hardly have been better. He and Verrochio had performed to specification, which ought to get Ottweiler and his employers off their necks, and managed to cover their tracks quite neatly along the way. It had been Byng's decision to depart for New Tuscany, and while Hongbo was genuinely shocked at what the Manties had done—and how easily they'd done it—no one could possibly fault him or Verrochio for it. And now Verrochio had gotten himself, and by extension Hongbo, on record as the civilian voice of reason in the face of spinal-reflex military pugnacity.

*Which is probably going to be a very good thing if it turns out that our good admiral has underestimated the Manties even half as badly as I think she has,* the vice-commissioner thought. *She's thinking in terms of standard reprisals against uppity neobarbs, something the Navy's done hundreds of times, whether it admits it or not. But these aren't your typical neobarbs, even based solely on what's happened already. Unfortunately, she doesn't even have a clue how different they are, and she's not prepared to listen to someone like Thurgood. After all, he's only Frontier Fleet. What could he know about fights between ships of the wall?*

"Well," Crandall didn't quite sneer, in response to Verrochio's protest, "you undoubtedly know the limits of your authority better than I do, Sir. However, I know the limits of *my* authority, and I also recognize my responsibilities. So, with all due respect for your need for Ministry approval, I have no intention of waiting for it."

"What do you mean?" Verrochio asked, his voice taut.

"I mean I'll be underway within forty-eight hours, Mr. Commissioner," Crandall said flatly, "and the Manties won't be happy to see me at all."

# Chapter Fifty-One

"WELL, THERESA?" Admiral Frederick Topolev said, looking at his chief of staff.

"Captain Walsh says we're ready to go, Sir," Commander Theresa Coleman replied. "And Felicidad's boards are all green."

Coleman nodded her head in the direction of Commander Felicidad Kolstad, Topolev's operations officer. It was odd, a corner of Topolev's thoughts reflected for far from the first time, that three of the four most important officers on his staff were not only all female, but all quite attractive, in their own very distinct ways. Although, perhaps, that attractiveness shouldn't have been such a surprise, since all of his officers were the products of alpha, beta, or gamma lines.

At the moment, Kolstad was concentrating all of her own attention on the readouts which showed the exact position of every unit of Topolev's task force, literally down to the last centimeter. All twenty of his ships were tractored together into two big, ungainly formations, nine hundred kilometers apart, as they floated with the closest thing possible to a zero velocity relative to one another and to the normal-space universe they'd left three months earlier.

"All right, people," Topolev said as calmly as he could, "let's do this."

"Yes, Sir," Coleman acknowledged, and passed the order to Captain Joshua Walsh, MANS *Mako*'s captain.

Absolutely nothing seemed to happen for the next two or three minutes, but appearances were deceiving, and Topolev waited patiently, watching his own displays, as Task Force One of the Mesan Alignment Navy translated ever so slowly and gradually back into normal-space.

This maneuver had been tested against the Mesa System's sensor arrays by crews using the early *Ghost*-class ships even before the first of the *Shark*-class prototypes had ever been laid down, and Task Force One had practiced it over a hundred times once the mission had been okayed. Despite all that, Topolev still cherished a few reservations about the entire operation. Not about the abilities of his people, or the technical capabilities of his vessels, but about the timing.

*And about the fact that we were never supposed to carry this out with the* Sharks *in the first place, Freddy,* he reminded himself. *Don't forget* that *minor point! This was what the* Leonard Detweiler *class was supposed to be for after the* Sharks *proved the basic concept. They weren't supposed to carry out the actual mission themselves; they were supposed to serve as training ships for the crews of the ships that* would *execute the mission.*

He felt himself scowling down at his console as the familiar, worn-out thread of worry trickled through the back of his mind. He banished the expression quickly—it was hardly the confident, calm look his officers needed to see at this particular moment—and wished he could banish the worry with equal speed.

No one seemed to have noticed his momentary lapse, and his own concern smoothed into concentration as readouts began to slowly flicker and change. Both groups of his ships slid gradually, carefully towards the hyper wall, making the slowest possible translation back into normal-space.

It was physically impossible for any ship to cross the hyper wall without radiating a hyper footprint, but the *strength* of that footprint was—to a large extent, at least—a factor of the base velocity the ship in question wanted to carry across the wall. The alpha translation's bleed factor was roughly ninety-two percent, and all of that energy had to go somewhere. There was also an unavoidable gravitic spike or echo along the interface between the alpha bands of hyper-space and normal-space that was effectively independent of a ship's speed. Reducing velocity couldn't do anything about that, but a slow, "gentle" translation along a shallow gradient produced a much weaker spike, as well.

No translation, however slow and gentle, could render a hyper footprint too weak to be detected by the sort of arrays covering the Manticore Binary System. Yet arrays like that, because of their very sensitivity, were notorious for throwing up occasional "false positives," ghost translations that the filters were supposed to strain out before they ever reached a human operator's attention. And the most common ghosts of all normally appeared as a hyper footprint and an echo, which was precisely what Topolev's maneuver was supposed to counterfeit.

Under normal circumstances, there would have been very little point to deceiving the arrays where a simple hyper footprint was concerned, given the fact that those same arrays would almost certainly have picked up the impeller wedge of any ship headed towards the system. Even the best stealth systems were unreliable, at best, against a sensor array which could measure eight or nine thousand kilometers on a side, and *Manticore's* long-range sensors were even larger—and more sensitive—than that. Closer in, where the gradient of the stellar gravity well provided background interference and there were dozens of other gravity sources to clutter the landscape and turn the master arrays' very sensitivity against them, yes. The really big arrays were all but useless once you got within a light-hour or so of a system primary or a wormhole junction. That was where the shorter-ranged sensors aboard warships and recon platforms took over, and with good reason. But this far out was another matter entirely. Really good first-line stealth systems *might* manage to defeat the big arrays at this range, but no betting man would care to risk his money on the probability.

Fortunately, Frederick Topolev had no need to do anything of the sort.

It seemed to take much longer to complete the maneuver than it had in any of the training exercises, although the time displays insisted it really hadn't. Personally, Topolev suspected the damned clocks were broken.

"Translation completed, Sir," Lieutenant Commander Vivienne Henning, his staff astrogator, announced. "Preliminary checks indicate we're right on the money: one light-month out on almost exactly the right bearing."

"Good work," Topolev complemented her, and she smiled with pleasure at the sincerity in his voice. He smiled back, then cleared his throat. "And now that we're here, let's go someplace else."

"Yes, Sir."

The twenty *Shark*-class ships, each about midway between an old-fashioned battleship and a dreadnought for size, deactivated the tractors which had held them together. Reaction thrusters flared, pushing them apart, although they didn't seek the same amount of separation most starships their size would have. Then again, they didn't need that much separation.

A few moments later, they were underway at a steady seventy-five gravities. At that absurdly low acceleration rate it would take them a full ninety hours—almost four T-days—to reach the eighty percent of light-speed that represented the maximum safe normal-space velocity permitted by available particle shielding, and it would take them another three T-weeks, by the clocks of the rest of the universe, to reach their destination, although the subjective time would be only seventeen days for them. Another ship of their size could have attained the same velocity in a little more than *thirteen* hours, but that was all right with Admiral Topolev. The total difference in transit time would still be under six days—less than four, subjective—and unlike the units of his own command, that hypothetical other ship would have been radiating an impeller signature . . . which his ships weren't.

"What've you got for me, Clint?"

Lieutenant Clinton McCormick looked up from his display as his supervisor, Lieutenant Commander Jessica Epstein, appeared at his shoulder. McCormick liked Epstein, but he sometimes wondered why in the world she'd ever decided to pursue a naval career. Born and bred on Gryphon, the dark-haired lieutenant commander was an avid backpacker, camper, and birdwatcher. She also liked cross-country running and marathons, for God's sake! None of those hobbies were particularly well-suited to the constrained dimensions found on the insides of spacecraft.

At least her assignment to *Hephaestus* meant she spent her time someplace big enough that there were actually personnel tubes, not just treadmills, set aside for the use of people who wanted to jog or run, but she clearly still had a lot of excess energy to burn off. Most other supervisors would simply have requested that McCormick shunt his data to their console, but not Epstein. She wanted any excuse to get out of her command chair and move around, which explained why he found her peering over his shoulder at his display in the big, cool, dimly lit compartment.

"Probably nothing, Ma'am," he told her now. "Looks like a ghost to me, but it popped through the filters. Right here."

He used a cursor to indicate the faint, almost invisible light splotch, then zoomed in. At maximum zoom, it was evident that there were actually *two* light splotches, each tagged with the time it had appeared, and Epstein grimaced at the telltale sign of a ghost footprint.

"I take it that this thing was strong enough the computers classified it as a genuine possible?" she said.

"That's what happened, all right, Ma'am," McCormick agreed.

"Well, better safe than sorry." Epstein sighed, then flicked her head in a sort of shorthand shrug. "I'll kick it upstairs, and they'll roust out some poor cruiser or destroyer division to go take a look."

"Hey, they ought to be grateful for us for finding them something to do instead of just sitting around in orbit," McCormick replied, and Epstein chuckled.

"If you think that's the way they're going to react, should I go ahead and tell them who spotted this in the first place?"

"Actually, now that I've thought about it, Ma'am, I think I'd prefer to remain anonymous," he said very seriously, and her chuckle turned into a laugh.

"That's what I thought," she said, then patted him on the shoulder and turned to walk back to her own command station.

Given the range on the possible footprint, the datum was over twelve hours old. Footprints, like gravitic pulses, were detectable by the fluctuations they imposed on the alpha wall interface with normal-space, which meant they propagated at roughly sixty-four times the speed of light. For most practical purposes, that equated to real-time, or very near to real-time, but when you started talking about the detection ranges possible to Perimeter Security Command's huge arrays, even that speed left room for considerable delays.

It seemed like an awfully long way to go for very little return. There'd been no sign of an impeller wedge, which meant no one was out there accelerating towards the star system. If there'd been an actual hyper footprint in the first place—which Epstein frankly doubted was the case—it had to have been some merchantship coming in with appallingly bad astrogation. Whoever it was had popped out of hyper a full light-month short of his intended destination, and then promptly (and sensibly) popped right back into hyper rather than spending the endless weeks which would have been required to reach anyplace worthwhile under impeller drive. And when she did arrive in the star system, or at the Junction, she wasn't going to tell a single solitary soul about her little misadventure. That kind of astrogation error went beyond simply embarrassing to downright humiliating. In fact, if Astro Control had hard evidence of a *Manticoran* astrogator who'd been that far off, they would undoubtedly call her back in for testing and recertification!

But, as she'd said to McCormick, better safe than sorry. That could have been the motto of Perimeter Security Command instead of the official "Always Vigilant," and Epstein, like virtually all of the officers assigned to PSC, took her responsibilities very seriously indeed. They were there, maintaining their endless watch, precisely to make sure everyone *knew* they were, which meant no one would even make the attempt to evade their all-seeing eyes. Checking out the occasional ghost was a trivial price to pay for that.

Commander Michael Carus, the commanding officer of HMS *Javelin*, and the senior officer of the second division of Destroyer Squadron 265, known as the "Silver Cepheids," sighed philosophically as he contemplated his orders.

At least it was something to do, he supposed. And he wasn't surprised they'd gotten the call. The squadron had earned its name from its demonstrated expertise in reconnaissance and scouting, although he'd always wondered if it was *really* all that appropriate. Cepheids were scarcely among the galaxy's *less* noticeable stars, after all, and recon missions were supposed to be unobtrusive.

"Here, Linda," he said, handing the message chip to Lieutenant Linda Petersen, *Javelin*'s astrogator. "We're going ghost hunting. Work out a course, please."

"To hear is to obey," Petersen replied. She plugged the chip into her own console, then looked over her shoulder at Carus.

"How big a hurry are we in, Skipper?" she asked.

"The datum is already almost thirteen hours old," Carus pointed out. "I feel sure our lords and masters would like us to go check it out before it gets a bunch older. So I'd say a certain degree of haste is probably in order."

"Got it, Skip," Petersen said and began punching numbers. A couple of minutes later, she grunted in satisfaction.

"All right," she said, turning her chair around to face Carus. "This is going to be a really short jump, Skipper. Not quite a micro-jump, but close, so if we build up *too* much velocity—"

"Once upon a time, in the dim mists of my youth, all of, oh, three years ago, I was an astrogator myself, my daughter," Carus interrupted. "I seem to have a vague recollection of the undesirability of overrunning your translation point in a short hop rattling around somewhere in my aging memory."

"Yes, Sir," Petersen acknowledged with a grin. "Anyway, what I meant to say is that I'd just as soon not get much above forty-two thousand KPS as our base velocity. That gives us a total flight time of about three hours—a tad less than that, actually—if we hit the theta bands."

Carus nodded. As he'd just said, he'd been an astrogator himself, once, and his own mind ran through Petersen' decision tree. Translating steeply enough to hit the theta bands in a relatively short hop like this would probably take a couple of hours off the ships' hyper generators and alpha nodes, but it wouldn't be too bad.

"Figure about five hundred gravities?" he said.

"That was what I was thinking. Take us about two hours to hit our transit velocity at that rate. I don't see any point pushing it harder than that and risking overrunning the translation point at the other end."

"Sounds good to me," Carus said, and turned to his communications officer.

Three hours later, the destroyers *Javelin, Dagger, Raven,* and *Lodestone* arrived at the ghost footprint's locus and began to spread out.

"You and Bridget take the outer perimeter, John," Carus said, looking at the trio of faces on his divided com display. "Julie and I will take the inner sweep."

"Understood," Lieutenant Commander John Pershing of the *Raven* acknowledged, and Lieutenant Commander Bridget Landry, *Dagger*'s CO nodded.

"Which of us plays anchor?" Lieutenant Commander Julie Chase asked from *Lodestone*'s bridge, and Carus chuckled.

"Rank hath its privileges," he said just a bit smugly.

"That's what I thought," she huffed, then smiled. "*Try* to stay awake while the rest of us do all the work, all right?"

"I'll do my best," Carus assured her.

"Almost exactly on schedule, Sir," Commander Kolstad observed. "Nice to have punctual enemies, I suppose."

"Let's not get too overconfident, Felicidad," Admiral Topolev responded, giving her a mildly reproving look.

"No, Sir," Kolstad said quickly, and he allowed his slight frown to turn into an encouraging smile, instead.

If he were going to be honest, Topolev supposed, he wasn't immune to the ops officer's sense of euphoria. In the roughly seventeen hours since their arrival, their velocity had increased to better than forty-five thousand kilometers per second, and they were almost a hundred and thirty-eight million kilometers closer to their destination. Under most circumstances, 7.6 light-minutes wouldn't have seemed like very much of a cushion against military-grade sensors. Especially not against *Manticoran* military-grade sensors. The Mesan Alignment had plowed quite a few decades—and several trillion credits—into the development of its own stealth technology, however, and the MAN was at least two generations ahead of the Solarian League in that capability. Their analysts' best estimate was that their stealth systems were equal to those of Manticore at a minimum, and probably at least marginally superior, although no one was prepared to assume anything of the sort. But as the Manties' own Harrington had demonstrated at a place called Cerberus, the key element in any passive detection of a moving starship was its impeller signature . . . and Task Force One didn't *have* an impeller signature.

The Royal Manticoran Navy was the enemy, and Frederick Topolev was prepared to do whatever it took to defeat that enemy, but neither he nor Collin Detweiler's intelligence services were prepared to *underestimate* that enemy or permit themselves to hold mere "normals" in contempt. Especially not given the RMN's combat record over the last twenty years. The MAN was almost certainly the galaxy's youngest real navy, and its founders—including one Frederick Topolev—had studied the Manties, and their officer corps, and their battle record with painstaking attention. They'd learned quite a few valuable lessons of their own in the process, and the admiral knew the crews of those destroyers were firmly convinced they'd been sent out here to investigate a genuine ghost. If anyone had thought anything else, they wouldn't have sent just four destroyers to check it out. But he also knew that, routine or not, the crews of those ships were doing exactly what they were supposed to be doing. He recognized the standard search pattern they were running, knew their sensor crews were monitoring their instruments and their displays intently. If there was anything out there to find, those destroyers would find it.

Except that no one in the entire galaxy knew *how* to find it. Knew even how to recognize that there was something out there *to* find. And so, despite the absurdly low range, and despite his own ships' ridiculously low top acceleration rate, Topolev felt just as confident as he looked.

# Chapter Fifty-Two

"I WISH I COULD SAY I was surprised," Elizabeth III said in tones of profound disgust as she flipped her hard copy of her cousin's report of the Second Battle of New Tuscany onto the same conference table in the same conference room. The initial report had arrived three days ago, with the news of Josef Byng's stupidity and the destruction of his flagship. That had been bad enough, but the rest of what Michelle had turned up after the battle was even worse, and the queen shook her head, her expression tight with anger.

"The Sollies have resented us for years," she continued harshly, "and we've walked on tiptoe around them for as long as anyone can remember. I guess something like this *had* to happen sooner or later, even if the timing could have been a lot better. In fact, I suppose the only thing I'm really surprised about is who seems to have arranged this entire—what's that charming military phrase? Oh, yes. This entire *cluster fuck*."

The treecat on the back of her chair shifted, his ears half-flattened, his needle-tipped claws extending far enough to sink into the chair's upholstery, and everyone in the room could hear his soft hiss as his rage mirrored his person's. Obviously, whether Elizabeth was surprised or not, the events at New Tuscany—and the fact that there truly had been no survivors from Commodore Chatterjee's murdered destroyers—had been enough to whip her fury to a white-hot heat even before the confirmation of outside manipulation had reached her.

The other two treecats present were less overtly infuriated than Ariel was, but neither of them was immune to the human anger—and anxiety—swirling about them. They were, however, somewhat farther away, and Prime Minister Grantville, sitting beside the Queen, kept a wary eye on Ariel as he shook his own head.

"I don't think there's any such thing as 'good timing' for a confrontation with the Solarian League, Your Majesty," he said, speaking rather more formally than was his wont. "On the other hand, as you've just said, it's not exactly as if there were any tremendous surprises here, is it?"

"I can *always* be surprised by Solly stupidity, Willie," Elizabeth said bitingly. "I shouldn't be, I suppose, but every time I think I've seen the stupidest thing they could possibly do, they find a way to surpass themselves! At least this particular idiot's taken himself out of the gene pool. It's a pity he had to take so many others with him!"

"I agree, Your Majesty," anger of his own rumbled around in Sir Anthony Langtry's voice, "and the fact that those flaming idiots in Chicago still haven't officially responded to our initial note only proves your point."

He shook his head in disgust. The note in question had reached Old Terra three weeks before this meeting, yet there'd still been no response at all from the League's Foreign Ministry.

"Of course it does, Tony," Grantville acknowledged. "Still, I stand by my original point. This is something we've all seen coming—or at least as a serious probability—ever since we found out Byng had fired on Chatterjee in the first place."

"Oh, I don't know, Willie," his brother said, reaching out to stroke Samantha's soft ears as the 'cat pressed against the back of his neck, "I think this minor matter of the sixty or so Battle Fleet superdreadnoughts Vézien and Cardot were so eager to tell Mike about could probably come under that heading. Surprises, I mean."

"Assuming they're really there, Hamish," Grantville pointed out.

"Personally," Elizabeth said, "I'm less worried about sixty obsolete Solarian superdreadnoughts than I am about the several hundred modern, *pod-laying* superdreadnoughts the Peeps still have. You're right, Willie. We've discussed the Sollies almost to death. I'm not saying we've figured out what to do with them yet, even if I do feel a little bit better in that regard than I did a month or so ago, but I think we may have let ourselves get overly focused on them. I mean, whatever kind of threat the Solarian League may pose in the long term, it's the Peeps we have to worry about now. So while I'm perfectly willing to admit that the League may be the greater danger in absolute terms, I think we need to focus on removing the threat we *can* remove as quickly as possible."

She looked at White Haven, her eyes sharp.

"When we received our first report about Commodore Chatterjee, Willie asked you and Sir Thomas about our ability to hit Haven now, hard and fast, hurt them enough to make them realize they had no choice but to surrender outright. You seemed to think it would be feasible within a couple of months' time. I realize that was less than *one* month ago, but could we do it *now?* And could we hold off the Sollies in Talbott while we do it?"

For the first time in his naval career, Hamish Alexander-Harrington felt an almost overwhelming temptation to temporize and dodge a fundamental question. But however great the temptation, he was still Elizabeth Winton's First Lord of Admiralty, and he met her eyes squarely.

"I've deliberately kept my hands off of a lot of the operational details," he said. "The last thing Tom Caparelli needs is to think he's got a backseat driver—and one who's a civilian, now—trying to grab the controls away from him, so he and I have both tried very hard to respect one another's spheres of authority. Having said that, though, I think the answer is probably that, yes, we could punch out the Haven System with what we have available right now. If we want to do it before we find ourselves up against the Sollies, though, and considering transit times and everything else, we'd have to use Eighth Fleet, which would mean uncovering the Home System at least temporarily. I don't much care for that thought, but I think enough of the new construction would be available at or almost at combat readiness to cover the gap, and we've made better progress than I really anticipated in getting the system-defense variant of Apollo into service.

"In addition, however, there's another timing issue involved. If there really are Solly SDs in Talbott, we can't afford to have our main striking force weeks away from the home system when they finally make their presence felt. That means that if we decide firmly in favor of taking the military option against Haven first, we'd have to launch the op *now*—immediately, without any effort to talk to the Peeps first—and that it would have to be militarily *decisive*, in the shortest possible period of time. If we present any ultimatums, they'd have to be delivered from the flag bridge of a fleet actually in position to attack, with no time for the other side to think about them or digest the implications ahead of time. Which, frankly, makes it much less likely, in my opinion, that they'd be willing to stand down without a fight. Faced with the same situation, *we'd* certainly be more likely to fight than just roll over, so I suspect we'd have to pretty much wipe out Capital Fleet before they were ready to give in. And we might well have to actually go ahead and really take out most or all of their infrastructure, as well."

The fourth and final human being present for the conference stirred slightly in her chair beside him, but he kept his eyes resolutely focused on the Queen. He already knew exactly how his wife felt about the notion of turning the Haven System into a scrapyard.

"As I say," he continued, "we could punch out Haven. But you asked me a two-part question, and my answer to the second half of it—whether or not we can hold off the Sollies in Talbott while we do it—is that I simply don't know. That's why I say we can't afford to take the time to send diplomatic notes back and forth first, if we're going to set up to attack the Haven System at all.

"Having said that, however, I also have to say that, judging from my preliminary read of the technical appendices of *this* report, I think all our estimates about how outclassed the Sollies' deployed equipment is may actually have been overly pessimistic. But they've got a lot of ships, Elizabeth. And whatever our long-term prospects might be, if they've actually got that many superdreadnoughts deployed in proximity to the Talbott Quadrant, then Mike's and Khumalo's ability to fend them off with nothing heavier than battlecruisers is . . . doubtful, to say the least. If the Sollies have that many wallers available, and if they decide to respond the way it sounds very much like this Admiral Crandall would be likely to, we could find the new systems in the Quadrant burning to the ground at the same time *we're* off hammering Nouveau Paris."

"But as Willie just pointed out, we don't even know those superdreadnoughts *exist*," Elizabeth retorted. "All we have right now is what amounts to hearsay evidence from a bunch of New Tuscans who admit they were part of a strategy to smash the

Quadrant before it truly has its feet under it. Forgive me if I find information they're offering as some sort of quid pro quo to keep us from leveling their system around their ears less than totally convincing. It certainly hasn't been *confirmed* yet!"

She glared down at the hard copy of the report again for a heartbeat or two, then raised her eyes to White Haven once more.

"And where the question of timing is concerned, frankly, I won't exactly cry myself to sleep if we do have to send our ultimatum to Pritchard along with Honor. If they're too pigheaded to see reason and surrender, it'll be on their heads, not ours. And let's not forget that not only are they the people who *started* this war, but they're also the ones who sabotaged their own proposed summit and then launched an all-out attack on *our* home system." The Queen's brown eyes glittered fiercely. "I think we all know who the real enemy is, and it's a hell of a lot closer than the Sol System. Can we afford to allow a hypothetical fleet of super-dreadnoughts, which might not really be there at all, to paralyze our strategic thinking and push us into taking our eye off the *real* enemy when we finally have the chance to finish the Peeps off once and for all?"

"I think we have to assume they *are* there," a soprano voice said. It was quiet, that voice, but there was something about its timbre, a hint of steely determination, and Elizabeth's eyes swiveled to the speaker.

"First, we have to assume that because it's our responsibility to make the most pessimistic assumptions," Honor Alexander-Harrington continued. "But, second, I think they really are. I think we've fundamentally underestimated Manpower's capabilities, and believe me, that's a much bigger surprise, as far as I'm concerned, than the fact that a stubborn, arrogant Solarian admiral wouldn't see reason and got his flagship's entire crew killed as an exercise in sheer stupidity. All of which makes me wonder—again—just how sure we really *are* about who the real enemy is."

"Honor, I know that you've thought—" Grantville began, but Honor cut him off with atypical brusqueness.

"Willie, I'm tired of people making allowances for what I think and why I think it. Yes, I've been in closer contact with the Ballroom—and with Anton Zilwicki and Victor Cachat"—Elizabeth's face tightened visibly at the second name, but Honor's voice didn't even pause—"than anyone else in this room. And, yes, my family history predisposes me to hate Manpower with every fiber of my being. All of that's true. But I am sick and tired of people who persist in using those facts to justify their refusal to look at the evidence because it doesn't suit *their* preconceptions."

"Meaning exactly what, Honor?"

Elizabeth's voice was sharp, and the look in her brown eyes was hard, as close to a glare as she had ever turned upon Honor Alexander-Harrington. But Honor looked back without flinching.

"Meaning, Elizabeth, that I've been telling you literally for months that it made absolutely no sense for the Havenites to assassinate Admiral Webster or try to kill Ruth and Berry. I'm not going to dispute with you over who did what to our prewar diplomatic correspondence, although I realize you know I don't think that's quite as open-and-shut as a lot of people seem to believe, either. But I'm telling you, Eloise Pritchart doesn't go around having people killed just for the fun of it, and she is *not* an idiot! If she'd actually wanted to derail her own summit meeting and killing Admiral Webster looked like the only way to do it, she would have found somebody one *hell* of a lot more deniable than her own ambassador's driver to pull the trigger."

White Haven managed not to cringe, but he didn't need Honor's empathic talent, or even Samantha's and Nimitz's soft hisses, to realize just how angry his wife truly was. She hadn't raised her voice, hadn't given the least indication of disrespect by tone or mannerism, but in a service not exactly noted for the pristine purity of its language, "the Salamander" was renowned for the fact that she *never* swore.

"That opinion isn't shared by the majority of the intelligence community," Elizabeth replied in a tone which made it obvious she was trying to throttle her own emotions.

"That isn't quite correct," Honor said flatly. Elizabeth's nostrils flared with anger, but Honor was no longer a mere cruiser captain meeting her monarch for the first time, and she continued without hesitation.

"That opinion *wasn't* shared by the majority of the intelligence community *at the time* and given what they knew then because they'd concluded that they couldn't think of anyone else with a motive.

"But we know things *now* we didn't know *then*, and not just the stuff Mike's just discovered at New Tuscany. There's Lester Tourville, for one thing. You know I know he was telling me the truth when he said that when Thomas Theisman originally briefed him for Operation Beatrice he told him no one in Pritchart's administration had expected to be resuming operations. That that was the reason they didn't start assembling his strike force until *after* we'd walked away from the summit talks. Of course Theisman could have lied to him, and of course it could still have been some kind of rogue operation launched by someone without Theisman's or even Pritchart's knowledge, assuming the someone in question had some personal reason to prevent the summit. So even granted that Tourville's been telling us the truth, and that Theisman told *him* the truth, there's still been the question of who else had a motive.

"Well, I submit to you that it's just been amply demonstrated—*again*—in New Tuscany that there *is* someone else with a perfectly good motive, and that someone is Manpower, Incorporated. Admiral Webster was hammering them on Old Terra; Berry is a symbol of everything they hate; the very existence of Torch is an affront to them; the weapon of choice for that attack was a *bioweapon*; and they're busy trying to get us—successfully, I might add, from all appearances—into a shooting war with the Solarian League. For that matter, according to Mike's report, one of their operatives just casually killed more than forty thousand people in New Tuscany to help their efforts along! And let's not forget that fleet of StateSec rejects that *Manpower* subsidized for an attack on *Torch*. I'll concede that I still don't know how they managed to respond that quickly to shoot down the summit, unless they've got enough penetration in Haven to have found out about it at least a couple of weeks before we did, but I'm not prepared to simply assume they couldn't have that kind of penetration. Not in the face of everything else we are finding out now! And do you think for one moment, Elizabeth, that Manpower isn't aware of how you feel about Haven? Or that they wouldn't be willing to play any card they could to get what they want?

"Yes, we're at war with the Republic of Haven. And, yes, they fired the first shot. And yes, they even launched the attack on our home system, and a lot of people have been killed. A lot of people *I* knew, people who weren't just professional colleagues but who'd been friends of mine for *decades*. Friends who'd literally risked their lives against impossible odds to save *mine* when they didn't have to, if you'll remember that little jaunt to Cerberus. So, believe me, I know all about anger, and I know all the reasons for distrust and hostility. But look at the evidence, for God's sake. Mike hit it exactly in her report—Manpower is operating *like a hostile star nation*, and *we're* the object of its hostility! Worse, it's got a hell of a lot more resources than we ever thought it did, even if it's hijacking some of them from the Sollies. And—" her almond-shaped, dark brown eyes pinned Elizabeth into her chair "—if there's anyone else in the galaxy who's even more inclined than the Legislaturalists or Oscar Saint-Just's State Security ever were to use assassination as a tool, it's Manpower.

"I admire you, and I respect you, both as my monarch and as a person and a friend, Elizabeth, but you're wrong. Whatever you may think, the *real* threat to the Star Empire at this moment isn't in Nouveau Paris *or* Old Chicago at all. It's in the Mesa System . . . and it's in the process of destroying the Star Kingdom *you're* responsible for ruling."

The tension hovering in the conference room was hard enough to chip with a knife as the two women locked eyes. And as those two sets of brown eyes met, Elizabeth Winton realized something emotionally that she'd long since recognized intellectually. Something Honor's analysis of any possible confrontation with the Solarian League had driven home in this very room only three T-weeks earlier.

Honor Alexander-Harrington had become the closest thing Elizabeth III had to a true peer. Admiral, Countess, Duchess, and Steadholder, the third ranking member of the Star Empire's peerage, a ruling head of state in her own right, and someone who had been born to none of those titles and identities. Someone who had won them. Who'd paid for them in the cold, hard cash of combat, in the loss of people for whom she cared deeply, in all the thousands of deaths—enemy and friend alike—she had taken onto her own conscience in the service of Elizabeth's kingdom, and in her own blood. Someone who had received many of those titles and honors from Elizabeth's own hands because she damned well *deserved* them.

And that peer—the person, Elizabeth realized now, whose absolute integrity and whose judgment *on every other question* she most trusted—disagreed with her on this one.

For several endless seconds, it felt as if the people around the table had forgotten to breathe, but then Elizabeth inhaled sharply, deeply, and shook her head like a boxer shaking off a hard left jab.

"I know you and I haven't seen eye-to-eye where the Peeps are concerned for a long time now, Honor," she said quietly. "I've tried to pretend we did. I've tried to ignore the fact that we didn't. And when I couldn't do that anymore, I've concluded that your personal acquaintance with people like Theisman and Tourville has affected your judgment. I still think that's possible, as a matter of fact. But—"

She paused, and silence hovered once more for several heartbeats before she spoke again.

"*But*," she continued, "maybe *I'm* the one whose judgment has been affected. You know why that might be true—better than anyone else, I suspect. And you're right, we do know things now that we didn't know then. As you say, there's still the problem of how they could have set up something like this so quickly—just the distances involved should have made it impossible. But"—her expression was that of a woman whose stubborn integrity was at odds with deeply held beliefs—"the explanation really could be as simple as their having someone close enough to Pritchart to know what she was thinking ahead of time. I still don't know how they could have known I'd pick Torch for the site of the summit, but if you're right—if it was a case of someone trying to manipulate me because they knew how I'd react to an assassination attempt anywhere—Torch would have been a logical target for Manpower. It could just have been serendipity that it was also the prospective site for the summit."

She inhaled deeply and shook her head.

"And you're right about what Mike's uncovered out at New Tuscany. Whether Manpower was involved in what happened to Admiral Webster and what happened on Torch or not, they're clearly on the brink of getting us into an actual war with the Solarian League. Yet even if my judgment's been less than perfect, and even if it is essential for us to regard that as a far greater *long-term* threat than Haven, that doesn't mean we don't have to deal with the Peeps before we can respond to the Sollies. And in addition to that, I have to think about how Pritchart is likely to respond when she finds out about what's happening in the Quadrant. When she realizes we're facing war with the Solarian

League all over again, she's certainly going to realize we can't fight both of them at once, as well. After what happened in the Battle of Manticore, after that many dead, who knows what she's likely to demand—or do—under those circumstances? We don't even know what she was prepared to offer or demand at her proposed summit, far less what kilo of flesh she'll demand as her price for peace at *this* point. You say it's our duty to assume those super-dreadnoughts really exist. Well, it's *my* duty to assume the Peeps would rather have victory than accept defeat, as well."

"Yes, it is," Honor agreed quietly. "But let's suppose you manage to impose peace on your terms. What are those terms going to be? Remember what we talked about here less than a month ago. Sir Thomas gave you the Admiralty's plan for defeating and occupying the Solarian League. Do you really think we could do the same thing to Haven, as well? Especially if we found ourselves trying to do both of them at once?

"We don't even know where Bolthole is, Elizabeth, so even if we demanded that they scrap their entire existing fleet, we can't take out their biggest and best yard with some sort of long-range strike. And it also means we can't picket it to make sure their fleet *stays* scrapped. So the Republic of Haven is still going to have a navy—and that navy's still going to be the only other major fleet with podnoughts—when we turn around to face the Sollies. We all know how well that worked out last time around. But let's suppose we *do* know where Bolthole is—that we demand its location as part of the surrender terms and then go blow the crap out of it. What happens then? If you impose punitive peace terms at knife-point because of the temporary advantage Apollo gives us, you've still got to come up with the hulls and ships to *enforce* those terms afterward . . . at the same moment when you're fighting for your life against the League.

"Do you really want to trust that we'll somehow be able to build a fleet big enough to handle both of those chores *at once*? And do you really think Pritchart—or, more likely, some other Havenite administration—wouldn't go right ahead and stab you in the back at the first opportunity? Or even simply offer 'technical assistance' to the Sollies to help them close the gap between their capabilities and ours even faster? And if you impose those terms by blowing the Haven System's infrastructure apart, and by killing thousands more of their naval personnel when they can't even shoot back effectively, I can absolutely guarantee you that *any* Havenite administration is only going to be licking its chops while it waits for the best possible moment to hit you from behind."

"So what do you suggest instead?" Elizabeth asked. Honor's eyes widened slightly at the queen's reasonable tone, and Elizabeth chuckled harshly. "Step up to the plate, as I believe they say on Grayson, Duchess Harrington. You've just done the equivalent of spanking me in public—well, in semi-public, at least—and I may have deserved it. But if you're prepared to tell me I've been wrong, then I'm prepared to tell you to suggest something better!"

"All right," Honor said after a moment. "I agree that we've got to be able to face one opponent at a time. I don't think anyone in this room, or anyone in the entire Navy, *wants* to fight the Sollies. Not if they have even the faintest conception of just how big, how powerful, the League is, anyway. I don't care what any of us said about potential Solarian weaknesses, or possible political strategies or opportunities. The truth is that none of us can know if any of that analysis was truly accurate, and only a lunatic would willingly risk the very survival of her star nation on *possibilities* if she had any other option at all!

"But, having said that, I think we have to *position* ourselves to fight the SLN, whether we want to or not. And that means reaching some sort of settlement, whether it's diplomatic or military, with the Havenites first. I've never disagreed with you there. But I think that rather than blowing still more of their ships out of space, and rather than destroying still more of their infrastructure, we ought to tell them *we* think it's time to talk. Hamish is right about the timing if we decide to launch what amounts to a preemptive strike, but remember what Pritchard did when *she* had the advantage because of what was happening in Talbott. She didn't shoot first, she offered to *talk*, and I genuinely believe she's telling the truth when she says *she* didn't set out to derail the summit.

"So I think it's time we show Haven *we* can forego an advantage in the interests of peace, as well. We defeated them decisively here in Manticore, despite our own losses, and they know it. By now, they know we could destroy the Haven System any time we chose to, as well. So I suggest that we hold Eighth Fleet right here, close to home, in case we do end up needing it in

Talbott. Instead of sending me to Nouveau Paris to hold a pistol to their heads and *make* them sign on the dotted line, send an accredited diplomat, instead. Someone who can tell them that *we* know we can destroy them, too, and that we're prepared to do it *if we have to*, but that we don't want to *unless* we have to. Give them the option and let them have a little time to think, a little time to approach the decision with dignity, Elizabeth, not just because they're lying face down in the dirt with the muzzle of a gun screwed into the backs of their necks. Give them the chance to surrender on some sort of *reasonable* terms before I have to go out and kill thousands of more people who might not have to die at all."

"It's time, Admiral," Felicidad Kolstad said.

"I know," Admiral Topolev replied.

He sat once more upon *Mako's* flag bridge. Beyond the flagship's hull, fourteen more ships of Task Force One kept perfect formation upon her, and the brilliant beacon of Manticore-A blazed before them. They were only one light-week from that star, now, and they had decelerated to only twenty percent of light-speed. This was the point for which they had been headed ever since leaving Mesa four T-months before. Now it was time to do what they'd come here to do.

"Begin deployment," he said, and the enormous hatches opened and the pods began to spill free.

The other units of Task Force One were elsewhere, closing on Manticore-B. They wouldn't be deploying their pods just yet, not until they'd reached their own preselected launch point. Topolev wished that he'd had more ships to commit to that prong of the attack, but the decision to move up Oyster Bay had dictated the available resources, and *this* prong had to be decisive. Besides, there were fewer targets in the Manticore-B subsystem, anyway.

*It'll be enough*, he told himself, watching as the pods disappeared steadily behind his decelerating starships, vanishing into the endless dark between the stars. *It'll be enough. And in about five weeks, the Manties are going to get a late Christmas present they'll never forget.*

# JAYNE'S

## INTELLIGENCE REVIEW

**Historical and Technical Database**

Packet Update 47.1922.36-B

QUERY: TALBOTT CLUSTER
SUB-SET: SKM/RMN
SOL/SLN

FILECAT: NAVY/SHIP, WEAP

SUBSCRIBER ID: 1983.08.30

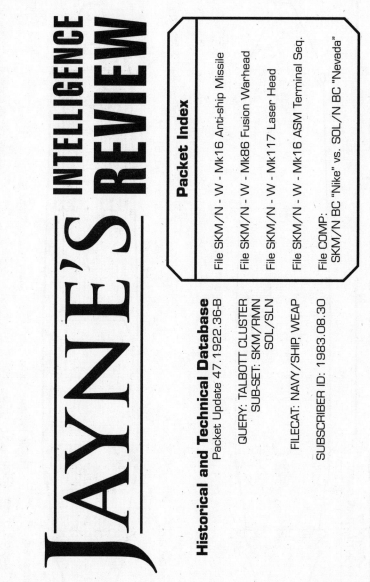

### Packet Index

File SKM/N - W - Mk16 Anti-ship Missile

File SKM/N - W - Mk86 Fusion Warhead

File SKM/N - W - Mk117 Laser Head

File SKM/N - W - Mk16 ASM Terminal Seq.

File COMP:
SKM/N BC "Nike" vs. SOL/N BC "Nevada"

# Mk16 Anti-Ship Missile

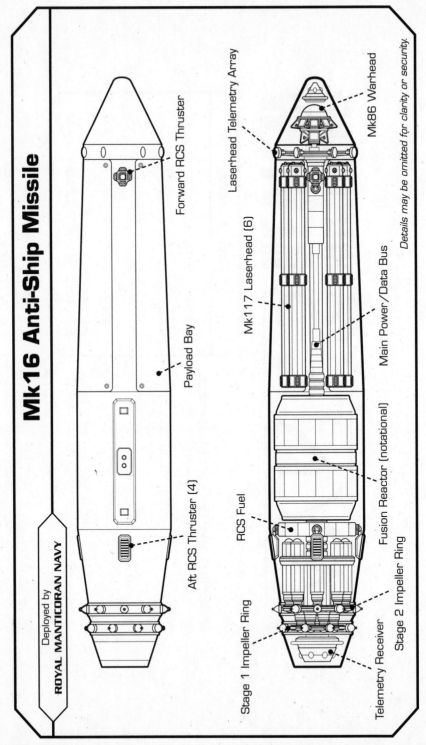

Deployed by
**ROYAL MANTICORAN NAVY**

Forward RCS Thruster

Payload Bay

Aft RCS Thruster (4)

Laserhead Telemetry Array

Mk86 Warhead

Mk117 Laserhead (6)

Main Power/Data Bus

Fusion Reactor (notational)

RCS Fuel

Stage 1 Impeller Ring

Stage 2 Impeller Ring

Telemetry Receiver

Details may be omitted for clarity or security.

# Mk86 Fusion Warhead

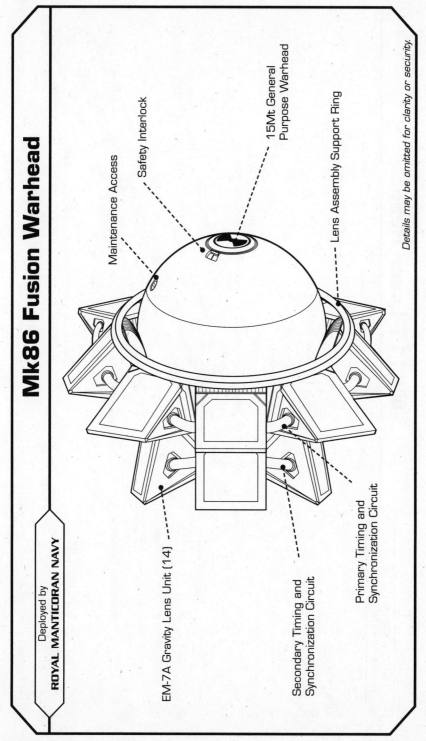

Maintenance Access

Safety Interlock

15Mt General Purpose Warhead

Lens Assembly Support Ring

EM-7A Gravity Lens Unit (14)

Secondary Timing and Synchronization Circuit

Primary Timing and Synchronization Circuit

Deployed by
**ROYAL MANTICORAN NAVY**

*Details may be omitted for clarity or security.*

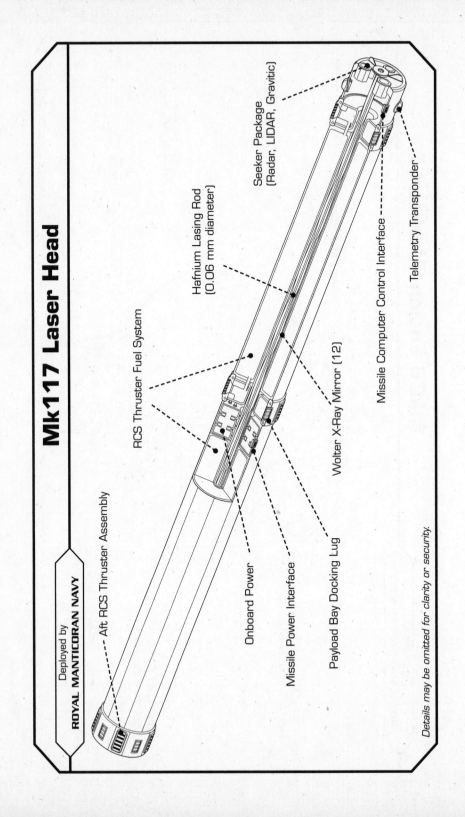

# Mk117 Laser Head

Deployed by
**ROYAL MANTICORAN NAVY**

Seeker Package
(Radar, LIDAR, Gravitic)

Telemetry Transponder

Hafnium Lasing Rod
(0.06 mm diameter)

Missile Computer Control Interface

RCS Thruster Fuel System

Wolter X-Ray Mirror (12)

Aft RCS Thruster Assembly

Onboard Power

Missile Power Interface

Payload Bay Docking Lug

*Details may be omitted for clarity or security.*

# Mk16 Terminal Sequence - Maneuvering

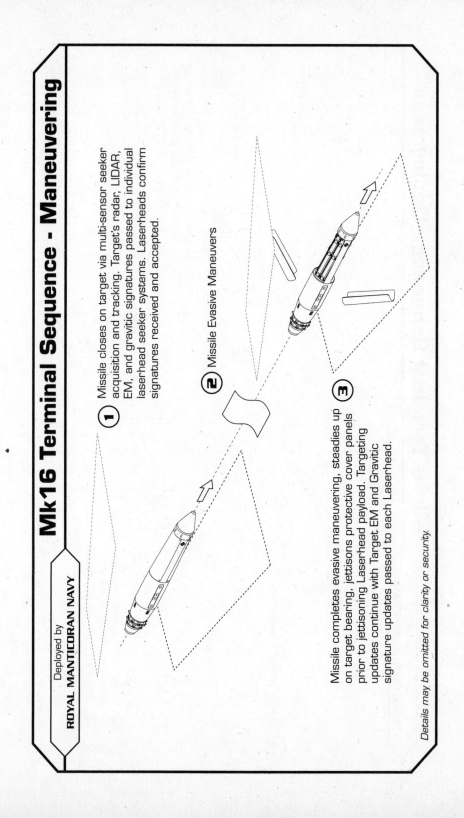

1. Missile closes on target via multi-sensor seeker acquisition and tracking. Target's radar, LIDAR, EM, and gravitic signatures passed to individual laserhead seeker systems. Laserheads confirm signatures received and accepted.

2. Missile Evasive Maneuvers

3. Missile completes evasive maneuvering, steadies up on target bearing, jettisons protective cover panels prior to jettisoning Laserhead payload. Targeting updates continue with Target EM and Gravitic signature updates passed to each Laserhead.

*Details may be omitted for clarity or security.*

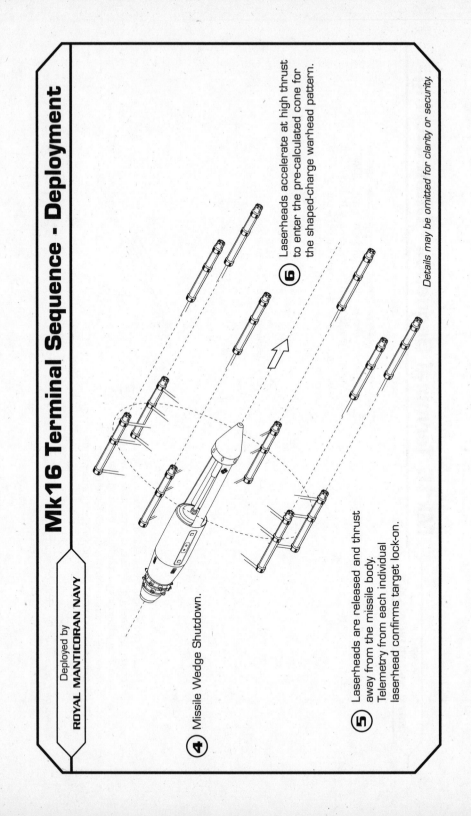

# Mk16 Terminal Sequence - Deployment

Deployed by
**ROYAL MANTICORAN NAVY**

④ Missile Wedge Shutdown.

⑤ Laserheads are released and thrust away from the missile body. Telemetry from each individual laserhead confirms target lock-on.

⑥ Laserheads accelerate at high thrust to enter the pre-calculated cone for the shaped-charge warhead pattern.

*Details may be omitted for clarity or security.*

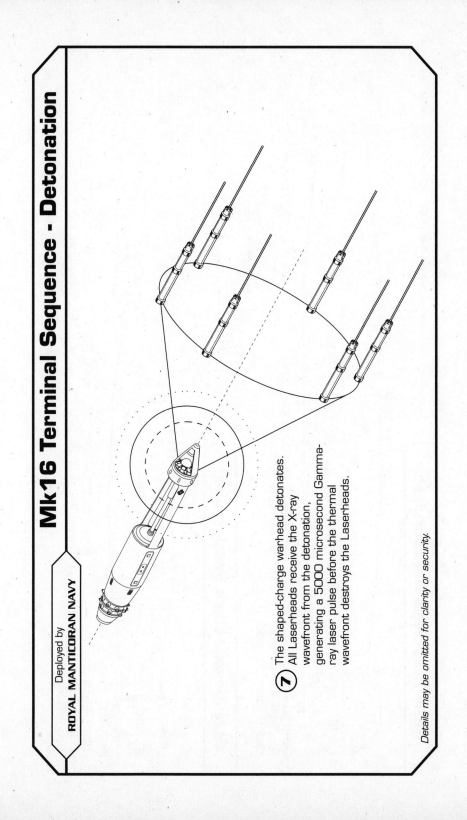

# Mk16 Terminal Sequence - Detonation

7. The shaped-charge warhead detonates. All Laserheads receive the X-ray wavefront from the detonation, generating a 5000 microsecond Gamma-ray laser pulse before the thermal wavefront destroys the Laserheads.

*Details may be omitted for clarity or security.*

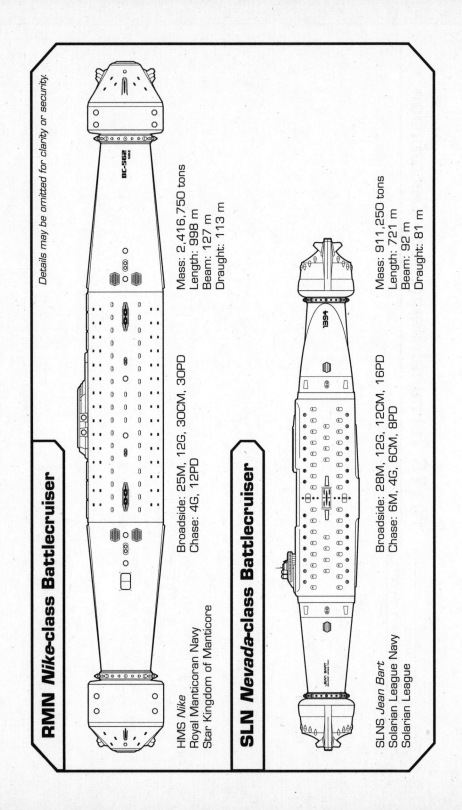

## RMN *Nike*-class Battlecruiser

BC-562
NIKE

Mass: 2,416,750 tons
Length: 998 m
Beam: 127 m
Draught: 113 m

Broadside: 25M, 12G, 30CM, 30PD
Chase: 4G, 12PD

HMS *Nike*
Royal Manticoran Navy
Star Kingdom of Manticore

## SLN *Nevada*-class Battlecruiser

1394

Mass: 911,250 tons
Length: 721 m
Beam: 92 m
Draught: 81 m

Broadside: 28M, 12G, 12CM, 16PD
Chase: 6M, 4G, 6CM, 8PD

SLNS *Jean Bart*
Solarian League Navy
Solarian League

# JAYNE'S INTELLIGENCE REVIEW

## PACKET END

Packet Update 47.1922.36-B

QUERY: TALBOTT CLUSTER
SUB-SET: SKM/RMN
SOL/SLN

FILECAT: NAVY/SHIP, WEAP

SUBSCRIBER ID: 1983.08.30

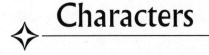

# Characters

**Aberu, Captain Ingeborg**, SLN—operations officer, Frontier Fleet Task Group 3021.

**Abruzzi, Malachai**—Permanent Senior Undersecretary of Education and Information, Solarian League.

**Adenauer, Commander Dominica**, RMN—operations officer, Battlecruiser Squadron 106; later operations officer, 10th Fleet.

**Agnelli, Chief Steward Joanna**, RMN—Aivars Terekhov's personal steward.

**al-Fanudahi, Captain Daud ibn Mamoun**, SLN—a Battle Fleet analyst assigned to the Office of Operational Analysis.

**Alcoforado, Captain Filipa**, RMN—CO, HMS *Theseus*. Shulamit Onasis' flag captain.

**Alonso y Yáñez, Fleet Admiral Engracia**, SLN—CO, Frontier Fleet, Solarian League Navy.

**Alquezar, Joachim**—Prime Minister of the Talbott Quadrant, leader of the Constitutional Union Party.

**Anisimovna, Aldona**—Manpower Inc. board member; a senior operative of the Mesan Alignment.

**Appleton, Lieutenant Martin**, RMN—XO, HMS *Roland*.

**Archer, Sir Roger Mackley**—"Gwen" Archer's father.

**Archer, Lieutenant Gervais Winton Erwin Neville ("Gwen")**, RMN—Michelle Henke's flag lieutenant.

**Armstrong, Captain Victoria ("Vicki")**, RMN—commanding officer HMS *Artemis*; vice Admiral Gold Peak's flag captain.

**Askew, Lieutenant Maitland ("Matt")**, SLN—assistant tactical officer, SLNS *Jean Bart*.

**Attunga, Marguerite**—a reporter for Manticoran News Service, Inc.

**Bardasano, Isabel**—Jessyk Combine cadet board member; senior intelligence specialist, Mesan Alignment.

**Billingsley, Master Steward Chris**, RMN—Michelle Henke's personal steward.

**Blaine, Vice Admiral Jessup**, RMN—CO, Task Force 302, Lynx Terminus Station.

**Boltitz, Helga**—Henri Krietzmann's senior personal aide.

**Bouchard, Lieutenant Commander Jerod**, RMN—astrogator, HMS *Artemis*.

**Bourget, Commander Hildegard ("Hildy")**, SLN—XO, SLNS *Jean Bart*.

**Boutin, President Alain**—System President, New Tuscany.

**Bouvier, Captain Adelbert**, RHN—Republic of Haven Navy POW camp liaison responsible for Camp C7.

**Braga, Lieutenant Commander Antonio**, RMN—staff astrogator, Battlecruiser Squadron 81.

**Brangeard, Lieutenant Toussaint**, RHN—CO dispatch boat RHNS *Comet*.

**Brescatore, Captain George**, RMN—CO, HMS *Sabertooth*.

**Breshnikov, Captain Adolf**, SLN—CO, SLNS *Restitution*. Evelyn Sigbee's flag captain.

**Brinkman, Chief Steward Clorinda**, RMN—Naomi Kaplan's personal steward.

**Bristow, Lieutenant Oliver**, SLN—sensor officer, Meyers Astro Control.

**Brulé, Anne-Louise**—an employee of the New Tuscany Ministry of Information.

**Brunner, Lieutenant Simon**, RMN—astrogator, HMS *Reprise*.

**Byng, Admiral Josef**, SLN—CO, Frontier Fleet Task Group 3021.

**Cardot, Alesta**—Minister of Foreign Affairs, New Tuscany.

**Carlson, Captain Frederick**, RMN—CO, HMS *Quentin Saint-James*. Sir Aivars Terekhov's flag captain.

**Carmouche, Captain Tanguy**—a fictitious New Tuscan merchant captain portrayed by Oliver Ratté.

**Carus, Commander Joseph**, RMN—CO, HMS *Javelin*; SO, Destroyer Division 265.2.

**Casterlin, Commander Sterling**, RMN—astrogator, Battlecruiser Squadron 106; later astrogator, 10th Fleet.

**Challon, Armand**—Deputy Minister of War, New Tuscany.

**Challon, Victor**—a powerful oligarch and politician in the New Tuscany System Parliament.

**Chandler, Commander Ambrose**, RMN—Augustus Khumalo's staff intelligence officer.

**Chang, Rear Admiral Liam**, SLN—CO, Battlecruiser Squadron 302.

**Chase, Lieutenant Commander Julie**, RMN—CO, HMS *Lodestone*.

**Chatterjee, Commodore Ray ("Bear")**—CO, Destroyer Squadron 301; SO, Destroyer Division 301.1.

**Cheng, Admiral Hai-shwun**, SLN—CO, Office of Operational Analysis, Solarian League Navy.

**Chernevsky, Anastasia**—head of naval research and development, Mesan Alignment.

**Clifford, Petty Officer First-Class Cheryl**, RMN—acting quartermaster, HMS *Hexapuma*.

**Coker, Petty Officer2/c Alan**, SLN—sensor technician, Meyers Astro Control.

**Coleman, Commander Theresa**, MAN—Frederick chief of staff, Task Force One.

**Colenso, Admiral Jennifer**, MAN—CO, Task Force Two.

**Conner, Captain Jerome**, RMN—CO, HMS *Penelope*. Senior officer, Battlecruiser Division 106.1.

**Cortez, Admiral Sir Lucian**, RMN—Fifth Space Lord, Royal Manticoran Navy.

**Cramer, Commander Wesley**, RMN—CO, HMS *Devastation*.

**Crandall, Fleet Admiral Sandra**, SLN—CO, Task Force 496.

**d'Arezzo, Midshipman Paulo**, RMN—assigned HMS *Hexapuma* for midshipman's cruise.

**Da Orta e Diadoro, Jacinta**—Interior Minister, Solarian League.

**Dallas, Commander Albert ("Al")**, RMN—XO, HMS *Artemis*.

**Danville, Surgeon Lieutenant Pryce**, RMN—ship's surgeon, HMS *Tristram*.

**Denton, Lieutenant Commander Lewis**, RMN—CO, HMS *Reprise*.

**DesMoines, Commander John**, RMN—CO, HMS *Roland*. "Bear" Chatterjee's flag captain.

**Detweiler, Albrecht**—CEO, Mesan Alignment.

**Detweiler, Benjamin**—Albrecht Detweiler's son; Mesan Alignment director of military affairs.

**Detweiler, Collin**—Albrecht Detweiler's son; Mesan Alignment director of intelligence operations.

**Detweiler, Daniel**—Albrecht Detweiler's son; Mesan Alignment director of nongenetic R&D.

**Detweiler, Evelina**—Albrecht Detweiler's wife; a senior genetic researcher for the Mesan Alignment.

**Detweiler, Everett**—Albrecht Detweiler's son; Mesan Alignment director of genetic R&D.

**Detweiler, Franklin**—Albrecht Detweiler's son; Mesan Alignment director of political strategy.

**Detweiler, Gervais**—Albrecht Detweiler's son; Mesan Alignment director of foreign affairs.

**Diego, Commander Wilton**, RMN—tactical officer, HMS *Artemis*.

**Drewson, Captain Ellis**, RMN—CO, HMS *Kodiak*.

**Duchovny, Captain Agafia Denisevna**, RMN—CO, HMS *Horatius*.

**Dusserre, Damien**—Minister of security, New Tuscany.

**Edwards, Lieutenant Commander William ("Bill")**, RMN—communications officer, Battlecruiser Squadron 106; later communications officer, 10th Fleet.

**Epstein, Lieutenant Commander Jessica**—senior tracking officer, Perimeter Security Command, Manticore Binary System.

**Fernandez, Lieutenant Commander Kyle**, RMN—communications officer, HMS *Artemis*.

**Filareta, Fleet Admiral Massimo**, SLN—CO, Task Force 891.

**FitzGerald, Commander Ansten**, RMN—XO, HMS *Hexapuma*.

**Flynn, Commander Sheila**, MAN—chief of staff, Task Group 1.1.

**Fonzarelli, Lieutenant Vincenzo**, RMN—chief engineer, HMS *Tristram*.

**Foreman, Commander Clement**, MAN—operations officer, Task Group 1.1.

**Garcia, Rear Admiral Jane**, RMSN—senior officer, Monica Traffic Control.

**Gold Peak, Countess**—see Michelle Henke.

**Gold Peak, Admiral**—see Michelle Henke.

**Goulard, Commander Rochelle ("Roxy")**, RMN—CO, HMS *Kay*.

**Guédon, Admiral Josette**, NTN—chief of naval operations, New Tuscan Navy.

**Gutierrez, Lieutenant Mateo**, Owens Steadholders Guard—Abigail Hearns' personal armsman.

**Gyulay, Shona**—Prime Minister, Solarian League.

**Haftner, Abednego**—Henri Krietzmann's chief of staff.

**Halstead, Captain Raymond**, RMN—one of Project Apollo's project officers.

**Harahap, Damien**—a former officer of the Solarian League Gendarmerie now working for Valery Ottweiler.

**Harrison, Commander Dwayne**, RMN—tactical officer, battlecruiser HMS *Ajax*.

**Hearns, Lieutenant Abigail**, GSN—Miss Owens. Assistant tactical officer, HMS *Hexapuma*. Later tactical officer, HMS *Tristram*.

**Hemphill, Admiral Sonja**, RMN—Fourth Space Lord, Royal Manticoran Navy.

**Henke, Vice Admiral Gloria Michelle Samantha Evelyn**, Countess Gold Peak—Elizabeth Winton's first cousin; fifth in succession for the throne of Manticore; CO 10th Fleet.

**Henke, Rear Admiral Gloria Michelle Samantha Evelyn**, Countess Gold Peak—CO, battlecruiser squadron 81. Later vice admiral.

**Hennessy, Lieutenant Commander Coleman**, RMN—Sonja Hemphill's chief of staff.

**Henning, Lieutenant Commander Vivienne**, MAN—staff astrogator, Task Force One.

**Hongbo, Vice-Commissioner Junyan**—Lorcan Verrochio's senior OFS subordinate, Madras Sector.

**Horn, Commander Alexandra ("Alex")**, RMN—XO, HMS *Ajax*.

**Houseman, Commander Frazier**, RMN—XO, HMS *Penelope*. Acting chief of staff, Battlecruiser Division 106.1.

**Huppé, Honorine**—Minister of Trade, New Tuscany.

**Hurskainen, President Stanley**—President of the Mannerheim System Republic.

**Imbar, Efron**—a reporter for Star Kingdom News.

**Inbari, Lieutenant Commander Mazal**, RMN—staff astrogator, Cruiser Squadron 94.

**Jackson, Lieutenant Thor**, RMN—astrogator, HMS *Roland*.

**Jackson, Lieutenant Aphrodite**, RMN—electronic warfare officer, HMS *Reprise*.

**Jacobi, Captain Rachel, MAN**—CO, freighter *Wallaby*.

**Jeffers, Lieutenant Sherilyn**, RMN—electronics warfare officer, HMS *Tristram*.

**Jenkins, Captain Vladislava, SLN**—logistics officer, Frontier Fleet Task Group 3021.

**Johansen, Lieutenant Commander Barnabé**, RMN—astrogator, HMS *Quentin Saint-James*.

**Kaminski, Lieutenant Albert**, RMN—communications officer, Battlecruiser Squadron 81.

**Kaneshiro, Missile Tech 1/c Naomi**, RMN—missile tech, HMS *Tristram*.

**Kaplan, Commander Naomi**, RMN—tactical officer, HMS *Hexapuma*. Later CO, HMS *Tristram*.

**Karlberg, Commodore Emil**—senior officer, Nuncio Space Force.

**Kenichi, Captain Otmar**, RMN—CO, HMS *Marconi Williams*.

**Khumalo, Vice Admiral Augustus**, RMN—senior officer, Talbot Station.

**Kingsford, Fleet Admiral Winston Seth**, SLN—CO, Battle Fleet, Solarian League Navy.

**Kittow, Captain Joshua**, RMN—XO, HMS *Quentin Saint-James*.

**Kolokoltsov, Innokentiy Arsenovich**—Permanent Senior Undersecretary for Foreign Affairs, Solarian League.

**Kolosov, Lieutenant Peter**, RMN—XO, HMS *Reprise*.

**Kolstad, Commander Felicidad**, MAN—operations officer, Task Force One.

**Krietzmann, Henri**—Minister of War, Talbott Quadrant.

**L'anglais, Captain Prosper**—CO, New Tuscan merchant ship *Hélène Blondeau*.

**Lababibi, Samiha**—former President of the Spindle System; Treasury Minister, Talbott Quadrant.

**Landry, Lieutenant Commander Bridget**, RMN—CO, HMS *Dagger*.

**Laszlo, Commodore András**—senior officer, Spindle System Navy.

**Laycock, Captain Mariane**, RMN—CO, HMS *Julian Lister*.

**Le Vern, Lieutenant Herschel**, RMN—logistics officer, HMS *Quentin Saint-James*.

**Lecter, Captain (JG) Cynthia**, RMN—chief of staff, Battlecruiser Squadron 106; later chief of staff, 10th Fleet.

**Lewis, Commander Ginger**, RMN—chief engineer, HMS *Hexapuma*.

**Lewis, Commander Stillwell ("Stilt")**, RMN—operations officer, Cruiser Squadron 94.

**Low Delhi, Baroness**—see Admiral Sonja Hemphill.

**Lynch, Commander Horace**, RMN—tactical officer, HMS *Quentin Saint-James*.

**MacArtney, Nathan**—Permanent Senior Undersecretary of the Interior, Solarian League.

**MacKechie, Major Esmé**, RMMC—CO, Marine detachment, HMS *Artemis*.

**MacMinn, Captain Eachann**, RMN—CO, HMS *Duke of Cromarty*.

**MaCuill, Captain Willard,** SLN—staff communications officer, Frontier Fleet Task Group 3021.

**MaGuire, Master Chief Alice**, RMN—bosun, HMS *Ajax*.

**Manfredi, Commander Oliver**, RMN—chief of staff, Battlecruiser Squadron 81.

**Markussen, Leontina**—Minister of Education and Information, Solarian League.

**Maslov, Lieutenant Isaiah,** RMN—EWO, HMS *Artemis*.

**Masters, Captain Eric**, MAN—CO, MANS *Chameleon*; Karol Østby's flag captain.

**Matsuko, Dame Estelle**—Baroness Medusa, Imperial Governor, Talbott Quadrant.

**McClelland, Commander Martin**, MAN—staff electronics warfare officer, Task Force One.

**McCormick, Lieutenant Clinton**, RMN—tracking officer, Perimeter Security Command, Manticore Binary System.

**McGill, Lieutenant Heather**, RMN—tactical officer, HMS *Reprise*.

**McIver, Commander Dabney**, RMN—chief of staff, Battlecruiser Division 106.2.

**Medusa, Baroness**—see Dame Estelle Matsuko.

**Metcalf, Jansen**—Mesan ambassador to New Tuscany.

**Mikhailov, Captain Diego**, RMN—CO, HMS *Ajax*.

**Miskin, Commander Edward**, RMN—CO, HMS *Galahad*.

**Mizawa, Captain Warden**, SLN—CO, SLNS *Jean Bart*; Josef Byng's flag captain.

**Molyneux, Lieutenant (JG) Gladys**, RMN—junior tactical officer, HMS *Tristram*.

**Monahan, Ensign Rachel**, RMN—midshipwoman assigned to midshipman's cruise, HMS *Reprise*.

**Montella, Lieutenant Atalante**, RMN—communications officer, Cruiser Squadron 94.

**Morgan, Captain (JG) Frank**, GSN—CO, HMS *Gawain*. Jacob Zavala's flag captain.

**Musgrave, Senior Chief Petty Officer Franklin**, GSN—bosun, HMS *Tristram*.

**Myau, Surgeon Lieutenant Zhin**, RMN—ship's surgeon, HMS *Quentin Saint-James*.

**Nagchaudhuri, Lieutenant Commander Amal**, RMN—communications officer, HMS *Hexapuma*.

**Nelson, Rear Admiral Gordon**, SLN—CO, Battlecruiser Squadron 201.

**Ning, Captain Kwo-Lai**, RMN—CO, HMS *Romulus*.

**Noorlander, Harbrecht**—Treasury Minister, Solarian League.

**O'Malley, Vice Admiral Quentin**, RMN—CO, Task Group 302.1.

**O'Reilly, Lieutenant Wanda**, RMN—communications officer, HMS *Tristram*.

**O'Shaughnessy, Gregor**—Dame Estelle Matsuko's senior civilian intelligence analyst.

**Ødegaard, Lieutenant Commander Mateuz**, RMN—staff intelligence officer, Cruiser Squadron 94.

**Olson, Lieutenant Commander Lori**, RMN—operations officer, Destroyer Squadron 301.

**Onassis, Commodore Shulamit**, RMN—senior officer, Battlecruiser Division 106.2.

**Orban, Surgeon Lieutenant Commander Lajos**, RMN—ship's doctor, HMS *Hexapuma*.

**Østby, Commodore Karol**, MAN—CO, Task Group 1.1.

**Ottweiler, Valery**—a senior diplomat for the Mesa System.

**Oversteegen, Rear Admiral Michael**, RMN—CO, Battlecruiser Squadron 108.

**Pélisard, Nicholas**—Minister of War, New Tuscany.

**Pershing, Lieutenant Commander John**, RMN—CO, HMS *Raven.*

**Petersen, Lieutenant Linda**, RMN—astrogator, HMS *Javelin.*

**Pettigrew, Sensor Tech 1/c Isaiah**, GSN—sensor tech, HMS *Tristram.*

**Pickering, Captain Henry**, RMN—CO, HMS *Daedalus.*

**Pope, Commander Tom**, RMN—chief of staff, Cruiser Squadron 94.

**Quartermain, Omosupe**—Permanent Senior Undersecretary of Commerce, Solarian League.

**Rajampet, Fleet Admiral Kaushal Rajani**, SLN—chief of naval operations, Solarian League Navy.

**Ratté, Oliver**—an employee of the New Tuscany Ministry of Information.

**Razumovsky, Captain Lex**, RMN—CO, HMS *Malachai.*

**Redmont, Admiral Pierre**, RHN—CO, "Bogey Two," Battle of Solon.

**Redondo, Consuela**—a reporter for the Sphinx News Association.

**Richardson, Lieutenant Osama**, RMN—chief engineer, HMS *Reprise.*

**Roach, Captain Hal**, RMN—XO, Charleston Center for Admiralty Law.

**Rochefort, Lieutenant Léopold**, NTN—communications officer aboard space station *Giselle.*

**Roelas y Valiente, Marcelito Lorenzo**—Foreign Minister, Solarian League.

**Ronayne, Brangwen**—Attorney General, Solarian League.

**Rützel, Lieutenant Commander Tobias ("Toby")**, RMN—CO, HMS *Gaheris.*

**Sackett, Commodore Lemuel**—senior officer, Montana system Navy.

**Sarkozy, Surgeon Lieutenant Ruth**, RMN—ship's doctor, HMS *Vigilant*, transferred to HMS *Hexapuma* following Battle of Monica.

**Sarnow, Admiral Mark**, RMN—senior officer naval forces assigned to the Silesian Confederacy.

**Saunders, Captain Victoria**, RMN—CO, HMS *Hercules*.

**Schroeder, Captain Federico**, SLN—staff astrogator, Frontier Fleet Task Group 3021.

**Seacrest, Captain (JG) Ellen**, RMN—CO, HMS *Lancelot*.

**Séguin, Captain Gabrielle**, NTN—CO, NTNS *Camille*.

**Shaw, Captain Terrence**, RMN—Sir Lucian Cortez' chief of staff.

**Shoupe, Captain Loretta**, RMN—Augustus Khumalo's chief of staff.

**Sigbee, Rear Admiral Evelyn**, SLN—CO, Battlecruiser Squadron 112.

**Simpkins, Lieutenant Hosea**, GSN—astrogator, HMS *Tristram*.

**Sloan, Chief Petty Officer Tamara**, RMN—HMS *Reprise*.

**Stackpole, Lieutenant Commander John**, RMN—operations officer, Battlecruiser Squadron 81.

**Sung, Commodore Roderick**, MAN—CO, Task Group 2.1.

**Sybil Moorehead**—Joachim Alquezar's chief of staff.

**Sywan, Mang**—Minister of Commerce, Solarian League.

**Szegdi, Commander Lindsey**, RMN—CO, HMS *Ivanhoe*.

**Taketomo, Kunimichi**—Minister of Defense, Solarian League.

**Taliadoros, Kyrillos**—Aldona Anisimovna's genetically enhanced bodyguard.

**Tallman, Lieutenant Commander Alvin**, RMN—XO, HMS *Tristram*.

**Teague, Captain Irene**, SLN—a Frontier Fleet analyst assigned to the Office of Operational Analysis.

**Teke, Captain Rachel**, RMN—CO, HMS *Slipstream*.

**Terekhov, Captain Aivars**, RMN—CO, HMS *Hexapuma*. Later commodore. (See Sir Aivars Terekhov, below)

**Terekhov, Commodore Sir Aivars**, RMN—CO, Cruiser Squadron 94. (See Aivars Terekhov, above)

**Wang, Astrid**—Innokentiy Kolokoltsov's personal assistant and chief of staff.

**Winton-Travis, The Honorable Frederick Roger**—CEO Of Apex Industrial Group; Elizabeth III's cousin; member of the Conservative Association.

**Wodoslawski, Agatá**—Permanent Senior Undersecretary of the Treasury, Solarian League.

**Wright, Commander Jason**, RMN—chief of staff, Destroyer Squadron 301.

**Wright, Lieutenant Commander Tobias**, RMN—astrogator, HMS *Hexapuma*.

**Xamar, Lieutenant Nicasio**, RMN—assistant tactical officer, HMS *Tristram*.

**Yang, Captain Sharon**, SLN—CO, SLNS *Resourceful*.

**Yao, President Kun Chol**—President and head of state, Solarian League.

**Zagorski, Chief Warrant Officer Sylwester**, RMN—logistics officer, HMS *Tristram*.

**Zavala, Captain Jacob**—SO, Destroyer Division 301.2.

**Zeiss, Commander Ursula**, SLN—tactical officer, SLNS *Jean Bart*.

**Zilwicki, Ensign Helen**, RMN—Sir Aivars Terekhov's flag lieutenant. (See Midshipwoman Helen Zilwicki.)

**Zilwicki, Midshipwoman Helen**, RMN—assigned HMS *Hexapuma* for midshipman's cruise. Later ensign. (See Ensign Helen Zilwicki.)